NIKOLAI: THE COMPLETE COLLECTION

BOOKS 1 TO 3

RUSSIAN MOB CHRONICLES

SHANDI BOYES

COPYRIGHT

Editing: Mountains Wanted Editing

Editing: Courtney Umphress

Cover: SSB Covers & Design

Photographer: Ren Saliba

Proof read by: Lindsi La Bar

ALSO BY SHANDI BOYES

*** Denotes Standalone Books**

<u>Perception Series</u>

Saving Noah *

Fighting Jacob *

Taming Nick *

Redeeming Slater *

Saving Emily

Wrapped Up with Rise Up

Protecting Nicole *

Enigma

Enigma

Unraveling an Enigma

Enigma The Mystery Unmasked

Enigma: The Final Chapter

Beneath The Secrets

Beneath The Sheets

Spy Thy Neighbor *

The Opposite Effect *

I Married a Mob Boss *

Second Shot *

The Way We Are

The Way We Were

Sugar and Spice *

Lady In Waiting

Man in Queue

Couple on Hold

Enigma: The Wedding

Silent Vigilante

Hushed Guardian

Quiet Protector

Enigma: An Isaac Retelling

Enigma Bonus Scenes (Two free chapters)

Twisted Lies *

Bound Series

Chains

Links

Bound

Restrain

The Misfits *

Nanny Dispute *

Russian Mob Chronicles

Nikolai: Representing the Bratva

Nikolai: Resurrecting the Bratva

Nikolai: Ruling the Bratva

Asher: My Russian Revenge *

Trey *

Nikolai: Bonus Scenes (10+ chapters from alternative POVs).

The Italian Cartel

Dimitri

Roxanne

Reign

Mafia Ties (Novella)

Maddox

Demi

Ox

Rocco *

Clover *

Smith *

RomCom Standalones

Just Playin' *

<u>Ain't Happenin'</u> *

The Drop Zone *

Very Unlikely *

False Start *

Short Stories - Newsletter Downloads

Christmas Trio *

Falling For A Stranger *

Enigma Bonus Scenes (Two free chapters)

Nikolai: Bonus Scenes (10+ chapters from alternative POVs).

One Night Only Series

Hotshot Boss *

Hotshot Neighbor *

The Bobrov Bratva Series

Wicked Intentions *

Sinful Intentions *

Devious Intentions *

Deadly Intentions *

Omnibus Books (Collections)

Enigma: The Complete Collection (Isaac & Isabelle)

The Beneath Duet (Hugo & Ava)

The Bad Boy Trilogy (Hunter, Rico, and Brax)

Pinkie Promise (Ryan & Savannah)

The Infinite Time Trilogy (Regan & Alex)

Silent Guardian (Brandon & Melody)

Nikolai: The Complete Collection (Nikolai & Justine)

Mafioso (Dimitri & Roxanne)

Bound: The Complete Collection (Cleo & Marcus)

WANT TO STAY IN TOUCH?

Facebook: facebook.com/authorshandi

Instagram: instagram.com/authorshandi

Email: authorshandi@gmail.com

Reader's Group: bit.ly/ShandiBookBabes

Website: authorshandi.com

Newsletter: https://www.subscribepage.com/AuthorShandi

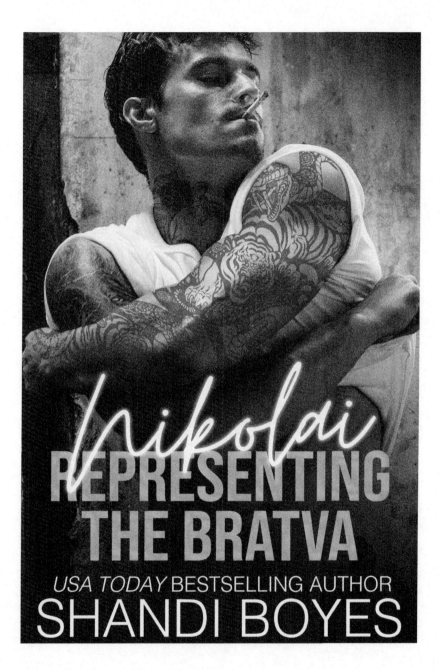

Nikolai
REPRESENTING THE BRATVA

USA TODAY BESTSELLING AUTHOR
SHANDI BOYES

FOREWORD

Please note in this series Nikolai refers to Justine as *Ангел*, which means Angel in Russian. He pronounces *Ангел* as Ahren.

This is not the correct pronunciation, but in *I Married a Mob Boss* (Rico's story), it states that Nikolai couldn't speak or read Russian as well as his siblings, and out of all the words he got wrong, this one stuck.

I think it's cute. I hope you do too.

Cheers,

Shandi xx

1

NIKOLAI

"**Y**ou have the right to remain silent..."
I drown out the rest of Detective Franco's frequently spoken statement. I've become a pro at being detained over the past four years.

My rap sheet is as long as my arm, yet I've not spent one night behind bars. I could compliment that to the wisdom of my family lawyer, Erik Monstrateo, but I could never be accused of being humble.

Thirty witnesses watched me pierce a beer bottle into a man's neck a mere second after I smashed it over his head, but despite all of that, I guarantee you none will come forward as a witness. They'd rather face prosecution for obstructing justice than rat me out because they know as well as the next man, the only way to stay alive in my industry is by keeping your mouth shut.

You don't live a hard and fast life as I have without amassing a reputation. Mine is now as feared as my brother's once was. I was the joker, the partier, the ultimate playboy, whereas Rico was all about facts, figures, and ensuring he only strayed as far as the leash his little kitty placed on him would allow.

It all changed when he was killed.

I hope those short weeks of marital bliss were the highlights of his life as all he has now are veins as cold as ice and the constant view of dirt.

Rico was executed by a Russian operative while endeavoring to keep alive a promise he'd made to his wife the night they wed. His death hit me like a wrecking ball. I was a fucking mass of destruction hell-bent on avenging his death no matter the cost.

We weren't close when he was killed, but I couldn't forget the years where our bond was tighter than one we would have achieved if we'd had the same blood. He protected me as well as I protected him until the person we needed protection from the most was each other.

Greed is a horrible thing, but it has nothing on vengeance.

My mother believed that more than anyone.

I arrived at Hopeton the afternoon of Rico's murder, ready for warfare. My operation nearly folded when the man responsible for killing Rico was found hanging in his jail cell shortly after his arraignment.

Carnage still prevailed, but it was off the FBI and local law enforcement radar. The Bobrovs were thirsty for blood, but revenge will forever triumph those seeking power.

Many of Kirill's men, including Viktor, the man I'm wordlessly commanding to stand down before he slits Detective Franco's throat, jumped ship when Kirill's fleet began to sink.

Viktor's desertion of the sanction he was born in has served him well the past three years as will his ability to follow orders when he backs away from Detective Franco with only the slightest groan.

Having one of my men kill Detective Franco would be the equivalent of snorting powdered sugar off a whore's breasts—unsatisfying and lackluster.

I'd rather toy with him for a little longer before showing him who really runs this town.

It isn't a man who earns forty thousand a year.

Besides, there's nothing wrong with having enemies. They ensure life remains interesting. If I've learned anything in my almost twenty-nine years, it is enemies who keep things honest. The men you class as family are who you need to watch the closest.

The man I call "father" assures this truth never strays far from my mind. He wanted a son. My mother birthed him his demise. He just doesn't know it yet.

After securing zip ties around my wrists, Detective Franco yanks me to my feet. While he walks me to his unmarked cruiser, I take in the tossed-up nightclub.

Like all fights I commence, my crew was eager to back me up. Several members of the Petretti crew lie lifeless on the battered wood floors of a nightclub I purchased not long after my twenty-first birthday. The flutter in the bloody spit in the corners of their mouths reveals they're still breathing.

They're down for the count.

Knocked out.

Lucky to be alive.

They were given reprieve since they weren't the ones standing before the court.

When Rico died, I took up his position of judge, jury, and executioner for the Popov reign. It forced me to mature and look at things from another perspective, and it's the sole reason I only stabbed the plaintiff in the neck instead of slitting his throat as craved.

I issued mercy—shockingly.

It was the first time, and in all honesty, I don't see it happening again any time soon.

Leniency is for the weak.

I learned that the hard way thirteen years ago.

A blood-smeared grin curls my lips when Detective Franco advises me to watch my head a meager second before he slams it into the roof of his cruiser.

He's pissed. Justly so. It's not every day a law-abiding citizen chooses to slip into bed with a mafia prince.

I treated his sister like a real-life motherfucking princess, only palming her off to my men once I'd had my fill, which was a record-breaking eight hours.

Attachments don't work for me.

Never have.

Never will.

Despite Detective Franco's beliefs, his baby sister isn't being forced to stay at Clarks, my offsite compound two miles from the Popovs' heavily manned quarters. None of the whores are there against their will. They stay with the hope I'll make one of them my queen.

There's a fat chance of that ever happening, but as long as they keep my dick warm, there's no reason to kill their eagerness. The more I keep their hope alive, the better they serve my men. My crew works hard, so it's only fair they play hard as well. Hell is even hotter when you're surrounded by tits, ass, and blow.

Detective Franco wants to smash the smirk off my face with his fists when I say, "I'll be sure to tell Alice you said hello when I walk away without a conviction today... once I've finished fucking her in the ass, of course."

It takes four riot officers to hold him back from his patrol car, but no amount of muscle can withhold the dozen threats he issues me. He tells me I'm going to regret the day I was born and how he'll ensure I spend my remaining years in hell.

I could tell him I'm already here, but where's the fun in that?

2

JUSTINE

Twenty-eight arrest warrants and fourteen DUIs in the past two years alone, plus a long list of felonies that fill a four-page dossier, all achieved before his twenty-ninth birthday, which is only two short weeks away.

I drift my eyes to my mentor, Mr. Fletcher, bulldog defense attorney and general all-around badass. "How is he not serving thirty to life?"

He flashes me a ruthless grin, sending the giddiness in my head to my stomach. "Because he had a man like me working for him, but with his lawyer vanishing, we have a perfect opportunity to secure him on our books. We want this client, Justine, even more than Clay wants to bed the assistant district attorney."

Stumped for a better reply, I smile. I've only been interning at Schluter & Fletcher for the past three months, but I'm already aware of Clay's hope to get frisky with Sasha Sheridan. His interests are abundantly clear even when they're clashing in the courtroom.

Before I can issue a response respectful for a first-year law graduate, a female police officer cracks open a secure entrance in the Las Vegas PD arsenal of properties.

She scans our frozen frames while propping the door open with her curvy hip.

I'm not offended when her gaze lingers on Mr. Fletcher longer than me. For a man ten years my senior, he has looks rivaling those featured in *People's* sexiest man competition. He's handsome, with inky-black hair, unique-colored eyes, and a body someone who works eighty-plus hours a week shouldn't have.

"Mr. Fletcher. Ms. Walsh."

The unnamed officer's formal greeting indicates she's well-informed about the individuals she's sneaking into the secured premises. Our location is so guarded I didn't know it existed until Mr. Fletcher's Bentley pulled into the underground entrance.

Mr. Fletcher showcases another one of his famous traits: his schmoozing voice. "Roselyn, it's been too long. We should catch up for a drink soon."

He kisses Roselyn's cheek, convincing their pasty-white coloring to shift to a vibrant shade of pink.

Hair falls into my eyes when I greet her with a chin dip. After returning my wordless greeting, Roselyn gestures to a dimly lit corridor on our right. "This way." She shuffles her feet to face the dark hallway. "He's being processed for a lineup. Sasha is already on-site."

As I snap our potential client's textbook-size police file shut, Mr. Fletcher guides me inside with his hand on my lower back. My pulse quickens when we enter the windowless building. It's sooty and damp, even without a dust bunny in sight, but I'm unsure if that's the cause for the eerie sentiment thickening the air.

I've always been skittish about this part of my internship, but the butterflies in my stomach aren't the ones I usually face when combing police headquarters for prospective clients. It's tense and exciting at the same time—like I'm moments away from unearthing greatness or free-falling into disaster.

After a turbulent few years, I hope it's the former.

When we reach a reinforced door marked "private," Mr. Fletcher inputs a six-digit code into the electronic security lock before opening the door and gesturing for me to enter.

"It's showtime." His tone is as jazzy as his insinuation.

My heart races when I slip into the cramped space. Two men are dressed head to toe in black in the far corner of the room. Their attire is the unofficial color of law enforcement, so that's not the cause for my clammy response—it's their inquisitive glances and tantalizing grins.

I understand their curious gawks—it's not every day a twenty-five-year-old first-year intern presents as a lead attorney on a case—but their grins are a ball game I'm still unfamiliar with.

For the first fifteen years of my life, I was the epitome of a nerd. My nose rarely left the inside of a book. Only when I grew into my lanky legs and developed breasts most men notice long before my aquamarine eyes did my social status change.

My newly acquired assets not only crowned me Ms. Spring Fling two years in a row, but they also secured me an internship at one of the most lucrative law firms in the country.

I'm not saying Mr. Fletcher's business associate, Mr. Schluter, hired me solely because I fill a bikini top like no other, but the cut-throat cunningness I've witnessed from him the past two months has made me hesitant. Certain female assets can lure clientele even someone with Mr. Fletcher's ninety-six percent win rate can't secure.

Although I'm disgruntled I work in a chauvinistic industry stuck in the Stone Age, the fire in my belly to achieve goals I made four years ago ensures my feet remain planted on the ground. I moved to Vegas to be trained by the best. I'm doing precisely that under Mr. Fletcher's wing.

He trains his interns with a hands-on approach. He brainstorms out loud and includes us in every decision he makes. It's an invigorating learning curve that holds more value than three years in law school.

Legal defense isn't for the faint of heart. You dodge grenades thrown by clients, all while representing them to the best of your ability. It's an exhausting and demoralizing position, but one I'm growing to love more than breathing.

When the gleeful glint in the detectives' eyes shift to disdain, I slide my hand down my fire-engine-red skirt. I must have a stain I haven't noticed. Otherwise what would be the cause of their sudden change in demeanor?

The reasoning behind their expressions comes to light when Mr. Fletcher stops at my side. Criminals love Mr. Fletcher. Detectives... not so much. More often than not, he has his clients' convictions thrown out before they enter a courtroom. He's shrewd, emasculating, and the first man I'd call if I were ever arrested.

"Justine, this is Bill Hammond and Joe Franco." Mr. Fletcher waves his hand to the gentlemen gawking at me, their glances nowhere near friendly. "Bill and Joe, this is Justine, a soon-to-be junior associate at Schluter & Fletcher."

My heart beats triple time at his mention of career advancement. When interviewed for my position, I was informed my internship would last a maximum of twenty-four months.

Although I was turned off at the idea of moving across the country for a non-permanent role, nothing could sway my decision to accept the position. Months of research couldn't alter the facts. Schluter & Fletcher is the best criminal defense firm in the country, so this is where I need to be.

Not long after I accept a handshake from Bill and Joe, a young man with a battered face enters the room on the tail of Assistant District Attorney Sasha Sheridan. The extensive injuries to his face make his age hard to identify, but I'd guess he is in his late twenties, early thirties. His crew-cut hairstyle barely conceals the gang-related tattoos etched on his skull, and his green eyes are lifeless and hollow.

His gang affiliation is evident even without the Roman numerals tattooed on his right cheek. Before they disbanded three years ago, the Petretti crew were well-known in my hometown of Hopeton, Florida. I've heard rumors that they aimed to revive the debunked group, but this is the first solid proof I've seen since the death of their leader. The complainant's cheek tattoo looks fresh, like he recently joined their faction.

After issuing Mr. Fletcher a nasty stink-eye that reveals their numerous battles over the past ten years, Sasha directs her client to a glass wall blocked out by a sizable red curtain. The client we want to secure is standing behind that two-way mirror with an additional four or five inmates brought in tonight.

Las Vegas County PD is the most bustling department I've seen in my short law career. You'd think weekends would be their busiest nights. They aren't. Thrill seekers, gamblers, and locals understand that weeknights are ideal for creating a ruckus. If they want their case brought before the judge prior to a weekend stint in lockup, Thursday afternoon is the absolute cutoff time to be arrested.

Our client's participation in an all-out brawl late Friday afternoon has me curious about his motive. His criminal file reveals he's a born-and-raised Nevada resident, so he must be aware his brush with the law this afternoon will see him spending the July Fourth weekend in a four-by-four concrete cell with a lidless toilet and twenty-four-seven surveillance.

I'm stumped as to why he'd take the risk. Is he hoping his unlawful ways will excuse him from the weekend festivities? Or is he so confident in his legal team that he has no cause for worry?

Mr. Fletcher's deep timbre drags my thoughts back to the present. "Justine?"

When I peer at him with a quirked brow, he nudges his head to the glass petition expanding the entire left side of the room, soundlessly requesting I follow him.

Within seconds, our position mimics the one I've witnessed numerous times in the past several months. The defensive team stands on the left, while the ADA, her client, and the lead investigators on the case stand to our right.

Usually a judge would have a prime position in the middle of the congregation, but since this is a lineup and not an arraignment, that space remains empty.

I breathe out slowly, easing the nerves fluttering in my stomach. Although I'm conscious the defendants can't see me, a peculiar sensation overwhelms me. I've never understood fearful excitement, but I'm confident that's what I am experiencing. It's an enthralling feeling that could grow as addictive as a jury siding with the defense on a seemingly un-winnable case.

I jump out of my skin when Mr. Fletcher leans into my side and mutters, "Number five." He keeps his voice low, ensuring the complainant doesn't hear his disclosure of our client's identification. "Nikolai, a Russian mafia prince."

As I lick my dry lips, my eyes drift down the line of defendants, only stopping when I reach suspect Number five. My heart rate turns calamitous when my gaze connects with a pair of icy-blue eyes staring straight at me. Nikolai's stare is so direct I glance over my shoulder, certain he's staring at someone behind me.

He isn't.

Other than Mr. Fletcher on my left, our quarter of the room is void of another soul.

After soothing a scratch impinging my throat with a quick swallow, I scan Nikolai's body, uncertain which god-crafted feature to categorize first. He has the glare of the devil, the sneer of a murderer, and the body of an Adonis.

Hold on, what?

Even if my assessment is accurate, it's inappropriate to say about a prospective client. Integrity is my most vital asset, so I'm appalled by my judgment and confused as to why I blurted it without consideration. I don't look at men like that. Well, I do, just not during a lineup. My perving is generally reserved for men not facing attempted murder charges.

Excusing my peculiar behavior as a repercussion of a long week, I return my eyes to Nikolai. No matter how many ways I look at it, the ache of my pulse is warranted.

Nikolai is wearing nothing but ripped jeans and an unforgiving smirk. His bare feet are planted shoulder-width apart, and the sheet of cardboard he's holding in front of his tattooed chest barely covers the thick line of dark hair flowing from his belly button to the waistband of his designer briefs. His body is divine. Its only letdown is the faint bruises mottling his sun-kissed skin.

Even if I weren't aware of his extensive criminal history, his persona screams bad boy. His demeanor is so compelling that I'm certain women sense it from a mile away. He's the reason fathers buy guns and women buy sex toys. He is the ultimate representation of sex, intrigue, and mystery while also displaying he'll be your worst nightmare.

Although his face shows signs of a fight, his is nowhere near as battered as the man accusing him of assault. His left brow has a gash similar to one a beer bottle would make when struck across a temple, and his right cheek has two puncture wounds approximately the width of a dime.

His hands are bloody and bruised, though I'm confident not all the blood is his. His teeth are straight and white, and his stubble-covered jawline is ruggedly handsome. He has the perfect body for gracing the pages of *Men's Fitness* magazine—he merely needs to dull down his mafia sneer.

Even with his criminal activities more comprehensive than Mr.

Fletcher's clients combined, I'm sure he has no trouble attracting the ladies. I'm confident they vie for his attention as intensely as every defense attorney in this county would fight to secure him as their client.

It shames me to admit, but we're only in this room because Mr. Fletcher's schmoozing is as fierce as his astuteness. If it weren't, we'd be camped out in the foyer with the other fifteen-plus defense attorneys we passed on our way to the concealed entrance of this building.

My eyes stray from Nikolai's unruly spiked hair to the ADA when she questions, "Can you identify the man who assaulted you today?" She peers at the complainant, whose face has grown gaunter since he entered the room.

As if sensing the direction of our proceedings, Nikolai's steel blue gaze drifts to the right. His extensive criminal history guarantees he's well-informed on how these proceedings unfold, but I'm still surprised by the accuracy of his stare.

Like when he peered at me, his gaze homes in directly on the complainant. He stares down his accuser, his glare more threatening than the veins bulging in his biceps.

I crank my neck to the side when the battered man answers, "No."

Sasha balks, shocked by his reply. I can understand her bewilderment. From the information disclosed during our commute, I was sure this case was a slam dunk for the prosecution.

Nikolai was arrested at the scene. His fingerprints are on the weapon used during the assault, and there are more than thirty eyewitnesses. Unless there was a major kerfuffle with the paperwork, the complainant is either mistaken or lying.

Sasha double-checks, certain she misheard her client. "Are you sure?"

The complainant nods. "Yep. I don't see him." His nerves are uncontained even with his short reply.

Joe rises from his seat and moseys toward the accused. "You don't recognize the man who assaulted you?" His voice is as swaggered as his stride. "The guy I dragged off you not even an hour ago isn't in that lineup?" He points his index finger to the glass partition, behind which a grinning Nikolai is standing, not the least concerned that his freedom is dangling on a fragile thread.

The complainant's throat works hard to swallow. "Nope. Don't see him. I swear."

Mr. Fletcher groans, recognizing our hope of securing Nikolai as a client is slim if he isn't positively ID'd in a lineup. Without being identified, he'll be scot-free before the ink on his fingers dries.

I shuffle on my feet so it appears as if I'm facing Nikolai, but I project my voice toward Mr. Fletcher. "Do you speak Italian?"

"What?" he replies, my voice too low for him to hear.

"Do you speak Italian?" I repeat, louder this time.

His brows stitch. "Some. I'm bilingual, just not as extensively as you."

A grin stretches across my face, pleased he perused my application before accepting me as his intern. Other than stating my multilingual talents on my resume, I keep my language fluency on the down-low, often finding my love of languages more valuable when people are unaware I can decipher what they're saying.

"Ask the complainant if he's prepared for the repercussions he'll suffer when his crew discovers he fears a rival."

Mr. Fletcher stares at me in confusion. I don't know if his perplexity stems from my request or how I'm aware of the complainant's gang affiliation.

I quote the infamous saying he utilizes anytime he's losing a disagreement. "Trust me."

After a roll of his eyes that looks more sophisticated than it should, Mr. Fletcher asks, "*Cosa dirà il tuo equipaggio quando scoprirà che temi un rivale?*" Conscious his Italian may not be as fluent as it once was, he speaks slowly.

The accuser's eyes snap to Mr. Fletcher, their anger doubling from the accusation that he's a coward. Although Mr. Fletcher didn't say that, the insinuation warrants his angered response.

The battered man's words fire off his tongue like venom. "I fear no one."

I inch back when he spits at Mr. Fletcher's feet. I inwardly sigh when his vile body product misses my exposed-toe pumps.

Mr. Fletcher's pricy shoes aren't as lucky.

When the complainant grins a blood-smeared smirk, thinking he has Mr. Fletcher panicked, Mr. Fletcher straightens his spine and rolls his shoulders.

He has four older brothers. Nothing intimidates him.

"If you have nothing to fear, you'll be honest." He steps over the spit not coating his shoes. "You know the man who trampled your face is standing behind that glass. You're just too scared to admit it." His tone is drenched with a superiority you'd expect a man of his stature to hold. "If you want to return to your crew as a hero, take down a rival instead of cowardly covering for one."

Sasha attempts to cite an objection to Mr. Fletcher goading her client, but she's so stumped by him aiding her case that her mouth remains tight-lipped, leaving only her eyes to express her condemnation.

"What do you have to fear? By the time he's out on bail, you'll be with your brothers, talking up how you took down a member of the Popov crew."

The complainant's eyes flare with disbelief. "I won't have to testify?"

Although his words are strong, the quiver in his jaw gives away his true defense. He's petrified. I can't blame him. I've only been subjected to our client's aura through bulletproof glass, and my insides haven't stopped shaking. He gives the impression of a man not to be messed with... unless you plan to eat via a straw for the rest of your life.

The plaintiff glares at Mr. Fletcher without remorse. "If this goes to trial, I won't testify. I'm not a snitch."

Sasha attempts to reply to her client, but Mr. Fletcher beats her. "You'll only testify if this case goes to trial. I guarantee that will not happen. This case is cut and dry. It won't reach preliminary stage."

His guarantee may seem fraudulent to an outsider, but I believe every word he speaks. He'd rather lick the shoes of the detectives glaring at him than have Nikolai sit before a jury of his peers. He'd even sacrifice his firstborn child. That's how influential a client like Nikolai is for a firm like Schluter & Fletcher. He's a defense attorney's equivalent of finding the pot of gold under the rainbow. He and his criminal tendencies are an endless money pit.

"All right." The complainant gingerly nods. "I'll admit, I see the accused behind the partition."

Sasha's shoulders loosen as her eyes drift to the detectives on her right. She smiles at them, revealing her every wish has been granted. I also smile, pleased we coerced the complainant into submission while praying our win will smother the worry brewing in my gut.

Tonight, we had a victory.

My intuition is warning me I can't make the same guarantee for the rest of the weekend.

3

NIKOLAI

"Where the fuck is Erik?"

I speak to the officer guiding me to a conference room in Russian to ensure no one overhears us. The eye tattoo peeking out the cuff of his long-sleeve shirt identifies that he's one of us, much less the Soviet Union flag hidden in the cornea of his realistic tattoo. They're indicators of his bratva ties. The eye means he's forever watching, and the flag sanctifies where his loyalties lay.

It isn't with the men in blue surrounding him.

After taking a sharp left, he replies in Russian, "Numerous attempts to contact him have failed to yield results."

He takes another left before steering me toward a room I'm all too familiar with. It's where I gave Carmichael enough evidence to convict Vladimir, the man who raised me, to three lifetimes behind bars.

Alas, I was the only fool who faced prosecution all those years ago.

"We're trying another angle." He coughs to cover his whispered words when our trek has us veering past Carmichael and the redhead I spotted earlier on the other side of what was meant to be a two-way mirror.

Since the transmittance of light hadn't altered, I didn't solely see the quiver of the plaintiff's thighs when my eyes locked with him, I was also bombarded with the features of a beautiful scarlet-haired woman.

Her expression when we undertook an intense stare-down was angelic, almost too pure, but there was a hunger in her eyes that revealed she was thirsty, and it had nothing to do with the fact we're in the middle of a desert in the peak of summer.

As I walk past the redhead eyeballing, her breathing becomes shallow and mouse-like. She's even more fascinating up close. Her lips are meaty and sheened with the slightest bit of gloss, her nose is as petite as her frame, and her tits gain more than the attention of my cock. They also have the eye of a handful of male officers as well.

Officers who'll be dead by the end of the day if they don't adhere to the voiceless threats beaming from my slit gaze.

I don't know what it is about this woman, but she's spiked an instant fascination out of me. I usually don't give a fuck about anyone, but I'm more than curious to unearth the cause of the slightest sliver of silver on her neck.

The faintness of her scar exposes her injury occurred a few years back, but she's concealed it in a way that reveals she's not a fan of it being seen.

She shouldn't be ashamed of it.

Scars are medals of bravery.

I wear mine with honor.

When the once-bustling corridor empties, I flare my nostrils so I can suck in the redhead's scent. It is as intoxicating as my impish mind predicted. She smells like a mix of roguishness and innocence, like a dream in the middle of a nightmare.

She doesn't belong here, but I plan to keep her here anyway.

When my entrance into the holding room sees her drawing in her first breath in almost ten seconds, I slant my head to hide my smirk.

I want to say this is the first time I've made someone forget to breathe, but if a peacock doesn't fan his feathers, who will?

After shuffling to the king's spot at the end of the long table, I slump into an office chair before raising my eyes to the unnamed officer.

He senses my command before I can announce it, and even

quicker than that, the shackles circling my wrists and ankles are dumped on the floor.

Even with four heavily armed riot officers in each corner of the large space, I could leave now if I wanted.

I would if I weren't feeding off the friction in the air like a crack addict seeking his next high.

I was born and bred in Vegas, so I will die before I'll ever side-step the chance to do something risky. Whether it's my life at stake or someone else's, the thrill associated with watching the danger unfold can't be achieved any other way.

People say murderers are the lowest of the low, but have you ever wondered what brought them to that place to begin with? Most parents raise their sons to be sports stars and musicians. Mine raised me to be a cold-blooded killer.

We all have our place in the world.

Mine just happens to be in your nightmares.

"*дымы.*" One word, and a packet of cigarettes and a lighter slide across the table from the other end.

After plucking a cancer stick from the recently opened packet and placing it between my lips, I raise my eyes to my gift recipient. I'm not surprised when the steely blue eyes of Detective Joe Franco reflect back at me. We were pulled apart by his peers long before we had finished our 'conversation.'

His threat was only dispersed in pieces.

Mine is already in production.

"If you are here to make amends, you're too late. *Это отправлено отплыл давно.*"

He tries to act nonchalant to my reply like he doesn't understand a word I speak. His poor acting skills are one of the reasons he should have never worked as an undercover cop.

Detective Franco and Bill Hammond are one of the many law enforcement officers who unsuccessfully bid to infiltrate the Popov compound over the last decade. They got as far as the front door before I sniffed out the rats hiding beneath sleeves of tattoos and scarred faces.

They left with additional scars, but their lives were spared as a warning to others what would happen if they dared to double-cross the true owners of Las Vegas.

After mockingly sniffing at Detective Franco, goading him to start what we didn't finish, I shift my eyes to a female police officer whose hips were designed for fucking. They're curvy and round but nowhere near as tempting as the redhead's in the hall. I've seen her around, but her name is slipping my mind.

Thank fuck name tags were invented.

From the way Detective Hammond stands protectively at Roselyn's side, I'm going to assume he doesn't realize the gleam in her eyes isn't there for him. She wants a bigger piece of the pie than he can offer her—the cream of the criminal justice crop. She wants the number one defense attorney in the country, and she's willing to face a firing squad just for the chance to warm his sheets.

Although I'd rather Carmichael live a miserably bleak existence, if Roselyn is occupying his time, I'll have a better chance at pretending I didn't notice the vein in his neck pulsating faster when the redhead leaned into his side. Then perhaps my wish to kill him will simmer to the back of my mind for a few weeks. Waters are already tempestuous, so I shouldn't add a murder conviction into the mix—regrettably.

Roselyn takes in a sharp breath when I reveal how easy it is to triumph your competitors by staying one step ahead of them. "What does Carmichael want?" When her lips twitch like she's preparing to lie, I warn, "Lying to me is punishable by death. Is your wish to scour your nails down Carmichael's back really worth your life?"

The silence in the room proves what I've always known. Wearing a badge doesn't mean your life is more valuable than the person next to you. Roselyn's life was threatened in front of six of her peers, yet not a word is spoken in her defense. Detective Hammond looks like he wants to jump in, but he's too stunned by Roselyn's lack of denial to fathom a reply.

"Who said Vegas is where chivalry goes to die?"

While smirking like a smug prick, I light the cigarette hanging out of my mouth, drag a long drawl of nicotine-laced smoke into my lungs, then return my focus to the officer who's more undercover than anyone in this room. "Grant Carmichael five minutes of my time." The excitement brightening Roselyn's face dulls when I add, "But the redhead will lead our exchange. If she doesn't, my talk with Carmichael will end with him losing his life."

Over our conversation and my inability to act passé about my interest in Carmichael's new lap dog, I stab out my half-smoked cigarette on the armrest, slouch low in my chair, rest my bare feet on the tabletop, then shut my eyes, blocking out the world I'm more than ready to rule once my vengeance has been achieved.

Only a stupid man believes he'll live forever, and only a jaded one wants to. I'm neither stupid nor boring, and I can't wait for the unnamed redhead to become aware of that.

4

JUSTINE

When a knock trickles in my ears, I stop splashing cool water onto my cheeks.

"Nikolai has been charged and processed for departure to Clark County Detention Center. He's in a holding room, waiting for his legal team to be brought in. Roselyn has secured us five minutes with him. The team is ready to move in."

"Okay. Just a minute," I reply to Mr. Fletcher.

While patting my face dry with a paper towel, I raise my eyes to the vanity mirror. Although I'm running on less than three hours of sleep, my eyes are surprisingly bright, enhanced by a set of thick lashes my Italian grandmother gifted me. My cheeks are rosy, compliments of the numerous dashes I make between the courthouse and Schluter & Fletcher every day, and my hair is a vibrant red. I look well put-together... if I could hide my dilated eyes.

Even spending the past hour pacing the halls hasn't eased the knot in my stomach. It's so tight I feel ill. Although coercing a client is nothing new for a defense attorney, something about this feels wrong.

Aren't we meant to protect our client under the presumption of innocence until proven otherwise? Not throw him to the wolves while we watch from the sidelines.

The turbulent storm inside me doubles when my eyes take in

the two red scars on my right shoulder. My marks have faded with the years, but they're a clear reminder of why I sit across from men like Nikolai every day when all I'd wanted to be was an architect when I grew up.

This isn't about me.

It is about him.

Breathing out my nerves, I adjust my hair to sit in front of my shoulders before I exit the washroom. My quick strides down the hall falter when I feel the heat of a gaze. Mr. Fletcher is scanning my body—not once but twice.

Attraction regularly fires between us, but my wish to keep our relationship professional means I've never acted on it.

Don't misconstrue my confession. My days are filled with flirty comments, brief touches, and enough electricity to light up the billboards on the strip. Still, it's nothing more than a playful banter associated with a flirtatious work environment.

My desire to keep our relationship professional is why I call him Mr. Fletcher. His formal title reminds me that he is my supervisor—not a prospective bed companion.

Although the way he's eyeing me now, with fascination brimming in his heavy-hooded gaze, I'm beginning to wish my work ethic wasn't so strong. I can't remember the last time I had a fun-filled, no-strings-attached exchange with a member of the opposite sex.

"Ready?" Mr. Fletcher asks when I join him in the hallway, my steps spirited from his amorous glance. "It's time to bring home the bacon."

"If Nikolai's rap sheet is anything to go by, we're about to bring home the entire pig."

Growling at my assessment, Mr. Fletcher opens the frosted glass door he's standing next to. Testosterone smacks into me hard and fast when I step into the spacious room. Four heavily armed guards fill each corner of the square-shaped space, but they aren't the cause of the virile scent depriving the air of oxygen. It's the man with glacier-blue eyes and a distinct aura of danger.

Nikolai sits at the end of a large boardroom table. His bare feet rest on the tabletop, and his arms are crossed in front of his slow-rising torso. He's lazed back in an office chair, relaxed and without worry. I would assume he's sleeping if his ticking jaw didn't announce he's detected our presence.

For a man facing a seven-year prison sentence, he's way too cocky for my liking. Confident clients are the hardest to work with. When their dominant personalities clash with Mr. Fletcher's commanding persona, more times than not it turns into a battle of the alphas instead of maintaining the integrity of the game. I hope to be proven wrong this time, but my intuition is usually spot-on.

Once three junior associates from our firm join us, Mr. Fletcher braces his palms on the tabletop. "Mr. Popov, my name is Carmichael Fletcher. I'm a defense attorney at—"

"I know who you are." Nikolai's deep accented voice is molten enough to singe. It's gritty and raw, with a touch of sexiness I can't help but notice.

After returning his feet to the floor, Nikolai raises his head. Air snags halfway to my lungs when our gazes collide for the quickest second. Our eye contact is brief but long enough for me to declare he has the beauty of a shark: visually appealing but with a dangerous edge that warns you not to get too close.

"I'm not interested in anything you're selling." His tone indicates today isn't his first meeting with Mr. Fletcher. "Wasn't interested thirteen years ago. Sure as hell ain't interested now."

My heart beats in an unnatural rhythm when he slants his head to the side and locks his arctic gaze with mine. He stares at me for mere seconds, but it feels like the earth circles the sun many times. His gaze is familiar yet concerning.

"Unless you're offering an incentive to sweeten the honeypot, the five minutes Officer Roselyn negotiated with Carmichael in the hope of slipping between his sheets is up."

I gasp, shocked by his suggestion that we negotiate. I am interested in discovering how he believes I can sweeten the honeypot, but wanting to be professional, I harness my curiosity—barely.

Upon taking my silence as a rejection, his tapered gaze strays back to Mr. Fletcher. "The door is that way." His jerked chin boosts his dismissal.

Mr. Fletcher stands tall at the end of the boardroom table, not threatened by Nikolai's slit-eyed gaze. Nothing against Mr. Fletcher—he's a brilliant defense attorney and an even better mentor—but he must be insane. Nikolai's vast police file shows he's not a man to mess with, and his scowl deepens by the second.

Worry burns my esophagus when Mr. Fletcher alters his plan of attack. "Now is not the time for stubbornness, Nikolai. You were positively identified in a lineup. Your fingerprints were found on the shattered bottle lodged in the neck of the claimant, and the DA has video evidence of the alleged assault."

I can only assume his last declaration is an assumption, as no video data was noted in the chain of evidence. Considering how many surveillance cameras line the Vegas strip, some evidence could have been recorded, but with Nikolai's family's reputation so fierce all his previous arrests were swept under the rug when they reached preliminary charges, I doubt the footage will remain uncorrupted for long.

"So?" Nikolai slumps into his chair, confident he's holding the trump card. "Are you advising me to be worried?"

"Yes," Mr. Fletcher replies. "Unless you're a foolish man, you should pay careful attention to every word I speak. I am your only guarantee of leaving this room without shackles cuffed to your wrists. The courts close in less than an hour. If you don't do everything I suggest, you'll be holed up in here the entire long weekend instead of sniffing crack from a hooker's tits while fucking another in the ass."

My heart slips into my stomach. I've heard him quote similarly ballsy statements over the past three months, but this one feels different. It's more personal, and, in all honesty, sleazy.

I tuck away my bother when Nikolai connects his eyes with mine. His gaze is brimming with condescending amusement. "What do you think, *Ангел*? Should I follow his every word to a T?"

When Mr. Fletcher attempts to answer on my behalf, Nikolai slices his hand through the air, stalling both Mr. Fletcher and my heart.

"I want to hear what she has to say, considering my decision will impact her as much as it will me."

My brows stitch, displaying my confusion at his statement.

How will his decision affect me?

Spotting my bewilderment, Nikolai smirks a grin that does stupid things to my insides. "If I agree for Carmichael to be my counsel, his celebration will entail a part of your body wrapped around his cock, so I'm interested in discovering if that is something you want or something you've already had?"

I anticipate my colleagues to react with shock, so you can imagine my bewilderment when they don't bat an eyelid.

The only one left breathless is me.

I thought the mutual attraction firing between Mr. Fletcher and me was well-concealed.

Clearly my assumptions were wrong.

Even a man as conceited as Nikolai spotted the attraction between us. I don't know if I should be pleased or panicked by that notion.

While snickering at my slack-jawed response, Nikolai snags a cigarette packet out of his jeans pocket. His arms flex when he lights the white stick dangling between his quirked lips.

"I knew I remained shirtless for a reason," he mutters, noticing the direction of my gaze. "Up here is for the thinking. Down there's for the dancing."

He taps his index finger on his temple. Thankfully he leaves the second half of his statement for me to decipher on my own.

I shift my eyes to the side, mortified he caught my perverted gaze. He finds my pitiful defense maneuver amusing. His heavenly gruff chuckle rolls over me like liquid ecstasy, hitting every one of my hot buttons.

"I always thought red was the color of the devil. Now I'm not so sure."

The dampness between my legs doubles when his eyes scan my inflamed neck and cheeks. After tossing his cigarette pack across the table to me, he sinks into his chair before taking a substantial draw on his now-lit cigarette.

As smoke billows out of his nose, he stares at me as if I am the only person in the room. For years I've dealt with looks of pity, but his heavy-hooded gaze has nothing to do with sympathy. His watchful stare bombards me with reckless thoughts—*desperate thoughts*.

I want to deflect his attention, but I'm unsure how. So, instead, I stand frozen, stunned that a man I hardly know can muddle my usually clear head. I shouldn't be shocked. As I stand across from

Nikolai now, mindless with need, I'm having a hard time recognizing myself.

When Nikolai's tongue clears a drop of ash from his bottom lip, the cocky glint in his eyes triples. "Not yet happened, but you're not against the idea." His jaunty tone strengthens his interpretation of my non-relationship with Mr. Fletcher. "Trust me, we'd have a lot more fun." A bold wink seals his pledge.

Determined to show I'm not the naïve imbecile I've been portraying the past ten minutes, I straighten my spine.

Nikolai's icy gaze sparkles with challenge when he spots my determined stance. He silently goads me, daring me to protest his insinuation that I want to get freaky with my boss.

I use his ignorance of the rules as a deflection. "This is a government building. You're not allowed to smoke in here."

Unmoved by my sneer, he takes another hefty suck on his cigarette. Once his lungs are brimming with smoke, he mutters, "This building is situated on grounds I own in a town I rule. I can do whatever the fuck I want." His teeth graze his bottom lip as he adds, "Even you." His last sentence is so soft that if the pulse in my pussy didn't intensify, I wouldn't have known he said it.

When the glint in his eyes turns blinding, I cross my arms in front of my chest and drop my gaze to the tabletop. I'm not here to engage in a battle more brutal than the Cold War. I'm here purely in a professional capacity.

Unappreciative of the early white flag in our battle, Nikolai drums his knuckles over the exact spot I'm staring at, soundlessly requesting my focus back to him.

"Smart and beautiful," he mutters when I return my eyes to his. "Who would have known?"

The long chain of smoke spilling from his quirked-with-amusement lips burns my eyes, but I keep my arms glued to my chest, refusing to bow to his arrogance for the second time in less than a minute.

Once bitten, twice shy.

As silence creeps on us, the air thickens. The tension between us is so hot you'd swear we're the only two occupants in the room. It's as if God is sparring an angel against a devil to see who will reign supreme. It's a pity God failed to get the memo that I'm anything but saintly.

My eyes dance between Nikolai's when he mutters, "There are devilish thoughts in the most angelic minds, *Ангел*." The gleam in his eyes switches to one I don't recognize before he continues. "I can't wait to hear yours."

Although shocked he read my inner monologue, I don't get to showcase my bewilderment. I'm too busy calming my heart rate from Michelle unexpectedly whispering in my ear, "What's an *Ahren*?" I was so fixated on identifying the glint brightening Nikolai's eyes that I failed to notice her sneaking up on me.

It's the fight of my life to drag my eyes away from Nikolai, but when I do, I notice the green flecks in Michelle's hazel eyes are barely visible since her pupils are swamping her cornea. Her lips are cracked from running her teeth over them, and her cheeks are hollow and white. She appears as confronted as I am about meeting a mafia prince in the flesh.

Although, I'm confident her insides are quaking with unbridled fear. Mine aren't entirely based on distress—I'm also aroused. Don't ask me to swear on a Bible, but I'm certain fearful excitement is the cause of the heat creeping up my neck. As is the shameless glance of a blue-eyed devil.

"He's called you *Ahren* numerous times, so it can't be an accidental slip in name," Michelle says, promptly reminding me I never answered her question. "Do you know what it means?"

Before a syllable is fired off my tongue, Nikolai's sexy voice trickles into my ears. "How far are you willing to go to secure me as your client? Will you dance with the devil? Or sleep in Satan's bed?"

I return my eyes to Nikolai, anticipating his focus to be fixed on Mr. Fletcher.

It isn't.

His eyes are arrested on me, as dark and haunting as ever.

I remain quiet, dazed. My response makes me look daft, but I have no plans to alter it. His eyes reveal what his negotiations pertained to. I'm simply unwilling to fall for his latest power trip.

Nikolai's tongue runs over the small cut on his top lip as he revels in my muted response. I swear, his pupils expand when the tangy flavor of blood overwhelms his taste buds.

"I'm tempted as fuck to discover how loud you scream, but are my desires potent enough to work with this *идиот*? I already have one lawyer breathing down my neck; do I really want another?" Nikolai mutters more to himself than me.

I tighten my arms over my chest, praying it will hide my body's inane reaction to discovering he finds me tempting. My lack of sleep must be playing havoc with my mind, as I've never been so poorly misguided.

Mr. Fletcher snaps my attention back to the task at hand. "You know I don't play fair, Nikolai. Fair is not a word in my dictionary. Justine was brought in to entice your less astute head. Clearly her presence has piqued your interest."

My jaw slackens as my eyes rocket to Mr. Fletcher. I knew I wasn't hired solely because of my perfect bar scores and exemplary attendance record, but still, having him admit it in front of a client is shocking and, if I'm being honest, demoralizing.

"But Justine isn't just a knockout. She's the shrewdest member of my team. If you don't want to sleep in a cell this evening, she's your signed guarantee that will not happen. Not maybe. Not possibly. Will not happen," Mr. Fletcher continues, dampening the anger bubbling in my veins.

"I have an attorney. I don't need another," Nikolai replies with his narrowed gaze rapt on Mr. Fletcher, his voice the most vicious I've heard.

With a rueful grin revealing he's about to play his most lethal hand, Mr. Fletcher slides a piece of paper across the table to Nikolai. "Perhaps this will change your mind on who you want representing you."

If I could tear my eyes away from the veins thrumming in Nikolai's neck, I'd be enticed to discover what hand Mr. Fletcher just dealt, but since I'm stuck in a panicked trance, I keep my eyes locked on Nikolai, equally appalled and confused by my ditsy response.

My reaction can't be helped. The same peculiar feeling I got when walking into our secure location this afternoon is knotting my stomach again.

After what feels like an eternity, Nikolai drops his gaze to the sheet of paper he's clutching. Hostile silence deprives the air of oxygen as he reads the text on repeat. The longer he scans the document, the tighter he grips the paper.

Confident he has the facts straight, he raises his head and drifts his eyes to me. His gaze is more ruthless than any I've seen.

I stand taller, vainly trying to portray I'm not intimidated by his glance.

It's all a ruse. I'm shaking so much I feel like I'm on one of those vibrating machines at the gym. You know, the ones that jiggle the cellulite off your thighs. I won't need to visit my trainer for a month with how much I'm internally shaking. That is how wrathful Nikolai's glare is.

After he scrapes his hand across his chin, Nikolai's eyes stray to Mr. Fletcher. The volatility in them doubles when he warns, "If this is found to be untrue, the smile you're wearing will drop two inches when I slit your throat and watch you take your last breath."

His voice gives no indication his threat was meant to be playful. He is as upfront as his warning tone relayed.

Not intimidated by Nikolai's threat, Mr. Fletcher guarantees, "You have my word. What I'm presenting is true."

My eyes lower to the piece of paper when Nikolai dumps it on the tabletop. Although it's scrunched into a heap, I can still read one sentence inscribed on it.

Erik Monstrateo—FBI Agent No: 1183429

Air traps in my throat, stunned Mr. Fletcher dug the grave of a former colleague and friend. Erik left Schluter & Fletcher the month before I arrived in Las Vegas, but his essence is still embedded in my office's bones.

"Okay."

Nikolai stubs out his cigarette and stands from his chair. His meekest movement has the armed guards sitting on edge, cautious of his every move.

"You have one chance to prove your worth. If all charges against me are dismissed, I'll sign you as my counsel." Mr. Fletcher strives to interrupt Nikolai, but he continues speaking, foiling his endeavor to assert I'm only a first-year intern. "No misdemeanors, plea bargains, or community service. All charges are to be dropped without record."

"And?" I query when his demands seem unfinished.

I don't know the man standing in front of me—before reading his dossier during my travels to Las Vegas PD, I'd never heard of

Nikolai Popov—but something in his eyes tells me his list of demands is not yet finalized.

"And..." Nikolai draws out his one word as if it's an entire sentence.

My pulse thuds in my ears when he veers around the table and heads in my direction. His swagger is pompous and reeks of attitude. I'm certain a man of his stature, much less looks, wouldn't lack confidence, but I'm still stunned by his sheer self-assurance. He's so cocky I doubt he needs assistance with his latest debacle. We walked into his trap, gifting him a new set of toys to play with.

My breaths turn ragged when he stops to stand in front of me. His eyes are even more exquisite up close, as are his sculptured face and shirtless torso. The stubble on his chin can't dampen the razor-sharp cut of his jawline, and his lips appear as soft as a cloud.

When he sniffs my hair, Mr. Fletcher signals for the guards to move in. I raise my hand in the air, requesting them to stand down.

Years of studying criminal masterminds award me with the knowledge that this is a tactic Nikolai uses to siphon out the weak. If I fail this test, he will move on to the next set of pawns waiting in the wings, contending for his attention.

Furthermore, I'm not afraid of him. He intimidates me more than any man before him, but something deep in his eyes stops fear from being my first response.

The scent of cigarettes and alcohol lingers in Nikolai's wake when he drags his nose down my neck before trailing it along my collarbone. His attention mists my skin with sweat and moistens my panties as well.

I pop my eyes back open when I lose the heat of his touch. He stares straight at me, his gaze unwavering and without reservation. I've always wondered what victims of crime felt in the hours leading up to their assault. Now I know because I just experienced it firsthand.

While tracing his index finger over the goosebumps mottling my wrist, Nikolai shifts his focus to Mr. Fletcher. "If you get within an inch of her, I'll cut off your cock and feed it to you."

Since his attention returns to me so quickly, he fails to see Mr. Fletcher's response to his warning. A man who dishes out threats like Halloween candy doesn't need to see Mr. Fletcher's reaction to know it exists. He can smell the fear leaching off his skin. It's potent and strong, nearly as intoxicating as Nikolai's ruggedly virile scent lingering in my nostrils.

My pulse quickens when Nikolai pinches my chin to return my devotion to him. His heavy-lidded stare is more intimidating than any I've experienced—icy, pulse-quickening, and terrifyingly delicious.

"And don't think I won't know if he touches you, Justine." He purrs my name in a throaty rumble, making it sound more feminine than it is. "I smelled your purity. I'll know if it changes." He whispers his last two sentences as if they are only intended for my ears.

I nod, spinelessly agreeing with his assessment. It isn't because I'm fearful Mr. Fletcher will lose a beloved member of his body. Nikolai's statement was laced with so much confidence that I'm not willing to test its accuracy. His eyes expose that he'd rather slay a man than be seen as a fool.

Nikolai smiles unabashedly, pleased by my cowardly agreement. When he steps back, I secure my first breath in what feels like several minutes.

"Let's get this wrapped up. I have 'supposed' crack to be snorting."

He stalks to the other end of the room by walking backward, his watch unwavering.

The junior associates jump to his demand, neglecting to notice he didn't disclose whose chest he'd be snorting crack from. They flurry around the room, oblivious to the fact Nikolai's eyes are filling in the gaps his mouth failed to speak.

Although his lusty eyes relay every thought streaming through his head, he articulates his notions out loud, ensuring I can't mistake his eyes' silent admission. "Don't make plans this weekend, Ангел. Your calendar just got blacked out by the man determined to read your wicked thoughts."

He smirks in a way I've only seen once before—when I went head-to-head with Satan.

"Nikolai was drinking at the same bar as the accused. That alone will dismiss his fingerprints on the bottle lodged in the complainant's neck. Unless they have surveillance footage or a witness willing to side with the complainant's account of events, it's the accuser's word versus our client's. No judge will let that pass."

My tone is more confident than my facial expression. I've spent the past forty minutes ensuring a minimum of four inches between Mr. Fletcher and me, and my exhaustion is more apparent than ever.

Mr. Fletcher shrugs, his tiredness after a long week also evident. "The vault-load of evidence the DA has isn't our concern at the moment. It's ensuring our client doesn't spend Fourth of July weekend in lockup."

"Nikolai can afford bail, so why aren't we proceeding to a bail hearing?" My eyes roam the exorbitant amount listed at the bottom of Nikolai's financial statement. "Even if the judge demands a record bail amount, it isn't above our client's means. I doubt he'd bat an eyelid at a multimillion-dollar term."

Mr. Fletcher slumps into his chair before his eyes drift to Nikolai. I don't follow his gaze. I've felt the heat of Nikolai's eyes on me the past forty minutes, so I'm confident he's watching me. You can't mistake the heat of covetousness.

"With Nikolai being positively identified in a lineup and having a criminal record that rivals inmates on death row, I don't see a judge agreeing to any bail terms presented. If it were a DUI or a misdemeanor, different story, but this is an attempted murder charge. The complainant has thirty-three stitches in his neck, and he identified his attacker. Our chances of securing bail are slim to none."

"What about house arrest? Nikolai won't technically be incarcerated and wouldn't be tempted to skip bail. Then we will have the long weekend to work through the obstacles in front of us." Michelle adds to the ideas bouncing between Mr. Fletcher and me.

Mr. Fletcher's lips purse. "I considered that, but only one judge approves house arrests in Nevada."

Michelle scoots to the edge of her chair, her interests unmissable. Michelle is an attractive twenty-nine-year-old female with platinum-blonde hair, olive-green eyes, and a trim body, but shockingly, not once in the past forty minutes has Nikolai's focus diverted to her.

Should I be flattered or insulted by that notion? Is Nikolai watching me to entice flattery? Or is he trying to scare me? Considering every time our eyes subtly meet across the room, he smirks, I'd say it's the latter.

Michelle's enthusiasm is doused when Mr. Fletcher grumbles, "That judge is currently sipping champagne on a chartered jet, returning from a four-week writing retreat in Honolulu."

I sigh, hating that forty minutes of tossing around ideas hasn't unearthed a way to fix the error I made encouraging Mr. Fletcher to goad the complainant into identifying Nikolai. We wouldn't have a case without the complainant formally pressing charges, but it doesn't ease the guilt weighing heavily on my shoulders.

Seeking a way out of our predicament, I snag my iPhone from my bag to research Nikolai's former charges. His previous defense attorney was a brilliant man, but even someone with Erik's expertise would have had a hard time getting his client off his numerous previous charges, so there must be something we're missing.

My heart thumps my ribcage when a notification flashes across the screen of my cell.

"Were you referring to Judge Ryder?" I ask Mr. Fletcher, my voice high with excitement.

When he nods, I disclose, "Judge Ryder's flight landed fifteen minutes ago. With weather forecasts grim, it was either fly out six hours earlier than planned or wait for the storm to pass."

"He decided to fly out early," Mr. Fletcher intuits, his lips curling into a grin. "He's always been an inpatient old bastard."

With a smile, I nod.

"With the right amount of persuasion and an incentive or two, he could be in chambers within ten, fifteen minutes max," Michelle exclaims, her pitch higher than usual.

Mr. Fletcher jackknifes into a half-seated position, startling me. "Get Judge Ryder's wife on the phone." He points to Trent, a junior associate at Schluter & Fletcher.

Mr. Fletcher's eyes drift to Michelle, spearing her in place with his soul-capturing gaze. "I need the most expensive bag of golf clubs on the strip, and I needed them five minutes ago."

Beaming, Michelle smiles before lurching from her seat. She

exits the interview room with a bounce to her step that mimics the thump of my heart.

Kirk leaps into action when Mr. Fletcher's attention locks on him. "Transport. I'm on it," he perceives, reading the demand from Mr. Fletcher's eyes. He darts out of the interrogation room, leaving only three people: Mr. Fletcher, Nikolai, and me.

Wanting to showcase that his impressive pull doesn't solely work on members of the opposite sex, Mr. Fletcher removed the armed guards within seconds of Nikolai agreeing for us to counsel his case. Considering we've gone from ten members to three, the room feels surprisingly claustrophobic.

"We need to fill in the house arrest forms, have them signed by Nikolai and endorsed by the DA before lodging them with the court within fifteen minutes," Mr. Fletcher mumbles, his words forced out of his mouth in a hurry.

"Eleven," I correct, glancing at the wall clock that reads 4:49 p.m.

He grumbles a cuss word while snagging his briefcase from the ground. After seizing a five-page document from a hidden pocket, he thrusts it onto the desk in front of me. He rummages so recklessly in the breast pocket of his blazer for his lucky pen that a cotton thread popping breaks the silence between us.

Once he has everything in place, Mr. Fletcher shifts his focus to me. "If this works, I'll begin preliminaries on your brother's case this weekend."

I want to scream. I want to slap Mr. Fletcher's cheeks and smack a sloppy kiss right on his grinning lips, but instead, I tuck away the flare of excitement it causes and timidly nod. This is everything I've ever wanted, but I can't get too excited. First, I must ensure a known criminal doesn't spend a night in lockup. Then I'll pop open the bottle of chardonnay chilling in my fridge and toast my success.

After pressing a kiss to my temple, Mr. Fletcher leaves the room, loudly shouting for an update on the location of the assistant district attorney, Sasha, on his way.

5

NIKOLAI

Tick, tick, boom. Carmichael is a dead man walking.

Celebratory kiss or not, I warned him what would happen if he got within an inch of Justine. He failed to take my threat as literal. I'd kill him now if his quick departure didn't present a perfect opportunity to sample the lips that have been teasing me the past forty-five minutes.

I could have ended the game sooner by giving Justine Judge Santos's contact details, but not only is my trust low after my Russian operative confirmed Carmichael's claim about Erik being an FBI agent, but I've also grown a sudden fascination with this side of the law.

The saying, "you can lead a horse to water, but you can't make it drink," doesn't resonate with Justine. Not only did she lap up every drop in the dish I left out for her, but she's also watching me via hooded eyes, pleading for another serving.

I told you she was thirsty.

My crew calls me The Snake because of my ability to sneak up on my targets unaware. By the time they know I'm coming, my knife is already halfway across their throats.

Justine is too smart for that. She senses my presence long before I can brush away the weighed-down curl hiding the scar I spotted earlier.

As she stills, her breathing turns choppy and loud. She stares at the chair I left neatly tucked under the table, her scent imposingly strong. I want to arch her over the table, hike her fire-engine red skirt over her thighs, then eat her cunt as I'm sure it's never been eaten, but I can't. This room has eyes, and I'm not their handler.

Usually that fact wouldn't bother me. Gangbangs are more about the number of eyes on you than how many participants there are, but for some reason, a voice in my head is begging for me not to treat Justine like I do the whores at Clarks. It thinks she's special, that she should be treated like a princess, and for some fucked-up reason, the devil on my shoulder agrees with its less evil counterpart.

There's no doubt Justine is threatened by me. The misting of sweat on her skin proves this without a doubt, but she doesn't fear me. She's afraid she finds me attractive and is cautious about the trouble I bring to the table, but curiosity is still her strongest emotion of them all.

It's for the best. My persuasive techniques almost always end with body parts being sunk into a deep watering hole.

When a creak sounds through my ears, I look up. My endeavor not to railroad Justine into submission flies out the window when I spot her race for the door. She can't trust herself to be alone with me, and for once in my life, I'm inclined to agree with her.

A squeak pops from her mouth when I reach the door a mere second faster than her. I slap it shut with my palm before using my other hand to silence her squeals. She's not screaming to alert the guards she's in danger. She is shocked about how agilely I moved.

"My crew calls me The Snake. So do the Ангел I bed." I take a moment to relish in her scent before leaning into her even more. "But you, my sweet Justine, you can call me Сатана."

The nicknames I chose are perfect for us. She's an angel seeking chaos, and I am a demon seeking peace. Together, we will be explosive.

After burrowing my nose into her molten-red hair, I squash the fear I feel pulsating through her veins with my body before warning myself to slow the fuck down. My eagerness is making me rush, which will only give me half the thrill. With this being the most playful I've felt in years, I don't want it over quickly.

"I won't hurt you, Justine."

My eyes bounce around the room, confused as to who spoke those five words. They projected from the direction of my mouth, but my voice was unlike anything I've ever heard. It was almost protective like Justine has my sworn pledge that she'll forever be safe.

She doesn't. But it isn't her life at risk. It is her sanity.

When her squeaky breaths stop whistling through my fingers, I press my lips to the shell of her ear. "If I remove my hand, will you squeal?"

My stomach's response to the moisture sliding down her cheeks when she shakes her head is new. I usually see tears as a sign of weakness. Everyone uses them—men, children, women determined to break you. My mother was the worst of them all. Even while throwing me to the wolves, she shed crocodile tears, so I should be more angered by Justine's tears than frustrated by them.

With my past weighing down my faith, I snarl, "Don't break my trust, Justine," before lowering my hand from her mouth to the vein fluttering in her neck. When she keeps her word, I get honest. "I thought we had a connection, but when I came to offer you assistance, you bolted for the door without even saying goodbye. It's rude to run off without first issuing a farewell. That's your second strike of the day. One more, and I don't think we can be friends. You might be too naughty for me."

She sucks down a big breath before raising her sinless eyes to my corrupt ones. "I wasn't meaning to be impolite. I was just rushing to have these documents lodged with the court before 5 p.m. Unless you want to spend the next three nights in lockup, you need to let me go."

The growl her scent rumbled in my chest escapes when I murmur, "I think the pleasure would outweigh the penance."

I grind my stiffened shaft against her ass to ensure she can't mistake what I'm referencing. It sparks more than need in her eyes.

She's begging to be resurrected from the dead. To live. And fear isn't rousing her pleas. It's me.

"I'm flattered you think I'm worth spending three nights in a concrete cell..."

Her reply shifts to a moan when I bring my lips close enough to her ear, tiny beads of condensation are left in the wake of my zealous breaths. When the scent of her hungry cunt lingers in my nostrils, my zipper bites the head of my cock. Despite an audience, he wants to sink into her heat.

"I don't *think* you'll be worth three days in lockup. I *know* you'll be worth it."

I bite her earlobe, wordlessly warning her how close to the edge I am. I'm teetering dangerously, trapped between wanting to rule my empire and slaying anyone responsible for me not taking her now—Vladimir included.

Pretending a hard and fast fuck in one of Las Vegas PD's many holding rooms is worth scarifying the vengeance I've been striving for since I was sixteen is fucking ludicrous, but it's also the most honest I've ever been. That's how bad I want to hear Justine screaming my name. I climbed the mountain, I reached the summit, now I'm dangling one foot over the cliff edge to prove my life is edgier than it is mundane.

I could have both her and my revenge, but that would need a commitment from both sides of the fence.

The angel and the demon.

Heaven and hell.

Her and me.

I'd have a better chance of coercing her to dance with the devil if I hadn't marked her with my teeth.

After soothing the angry red welt on her fleshy skin by sucking it into my mouth, I ask, "Do you want to leave? Or shall you stay and let me play?"

Shock is the first thing registered on her face. It's quickly chased by innocence. "Leave."

Her reply is short, but it does little to douse the fire roaring in my gut. I can smell the excitement slicking her skin and feel the lusty heat blazing through her body. She wants this, but she's just too afraid to admit it.

"If you truly want to leave, *Ангел*, all you need to do is say goodbye."

Goosebumps follow the trek my hand makes when I drop it from the throb in her throat to the one between her legs. I don't touch her without permission. Rape is Vladimir's pleasure of choice, not mine, but I keep my fingers a mere inch from the area I feel growing more heated with every second she spends pinned to the door.

"You have to the count of five." I'm being lenient. Usually I don't issue a warning before ending someone's life, but since this is different—I more want to steal her life rather than cut it short, and I'm open to trying something new. "If you haven't bid me farewell by then, I'll start my weekend by discovering if you're a true redhead. Five... Four... Three—"

"Goodbye." Her voice is as impish as the devil on my shoulder goading me to listen to him.

You don't ask, he says. *You take.*

"Louder." Because if an angel can't steer me in the right direction, she won't leave this room in one piece.

Justine's throat works hard to swallow before she mutters, "Goodbye, Nikolai."

I groan. It's full of disappointment.

I'm not the only one disheartened. When I step back, unpinning Justine from the door, her sigh has the devil on my shoulder calling me a soft cock.

I'll show him.

"Turn around. No one says goodbye without a farewell kiss. Not even your boss could leave this room without putting his lips on you." My tone is the one that generally comes out of my mouth—it's gruff and full of command. "Hurry, *Ангел*. The courts close in five minutes, not only trapping me in here for the long weekend but also costing you the chance to have Carmichael I'm-going-to-gut-him-alive Fletcher defend your brother."

Justine sucks in a sharp breath, shocked I know about her brother's incarceration. I don't know why. I haven't taken my eyes off her for a second, so I know every word she and Carmichael shared.

"Now four and a half minutes."

Unsure about the authenticity of my threat, she spins around to face me. Since I'm standing so close to her, she can't rotate without grinding herself against the area of my body still maintaining its own pulse.

When her eyes lift to mine, cockiness thunders through me. If she wants me to believe her wish to flee me is legitimate, she needs to have a word with her eyes. They're flaring with hope, although it's barely seen through the yearning clouding them.

Smirking, I tap my index finger on my right cheek. Not needing further prompting, Justine leans forward to press her lips where I'm pointing.

Incapable of reeling in my domineering personality, I crank my neck to the side in just enough time to force her mouth onto mine.

6

JUSTINE

W hen a bolt of electricity sparks through my puckered lips, I freeze. The charge surges down my throat before clustering in my flipping core.

I yank back, astounded by the sheer power of the zap.

My movements are so abrupt my head rams into the glass door with force.

Wincing in pain, my hand darts up to cradle the throb in my skull. My accident gains the attention of the armed guards moseying in the hall. When Nikolai spots the guards' distorted shadows charging for us, he seizes my wrist in a vice-like grip and yanks me into his body.

Panic would usually be my first response to being abruptly grabbed, but shockingly, I feel no fear.

Hot air blasts my hair when the thick reinforced door veers past my skull with only an inch to spare. I draw in rattled breaths as my eyes dart between Nikolai's. If he hadn't pulled me into his chest, I could have been injured by the wildly flung door.

"Thank you," I whisper, a better reply beyond me.

The wild beat of my heart doubles when a genuine smile stretches across Nikolai's face. It's even more appealing than his ruthless smirk.

When two high-powered assault rifles dot his chest with red, he releases me from his grip and paces backward, only stopping when he reaches the chair I knocked over during my attempt to flee. He lifts the chair from the floor and sits, his movements more agile than a ballerina performing on a Paris stage.

The unidentifiable glint his eyes have carried the past hour fades when he connects them with the two guards. "Your disrespect won't go unnoticed," he sneers in a low, pussy-quaking tone.

He continues reprimanding them in Russian, but with my name being shouted from outside the room, I fail to hear the rest of his scold.

Mr. Fletcher's frame fills the doorway not even two seconds later. He absorbs my inflamed cheeks and wide eyes as I muster a fake smile.

"Everything okay?" he queries as his worried gaze drifts between Nikolai and me.

I forcefully nod. "Uh-huh."

My eyes swing sideways when Kirk reenters the interrogation room, his arrival as hurried as his words. His excited mumblings are thwarted when Mr. Fletcher raises his finger into the air, silencing him.

"Are you sure everything is okay, Justine?" Mr. Fletcher paces toward me, his worry unconcealed. "You're very pale. Whiter than usual."

He brushes his hand over my heated cheek, revealing our contrasting body temps. I've only just registered his remark on my fair skin coloring when a furious growl rumbles around the room, causing both my heart and pussy to shudder.

Mr. Fletcher's hand falls from my face as his eyes sling in the direction the growl resonated from. Nikolai is standing at our right. His fists are balled as tightly as his jaw is clenched, and his eyes are narrowed.

I step away from Mr. Fletcher, mindful that even being surrounded by armed guards won't stop a man like Nikolai from serving justice.

A ghost of a smile cracks on Nikolai's face, smitten by the foot of air lodged between Mr. Fletcher and me. As a guard guides him out of the room, he snarls at Mr. Fletcher. "Don't underestimate me, Carmichael, or this time, your stupidity will cost you your life," he warns, his voice as violent as his snarl.

My brows scrunch when Mr. Fletcher nods. His gesture was quick, but its swiftness didn't lessen its impact. I had a feeling Mr. Fletcher and Nikolai had met before. Now I have proof to back up my intuition.

When Nikolai enters the corridor, Mr. Fletcher connects his eyes with mine. "Do you want to work on this case, Justine?"

"Yes," I answer. "Do you? I'm not the one who had my life threatened by a mafia prince."

He nods without hesitation. "It's thirteen years later than I would have liked, but I'm not walking away again."

A million questions filter through my brain, but I can't get one of them to fire off my tongue. Luckily, Mr. Fletcher continues speaking, saving me from the embarrassment of flapping gums. "If this case will stir up old memories for you, Justine, I'd rather you sit this one out. We have a backlog of clients dying for someone with your criminal knowledge to peruse their files. You can work on those until—"

"I'm not giving up this case, Carmichael," I interrupt, cutting him off mid-sentence.

He glowers at me in shock. I don't know if his dropped jaw arises from my determination to remain on this case or because I called him by his given name for the first time.

"Nikolai's interest in you won't taper. The instant you denied him, you became a challenge," he warns, his tone more friendly than professional.

"I know," I reply, nodding. "I can handle it. I can handle him."

I inwardly sigh, grateful my voice held the confidence I wanted it to exude. Nikolai's attention does replicate advances I've been unappreciative of in the past, but the retainer I will receive working on his case warrants an unrestrained reply. The goals I've been aiming for the past four years will now be within reach, so nothing said or done will alter my decision.

After reading the honesty in my eyes for a few moments, Mr. Fletcher says, "Okay, then let's do this."

His eyes stray to Michelle, who is lugging a set of sparkling golf clubs down the corridor. "Golf clubs?"

"Check!" Michelle declares loudly, giggling at the obvious, before turning to me and seeing my bug-eyed expression. "I keep a spare set in my trunk in case of emergencies."

Mr. Fletcher's bright smile reveals Michelle's out-of-the-box approach will be immensely rewarded.

"Transportation?" Mr. Fletcher queries, his tone high with hope.

Kirk cups his cell phone with his hand. "Two will ride with Nikolai in the transportation van, while the rest will follow in your town car." He waits for Mr. Fletcher to nod in acknowledgment before he returns to barking commands into his cell. I swear, I've rarely seen him without an electronic device the three months I've known him.

"Judge Ryder?" Mr. Fletcher leaves the interrogation room to find Trent in the bustling corridor.

Although Nikolai's arrest is as regular as me eating waffles on Sunday, his presence has drawn a crowd of onlookers. Even a plain-clothed officer is snapping a picture of him being guided into the back of a transport van, idling at the end of the hallway.

My eyes stray from Nikolai when Trent suddenly bursts into the hallway. He has a shit-eating grin stretched across his face and a set of excessively waggling brows. "Mrs. Ryder requested I thank you for the Hawaiian adventure and to advise that she looks forward to issuing her gratitude in person when she hand delivers Judge Ryder to his chambers in T minus three minutes."

Mr. Fletcher fist pumps the air. "Yes, now all we need is the paperwork."

The room shrinks in size when everyone's eyes snap to mine.

"Yep. I'm on it," I lie, loathing that I turned up to the celebration minus a gift.

"All right. Let's do this," Mr. Fletcher claps his hands together while saying, "It's time to..."

"Bring home the bacon!" the team shouts in sync.

7

NIKOLAI

W hile Carmichael fusses over Justine more than his junior associates, unaware each second of attention is slicing years off his life, I slide the five-page document I 'borrowed' from his briefcase out of my jeans pocket.

Although I spent the last fifty-five minutes ensuring there was a minimum of three inches between Justine and Carmichael, I quickly caught on to their plan to have me placed on house arrest until they find a 'legal' way to get me off my charges.

Once again, I could lay all my cards on the table, but where would be the fun in that?

This will be more fun. I need to be alone with Justine to see if the groove between her brow will smooth from my touch or deepen.

My plan could backfire, but tell me one person who doesn't anticipate an unexpected houseguest for the Fourth of July weekend?

After being guided into a transportation van idling at the curb by Daniil, a Russian operative who's fronting as a police officer, I'm given a two-minute window to get things in order. Usually this is where I call in the clean-up crew who'd do *anything* necessary to free me from conviction—including storming a heavily-manned Police Department.

However, with my mood the most playful it's been, I switch tactics. I still dial a frequently called number on the burner cell Daniil slipped into my hand during our short walk from the holding room to the van, my demands are just different.

"You want me to do what?" Trey, my number two, asks down the line, certain he heard me wrong.

I scrub at the day-old stubble on my chin before breathing out slowly, "Have a guard on standby to switch out my house arrest documentation with the one I'm about to forge before it reaches the judge."

I hear Trey's smile over the phone. "I heard what you said. I'm just a little lost on why you want me to do that." As quickly as his confusion arrives, it leaves. "The rumors are true. Fresh blood is balancing on the balustrade between good and evil. Are you hoping she'll unearth a little bit of good in that black soul of yours? Or are you hoping to unearth her dark side?"

My tongue peeks out between my teeth as I struggle to hold in my snicker. "More like I want to fuck her as I'm sure she's never been fucked."

"Yeah, yeah, Nikolai. Keep telling yourself those lies. If all you wanted was a night of fucking, you would have gone to Cliché."

Cliché is a strip club I co-own with Trey. Its title explains our establishment well. It's like every other strip club known—owned and operated by gangsters.

Ignoring the niggle of doubt in my gut that Trey is right, that this is about more than a weekend fuckfest, I get back to the task at hand.

I'm about to ask him to search the Popov's database for Justine's address, but before I can, a double-tap hits the van's rear window, signaling I must cut our conversation short.

"Flock is about to fly. See you in five."

Not giving Trey the chance to reply, I disconnect our call, yank the battery out of the back of the burner phone, then crush it between my foot and the checkered metal beneath my feet.

I've only just flicked the mangled shards of glass and plastic under my seat when the back door of the transport van swings open and a guard as wide as he is tall enters.

He grunts at me, acting impassively. His performance is a waste of time. I can smell a traitor a mile out. His unpolished shoes are the first hint he'll turn on a dime for the right amount of coin and so are his wrinkled clothes. Only someone who doesn't care about their job gets lax about their appearance.

Why do you think I get around in ripped jeans and designer shirts?

"The redhead in the hall..." I unfold the paper I removed earlier, run my hand along the crinkles to smooth them out, then pass it to the officer, confident I have a conspirator at the ready. "I need her name and contact details added to this form. Now." I count his pulse before placing my offer on the table. "A five thousand dollar buy-in at the craps table in the high-rollers suite of my casino."

To an ordinary man, my offer seems generous. High-class hookers go for less than what I'm bidding for Justine, but five thousand dollars is chump-change compared to the amount of money my casino launders each night.

"Five *thousand* dollars?" He's seeking confirmation. However, the quickest lick of his dry lips reveals his decision is already made.

"You better hurry. If she arrives before her information does..." I nudge my head to Justine, who's making her way down the corridor, using her hand as a notepad so she can fill in my forms before we arrive at the courthouse. "My offer will be removed." I lift and lock my eyes with his. "As will your tongue. *Мертвец не может ничего сказать.*"

His throat works through a stiff swallow before his head bobs up and down, proving he's smarter than he looks.

My threats aren't idle.

While Carmichael stands outside the idling transport van, nervously tapping his foot as he waits for Justine to finalize my house arrest documentation, the guard recites Justine's home address to me. I had planned to make him fill in the form, but he's shaking so violently, I don't want to run the risk of the judge not understanding his no doubt chicken-scratch writing.

"We need to go, Justine," Carmichael begs her at the same time I peg my pen at the guard's head. I could keep it, they make handy weapons, but I need my hands empty for the swift one I'm about to pull on Justine when Carmichael steers my ruse in a direction I never saw coming. "Finish them during the commute. Kirk, swap places with Justine."

My jaw ticks when Carmichael hoists Justine into the van by the tops of her arms. His hands aren't his cock, but I'm still tempted to cut them off for getting within an inch of a woman he doesn't have the right to smell, much less touch.

Even if Carmichael and I hadn't met earlier, I still wouldn't like him. He's one of those men who has you plotting their demise within minutes of meeting them, the urge growing more rampant the more time you spend with them.

If he hadn't become a lawyer, I guarantee he would have been a serial killer. He has the psycho tenancies most men have but he hides them with an expensive suit and worthless words.

Once we're joined in the van by an additional three riot officers, we commence the most direct route to the courthouse. The instant I was arrested, Trey organized for my crew to line every route known to mankind. If I want out, I merely need to brace my tattooed hand on the 'supposed' bulletproof glass above my head, and my crew will jump into action.

I was born craving carnage. Chaos, death, and sidestepping justice is all I know. So usually the urge for destruction would have had me placing my hand on the glass over two miles ago.

Alas, a boring life is as meaningless as a moral one. I'll still get the thrill I'm chasing tonight. It will just come from a pretty molten-haired woman with unique-colored eyes.

I stop sucking in Justine's scent that grows stronger with each second I stare at her when she shouts, "Done."

Her eyes pop up from the documents to me. They're as dilated as predicated, heavy with need. A lesser man would believe her excitement stems from her being the only female in a tin box brimming with testosterone, but I know that isn't the case. She's forgotten everyone else in the van. As far as she is concerned, it's just her and me.

"Now you just need to sign it."

"Do not approach the detainee," an armed guard roars when she attempts to hand me the paperwork.

When Justine recoils in fear, blood furiously pumps through my veins to cool my skyrocketing body temperature. I'm shackled to the floor, but no amount of metal will save him. One look, and a bounty will be placed on his head the instant I leave this van.

I hope he kissed his family goodbye this morning because it was for the final time.

I work my jaw side to side when Justine says, "I just need a signature on the bottom of these forms."

She's shaking so hard, my house arrest documents shudder along with her words.

Usually I'd relish in the fear, but since it's coming from her, I'm fucking ropeable.

"It's just a few pieces of paper and a pen. What harm can be done?"

The guard snarls at Justine before jerking up his chin, wordlessly approving her request. I could let this be the end of it—he's a dead man no matter how much he pleads—but our exchange not only presents the perfect opportunity to warn him about the wrath he's about to face, but it also gives me the chance to commence my ruse long before we reach the courthouse.

"Ten seconds," I murmur while removing the documents from Justine's grip.

Justine chokes down her annoyance before asking, "What?"

While her wide eyes dance between mine, seeking an answer to my riddled comment, I switch out the sheet of paper responsible for incarcerating me at the Popov compound until my case is presented to the courts with the one I filled in. I don't bother darting my eyes between the many pairs I feel watching me because even if they witnessed my not-so-inconspicuous swap, none of them are brave enough to confront me about it. Guaranteed.

"Ten seconds." I bend the edges of the paper so my unstapled sheet appears to have been clipped with the original ones before saying, "That's all it takes for me to kill a man with a pen."

The true scope of Justine's innocence is exposed for the world to see when she replies, "Oh." I was anticipating a 'gross,' 'eww,' or a hard swallow. They're typically the responses I get when talking about murder as if it's an everyday occurrence.

She didn't even bat an eyelid.

Keen to unearth more of her quirks, I keep our conversation light. "What am I signing?"

My jaw clenches so firmly when Carmichael says, "It's a petition for you to be placed under house arrest until better circumstances can be arranged." My teeth will be ground to nubs by the end of today.

"I wasn't asking you." My sneer sounds as if it was delivered straight from hell. "I was asking Justine, *my* defense attorney."

Justine appears shocked by the possessiveness in my tone. She's not the only one. Usually I only look out for number one—me. But instead of panicking about it, she explains, "It's as Mr. Fletcher stated, an application for house arrest."

Hating the low hang of her head, compliments of Carmichael-I'm-going-to-gut-him-alive- Fletcher's observant stare, I remove the strands of hair fallen in front of her eye before slanting my head to block Carmichael from her view.

"Your eyes show the confidence you fail to exude. Don't hide them from me."

When she nods, I keep the boost her submissiveness fed my ego on the down-low by pretending to peruse the house arrest documentation as if it's the first time I've agonized over one.

I need to take a moment to consider my next step. I live my life a million miles an hour, knowing it could end at any moment, but this is the first time I've thrown an outsider into the chaos. My crew faces a grueling initiation process to ensure they understand the dangerous world they're entering as do the whores who service them after a gory day, so why am I not giving Justine the same leeway?

I don't ask for shit. I take what I want and bring fury down on those who dare to keep it from me, but for some fucked-up reason, I want this to be Justine's decision.

I guess even those born evil don't realize how much they want something until they risk having it taken from them.

After removing my thumb from Justine's address scribbled across the paperwork, I ask, "Is this what you want?"

As Justine's throat works hard to swallow, she raises her eyes from her address written in thick black ink to me. "It isn't about what I want, Nikolai." The professionalism in her voice is replaced with the pitch of a woman desperate to break away from her dull existence when she adds, "This is about you and what's in your best interest."

While returning her wanton stare, I take a moment to consider the consequences of my actions. Since it's not something I often do, it is a long, drawn-out thirty seconds. Roman, my somewhat advisor, would be proud *if* I had given the voice of reason in my head more than two seconds to plead its case. I'm listening to the sadistic one instead, the one that usually sees me facing a line-up instead of a three-day long weekend in a stranger's bed.

It could be worse.

A grin tugs at my lips when my request for a pen doubles the throb in Justine's neck. Her response is understandable. I told her only seconds ago how I can kill a man with a pen in ten seconds, yet she still hands one to me. If that doesn't prove she wants this as much as me, I don't know what will.

Evil is a power only the good are afraid to harness. The hesitant gleam Justine's eyes get every time she looks at me reveals she knows this better than anyone. She's mostly good, but I guarantee there's a little bit of black inside her dying to be nurtured to its full potential, and who better to bring out that side of her than darkness itself?

As the van comes to a stop in the front of the courthouse stairs, I hand the signed house arrest documentation and pen to Justine. She murmurs her thanks as my shackles are unlocked, and I'm guided out of the van by the man responsible for throwing her into hell with me.

Even from a distance, I see suspicion form in Trey's eyes when the courthouse bailiff's pat-down fails to find the document he's meant to switch before he hands it to the judge.

I don't know what he sees on my face, but it increases the smug grin plastered on his.

After arching my brow at him, demanding he take his eyes off Justine's ass before I gouge them out with a fork, I nudge my head to the officer who felt the need to enter a war he didn't belong in.

Trey jerks up his chin, advising he understands my request before straying his eyes to Dion. Two seconds after their quiet word, Dion slips into the driver's seat of a blacked-out Escalade, and just like that, Officer Lennox's life expectancy is shortened from years to hours if Dion is feeling playful. He only tortures them when he's bored. If he is entertained, Officer Lennox won't make it a mile from where he stands.

As I'm chauffeured up the stairs of the courthouse, the media circle me like starving sharks. It's like this everywhere I go. Evil may be the root of pain, but it is also the stuff of legends. Love it or hate it, for as long as Earth has rotated the sun, key members of the underworld have been seen as celebrities.

We make it into the courtroom with only a minute to spare. A judge with bushy brows and a wonky smirk sits at his podium, wrongly believing he's the ruler of this town. Sasha, a woman as eager to jump ship as Carmichael was almost thirteen years ago, is positioned on the right side of the courtroom, and Justine, Carmichael, and I take up the left.

I'm not surprised to discover the seat next to the ADA is empty. The plaintiff's lack of respect reveals he's nothing but a bottom feeder in a rivals crew.

It doesn't mean I'll let his snitching ways be forgotten, though. If Dimitri doesn't sniff him out as the rat he is, I'll send some of my men to Hopeton to aid in the extermination of his rodents.

When Carmichael commences proceedings by crawling so far up the judge's ass, we'll need a tire wrench to get him out, I cradle my head in my hands. "Judge, the Hawaiian sun did wonders for your complexion."

I take a mental note to add this judge's name to a list of potential replacements for when Judge Santos retires when he sees straight through Carmichael's bullshit. "Yes, yes, Carmichael. Save your yakking for my wife. She's waiting for you outside."

My knowledge of Carmichael's relationship with the judge's wife is unknown, but if the whitening of his gills is anything to go by, the judge didn't marry his wife for her looks.

After being granted permission to approach the bench, Carmichael hands the judge the doctored request for my house arrest. "Our client's request for house arrest has been signed by the defendant and endorsed by the DA's office." Sasha gasps in a sharp breath when he waves his hand at her nonchalantly. They fucked, and he snuck out while she was asleep. I guarantee it. She wears the look of a scorned woman well. "With lockup overrun with rowdy school leavers, one less occupant is best for all involved."

The judge's old-timer eyes shift to Sasha, who's still reeling over Carmichael's hand thrust. "Are Mr. Fletcher's claims true, Ms. Sheridan? Are you siding with the defense so their client can be bailed under the condition of house arrest?"

"Yes, but our agreement is merely to stop Mr. Fletcher's client from coercing drunken fools into becoming members of his... associ-ation." I hit her with a frisky wink when her eyes drift my way during the last half of her statement. If the hue on her cheeks is anything to go by, she doesn't just want to defend criminals, she wants to be bedded by them too.

The pulse of victory drums through my veins when the judge says, "Very well. With both parties agreeing to the terms as stated, I have no reason to decline your request, Mr. Fletcher."

As the crowd filling the chambers whispers their surprise about the judge's verdict, blood floods my cock. Its inflation has nothing to do with the vehement eyes of the ADA watching me under hooded lids and everything to do with Justine's breaths hitting my neck. Her excitement is as stealthy as mine. We just have different reasons to be excited. She thinks today's victory awards her the privilege of being my counsel. It does, but it's only one of the many perks I plan to award her with.

"However..." My eyes snap to the judge, my gaze set to kill. I hate stipulations as much as I despise the men who feel they have the right to issue them. "I'm only agreeing to the request for house arrest because the defendant is not being housed in any compounds associated with him or with any known associates of his."

When Carmichael's eyes rocket to Justine, wordlessly demanding an explanation to the judge's comment, it is the fight of my life to hold in my grin. It's pulling at my lips, begging to be freed as much as my cock wants out of my jeans.

I lose the chance to hold back my grin when the judge says, "I hereby sentence Nikolai Popov to serve bail under the terms of house arrest at Unit 23, 431 West Lucy Lane, Las Vegas," so I set it free.

As the color drains from Carmichael's cheeks, Justine leaps up from her chair. "That's not the correct address. You've made a mistake."

I almost order my second hit of the day when the judge glares at Justine as if she's simple. The only reason I don't is because the hellion I see hiding deep within Justine's eyes jumps to her defense before I can. "Please check. Someone has made a mistake. If not you, someone else."

"I don't make mistakes, young lady."

Except the one you just did.

"And if another insult leaves your lips, I'll hold you in contempt of court."

I watch Justine for several long seconds, knowing she has the gall to fight more but also aware she won't. She isn't backing down because she's a coward but because she knows angels can fly no matter how heavy the burdens on their shoulders are.

8

JUSTINE

My eyes lift when Mr. Fletcher enters the meeting room I'm pacing. The minuscule portion of hope I've been clutching the past thirty minutes vanishes into thin air when he shakes his head.

"Judge Ryder understands an error was made, but with the courts closed until Tuesday morning, he legally cannot move on his judgment."

I slump into the chair and cradle my head in my shuddering hands. "I can't believe I was so stupid. Who puts their address in the defendant's details?"

Assuming my question isn't rhetorical, Mr. Fletcher takes the empty seat next to me. "We all make mistakes, Justine."

I glare at him, requesting he provide an example of when a member of his staff acted so heedlessly.

The tightness across my chest constricts when his eyes drop to his shoes. "Maybe not to this caliber, but it happens."

I may have believed his false admission if he were looking at me.

I scrub my tired eyes before locking them with Mr. Fletcher's. "Can Nikolai stay at my residence while I camp at a hotel?"

My choppy words show I am aware of the answer to my question. My career title was the collateral Judge Ryder needed to agree with the defense request for house arrest. By separating Nikolai from the mafia lifestyle he was raised in, the chances of him following his bail terms significantly increase.

Although the address was filled out in error, it could also be considered a godsend. Without my address on the application, Schluter & Fletcher would have never secured Nikolai as a client, as our agreement would have been void the instant he was incarcerated.

Mr. Fletcher's eyes follow me when I stand from my seat. "Where are you going?"

"I have a guest to prepare for." I gather my belongings from the table before pivoting around to face him. "I've got knives, scissors, and razors to take care of."

Mr. Fletcher leaps to his feet, the expression on his face anything but pleasant. "The sheriff's department will take care of that."

"I know," I interrupt, nodding. "I'm talking about the instruments I plan to stash under my mattress to protect myself."

I aim for my voice to come out playful, but the fear curled around my throat dulls my efforts. I'm not scared of Nikolai. I am petrified at how quickly my walls crumble around him. He's the equivalent of a stranger, yet my body thrums with excitement every time he's within touching distance of me.

When a flare of panic ignites in Mr. Fletcher's eyes, I assure him, "I'm joking. I just loathe delayed gratification. The quicker this weekend begins, the quicker it will be over."

The worry in his eyes lessens.

"Besides, the more time you sit here comforting me, the less time you'll have to work on my brother's case."

The weight on my shoulders eases when he nods. "Kirk is transferring Maddox's records to my home office as we speak. I'll begin working on an appeal tonight."

Unable to contain my joy, I lean in to kiss his cheek. My puckered lips freeze within an inch of his face when Nikolai's threat filters through my mind.

Shame thickens my blood when I air kiss Mr. Fletcher's cheek instead.

Am I truly that stupid that I think a stranger would know I kissed another man's cheek?

Shutting down my worrisome thoughts for a more appropriate time, I align my eyes with Mr. Fletcher's. "Thank you."

The nerves in my tone are unable to contain my glee. I've been striving for Mr. Fletcher to work on my brother's case since I started at Schluter & Fletcher.

"You have my number, Justine. Use it at any time." Mr. Fletcher projects his deep timbre through the rapidly closing door I'm gliding through.

"I won't need it," I shout back, my words confident. "You're not the only one with four older brothers."

I've got this. It is in the bag.

When Mr. Fletcher's throaty laugh booms into my ears, what once felt like a death sentence shifts to an awakening. If I survive the long weekend in the presence of a man whose ruthful glance turns me on as much as it antagonizes me, the possibility of my brother leaving the maximum-security prison he's been detained in the past four years may reach fruition.

"I've got this," I repeat out loud this time.

The commute from the courthouse to my apartment building has me fidgeting. It isn't solely nerves making me a jittery mess. It's the arctic-blue gaze of Nikolai staring me down. He hasn't spoken a word since I joined him in the sheriff's transportation van twenty minutes ago, but he doesn't need to speak for me to know what he's thinking.

He believes I placed my address on his house arrest documentation so he could make good on his promise of a weekend fling. I did no such thing. It was a mistake—a horrendously horrid mistake.

For one, I'd never risk losing my position at Schluter & Fletcher to dance beneath the sheets with a client, and two, I don't sleep with strangers.

"It was an accident," I insist for the umpteenth time. "I meant to put down your address, I was just—"

"Flustered." Nikolai's smug grin doubles when he spots the heat creeping up my neckline. "Don't be ashamed, *Ангел*. You have good instincts. You should be flustered. Scared. Praying to the gods you'll survive me." He whispers his last sentence with a risky edge that skyrockets my heart rate.

The fear clutching my throat lowers to my pussy when he adjusts the girth of his knees. His kneecap barely brushes my thigh, but my body reacts as if he's kneeling naked between my legs, moments away from ravishing me.

His meekest touches, however, aren't the sole cause for my heightened senses. It's the way he peers at me while doing it. I've never been on the receiving end of the glances he's given me all afternoon. He looks at me like he wants to devour every inch of me —over and over again.

If I weren't panicked about how one wrong move could be fatal for my family, I'd strive to keep the gleam in Nikolai's eyes forever. His motives may not be pure, but who doesn't want to be treated as if they're the most valuable jewel in the world?

"His defense attorney," I grumble under my breath.

While the sheriff's department sweeps the floor of my building, Nikolai and I remain seated in the transport van. The bristling of tension between us grows with every beat of my heart. It grows until it reaches a point I can no longer ignore. My skin slicks with sweat, and my insides do a weird flippy thing.

Nikolai's gaze drops to my neck before slipping over my paper-thin satin blouse. Air hisses through his teeth when he spots the buds of my nipples. I shouldn't get satisfaction from his attentive stare, but I do. Nikolai Popov is clearly a breast man.

"Soon, Ангел. Very soon," Nikolai promises when he notices me squirming in my seat.

Cocking his head, he returns his eyes to mine. He doesn't speak, letting his shadowed gaze reveal his intentions instead. His thoughts are as sinful as the ones streaming through my depraved mind.

I freeze, distressed by my body's positive reaction to his threat but unable to help it. I'm a woman with needs, and his attention is making me reckless—mindless. My mind is spiraling with endless possibilities, none suitable for an attorney and her client. Nikolai's manly scent is doing wicked things to my libido, and I can barely smell it over the lust in the air. I was confident nothing would awaken my libido's prolonged stint of abstinence, so although I'm disturbed it has chosen now to be aroused, I'm still grateful for its return.

I mentally slap myself. To survive this weekend, I need to be a cutthroat law intern, not a young woman whose cheeks flame every time her gaze collides with a pair of icy-blue eyes staring at her with zeal.

When I'm given the nod of approval to leave the van, I crack open the sliding door and clamber onto the sidewalk as fast as my quivering legs can. For the first time in months, my lungs relish the bone-dry heat of Las Vegas. With the sexual tension thrumming between Nikolai and me so muggy, my lungs felt like they were drowning with every breath I gulped.

With four armed guards, an attendant, and a shackled prisoner, the elevator ride to the fifteenth floor of my apartment is torturously long. Even with Nikolai flanked by armed guards, our friction is intense. My nape drips with sweat, and my heart beats wildly.

When the elevator dings, announcing our arrival at my floor, I charge out of the small confines. My need for fresh air is more extreme than when Nikolai clamped his hand over my mouth. I'm startled by my body's responses today. I've spent hours interacting with clients in tiny four-by-four cells, and I've never been bombarded with the claustrophobia I'm experiencing now.

My wobbly stride increases with every step down the dimly lit hall. I've always been house-proud, but with most of my wage set aside to fund my brother's legal fight, my apartment isn't as glamorous as the residence I was raised in.

When I shove my key into the lock and swing open my apartment door, I'm pushed aside by one of the parole officers. He's so eager to rummage through my small space he must have misplaced his manners.

"смотри это," Nikolai sneers under his breath as he uses his torso to steady my footing.

I issue him my thanks with a tight smile, praying it will hide my flaming cheeks. I knew from seeing him shirtless this afternoon that his body would be firm, but I had no idea how built he was. His athletic body is compact and tight, showcasing every cut muscle in glorious detail.

After enhancing his threat with a snarl, Nikolai shadows me to the corner of my cramped living room. His eyes drift around the space, taking in the unique qualities of my retro seventies apartment.

Although my apartment is dated, like many things, its age has benefits. For the same price as a brand-new apartment on the same street, I secured a second bedroom and a massive eat-in kitchen. Although I'm years away from starring on *MasterChef*, my culinary talents have a chance of developing in my mammoth kitchen. If I could find a spare hour or two to cook in it.

"Nice." Nikolai's lips quirk. "Small as fuck, but nice."

I smile at his backhanded compliment.

Over the next twenty minutes, the patrol officers go crazy, ridding every nook and cranny of my apartment of illegal instruments. Although I am grateful their search is thorough, it would be nice if they handled my property with more diligence. My bric-a-brac items don't have a high monetary value, but no amount of money can replace their sentimental worth.

Not even five seconds later, I pray for a sinkhole to appear and swallow me when one of the officers ruffles through my lingerie drawer exposes that my lack of personal time has led to an extensive collection of self-pleasuring toys. Some are still in their original packaging. Others... they leave no suspicion on their appeal.

"Don't say a word," I mutter in warning when Nikolai swings his wide eyes in my direction.

Ignoring my sneered demand, Nikolai says, "Take them with you. Justine won't need them." He rocks on his heels, his arrogance at an all-time high. "She's got everything she needs right here." He doesn't need to grab his crotch to emphasize his statement.

The officer shrugs before dumping the drawer of sex apparatuses onto my bed. His hands delve through the vibrating butterfly clips, silver beads, and an epic black dildo as if it's something he handles every day.

"On second thought, maybe we should keep them," Nikolai groans under his breath.

His voice is full of command, but his tugging lips reveal his true composure. He's a lot more playful than I realized. Ruthless as a missile locked on its target—but playful nonetheless.

I crank my neck to the side when shredding jingles into my ears. An officer is yanking my couch cushions so roughly he has torn a corner seam.

"You do realize we're on the same team, right? I work in the justice system," I grumble, angered at having my privacy invaded in such an unjust way.

The blond officer with his hand shoved halfway down my couch grunts. "You're not one of us. If you were, you would have let that scum rot in jail," he sneers, proving he doesn't enjoy solely pushing women around—he gets pleasure from verbally taunting them as well.

"I didn't invite him into my home. It was a mistake..." Words fail me when a shimmer of silver catches my eye. Nikolai uses his thick forearm to conceal a letter opener he slipped off my writing nook.

"Put it back," I implore softly, afraid of what he's planning to do with it.

The letter opener isn't sharp or overly pointy, but I'm not willing to take any chances after Nikolai's disclosure of how quickly he can kill a man with a pen.

Acting like he didn't hear a word I spoke, Nikolai locks his eyes with the officer. "Only a coward makes threats from a distance," he taunts, his words as volatile as the veins bulging in his neck.

The unnamed officer straightens his spine. "Coward? You're calling me a coward?" He moseys over to join Nikolai and me, his walk full of arrogance. "I'll show you how much of a coward I am."

My hand darts up to muffle a breathless scream when he throws a jab into Nikolai's stomach. Nikolai doesn't flinch from the brutal blow he endured. He doesn't even grimace. He smiles an evil smirk that relays his every intention without a peep sounding from his lips.

"Is that all you've got?" Nikolai teases, his full Russian accent on display. "My дедушка hits harder than you."

My eyes dart to the officer's colleagues when his fists firm, praying they will stop him from issuing Nikolai his own form of justice. Although the non-offending officers' eyes spark with amusement from their exchange, they continue rummaging through my belongings, neither encouraging nor discouraging their team member's prejudiced punishment.

I launch into action when a second flash of silver topples past Nikolai's wrist. My frantic leap sees me landing in front of Nikolai's body, not only saving him from being struck a second time but also thwarting his attempts to gut the parole officer with the letter opener he's fisting in his unrestrained hand.

"If you so much as ruffle another hair on my client's head, I'll have you arrested for police brutality," I warn the officer, my tone guaranteeing my threat isn't idle. "You are not here to prosecute my client. You're here to sweep my house. If that has been done, I suggest you leave."

Although wary of what Nikolai's response will be to me interrupting his quest for vengeance, I will not stand by and watch another man assaulted without cause. I witnessed my brother's vicious arrest without speaking a word. I won't do the same thing a second time.

The offending officer sneers at me, the utter disgust on his face unmissable. Having no clue I saved his life, he snarls, "I'll leave a body bag with the receptionist. It will save me from carting one back here tomorrow."

After tossing a set of handcuff keys into my chest, he nudges his head to my front door, demanding his team follow his showy exit.

"Have fun with her," he mutters as his evil eyes connect with Nikolai's narrowed gaze.

Handcuffs falling onto wooden floorboards ring through my ears while the latch on my front door clicks into place. My heart launches into a mad beat when the heat of Nikolai's body curls around mine not even two seconds later. He once again moved so agilely that I barely registered his approach.

"You should have let me teach him a lesson," he murmurs into my neck as his arm wraps around my stomach. "Spineless men like him don't deserve to breathe."

My chest flattens on the wooden paneling of my door when he nudges my ankles apart with his feet. He slips his leg into the gap between my thighs as his hands roam my body. Air traps in my throat when he tugs my satin blouse out of my high-waisted skirt. I try to fire off a demand for him to stop. I'm screaming the word no on repeat in my mind, but Nikolai continues talking, lessening my inhibitions with every syllable he speaks.

"If my desire to taste you wasn't stronger than my urge to slit his throat, he'd be quivering his last breath right now," he mutters in my ear, his voice dangerous and thick. "But my needs are too strong to ignore. After years of pussy on tap, my cock grew bored. Nothing could gain its interest. Except you. One glance, and I was done. I knew I had to have you."

His words excite me more than I can explain.

"Then when you spoke... *Fuck*. In a room full of men, my cock turned to stone. I've never been so fucking hard." He grinds his pelvis into my backside, strengthening his statement. He's primed, jutted, and extended well past the swell of my lower back.

I remain quiet, trapped in a trance, dazed, and incredibly confused. My brain knows this is wrong, but my body reacts positively to every touch Nikolai awards it with. It silently moans when the scruff on his chin digs into my collarbone as he nips at my neck. My hips match the rhythm of his grinds when he rubs his erection on my ass, and the heat between my legs competes with the lust heating my veins. But even with this feeling oh-so-good, I also know it's wrong—very, *very* wrong.

"Stop. We can't do this. This isn't right. I'm your attorney," I mumble when guilt crashes into me.

"We're making the best out of a bad situation. How can that be wrong?" he replies as his hand slips under my bra to cup my engorged breast.

He expertly tweaks my nipple, proving my assumption of his sexual capabilities is spot on. He's barely touching me, but my orgasm is hovering, threatening to erupt at any moment.

Hearing my husky moans, Nikolai murmurs, "Tell me again you want me to stop."

My lips twitch, but my pleas remain entombed in my throat. I'm so clouded by lust that I doubt anything could burst the heady bubble surrounding me.

I freeze when his free hand moves toward an area that will expose my true desires. If he feels how damp my panties are, any chance of stopping our exchange will be thwarted. I don't know if it's something I should encourage or discourage.

"Stop. I need a minute to think. Oh god, Nikolai. We can't do this—"

My blubbering rant tapers off when he groans at the mention of his name. From his reaction, you'd swear he's never heard his name moaned before. With a panty-wetting face and mouth-watering body, I highly doubt that is true.

"You want me to stop?" He tries to hide the disappointment in his tone. He would have miserably failed if it weren't for the covetousness thickening his timbre.

"No. Yes. I don't know." My words are whimpered with confusion.

I can't believe the opposing viewpoints pumping into me. Is it possible I'm so incredibly aroused my morals have been left for dust? Or do I genuinely believe there's something so great sparking between Nikolai and me that I'm willing to give up everything to find out what it is?

Suddenly, I stiffen like a board, disturbed by my stupidity. Nikolai is a client. There can never be anything more between us than an attorney-client relationship. Furthermore, it was my unwillingness to be another notch on a severely serrated bedpost for my current predicament.

It's also why I've lived the past four years riddled with guilt. I have no doubt one night with Nikolai could erase months of horrid memories, but it would never be substantial enough to push aside the love I have for my family. My brother sacrificed his life for me, so I must do the same for him.

"Stop, Nikolai. Please stop." I arch my spine, pushing back from the door I'm pinned against. My fight is a pointless endeavor. A woman my size is no contest against a man as virile as Nikolai.

Deciding this may be the one time words will triumph over actions, I say, "This isn't what I want. This isn't why I brought you here. It was an accident. A mistake. I was flustered. Have you never had a lapse in judgment before? Have you never made a mistake?"

My words blurt out of my mouth so hard and fast that I fail to notice Nikolai's exploration of my body ceases. Although his hand remains cupped around my breast, his index finger and thumb are no longer rolling my nipple into a stiff peak.

"A mistake?" he mimics, his voice the deepest I've heard. It sounds as if it were delivered straight from hell.

A throaty gargle overtakes the beat of my heart when his hand slips into my panties to cup my pussy. He deeply exhales, ruffling my hair with his breath when he feels how damp my pussy is.

"This doesn't feel like a mistake." His words are as dangerous as quicksand. "This feels like a game. A taunt. I don't play games, Ангел, not ones that don't involve a weapon." His tone is so low only a hint of Russian heritage echoes in his reply. "Is this a mistake or a game?" His deep voice is dampened with confusion.

"It's neither. I'm as confused as you..."

Any further explanation I'm planning to give is pushed aside when his thumb grazes my clit. One touch and I'm done. I'm burning up everywhere. My urge to climax grows so fast that I feel like I'll erupt like a volcano at any moment.

"You're dripping," Nikolai mutters as the confusion in his tone is stripped away, leaving nothing but pure, unbridled lust.

My head lolls onto his shoulder when his finger slides into my aching pussy. It hugs his thick finger, encouraging his pursuit no matter what objections my brain cites. I need this more than I need to breathe. I need the release. I need to lose control. I need to be the old Justine for just one night.

"Please... Oh god. Please, Nikolai," I shamefully moan when the tip of his finger stops within half an inch of the sweet spot inside me, my needs too intense to ignore.

He groans before his finger flicks the sensitive region begging for his attention. He works my body like he intimately knows it, finger-fucking me at a pace slow enough that no friction can be felt but fast enough any possibility of staving off my orgasm is impossible.

I lean into his body when my quaking legs cannot hold our combined weight. He takes advantage of my new position by worshiping my neck with as much attention as he is bestowing on my pussy. Every touch has my climax soaring, building so rapidly that it's frightening.

How is it possible a stranger knows my body so well he has me on the brink of ecstasy within a matter of seconds? It's genuinely outstanding how well in tune he is with my body.

My breathless moans turn noisy when Nikolai mutters, "Let me hear your screams. Perhaps if the world hears how much you're enjoying this, your brain will acknowledge your body's pleas a little sooner next time."

His cock pulses against my ass as his pursuit to unravel me ramps up a gear. I spread my thighs wider, giving him unlimited access to my soaked pussy. My skin grows hotter as my throat dries. This feels so much better than I could ever explain.

It feels so good I do something I haven't done in years.

I start singing a wickedly dirty song.

"Oh god, yes. There. It feels so good. Please. Yes. *Yes.* Yes!"

He grinds into me harder, his quest for release as potent as mine. "That's it. Nice and loud. I want to hear your screams ringing in my ears for days."

I continue moaning without shame, not the least bit embarrassed.

I'm aching for him.

Dripping for him.

I'm about to lose every one of my morals for him.

When the pad of Nikolai's palm slams down on my throbbing clit, I'm done. Sparks ignite in my womb as my pussy clenches around his thrusting finger. I snap my eyes shut as shudders overwhelm every inch of me. I'm moaning on repeat, my words as stuttered as my heart rate.

I've never experienced something so intense, so wild, so climactic. My orgasm sucks the life right out of me. I'm left panting without reserve, grateful Nikolai's hold on my hip has saved me from tumbling to the floor.

It takes me minutes to return to the land of the living, and even when I do, I'm still dazed with arousal. I feel woozy and free, like I have the world at my feet. Who knew a mind-hazing orgasm could eradicate years of negativity?

The hotness of Nikolai's breath fans my sweat-slicked neck when he says, "Turn around. Let me see what I've done to you."

His rough voice leaves no room for argument. It also gives me my first hesitation of the past ten minutes. It's a prompt reminder that our exchange isn't a romp between two consenting adults seeking release after a tiring week. He's my client, and a replica of the man who instigated my family's demise.

"I can't," I barely whisper, my voice scratchy from the screams I released during ecstasy.

He stiffens for the quickest second, revealing that he heard my mumbled comment. "Can't or don't want to?"

Mercifully, I'm saved from answering him when a feeble knock sounds at my door, closely followed by, "Justine, honey, are you there?"

9

NIKOLAI

Justine's cunt clenches around my finger when I growl, "Ignore it."

I could barely hold back the urge to claim her in a room full of cameras, so you can imagine how potent my cravings are now. It's the equivalent of putting an addict in a room full of cocaine and telling him not to sample the goods.

It would never happen.

Some of the annoyance heating my blood dampens when Justine cranks her neck back to peer at me. Her eyes are sparked with lust, but that isn't the only thing firing in them.

There's also life.

"You want to spin around, but you can't." My lips tug into a smirk when she tries to deny my comment with a brisk shake of her head. "The most dangerous lies are the ones you tell yourself, *Ангел.*"

Her lips twitch in preparation to refute my remark, but a person with an obvious death wish interrupts us for the second time. "Justine? Honey? Is everything okay?" She pauses for a moment, most likely to fix her dentures back into place to stop her questions from coming out with a whistle. "I know you're home. I heard you..." My cock stirs all over again when Justine's cheeks redden at the interrupter's second pause. "Do you want me to call the police? I saw the men entering your apartment. I'm really worried."

Preferring to keep my whereabouts unknown by my father, I withdraw my hand from Justine's soaked panties before stepping back, unpinning her from the door.

My voice is rough with endorphins, but it still holds its usual arrogance when I growl, "Get rid of her."

Justine's address may be on my house arrest documentation, but Vladimir knows as well as anyone that proof is in the eye of the beholder. He won't believe I placed myself under house arrest at my defense attorney's apartment any more than I'm shocked I cooked up the idea. This is the first time I've been led by my cock, and look where it's gotten me?

The teeth marks of my zipper are imprinted in my cock.

When the person responsible for the interlude in our activities knocks for the third time, Justine straightens her clothing before swinging open the door. An old bitty with a headful of silver curls falls forward at a rate too quick for her chubby feet to keep up with.

She doesn't have far to fall—she'd be lucky to be four feet tall—but Justine saves her from landing on the tiles of the entryway by grabbing the tops of her arms.

"Whoa, careful," Justine mutters to her guest.

Just as quickly as her guest's hands shoot up to check none of her ringlets bobbed out of place, Justine has her back on her feet.

The whistle I heard earlier amplifies when the lady I'd guess to be mid to late seventies says, "Sheesh. You had me worried, honey. I wasn't sure if you had company or if these old girls were playing tricks on me." She taps on a hearing aid curled around her ear. "It's been a while since I've heard those noises come from this apartment. I honestly couldn't tell if they were cries for help, or if you were..."

Her words trail off when I fail to stifle my chuckle. I'm not embarrassed she heard Justine's cries of ecstasy. I am fucking stoked even someone as ancient as her recognizes the moans of a woman in need. If she has the ability, perhaps it won't take me as long to coerce Justine into a second 'entrapment' against her front door.

"Oh, excuse me, young man." She's fast, but I don't miss her quick scan of my body before her eyes rocket back to Justine.

They're even wider than her circled lips. "I best let you get back to it."

When she pivots on her heels, preparing to exit, Justine slams her front door shut, endangering her life. Archaic old lady or not, nothing will stop me from making Justine mine tonight.

"Oh, no, don't leave. We're not doing anything you can't participate in." When the elderly lady eyes Justine like she wasn't born many moons ago, Justine coughs out the most pathetic excuse I've ever heard. "I stubbed my toe. It really hurt." She curls her arm around the interrupter's shoulders before ushering her into the living room. "We're long overdue for an official introduction."

"Are you sure I'm not interrupting something?" Justine's elderly guest is acting as if she wants to leave, but her bouncing eyes say otherwise. She's been dying for this moment for months. I guarantee it.

"I'm not a patient man. Make this quick," I growl at Justine in Russian, eyeing her with the eyes of both a murderer and a desperate man.

Justine's head bobs half an inch when her guest breaks away from her side. "Oh, dear, are you hurt?"

I'm so shocked when she grabs my face to inspect the wounds my all-in brawl caused, I represent a *ублюдок* with half a cock. No one handles me without asking, but she's not really handling me, is she? She is trying to take care of me.

My assumptions are proven accurate when she drifts her eyes to Justine and asks, "Where's your first-aid kit? If we don't address his injuries, they may scar." My zipper stops biting my cock when she returns her eyes to mine. They're brimming with unhidden admiration, and they make my skin crawl. I may fuck whores, but I still have standards. "We wouldn't want any nasty little marks ruining such a handsome face."

When she claps her hands together two times, Justine jumps into action. She races across the living room, forgetting the excuse she used to cover up her cries of ecstasy.

I stop summarizing the many ways I can force Justine's visitor to take a leave of absence when she mutters under her breath, "Stubbed toe, hey."

The redness on Justine's cheeks deepens from her guest's leering comment, but she continues her mission to fetch the first-aid kit from the bathroom, unwilling to test her ability to think on the spot against a woman as quick-witted as this silver-haired hellion.

In a record-breaking three seconds, Justine thrusts a new first-aid kit into the chest of our interrupter. "Here you go."

I eye the elderly lady in confusion when her chin hair wobbles along with her pencil-thin brow. Is she requesting me to sit on the couch brushing the back my knees, or are her nighttime suppositories not working as intended? I'm truly unsure. Her angry face is identical to the one Roman makes when he's constipated.

When Justine mouths a quick, "please," I realize it's the former, but before I can act on her request, Justine snatches a cotton ball out of the elderly lady's hand, shoves me into the armchair with force, then mumbles, "Let me, Ms. Aaronson."

The burn scorching my face is forgotten when Ms. Aaronson scolds Justine about her rough application of the iodine. "Gentle dabs."

She displays what she means on a handful of smaller scratches on my cheek before leaving Justine to handle the bigger ones. She's clearly smarter than she looks. If she had hurt me, unintentionally or not, I don't know how I would have reacted. Violence is usually my go-to reaction—I punish first, ask questions later—but I don't see myself facing the same conflict with Justine. I don't know why. The thought just doesn't anger me as you'd expect.

"Much better," Ms. Aaronson praises Justine when she blows on a cut in my left brow I didn't know existed until now.

I'm going to assume the gash is compliments of Detective Franco guiding me into the back of his unmarked cruiser. I was having too much fun goading him about his sister to worry about a little sting to the forehead.

I watch Justine closely when a ghost-like smile stretches across her face. The woman seated across from me isn't a wannabe defense attorney or a woman on the verge of a climax. She's just her —an angel trapped in a void she doesn't know how to get out of but is still capable of spreading her wings to help others.

As the bright gleam in her eyes lessens their blackness, a faint pink hue creeps across her milky white skin.

"Do you know your smile extends all the way down here?" I brush the back of my hand down the silky-smooth skin high on her inner thigh. My cock aches to sink into her when the faint red coloring inflames from my briefest touch. "As does your excitement."

I slump into my chair with a laugh when Justine backhands my chest. Her slap is the equivalent of a fairy tap, but the playfulness it arrives with denotes fireworks in her eyes. She's grappling to reach the top of the food chain, and I'm on the verge of letting her win.

"Unless you want these stabbed in your eye, I suggest you sit still." She snaps together the stainless-steel tweezers she's been using to remove slivers of glass from my wounds, unaware they're the perfect instrument for that exact job.

"Without pain, there is no pleasure." Heat skates through my body hard and fast when her knees curve inward at my reply.

Although she's clearly affected by my accurate statement, she maintains a cool head. That might have more to do with the fact Ms. Aaronson is eyeballing our exchange like she's the head surgeon of my heart transplant.

If she is, she's wasting her time.

I don't have a heart.

Once Justine has half a dozen shards of glass sitting in a makeshift surgeon's dish most people would call a soap dish, she places down the tweezers so she can inspect her handiwork. Her face is whiter than it was earlier, but her eyes remain bright.

She's halfway through her assessment when Ms. Aaronson thrusts a three-strip of Band-Aids into her face. "Better cover up the wounds to stop any nasties," she whistles through her false teeth.

I groan as my dick softens. I can feel blood dribbling down my face, but there's no chance in hell I'll ever wear a Band-Aid.

When I say that, Justine's eyes rocket back to mine, stunned by the menace in my tone. "It's just a Band-Aid."

"Exactly," I snap back, my voice one I haven't used the past hour. "It's a fucking Band-Aid. I don't do Band-Aids."

Unaware this is a fight for two, Ms. Aaronson butts in, "If we don't cover the wound, it will scar."

I'm about to tell her I don't give a fuck if it's capable of healing my black soul, I'm not wearing it, but Justine's quick rip of the material surrounding the Band-Aid stops me.

Acting oblivious to the threat I know she sees in my eyes, she snags a pen from the coffee table, pulls the Band-Aid out of its packaging, then jots something down on the no longer sterile strip.

When she pivots the Band-Aid around to face me a few seconds later, I forget we have company when I read what she wrote across the brown strip.

Bad boy.

What did I tell you? The good girls always want the bad boys.

Confident she's subdued the moody beast inside of me, Justine mutters, "Now it's not just a Band-Aid. It is a kick-ass accessory any *man* would be proud to wear."

Although I'm always up for an argument, the fact she called me a man weakens the desire. With most of the men in my industry decades older than me, for years, I was known as 'the kid.' That all changed when my knife showed them how much I hated it. I didn't have a childhood, so how could anyone give me a childish nickname?

Justine sucks in a relieved breath when I jerk up my chin, granting her permission to place the Band-Aid on the gash above my left brow. I don't usually give in, but there's a flare in her eyes advising she'll pay restitution for my agreement before dawn.

It, along with my cock, would have me agreeing to anything.

Once Justine has the Band-Aid in place, I shift my eyes to the mirror on the other side of the living room. I stare at myself, lost as to who is peering back at me. It isn't the brown sterile strip stretched across my brow deceiving my mind, it is the light in my eyes. They're usually black pools of death. Tonight is the first time they appeared the color of the coolness that slides through my veins.

My eyes return to Justine when she asks, "Have you never worn a Band-Aid before?" Her voice is low, panicked as to how I will reply.

My racing heart can be seen in the flutter of the pulse in my neck, but its fast beat isn't necessarily in anger. I'm more confused than anything.

When Justine arches her brow, patiently awaiting my answer, I say, "No, I haven't. My father believes scars are medals and dressing wounds is for the weak."

I learned fast not to hide the scars Vladimir gave me as a child, or he would have given me ones I couldn't hide. Wearing scars on my sleeves saved them from being worn on my face.

"Is that why you wear these with pride? To prove your strength?"

The light in Justine's eyes fade when I trace my fingertip over a faint scar on her shoulder. It's larger than the tiny one on her neck and covered with a generous amount of concealer.

"My scars have nothing to do with courage, Nikolai." Justine closes the first-aid kit with a snap before standing from her seat. "I have them because a man as hideously misguided as your family wanted to teach me a lesson."

My back molars smash together, but Ms. Aaronson's thunderous balk keeps my response hidden from Justine. "They were put there against your wishes?"

I stare at Justine, silently begging for her to deny Ms. Aaronson's claim, to say she wasn't marked by another. A car accident, a boating incident, a wayward fucking missile, I'll take any of those excuses over Ms. Aaronson's assumption she was deliberately hurt. If I find out her scars were manmade, my hitlist will be endless. I won't just take down the man responsible for her marks, his entire family will become extinct.

Hate so black it scorches my skin burns through me when Justine dips her chin in confirmation of Ms. Aaronson's question.

Just like me, she was scarred by another.

Just like me, she had her wings clipped.

Just like me, she'll have her revenge.

I'll make sure of it.

When the tension hissing in the air becomes too much for Justine to bear, she attempts to dart into the bathroom at the back of her living room. I seize her wrist before she gets one step away from me. I'm barely touching her, but I'm confident she can feel the angry current surging through my veins and the promise it comes with.

We were strangers mere hours ago, but that won't stop me from protecting her. Friends can become enemies as quickly as a once-stranger becomes your everything.

The brave woman in front of me is living proof of this.

"*Ангел*..." I force out through the anger clutching my throat when she yanks her wrist out of my hold before spinning on her heels and sprinting into the bathroom she was racing for earlier.

The brutal bang of the bathroom door startles Ms. Aaronson enough I'm reminded that Justine's devastation isn't solely being witnessed by me.

I hate that.

Acting happy when you're on the verge of breaking is an admirable strength, but I don't want Justine to act when she's around me. The only time she's been honest with herself today was when her juices were coating my palm.

That's why I've been so desperate to get her alone because I knew I had a better chance of lowering the barriers I'm certain she erected years ago if it was just the two of us.

"Oh, dear. I think I made her upset. I should go check on her."

Ms. Aaronson's wobbly strides stop halfway to the bathroom door when I rocket out of my chair to block her with my thumping-with-anger frame.

"I think you've done enough." I don't mean for my voice to come out with the fury it does, but I don't regret it when it replaces the remorse in Ms. Aaronson's eyes with fear. It stops her from chasing down Justine and has her at my complete mercy.

Conscious of her earlier threat to call the police, I lower the severity of my tone while bringing out a side of myself I haven't seen in years—the swooning side.

"Do you know what Justine needs right now?" Ms. Aaronson peers up at me with her big rheumy eyes out in full force. "The type of comfort you can't get from words. She needs carbs, calories, and c—"

"Chocolate," Ms. Aaronson interrupts, grinning.

I was going to say cock, but I'll go with her reply if it ups the ante of her leaving sooner rather than later.

Ms. Aaronson's pencil-thin brow pops up along with her index finger. "And I know the exact thing that'll bring back the rosy coloring to her cheeks."

Now I'm one hundred percent certain I should have said cock.

I'm reminded the wrinkles on Ms. Aaronson's face aren't lifelines when she says, "Pancakes. Pancakes make everything better."

I almost dip my chin in agreement, but her race for the swinging door that leads to Justine's kitchen stops me.

"Where are you going?"

"To make pancakes, silly." The 'S' of silly whistles through her false teeth.

I race to catch up with her. "Can't you make them in *your* apartment?"

She continues for the kitchen, but mercifully, her shuffles are so slow, her dated hearing aids have no issues picking up my question. "Can't. Got no sugar or eggs."

"Then I'll get you some."

Her tattered dressing gown floats across the floorboards when she spins around to face me. "It's too late for that. The local grocer is closed."

I choke out a laugh. "This is Vegas. Nothing is *ever* closed in Vegas."

Her flabby lips twist, but she doesn't argue with me. It's for the best. My patience is stretched thin.

"If I can get you the ingredients needed, can you make them in your apartment?"

Why the fuck am I negotiating? She either does what I ask or dies.

I don't barter.

After banding my arm around Ms. Aaronson's chubby waist, I guide her to the door—forcefully. "I'll get you what's needed, then, if Justine is up for it, she'll join you for a *late* brunch tomorrow morning." Late because Justine and I have more than just the issues of my cock to tackle tonight.

I'm not surprised when the opening of Justine's front door occurs with the shuffling of an expensive pair of black boots. Roman doesn't back down as readily as my crew. That's probably more due to the fact he's my mentor than a soldier hoping to climb the ranks. He challenges me as much as I grate on his last nerve.

Ms. Aaronson brings out all her tricks when Roman steps out of the shadow covering his face. As she takes in his six-foot frame, cut jaw, and deadly black eyes, she appears more and more like a lady on the brink of climax. When she drags her teeth over her lower lip, my stomach's cramps have me grateful I skipped lunch.

"Oh, hello there, young man." She bats her lashes that are as glistening as much as the sweat mustache on her top lip. "What are you doing hiding out here?"

Roman chokes on his spit when I say, "He's here to take you to the store."

I can see the fight in his eyes, smell his wish for an argument on his skin, but since he knows better than to second-guess anything I tell him to do, he gestures for Ms. Aaronson to lead the way. "After you."

She slices her hand through the air, pretending she's not on the verge of coronary failure before saying, "Sheesh, slow down, young man. I need to get my purse first."

While wiggling his finger in his ear to ease the damage Ms. Aaronson's high-pitch squeal caused to his hearing, Roman strays his eyes to mine. He doesn't speak, but I see the demand in his slit gaze.

I owe him.

10

JUSTINE

After taking a few minutes to calm the erratic beat of my heart, I wash my hands in the sink before leaving the bathroom I've been hiding out in the past twenty minutes. Although confident neither Nikolai nor Ms. Aaronson will believe I've been using the facilities this long, I refuse to be called out as a liar twice in under thirty minutes.

As I pace into my living room, my eyes categorize the empty space. A man with an aura as distinct as Nikolai's could never be doused, much less a lady who reeks of nosey-nancying like Ms. Aaronson, so I'm truly at a loss as to where they've gone.

My head rockets to the side when a lock clanking into place booms into my ears. Nikolai is standing in my foyer—all alone. My heart lodges in my throat when I spot Ms. Aaronson's plump shadow through the sheer curtains in my living room. She completes the trek between our apartments in two point five seconds, utterly oblivious to the dangerous situation she has left me in. I could barely deflect Nikolai's interest when she was two feet away from me, so what chance do I stand now?

Nikolai pivots around to face me, his moves as haughty as the flare in his eyes. "Ms. Aaronson wishes for me to pass on her apologies for the interruption, and she has assured me it won't happen again. No matter how loud you scream." A ghost of a smile spreading across his face during his last sentence lessens the severity of it.

"I don't know where to start," he mutters as his eyes drift over my shoulders before sweeping past the budded peaks of my nipples. "At the event we were undertaking before Ms. Aaronson arrived, or the secrets your twenty-minute bathroom break were hoping to conceal."

My throat works hard to swallow as panic engulfs me. There's no doubt I am attracted to him, but nothing can come of it. We are from opposite worlds—even more than he realizes.

My well-used flight mechanism kicks in when Nikolai pushes off his feet and heads in my direction.

I scan the room, seeking a solution to my predicament.

The more my eyes examine my dingy apartment, the more my energy drains. Other than the Juliette balcony hanging fifteen floors above the in-ground pool, Nikolai's six-foot-plus frame is blocking my only viable exit.

Although fleeing is against the terms of Nikolai's bail, sleeping on an outdated couch in the foyer of my building isn't. It will be a restless three nights, but if it's the only solution to stop me from making another foolish mistake this weekend, I must take it.

Yes, I inwardly chant when a brilliant idea pops into my head.

Acting as if it isn't ludicrous for a grown woman to bolt from a prospective bed companion, I sprint toward the couch Nikolai was seated on when I dressed his wounds. My years of track come in handy when I vault over the springless chair, perfectly dismount, and then charge for my bedroom door.

"There are spare blankets and towels in the linen closet. Help yourself to anything in the fridge. I'm not hungry. I'm going to have an early night. I'll see you in the morning," I blubber out breathlessly as I race across my living room.

My peek-toe pumps lose their grip on the wooden floorboards when I slide to a stop inside the master suite. I shut my bedroom door and plaster my back against the thick wooden paneling. I curse my easy-going demeanor when my constant turn of the lock fails to latch it into place. If I had chased down the super, who guaranteed my door would be fixed before I moved in, I'd have more than a panel of wood between me and a mafia prince.

My chest thrusts up and down when a dark shadow extends

past my feet. Although Nikolai is as quiet as a church mouse, I can feel his presence through the door. It's as muggy and intense as it was when we sat beside each other in the transport van earlier tonight.

Tension develops in the air, motivating me to say, "After my performance in the foyer, I know you have no reason to believe me, but it's best for all involved if we pretend tonight never happened. I am your attorney, Nikolai. Ethically, we can only have a client-attorney relationship."

When Nikolai fails to respond to my suggestion, my eyes drift to the door handle, expecting it to twist at any moment.

It doesn't.

It remains perfectly still, not even giving the slightest wiggle in the lead-up to Nikolai's shadow disappearing beneath the door.

My shoulders slump as I sigh softly. It's more a disappointed sigh than a pleased one.

To be safe, I hook my ankle around the wooden chair near my dressing mirror. Its feet scrape across the wooden floorboards when I drag it to stand in front of me. Keeping my weight on the door, I ram the arched back of my chair under the door handle, effectively locking Nikolai out of my room. And myself in it.

After rattling the door to ensure it is adequately restrained, I stroll to my bed. My steps are heavy, weighed down by the guilt besieging me. Not just from four years ago, but from tonight as well.

I'd love to give Nikolai a reason for my contradictory responses, but I wouldn't know where to start. I don't think a man as dominant as Nikolai would appreciate the well-used "It's not you. It's me" line I've given every man I've dated the past four years. Even if it's true, no one ever believes me.

11

NIKOLAI

My blood boils when the winded grunt of the bottom-feeder I have nailed to the brickwork of Justine's apartment registers as familiar. It's pathetic and weak even with its owner being a direct descendent to one of the longest-serving criminal entities this side of Russia.

Sergei may have Popov blood, but he will *never* be a true Popov. He's too weak, too *трусливый*. After what he did to Rico, his limbs should be feeding fish in the bottom of the ocean, not lurking outside of my attorney's apartment.

I revel in the feeling of his pulse weakening for several long seconds since his snoop lost me the chance to refute Justine's fabricated statement before loosening my grip on his throat.

When I fully relinquish him from my hold, he falls to his knees to suck in some much-needed breaths. His lungs are heaving as much now as they did when I stunned him with a quick left-right-left combination before ramming him into the brickwork outside of Justine's bedroom. I should have killed him, but there were too many onlookers to pretend his death was in self-defense.

"What are you doing here, Sergei?" I sound calm even with my insides engulfed by fury. He was right there, peering through the glass door of Justine's balcony, closer to her than I was.

That's unacceptable.

After another three wheezy breaths, Sergei says, "He sent me to check on you."

"He?" I know who he means, but I just want to test where his loyalties lie. If they're with Vladimir, he'll die even with witnesses. If they aren't, I'll save his death for a few more days.

I can't say weeks as that's not a guarantee I can give a man as worthless as Sergei.

Sergei's life is spared for the night when he mutters, "Vladimir. He doesn't believe Trey's recollection of events. He sent me here to check."

"What did Trey tell him?"

He gasps in another breath before releasing it with a half-truth. "That you're hiding out until Terry Lennox's homicide dies down."

It takes me a few moments to recall who Terry Lennox is, but when I do, I can't help but smile.

Dion must have had plans because Officer Lennox's death was even quicker than I anticipated.

I fold my arms in front of my chest, fighting the itch to kill while also acting ignorant to the numerous pairs of eyes on me. My face is well-known in this town. It's almost as infamous as my reputation. "Why didn't Vladimir believe Trey's story? He encourages silence after punishment."

I know this firsthand. It's what he did after sentencing me to be beaten to death at the tender age of sixteen. Ignorance is very much Vladimir's strong point.

When Sergei kicks the monitoring bracelet on my ankle, I work my jaw side to side. "Daniil is on Vladimir's payroll."

I'm not asking a question. I'm stating a fact.

Sergei is too dumb to know that, though.

"Yep. Had him trace the device when you failed to show up at the compound after dusk."

Now I'm even more grateful at my inability to deny my cock its every wish. If I hadn't, Vladimir might have discovered the Popov compound isn't the only facility I'm working. He doesn't know about Clarks, my off-site complex. No one outside my inner circle does. Not even Sergei, and he's technically family. His mother and my mother were cousins.

I say 'were' because they're both dead, victims of the same man. Vladimir.

"How long do I have?" When Sergei appears stumped by my question, I simplify it for the dumb fuck. "In other words, how many lap dances do I need to organize for you at Cliché before you run back to Vladimir with your tail between your legs?"

When he smirks, I'm enticed to lower his grin by several inches. "Come on, Niki, even I know she's worth more than a handful of lap dances."

Calling me 'Niki' already has me wanting to slit his throat, not to mention the gleam his eyes get when they rocket to the glass sliding door of Justine's bedroom. Since her curtains are made of lace, and her bedroom light is on, we can see her moving around her room, preparing to go to bed.

If hate weren't holding my emotions hostage, I'd smile at the flimsy chair Justine notched under her door handle. Alas, it's rare for pleasure to come before business, even with my night starting out as a bit of both.

After stepping to the left, blocking Justine from Sergei's impish glare with my brooding frame, I ask, "If you don't want the star treatment at Cliché, what do you want?"

A gleam I know all too well shines in his soulless eyes when he rubs his hands together. If he thinks he's getting a slice of Justine, he's dead fucking wrong. I don't share my favorite whores, so there's no chance in hell I'll share Justine. For one, she isn't a whore, but even if she were, I'd never share her with a *ублюдок* like Sergei.

My outer appearance doesn't give away my shock when Sergei growls, "Nina," a few seconds later, but my insides sure do.

Nina was my favorite whore—*was* being the prominent part of my reply. I haven't tasted Justine yet, but I have no hesitation in saying she'll make Nina's loss worthwhile. I wasn't lying when I said my cock grew bored years ago. Nina is the equivalent of every Russian man's wet dream. However, my dick doesn't twitch at the thought of her lips circling it. Justine's pillowy lips, though... I'm hard now just recalling how delicious they tasted, much less the idea of them sliding down my shaft.

"Consider Nina yours."

Sergei steps back, shocked, aware Nina was once off-limits.

This is different.

I'm not sharing Nina.

I'm giving her to Sergei.

"I'll have her delivered to you within the hour. But..." I step closer to him, chest to chest, eyes to eyes. "If she shows up dead tomorrow, you'll be buried alongside her tomorrow afternoon."

His smirk reveals how stupid I am being. I've always believed it is better to risk everything than walk away with nothing just to play it safe, but it isn't solely my life at stake here. It is the woman I'm endeavoring to protect after she's already been hurt, the one who doesn't appear to trust anyone.

It's all about the angel who walked through the gates of hell unscathed. Because if she can do that, perhaps she can show the devil the right way out.

I wait for Sergei to enter the elevator at the end of the outdoor corridor before yanking my cell phone out of my pocket. It's cracked like an Easter egg, compliments to my arrest, but it will get the job done.

My boiling anger dulls to a simmer when Trey answers my call two rings later. "If you're hoping to send me on a grocery expedition like Roman, you're shit out of fucking luck. I'm not your lackey."

I twist my lips to hold back my smirk. "The title is negotiable." Once his laughter lessons, I advise him the real reason for my call. "I need Nina delivered to Sergei within the hour."

I hear the groan of a woman on the brink of orgasm before Trey says, "You're loaning Nina to Sergei?"

From the ruffling of sheets and a faint 'come back to bed, baby,' I can only assume he is being entertained at either Clarks or Cliché.

"No." I shake my head, even though he can't see me. "I'm *giving* her to him."

"Fuck." More ruffling, most likely Trey tugging on a pair of jeans. "Vladimir didn't buy my excuse?"

I smirk, not surprised he understood my request without me needing to spell out all the details. He's good like that. Always one step ahead.

"No, he didn't."

"Need decoy?"

I stray my eyes to Justine, who is pulling back the sheets on her bed. "No. I need you to deliver Nina to Sergei. Her delivery will give me a couple of hours—"

"And gain you more blood on your hands..." Trey's words trail off when I growl. "Sorry, Nikolai, but this is Sergei we're talking about." A car door creaking open booms down the line. It's quickly chased by the rumble of a motor. "He swears he doesn't have a thing for necrophilia. I don't believe a fucking word he speaks."

He's not the only one.

"I told him he'd be buried with Nina if he killed her."

"Do you really think that'll stop him?" he huffs out with a grunt.

He isn't technically asking a question, but I answer him anyway. "Probably not. That's why you're going to deliver Nina, then make yourself comfortable."

I can't see Trey, but I can imagine his smile when silence resonates down the line. "Sergei has been seeking a way into your crew for years."

"And you're going to make him believe he's in with a shot. Greed is Sergei's drug of choice. He'd choose it over lust any day of the week."

"Should you be encouraging him down this path, though, Nikolai?" He sounds worried. Justly so. Sergei is even more unhinged than me.

I scrub at the stubble on my chin as my eyes once again stray to Justine. She's in her bed now, sleeping on top of the bedding since it's too humid to slip beneath them. Even with my attention being shot down more than welcomed, my thirst for her is undeniable. I crave her like I already know what she tastes like.

The fucked-up thoughts in my head should frustrate me more than they do, but for some reason, they don't. A life without challenges is boring and convincing an angel to side with a devil is far from tedious.

I watch Justine for a few more seconds before shifting my focus back to my conversation with Trey. "I don't have much choice. Vladimir has already walked us down this path. At least this way, I get a few hours of reprieve."

"True." Trey's big exhale rustles down the line. He's not one hundred percent convinced, but since he is minus a better solution, he's going to run with mine. "If Sergei falls for it, what do you want me to do with Nina?"

I take a moment to consider a reply. It's nowhere near long

enough considering the short period of time I've known Justine. "Offer her an out. If she wants it, buy her a one-way ticket to LA. If she doesn't, make sure she is aware our agreement is terminated."

"Look at you, acting all grown up." My swollen chest shrinks when he adds on with a laugh, "If only you could get rid of your fiancée just as easily, eh?"

Yes, I'm engaged.

No, it's not up for discussion.

It was a stupid mistake I made years ago while high, and I'm still fucking paying for it. I'd cut ties now if it wouldn't cause severe implications to plans I've had in the works for years.

Alas, even princes have to occasionally do shit they don't want to do to keep the wheels turning.

"With all the weaponry trade we've conducted the past six months, have you found a vanishing potion yet?"

Trey's reply is more honest than deceitful. "Yeah, it's called a bullet."

After talking shop with Trey for almost twenty minutes, I make my way back into Justine's retro apartment. Our conversation didn't stray far from the ones we've had many times the past six months, except this time, I requested my personal life to be included in our efforts to keep Vladimir in the dark about my business proposals. There will be less chance of an ambush if we watch Vladimir as closely as he forever watches me. I hate needing to be cautious, but I prefer it over being dead.

I dump my cell phone onto the table housing the letter opener Officer Prentice almost had a meeting with before heading for Justine's bedroom door. I know her door isn't locked. Not only did I fail to hear the locking mechanism slide into place when she slammed it shut, but the barrel of the lock is drilled out. It makes the perfect peep hole, which I look through not even two seconds later.

Justine's strengths shine when I notice the rise and fall of her chest. She's sleeping peacefully, blissfully unaware of the chaos homing in on her.

I could let her rest, but I can't execute a perfectly laid-out plan with patience.

I also need to shut her blinds before anyone gets a sneak peek of the luscious thighs exposed by the high rise of her skirt.

The rusty hinges on Justine's door would buckle under the force of my boot in no time, but then I'd run the risk of waking her, so, instead, I carefully apply pressure to the door handle until the mechanism stopping it from twisting warps.

Just before the foldable chair Justine placed under the door-knob collapses with a bang, I push open the door enough I can catch it in my hand. Word to the wise—if you want to keep a bad man out of your room, don't barricade your door with a foldable chair. You may as well leave it open and pretend you locked it.

Once Justine's curtains are closed, I move to the side of the bed she's sleeping on. She stirs when I track my finger over a mottled scar on the back of her right knee. It doesn't replicate any of the burns and marks my body holds. It's angry and stretched as if her skin was shredded by an immense amount of force.

The span of her scars and their odd shape keep me fascinated for several long minutes. I'm not surprised. Scars tell a million stories, and I'm dying to hear hers.

"You've just got to be brave enough to share them with me, Ангел."

While staring at her angelic face, I count backward from ten, knowing I should leave when I reach zero, but aware that's unlikely to happen. Vladimir is already watching, so now I must watch too. I watch the way Justine's lips part when she takes in shallow breaths and the paleness of her cheeks since she is unaware she's caught my eye. I watch a red blush creep from her knees to her nape when the desire to touch her becomes too much to bear, and how her breathing grows along with her body's hue when she senses my touch. Then I watch her some more just for the hell of it.

I should wake her so I can finish what I started on her front door. I should spread her thighs wide, snap off her no-doubt still soaked panties, and eat her cunt as if I've never been fed. I should fuck her until her body is so flushed with heat, her scars will fade in its fiery-red coloring, but I can't. Not only must I remain alert in preparation for Vladimir's next move, but there's also something so surreal about seeing an angel in the flesh, I can't act on any of the inane thoughts in my head.

Rico said years of misery would be undone by a reward I'd never anticipate. I assumed it would be of monetary value. I had no clue it would be in the form of an angel.

12

JUSTINE

The grumbling of my stomach overtakes the sizable tiger-like yawn ripping through my mouth. Rising from my slumped position, my hand darts up to rub the sleep from my eyes. A waffle-knit blanket my grandma knitted for me when I left for college falls from my body when I scoot to the edge of my bed.

With my bladder declaring its desire to be emptied, I must ignore the screams of my temples for more sleep and shuffle to the bathroom. The sun beaming into the living room announces it is morning, but my body is acting as if it has barely slept an hour.

My bare feet are noiseless as I enter the foggy bathroom across from my bedroom. I can't tell if it's a hazy morning hampering my vision or the goop in my eyes from a measly few hours of sleep.

After finishing my business, I flush the toilet before shuffling to the sink to wash my hands. I'm so zonked I don't register the sound of running water until a loud shriek follows it.

I startle to within an inch of my life when a male voice screams, "Jesus fucking Christ."

My eyes bulge out of my head when a wet—and head-to-toe naked—Nikolai dives through the shower curtain pulled across my bathtub. With my mind fritzed from a lack of sleep, I completely forgot I have a houseguest.

In no time at all, the temperature in the room doubles, the mugginess evenly distributed between the scalding water the flushing toilet caused to Nikolai's shower and the magnificent image of him stripped bare.

"*Утро*, Justine," he greets me when he notices me standing at the side and gawking without remorse. His voice reeks of attitude, as does his composure.

I can understand his cockiness. His body is mind-blowing. Not even the inclusion of an ankle monitor on his right leg can detract from the sweat-producing visual. Droplets of water careen through six indents in his stomach before rolling past a large tattoo weaved around his right hip and halfway down his thigh. The teasing portion of a V muscle I spotted yesterday is on full display, proudly arrowing in on a section of his body that would put any man to shame.

"My god, is that a python?" I question, my words as colorful as my cheeks.

"It's a dragon," Nikolai corrects, assuming I am referring to his tattoo.

I'm not. I try to tear my eyes off his cock. I miserably fail. The instant my eyes deviated past his mid-section, I was thrust into an idiotic trance. I've heard the size of a man's hand is a good predictor of the size of his cock, but I had no idea it was true. Nikolai's hands are massive, his fingers long and pussy-clenching thick.

When he notices the direction of my gaze, the heat in the room doubles. "Be careful, *Ангел*," he warns, his voice sultry and smooth. "A dragon has never died from a snake bite, but that doesn't mean it shouldn't be wary of the snake. Venom isn't a snake's only danger."

My eyes rocket to his face when his cock stiffens. He stares at me, the direction he wants to take our exchange unmissable in his heavy-lidded gaze. The hunger in his eyes is as wild as it was last night—if not more rampant. He looks like a man about to go on a hunt, and I'm his prime target.

As he slowly advances, I shift my eyes to the side, striving to break free from his enthralling aura. My pulse quickens when I catch my reflection in the vanity mirror. Now I understand Nikolai's unbendable approach. My brain is screaming, No. No. No, but my blushing cheeks, dilated eyes, and parted lips are clamoring for the opposite. My body is screaming, Yes. Yes. Yes, while demanding he take me now, immediately, and without delay.

My body wants him—badly.

The desires playing havoc with my mind vanish when the glistening of dog bites reflects in the vanity mirror. With the bathroom lit by fluorescent lighting, the scars on my body are more prominent than ever. Their ghastly appearance pushes a pledge I made years ago to the forefront of my mind and remind me that I'm not worthy of a man as handsome as Nikolai.

It may be extremely shallow of me to think this way, but it's true, and since I place a high value on honesty, it must be adhered to.

Wanting to leave the bathroom before Nikolai discovers the marks on my shoulders are tame compared to the rest, I charge for the door. My frantic pace has me kicking the bin under the vanity sink, but I continue my mission, my pride too fragile to sustain another rejection.

Air snags in my throat when Nikolai outwits my exit. I wail and kick when he wraps his arm around my waist and draws me to his bare torso. My trepidation has more to do with his reaction to my imperfections than actual fear.

Nikolai's hot breath fans my ear when he says, "You like what you see, yet you continually deny me. Why?"

"Who says I like what I see?" I snap back, my determination to flee surpassing my manners.

Desire floods me when he rocks his hips forward, dragging his erection along the globes of my ass. My eyes bulge when a husky moan unwillingly seeps from my lips.

"Tell me again you don't like what you see," he mocks, his tone too arrogant for my liking. "You want my cock nearly as much as I'm dying to slide it between your lips."

His words are hoarse, like the thought of me sucking his cock has his mouth drying up.

My lips twitch, preparing to deny his statement, but he squashes his finger against my mouth, outwitting my attempts.

"Before you speak, be warned. If you lie to me again, I'll tie you up and bring you to the brink of climax—over and over again—only stopping when my cum is covering every inch of you. Then I still won't let you come, no matter how much you beg."

I sag against his chest as excitement steamrolls through me.

Wait, what? When have I ever been aroused by filthy talk?

His erect cock digs into my backside. "I won't chase someone who doesn't want to be chased. Do you want this? Yes or No."

I nearly nod until the quickest glimpse of my reflection swallows my reply.

He's not the problem. I am.

"No, I don't."

Since I'm staring at my reflection, my response sounds honest.

When Nikolai places me on my feet, I keep my eyes front and center, not trusting my lust-driven heart to follow the prompts of my street-smart brain.

Not long later, the shower curtain opening sounds through my ears. I wait a beat, giving my body time to correctly identify the noise of water running over flesh before I crank my neck back. My hearing didn't falter. Nikolai is once again in the shower.

Although the sheer curtain does a good job of keeping the water in the tub, it neglects to conceal Nikolai's pussy-shuddering frame from my perverted eyes. My pussy clenches when I follow the water running down his perfect body, only stopping when it reaches his midsection.

I fail to stifle a groan when Nikolai fists his stiffened shaft. He slides his hand to the base before slowly returning it to the tip. My brain screams for me to look away, but my heart refuses to comply. The visual of him stroking his cock is... I don't have a word to explain it. Mind-boggling. Hypnotic. I'll-never-forget-it, out-of-this-world-unreal.

"Why watch when you can join, *Ангел?*" Nikolai's voice is as hard-lined as his cock.

It's the fight of my life to make my eyes snap to the floor when he adjusts his position, awarding me an uninterrupted view of the pussy-clenching visual. The only reason I do is the sheer arrogance beaming from his eyes. It's as thick and unforgiving as the veins feeding his magnificent cock.

"You're responsible for this. Your eyes, your lips, your body." His strokes quicken with each word he speaks. "I couldn't sleep thinking about how good you'd feel wrapped around my cock. That's why I was in the shower, seeking release. If I didn't do something, I would have slipped under your knitted blanket and taken you while you slept."

My eyes snap to his as shock rockets through me. How does he know I slept with the blanket my grandmother knitted me when I left for college? I freeze as another reality smacks into me. My chair wasn't lodged under the door when I trudged to the bathroom.

I glare at Nikolai, my anger overtaking the lust curtailing me. "You were in my room." I'm not asking a question. I am stating a fact.

He winks as his cock thickens more. "You're even more beautiful when you're sleeping."

I roll my eyes, disgusted at both Nikolai and myself. I can't believe I've become so lust-hungry I'm standing in the bathroom, watching a man stroke his cock, instead of working on a way to ease my family's turmoil. The perfect solution to end the drama killing my family is standing in front of me, fisting his cock. But instead of seizing the opportunity Nikolai's arrest presents me with, I'm acting like a lust-crazed idiot more determined to have her pent-up sexual frustration released than her flesh and blood. My grandmother would be rolling in her grave if she could see me now.

With my head held high, vainly acting uninterested, I leave the bathroom. Every step I take is a torturous feat.

"If you haven't finished in twenty minutes, I'm switching off the water heater," I warn, my voice wielding uncharacteristic wrath.

With that, I shut the bathroom door, locking in the rough chuckles of a mafia prince breathless in ecstasy.

13

NIKOLAI

"We've held him off for as long as we can, Nikolai. We can't delay the inevitable for a second longer."

I glare at Roman, the playfulness I exuded in the shower two hours ago long forgotten. Wrangling Ms. Aaronson back into her apartment thirty minutes ago already had my mood slipping, and now Roman has gone and fucked it up entirely.

"I have a monitoring bracelet on my ankle. How far does he expect me to get?"

Roman scoots to the edge of his chair in the dining nook of Justine's kitchen. "You know how Vladimir has been since Rico's death. He doesn't trust anyone." I'm about to say his lack of trust occurred long before Rico's untimely demise, but Roman continues talking, thwarting my endeavor. "He's also aware a tracker won't stop you."

He's right, but it doesn't make his confession any easier to swallow.

What he says next, though, sure does. "And while he's occupied ensuring your whereabouts are known at all times, we'll have the opportunity to slip an operation under his nose without his consent."

Smirking, he slides a manila folder to my side of the table. It's similar to the one he left on my bed last night, but the target's name is different. It belongs to the officer who bullied Justine mere minutes before he attempted to goad me into spending the long weekend in a holding cell.

While perusing Officer Prentice's file, I say, "I thought you wanted to let his 'mishap' slide?"

Roman argued that exact point last night when I requested him to compile a file on Officer Prentice. He thought I was starting a war that didn't need to be fought and assured me he'd find a way for Officer Prentice to learn the meaning of the word 'manners' without me needing to get involved.

I wasn't fucking happy, but with Vladimir already having me burning the candle at both ends and the media circulating a story about the death of a long-serving Las Vegas judge, I gave Officer Prentice a few days of amnesty. He will still be punished, just not until Justine has my charges expunged, which will now be in a legal manner since the media was referencing the judge I have on my payroll—*or should I say had?*

Judge Santos was found deceased in his home late last night. Reports aren't saying how he died, but if the photographs I have of him in my safe at Clarks are anything to go by, I'm going to assume he was asphyxiated during sex. He liked things kinky and considering his flavor of the month was usually an unsuspecting male teen willing to do anything to stay out of jail, he's lucky to have lasted as long as he did.

If he even suggested that type of plea bargain with me when we met shortly before my eighteenth birthday, I would have killed him where he stood. Alas, not all teens are as ruthless as me. They're also not as smart. They have no clue the judicial system here is so overcrowded, the chances of them spending a night in jail for a misdemeanor are extremely low—almost as low as my mood drops when a handful of photos slip out of Officer Prentice's file. He doesn't just bully women. His quirks extend to kids too.

"How old is she?"

Roman's worldly eyes lift from the photo of a badly battered girl I'd guess to be early teens to me. "Fifteen. These images were obtained during her arrest for soliciting." He opens a second folder with as many pictures as the first one, although grainier. "These are the ones from a surveillance camera in the alleyway an hour before she was arrested."

My jaw ticks when he hands me the photographs. The girl barely had a scratch on her before Officer Prentice approached her. Her cheeks only get busted up after he moves her into a shadow in the corner of the frame.

The timeline of images is already enough to get my blood boiling, but what Roman says next utterly annihilates any sense of normality. "I had his plates run through our surveillance system. Excluding the occasional piss in the alleyway, Prentice hasn't left his vehicle parked on the corner of Malor and West Lucy."

"West Lucy?" When Roman dips his chin, my blood pressure skyrockets. "He's here? Staking Justine's apartment?"

"That's the thing," Roman says, his tone low. "He's not on the roster for any drive-bys or surveillance in this region. No one is. Judge Ryder didn't request surveillance as part of your house arrest, which means he's only here for one reason."

"He's toying with me." I drag my hand along my jaw, tracking the tic there when an even more perverse thought enters my mind. "Or he wants to toy with Justine."

I've never heard my voice as hot and violent as it is now. It truly seems as if it was delivered straight from hell. Its change in temperament is understandable. Officer Prentice didn't just beat the teen he arrested, he did it while forcing her to perform a sex act on him.

If he thinks he'll achieve the same outcome here, he's shit out of luck.

I'll slit his throat before he gets within an inch of Justine.

When Roman spots the grave expression on my face, he slides the file back to his side of the table before standing from his chair. "I'll call in the crew and get this taken care of."

By 'this' he means Officer Prentice.

I slap my hand down on the file, stopping his hasty retreat. "No. I'll handle it. This is personal, which means it's my responsibility."

Roman glares at me funny, but before he can voice a single smidge of the confusion I see in his eyes, a commotion at the side gains our attention. Justine has been thrust into the kitchen by Viktor. Her eyes are wide and frightened until they lock on me. Even scared, she's already aware I'll never let anyone hurt her.

"I found her snooping outside."

Justine shakes her head, denying Viktor's claims. "I wasn't snooping."

My back molars become friendly when Roman says, "Nikolai is busy, Justine. Go wait in his room until he is ready for you—"

The confusion in his eyes doubles when I cut him off by slicing my hand through the air. Usually women are forbidden from any Popov meetings, even ones as simple as today. But Justine isn't like the women at the Popov compound. For one, she's not a whore, and I'll kill anyone who dares to say differently, and two, this is her realm as much as it is mine.

Roman's throat works through a hard swallow when I say, "She's fine, Roman. Let her be."

When I stand from my chair to head Justine's way, a tiny vein in her neck works overtime. She dressed differently than she was this morning. She's switched out her business attire for a fun, flirty look. The teasing length of her shorts has me dying to see more of her long legs, and her shirt is modest but fitted, meaning I have no issues taking in the way her nipples bud more the closer I get to her.

When I finish bridging the gap between us, I notice a slight alteration to her scent. It's still seductive as fuck, but it has matured, like our grapple in the bathroom fortified a steel rod in her back. She's aware she doesn't belong in the dark and dangerous world I'm endeavoring to pull her into, but she also knows she doesn't belong outside of it either.

No wonder why I'm so conflicted. Justine's emotions are as contradicting as my sudden urge to be her knight in shining armor. I want to say my protectiveness stems from knowing she's damaged like me, but it's more than that. She has more depth than her outer shell portrays. I just need to get her alone to work out what it is.

Justine is tall for a girl, bringing her only a few inches under my six-foot-two height, but I feel like a giant when I stand in front of her. It isn't because I'm wearing boots and her feet are bare. It's from the way she peers up at me with innocent yet seductive eyes. They're as soft as the clouds angels dance on but capable of provoking the deadly fury of a devil.

I'm tempted as fuck to see if her skin will sizzle under my touch as much as the gleam in her eyes fires whenever I'm in her presence, but I can feel the eyes of my men on me, so instead of touching her like I really want to, I keep my hands balled at my side.

Let me tell you, it's a fucking hard feat.

My struggles are heard in my words when I ask, "What do you need, *Ангел*?"

"Umm..." She scans the room, as overwhelmed by the tension crackling between us as me. With how roasting it is, she says the last thing I'm anticipating. "I was just wondering if you needed anything at the store?" She jerks her chin to a door I'm assuming is a pantry on our left. "There is barely enough in there to scrape together a meal, let alone three days' worth, so I thought I should go gather some supplies."

"You're running to the store?" Hesitation thickens my tone, but Justine seems oblivious to it. As she nods, her eyes flare with excitement, pleased I'm falling for her ruse. I'm not, but I'm happy to play along. "To gather supplies?"

When she nods again, a rueful smirk tugs my lips high. Although I'm dying to taste her, a trip to the store is best for all involved. While she's out, I can handle Officer Prentice's crimes without needing to expose her to my heinous world just yet. She has the strength to rule an empire, but I don't want to frighten her until the fire in her eyes is fully relit.

"Are you going to feed me, *Ангел*?"

My nostrils flare when the need in my voice causes Justine's knees to pull together. Her scent wipes the chaos from my mind, foolishly leading me to believe being her savior will far exceed the losses I will endure—even more so when she whispers, "Yes." She does a quick swallow to force down her lie before adding, "Food. Only food."

I let her fib slide with a smile. "We'll see."

When I crank my neck to Roman, he tosses me a wad of cash out of the bundle Cliché earned last night. Its rolled-up appearance hides the fact a majority of it was tucked in the sequined panties of over three dozen strippers. The women in my club keep their tips *after* they've been thoroughly cleaned by my crew, and no, I'm not referencing the dirty mitts of my clients. I only have legitimate businesses for one reason—to hide the transactions I don't want the law to see.

While yanking three one hundred dollar bills out of the bundle,

I nudge my head to Viktor. "Take Viktor with you. He'll keep you safe."

The playfulness heating my veins gets a second dose when Justine snorts. "I'll be safer without him in my presence."

Her sass takes a backseat when I mutter, "Now that he's aware of who you are, he'd slit his own throat before he touches you again."

Viktor looks surprised by the protectiveness in my tone, but he nods his head nonetheless, aware of the repercussions if he dared to second-guess me. "Y-y-yes, boss. I-I'll take her to the store. I'll keep her safe."

I tuck the bills into the pocket in Justine's shorts before returning my eyes to her face. "Go to the store, get what you need, and then come back here immediately."

The possessiveness in my tone has her jumping to my command. "Okay."

After a quick grin, she spins on her heels, preparing to leave. She barely gets two steps away when my growl of her nickname has her freezing halfway through the swinging door.

"Are you forgetting something?"

When she cranks her neck back to me, I tap my cheek. Her breathing grows excited as she swings her eyes to my crew. If she's hoping they'll jump in and save her, she's seeking help from the wrong people. My men wouldn't challenge me on my best day, much less provoke me when I'm the most vulnerable.

As Justine drifts her massively dilated eyes back to mine, her chest rises and falls three times. My cock thickens painfully quick when she stammers out, "Attorneys don't kiss their clients goodbye."

She's once again telling me no, but her body is on the opposite end of the spectrum. Her nipples are hard enough I'm afraid they're about to break through her shirt, and the syrupy goodness my cock is dying to have coating it doubles in strength.

Fight as she may, not even she is safe from the chaotic storm brewing between us.

I step closer to her, budding her nipples even more. "Then I guess I better get a new attorney... as I'm planning on doing a whole lot more than kissing you."

It's the fight of my life not to gorge on her now when the

quickest brush of my lips on her cheek buckles her knees. She's hot all over, her needs as desperate as mine. I'm so eager, if the images I scanned earlier weren't replacing the teen's face with Justine's, nothing would stop me. Alas, this stranger became my everything as quickly as my family became my enemy.

Both were brutal, unexpected events.

I'm just hoping this one doesn't end as gorily.

14

NIKOLAI

"He won't get close enough to touch you, I swear." Maya peers up at me, blinking and mute. She's panicked about my request for help but mindful her assistance will be greatly rewarded. "I need someone who matched the description of his previous victims at short notice. You were the perfect candidate. He likes them..." I stop before I say *small and malnourished like you*. I want her help, not remind her about how poorly Vladimir treats his children.

Maya is my half-sister—well, she would have been if I had Vladimir's blood as my mother led me to believe. Her mother was a French tourist who was as blinded by Vladimir's dark insides as she was the bright lights of Vegas.

Vladimir pulled all his best tricks on her—a promised penthouse with views of the strip, a sleek new ride, and a sworn oath to end his promiscuous ways.

All she ended up with was a dungeon-like room in the basement of the Popov compound and three children who are treated more like slaves than family.

Although Rico endeavored to help as many as he could before he was killed, the effort was bigger than anyone could have comprehended. Over the past fifty years, Vladimir has had many whores. With his view on protection as lax as his ideas on equality for women, his offspring grew exponentially each year. The age of his children extends from forty-three to six weeks old, his latest daughter compliments of the twenty-three-year-old Scandinavian woman he purchased on the black market in the middle of last year. Their daughter wasn't immaculately conceived, nor was she born in the safety of a hospital.

If the last reports are accurate, her conception and birth traumatized her mother so much, Vladimir is on the verge of sending her to live with Maya's mother in the underbelly of the Popov mansion. It is gruesome, but it's a better outcome than the one Vladimir's other insubordinate whores were handed. Her life will be spared, although I can't guarantee it will be full of rainbows and sunshine.

I'm pulled from my thoughts when Sergei enters Justine's dining room on Trey's heel. I hate that I'm being forced to bring Sergei into this, but he is a master at removing tracking devices without alerting the authorities. The scope of my ankle bracelet perimeter should include the alleyway where Officer Prentice is about to meet his timely demise, but I'd rather local law enforcement officers not know I was in the alleyway at the time of their fellow officer's death.

It's easier to get off a murder conviction when you have a solid alibi, hence the reason Justine's apartment is being swarmed by my crew members and the whores who keep them occupied during stints of chaos.

After slumping into one of the chairs squashed around the dining table, I hook my foot onto the warped wood, then nudge my head to the swinging door. "Go with Trey, Maya. Lia brought some clothes for you to change into."

I need to get things moving. Justine left nearly twenty minutes ago. If she shops as quickly as she comes, I don't have a minute to spare.

After giving me a warning look, announcing his unease about my plan, Trey guides Maya into the living room where Lia is waiting. I had originally intended to use Lia for my ruse. She's another one of Vladimir's many daughters, but instead of cowering in the shadows like Maya, waiting for the scraps Vladimir's sons leave behind, she fights for her share. Not even a run-in with Satan himself saw her knees knocking in fear. All it did was make her more determined.

Lia will never be seen as an equal in the ruthless, male-dominated world she was born in, but she has earned the respect of siblings the past ten years. Some say that's compliments to her sharing my bloodline, but I'm not so quick to agree. She has the determination and grit of our mother and refuses to settle for anything less than perfection.

Regrettably, those traits made her unsuitable bait to lure Officer Prentice out of his car parked on a pedestrian-littered street, so I had no choice but to look elsewhere.

Maya is the perfect candidate. Her short height and petite frame make her appear years younger than she is, and she gives off the vibe of a woman beaten into prostitution—Officer Prentice's ideal plaything. His run-in with a teen prostitute last month wasn't his first soirée with underaged women. His unknown 'record' is almost as long as mine.

With my blood hot with annoyance, I lock my eyes with Sergei's almost black gaze. If the bags under his eyes are anything to go by, he didn't mourn Nina's decision to return to LA for long. Since he wrongly believes he's 'one of the crew' now, he used his membership to the exclusive club to his advantage. He only left Cliché because Trey dragged him out of there at my request.

"What will it take to get this removed?"

Sergei twists his fat lips as I wish I could his neck. "These units aren't worth the materials used to make them." He yanks my foot to the left before slowly dragging it to the right. "The GPS portion of the tracker doesn't work everywhere, so if you're staying close to base, you don't need to remove it. Just hit it on the brickwork a few times to weaken its signal."

"Who said I'm staying close to base? You know me, Sergei. Forever restless." My voice is calm and collected even though I'm anything but. He's digging for information he's not privileged to know, and I don't fucking like it.

Sergei smiles a slick grin, loving my ruffled appearance. "Just assumed, that's all. From your eagerness last night, I thought it would be a day or two before you'd go back to your old ways." He twists his lips again, this time more in mockery than amusement. "Perhaps her cunt isn't as sweet as the generous swell of her tits."

He watches my hands ball into fists before continuing, "Or perhaps you didn't fuck her how she needs to be fucked... hard and brutal like the many whores before her."

Snickering at my narrowed eyes, he threads a thin wire-like contraption through little loops in the side of my tracker. He thinks his birthright will excuse his arrogance.

He's dead fucking wrong.

I don't care who you are. If you disrespect me, expect to die.

After fiddling with my ankle monitor for a few seconds more, Sergei raises his scheming eyes to mine. The bigheaded glint in his eyes tells me he has no clue how thin the ice is beneath his skates. "I bet it would only take a cut or two to have her whimpering beneath me."

A jeering grin touches his lips when I fail to respond to his rile. He knows he has me wedged between a rock and a hard place. Without him, my ankle monitor will remain, and Officer Prentice will get off his charges scot-free, but by keeping him around, I need to remain cautious because his crimes are as vile as the man I'm attempting to prosecute.

He doesn't just cut women.

He kills them too.

With my annoyance hidden as well as I plan to hide his body, Sergei returns to disarming my ankle monitor. You'd think he'd need more than a thin piece of wire, a bolt, and a nut to get the job done, but within minutes, the lock mechanism pops open without the tracking light missing a beat, and I have Sergei nailed to the wall of Justine's kitchen by his scrawny fucking throat.

He claws at my hand like a girl when my death-like grip stills his legs. His pulse is fading fast, the light in his eyes almost diminished in under a minute.

"How many times do I have to tell you, Sergei? How many times must I warn you about goading me the way you do my brothers?" I tighten my grip, loving the blue tinge of his lips that are attempting to disperse the same excuses he always gives me. "You were joking, right? Just playing. Having fun. You're my cousin, my blood, so I should know you didn't mean to upset me with your comment. You were keeping things interesting, right?" I sing, canarying the excuses he constantly gives me.

My clutch on his throat prevents him from nodding, but not even being on the brink of death can hide the agreement in his eyes.

"But the thing is, Sergei, you didn't just disrespect me this time around. You disrespected her." When his eyes bulge, seemingly confused, or perhaps because I'm squeezing his neck too tight, I endeavor to squash his confusion. "You called Justine a whore."

It's virtually impossible for him to do, but he manages to shake his head in denial.

"You may not have straight up said it, but you implied it." *And it pissed me off more than I can explain.*

I've been surrounded by whores my entire life. I was raised by them, fed by them, and fucked many of them, but hearing Justine being called a whore caused something inside me to snap. Sergei is family and killing him guarantees I'll be dead by the end of the week, but no matter how much the voice inside my head demands for me to loosen my grip, I can't. I'm nobody's savior, but I sure as fuck want to be Justine's.

By killing him, I'll terrify them all.

By freeing him, I'll terrify no one but myself.

Usually I'd end a life without a second thought, but even with hate heating my blood so much it turned black, I know there's more at stake here than just the repercussions of my actions. Every decision I make from here on out will affect Justine as much as it does me. I told my men she's off-limits, and I warned them what would happen if they so much as look at her the wrong way, so I'm just as confident it won't be solely them questioning why I sentenced Sergei to death years after his crimes. Vladimir will make inquiries as well.

With that in mind, I loosen my grip on Sergei's neck before issuing a threat I'll uphold no matter how affluent his DNA. "If you touch a single hair on Justine's head, I'll slit your throat and leave your body for the vultures because even a shallow grave in a roadside ditch is too good for you."

As Sergei slumps to the floor to suck in some lung-deprived breaths, I push through the swinging door of Justine's kitchen, more than eager to get the party started.

"Let's go. I want Prentice's blood hosed off the sidewalk before Justine returns from the store."

After snatching the letter opener off Justine's desk, I make a beeline for the door with Trey, Roman, and Maya closely shadowing me. Even with my emotions belonging to those of a stranger, I know who I am.

I am not a vigilante or an adversary of the devil.

I am Nikolai, Russian Mafia Prince.

15

NIKOLAI

My steps into Justine's guest bedroom slow when I detect I am being watched. I'm used to being eyed, men want to be me, women want to be bedded by me, but this stare is different. It's pronged with admiration, but it has no infatuation attached to it—thank fuck. That would have been awkward considering the watchful gaze is coming from my sister.

Lia acts unaffected by the blood-splattered clothes and boots dumped at the end of my bed. She's accustomed to the gore associated with our childhood. Sometimes, she was even the perpetrator of it.

With my exchange with Sergei still in the forefront of my mind, Officer Prentice's death was swift and unpleasurable. The stab wound I inflicted to his chest bled more than I anticipated, but that had more to do with the fact Justine's letter opener wasn't as sharp as I'd hoped.

Don't get me wrong, it got the job done, but my knife usually leaves my face blood-free. Since that didn't occur this time around, I had no choice but to shower for the second time before midday.

I finish drying droplets of water on my chest before dumping my towel onto the bed housing Lia's backside. "Where's Maya?"

Lia twists the top half of her body to face the wall, granting me the privacy to tug on a pair of boxers and jeans while she says, "Trey is taking her back to the compound. She's a little shaken up, the poor thing." She'd seem more sincere if she weren't picking at the varnish on her nails. "I really wish she would have accepted your offer to move her out of the compound. She'll never have a life if she remains under Vladimir's reign."

I jerk up my chin, agreeing with her. "She would have given it more thought if it weren't for her mother. She's still under Vladimir's spell."

I inwardly laugh at Lia's gag. Even with her sharing Vladimir's DNA, she loathes him almost as much as me. I'm not surprised. Our mother continually placed Vladimir before us when we were children.

Lia is four years older than me and was despised by our mother on sight because she was born without the required equipment between her legs needed for her to become the next heir of the Popov entity. That honor went to Rico, who was born three weeks after Lia.

"You can't fix stupid." After checking the coast is clear with a quick glance my way, Lia pivots back around to face me. "Did he cry actual tears?" She clasps her hands together like she's watching a sappy movie. "I bet he did. The cry-for-my-momma vibes were pumping out of him when you grabbed him unaware."

I arch a brow in suspicion. "You watched me serve Prentice his punishment?"

"Of course." A hint of her husband's English heritage highlights her tone when she attempts to act innocent. I say 'attempt' as it isn't a look Lia can pull off without an immense amount of acting. "Adrian said a direct hit to the precordium almost always results in death, but he won't let me put his theory into practice." She sighs like she's annoyed her husband saddled her down with responsibility and kids, where, in reality, she adores him. "Talking about theories, I better get back on deck before the next shipment comes in. Adrian's men still believe compromises begin with words. Us Popovs know busted kneecaps work much better."

She stops gathering her purse from a set of drawers on her right when I say, "I promoted Adrian to head of operations at Knightsbridge." Her eyes dart between mine, but she's too stunned to speak. It's for the best as my terms aren't up for negotiation. "We need someone with his skillset while endeavoring to overtake Davies's operations on that side of the continent."

She doesn't buy the lie I am selling as she knows this has nothing to do with business. "You said a move was years away, Nikolai. That you'd give us plenty of notice."

"Things change—"

"Not in a weekend. Jesus." Nothing but unbridled panic is heard in her tone, aware that this is more than a wish to coerce my attorney into my bed. This goes way deeper than that. "Are you sure you're ready for this?"

Nodding, I brush the back of my index finger across her cheek to wipe away a blob of moisture balled there. She is as surprised by her tears as I am by my chivalry. Kindness was not a trait our mother instilled in us.

After clearing her cheeks of moisture, she steps closer to me, her eyes begging. "Let us stay. Let us help your campaign."

"No, Lia. We discussed this. Adrian and you were to move back to the UK before I commenced my bid for Vladimir's throne." As images of her punishment the last time she sided with me over Vladimir flash before my eyes, I step back, placing distance between us. We're not overly close, but I still don't want to see her hurt. "If you won't do this for Adrian, do it for your girls."

It's low of me to bring her daughters into this, but I know they're the only things needed for her to agree to my request. Lia is all about blood and gore until her eyes lock on her twin girls. They are three years old, yet they've never met their grandfather. Lia would fall onto a knife before she'd ever introduce her daughters to the monster from her nightmares.

"Fine. I'll go. Adrian's parents have been expecting us for months." She wipes her wet cheeks again, straightens her spine, then locks the dark brown eyes she was gifted from her father with mine. "But if you don't get the job done, I'll come back and do it for you."

When I dip my chin, she moves to a mirror tacked to the wall to check her face. Her knees are shaking so much she can barely walk, but she puts on a brave front. The last thing she'd ever want is for my crew to know she's rattled. It took her years to gain their respect, and she won't let it slip for anything.

While she clears away a minute sliver of mascara smeared

under her eyes, I move to the cracked open door of Justine's guest bedroom, stunned that the almost deafening buzz of my men has dulled to barely a murmur.

They still have the tits of my whores in their mouths and my drugs running through their veins, but their eyes are rapt on the same thing—Justine.

She's also mine. My crew is just unaware of how far my fascination extends.

The same can't be said for Lia. It only takes her noticing the narrowed squint Justine's eyes get when she walks out of my room to know the real reason I've brought motions into play to take back what's mine years earlier than predicted.

"Is that her?" When I nod, Lia's smile heats my cheek. "I see in her eyes what Rico saw in yours. She's not lost. She just needs to learn not all crowns are made from rhinestones and gems... some are from determination and courage."

I nod again, agreeing with her. "I can see the fire in her eyes. She just needs someone to relight it."

I realize I said my comment out loud when Lia says, "You can do that for her, Nikolai. You did it years ago, and you can do it again, except this time, you'll get more than the admiration of your big sister for your efforts."

When I roll my eyes, Lia's breathy chuckle fans my neck. She knows she is treading water in a shark-infested ocean, but since she's also aware Adrian will have her bags packed before she's returned home, she is willing to test the waters.

"Call me if you need anything."

She waits for me to jerk up my chin before planting a goodbye kiss onto my cheek. Her lips barely touch my skin, but her contact is enough to burn jealousy through Justine's veins. She watches us from across the room, the bags of groceries held close to her chest, incapable of hiding the frantic thrust of her lungs.

Jealousy has never looked so good.

After watching Lia's trek out her front door, Justine returns her eyes to mine. I could act ignorant to the possessiveness flaring through her unique colored eyes. I could pretend the same annoyance isn't knocking at my chest from my men eyeing her like she's a feast they're about to gorge on, but since this is as new to her as it is me, I slant my head and arch a brow, placing the ball back into Justine's court.

When she returns my serve with a dramatic exit, I attempt to follow her. I barely make it one foot when the woman I see in her eyes stops my feet as quickly she does my heart. Her scorned stare is wicked and proves what I've always known. Only a woman worthy of a throne can switch from being numbed by jealousy to a straight-up gangster in under a second.

My focus shifts from the swinging kitchen door to Roman when he stops at my side. His brows are dotted with sweat, and his sleeves are rolled-up to his elbows. With his suit jacket nowhere to be seen, I'm going to assume he got blood on it while moving Officer Prentice's body from the alleyway of Justine's building to his final resting place.

"Everything good?"

Roman jerks up his chin. "He won't be found any time soon."

"And the surveillance we uncovered?"

He tilts closer to me to ensure we don't have any unwanted ears listening to our private conversation. "Trey is placing it into the right hands. If the rumblings are anything to go by, his colleagues will consider his quick death merciful."

My jaw tics. I hate that his death was quick and unsatisfying, but Viktor had advised he was en route with Justine, so I didn't have much choice. I doubt jealousy would have heated Justine's cheeks if she knew I had murdered a man for her.

Some of my annoyance slips away when Roman discloses why the men who worked alongside Officer Prentice won't mourn his death. "One of the girls on the tape was Bill Hammond's niece. She wasn't a prostitute. She merely took a shortcut down an alleyway on the way home."

A grin tugs on my lips. I'm not happy Detective Hammond's niece was assaulted, but it feels good knowing one less rapist is on the streets.

My smile slackens when Roman hands me a sheet of paper. "What's this?"

He keeps his eyes front and center. His face gives nothing away. "You asked for additional information on Maddox's arrest. With his criminal record doctored to the point of being worthless, I dug a little deeper." He drops his knowledgeable eyes to the sheet of paper I'm grasping. "This isn't exactly what you were after, but I figured you'd be interested in what I uncovered. There could be rules in play here we were unaware of."

Through fettered brows, I take in the document he handed me. It's a grainy photograph. However, no amount of pixilation can hide Justine's alluring features. She appears a few years younger than she is now, and her shoulders aren't weighed down with burden. She's standing across from a man with eyes as icy as mine and blood tainted with just as much evil.

"Is this it? A shared umbrella on a rainy afternoon?"

The chances of me ignoring my tightening jaw fly out the window when Roman shakes his head. "No. There were a handful of dates. Dimitri seemed to have quite the fascination with her."

I work my jaw side to side to loosen up my next set of words. "How long ago?"

"A couple of years."

With Roman not getting to the point as quickly as I like, I force him there. "Around the time of Justine's hospitalization?"

He waits a beat, unsure how to confirm my suspicions without sending me into a rage. "It appears as if they were on a date the night of her admission."

Air whizzes out of my nostrils as I suck in deep breaths, endeavoring to cool the fire incinerating my veins. "He hurt her."

I'm not asking a question—I'm stating a fact.

Well, so I thought.

"No. From the intel I've gathered, Dimitri isn't at fault here."

"She was hurt under his watch, Roman. How is this not his fault?"

He peers at me with pleading eyes, imploring for me to calm down. "I'm not saying his conscious is clear, but there's more to this than either of us know, so jumping to conclusions won't help anyone." He shifts on his feet to face me. The worry on his face is the same as it was when he unshackled me from my torture chamber thirteen years ago. "You've only just met this girl, Nikolai. Are you sure the benefits will exceed the repercussions?"

"Yes," I answer without pause for thought, speaking truthfully for the first time in years.

I can't explain my immediate desire to protect Justine any more than I can deny it. She riveted me from the moment I saw her, and the more I unearth about her, the more captive I become. Her scars, the fight in her eyes, and the way she should be scared but isn't are as appealing as her angelic face and cock-thickening body.

When I look at her, I remember a young, naïve teen who tried to do the right thing and was chastised for it in the most unimaginable way. We've endured the same torment. She just chose good over evil. I picked whichever team guaranteed I'd live.

For years, I believed that was siding with the devil.

Now, I'm not so sure.

My life isn't any better than Justine's.

I just pretend it is.

Unease highlights my tone when I say, "I need more information. Times. Dates. If Dimitri's fascination is still current."

Roman nods, acknowledging he understands my request without me needing to spell it out for him. I need to know if Justine is in debt to the Petrettis.

"I'll do that while you catch up on some sleep."

I shoot Roman a wry look. Sleep is the last thing on my mind.

He tries to act unaffected by my scorn. He'd have a better chance of me believing him if his Adam's apple weren't bobbing up and down in rapid concession. "You either sleep while the devil is appeased or later when he's walking the gallows. I don't know about you, but I'd rather the former."

He has a point—regrettably.

Upon seeing the acknowledgment in my eyes, he tosses my dismantled ankle bracelet into my chest before making his way to the living room. I stop him before he gets two steps away from me. "Make sure Justine is aware she either stays in the kitchen or her room until I awake and ensure the men know those domains are off-limits." Roman smiles like the hard-ass warden he is, more than eager to hand out my rulings. "Ensure they understand the order is coming directly from me. I don't want them messing with Justine. If they mess with her, they mess with me."

I trust my men, but there's a churning in my gut that won't quit —even more so after what Roman exposed. If the Petrettis consider Justine their property, my fight just took on an entirely new meaning.

It doesn't mean I'll back down, though. Good soldiers fight for

the system. Bad soldiers fight for themselves.
Can you guess which team I belong in?

16

JUSTINE

The chaotic scene in my living room is even more dreadful than the midday sun that pelted my shoulders as we trekked the two blocks from a parking garage to my apartment building. Parking has always been an issue in my location, but with it being the first day of a long weekend, it's even more unbearable than usual.

The handful of Popov crew members left lingering in my kitchen this morning has grown dramatically. Every surface in my living area has a backside on it. Unfortunately, not all of them are male. A selection of women are nestled between the men, most void of essential clothing.

When two heavy-breasted ladies spotted Viktor upon our return, they squealed loudly before prancing over to greet him with sloppy kisses.

Their overzealous attention had me wondering if they were the cause of Nikolai's wet hair.

He showered this morning, so why would he need to bathe again so quickly if he wasn't undertaking strenuous activities during my absence?

A knot forms in my stomach when I recall the pretty, petite brunette with dazzling chocolate eyes and flawless skin who exited the bedroom Nikolai had his shoulder butted against. Although she

was dressed more respectfully than the other females in attendance, I couldn't control the awful thoughts that plagued me.

With my middle school years spent hiding from vicious bullies
and then my college days haunted by similar unwanted attention, I
can't testify that it was jealousy plaguing me, but I'm reasonably
sure that's what it was. I felt clammy and hot, even though I was
shivering, and I had a ridiculous desire to yank the brunette away
from Nikolai.

If this wasn't jealousy, the Pope isn't Catholic.

I try to let go of my anger by thinking back to my dad's laid-
back attitude and carefree nature. I was just like him before unan-
ticipated events altered my life course.

Life was good.

Life was easy.

I'd give *anything* to go back to that life.

Adulthood is already daunting, but when it thrusts you into an
unknown world, daunting is too tame a word to describe it.

Everything changed with a simple smile. Not solely for me but
my family as well.

It's frightening how one humble mistake can cause the biggest
ripple.

Four years ago, it was a smile.

This weekend, it was the accidental misplacement of an
address.

Both blips are as significant as the other.

With a huff, I dump a loaf of bread on the counter with more
aggression than needed. I don't know what's angering me more:
Nikolai's crew treating my private abode like a cesspool of desecration, or the sick jealousy playing havoc with my thoughts.

Considering that the churning of my stomach ramped up
during my last confession, I'd say it's the latter, which is utterly
ridiculous since I have no claim to Nikolai.

It's days like today I wish I didn't get the smallest slice of my
mother's personality. She's the risky rule breaker, the one who
believes all rules have room to be bent. Although, I doubt even
someone as unpredictable as her would have acted as unstable as I
have this weekend.

After emptying one bag of groceries, I pivot toward the second.
My heart rate spikes when I notice how deserted my kitchen is. It's

not slightly empty compared to my bursting-at-the-seams living area. Deserted—*deserted*.

The heat of so many bodies crammed into one space must be disgusting, so why aren't Nikolai's guests taking advantage of every area available?

"Because they can't fuck in a kitchen, Justine," I grumble to myself.

Striving not to let jealousy get the better of me, I set to work unpacking the rest of the items I purchased. With it being my first trip to the market in nearly a month, I have a lot of items crammed into two little bags.

I've nearly packed away all the groceries when a deep voice asks, "Did you get bacon? Nikolai loves bacon."

I clutch my chest, startled someone snuck up on me unaware. I've been accused many times of having eyes in the back of my head, as I'm notoriously vigilant.

Once I settle my irregular heart rate, my eyes drift from the fridge to the only entrance to my kitchen. The gentleman seated beside Nikolai this morning is standing inside my swinging door. His veined arms hang loosely at his side, and a shy smirk is etched on his face. Although his eyes don't house the same arrogance of his associates partying in my living room, his aura alludes that he is not a man to be messed with. I can't tell if he is a friend or a foe.

When he stares at me, promptly reminding me that I failed to answer his question, I jingle a paper parcel, allowing the deli-wrapped bacon to answer on my behalf. I'd like to articulate a better response, but with jealousy clutching my throat, words are eluding me.

As I close the fridge door, the unnamed man enters the kitchen. "My name is Roman. It's a pleasure to meet you, Justine," he greets, offering me his hand to shake.

I accept his gesture cautiously. His eyes are soul-baring, showing he's a man who has lived many lives in one, but they also reveal that not all his memories are pleasant. Roman is a handsome man I'd guess to be mid-to-late fifties. His dark hair has a sprinkling of gray woven throughout, and his worldly eyes are green. He presents as a man who values fitness. Even the loose fit of his collared shirt can't hide the ridges of his chest and stomach.

I brace my back on the kitchen cabinet. "Hi."

Roman returns my greeting with a chin dip before advising, "Nikolai has requested that you stay in the kitchen or your room during the festivities." His facial expression is more forgiving than his austere tone.

My spikes hackle as anger overwhelms me. "Why?" I blurt out before I can stop myself. "Is he afraid I'll interrupt him and his posse of women?" The viciousness of my tone leaves no doubt I'm enraged by jealousy.

Roman shrugs, sending my annoyance to an all-time high.

"Tell Nikolai he has no cause for concern. I have no intentions of participating in the festivities." *Or ever speaking to him again.*

Spotting the scorn creeping up my neck, Roman asks, "If you could pick, how would you prefer to be seen by Nikolai? As a housemaid or a whore?"

The horrified expression on my face doubles as my stomach churns in contempt. He asked his question without remorse, as if it's perfectly normal to sanction women in those two groups.

"Is there another option? Because those choices suck."

I grimace, suddenly mindful I'm unleashing my anger on the wrong person. Although I'm disturbed by how women are viewed in the Popov family, Roman isn't the cause of the rage disintegrating my veins. It's the devil with the tempting blue eyes and an even more sinful body.

Thankfully, Roman doesn't flinch at my snippy comment. He takes it in stride, not the least bit affected. "Not in this industry, there isn't." His tone is flat and missing emotion. "But I'm not here to argue the rights of women. I'm here to pass on Nikolai's request."

I roll my eyes, appalled by his nonchalant response. "Rights? They would have to have rights for us to argue about them," I grumble, my annoyance too strong to contain.

"Love it or hate it, whores belong out there. Housemaids belong in here," Roman retorts, nudging his head to my swinging kitchen door, his tone simmering to a slight sneer.

Following his gaze, I realize what he is saying is true. It might be unjust and vile, but I don't belong out there. None of the women in my living room are appropriately dressed, and the ratio of men to women is one to five. I didn't survive a second in that environment years ago. I don't see it ending any differently this time around.

My attention strays back to Roman when he adds, "Besides, no one will be game to touch you in this domain, so it's safer for you to stay here."

"What if I want to be touched?" I snap before I can leash my spiteful tongue.

I'm far from wanting any form of contact, much less a sexual exchange, but the bitter jealousy eating me alive spoke before I could shut it down.

I'm not expecting Roman to reply to my snapped comment, so you can imagine my surprise when he says, "Then I suggest you choose wisely, as any man you touch will be buried in a shallow ditch within minutes of your exchange. Nikolai has never placed dibs on a woman before you."

If he's hoping his statement will fill me with gratitude, he needs another tactic. I'm more annoyed now than when I was plagued with horrible thoughts on the many ways Nikolai and the brunette entertained themselves while I was away. Being treated as a commodity catalyzed my family's downward spiral. If I hadn't attracted the eye of a man who chose fear over respect, my brother wouldn't be rotting away the best years of his life in a high-security penitentiary.

The hairs on my nape bristle when Roman leans across my body to secure a bottle of beer from the fridge. "If you truly want to get out of this situation unscathed, keep your head down and your ears closed. A blind mute has never had a problem with the mob."

Stealing my chance to reply, Roman exits the kitchen as stealthily as he entered it.

17

JUSTINE

When the protests of my hungry tummy grow too great to ignore, I rise from the eating nook in the corner of my kitchen, shut down my laptop, and then pace to my walk-in pantry. I've spent the last several hours weeding through the mammoth pile of evidence from Nikolai's case that Mr. Fletcher emailed me this morning.

My determination to retain Nikolai as a client surpassed my jealousy when Mr. Fletcher's brief contact granted me an update on my brother's defense. Like all knowledgeable defense attorneys, the circumstances of my brother's arrest and the swiftness of his court case have Mr. Fletcher's interest immensely piqued. So much so his sleep was as lacking as mine.

My brother went from being a free man to being incarcerated in a maximum-security prison in under a month. If that isn't cause for an appeal, I don't know what is. Mr. Fletcher's guarantee he won't stop working on my brother's case until his verdict is overturned had me pledging I'd do everything in my power to secure Nikolai as a client for Schluter & Fletcher. Although my promise wasn't as determined as Mr. Fletcher's, he accepted it as if it was.

While having a lazy stretch, I enter my pantry, eager to hunt down the emergency-only candy bars I keep hidden in the back.

This is an urgent situation. Three meals dwindling to one has my blood sugar declining as much as my ego has the past three hours.

Although I'm grateful for Roman's guarantee that the kitchen would be a safe alternative to the all-night bender in my living area, I'm still disappointed Nikolai shunted me from the festivities. I feel like I'm in high school all over again. I'm fine to hang out with at lunch but not popular enough to secure an invitation to social events outside of school.

My hunt for the sugar-crammed snacks halts when a shimmer of light captures my attention. I barely see its faint blink behind the year's supply of rice my mom purchased during our first grocery trip in Las Vegas. She's always been a "store it for a rainy day" type.

Tinned fruit, cans of Spam, and a bag of rice that could feed a village are stacked in the back corner of my pantry. I would have never spotted it if it weren't for the vibrancy of the screen in the dimly lit space.

After glancing over my shoulder to ensure I'm alone, I remove the device from its hiding spot. It's the size of an iPad mini but three times its thickness. It reminds me of the surveillance instruments used in war movies. It's so sturdy a tank could run over it, and it wouldn't buckle.

Unease builds when recognition dawns on why the footage displayed on the screen seems familiar. It's broadcasting a live feed of my living room. I know it's live, as my apartment has never seen so much action.

The noise booming through my kitchen door the past several hours gave me a hint of what was happening, but this footage showcases the ruckus in a new light. It's even more villainous than I'd presumed.

I take a moment to settle my anger before dropping my eyes to the command prompts at the bottom of the screen. I've never been overly techie, but my lack of computer skills isn't an issue with this device. It's as basic as they come. It has the standard buttons every girl knows: play, pause, rewind, and fast forward.

The only thing I can't fathom is how to switch the screen between the numerous surveillance areas broadcasting in little boxes at the top of the monitor. The main image televised is of my living area, but I'm more interested in the live feed in the top left-hand corner. The one that shows a shirtless Nikolai sprawled across the bed in my guest room—all alone.

I inwardly cheer when my frantic taps on the screen switch the feed to the one I want. I watch Nikolai in silence for several moments, shocked he seems pleased at being excluded from the festivities. His arm is braced across his eyes, and his chest rises and falls in a rhythm that indicates he's asleep. He looks comfortable in my domain, as if he's always belonged here.

I guess his laid-back approach shouldn't be surprising. From what I've read the past few hours, he has barely had a moment of quiet in the past fifteen years. If he's not dodging prosecution, he's being groomed to become the next king of the Russian mafia.

I don't know which fact is more disturbing. Usually it takes great respect for a son to follow in his father's footsteps. My dad was immensely proud when my eldest brother followed in his shoes —but Nikolai didn't have a normal upbringing. He grew in the shadows of a cold-hearted and vindictive man.

Vladimir Popov is a vile, worthless man who doesn't deserve to share the same air as his numerous children. The hideous things I unearthed about him the past two hours are stomach-churning. There are multiple reports of him torturing, maiming, and beating his own flesh and blood, so imagine the atrocity he inflicts on people he doesn't consider family.

Although Nikolai's extensive criminal record is shocking, it's now understandable. A monster raised him. It doesn't excuse his behavior, but it's a plausible defense any attorney would be foolish to overlook. It swayed my opinion of him immensely, so who's to say it won't do the same with a jury of his peers?

After taking longer than I care to admit stalking Nikolai, my finger moves to the rewind button. With unwarranted jealousy strangling my heart, I can't harness my curiosity for a second longer. If this surveillance device was installed during my trip to the grocery store, it may reveal the cause of Nikolai's obsessive showering regimen.

I'm about to tap on the rewind button when the creak of a door sounds through the device. Two scantily clad women enter Nikolai's room, their faces a unique mix of fear and excitement. Since Nikolai is sleeping, he fails to respond to their sneaky approach.

When they reach the foot of his bed, they peer at each other, soundlessly discussing their next move. Bile burns the back of my throat when they pull their midriff shirts over their heads before slipping their skirts down their thighs.

In sync, they crawl onto the mattress, one on each side of Nikolai's slumbering frame. Nikolai stirs when they rake their nails through the faint hairs trailing from his belly button to the seam of his jeans. Their pace is slow and teasing but leaves no suspicions of their intentions.

Blood floods my heart when the brunette on Nikolai's right undoes the button on his jeans and slides the fly down. With her index finger pressed against her lips, she encourages the blonde to slip her hand into Nikolai's boxers. She does without protest, her excitement unmissable even when projected through a grainy monitor.

I snap my eyes to the floor, mortified when Nikolai releases a faint moan from their contact. I'm bombarded with sick jealousy, making it hard for me to breathe. I have no claim to Nikolai, but it's the fight of my life not to storm out of the kitchen and drag those women off him. I'm consumed with such unbridled jealousy I feel ill. The slosh sitting in my stomach is winding up my throat, begging to be released, and my body is shaking.

I jump in fright when a furious Russian roar booms through the security apparatus's speakers. "Get the fuck out! You were told this domain was out of bounds."

With my heart in my throat, I return my eyes to the screen. Nikolai's face lines with anger as he jumps off his bed like it's on fire. As he throws a shirt over his torso, his icy-blue eyes shoot daggers at the two females frozen in the middle of the mattress.

His unnamed companions' bewildered expressions grow when he grips the tops of their arms and forcefully removes them from his room. Although it would have been polite for him to wait until they were dressed, I can't stop the glee surging through me. I don't love his beastly disrespect for women. I'm simply appreciating the contents of my stomach staying in their rightful spot.

Yeah, right.

The women stand frozen outside Nikolai's door, watching him snag their clothing from the floor before tossing them at their feet.

"Disobey me again and I'll send you to live with Yakor,"

Nikolai warns, his voice hoarse from his unexpected awakening. "He'll beat the disrespect right out of you."

Fear strikes the brunette's features, but it doesn't stop her from saying, "Nikolai, darling, it's me, Alyna. I brought Luyca—one of your favorites." She stares at Nikolai in shock, utterly baffled by his rejection.

She isn't the only one stunned. After spending several hours knee-deep in Nikolai's private life, I was certain he'd welcome their attention with open arms. Nikolai's life has been splashed across the papers for the world to see his entire adulthood, and it's obvious his escapades with the opposite sex are as extensive as his criminal tendencies.

Nikolai glares into the brunette's eyes, his stare hot enough to melt ice. "I'm. Not. Interested." He growls each word with spine-chilling enunciation.

After issuing another threat using solely his eyes, he slams his bedroom door shut. I watch him in silence, numb with an equal amount of shock and euphoria.

Did he reject them for me? Or...

My inner monologue trails off when Nikolai suddenly glances up. Like the afternoon of his arrest, he stares straight at me, his gaze pulse-quickening and wrathful. The accuracy of his stare is shockingly precise, and even through a computer device, it makes me squirm with need.

My heart thwacks my ribcage when the most wickedly delicious smile stretches across his face mere seconds before he strides out of his room. My stomach gargles, warning me I'm moments away from his arrival.

As I fight to switch the live feed back to its original screen, my pulse thuds in my ears. The device is as uncooperative as my heart has been the past sixteen hours.

"Come on, please," I mumble when the device remains frozen on Nikolai's room.

My heart rate spikes when the creak of my kitchen door filters into the pantry.

Crap!

In a flurry, I switch off the surveillance device and store it in its rightful place, hopeful its restart will take it back to its original screen. My eyes frantically dart around the pantry, seeking an item

I can pretend I was searching for before I leave my hiding space. Although I can't see the person whose shadow is expanding halfway across the tiled floor, the prickling of my nape identifies him.

"Hey," I greet Nikolai, whose shoulder is propped on the wall opposite the pantry. "Hungry?"

Ignoring the roasting heat of his suspicious glare, I pace to the stove to prepare the sour cream and chives pasta packet I found lodged in the back of the pantry.

He remains quiet, his gaze never leaving mine as I secure the milk, butter, and jug of water from the fridge. His stare has me burning up everywhere, but I act unresponsive. He doesn't need more fuel stoking his over-stacked fire.

I've just dropped a scoop of butter into a cup of milk when the warmth of a torso heats my back. "You went to the store for an hour, and all you came back with was a box of pasta?" He is standing so close that his breath leaves a circle of condensation on my neck.

"No."

My reply is choppy from the excited shudder running down my spine. Even knowing I shouldn't be attracted to Nikolai doesn't change the facts. He is a handsome man any red-blooded woman would have a hard time ignoring.

"There are ample supplies in the fridge if you're hungry," I advise, nudging my head in that direction. Thankfully, this time around, my sentence is delivered confidently.

Nikolai gathers my hair to the side, exposing my neck to his five o'clock shadow. I try to act unaffected by his closeness, but the goosebumps on my nape give away my excitement.

"You smell good enough to eat. Perhaps I should eat you?" he murmurs into my ear, his voice sinful enough to poison an ethical mind. It's husky and drenched with sexual ambiguity.

I take a few seconds to calm the fire before I can stammer out, "I doubt I'd be nutritious enough to sustain your appetite for long." I aim for my tone to be playful, but it has a dash of bitterness in it.

My contradictory responses can't be helped. Nikolai is lavishing me with attention I'd never tire of, but his unexpected arrival came with more than I bargained for. Not only is my house being desecrated by drunken fools and topless women, but my apartment has been bugged with surveillance cameras.

The anger clogging my heart could push me into coronary failure, and don't even get me started on the unknown brunette clinging to Nikolai upon my return from the store.

He rejected the two unnamed beauties' advances, but was that for me or because he was exhausted from his earlier guest's antics? The way the pretty brunette was cozying up to him shows they're more than friends, but hours of research have left me no closer to unearthing their connection.

Although she was spotted in numerous surveillance photos with Nikolai in the past three years, her identity is better guarded than a bank vault. I wasted valuable time I should have used on Nikolai's case, and I still have no clue who she is.

"Is this sexual tension or anger?" Nikolai asks, noticing how tight my shoulders are.

"Both," I grumble before I can stop my words.

He laughs into my neck, stupidly exciting me even more. "I can fix that." He grinds his stiffening crotch against my ass, ensuring I can't mistake his solution. "All you need to do is ask," he confides before sucking my earlobe into his mouth.

My knees curve inward as lust warms my insides. For a man who has a flurry of women vying to warm his bed, his eagerness to nibble on my neck makes me feel treasured, but it isn't persuasive enough to diminish my anger.

"And my other dilemma? What's your solution for that?" My eyes stray to the door, which is doing a poor job of concealing the ruckus in my living room.

I sigh, disturbed I let my heart speak before my brain. I should be demanding an explanation for the surveillance devices installed in my apartment without my permission, not seeking a solution to stop more naked women from sneaking into Nikolai's room.

Nikolai's lips freeze halfway down my neck before his eyes mimic the direction of my gaze. "They're my men, Ангел. They go where I go." If it weren't for the nick of disappointment in his tone, the tartness of his reply would have agitated me more.

"And the women?" My voice leaves no doubt that I'm enraged with jealousy. "Do they go where you go as well?"

Even though I can't see him, I know he's smiling. I can feel it deep within my bones.

"You're sexy as fuck when you are jealous," he barely whispers, his voice a throaty growl.

"I'm not jealous," I fight back, rolling my eyes.

Acting as if I didn't speak, his finger treks from my ear to my collarbone. "Your skin flames with heat when your little green monster raises its head." The cockiness radiating out of him doubles when the skin he traces blushes with a vibrant pink hue. "Most men would think you are embarrassed, but I know the real cause for your blooming color and seductive scent."

The air in my lungs leaves in a brutal grunt when his hand brushes the back of my right knee. He barely misses two hideous scars no amount of makeup can hide. "Unlike your face, this area only flames when you're angry." He stops for a second, his breathing coming out in ragged pants. "Or turned on."

Hotness spreads through me. I'm stunned he's been watching me so closely he's already learned the prompts of my body. With my pasty-white coloring, it only takes a crude comment to instigate a horrid case of blushing, but only those closest to me know the back of my knees gives away the real reason for my flushed appearance.

My body temperature triples when Nikolai bends his knees to meet me eye to eye. "I sure fucking hope you're blushing because you're turned on. I'm not a patient man, and I am beyond ready to have you beneath me."

I try to speak. Nothing but air bubbles come out. I'm stunned and incredibly aroused a man as handsome as Nikolai wants me, but I can't act on the prompts of my body. My heart and brain need to speak the same language. Right now, that isn't happening. All I hear is confused gobbledygook. I'm a smart and intelligent woman, but all my common sense seems null and void in Nikolai's presence.

Unappreciative of the awkward silence, Nikolai spins me around to face him. His movements are so quick I don't have a chance to protest before I'm facing him head-on.

When his hankering eyes connect with mine, the heat turns unbearable. His eyes are shining with pure, rampant lust, leaving no doubt every word he speaks is true.

I embarrassingly squirm, incapable of controlling the manic pulse between my legs. I'm both disturbed and nervous by my response.

Reveling in my capricious reaction, Nikolai groans, "If I were a man who took what he wanted without asking, I'd be fucking you where you stand, proving there's no reason for your jealousy."

A thousand wicked thoughts stream through my mind when he steps closer to me, filling the tiny gap of air between us. It's a struggle to fight off the lust burning me alive when he murmurs, "There's only one woman I want wrapped around my cock, Ангел. It isn't my sister."

"The brunette was your sister?" I blubber out, my words high with dazed excitement.

He doesn't respond to my question. He doesn't need to. I can read the truth in his eyes. That's why they had such an obvious connection. They're related—by blood!

The heat on my neck creeps to my cheeks when his finger glides over my budded nipple. It blooms even harder under his touch. He smiles, loving my body's inability to deny his touch.

"The good girls always want to tame the bad boys. But what happens when the good girl likes the bad boy just the way he is, but she's too afraid to admit it?" He steps back, freeing me from throwing my internship down the toilet. "Soon, Ангел. Very soon," he murmurs when he hears the groan I failed to stifle from the loss of his contact.

His smirk adds to the mess between my legs when he snags the unopened pasta off the counter and moseys to the pantry.

Before he enters, he spins back around to face me. "Perhaps if I fill your stomach, you'll let me gorge on you."

J ustine doesn't reply. She doesn't need to. Even angels know better than to second-guess the devil.

While I switch out the pasta for potatoes, steak, and fresh vegetables, Justine clears away stacks of paperwork from the kitchen table. From the thickness of the files, I'm going to assume getting me off my charges was her main focus over the past three hours.

Since I'm curious to see how deep her dig went, I ask, "Did you discover anything interesting in my records?"

"Umm..." She spins to face me, her nose screwing up like it does in her sleep. "I wouldn't necessarily say interesting."

I can't help but smile at the panic crossing her face. She didn't mean to insult me, but she can't help but be honest.

It's another trait I'm not familiar with.

"My brother always said the best way to learn about someone is to go directly to the source. Perhaps you should give that a go?" I hate talking about myself, but if it slides us toward a conversation we'll need to have at some stage this weekend, I can place my neurosis on the backburner for an hour or two.

"Okay."

Justine drags her sweaty hands down her denim shorts before joining me at the counter. While washing dirt off potatoes in the sink, she asks me a range of questions I assume most people stumble over during a first date. They're not overly probing, but they reveal she's not knowledgeable on many aspects of my industry, which convinces me her time with Dimitri was brief.

Short enough to save her from being classed as his? I don't know yet. But I am determined to find out.

I stop calculating my next move when Justine asks me to hand her a peeler. "A what?"

Her smile could bring a man to ecstasy without touching him. "A potato peeler." As humor glows in her eyes, her mischievous grin grows. "You do know what a potato peeler is, don't you?"

Laughter would usually result in bloodshed, but since it's coming from Justine, and it is more in happiness than contempt, I subdue my anger by switching the humor in her eyes to lust.

After pulling her waist-length hair away from her neck, I rest my stubble-covered chin on her shoulder blade. "I was raised in a household that believes—"

"Women are either maids or whores. I'm aware."

Her eyeroll freezes halfway when I press my lips to the throb in her throat so I can count her pulse. "Not all women belong in those categories." I savor the shudder that rolls down her spine when my desire to taste her becomes too much to bear. My tongue only tracks across her skin for the quickest second, but the moan she releases makes it seem much longer. "Some are angels." I bite and nip at her neck without a protest sounding from her mouth. "And others are queens." I suck on her skin firm enough to leave a mark but soft enough she has no idea on the evil attempting to claim her. "You, my sweet *Ангел,* were born to be both."

When she leans into my embrace, instead of repelling from it, I wedge my hand between her and the counter I have her squashed against. The silky-smooth skin on her stomach flutters under my touch, but unlike last night, she doesn't voice a protest when I slide my hand toward the heat between her legs.

The same can't be said for me when Trey unexpectedly bursts into the kitchen. I growl out my annoyance, which heats Justine's skin almost as much as my mouth.

The irritated expression crossing Trey's face switches to leering when Justine uses his interruption as an excuse for an interlude in our exchange. After slipping my hand out of the waistband of her shorts, she squashes her breasts against my arm to gather a plastic-looking thingamabob out of the drying rack on my left.

Ignoring how the quickest brush of her tits on my arm has my cock acting as if he hasn't sampled his first cunt, she commences peeling the potatoes she just washed. I may have believed her calm, collective ruse if the needy scent of her cunt wasn't thickening my cock even more than the budded peaks in her shirt.

Trey's interruption better be important.

If it isn't, he's a dead man walking.

"The marinade on the steak, what is it?"

Justine pushes her half-consumed plate of steak, mashed potatoes, and steamed vegetables to my side of the table before raising her greedy eyes to mine. She looks just how she would have looked if Trey hadn't interrupted us—thoroughly satisfied.

The yearning in her eyes detonates when I murmur, "I've only tasted one thing more delicious than this steak..." I pause when the hunger in my tone enflames her cheeks. "Fuck, *Ангел*, I love the way you blush. If there weren't cameras watching my every move, I would be spreading you out on this table and eating you for dessert."

Although Trey's interruption could have been held off for an hour or two, it was for the best. I was so eager to feed on the lust teeming between Justine and me, I completely forgot about the cameras watching my every move. Trey's arrival reminded me I wasn't just risking my crew seeing Justine in a vulnerable state, I was placing her on Vladimir's radar as well.

For my entire life, anything I ever wanted, Vladimir took. The love of my mother. The devotion of my siblings when he grew worried our bond was becoming unbreakable. If I so much as showed an interest in something or someone, he made it his.

I scoot closer to Justine, squashing her into the far corner of the dining nook. Vladimir's surveillance is top of the line, but not even the most advanced equipment can record through concrete support beams.

Needing my hands on her in some way, I twist a piece of Justine's hair around my finger. It's as silky and as smooth as her pasty-white skin. Something so simple shouldn't appease the hesitation I'm certain I was born with, but for some reason, it does.

Justine reads the carefreeness in my eyes in the wrong manner. "You can trust me, Nikolai. Anything you say won't leave this room."

My lips twist into an uneasy grin. "If only that were true." I keep my voice low enough the poor-quality microphones in the cameras won't pick up my reply. "I don't trust anyone, *Ангел*. The devil was once an angel too." Hating the fear trickling into her greenish-blue eyes, I veer our conversation back onto mutual territory. "Now tell me about the marinade on the steak before I spend my afternoon hunting for a much more succulent recipe."

I anticipate for her to respond to the fight in her eyes, so you can imagine my surprise when she jests, "If you want my nonna's secret recipe, I'd first have to kill you."

"Nonna? So you're Italian?" Shock resonates in my tone. She could only be paler if she was a vampire.

When she answers my question with a simple 'yes,' I say, "Then where did you get your red hair and pasty-skin tone from?" I tug on the strand of hair I was twisting earlier, causing an avalanche of curls to cover the slivers of silver on her shoulders.

Her blistering smile has me once again forgetting we have an audience. "My dad is Italian, but my mom is Irish." My teeth grow envious of hers when she drags them over her plump bottom lip. "I look very much like my mother, but I have the personality of my father. Probably doesn't help that I have four older brothers, so I'm a little bit of a tomboy."

"From what I'm seeing, you're all woman." I'm not lying. Her tits alone would have the strongest man's knees bowing.

Her smile turns blinding. "You wouldn't be saying that if you saw my childhood pictures. I wore boy's clothes and even had a boyish haircut."

A grin curls my lips. I saw the photos. I'm aware of the travesty.

Justine proves she is as smart as she is beautiful when she asks, "But you already know that, don't you?"

I drag a napkin across my mouth to hide the tic in my jaw before locking my eyes with hers. "I know many things, Justine, but

I prefer hearing them directly from the source." Her chest expands when her name leaves my throat in a gravelly whisper. "You'll never believe how quick a fact becomes a lie when it's passed through many lips."

Not an ounce of panic resonates in her tone when she asks, "Exactly how much do you know about me?"

She knows I'm not a threat to her.

Not physically, anyway.

Needing to occupy my hands before I use them to peel down her shorts and eat her for dessert, I dig a pack of cigarettes from my pocket, place one between my lips, then offer one to Justine. When she shakes her head, I light the cancer stick balancing precariously between my lips before tossing the packet and lighter onto the tabletop holding leftovers of the meal we just shared.

I've always been overly cocky, and it's displayed in an unfavorable light when I mutter, "How's this for knowledge? You're the youngest of five siblings. You were born and raised in Hopeton. Your mom works as an engineer, and your father is a pilot. Unlike three of your older brothers, you didn't follow your parents' footsteps. You first branched out into the world of architecture, but your third year in college saw you changing your career path to the corrupt and dangerous world of law." I start at the points that don't make my blood boil before moving to the big stuff. "Your peers were shocked by your decision. All they saw was a shy little mouse. No one thought you would grow into the woman you have become. Not even Dimitri."

She rapidly blinks at the mention of my enemy but remains as quiet as a church mouse. I don't know if her silence appeases me or pisses me off. It could be a combination of both. She doesn't give off the vibe of a scarlet woman, but she's fucked with my head so well in an impressively short time frame, I'm not even sure if I should trust myself, much less my instincts.

I strive to keep anger out of my tone when I ask, "How long have you known Dimitri Petretti?" I fail like a fucking loser.

Justine licks her quivering lips before answering, "I've known Dimitri all my life... but we only became *acquainted* a few years ago."

The way her tone dipped when she said 'acquainted' reveals

she classes him as more than a friend. I wouldn't necessarily say they've fucked, but there's more to them than a casual familiarity.

With my blood hot with anger, our conversation switches to an interrogation awfully quick. "Dimitri has always had a fascination with redheads, so I'm not surprised you caught his eye. I just can't work out why he'd ever let you go."

"It wasn't his choice." The anger slicking my skin with sweat triples when moisture floods her eyes. "A man can voice his interests all he likes. It doesn't mean his feelings will be reciprocated."

Although I agree with her, I know that isn't how things work with the men in my profession. "That's not the way things work in this industry. When we say jump, you're supposed to ask how high. It isn't about what you want. It's about what we crave." The anger burning through her impressive eyes reveals more than her words ever could. "Your brother saved you from Dimitri. He fell on the knife to remove you from Dimitri's radar."

I'm not seeking confirmation, but Justine answers me as if I am. "Yes, but I don't have proof. Maddox won't talk. He refuses—"

"He will die if he talks. If not by the hands of a Petretti member, by one of my own crew."

I don't mean to be a brute. I just want her to know her ideas on the life her brother is living in isn't close to what she thinks. If he sided with the Petrettis, then goes against them, he will die. This isn't a possibility. It is a fact. That's how the underworld works.

The dishware rattles when Justine slaps her hand on the tabletop. "The Petrettis are rivals of the Popovs. Why would you side with them?"

"A snitch is a snitch. He belongs to no team."

She pushes back from the table, her face disgusted. "Maddox didn't do what he is accused of. He's innocent."

I stare up at her, hating the disappointment in her eyes, but determined to show her the way things truly work before she's thrown in the fire with Maddox. "He may not be a murderer, but he is not innocent. When you play with fire, you risk getting burned. He got burned."

The first chink in Justine's shield blisters when she snarls, "Maddox is in jail because a man as vile as your family didn't understand the word no. He didn't play with fire. He protected his baby sister from a monster! Wouldn't you do the same for your sister?"

My face reddens with anger when I recall the punishment I faced when I placed myself between Vladimir and Lia during one of his many tirades. It is heard in my reply when I quote the words he spoke to me that day almost twenty years ago. "That is not the way things work. Everyone in this industry has a place, and the predicament of one woman should never fracture the order."

Justine glares at me with the same disdain Vladimir's eyes held that wintry afternoon. "Your mother should be ashamed she raised such an abhorrent, heinous, worthless man—"

"My mother is dead."

With her mood as erratic as mine, Justine shouts, "Lucky her!"

I stand from my chair, torn between washing her scornful words from her mouth with my tongue or my cock. *Perhaps I should do both?*

I settle on neither when the quickest flash of red captures my attention. The prickling of the hairs on my arms assures me we're being watched by Satan himself. This wasn't a test he organized, but I will be graded on it either way.

Although Vladimir would prefer me to respond to Justine's disrespect with violence, I use words instead. "If you were anyone else, you'd be suffering the consequences of a bitter tongue."

She doesn't balk at the danger in my tone. She doesn't even cower. She merely tugs down the collar of her shirt to expose the scars I traced last night before murmuring, "You don't think I'm already suffering, Nikolai?" Her watering eyes bounce between mine. They're brimming with tears, but not a single one falls when she says, "Two weeks after saving me from being mauled by a dog on the Petretti compound, my brother was arrested for murder. Nothing you could do would ever pain me more than that, so rest assured, Your Highness, I'm already suffering."

Her confession hits me like a ton of bricks, but before she spots my murderous expression, she gathers our dishes off the table and tosses them into the overflowing sink, unmoved when one porcelain plate cracks under the force of her throw.

Conscious I'm being watched, I ensure my face reflects unbridled anger even though my whispered words are anything but.

"Your brother may be in jail, *Ангел*, but he is more free now than he would have ever been in the Petretti crew."

Stealing her chance to reply, I push through the swinging door, race across the party-like atmosphere in the living room, then get up so close to Roman's face if he wasn't aware of the ingredients Justine seasoned our steak with, he is now.

"She was mauled by a dog, Roman!" My whispered sneer coats his face with my spit. It's vile and disgusting, but considering I'm on the verge of snapping someone's neck, it is the lesser of two evils. "By a fucking dog on the Petretti compound!"

I never realized how violent words could be until now. Mine are more deadly than both my knife and my fists. They're capable of killing, and I know the perfect person to inflict them on—Dimitri Petretti.

When my sneered words reach Roman's ears, he moves to the boom box in the corner of the room. After dragging the volume dial to the highest setting, he locks his eyes with Viktor, who's standing guard at the door I just rocketed through at the speed of a bullet. They don't speak, but not even two seconds later, Viktor smashes his fist in Jay's face, knocking him into a group of my men huddled around the couch.

And just like that, an all-in brawl commences.

With the camera in the living room shifting to take in a fight promoters would pay top dollar for, Roman yanks me to into the bathroom that's in the far corner of the compact space. "Speak now and do it quickly."

Understanding his ruse, my brain switches from personal to business in under a second. "Justine said two weeks after Maddox saved her from being mauled by a dog on the Petretti compound, he was charged with murder."

"Coincidence?"

I shake my head. "Not according to Justine. She believes it's linked, and in all honesty, so do I. Dimitri wouldn't have stopped her punishment unless it was for a good reason. Maddox must have offered something substantial."

Roman sucks in a sharp breath. "Like murder?"

I work my jaw from side to side before dipping my chin. Justine thinks Maddox is innocent, but she doesn't know how far siblings go for one another when their life is placed up for negotiation. I held a knife to Vladimir's throat after he ordered for Rico's back to be burned with acid, and we didn't even share the same blood.

Roman drags a hand down his tired face, as lost as me on where we go from here. "I can reach out to some contacts I have, but I don't see it doing any good. If Maddox is serving Justine's punishment, the Petrettis have no reason to seek additional retribution from Justine."

"I'm not worried about any outstanding debts. I can handle that. I want to know why Justine was punished to begin with."

"Nikolai—"

"No, Roman," I interrupt, refusing to hear the same excuse he always gives for the fucked-up world we live in. "I *want* to know." I swish my tongue around my mouth, loosening up my words. "I can't help her if I don't know what happened to her."

A glint flares through Roman's eyes. It could be pride. It could be disgust. I honestly don't know. "Okay. I'll see what I can find out. While I do that..." he nudges his head to my men brawling in the living room like they won't have each other's back the next time we go to war, "... you can sort out that mess."

He races for the door, leaving me defenseless to a large group of drunken, rage-fueled men. With how hot my blood is with anger, unlike the weeks after my sixteenth birthday, I'm looking forward to this challenge.

A dog will look down when they've done wrong, but a snake will always look you in the eyes, even when he is the perpetrator.

19

JUSTINE

My tears about my fight with Nikolai are brief. Long enough to grieve the pain my poor judgment caused my brother but not long enough to forget why I'm in Las Vegas to begin with.

Private DNA testing, traveling to interview witnesses, and gifts used in bribery make the defense of the innocent a costly endeavor. Although the Petretti crew was nearly defunct after its founder, Col, was killed during an FBI sting four years ago, their influence in our hometown is stronger than any monetary value I could offer.

But that doesn't mean I'll give up. I'll continue working on my brother's case until he's released and his conviction overturned. I'll fight for his freedom with every breath I take. I will not give up.

I place a scrubbed frying pan into the drying rack when the creak of a door sounds through my ears. I roll my shoulders and level my breathing, preparing for the next hairpin curve on the vicious rollercoaster Nikolai and I have been riding the past twenty-four hours.

God—has it truly only been twenty-four hours? The emotions pumping into me make it seem like forever.

Suspicion arises when my body fails to respond as it usually does in Nikolai's presence. There's no crackling of electricity in the air, and the hairs on my nape remain stagnant. Although my intuition still alerts me to be cautious, I sense more danger than before.

When I crank my neck to the side, my full gaze meets with a pair of black, almost lifeless eyes. An unnamed man is standing at the foot of the table where Nikolai and I shared a meal nearly thirty minutes ago. Like almost every man I've had the displeasure of meeting this weekend, this stranger's aura impels negative thoughts. His fists are clenched at his side. His mouth is set in a straight line, and his gaze is as stern as stone.

"Is there any left?" He jerks his chin to a plate of food on my island counter.

I nod. "Help yourself." I keep my voice friendly, even though I am feeling anything but.

The stranger's slit-eyed gaze glares at me. "I'd prefer you serve me," he insists, treating me as if I am worthless.

Anger works its way from my stomach to my throat, but not trusting his lifeless eyes, I secure the plate of leftover food before gesturing for him to take a seat. With an arrogant snarl, he sits in the chair on the far right-hand side of my dining nook. From his vantage, his view of the kitchen is uninterrupted.

The rattling plate exposes the shudder raking through my body when I set the food down in front of him. "Beer," he commands, his snarled tone failing to excuse his bad manners.

Not trusting the stranger's motives, I save the roll of my eyes until I'm facing the fridge. After acquiring his requested beverage, I pop it open and place it on the coaster beside his plate. He grunts, rudely dismissing me so he can eat in peace. With a grumble, I return to the dishes I was washing.

"When we first arrived, we were advised this domain was out of bounds," the stranger says a short time later through a mouthful of steak. "I guess Nikolai's interests in you have waned since there's no longer a man guarding the door."

His comment bestows upon me a severe bout of indigestion, but I keep my worry unknown, ensuring he won't smell my fear. While shoveling food into his mouth, the strange man keeps his narrowed gaze arrested on me.

It isn't that I can see his eyes. It's because his gaze is so tumultuous my nape is dripping with sweat.

A short time later, in the corner of my eye, I watch him throw a chunk of steak onto his plate. "If you taste as bland as this meat, I understand Nikolai's disinterest."

"I am an attorney, not a cook," I mumble, the unease clutching my throat not enough to stop me from retaliating against his rudeness.

My throat works hard to swallow when he stands from his chair and steps away from the table. "An attorney, hey? You've got looks and brains. An odd combination for Niki's whores."

His haughty tone makes my fear climb, but my fighting instincts have me saying, "I am part of Nikolai's defense team. Not his whore. Anything happening out there has nothing to do with me."

A deep rumble fills the kitchen. It takes me a second to realize it's the stranger's laughter. It isn't a happy laugh. It's as villainous as the high and mighty gleam darkening his eyes.

"You've got attitude. I like that. The fighters keep things interesting."

Flashes of my past tear through my brain, holding me captive. As fear envelops every inch of my body, I dart my eyes to the swinging door, praying someone will walk through it.

My anxiety is so high that I'd rather endure another verbal slinging match with Nikolai than be eyed as I was four years ago.

My stomach recoils when the stranger growls, "The louder you scream, the harder I'm gonna fuck you." When he glares into my eyes, his every intention is revealed in sickening detail, all of them as disturbing as his abhorrent face.

When my fight-or-flight mode kicks into gear, my eyes dart to the door so I can calculate my most viable exit. My stomach swishes when I realize my steps to the door are double the stranger's. No matter how fast I run, I'll never beat him to the door.

As my back splays against my kitchen cabinets, I frantically search for an object I can defend myself with. I'm not going down without a fight this time.

I cuss out the sheriff's department under my breath, loathing that their removal of dangerous weapons was so thorough I can't find a weapon. Recognizing I'm not leaving this room unscathed no matter what I do or say, I charge for the door.

A squeal bubbles up my chest when the man's thick arm curls around my waist. I kick and thrust while screaming for help at the top of my lungs, praying my loud pleas will be heard over the thumping of bass in my living room.

The man tightens his grip around my waist so much he winds me. "I haven't even started yet, and you're already screaming."

He flings me across the room as if I am weightless, sending me crashing into the drying rack with a thud. Shards of porcelain spray across the floor when the plates Nikolai and I used shatter on the tiled floor.

"Come on. Fight me, bitch. It just makes me harder," he sneers, his hot breath hitting my ear when he curls his body over mine.

With one hand clamped over my mouth, muffling my screams for help, his other hand yanks down my shorts. With my mind hazing between the past and the present, I frantically claw at him. My sharp nails break the leathery skin on his hands, but nothing I do impedes him. He tugs on my shorts so hard the steel fastener soon bursts open under the pressure.

Remembering the self-defense classes Maddox taught me in the weeks before his arrest, I throw back my head and stomp down hard on my attacker's foot. The man howls in pain when the heel of my stiletto pierces the fake material of his polished dress shoes.

Using his imbalance to my advantage, I ram my elbow into his ribs before dropping it to his crotch.

A feral grunt seeps from his mouth when my aim on his family jewels showcases its perfection. He falls to his knees, the anger on his face pushed aside for pain.

"You fucking bitch!" His loud voice forces more flashbacks into my mind, but with sheer determination moving my legs, I race for the swinging door.

My house is crammed with mafia kingpins and women barren of souls, but I'd rather take my chances with them than continue tussling with a man without a heart.

My quick pace ends when the stranger snags my ankle and yanks me backward. "Where the fuck are you going? I'm not even halfway done with you yet."

20

NIKOLAI

Three busted eye sockets, one broken nose, and several sets of bloodied knuckles later, the fight Roman started finally comes to an end. My men have always been thirsty for conflict, but their edginess today reveals they can sense a storm on the horizon as well as me.

Things were volatile when Rico was killed, but it settled within a year, and it's been virtually clear sailing since then. Although Vladimir has dabbled in some deals I'd prefer our sanction not be associated with, if it kept his focus off me, I happily turn a blind eye.

Once the rightful order is restored and the true king is returned to his throne, I'll work toward returning the Popov entity to the glory it once was. That operation won't include totem auctions and underage prostitution rings.

My eyes stray to the front door of Justine's apartment when Roman enters it. I'm not shocked by the frustrated expression on his face, but I am apprehensive about it. He has daughters, so he's more empathetic to women than most men in my crew, but even if he wasn't, the expression on his face tells me I'm not going to like what he's unearthed the past thirty minutes.

I return Justine's upended couch to its rightful spot before joining Roman in the foyer. My strides are as uneasy as the twisting of my stomach. When I reach him, he hands me a black tablet. "There's no sound, but you don't need it to get an idea of the event."

I soothe the bile scorching my throat with a quick swallow before hitting play on the video. It commences with Justine and Dimitri walking into a moderate yet heavily guarded mansion. Although no date is cited, I'm certain it was before Justine was mauled by a dog because not only are her shoulders high, but she's also wearing a spaghetti strap top. Excluding the times I've pulled her hemline away from her neck, I've yet to see the skin she hides with long-sleeved, high neckline shirts.

"Was this footage edited?" I ask Roman when Justine's entrance at the Petretti compound is quickly chased by her exit only minutes later.

Roman shakes his head. "No. The timeline is correct."

My mood shifts to dangerous when the frame jumps forward several minutes. I can't see who is clutching Justine's arm, but their hold is as violent as the fury that thunders through me when she's shoved through a door at the end of a narrow staircase.

Excluding the spotlight of several camera phones, the room is almost pitch black. The poor lighting can't take away from the inhumane act occurring. Justine isn't solely being terrorized by a dog trained to kill, she's being taunted by the numerous spectators watching the event through protective glass.

I can't see their faces, but I guarantee you every one of them will be dead by the end of the month. Their laughter will switch to howls when I remove their voice boxes from the slit I slash across their throats.

When the beast mauling Justine rips a chunk of flesh off her rib, she falls to her knees. Mercifully, her low position on the ground presents the perfect opportunity for her to protect her face and neck. The wrong strike to the jugular would have killed her— although I'm reasonably sure she would have been begging to die by this stage. Stab wounds with rusty knives are immensely painful, so I can only imagine what it feels like to have your muscles shredded by the fangs of an animal.

"Who is he pleading to?" I ask Roman while pointing to the side of the screen that shows Justine's brother, Maddox, kneeling at the heel of a man wearing polished black shoes.

Since there's no sound, I can't hear what Maddox is saying, but I'm confident he's pleading. His eyes are wet, his lips are moving in quick succession, and he has the face of a man who'd murder to save his baby sister.

My jaw tightens when Roman says, "We don't know. We scoured several angles of footage. It never shows who he is."

"There's more than one video?"

"Yes." He licks his puffy black lips as he fights to ignore the furious tic in my jaw. "This was the less confronting of the half dozen."

Hate singes my veins. It is quickly followed by the warmth of vengeance. I told Justine she'd get her revenge. For the first time in my life, I plan to keep my promise.

I double-tap the screen, freezing it on the hand of the person Maddox is pleading to. Even with his face shadowed, I know he is a Petretti. The diamond and ruby 'P' ring on his right hand ensures I can't be mistaken. They're only given to direct descendants of the Petretti family.

I was gifted mine last month.

It was the reason for my confrontation with a Petretti crew member yesterday afternoon. Word is getting out about my true birthright quicker than I can silence the preachers, which has me wondering if the snitch is coming from my side of the battlefield.

Needing to end one war before I start another, under Roman's watchful eye, I restart the video. The 'P' ring is in a frame from its owner granting permission for Maddox to enter the cage his sister is being brutalized in. He races to her in a nanosecond, rips the dog off her with the same viciousness the dog instilled on Justine the past ten minutes, then lifts her bloodied body into his arms.

That's where the video ends, frozen on the frame of a lifeless Justine being carried out of the room coated in her blood. I've seen many sickening things in my life. I've taken lives—many of them— but this is by far the most horrendous thing I've ever seen. A bullet between the eyes is painless. A knife across the jugular causes a few seconds of pain. Justine's punishment may have only lasted ten minutes, but the pain and humiliation associated with it will never end.

I know this from experience.

Just as I hand the tablet back to Roman, a commotion from the kitchen gains my attention. I could brush it off as Justine being feisty with the dishware like she was earlier, but my gut is cautioning me not to be stupid.

After instructing Roman to find out who the owner of the ring is, I make my way to the kitchen. My speed increases when I hear three thumps in a row. It sounds like someone stomping their foot on the ground, just more in desperation than impatience.

When I break through the swinging door of the kitchen, the anger I'm barely containing reaches a fever pitch. Justine is on her hands and knees, crawling my way, and Sergei is holding his gushing nose together with his hand.

Although Justine isn't injured like she was in the video I just watched, the fear in her eyes sends my blood pressure through the roof.

"Ангел?"

Before she can tell me what the fuck is going on, Sergei stands from his kneeled position. "That whore kicked me in the face. I will slit her throat the instant I've finished fucking her."

He stares Justine down, his gaze threatening. I hope he likes what he is seeing, as her angelic face will be the last thing he'll ever see.

"Or maybe I'll slit your throat first, then I will have another hole to penetrate."

His words are as worthless as the man standing before her, but Justine doesn't know that. She scampers behind me so she can use my thighs as a shield. The terrified expression on her face sends rage exploding through me, making me the most unhinged I've ever been.

"You're dead!"

While charging the man who will die a death more painful than a thousand, I remove my trusty knife from my back pocket. Sergei squeals a blood-curling scream when I draw a vibrant red streak across his throat. I could have taken him down with one slice, but I want his wails heard across Vegas, warning others what will happen if they dare to mess with Justine.

The scent of fresh blood streams into my nostrils when I fist Sergei's sweat-drenched hair to yank his head back. He is on his knees like he was when I entered the kitchen, except now his hands are cradling the thin, yet life-threatening gash sliced from one ear to the next.

"*Носмотри на нее*," I sneer, my voice unrecognizable since it's seared with revenge. "Her angelic face will be the last you'll see when I send you to hell for touching what is mine."

I yank his head back further, wanting him to witness what I'm witnessing, to see the fighter climbing out of the trench and the angel set to expand her wings. He may have scared her, but she won't stay down for long. Her wings will cocoon her until she's ready to fly again—as will I—then she'll emerge stronger than she was before. Not even watching me murder a man will hinder her metamorphosis because only cowards stay down when they fall. The strong do whatever it takes to live—even placing their own heads on the chopping block.

When the nib of my blade digs into the vein keeping Sergei's brain alive, Roman shouts my name. He's standing to the left of Justine. His eyes are as wide and as terrified as they were when he handed me the tablet, but his fear is no longer solely focused on Justine. He's petrified for me as well, aware of the punishment I'll face just as much as he knows I've already made my decision.

Sergei is a dead man—nothing said or done will change that.

When Roman's worldly eyes fail to subdue me, he uses words. "Think of the repercussions of this with your father. Sergei is family. He may not have the Popov name, but he has the blood."

"I don't care if he has the blood of a Popov. His disgrace will not be tolerated! You don't disrespect me and not suffer the penance for your poor judgment." Blood gurgles in Sergei's throat when I yank his head back far enough his close-to-death eyes can lock with mine. "You were warned I'd slit your throat if you touched her. Unlike my brothers, my threats aren't idle."

I'm about to charge, sentence, and execute Sergei for his crimes when the faintest plea stops me. "Don't."

It didn't come from Roman. It came from Justine, who's slumped on the floor, shuddering through a massive surge of adrenaline and fear.

When I stare at her in shock, confused as to why she's pleading with me to give Sergei a second chance when I've already given him many, she says, "Two wrongs won't make a right."

Realizing there's only one person in this room capable of stopping me, Roman joins Justine's campaign. "Listen to Justine, Nikolai. She doesn't want this." He lowers his eyes to Justine. "Tell him this isn't what you want."

When he nudges his head my way, Justine returns her eyes to mine. They're still full of fear, but she's no longer in fear for herself. She's worried about me. "I don't want this." Her strength doesn't surprise me. I saw it in her eyes in under a second, but what she says next sure does. "No woman is worth a fracture in the order, remember? You said that only an hour ago."

My blood blackens, frustrated she took my comment as literal, but I'm also determined to show her differently. "He hurt you."

Red waves topple down her shoulders when she shakes her head. "No, he didn't. Look at me, I'm fine."

There's barely a scratch on her, but my mood is too hostile to realize that's a good thing. "He touched what is mine."

"I know," Justine replies, unfazed by the possessiveness in my tone. "But I'm fine. Look at me, Nikolai. I am perfectly fine. Sergei is the only one injured."

My focus shifts from the fading of Sergei's pulse to Justine when her attempt to stand has her wobbling as much as Sergei's knees. Roman's hands shoot out to settle her sways, but since her emotions are still fueled by fear, she shrugs out of his hold.

"Ангел..."

As the color from her face drains, she mutters again, "I don't want this."

When she careens toward the floor, I thrust Sergei out of the way. I catch her in my arms, but the movements of her head are too fast to avoid a collision with the floor. Her right temple hits the tiles with a sickening bang, fracturing a muscle in my chest I was certain died years ago.

As I pull Justine into my chest, Roman orders Trey and Viktor to remove Sergei from the kitchen. He's not foolish. He knows this is his one and only chance to save Sergei from the wrath of my blade—*for now.*

He won't be so lucky when Justine wakes.

"Get Dok."

My men part like the Red Sea when I walk through the trashed living room with an unconscious Justine in my arms. They look a little lost, unsure if they are coming or going. I can't blame them.

I'm a little stumped as well. I've never had the urge to protect someone as I do Justine. In all honesty, the need riddles me with guilt.

When I was ordered to place a hit on Rico's wife, I never stopped to evaluate what Rico would go through. I was too busy gauging what my punishment would be if I failed to follow through with Vladimir's request. I was already struggling to hide my true birthright from those who'd use it against me, so the last thing I wanted was to be placed on any team that wasn't Vladimir's.

It was only after witnessing Vladimir's lack of grief about Rico's murder did my thoughts change. Your teammates aren't your family. It's the people who walk through the gates of hell beside you as they trust you're not dragging them there for no reason.

"What happened?" Dok asks, following me into Justine's room.

I place Justine onto her mattress, cover her with a knitted blanket for modesty, then pivot around to face Dok. "She hit her head when she fell."

When he steps toward Justine's bed in preparation to assess her, I puff out my chest, wordlessly warning him about the fury he'll face if he so much as causes her to whimper. My mood is so erratic, I can't trust a single groan won't have me snapping necks. Considering Dok is one of the rare good ones, I'd hate for him to endure the punishment I plan to finish issuing Sergei the instant I know Justine is okay.

Dok's Adam's apple bobs up and down, proving he heard my silent caution. "I doubt she is concussed, but if she is, rest is the best possible solution. Is she running a fever?"

I shake my head. When I carried her to her room, her body was minus the heat that blazes through it whenever I'm in her presence. It's partly responsible for the spike in my pulse. I love the way she responds to my touch, but Sergei's filthy motherfucking hands ruined that.

"Then let her rest. We will reconvene when she wakes..." Dok's words trail off when Roman enters the room. He doesn't say anything. He merely runs decoy with the hope Trey and Viktor can carry a slumped Sergei through the living room without incident.

"Is he dead?" The low hang of Sergei's head has me hopeful.

Roman waits for the front door of Justine's apartment to close with Sergei on the other side before shaking his head. He shouldn't look so smug. A stay of execution only delays the court's order. It doesn't overturn it.

"Hide him well, Roman, because his life will be the first I claim when she wakes."

Ignoring Roman's silent pledge for me to reconsider, I return my focus to Justine. I watch her like I did last night, shocked only twenty-four hours has passed since we met. I don't know why I'm surprised. The longer you dance with the devil, the longer you remain in hell.

The same can be said for angels.

21

NIKOLAI

R oman holds Dok back when Justine groans approximately
an hour later. As her hand shoots up to rub the bump her
collision with the floor caused to her right temple, her
eyes flutter open. They float around her room before they eventually stop on me. The pained expression on her face claws at my
chest in a way I've never experienced.

I don't do attachments.

Usually I'm in and out in a matter of hours.

This is different.

Not only is the way she's looking at me producing a foreign
sound from my chest, but it also has me expressing emotions I was
certain I was born without. I don't just want to protect her and keep
her safe, I want to give back the dignity she lost when she was
mauled by a dog. I want to earn her respect without scaring it from
her. But even more than that, I want to keep her forever.

An angel doesn't belong in hell, but they've opened their doors
once before, so who's to say they won't do it again?

Justine breathes nosily out of her nose when I scoot closer to
her. "I won't let anyone hurt you."

I have the respect of hundreds and am feared by thousands, but
I feel the most powerful I've ever felt when she mutters, "I know."

When I cup her cheeks, a little vein in her neck works overtime. "How are you feeling?"

Not giving her the chance to reply, I brush away the curl covering the bump on her right temple so I can inspect it. She stills when her molten-red locks fall from her shoulders far enough the bite marks she referenced earlier today are exposed, but she knows better than to hide them from me.

The skin stretched over the marble-sized lump is faint purple in color, however, it didn't crack under the pressure. Its flat appearance has me skeptical it's the sole cause of her unconsciousness. A lagging sleep schedule may also be at play. She looks more tired now than she did last night, which is understandable. Fighting off a man double your size is exhausting no matter how strong your will.

I also know this from experience.

My words are gravelly when I ask, "Does your head hurt?"

Justine takes a moment to compile a response before shaking her head. I don't need a doctorate in medicine to know a knock to the head isn't responsible for her delay. She's speechless because my hands are on her. I like that even more than the way the fear in her eyes subsides the longer I sit across from her, stroking her cheeks.

"I can give you something to take the edge off if you'd like?"

It doesn't take her as long to respond this time around. She nods —rather briskly.

Ignoring the cocky bastard inside me itching to fan his feathers, I hold out my hand palm side up to Dok. He places two of the Xanax tablets he found in the medicine cabinet in Justine's bathroom into my palm before rejoining Roman by the door. The date on the prescription label states it was filled over two years ago, and the number of pills inside the canister reveals Justine doesn't use them in day-to-day life, but something in her eyes tells me she needs more than a stiff drink to see her through this.

"Drink slowly, *Ангел*," I instruct when she downs the tablets with half a glass of water. "We don't want your food coming back up."

The heaviness on my chest is pushed aside for smugness when she switches her gulps to tiny sips. Once the glass is empty, she hands it back to me. I place it onto the bedside table, stand to my feet, yank the sheets out from under her bottom, then nudge my head to her pillow.

Hearing my silent command, she slips between her sheets without a single protest. Her obedience has me tempted to join her. I would if I didn't feel the eyes of Roman and Dok on me. They're eyeballing me like I'm doing one of the many inane thoughts in my head. Justine was assaulted. I should not be having the thoughts I am.

Heat races across Justine's chest when my wish to touch her becomes too much for me to bear. I drag my finger down her cheek, across her collarbone, and past her budded nipple before I raise my eyes to her face. You have no idea how hard my next set of words are to articulate when I spot the lust gleaming in her eyes. I want to stay but leaving is the right thing to do. I know better than anyone how one wrong move could fuck everything up. Since that's the last thing I want, I listen to the silent pleads Roman has been throwing my way the past hour.

My voice is low and dangerous when I say to Justine, "I'll be right outside your door if you need me."

I wait for Justine to nod before gesturing for Roman and Dok to leave before me. When the door creaks shut, I drop my eyes to Justine's chest. The heaviness weighing mine down lightens when I notice how firm her nipple still is. I love how she responds to my meekest of touches, her desires more potent than her fear.

Even spooked, fear will never be her strongest emotion around me.

Need will be.

"Soon, *Ангел*. Very soon," I promise before pivoting on my heels and leaving her room, acting ignorant to the disappointed sigh escaping her lips.

If I don't leave now, I never will. Then, not only will Justine be placed on Vladimir's radar, but I'll also triple my fight to bring Sergei before the courts for his crime.

While closing Justine's door, I seek Dok's gaze. Like most of my men, he reads the command in my eyes without me needing to speak. "From the width and depth of her bump, I'd say it's a superficial wound. Her eyes were responsive, and she was clearly alert, so I don't see her having any long-term side effects from her fall."

"Unlike Sergei."

Roman shoots me a wry look. It does little to settle my itch to kill. I told Sergei I'd slit his throat if he touched Justine. I don't disperse threats I can't execute. I'll just need to be inventive since Sergei is being sheltered by the last man I expected.

"If Justine wakes, come get me."

Nodding, Dok takes a protective stance in front of Justine's bedroom door. Confident he won't let me down and more trusting of my men now Sergei is gone, I push off my feet and head to the kitchen. Roman shadows my stalk. I can hear his brain ticking a million miles an hour, but he remains quiet while I hunt for the device I know he hid in the pantry, untrusting of my surly mood. I don't blame him. I can't recall the last time I was this worked up.

When I find a tablet similar to the one Roman handed me earlier stashed behind a year's worth of rice, Roman attempts to snatch it out of my grasp. I glare at him, warning him I'll rip him into motherfucking shreds if he doesn't back the fuck up.

Roman is like a father to me, but my mood is hostile. I'm the most unhinged I've ever been, so now is not the time for him to 'mentor' me.

After holding his hands up in defeat, Roman yanks out a frail wooden chair from beneath the dining nook, spins it around, then straddles it backward. His face is as hard as stone and as impenetrable as the shield I plan to shroud Justine in.

His tough stance all but crumbles when Justine's fight to get away from Sergei blares through the speakers of the surveillance device. Sergei calls Justine a whore and goads her to fight him because her screams turn him on before he yanks at her shorts so fiercely, her button pops open under the strain of his tugs.

Considering Justine is barely half Sergei's size, her fight is commendable. She gives it her all to get away from him and was on the verge of winning before I intervened. The thought puffs my chest with pride, although it's barely felt through the anger turning my veins black.

My hands shake when I stab my finger on the rewind button so I can watch Sergei's crime repeatedly. Each second of reel convinces me my sentencing was right.

Sergei is going to die.

I *am* going to kill him.

Then I *will* parade his death for the world to see.

He hurt what is mine, so he will hurt for his stupidity.

When the video commences playing for the fourth time, Roman shouts, "Enough!" He stands from his chair, the veins in his tattooed arms pumping. "I get it. I understand, but will you stop fucking watching it?"

"He was going to rape her, Roman! He was going to kill her."

"I know, but watching it over and over again won't change the outcome. You stopped him, Nikolai, so stop torturing yourself as if you didn't." He snatches the tablet from my hand, tosses it onto the kitchen counter, then runs a shaky hand over his thick afro. "I understand the pain clawing at your chest. I feel the hurt poisoning your blood, but if you kill Sergei, Vladimir will—"

My angry roar bounces off the white-washed walls when I interrupt, "I don't fuckin' care what he'll do to me! I will suffer the injustice."

Roman is quick to shut down the panic detonating in his eyes, but I see it before he fully tucks it away. "He won't stop them this time."

"I wouldn't expect him to." I take a step closer to him, the air pumping out of my nostrils as chilly as my words. "But I'm not a sixteen-year-old boy anymore, Roman. I know how Vladimir thinks. I know what makes him tick, so I'm more than capable of withstanding his wrath."

A fatherly flare darts through Roman's almost black eyes when he says, "You are... but is Justine?"

His question jabs at me like a knife to the chest, stealing both the air from my lungs and the words from my throat.

The fury in Roman's eyes softens when he locks them with mine. He doesn't speak, he just lets me see the worry etched on his face. Justine is barely coping after her tussle with Sergei. She's not strong enough to endure the madness that comes from being drafted in a war against a man as evil as Vladimir.

She will be soon.

She's just not there right now.

Confident I understand his objective, Roman slaps my shoulder before giving it a firm squeeze. "You will sentence Sergei for his crimes. We just need to work out a way you can do that while keeping both you and Justine safe." I'm about to say *I can take care of myself,* but he continues talking, foiling my endeavor.

"Vladimir's family shares blood. Ours share burdens, Nikolai. This is our fight as much as it is yours."

Stealing my chance to reply, he squeezes my shoulder for a second time before stalking out of the kitchen, taking the tablet with him.

Several hours later, my eyes pop up from the weapon distribution schedule in front of me. Even with my agitation still on edge, business must continue as normal. I've been placing footholds around Vladimir's empire the past three years, and now more than ever, I need to ensure they're capable of withstanding the load I'm about to place on them. My competitors are weak, villainous men, but they protect their assets well—assets that will crumble when the monarch of their realm falls victim to my knife.

I stub out my cigarette into an ashtray when Justine's head pops out of her bedroom door. Since Dok is blocking her exit, she misses me signaling for him to stand down. She looks well-rested, so there's no need to keep her trapped in her room. I'm also interested to see how she interacts with my crew. I was born a mafia prince, and my entire life has been consumed by it, so I don't just need a woman strong enough to stand at my side, I need her to walk through the inferno of hell with me.

Justine has already done it once and survived without her wings smoldering from the heat, so I'm confident she'll do it again. Sergei's attack would have most women cowering for days. Justine only rested for a few hours. She battled the most vicious man in Vladimir's crew and came out without a scratch on her. If that doesn't prove to you she's an angel seeking chaos, I have no fucking clue how else to convince you.

The wish to kill that's been clotting my veins the past three hours clears away when Justine spots my stalk from the corner of the living room. Just as quickly as her angelic face calms my unease, my devilish one erases the worry lining hers.

I watch her move through the throng of people separating us with revered silence. Since her professional look has been switched for a more casual ensemble, she fits into my crew remarkably well. They don't touch her, and none of the men doped out on crack are stupid enough to mistake her for a whore, but they're quick to offer her a drink and for her to sit on the three-seater couch across from me.

"Thank you," Justine whispers to Gavril when he hands her what she assumes is a glass of water.

Although her words are crisp, I already suspect that Dok slipped her another two Xanax when I wasn't looking. Her eyes are almost too bright for the dullness of her cheeks. Her face replicates the one women wear when they leave my bed and the one men crave when sampling my drugs. She's here, just not entirely.

I hide my snicker with my glass when Justine's big gulp of her drink causes her nose to screw up. She just made a liar out of those people who say you can't taste or smell vodka. She's acting as if her throat is on fire, and it has my tongue wishing it could soothe the burn.

The inevitable is unavoidable. She will be mine. I just need to practice patience while my crew lays out some well-placed traps.

Sadly.

Justine and I sit across from each other for the next twenty minutes. The tension is as thick as it was when we rode in the sheriff's van last night, but for once, the stiffness doesn't have me craving a bloodbath. Her face alone ensures me the storm in my gut will only be tamed by her lips, body, and the scent I'm sucking in like her panties are an inch from my nose.

I'd give anything to bend her over the couch and devour her sweet little cunt like a man starved of taste, but since Vladimir is already questioning why there's a ten-minute gap in the footage from the surveillance cameras planted around Justine's apartment, I stay on my side of the living room, watching her like a creep.

Justine doesn't seem to mind. She maintains my eye contact while squirming like she did last night. The pressing of her thighs is as dangerous to my mind as her erotic scent. It makes me feel so reckless, I have no hesitation in saying torture will never bend my knees, but I bet Justine can.

We stare at each other for several cock-thickening minutes, our connection only lost when Alyna and Luyca slot into the minute gap on each side of Justine's thighs. They fiddle with her hair and touch her face as my hands are itching to, hopeful she'll share the secret on how they can regain my interest.

Justine hates their attention, but she'll never tell them that—not even when they drag her into the bathroom with a promise of a makeover. I don't want them to change her, she's fucking perfect the way she is, but since Satan is walking the gallows, I must maintain my watch from afar.

It looks like I'm working on a weaponry trade that will net the Popov entity $2.4 million, but not once do my eyes leave Justine. She handles Alyna and Luyca applying a heavy dose of makeup to her face without so much as a flinch, but the instant they move for her hair, she clams up. They want it high and off her face, but Justine doesn't want to give up her shield just yet, proving Roman's concerns were warranted. She's strong until someone tries to remove her armor.

Justine gives off the shyness of a mouse, but Alyna and Luyca learn otherwise, not even ten minutes later. Over their ploy of acting friendly with the hope of slipping between my sheets, Justine thanks them for their advice, scrubs the gunk off her face with a washcloth, then returns to the living room. While taking in the party-like atmosphere with wide, untainted eyes, she glides past the cabinet housing a range of board games, floats by the men playing *Nard* for an impressive amount of coin before she returns to the seat directly across from me.

I slant my head to hide my cocky grin. She's safer being surrounded by my men than being alone with me, but I fucking love that she thinks she isn't.

When the joining of her knees can't weaken her body's response to my stare, Justine downs vodka as if it is water. She tosses them back as regularly as I do, only stopping when I place my hand over her glass before Gavril can refill it for the fourth time.

When her eyes slit, a soundless laugh rumbles in my chest. She's more upset about being left out of the festivities than she is about her apartment being treated as if it is an underground nightclub on the strip.

I told you there are devilish thoughts in the most angelic minds.

"Do you want to dance on the table with Renata and Sophie, Ангел? Because if you continue drinking at the rate you are, that's where you'll end up."

She looks disappointed I know the names of the topless women using her coffee table as if it's the stage at Cliché. Or is it pride? With her pupils the size of marbles, I'm having a hard time reading her.

Heat treks through my veins when she mutters, "Would you be bothered if I did?"

"Not at all." With surveillance forgotten, and my cock as hard as stone, I balance on the edge of my chair. "But I'll clear the room first. Request a private show. I like my men, but I'll kill them all if even one of them sees you naked."

Her next set of words come out with a slur, but I'm skeptical alcohol is the cause of her stammered words. She's turned-on by my warning and loving my jealousy. "Who said I'd dance naked?"

She joins me in balancing on the edge of her chair. We've downed the same amount of alcohol, but her movements aren't as stable as mine since her veins are tackling both anti-anxiety pills and alcohol.

"You can be sexy with your clothes on. You just need to be inventive." Her face goes from playful to serious in under a second. "Is that why you stare at me like you do? Because you're being inventive?" She stumbles over her last word. "Or are you scared?"

"Nothing scares me, *Ангел.*" *Except the look you're giving me now.*

She wants to forget just for a night, but I'm stopping her from doing that.

I'm a *ублюдок.*

Even if Vladimir is watching, there's no reason she can't enjoy the festivities. He'll be less skeptical if she acts on the devilish thoughts in her head instead of the saintly ones.

The fine hairs on Justine's arms bristle when I lean over to fill her empty glass with the top-shelf vodka I'm drinking. It spills over the rim from the shudder that rolls down her spine when I say, "Keep your clothes on, or the death of every man in this room will be on your shoulders."

She nods. It's not in submission. It is because she knows my threats aren't idle.

Sergei is mere hours from discovering that himself, and Vladimir won't be far behind him.

22

NIKOLAI

Trey grins at me over the rim of his bottle of beer when I yank Justine down from the coffee table she's dancing on. She kept her word, she's dancing with her clothes on, but what she said earlier is true. You can be sexy with your clothes on, and she is sexy as fuck.

I trust my men. They have my back no matter how dangerous the target, but they're a bunch of horny fuckers who wouldn't feel an ounce of shame using Justine's seductive dance moves as inspiration while lessening the tension their whores can't.

There's an edge of seduction attached to women who don't flaunt their goods. The saying, 'what you can't see makes you want it more,' is absolutely on par with Justine, and no, I'm not just referencing her seductive-as-fuck body. The woman I see in her eyes is just as ravishing as the one who's been dancing up a storm the past hour.

Silence falls between Justine and me when I carry her into the kitchen. Sergei's blood is still spilled on the floor. It whitens Justine's gills as much as it sobers her up.

"I'll have that cleaned up in the morning," I promise through a growl, frustrated by the lack of spillage.

If there were more blood, I wouldn't have needed to seek confirmation if Sergei had succumbed to the knife wound I slashed across his throat. I would have known without a doubt.

After placing Justine's backside onto the kitchen counter, I toss a dish towel onto the blood, then move into her pantry. It's one of those old-aged ones you'd expect to find in the South during the slave era. It is the size of a bathroom and echoes from the emptiness down one end.

Once I have a loaf of bread, peanut butter, and a jar of jelly in my hands, I return to Justine's side of the kitchen. She's clearly drunk, but just like fear will never be the first emotion she displays around me, a belly full of vodka can't hide the lust in her bloodshot eyes either.

A ghost-like smile touches her lips when I slather two slices of whole-grain bread with a generous serving of condiments, shred it into two even halves, then hand one to her. "The carbs will help absorb the vodka in your gut."

Her half-smile switches to a full-blown grin when I rip through my half of our sandwich like I'm a savage. I'm hungry as fuck. My hunger just has nothing to do with food.

I swallow down the chunk of gooey bread without chewing before jerking up my chin, wordlessly demanding for Justine to follow suit. She hasn't eaten since lunch, which means there's nothing but vodka and Xanax in her stomach.

She takes a little nibble on the crust before rolling her eyes. "I'd rather greasy bacon."

"And I'd rather you naked and on your knees sucking my cock, but we can't always have what we want, can we?" I'm lying. If my actions weren't being monitored, I'd give her everything she wants —including my head between her legs.

Justine tries to hide the heat flaring across her face with her sandwich, but it does her no good. She's redder than the strawberry jelly sitting on her top lip.

When I clear away the blob of sugar with my thumb, her hot breaths fan my cheeks. I stare at the lips I've fantasized about sliding down my cock more times than I'll ever share while she peers at me with hungry, desperate eyes. Her stare alone is hot enough to tempt a devil into becoming a saint, and it has me thinking recklessly.

Leaning in, I drag my nose down the vein beating out a funky beat in her neck, confident its thump matches the one between her legs. When the scent of her needy cunt, which has gone from subtle to dangerous in less than a minute, fills my nostrils, I'm hard in an instant.

With my pulse as high as my wish to claim her as mine, I place my hands on Justine's thighs before spreading them wide enough for me to slot between them. While brushing the back of my hand down the heat making me mindless with need, I lock my eyes with Justine's. She returns my stare, knowing she should tell me to stop but aware she never will.

She wants this.

She wants it as badly as me.

Her breaths batter her ribcage when I curl my fingers around her neck. My hold is dominant but painless. The soft moan she releases when I tighten my grip assures me of this.

When I inch her mouth closer to mine, ever so slowly, yet also impatiently, warning alarms sound, consequences are assessed, but more than anything, need prevails. She'll be the most expensive trophy I've ever owned, but she'll be worth the risk, the torment... *my death.* If she survives me, she'll be strong enough to survive Vladimir. I am the devil incarnate, the spawn of all evil. I'm worse than Satan himself. I fear nothing—except how weak she makes me.

Fortunately for me, my weaknesses make me stronger. I won't let anything happen to Justine. I will protect her and keep her safe *after* I make her mine.

Our lips are an inch apart.

We're sharing the same breath.

Then disaster strikes.

Roman bursts into the kitchen, knowing all too well what he's interrupting. Not only does his arched brow fault his ruse, so the fuck does the device in his hand. It's showcasing a live stream from the camera perched high above my head.

"*Не говори ни слова,*" I warn him in Russian, even though I'm aware he doesn't speak a word. "Or I'll cut off your tongue and feed it to you."

Justine giggles when Roman rolls his eyes like a child. I really wish she wouldn't. I'm on the verge of killing him, and I'd rather do that without an erection. I've been called many things, but a deranged psycho will never be one of them.

Well, not tonight, anyway.

Justine's laughter shifts to a groan when I lift her off the counter, then nudge my head to the door still swinging from Roman's brutal push. "Time for bed."

For someone disappointed the fun is over, she follows my command remarkably quick.

I guess I didn't say she was going to bed alone, so she has no reason to fret.

Roman doesn't utter a syllable when I walk past him with a stumbling Justine in my arms. He doesn't need to. His worldly eyes convey the entire story, not to mention the file he's clutching like I want to do to his neck. It's stamped with the Wallens Ridge State Prison seal, and the stack of papers inside are missing the thick black lines Maddox's last file had, proving his time away from Justine's apartment has served me well.

"I'll meet you on the balcony." Although the tightness of my jaw chops up my words, Roman has no issues hearing them. He dips his chin before following my exit of the kitchen, snickering like his tendons aren't close to being sliced.

Even with Justine's apartment being the smallest I've stayed in, our walk from the kitchen to her bedroom seems longer than a marathon. She takes more steps backward than she does forward, but since I can't trust myself to touch her and stop, I guide her steps instead of forcing them.

She uses our closeness to her advantage. After pivoting around to face me head-on, she assesses my face as I plan to do her body when she's not drunk.

Just like her, my face is free from the scars of my childhood. It hides my stories well.

A massive surge of cockiness pelts into me when she slurs, "You're *sooo* pretty."

Her voice is the same cock-thickening one she generally uses, but it has an edge of playfulness to it, making me convinced it's been a long time since she let go of the reins. Almost as long as the last time she was fucked.

"I wish I had your lashes. They're *sooo* long they could reach the stars."

Once she's in the safety of her room, she breaks away from my side. "Woo!" she squeals as she dives onto the mattress.

With a laugh, I kick her door closed before pivoting around to face her. My cock knocks at my zipper when she commences removing her clothes. She drags her shorts down her milky-white thighs before fisting her long-sleeve shirt. When it joins her shorts on the floor a few seconds later, I ball my hands into fists, fighting like fuck not to touch her.

Her beautiful body ensures one taste will never suffice. It will have me craving another, and another, and another until we both end up in a ditch. I can protect her, but only if I remember the killer I was raised to be.

My beeline for the door slows when Justine murmurs, "Don't go. Please." My nails dig into my palm as painfully as my cock headbutts my zipper when she undresses while murmuring, "Stay with me. I don't want to be alone. I'm sick of being alone."

Her whispered words tug at my chest. They pull me into a dark place—a solemn hole. They hit me harder than any fist, whip, or chain has. A man like me has rules for a reason, but she has me wanting to break every one of them.

The thought pisses me off as much as it excites me.

When I shift on my feet to face Justine, I work my jaw side to side. She's lying on top of the bedding, looking as ravishing as she does innocent. "Climb under the sheets. There is no fucking way I can lie next to you looking like that and not touch you." My husky words reveal my wavering constraint. They are as hot and temperamental as Justine's sinful body. "And considering I won't take anything not willingly given, you need to get your fine ass under the sheets."

Mistaking the yearning in my voice as repulsion, Justine's lower lip drops into a pout before she slips under the sheets as requested. The cloudy haze dampening her eyes softens when I move to the opposite side of her bed to remove my boots and jeans. My boxers are incapable of hiding the response of my body. I'm thick and hard, and the crown of my cock is peeking out the top of the stretchy black material. Although the removal of my jeans doubles my fight, it sliced Justine's in half.

The instant my head hits the pillow, she scoots across the mattress until we meet eye to eye. "A perfect fit."

I thought being almost beaten to death would be the worst punishment I'd endure in my life. I was fucking wrong. Justine flattening her breasts against my chest is by far more taunting, and don't even attempt to get me to mention the heat of her cunt scorching my dick, or I'll kill you.

"See? Other than your extra-long legs, we're a perfect match."

A breathy chuckle rumbles in my chest when she murmurs a few seconds later, "Is the bed moving?" She looks like she wants to punch me in the stomach when she hears my laughter, but since that means she'd have to remove her tits from my chest, she's not willing to do that. "I swear, my head is foggier now than it was on my eighteenth birthday. I guess that's what I get for not drinking in almost a decade." When I arch my brow, she rolls her eyes. "My brothers were worse than my father. I would have had more freedom in a convent than my childhood home."

After snuggling into my chest, she tells me how her brothers had planned her eighteenth birthday celebration on the belief there'd be no alcohol involved. Excluding the part about her friend leaving with an abusive douchebag, it sounds like a typical eighteenth.

Well, I assume. I've never celebrated my birthday, much less had a party.

No one rejoices the devil's resurrection.

The gleam in Justine's eyes hardens when she says, "I'd give anything to go back to the days where my biggest worry was beating Maddox into the Jack-and-Jill bathroom we shared. He was such a free spirit, Nikolai. He wouldn't have harmed a fly."

I dip my chin, acknowledging I heard her, but I don't utter a sound. I don't want to rock the boat by pointing out that she said 'wouldn't have' as if Maddox's favorable traits are past tense. She has enough guilt in her eyes without me highlighting that she's secretly skeptical about her brother's innocence.

"If I had listened to him, he wouldn't have needed to step in." A hue stains her cheeks. This one is more in anger than lust. "I thought Dimitri saw me... the real me, but all he saw was a pretty doll for his display cabinet."

My knuckles pop when I clench my fists. Dimitri is on the other side of the country, but that doesn't stop me from wanting to beat the living fucking shit out of him. He hurt Justine in more ways than one, yet she's the one who got punished.

How the fuck is that okay?

By the time I've settled my anger enough that I can talk, I'm too late. Justine is asleep. The gentle rise and fall of her chest ensure I can't be mistaken, let alone her faint snores. Watching her sleep settles something deep within me. She truly looks like an angel when she lets go of the weight on her shoulders. The shadows beneath her eyes aren't as dark, and the groove between her brows isn't as deep.

She's peaceful.

Safe.

Protected.

More protected than she was when she got these.

The figure-eight pattern I trace over the bite-like scar she usually keeps hidden shouldn't be enough to wake her, but I forgot about the sexual tension that forever crackles between us. It could wake the dead.

Justine stares straight at me, her eyes vacant and sad as she once again places the needs of others above herself. It's a known trait of any survivor. "You have to help him, Nikolai. Maddox doesn't deserve the life sentence he was served any more than you deserve the one you were issued at birth." I'm not surprised she sees through the shield others can't. I just wish it was occurring after I had reclaimed my throne. "If he could just serve his time at Harborview, my guilt wouldn't be so intense. He wouldn't be free, but at least he'd be safe."

I stiffen when she burrows her head into my chest to hide the wetness streaming down her face. Tears are still new for me. I honestly don't know how to respond to them. For years, I thought they were a sign of weakness and manipulation, but that wasn't what reflected out of Justine's eyes before she buried her head between my pecs.

She's not crying because she's weak.

She's crying because she's been strong for too long.

The heartache heard in her sobs brings back the unfamiliar stab of protection I felt when watching the video of her assault. It has me wanting to cocoon her from the world, to protect her how her brothers endeavored to when she was young.

I never relied on anyone. Even your shadow leaves you when things get dark, but you can trust me when I say I'll stop at nothing to ensure the people responsible for Justine's pain feel her pain.

If a devil can't bend the rules of heaven for an angel to live her life in peace, he'll raise hell instead. My body wears the medals from the last time I stepped into the fire for another. This time the honor will be bestowed on the area where my heart once thumped.

23

JUSTINE

Groaning, I roll onto my side. My temples are throbbing so much that they feel like they will crack open my skull at any second. This ache isn't from being tired. It's more an external pain than an internal one.

Incapable of protesting the pounding in my head, I try to figure out where I am. The softness caressing my curves indicates I am in my bed, but a unique smell lingering in the air is misplacing my conception. I flare my nostrils and inhale deeply, eager to identify the smell.

I jackknife into a half-seated position when I realize it's a manly scent heightening my senses. My sudden movement makes a rush of nausea surge into my stomach, intensifying the thump in my head.

Clutching my temples, I circle the ache, numbing the urge to be sick. Once the desire to vomit has lessened, I flutter open my eyes. My heart rate kicks up a gear when I discover the cause of the intoxicating smell. A tattooed arm is splayed across my bare thigh, which is barely covered by the thin bed sheet.

Crap!

With my heart rammed in my throat, my eyes drift to the warmth heating my side. I don't need to see Nikolai's face to know it's him lying beside me. There's no mistaking his unique manly scent, and don't even get me started on his impenetrable aura.

My intuition is proven spot on when my eyes connect with a sleeping Nikolai. His eyes are snapped shut, and his lips are slightly ajar. With his usually unruly spikes flattened, wisps of dark hair curl around his sculptured cheeks. His jaw is relaxed, relinquishing the strain his face regularly holds, and his lips are minus his infamous pulse-quickening snarl.

My eyes' eager trek over the veins pulsating through his cut body stop when I reach the curve of his backside. His ass is barely peeking out of the bed sheet draped across his lower back, but it won't stop me from assuring you it's a spectacular visual.

Scarcely breathing, I scoot down the mattress so I can categorize Nikolai's gorgeous face more diligently. It's so surreal seeing him like this. He looks like an entirely different man when he's sleeping. He appears almost angelic instead of the evil villain dictated by his mafia prince title.

As I watch him in silence, tiny snippets of our exchanges trickle into my hazy mind. Our grind-up on my front door, our rendezvous in the bathroom, and the abrupt ending of our shared meal roll through my mind like a movie. My memory is so vivid it feels like I am reliving each moment. There's just one memory still hazy—how we ended up in the same bed.

My trip down memory lane ends when awareness of being watched washes over me. Nikolai's eyes are open and glancing straight at me. Unlike me, shock at discovering me lying next to him doesn't register on his face. He doesn't seem the slightest bit bothered by our casual sleeping arrangement. Actually, come to think of it, he looks smitten, like his greatest wish has finally been granted.

"*Доброе утро*, Justine," he greets me, his words groggy, proving he wasn't just resting his eyes.

"It is morning?" I ask, shocked I slept so long. I haven't slept more than five hours a night in the past four years. "That's why it's so quiet. Everyone is passed out."

A massive set of lines groove in Nikolai's forehead as he brushes a rogue strand of hair from my face. Air hisses out of my mouth when his fingertips briefly skim my right temple.

"*Мне жаль*," he apologizes. "Dok assures it's a superficial bump from your fall. There are no internal injuries."

My eyes expand to their full width when the cause for my bumped noggin filters through my brain. "Sergei." Bile burns the base of my throat.

My eyes missile to Nikolai's when he snarls, "Sergei should be grateful he's still breathing." He cracks his knuckles before swinging his legs off the bed. "If you hadn't fainted, he wouldn't be so lucky."

My worry for Sergei is pushed aside when his naked backside is thrust into my peripheral vision. I should be disgusted my libido is overruling my morally astute brain, but I'm not. Nikolai announced that Sergei is alive, leaving me free to ogle him like a shameful nymph. I haven't seen a backside this glorious since... *ever!*

I only remove my eyes from his ass when a pair of low-riding jeans covers the pussy-clenching sight. I sigh, mortified at my lack of professionalism. When he spins around to face me, all thoughts vanish. The pulse of my pussy grows wilder as my eyes zoom in on the V muscle the low rise of his jeans doesn't have a chance in hell of hiding. My god, his body is delicious. I doubt a million years would leave me tired of eyeballing it.

Noticing my brazen stare, Nikolai asks, "Do you look at all your clients like you do me, Justine?" My name rolls off his tongue in a throaty, rumbling purr.

Unable to utter a suitable reply, I shake my head.

The anger on his face slides away as an impish grin tugs at his lips. "Good. My hit list just halved."

I align my eyes with his when I fail to hear any humor in his reply. The reason for his lack of candor becomes apparent when our gazes collide. He had no intention of me taking his threat as facetious. He meant every word he said.

"What happened last night? Why can't I remember anything?"

Although my recollection of the events leading to my awakening remains hazy, I'm more using it to distract me from thoughts I shouldn't be having.

My clenched insides loosen when Nikolai throws a shirt over his head. "After you fainted, Dok checked you over. He guaranteed you weren't concussed but suggested we give you something to take the edge off." He smiles wickedly, causing my clit to ache. "I gave you something."

"You gave me something?" I quote through raised brows, my

words breathless. "What exactly did you give me that knocked me out for over twelve hours?"

Nikolai audaciously winks. "You weren't knocked out. You were alert." His brows waggle as his smile grows. "Not overly lucid, but very much alert."

His tone is playful, but all I hear is a heap of sexual ambiguity.

Like a freight train smacking into me, reality dawns. "Oh my god! Did we..." –I cough to clear my throat— "have sexual relations?"

He chuckles. I feel its hearty vibration all the way to my thrumming clit. "It's called sex, *Ангел*," he jests, his voice carrying through me like liquid ecstasy. "Just don't call it making love, as every man knows love is just lust misspelled."

I roll my eyes, acting like the need in my pussy didn't grow with every wicked word he spoke.

"Did we sleep together? As in, have... *sex*?" My rephrased question isn't any more convincing than my first childish one.

"Are you sore?" Nikolai's voice is throatier than I'd anticipated.

"No. But what does that have to do with anything?"

A squeal tumbles from my lips when he hooks my ankle and drags me down the mattress. My girly squeal switches to a shallow pant when he prowls up my body. Other than tugging the bed sheet into my neck to cover my scars, I don't cite an objection to his panther-like crawl. What woman in her right mind would? I have the man who fiercely protected me like I'm worth my weight in gold, glancing into my eyes as if I am his savior. I'd be mad to act ungrateful.

His pussy-pulsating trek stops when every inch of his body is pressed against mine. Although there's a bed sheet between us, my body acts as if there isn't. I can feel every inch of him—every mouth-watering inch. Our bodies align perfectly. Our eyes, chest, and crotch are in direct symmetry. It's as if we were made for each other. Two broken pieces molded to create one.

A wildfire burns through my womb when Nikolai rocks his hips forward, dragging his erect cock along the soaked seam of my panties. I pant, fighting with all my might not to scream the wicked thoughts streaming through my mind. It's a torturous effort.

"Are you sore?" he repeats, his deep voice strained with lust.

My reply snags in my throat when he thrusts his hips forward again, his second grind more controlled than his first. I moan softly, adoring the surge of excitement dashing through my body. My brain screams for me to withdraw from his embrace, but I cannot stop it. With the heat of his flesh dominating every inch of my body, my mind is blank, stuck in a lust-filled trance.

My pussy grows wetter when he grazes his teeth over my bottom lip. His bite isn't overly painful. It's more intoxicating than anything, even more so when he sucks my lip into his mouth to soothe the sting of his touch.

When he once again grinds against me, my lips part, allowing his tongue free passage to slide between them. I moan an indescribable grunt when the delicious flavor of his mouth engulfs my taste buds. His mouth is tangy and sweet and oh-so-manly.

Growling at my husky response, he drags his tongue along the ridges of my mouth before dueling it with mine. "Ah, fuck, woman, I didn't possibly think you could get any tastier," he groans into my mouth before kissing the living hell out of me.

My god—he is a man who knows how to kiss. The controlled and precise strokes of his tongue and the soft tenderness of his lips have my heart swelling as quickly as my panties dampen.

Mindless with need, I meet the strokes of Nikolai's tongue lick for lick. I give it my all, awarding his kiss with equal vigor. Our kiss puts me off balance—a snake isn't just luring me. I'm being wholly consumed by one.

By the time he pulls back, my jaw is aching and my panties are soaked.

As if appreciative of my breathlessness, his lips tug into a predatory smirk. "What drug could make you forget that?" he asks with his eyes arrested on mine.

"None," I reply without just consideration.

Our kiss was so unforgettable a million years won't erase it from my memory.

"Then there's your answer," he murmurs, his voice exposing I'm not the only one left winded by our kiss. He is as taken aback as I am.

As his heavy-hooded gaze drifts between my eyes and my mouth, he says, "If a kiss can make you forget your own name, imagine what a night of fucking will do."

My eyes dance between his, confused as to why his comment

made me equally euphoric and panicked. I've never had such a conflicting array of emotions pummeling into me. I want to forget I witnessed him stabbing a man in an anger-fueled rage like he does it every day. I want to forget the cruel words we've exchanged the past two days. But more than anything, I want to forget he is my client, and no matter how sparking our attraction is, nothing can come of it. For a moment, I want to be the old Justine—the one before my life was upended. I want to be me.

I still when Nikolai runs his thumb over the bite marks on my shoulder. "You ran the gauntlet instead of running to Dimitri's bed." His tone is informative, ensuring I can't mistake his comment for a question. "He's the reason you're marked."

With my heart in my throat, I gingerly shake my head. "Dimitri isn't to blame for my scars. He let me leave when I turned down his proposal. It was his father who chose my exit."

He curses under his breath as the tightness in his jaw firms. When his eyes connect with mine, they flare with molten heat. If the wrath of his anger was directed at me, I'd be a puddle of mush. That's how volatile the rage in his eyes is.

"You have my word nothing like that will ever happen to you again, Justine. I'll slit the throat of any man who dares look at you sideways. Family or not."

My mouth falls open. I'm shocked and incredibly aroused by his protectiveness. "Thank you."

It feels like the wrong thing to say, but when he smiles, I'm glad I said it.

It strikes me how big his hands are when he uses his thumb to wipe away a rogue tear descending my cheek. They're so large they nearly swamp my face. After clearing the small handful of tears my bursting eyes could not contain, he trails his thumb over my lips. The saltiness of my tears moistens my mouth, which is still parched from our kiss.

"I want you, *Ангел*," he confesses as his eyes bounce between my lips and my wide gaze. "I've never met a woman like you. You're smart, beautiful, and you don't scare easily. I'm not gonna lie. I'm fascinated as fuck to see how you thrive when you regain your confidence."

His words floor me. I've never felt this wanted before. But his words don't stop me from asking, "Is that why you're doing this? To help me regain my confidence?"

I groan greedily when he throws his hips forward, dragging his erection along my aching sex. "Nah. This is all for me. I'm so worked up I'll soon fucking explode. That's why I'm pinning you to your bed, stroking you with my cock. It's got nothing to do with building your confidence, and everything to do with me and my insatiable desire to have a part of you wrapped around my cock."

I don't reply to the slight dishonesty in his words. I can't. Lust is clutching my throat so firmly, stealing my ability to talk.

The desire making my pussy a sticky mess triples when Nikolai slants his head to the side to align our mouths. I calm my breathing and moisten my lips, my mind as determined as my body. I'm done fighting a desire bigger than Ben Hur.

Just before his lips touch mine, the shrill of a cell phone ringing breaks the silence between us, stopping his pursuit in an instant.

24

JUSTINE

Nikolai grumbles a Russian curse word under his breath as his neck cranks to glare at my phone. I'd be tempted to laugh at his solemn expression if I weren't consumed by unbridled anger from losing his utmost devotion.

"You should probably get that," he suggests, nudging his head to my cell phone vibrating on my bedside table. "It's been ringing nonstop all night."

After pressing an innocent peck to my pursed-with-worry lips, he rolls off me. I'm not going to lie. My body groans in protest.

Chuckling, he mutters, "Soon, *Ангел*. Very soon."

My libido shrivels up and dies when he stands from the bed and heads for the door. For every stride he takes, my bewilderment grows. I kissed a client. In my bed. Wearing nothing but a sheer thong and a push-up bra. If it wasn't the most incredible kiss I'd ever received, I'd be slamming on the brakes and setting some strict ground rules.

Wait. What?

One kiss can't erase years of hard work, can it? If it were any other man than Nikolai, I'd have no hesitation in saying no. Now I'm not so sure. I'm so damn confused. My interactions with him are like trying to untangle Christmas lights. For every knot I unravel, another forms in its place.

The confusion muddling my mind eases when I catch the quickest glimpse of my family portrait on my chest of drawers. I'm not here for me. I'm here for them.

Nikolai's strides halt halfway across my room. He freezes before pivoting on his heels to face me. Just seeing the vibrancy in his eyes vanishes the horrid neuroses surfacing in my mind. I'd kiss him again in a heartbeat if it guaranteed his eyes would keep the level of intensity they have now. He looks as if he has the world at his feet.

I inwardly snort. *He probably does.*

Lifting his hand to his lips, he twists, presenting a gesture frequently used to demand silence. Although confused by his request, I nod, trusting the glint in his eyes that promises my faith will be well-rewarded.

Smirking at my agreeing response, he points above his head. Following his gaze, I look up. My heart smashes into my ribs when I spot a pair of yoga pants dangling midair. They're hiding a black instrument that looks very similar to a surveillance camera.

My eyes rocket back to Nikolai when I recall discovering a surveillance device in my pantry yesterday. The grimace on his face shows he's the culprit for the surveillance device, but he is as disgruntled about them as I am.

Trust me? he mouths.

I nod without consideration. Although gruesome, how he defended me last night placed him on a small list of men I trust. He is the first man who doesn't share my last name.

He glances toward my balcony. "Outside," he faintly murmurs before his eyes stray to my cell phone.

I nod again, acknowledging his request to take my call outside.

Satisfied at my obliging nature, Nikolai winks before exiting my room. "I'm going to take a shower. Perhaps you'll join me after your call." He winks suggestively before pivoting on his heels. His pace is brisk but not quick enough for me to miss his avid scan of my body.

I stare at my door for several moments, shocked at the turn of events the past twenty-four hours. Yesterday was filled with so many contradictions it feels like a month has passed instead of one measly day.

I snap out of my thoughts when my cell phone hollers again.

Fumbling, I wrap my bed sheet around my sweat-slicked body, secure my phone from the bedside table, and then stand. The frantic beat of my heart, which I just settled, starts again when I glance down at my screen and notice who is calling. It's my dad. Worry clouds me. He only calls when it's a family emergency.

Swiping my finger across the screen, I press my phone to my ear while padding to my balcony door. "Daddy, is everything okay? Is it Maddox? Is he safe?"

My voice is doused with anxiety as guilt steamrolls back into me. I've been so tied up with Nikolai that I keep failing to recall why he is a guest in my house.

Ghastly Las Vegas heat blasts my face when I open my balcony door and slip outside. Since my thin bed sheet barely covers me, I stand in the far corner of the patio, not wanting to startle any neighbors enjoying a refreshing swim.

"Dad?" I query when he fails to answer me.

Some of the panic on my chest lifts when my dad grumbles, "Darn fandangle phone. Where is the volume button?"

My hand darts up to stifle a giggle. My dad is a brilliant man who can fly a jumbo jet with his eyes closed but can't work out the simplicity of a landline phone for the life of him.

"Justine, are you there, darling?"

My heart squeezes, adoring the heavenly deepness of my dad's voice. Since he isn't a fan of talking on the phone, I haven't heard his voice in nearly three months.

"Yes, Daddy, I'm here. Is everything okay? Is it Maddox?" I'm sure he can hear tears in my words.

Dad instructs my mom to get on the other line before he answers, "Everything is fine, darling. Maddox is fine."

I release the breath I'm holding in. It's quickly redrawn when my dad adds, "We received a call from Wallens Ridge State Prison late last night. Maddox was placed in isolation overnight. They're preparing him for transport."

"They're moving him to another location?" My voice is high with delighted shock.

With the population of Petretti crew members housed at Wallens Ridge the highest in the country, I've been petitioning for Maddox to be transferred to another prison for the past three years. Every request I lodged was denied within hours of being received.

"Yes, honey, they're moving him to Harbortown. He will be thirty miles from home. Can you believe it?" my mom chimes in, her voice cracking with emotion.

My mouth opens and closes, but not a syllable escapes my lips. My request to have Maddox transferred to Harbortown was denied because it's a medium security facility that doesn't have the features required to house a non-parole-eligible inmate. Even my close connection with a detective at the Ravenshoe Police Station couldn't get the warden at Harbortown to glance at my request, so I'm not only delighted by this development but also stunned.

"Justine, darling, are you there?" The deep shudder of my dad's voice conveys he's on the verge of tears just like me. "What's with this damn thing? Why won't it work?" He smacks on the speaker, blaming the phone for my lack of reply.

"It's not your phone, Daddy, it's me. I truly don't know what to say," I reply as a tear glides down my cheek.

"Actions speak louder than words, honey. So you better buy that boss of yours a big steak," my mom suggests with a giggle. Her laughter fills me with homesickness. It's been a while since I've heard her carefree laughter. Way longer than I would have liked.

"I will. I promise. The biggest steak you've ever seen."

"Or the whole damn cow," my dad adds, his smile radiating in his tone.

We laugh in sync, our joy reflected in our chuckles.

I squash my phone closer to my ear when my dad says, "I know I gave you a hard time about trekking across the country for this man, Justine, but I was wrong. You did well. You've done us proud, darling. Very, very proud."

More tears well in my eyes. As much as I knew my dad would always support me, he struggled when I told him my plans to move to Vegas. He already had one child torn away from him, so the thought of not seeing another for months at a time was more than he could bear.

"Thank you, Daddy. It means the world to me to hear you say that."

After guaranteeing I'll be kept informed on Maddox's transfer, I disconnect the call with my parents. Although my eyes are moist, only a few tears have trickled down my cheeks. My happiness is so overwhelming I'm unwilling to let anything ruin it. Not even a few measly tears.

My hands rattle when I punch in a well-used cell phone number. I can't believe in such a short period, Mr. Fletcher achieved something I've been endeavoring to do for years. I know he's a brilliant attorney, but this showcases him in a new light. It will be hard for any man to steal the torch I am about to shine on him.

"Good morning, Justine. Everything okay?" Mr. Fletcher sounds like I woke him up.

Riddled with guilt, I pull my phone away from my ear. My remorse doubles when I notice it isn't even 8 a.m. "Good morning. Sorry for waking you. In my excitement, I forgot to check the time," I greet him, grimacing.

A creak of an office chair sounds down the line, closely followed by the pants of Mr. Fletcher's breaths. "Have you found a way to get Nikolai off his charges?" he queries, his words hurried, as if he's running.

My lips twist. "Not yet. I'm close, though." That's a lie. I've spent more time dodging Nikolai's suaveness than working on his case.

The tap of feet padding stops as Mr. Fletcher says, "Oh. Then why are you calling me so early?" He sounds shocked about my eagerness to discuss anything not pertaining to work. His gasping response isn't unexpected. Neither of us has a social life.

"I wanted to thank you. I can't believe what you did. It's amazing. I'm in complete awe of you." My voice is laced with so much sentimental emotion I almost gag. "I've been striving to do that for the past three years. You did it in less than twenty-four hours..."

My excited gushing continues for the next several minutes.

When I inhale much-needed air, Mr. Fletcher mutters, "I don't know what you're talking about, Justine. What are you thanking me for?"

I smile, adoring his humble attitude. He has no idea how much Maddox's transfer means for my family. Instead of traveling eight hours to see him every second month, my parents can visit him weekly.

"Maddox's transfer to Harborview. My parents were contacted

last night. His application was approved," I inform Mr. Fletcher, my tone still gushy.

He breathes heavily down the line. "I didn't request a transfer." He stops for a moment. "Well, I am proposing a transfer, but the paperwork hasn't been finalized yet. It's sitting on my to-do list."

"Oh..." A better reply is above me. I'm as shocked as Mr. Fletcher's tone suggests. "Then who arranged it?"

Assuming my question isn't rhetorical, Mr. Fletcher replies, "I'm unsure. Who else have you informed about your brother's wish for a transfer?"

"No one. I don't talk to anyone outside of work. I don't know anyone in Vegas..." My words trail off when reality smacks into me hard and fast. *Nikolai.*

"Can I call you back?" I ask Mr. Fletcher. I disconnect our call without waiting for him to comply with my request.

I dump my cell phone onto my bed before securing a free-flowing summer dress from my wardrobe. I'm so eager to confront Nikolai about my flashback that I don't bother wrangling my hair or checking my face in the mirror. My pace out of my bedroom is frantic, causing my steps to stumble like a catwalk model wearing ten-inch heels after too many chardonnays.

My eyes snap to my bathroom door when I hear the distinct noise of a shower being switched on. I stand frozen outside the door for several seconds, contemplating what to do. If I enter the bathroom, I look like a hussy willing to do anything to secure her brother's freedom. If I don't, my questions will remain unanswered.

Like a flash of lightning illuminating a pitch-black sky, an idea pops into my head: the surveillance cameras.

My bare feet fail to gain traction on the wooden floor when I race toward my kitchen. I walk through the swinging door, not noticing the floor is void of crockery splinters until I'm halfway across the tiled space. I freeze at the same time my heart stops beating. My kitchen is clean—spotlessly clean. It's tidier than it was when I moved in. Come to think of it, my living room is sparkling as well.

"The Popov housemaids are the best of the bunch," says a deep voice at the side of the room, scaring the living daylights out of me.

Roman stands from his seat and heads in my direction. The smile on his face is as carefree as Nikolai's attitude this morning.

My stomach grumbles when he opens my oven door, displaying a feast fit for a king. Pancakes, sausages, bacon, eggs, and hash browns are being kept warm in an oven that still had its protective seal on the glass door as early as yesterday afternoon.

"The Popov housemaids made me breakfast?" I pace toward Roman, my stomach grumbling as ruffled as my facial expression.

He nods. "Yes."

"Why?" I cringe when my voice sounds like I'm peeved. I'm anything but annoyed.

His eyes are worldly as ever, but a sparkle of amusement swells in them. "Because Nikolai asked them to after ushering everyone out of your apartment."

My heart thuds in my chest. "Nikolai asked everyone to leave?" I don't know why, but I'd assumed they left of their own free will.

Roman nods again. His blasé response doesn't lessen its impact.

"Then why are you still here?" I sound like a demented teen, but I'm shocked by this development.

Although I am asking a question, I reach my conclusion before a syllable escapes Roman's mouth. "You're Nikolai's protector."

He shrugs as his lips crimp. "It's more of an advisory role than a protective detail. As you witnessed last night, Nikolai doesn't require protection."

I stare at Roman as my brain works through the facts. He did aid in stopping Nikolai from dishing out his own form of justice last night, but where was he when Nikolai lodged a beer bottle in the neck of another man? That seems like a pivotal time for an advisor to step in to me.

Seemingly reading the quiet questions streaming from my eyes, Roman explains, "The exchange between Nikolai and his accused Friday afternoon was family business. It was not my place to intervene."

I huff out a chuckle. "Family business? The man Nikolai attacked was from the Petretti crew. How could that be family business?" I air quote my last two words.

Roman smirks, fighting to conceal the worry rapidly forming in his glistening gaze. "That is also a matter of family business. One that isn't mine to share."

I huff again, louder this time. "Family ties didn't stop Nikolai from assaulting one of his own last night," I grumble, my mood noticeably more hostile.

I'm not angry at Roman. I'm confused by what this all means. I've heard comments that when you join the Popov or Petretti crew, you become a member of their family, but I've never heard the reference used for rival gang members.

"Are you sure of what you saw, Justine? From my vantage point, Nikolai appeared to be protecting one of his own." He steps closer to me, looming over me with his large frame. "You're under Nikolai's skin," he whispers, his voice barely audible over the hammering of my heart. "Usually I'd be pleased by that notion. But for a man with responsibilities like Nikolai, attaching himself to someone could mean death."

"He's not attaching himself to anyone," I mumble, my words hindered by the pulse in the back of my throat. I've only known Nikolai for days, but the thought of him being hurt cuts me raw.

The worry in Roman's eyes softens as he says, "Nikolai calls himself The Snake, as he must continually shed his skin to stay alive. I've yet to see him do that with you. That should mean something, shouldn't it?" Spotting the tears welling in my eyes, he says, "Ah... He's under your skin as well. This will make the fight a lot fairer."

He pivots on his heels and stalks to the door, leaving me stunned.

25

NIKOLAI

W hen the soap slips from my hand, I curse it as I did Roman's smug grin when Dok assured me Justine's faded memories have nothing to do with her fall and everything to do with her mixing anti-anxiety medication with alcohol.

Roman cited the same thing when he busted me sneaking out of Justine's room, but since he isn't a doctor, his opinion didn't count.

My veins will run dry before I'll ever admit I was wrong, so instead of telling Roman Dok agreed with his assessment, I told him to clean up the mess the Popov housemaids missed before entering the bathroom to have a quick shower. I don't want to wash Justine's scent off my skin, but I need to eradicate the funk halving its allure.

So much shit is happening right now—fucked-up crap that should have my cock taking a leave of absence, but no matter how often Roman warns me I'm walking into a tornado with my eyes closed, I can't get the fucking thing to stand down.

Even now, after placing myself on a flimsy limb to have Justine's brother transferred to the medium-security prison Justine mentioned last night, I'm as hard as a fucking rock.

Maddox's transfer is costing me millions, but I'm not worried about the money. Evoking the favor I did is unheard of in my industry, even more so when you are doing it for a man who has ties with your rivals.

Justine thinks Maddox is innocent, however, Roman's research the last two days reveals his record isn't as squeaky clean as he wants his family to believe. He wasn't just cruising by the Petretti compound and happened to stumble upon his sister's cries for help. He was there, as a participant, only switching from perpetrator to a savior once he realized who was being punished.

He did what needed to be done. He fell at the heel of a man undeserving of his respect, but what he did after that is where he went wrong.

If you take anyone's debt, no matter how small the liability, you'll be expected to repay the debt in full.

Maddox only kept one side of the deal.

He killed for Col...

...but he failed to pin his victim's murder on the appropriate person.

Even with Col dying years ago, until the debt has been fulfilled as cited, Maddox will remain indebted to the Petrettis, which, in turn, means his sister is as well. The thought alone should be enough to soften my cock, but alas, just like I know Justine's debt won't remain the Petrettis' for long, so does my cock.

The situation goes from bad to worse when I replace the insubordinate bar of soap with the shower puff hanging on the outdated faucet. I didn't add any body wash to the squishy pink puff. I didn't need to. The suds coating my skin aided in its glide over my body, much less the pre-cum seeping from my cock.

Instead of the shower puff washing Justine's scent from my skin, it coats me in it. The scent of her floral shower gel mixed with my manly, virile smell has my cock standing at attention as painfully as her delicious mouth.

I could shut off the faucet and pretend my nuts aren't aching. I could act as if the bathroom has a surveillance device like every other room in Justine's apartment. But instead of doing either of those things, I wrap my hand around my cock and give it a long, strangled tug, pissed I'm stroking one out in the shower like I'm twelve but loving the responsiveness of my dick.

Even by my hand, this is the best hand job I've ever been given.

As my tongue darts out with the hope of sampling a smidge of Justine's mouth on mine, I pump my fist in rhythm to the pulse I felt between Justine's legs. It's a brutally fast pace that would only feel better if each stroke was piercing my cock's head between Justine's plump lips. Or better yet, her no doubt tight cunt.

I increase the pressure of my thumb on the vein feeding my cock as a zinging sensation roars through my veins. My cock throbs with want, its need seeping from the crown. After balancing my empty hand on the dated yet spotlessly clean tiled wall, I lower my head under the stream of water. It flattens the hair on my head, glides over my tattooed pecs, then puddles around my fist sliding up and down my shaft.

The fast, frantic pace I stroke my cock has me chasing release even quicker than I did the first time I fucked a girl. I picture Justine standing in front of me, her fingers sunk into the glistening slit between her legs, her eyes closed. She'll match the strokes of my cock pump for pump, finger-fucking herself as erratically as her cunt is dying to suck at my dick.

I can imagine how the steam from the shower would increase her scent—so sweet and oh-so-tempting. She'd come with a whispered roar like she did on the door, her knees buckling a mere second before I transfer her weight onto my cock.

When I moan, it comes out with a growl. The image in my head is so erotic, my balls tuck in close to my body, preparing for release. While increasing the speed of my pumps, I close my eyes, enhancing the intoxicating visual gripping every inch of my sack. Justine is beautiful as she is, but the image of her peering up at me like she did after we kissed took her sexiness off the Richter scale. There's not a number high enough to describe the sleepy sex-kitten look her eyes get when she's on the cusp of ecstasy.

A kiss brought her to the brink of insanity.

A teeny tiny inconsequential kiss.

My kiss.

I thought the drugs my crew sells were the most potent on the market. I had no fucking idea lust is more dangerous than any of the white powders I sell, and that's before you add Justine's cock-thickening body into the mix.

I've only seen her in a bra and a pair of panties, but my imagination was enticing enough I'm stroking my cock in the shower instead of taking my funk out on my crew's many whores as I would have only two days ago.

My change in attitude is also why Justine's apartment is silent. The women I usually go through like underwear were the reason I kicked my men out a little after two this morning. They can be upset about me saying no and be opposed to the idea of me being a one-woman man, but they sure as fuck don't get to ignore a direct order.

I told them no. I told them I wasn't interested, but the instant I tiptoed out of Justine's room, they were on me like the tent my cock was pitching in my jeans was for their shelter.

It fucking wasn't.

Even now, while rubbing one out in the shower like a loser, their fake tits and surgically altered lips aren't being featured. All I can see is Justine. Her eyes. Her knee-bowing body. Her kissable, pouty mouth I can't wait to smear my cum over.

The thought of her peering up at me with cum on her lips is my undoing. I tighten my grip around my shaft before dragging my hand all the way down to the base. My cock pulsates in my palm as it brutally shreds me of any dignity I have left. I come with a growl, my entire body spasming as thick white seed pumps out of the crest of my cock. It's a never-ending orgasm, the backlog of cum compliments to a thirty-six-hour hard-on. It feels fucking great, even with it occurring without an audience this time around.

As the water jetting out of the showerhead cools, I loosen my grip on my throbbing shaft, but I don't fully free it from my grip. I give it another three gentler strokes, ensuring not only is every drop of cum pumped from my shaft but also allowing the water rolling off my back time to circle my cum down the drain.

26

JUSTINE

R oman's quick departure of the kitchen gave me plenty of time to consider his points. Nikolai is under my skin, but in a crazy, demented way I can't explain. I guess it's like drug addicts trying to justify their addictions. There's no sense or reason why someone is the way they are. Maybe my brain has a profound chemical imbalance, encouraging me to seek a more adventurous lifestyle.

My thoughts drift back to the present when the water heater switching off booms into my ears. Recalling why I'm standing in my kitchen, I push off my feet and continue my original mission before losing the chance.

A string of illicit curses topples from my mouth when my hunt for the electronic device results in my spilling a year's worth of rice onto the floor in my walk-in pantry. When I fail to locate the black box in its original position, I search every nook and cranny in my pantry.

I've only just delved my hand into the second shelf when a deep voice asks, "Are you looking for this?"

I straighten my spine and peer out of the pantry. Nikolai is standing at the opening, his grin as enticing as the food in my oven, begging to be devoured.

Spotting the surveillance device in his hand, I say, "No. I was looking for the maple syrup." I shift my eyes back to the pantry shelves, praying he won't see the deceit clouding them.

My breathing shallows to a pant when Nikolai leans over my shoulder to seize the bottle of maple syrup on the third shelf. Although his chuckle is soundless, the shaking of his torso advises of its arrival.

"Thank you."

I accept the bottle from his grasp and spin around. My change in position awards me with the scent of Nikolai's freshly showered skin. Not thinking, I snap my eyes shut and inhale deeply, relishing the smell of my soap on his skin. I forgot how intoxicating it is to smell yourself on another.

My eyes pop open when he says, "Imagine how good we will smell when our scents are intermingled the old-fashioned way."

My pulse quickens when he drags his nose down my neck, his whiff of my skin more undignified than mine.

A low, simpering growl rolls up his chest as he peers at me sideways, spearing me in place with his lusty gaze. "You smell like me."

My heart rate spikes as I swallow harshly. "Yes." My short word is incapable of concealing my heightened state. "I should probably shower?"

I don't know why my declaration came out sounding like a question.

He steps into my path, thwarting my endeavor when I attempt to sidestep him. Pretending I can't feel need dampening my panties, I narrow my eyes and step to the left. The girth in his jeans brushes me when he moves into my path again.

"Nikolai..." I growl in warning.

"Justine..." he replies, his voice as groggy as mine. It sounds as I imagine it will during ecstasy—all virile and hot. "I just came in my hand recalling the taste of your lips. What I wouldn't give for another taste."

Jesus Christ. How am I supposed to reply to that?

Mercifully, he continues talking, saving me from issuing a blubbering response. "A kiss for a pass," he suggests, his playful tone colored with lust.

My eyes rocket to his. He can't be serious, can he? I'm not five. This type of childish negotiation doesn't work for me. I grew up with four older brothers. I'm well-rehearsed on the tricks boys use to get what they want. The instant I kiss him, he'll devise another ruse to keep me holed up in the pantry.

Ignoring how the carefree glint in Nikolai's eyes makes me want to forget the world, I fold my arms over my chest and return his hankering stare. For every second that passes, the lusty flare in his eyes doubles.

"A kiss for the device," I request a short time later, nudging my head to the surveillance instrument.

My eyes bulge, stunned my IQ dropped so low I'm negotiating with him instead of demanding he move out of my way.

He licks his lips as he contemplates my suggestion. "No. A kiss for a pass, or you remain trapped in the pantry. With me. For eternity."

He takes a step closer to me, filling the microscopic snick of air between us as his tongue delves out to replenish his lips again.

The reasoning behind his obsessive lip licking is exposed when he says, "Your taste is fading from my mouth, and I'll be fucked if I can wait another two days to replenish it. Just a quick nibble. A little sample. I'll even keep my tongue in my mouth."

I glare at him when he doesn't attempt to hide the deceit in his tone.

"I'm your attorney, Nikolai. Our interactions are crossing a very clear line we're not supposed to cross," I mumble, using my only plausible defense.

I inwardly sigh. My voice couldn't be laced with more ambivalence if I tried.

He steps closer to me, stealing the air from my lungs with his impressive body. "You witnessed me stabbing a man, without calling the authorities. The line has already been crossed."

"Who said I didn't call the police? I could have been doing that while you were seeking release in the shower."

I inwardly curse. Why did I bring that up again? Oh, that's right. Because the thought of Nikolai stroking his cock sparks wild recklessness.

It's the fight of my life not to lean into his embrace when his finger follows the heat creeping up my neck. "Do you know your neck flushes every time you lie? Coincidently, it always happens when you deny my advances."

"Who said it's a lie? Maybe I'm embarrassed by your pathetic attempts of schmoozing." I snap my mouth shut, mortified at my snarky response. I'm so sexually frustrated I'm letting it drag down my mood.

Thankfully, he isn't the least bit deterred by my snarky comment. "Is that what you want, *Ангел?* Do you want to be wined and dined? You want me to treat you like a princess?"

I lock my eyes with his, wanting to ensure he doesn't miss the honesty in my eyes when I shake my head.

My first two dates with Dimitri were out of this world. He wined and dined me in the most elegant restaurants and showered me with expensive gifts. That should have been my first warning sign. Having a suit laundered and getting a fresh haircut are adequate ways to express an interest in your date, whereas booking out an entire restaurant and lavishing your date with custom jewelry is borderline possessive.

Don't get me wrong, away from his family, Dimitri is a pleasant man, but just like Nikolai, he was raised by a monster. It's lucky my introduction to his family happened early in our courtship. One meeting with his father was all it took to recognize I didn't belong in his world. I ended things amicably. Well, so I thought at the time.

Dimitri's father didn't take my rejection as well as Dimitri. He classed my refusal to date his son as a direct insult to him. He swore to make me so unattractive no man would ever want me. In some ways, he did. Although the bite marks on my skin will fade, the damage to my confidence will never be repaired.

Dimitri and Nikolai share a lot of qualities. Both are mafia princes. Both are handsome and unique in their own right. The only difference is Nikolai defended me when I was being attacked. Dimitri let it happen.

"Then what do you need?" Nikolai asks, drawing my attention back to him. "Tell me what it will take to get another taste of you, and I'll do it."

I stare at him, void of a response. He wants me so badly he's willing to do anything to have me?

"Don't play stupid. I know you want this as much as I do. I can feel it in my bones. Smell it in the air. Taste it on my lips." His minty breath wafts into my flaring nostrils. "I won't stop until I have you beneath me, so tell me what you need so that I can achieve that."

"A less dangerous job title." I smack my lips shut, stunned I said my inner monologue out loud.

When he throws his head back and laughs, I use his imbalance to my advantage. I slip under his arm and hightail it into the kitchen. Groaning, he adjusts the thickness in his jeans before shadowing me in the fragrant-smelling space.

Although my brain begs me to place distance between us, I keep my feet planted on the ground. Ignoring the insane connection bursting between us has gotten me nowhere fast, so it's time to face the music by confronting the issues head-on.

"During breakfast, I'd like to ask you some questions," I advise Nikolai while bobbing down to gather the food warming in the oven.

The hairs on my nape prickle when he asks, "What type of questions?" He once again snuck up on me so agilely that I didn't hear his approach.

He scoops the stainless-steel dish out of my hand, his movements so sleek he somehow manages to brush my inner thigh on the way past. With a cocky wink announcing he heard my quick breath from his touch, he heads to the table we ate at yesterday.

"Some are pertaining to your case... Others are more personal." I rush my last sentence.

After grabbing two plates and a set of forks from my kitchen cabinets, I mosey to the dining nook. My steps freeze halfway across the tiled floor when I realize how pointy my forks are. They're sharper and more pronged than the butter knives confiscated Friday afternoon, so why didn't I consider using them to protect myself yesterday?

I shrug off my query. If forks were classed as a dangerous instrument, the sheriff's department would have confiscated them along with the rest of my utensils.

"Twenty-six seconds," Nikolai advises, talking through the crispy bacon he is nibbling on.

"Hmm?" I ask, setting our plates on the tabletop before sitting across from him.

He drops his eyes to the forks sitting between us. "Twenty-six seconds. That's how quickly I can kill a man with a fork." He snags a fork off the table, points it at his jugular, then twists. "If the strike doesn't kill him, he'll soon choke on his own blood."

I push my empty plate out of my sight, no longer hungry.

Nikolai chuckles at my sickened expression.

"No remorse at all?" I ask, traumatized at his nonchalant response to a potential loss of life.

He shakes his head. "No. The men I punish are villainous, vile men who deserve to die."

"Kill, Nikolai," I correct. "It's not punishment when they're dead."

He shrugs, neither denying nor agreeing with my assessment.

While loading my plate with pancakes, he grumbles, "I don't like being interrogated, so let's get these questions over with as soon as possible; then we can enjoy the rest of our day." A waggle of his brows dampens the haughty arrogance in his tone.

After covering my pancakes with syrup and butter, he aligns his eyes with mine. He doesn't speak—he doesn't need to. His commanding gaze relays his every demand. I am to eat every bit of food in front of me without reservation. If I refuse, our exchange will be over.

I start our conversation on one fact that hasn't left my mind for thirty minutes. "Did you arrange for my brother's transfer to Harborview?"

He nudges his head at my plate of food, demanding I eat before he'll answer my question. I roll my eyes, feigning annoyance at his bossy demeanor. I'm not annoyed—I'm far from annoyed. I grew up with four older brothers. Dealing with bossy, testosterone-fueled men is as second nature to me as salty water in an ocean.

If I so much as mentioned the word "diet" in front of my brothers, I was interrogated until I gave up the source responsible for my slump in confidence, and then every meal I ate was scrutinized to ensure it gave adequate nutrition for someone of my age and height. My brothers' gazes lacked the lust Nikolai's eyes are carrying, but his stare is one I've been given many times previously.

When I pop a big chunk of pancake into my mouth, bending to Nikolai's unbreakable demand, he finally answers, "No, I didn't set up your brother's transfer."

My eyes rocket to his, certain I heard him wrong. I didn't. His eyes are open and honest. He didn't arrange for Maddox's transfer to Harborview.

"I asked Roman to do it. He did as instructed," he adds when he spots my baffled expression.

I ball up an unused napkin and hurl it at his thrusting chest. He chuckles as his focus returns to his overflowing plate of food. His chin is tucked into his neck, but I don't miss the curve of his lips when I follow his lead. I'm starving, but not all my hankering is for food.

A short time later, while pushing chunks of melting butter around my half-empty plate, I ask, "Why did you help Maddox, Nikolai? Your opinion on his case was highly notable last night, so why the sudden change of heart?"

"You asked for my help. I looked into it," he answers like it's no big deal.

"I asked for your help? When?"

Remaining quiet, he slides the surveillance device to my side of the table. I run a napkin over my hands, removing the sticky residue from my fingers before lifting it from the tabletop. Seemingly aware of the direction our conversation was going to take, the surveillance footage starts in the minutes leading to my fainting spell.

My swaying movements are as compelling in playback as they felt in real life. I am as white as a ghost and as wobbly as a drunk. Although Nikolai's crusade to catch me before I fall is impressive, the heaviness of my head plummeting to the ground is too swift for him to prevent, meaning my right temple brutally makes contact with the floor.

After scooping my slumped frame into his bloodstained chest, Nikolai exits the kitchen, leaving a white-faced Sergei withering on the floor. The crowd of primarily men covering every inch of my living room part when they spot Nikolai's approach. Some stare at him in admiration, whereas the rest peer at him in shock.

"That's Dok," Nikolai advises when he is followed into my bedroom by a man not much older than him.

I'm shocked. When Nikolai said my bump was inspected by a doctor, I anticipated a man in his mid-sixties with gray strands of hair and a rounded tummy, not a strikingly handsome young man with snow-white locks hanging past his ears, and a fit, cut body.

"Fast forward an hour," Nikolai requests before shoveling a forkful of scrambled eggs into his mouth.

I raise my eyes to his. "Why? So I can miss you spiking my drink?"

He smirks but doesn't deny my claim. I fast-forward the tape as suggested. Thank god, as the entire hour was filled with me passed out on my bed with an ashen-faced Nikolai sitting at my feet.

Although Nikolai's obvious agitation weakens the more the footage rolls, his protective stance never falters. No one gets within three feet of my bed—not even Dok and Roman—when I wake up dazed and confused.

After cradling my jaw to assess me as if he's a doctor, Nikolai hands me two white tablets. My brows furrow when I down the tablets without a snick of hesitation crossing my face.

"Is there any sound?" I ask Nikolai, who is eating his breakfast across from me.

Hearing our conversation may explain my willingness to trust so quickly. Usually it takes a lot to gain my confidence, so I'm stumped at how cooperative I'm being.

Nikolai removes the device from my hand and fiddles with the buttons. There has been a significant jump in the timeline when he hands it back to me. The sun setting through my curtains has been replaced with an inky-black sky.

My pupils expand when, "You're *sooo* pretty," booms through the speakers of the surveillance device. My voice is missing the drunken tone I have after too many shots of tequila, so I'm confident I'm not drunk.

"I wish I had your lashes. They're *sooo* long they could reach the stars." I inwardly gag, mortified at the seductive purr of my voice. Even not seeing who I'm schmoozing, I know it's Nikolai. He has the world's longest lashes.

Although peeved at my lack of self-worth in the footage, I will admit that I wear drunk well. The unique color of my eyes is even more noticeable with dilated pupils, and my pasty-white skin is accentuated with a golden hue from the alcohol squashing my inhibitions.

When I reach the part where Nikolai demands I climb under the sheets, I lift and lock my eyes with his. "Yet I wake up with you naked in my bed."

"The fewer clothes I had on, the more chance your scent would imbed into my skin," he replies, revealing he heard my mumbled statement.

I grimace when I return my focus to the tablet. I'm practically dry humping Nikolai while underhandedly announcing how perfect we are for each other.

"You can't trust a drunk," I mumble.

Nikolai's smile is brighter than the tablet screen. "No, you can't. But you can trust the word of a drunk. People are most honest when they're void of anxiety."

With no defense to his reply, I refocus on the video footage.

Flapping gums must be exhausting, because I blabber nonstop for twenty minutes before I finally fall asleep.

After switching off the tablet, I hand it to Nikolai. "What was in the white pills? If it's anything illegal, I need to know. Regular drug testing is mandatory at my firm."

Although I have a million questions running through my mind, I must start with the most critical one. If I lose my job, I lose any chance of having my brother's conviction overturned.

"You have nothing to worry about. Anti-anxiety pills are exempted from every test," Nikolai answers, his tone informative, as if he researched his answers.

"They were anti-anxiety pills?" I cringe when my girly voice bounces off my kitchen walls before shrilling back into my ears.

"Yes," he replies with a chuckle. "You're quite entertaining when you let go of your worries."

I burrow my head in my hands, wishing I could vanish from the world. I'm well overdue for a weekend bender, but I wish I had chosen better circumstances.

"Okay," I breathe out slowly, lifting my eyes to Nikolai. "First, thank you for arranging Maddox's transfer to Harborview." When he attempts to interrupt me, I talk faster, wanting to express myself before I lose the chance. "You may not have directly initiated it, but it would have never happened if you hadn't asked Roman to look into it. So, thank you."

He bows his head, accepting my gratitude with a sincerity I was certain he didn't hold.

"Second, I am attracted to you..." –The shit-eating grin spreading across his face makes what I am about to say so much harder—"but nothing can come of it. I am your attorney, Nikolai."

"That can be fixed."

"I am also not a girl who does casual sex. I don't necessarily need commitment, but I need feelings," I continue, pretending I didn't hear his snapped remark.

The smile is wiped straight off his face. "You need a heart to feel, Justine. I don't have one of those." His admission is so quiet, if he hadn't said my name, I would have assumed he didn't want me to hear it.

After setting his fork onto his half-eaten plate of food, he connects his eyes with mine. He stares into my eyes, showing me what he sees inside himself. A chill runs down my spine from the desolate cloud swamping his alluring gaze. He truly looks like a lost soul. He is dark and haunted but also real.

"Any man can be a monster, Nikolai, but only a monster who knows right from wrong can turn into a man. You were born into your lifestyle, but it only became your life when you let it."

He shakes his head, dismissing my claims. "No. This life was not my choice. It was my destiny. This is who I am. I am my father's son." He stands from his chair, his chest puffed high. "I am the devil reincarnated to rule my empire and slay the weak. I am Nikolai, prince of the Russian mafia."

He couldn't shock me more if he slapped me in the face. It isn't his arrogant words that have me choking back tears. It's the brokenness of his voice. If that wasn't a rehearsed line, I'm not Catholic.

Although frightened by his response, my campaign to alter his viewpoint doesn't falter. "Your family are not gods, Nikolai. They're mere men who'll meet with their creator on their final day like every other person on the planet."

His icy glare sends a chill down my spine. "You need to watch your tongue. Respect is a highly valued commodity in my family. It's more worthwhile than life itself."

I nod. "Respect is valued, but when it's gained with integrity, it far exceeds respect gained by force."

"Respect without fear is worthless." Nikolai's hot breath hits my lips.

"No. Respect derived from fear is worthless. Fear is forcing people to bow at your feet. Respect has them bowing of their own free will. They're two completely different things," I continue to argue.

When pain flashes in his eyes from my snarled comment, I lower the severity of my tone. "You know this. Deep down inside, you know what I am saying is true. Values are not taught. We are born with them."

My heart hammers so fast I'm afraid it will explode when the anger in his eyes fades for vulnerability. "That is easy for you to preach when you're not the one forced to toe the line. Shadowing his reign is the only thing keeping me alive. If I don't do that, I'll be buried right alongside my father. You don't have to understand the rules of this lifestyle, Justine, but I must abide by them."

I stare at him with confusion smeared on my face. His father isn't dead. The countless reports of him wreaking havoc on families from Las Vegas to Florida ensure I can't mistake this, so I'm genuinely at a loss as to what Nikolai means by his comment. Maybe he means it metaphorically? Like he will become as heartless as his father?

The moisture brimming in my eyes doubles when my gaze briefly collides with Nikolai's. His comment wasn't a metaphor. It was a statement relayed directly from his heart.

"Leave, Nikolai. Walk away and don't look back."

"I can't!" His arm flies across the table, sending our plates sailing to the floor. "Disrespecting Vladimir carries the penalty of death. If I leave, it will be at the cost of my life."

27

NIKOLAI

Needing to leave before I hammer another nail into Justine's coffin, I exit the kitchen at the speed of a bullet. My pace is so brutal, I send Roman sailing when I burst through the swinging door.

If I weren't already aware I had ears listening in on my private conversation, I am now.

"Call Vladimir. I want out."

Roman scampers to his feet before following me into the guest bedroom of Justine's apartment to watch me pack. To go where? I don't know. I just need to leave Justine's apartment before my fucked-up childhood conjures up ways for me to discover if I'm being played again.

She said *his* words—the same fucking words that almost got me killed, convincing me I'm either being screwed over by Carmichael for the second time, or he's under Justine's skin more than I realized.

Neither of my theories will end well for Carmichael.

He's dead no matter what.

28

JUSTINE

When the faint ring of a cell phone sounds through my ears, I stop rubbing at a kink in my neck. Confident it's coming from my bedroom, I commence my hunt. It takes shuffling through the mammoth load of paperwork sprawled across my bed before I find it under the photographic evidence from Nikolai's attempted murder charge.

My pulse quickens when my eyes drop to the screen and I discover who is calling. With everything that happened this morning, I forgot to return Mr. Fletcher's call as promised.

Riddled with guilt, I swipe my hand over my screen and squash my phone close to my ear. "Hey," I greet him. "Sorry I forgot to call you back. Things have been a little hectic here."

Although my statement is honest, my tone is smeared with dishonesty. Things were more than hectic at the start of my day, but the past five hours have been very somber. I haven't seen Nikolai since our exchange in the kitchen this morning.

When I approached his room to seek clarification on some notes documented by a detective on the scene, Roman advised me Nikolai didn't want to be disturbed and that any messages I wished to give Nikolai would need to be directed through him from now on.

I'm not going to lie. I'm peeved. Although our argument was brutal, I shouldn't be the only one left searching for crumbs to piece back our attorney-client relationship.

I sigh softly. If I were being honest, I'd admit I'm not solely seeking a way to fix our professional relationship. I also want to spend time with Nikolai.

When I interviewed for my internship at Schluter & Fletcher, I was asked why I wanted to be a defense attorney. I answered the same way every intern does, "I want to protect the innocent."

Only after my argument with Nikolai did I realize innocence doesn't just extend to people guiltless of a crime. It also reflects the men, women, and children who don't have a choice.

Nikolai doesn't have a choice. He was born and raised to serve his lifestyle. He knows no different. And if I hadn't seen snippets of the man he could be this weekend, I would have believed he had no chance of rehabilitation. Now I think he just needs someone to believe in him.

That's precisely what I've been trying to do for the past five hours.

On paper, Nikolai is presented as a ruthless and coldhearted leader who rules the Popov entity with an iron fist. But I believe the man who woke up in my bed this morning is the true Nikolai Popov. The angry, gruff mobster he displays in front of his crew is a persona he created to survive the ruthless life he was born into—I'm sure of it. And I believe I know why.

With Nikolai's parting statement fresh in my mind, my search of his records delved deeper than a standard examination. It took several hours, but my dedication was rewarded in a way I never expected.

A medical record from when Nikolai was eight discloses that his blood type is AB positive. His father's is O negative. Although there's a slim chance they're still related, Nikolai's confession early this morning leaves me doubtful.

Nikolai plays the part well, but I'm beginning to wonder if he truly is a Russian mafia prince.

My focus snaps back to the present when my boss calls my name. "Justine? Are you there?" His cell phone beeps when he pushes the buttons.

I lick my parched lips before muttering, "Yes, sorry. I spaced out."

Mr. Fletcher's chuckle eases the swishing of my stomach. "Glad to hear I'm not the only one dropping the ball this morning. Let's hope your frantic morning was more worthwhile than mine. Have you unearthed any flaws in Nikolai's case that will aid in the dismissal of his charges?"

"Not yet." Frustration echoes in my tone.

"I'm close, though," I lie when his disappointed huff sounds down the line. "The DA is presenting this case as if Nikolai assaulted the complainant without cause, but the evidence doesn't corroborate that. A portion of the surveillance footage Trent uploaded yesterday morning shows Nikolai and the complainant had a brief exchange an hour before the incident. After pleading with the club's owner, I've been granted access to their security feeds. I've been backtracking through old tapes for the past few hours, hoping to discover if Friday night was their first encounter. Although I can't swear on a Bible, I have an inkling they've met before."

My intuition could be wrong, but just like I'm sure Nikolai and Mr. Fletcher have met previously, I'm highly suspicious of the complainant's claim that a stranger attacked him. Nikolai's rap sheet is extensive, but I doubt even he would stab a man with a beer bottle all because he bumped into him during transit to the restroom.

"Okay. That's good. Suppose we can establish a relationship between the complainant and our client that he failed to disclose during testimony. In that case, we have a good chance of having his statement stripped from the DA's evidence," Mr. Fletcher replies, sounding impressed. "Forward all your notes and the access codes for the security monitoring to Trent. I'll have him run their faces through our facial recognition software. It will be a quicker process than viewing the tapes firsthand."

"All right. I'll do that now." I contemplate how to articulate my next question without sounding rude. It's a waste of time when I blurt out, "Why does Trent need my notes? They're not required for facial recognition."

My heart slithers into my guts when Mr. Fletcher sighs softly, a sigh that relays I won't like what he has to say. "You're off this case, Justine. If we secure Nikolai as a client, we have an immense opportunity to extend the handshake to other men in his industry. This is a goldmine for Schluter & Fletcher. We can't risk losing this opportunity if you fail to clear Nikolai's charges."

"I'm not going to fail." My words come out in a flurry. "I'm giving this case everything I have. You know this arrangement is as important to me as it is to you, Mr. Fletcher. I will not mess it up for anything. Or anyone." I scarcely whisper my last guarantee.

I grind my teeth together when my voice reveals I am on the verge of tears. The only thing keeping them at bay is the anger thickening my blood. Except for his little slip-up during our first meeting with Nikolai, Mr. Fletcher has not once treated me like a worthless commodity, so I am shocked by his sudden belief I am incapable of doing my job.

"This decision wasn't made lightly, Justine. I appealed the board's verdict with as much grit as you're displaying now. The matter is out of my hands. The board's vote was unanimous." Even hearing the truth in Mr. Fletcher's voice doesn't lessen the impact of his words.

Not willing to back down without a fight, I continue pleading, "Did you tell them this isn't what Nikolai wants? He requested I be the lead counsel on his case. If I don't continue, he may seek alternative arrangements..."

The remainder of my sentence is lost when he says, "Nikolai is aware you've been removed from the case. Consent was given over two hours ago."

Disappointment blemishes my skin with a vibrant red hue. "Then I guess everything is settled," I snicker, my pitch snarky. "I'll forward the online documents to Trent now. Then I'll arrange for a courier to collect the rest once our call ends."

The whooshing of multiple emails being forwarded nearly drowns out Mr. Fletcher's reply. "You know this isn't a reflection on your work standards, Justine. It's just—"

"Business. I know. It's fine." I inwardly smile, grateful I sound put-together when I feel anything but.

After jotting down the address he wants my paperwork couriered to, I disconnect our call, cutting off his farewell mid-sentence.

The papers scattered over my bed crinkle when I flop onto my back. I fight with all my might not to let disappointed anger envelop every inch of me, but it's impossible.

Before I stop to consider my actions, I scamper off my bed and march across my bedroom floor.

29

NIKOLAI

My eyes stray to Justine's closed bedroom door when Roman ushers Vladimir and three of his foot soldiers into the foyer of Justine's apartment. I doubt she'll come out of her room any time soon. She was pissed when Roman stopped her from talking to me hours ago, citing all contact must now go through him, and she's been holed up in her room ever since.

As Vladimir bridges the gap between us, he takes in Justine's outdated apartment. I was hoping my request for assistance would occur over the phone. I should have known better. Vladimir likes getting his hands dirty, even when it's helping a man he detests. He wouldn't be here if I didn't have something he needs, but with my blood pressure sky high, we'll keep that snippet of information for another day.

"Niki, you look well." Since we're minus the swarm of press who usually circles us when we are together, Vladimir doesn't lean in to kiss my cheek as he usually would. "Your new whore must have a tasty cunt, otherwise what reason would you have to stay holed up in this dump?"

The harsh twist of his lips tells me he's watched the surveillance from Justine's apartment more than once, so he's aware

I've yet to bed Justine. He's just mocking me since he failed to see the shake of my bones from him calling me Niki.

The last time he called me that was when he told me my brother had been killed by a rogue Russian operative. He smiled while telling me the news of Rico's murder, his face as joyous as a father announcing the birth of his first child.

"Your accommodation is usually more... *fragrant*. I can barely smell an ounce of lust in this room. It almost smells like death."

He's fishing for information he'll never get from me. He taught me how to act ignorant long before he showed me how you can kill a man without draining an ounce of blood from his veins.

My eyes shoot to Roman when Vladimir snickers under his breath. "Let's hope her cunt isn't as bland as her cooking because from what I heard, she could learn a thing or two about serving those above her."

Roman had a hacker remove the footage of Justine's attack and the aftermath that followed it, so how does Vladimir know about her exchange with Sergei?

Before attacking Justine, Sergei taunted her about her 'supposed' bland meal. Only someone who watched the footage would know that.

My jaw tightens when reality dawns. The wound to Sergei's throat clearly wasn't deep enough to shut his flapping gums. I'll be sure to fix the injustice the instant I return to the Popov compound, where Sergei is recovering from his 'injuries' in a room that was once Rico's.

The tick in my jaw lowers to my fists when Vladimir returns my focus to him. "What do you need, son? I don't have all day."

A blind man wouldn't miss the shudder that rolls down my spine this time around. I hate when he calls me son almost as much as I do when he calls me Niki.

After loosening the tight clench of my fists, I gesture for Vladimir to join me in my room, not wanting our conversation overheard by Justine. I anticipate for us to talk man to man, but I forgot that Vladimir doesn't know the meaning of the word. His goons follow him into my room, cramping the confined space even more than Justine's bulky furniture.

Once Roman shuts the door, I lock my eyes with ones as lifeless as death. Vladimir's dark chocolate eyes should have been my first clue he wasn't my father. I'd often wondered why I was his only child to have icy-blue eyes, but since he treated all his children as if he hated them, I didn't dig as deeply as I should have.

It was foolish of me, and I've not made the same mistake since.

With my body gripped with hidden tension, I say, "I've managed to secure an informant from the Petretti crew. He's been with them for a few years now and is deep enough to secure a lot more intel than your last lackey got."

Vladimir is smarter than he looks. He ignores my snipe at his failed attempts to infiltrate the Petretti crew the past three years by only acknowledging the useful information in my comment. "The transfer you organized was for an informant?" When I jerk up my chin, hiding my annoyance at how closely he's watching me, he scoffs. "He's serving life in prison. How could he possibly help us?"

He says 'us,' but he means him.

My walk to a set of drawers is done in silence, but when I toss open a file containing photocopies of the visitors register at Wallens Ridge State Penitentiary for the past four years, I hear a murmur of commendation rattle in Vladimir's chest. For every month of Maddox's conviction, there's a signature no amount of messy hand-writing can hide—D Petretti.

"Dimitri didn't even visit his brother monthly when he was incarcerated, yet he has plenty of time for a supposed bottom-dweller of his crew."

"Interesting." Vladimir steps closer to authenticate the docu-ments. They cost me a pretty picture to purchase, but they're worth every damn penny when Vladimir's approving murmur is audible this time around. "What is Prisoner 65281 incarcerated for?"

"Murder." I don't mention it was to fulfill his sister's debt. I only tell Vladimir what I want him to know. Maddox's connection to Justine will never be exposed, not even if I discover she's one of Carmichael's many tricks. "He won't be out any time soon, but his intel could be priceless."

It kills him to do, but Vladimir nods in agreement. "I agree." His trench coat scratches the floorboard when he turns to face me. "So, I will ask again, my boy, what do you need from me?"

Ignoring the tremor hitting my jaw, I say, "Judge Santos is dead."

Vladimir smiles a cruel and vindictive grin. "I heard. It was very unfortunate for *all* involved, wouldn't you say?"

My eyelid twitches as anger steamrolls into me. Only now am I realizing an underage boy didn't steal the light from Judge Santos's eyes.

Vladimir did.

With my thoughts elsewhere, I played right into his fucking hand. He didn't appreciate me stepping out on my own, so he devised a way to force me back home. By killing Judge Santos, I had to either face my charges like an everyday civilian or ask Vladimir for help. He knew I'd always choose the latter, which meant I'd be indebted to him even more than he thinks I already am.

I had planned to secure his help by wowing him with the possibility of an informant from his rival crew. Now Maddox is my only lifeline, and Vladimir fucking knows it.

One of the reasons my crew calls me The Snake is showcased when my annoyance rolls right off my scales. Now is not the time for me to lose my head. I've got enough people playing me for a fool. I can't add another to my list, especially when it's a *ублюдок* like Vladimir.

"I want to head to Florida and speak to my informant in person. I can't do that if I'm sitting in a holding cell, awaiting trial. I need my charges dropped."

Vladimir looks like I told him I'm giving him the millions of dollars in my bank account when he asks, "And you need my help to do that?"

It takes a good three seconds for me to lower my chin, and even then, it's as weak and as pitiful as the man I've been portraying the past four hours. "I had my case transferred to Mr. Schluter's side of his firm a couple of hours ago. Ernest is willing to do what's needed *after* you've given him the green light."

While Vladimir contemplates a reply, I sit on the end of my bed to run a hand down my tired face. I'm exhausted from a lack of sleep the past two days, but that's not the only thing making me restless. It's from dumping a woman I'm certain isn't evil into hell without first giving her the chance to explain herself. Justine said words identical to ones that almost got me killed, but that doesn't mean she understands their significance. Perhaps she does truly believe I deserve better.

My hand has only just fallen from my face when my bedroom door shoots open and Justine darts into the testosterone-filled space, oblivious to the danger she's thrusting herself into.

"You're a complete and utter idiot. I know we've said stupid things, done stupid things, and acted stupidly, but I am a professional, Nikolai. Nothing said or done would have ever affected my representation of you in court." Since her eyes are locked on mine, she fails to notice we have company. "Your inability to trust just cost you five to seven years of your life because what Carmichael said Friday was true. I'm not just the best attorney Schluter & Fletcher has seen, I was your only chance of having your charges dismissed. Because I see you, Nikolai... the real you. I would have defended your honor until my last breath."

Justine's breath catches in her throat when Vladimir mocks the speech that resurrected the dead organ in the middle of my chest. "Is that so, *Ангел?* You see the real Nikolai?"

30

JUSTINE

With my heart lodged in my throat, I swing my eyes in the direction of the voice. Standing at the side of my spare bedroom, wearing a thick black trench coat, is a man whose eyes are as dark as his poor choice of summer attire. His salt-and-pepper hair is slicked back on his thick skull, and his lips are curled into a snarl.

Even though I've never met the man glaring evilly at me, I know who he is. He is Vladimir Popov, the mob boss of Las Vegas and the monster who raised Nikolai.

After Vladimir's sullied eyes rake over my body in spine-tingling detail, he returns them to my face. "Maybe we should have kept her on as counsel. It would have made the trial more entertaining for all involved."

The three men surrounding him follow his lead when he laughs as if his comment is funny. My lungs begin accepting oxygen again when Vladimir signals for the men pointing guns at me to stand down. I've barely inhaled an entire breath when he heads my way.

I spot Nikolai rising from his bed in the corner of my eye. The fury on his face makes my skin slick with sweat even more than the fire in his eyes. His gaze is murderous and rapt on his father.

When he attempts to thwart Vladimir's prowling approach,

Roman splays his arm across his thrusting chest, halting his endeavor. They get into a tussle, but with every pair of eyes in the room glued to Vladimir, no one but me notices their exchange.

Clutching Nikolai's shirt in a firm grip, Roman mutters something in his ear. His voice is so soft I can't hear what he is saying, but whatever he is muttering must be unpleasant, as the agony in Nikolai's gaze turns vicious.

My eyes drift away from Nikolai when Vladimir stops to stand in front of me. "As fine as a rose petal, but with the intensity of a huntress. You'd be a lot of fun," he say, his eyes as desolate as his heavily accented words. "But no woman disrupts the rightful order. Not even one as pretty as you."

After tracking his thumb down the pulse in my throat, Vladimir slings his eyes to Nikolai. "Is she yours, Niki? Is she the reason you tried to slit your cousin's throat?" He sneers out Nikolai's name as if it's a derogatory word. "You're letting a woman weaken you like Rico did. I thought I raised you better than that." I don't know who Rico is, but Vladimir hissed out his name as if it scorched his throat.

Panic engulfs every inch of me when Nikolai replies, "She isn't mine." His throat works hard to swallow before he adds, "She isn't anybody's. Sergei has been stepping out of line for years. I simply put him back in his place."

Nikolai silently requests that Roman corroborate his statement.

My heart slowly creeps back down my windpipe when Roman says, "Sergei disrespected Nikolai. He was punished for his insolence, not a whore."

Vladimir eyes his son with skepticism, his mistrust highly notable. "So you wouldn't mind if I made her my whore?" His lips twitch as he struggles to contain his rueful grin.

When Nikolai deliberates for half a second, I beg, "Please."

Who is this man? Only this morning he promised no one would ever hurt me, but now he stands in front of me, contemplating his father's suggestion of making me his whore like it's a perfectly acceptable thing to do. I'd spit at his feet if I wasn't engulfed in fear.

Ignorant of my appeal, Nikolai drifts his eyes back to his father. "Would you like her? You can have her if you want. As a gift, perhaps?" he asks in Russian, his tone unlike any I've heard him use. It was shallow and weak, a stark contradiction to the man he is.

Moisture burns my eyes as my heart falls from my ribcage. I

can't believe I stupidly thought Nikolai wasn't the man his file portrays. This proves what the pessimists always preach. A leopard can't change its spots.

As he notices my distressed look, the haughty gleam in Vladimir's dark gaze doubles. He feeds off my fear, loving every tremor shuddering through me. He takes his time appraising my ashen face before his dedication drops to my body.

I've never been more grateful for the bite marks on my arms when the lusty expression on his face switches to disgust. He glares at the red indentations maiming my skin, deepening them more with his wrathful gaze.

"She's marked! That makes her worthless!" he spits out in disgust, the words fired off his tongue like venom. "I could have looked past her lack of innocence to witness her face in ecstasy, but I've tasted the richest wine, and I refuse to settle for anything less than perfection."

My breathing spikes when Vladimir runs the back of his hand down my cheek, wiping away a tear. I fought with all my might to hold in my tears, but when his words echoed what I've been waiting to hear the past four years, they spilled over before I could stop them.

Vladimir releases a throaty moan when he sucks the salty droplet off his finger. "It's a pity you're marked. If your cunt tastes as sweet as your tears, we could have had a lot of fun."

Even though I'm not looking at Nikolai, I know he balks at his father's crude statement. His movement was so rigid the air rippled.

I secure my first breath in what feels like ten minutes when Vladimir steps away from me. "Thank you for the offer, Niki, but I must decline your invitation."

Not bothering to issue a farewell, Vladimir hightails it to my front door. The three heavily armed men follow closely on his coattails.

The instant my apartment door slams shut, Nikolai's hand curls around my quaking jaw. His body is hot and brooding, nearly as tumultuous as mine. I yank away from his embrace, sickened he failed to defend me as promised.

"I'll slit the throat of any man who dares look at you sideways.

Family or not," I quote with devastation dangling off my vocal cords. "You're such a liar."

Nikolai growls, angered by my insult. Normally, the fury in his tone would have me cowering away, but not this time. Call me stupid, but I know he won't hurt me, so it gives me free rein to unleash my vicious tongue.

"Why did you do that? Why did you offer me to him as a gift?" My anger is so intense it chops up my words, making them weaker than I had hoped.

He stares at me, shocked I understood what he said to his father.

"I can speak thirteen languages, Nikolai—including Russian. Perhaps you would have discovered that if you hadn't thrown me away like trash."

"I offered you to him to save you from him," he whispers, his words barely audible.

I laugh. It's a torturous chuckle that exposes that my heart is still sitting at my feet.

"Don't treat me like an idiot! I know what your father is like. I know exactly what he would have done to me if he had accepted your offer."

Fury lines his face as his fists clench into balls. "He wouldn't have touched you. I wouldn't let him touch you like that. I'd kill him before I would let him touch you." His voice grows louder with every sentence he speaks.

"You offered me to him!" I shout, my words croaky from the absolute despair clutching my throat. "You gifted me to a man who sells his daughters to the highest bidders and tortures his sons as if they're animals!"

When a fresh batch of tears trickle down my cheeks, Nikolai wraps me up in a tight hug. "I offered you to him to save you," he mutters into my hairline. "If I thought there was any chance he would have accepted my offer, I would have never said it."

I pound on his chest, sickened by his continued denial.

If he can't see how wrong this is, he's beyond saving.

"Don't touch me," I sneer, pulling out of his embrace and high-tailing it to the door. "You lost the right to touch me the instant you offered me to that monster."

"Justine..." Nikolai growls in warning.

The vicious snarl of his tone sends horrid memories rushing to the forefront of my mind, but I continue with my trek, more determined than ever. This exchange is different from my last tussle with a mafia prince. No vicious animals are forced to follow their owner's command or die.

My shaky steps falter mid-stride when he says, "If Vladimir knew how much I want you, he would have taken you away from me. If not for himself, for someone else. He has been that way my entire life. Anything I love, he takes. I only offered you to him because I knew he wouldn't take you. Vladimir craves perfection, so I used anything to save you from him."

The swishing of my stomach amplifies when it dawns on me what he's saying. I feel sick—horribly ill. Although grateful the marks mottling my skin saved me from a man as horrid as Vladimir, hearing Nikolai say I'm not perfect hurts more than I can explain. I stupidly thought he was the first man not bothered by my scars.

Clearly I was wrong.

I can't stay here and let him watch me cry, so I continue marching to my bedroom.

"Justine," Nikolai shouts, following after me.

When he snags my wrist in a vise-like grip, my free hand flies wildly through the air, only stopping when it brutally connects with his face.

31

NIKOLAI

J ustine's slap rattles both my teeth and the devil I'm trying to keep contained. I was raised by violence, so it's my quick go-to when I'm spiraling out of control.

I'm trying to be different this weekend. I want to be the man Justine sees when she looks at me for just a day—even if it kills me.

My grip on Justine's wrist tightens as I talk through the anger clutching my throat. "Don't ever hit me." My words are as violent as the abuse I endured during my childhood.

I've been burned, stabbed, shot, beaten with fists, sticks, and chains, but nothing hurt me as much as my mother's hand colliding with my cheek. She was my blood, the only person I ever loved without wondering what she wanted from me, but not even that was enough for her. She abused me as much as Vladimir.

"I'm sorry," Justine mutters on a sob as tears flow down her cheeks. "I shouldn't have hit you. No one has the right to put their hands on another. I let my emotions get the better of me, and I'm sorry for that."

Sorry is another word people use without significance. They rarely mean it, and it's only expressed once it's too late. The damage has already been done.

Justine's apology didn't sound worthless. It was the most

genuine I've heard. There was no malice in her tone when she spoke, and her eyes aren't just full to the brim with moisture, they're also crammed with remorse.

She's as sorry she slapped me as I am about hurting her.

I shouldn't have used her scars to free her from Vladimir's madness. I should have shielded her from him as I plan to from here on out.

Roman peers up from his shoes when I ask him to leave. As he takes a step toward me, the worry on his face becomes unmissable. "Your father, Nikolai. You know what he is like after Rico. Disobeying his direct order could result in—"

"I'll deal with him," I interrupt, my hostile voice warning him my mood is already on edge, so he'd do best not to test me. I've never struggled with my emotions as I am now. Usually I give a demand, and you either follow it or die. Today, the only thing I want to kill is the pain in Justine's eyes.

After a stretch of intense silence, Roman asks, "Will the benefit outweigh the penance?"

He has asked that question many times in the past decade. Not once have I been able to answer yes. This time is different. Justine is unlike any woman I've ever met. She's smart, beautiful, and when her eyes aren't filled with pain, she sees the real me, the man I hide from others.

Although hurt continues reflecting from Justine's eyes, its rate slows when I drag my thumbs across her cheeks to clear her tears. I don't know if my touch is responsible for the flare of hope drying the wetness in her eyes or what I say while touching her. "Yes. Do I not deserve a night of pardon after all the years I've served?"

I killed for Vladimir, and I forgot who I was for him, so I deserve more than one lousy night, but if that's all I can get, I'll take it. A lifetime of apologies won't fix the mistakes I've made, but one night of showing Justine who I really am is a great start.

Roman's eyes hold the sentiment they did when my shattered ankle was set without anesthetics when he mutters, "You deserve that and so much more."

After dipping his chin and wishing me luck, he exits Justine's apartment without so much as a backward glance. Strangers would believe he's leaving me high and dry. I trust that he'd never do that. He will put measures in place to ensure my one day off isn't interrupted because he knows I'll come out the other end more powerful than I've ever been.

A grin tugs at my lips when Roman's deep timbre booms through Justine's rapidly closing door. "You know how to reach me. Contact me when you're ready."

When the latch on the front door clicks into place, announcing we're alone, I commence rebuilding my empire by removing the tears slipping down Justine's face. Even a devil needs a queen at his side when he takes his throne, and bratva queens don't cry when they're hurt by their enemies. They annihilate them.

Once Justine's face is free of moisture, I plop her backside on the couch so she's out of the way while I remove the one object I know will foil my attempt to make things right—the surveillance equipment monitoring every inch of her apartment.

"Wait here."

Although confused by my quick change in demeanor, Justine nods, agreeing with my request. Her chin has barely lowered an inch when I drag the armchair I sat on last night while watching Justine dance up a storm to the far corner of the living room.

An idea of the madness I want Justine to be a part of is showcased in an unfavorable light when the electrical cord maintaining the live feed breaks through the crown molding in the living room.

"They were hardwired?" Justine mumbles, shocked.

Nodding, I cut through the wire with my knife before moving for the camera in Justine's room. It's still covered by her yoga pants, but that won't stop its microphone from being activated.

While removing the blinking red contraptions from Justine's dead-silent apartment, I feed off the torment slicking my skin with sweat. Before ending the live feed with my knife as I plan to do to Vladimir's life, I smile down the lens. Each condescending smirk should add another nail to my coffin, but I was raised by a master manipulator, so I know all his tricks.

I have something Vladimir needs. I'm his golden ticket to a power he's been striving for his entire life. Without me, his greatest wish will never come true. Not only does that knowledge free me from the fear of persecution, but it also changes my game plan in an instant. Vladimir will still class what I'm doing as disobedient, but he will also respect it because, as far as he is concerned, I'm being the man he raised me to be.

With my veins as icy as my blue eyes, I stare down the camera lens in Justine's kitchen before singing a nursery rhyme no one but Vladimir will understand. "Send the angel to the devil's bed, hold her, cherish her, then cut off her head. She danced with Satan, and now she is dead, all for lying in the devil's bed."

Every one of Vladimir's men understands Russian. They just have no clue what his rhyme means. It isn't about good or evil or coercing an angel to dance with death. It's a warning to Vladimir's sons on what will happen if they let a woman fracture the rightful order. They can be bedded by the devil and cherished by him, but the instant they dance with Satan by placing themselves between him and the spawn born solely to protect him, they'll lose their lives by the devil they've fallen in love with or die alongside him.

I'll never let anyone hurt Justine. I will protect her how Dimitri failed to do years ago, but I can only do that by convincing Vladimir she means nothing to me. Reciting Vladimir's rhyme adds to the ruse Roman and I pulled on him earlier. When he hears it, he will believe Justine is nothing more than a night or two of entertainment and that the words I spoke moments ago were said to trick her into my bed.

I meant every word I spoke, but I'm happy for Vladimir to think otherwise. Then, once Justine is off his radar, I'll play the game with the ruthlessness it deserves, and I will win.

The crown.

The throne.

The queen.

They will all be mine.

As will Vladimir's life.

Once I have the dismantled surveillance cameras in my hand, all seven of them, I request Justine to follow me into the bathroom. The air turns roasting when she immediately jumps to my command. Her steps are shaky, but a gleam in her eyes has me skeptical fear isn't solely responsible for her wobbly knees.

The strong don't cower when fear comes knocking. They welcome it with a smile.

When I dump the cameras into the bottom of the bathtub before twisting on the faucet full pelt, Justine gasps in a sharp breath. She watches me with her mouth hanging open when I climb into the tub to crush the small black devices with my boots, preferring to be cautious than be played for a fool for the second time today.

Just because the devices were hardwired doesn't mean they don't have backup batteries. My men were caught out by a rival once before. They learned from their mistake.

Once the recording apparatuses are as shattered as the expression on Justine's face when I offered her to Vladimir as a gift, I stray my eyes to Justine's. "Happy?"

She's lost as to where I'm going with this, but since she's more trusting than scared, she nods her head. Slanting mine to the side to hide my smile, I climb out of the bathtub and make my way to her. As I did the last time we tussled in this very room, I drastically reduce the length of my stride, giving Little Red Riding Hood plenty of time to escape the Big Bad Wolf.

Unlike our last soirée, Justine doesn't seek the closest exit. She holds my gaze as I bridge the gap between us, her breathing as unhinged as my desire to show her she's perfect.

A floral scent stirs my cock when I grip the hem of her dress to pull it over her head. The thin cotton material falls to the floor with a whoosh, concealing the whistle of my lungs from the hurried breath I suck in. I'm not gasping in horror but struggling to maintain a rational head.

Her body... Fuck. Me.

I'm a goner.

I want her now more than ever.

Her perfect tits, milky white hips, and the scant little pair of panties she's wearing have me wanting to forget why I'm stripping her bare. I want to sample the scent growing stronger with each second ticking by. I want to fuck her until the embarrassment in her eyes disappears, but since I know that will tiptoe her closer to the madness I'm endeavoring to save her from, I listen to the head on my shoulders instead of the one headbutting the zipper in my jeans.

It's a fucking hard feat.

A vibrant pink hue creeps across the thrusting globes I'm struggling to ignore when I press my lips to a bite mark on Justine's right shoulder. "Perfect." I drop my lips to the tear that forced her onto her knees during her mauling. It's as silky as the skin on her stomach but glittered with strength. "Perfect."

When I fall to my knees, a smirk curls my lips. I've always believed it is better to die than show weakness by kneeling. Clearly, I had no clue the power associated with kneeling before a woman whose only weakness is you. I may be on my knees, but I am the most lethal I've ever been because nothing will stop me from protecting this woman. Not a million bullets or the Almighty himself.

Nothing.

"Perfect," I mumble against two smaller bites on the back of Justine's knee.

I kiss every bite I know of and a few she kept well-hidden, before standing to my feet and locking my eyes with ones that aren't as pained as they were minutes ago. "I previously said you'd be worth three nights in lockup. I was wrong. You're worth so much more than that. You're perfect, Justine. Don't ever let a monster like Vladimir lead you to believe any different."

I anticipate the lust depriving the air of oxygen to thicken from my confession. All I get is more torment. She wants to believe what I'm saying, but her exchange with Vladimir didn't just dent her ego, it stole her trust as well.

Justine stiffens like a board when I spin her around to face the vanity mirror. It's one of those old-school Hollywood ones with over a dozen lightbulbs covering a rectangular wooden frame. The bright lights illuminate her pale skin, making her glow as if she truly is an angel.

"Look in the mirror and tell me what you see." When Justine shakes her head, I tighten my grip around her waist before repeating my demand in a manner she won't be able to refuse. "Look in the mirror and tell me what you see, or I'll bend you over the tub and fuck you so mindless, you'll submit to my every command without stopping to think."

I understand this is hard for her to do, but I need her to see the woman I do before she's swallowed by a blackness so thick, no amount of purity will clear.

When Justine's eyes remain arrested on the floor, my dominance gets the better of me. "Five... four... three... "

My words trail off when her eyes slowly lift to our reflections beaming from the retro mirror. At the start, she stares directly at me, her focus only shifting when the contrast between our bodies becomes too great for her to ignore. Her eyes shoot in all directions as they take in the way my large frame swamps her tiny one. Her skin looks super pale against the darkness of the ink covering most of my body, and although both our eyes have shades of blue, hers are too angelic to ever appear evil.

"We look like night and day. Darkness and light—"

"Angel and devil," I interrupt.

As confirmation flares through Justine's impressive eyes, I pull her molten-red hair away from her shoulders. My hold around her waist allows me to feel the surge of her pulse when the bright lights emphasize the slivers of silver in her scars, but she remains as quiet as a church mouse.

After locking my eyes with the mirror, I ask, "What do you see now?"

Justine's pupils swamp her corneas when she mumbles, "I'm not who I used to be, Nikolai..." Her words are replaced with a squeak when our eyes collide for the quickest second. The thirst I saw in her heavy-hooded gaze the day we met is unmissable in mine. Scars or not, I want her. She's beautiful—a true gift from heaven.

"Nothing changed, *Ангел... nothing.*"

When disbelief remains in her eyes, I set her back onto her feet before taking three steps backward. Her lips twitch like she wants to question my retreat, but before a word can spill from her pouty mouth, I yank my shirt over my head by the tag at the back before popping open the button on my jeans and sliding down the zipper.

Once I'm as naked as Justine's vulnerability makes her, I raise my eyes to Justine's face. She's still facing the mirror, but her eyes haven't left mine the past two minutes. "Turn around."

It's a hard struggle to conceal my smugness when she follows my order without batting an eyelid. Once again, she's not being submissive. She's just being open to the idea not everyone is out to hurt her.

I wait for her eyes to stop scanning my body before saying, "Come here."

I can't hold back my smile when she whispers, "No. I'm safer here," so I set it free. It doubles the heat on Justine's cheeks while ensuring me I'm on the right path. This is all new to me. I've never done anything like this before. I've only ever placed myself first.

That's set to change now.

"I guess I'll come to you, then." When I take a step forward, Justine takes a shaky one back. "Don't run unless you want to be chased, Ангел." My growl of her nickname reveals how far out of my depth I am. I'm struggling just as much as Justine. I'm just too fucking stubborn to back down. "I will chase you no matter how fast you run because I know that's what you want."

My cock throbs with want when my threat freezes her feet. She watches my stalk across the room with wide, hungry eyes, proving she doesn't just want to be chased, she wants to be devoured as well.

I'll give her what she wants *after* showing her only the most courageous people have scars.

Some wear them on the body.

Others wear them on their hearts.

Justine wears hers beautifully.

While peering into Justine's eyes, I gather her hand in mine before tracing it over the tattoo just to the left of my six-pack. Tears pool in her eyes when it dawns on her why the scales in the dragon's head look real because they are. My dragon tattoo conceals over half a dozen scars of which sizes differ as much as the reason I have them. Some are grazes from being dragged, others are cigar burns, and the main one is from the acid on Rico's back soaking into my hip when I struggled to keep him on his feet while moving him from the dungeon he was tortured in to his bedroom.

The second scar I show Justine is the one Rico gave me after he learned I organized for his wife to be raped and killed. When he used my knife against me, I did nothing to stop him. I tried to lessen the severity of the blaze when I ordered Blaire's hit, but I still played with fire, so I deserved to get burned.

After showing Justine a handful of less memorable scars on my back and chest, I lower her hand to the gravelly skin stretched across my right rib. This scar is more notable than the rest because it's a reminder that no amount of fear will ever abolish my sins. I can beat them until their skin is as black as mine was when I was tortured. I can whip their backs until their blood pools around their feet, and I can stomp on them until their bones break under the pressure, but there is one thing they stole from me only now am I realizing no amount of retaliation will return.

My freedom.

I thought they broke me thirteen years ago.

I thought they stole my wish to live even more than the hell I was born in.

I thought I was worthless.

I know better now.

Time didn't heal my wounds. Showing an angel her scars mean she is stronger than the person who tried to break her did. The wounds of our battles reveal how hard we fought to survive. We didn't break, cower, or give up. We rose above the ashes and conquered the beast.

We chose to live.

With my chest sitting as high as my determination to show this beautiful woman just how perfect she is, I lock my eyes with Justine's and ask, "Do you see me any differently now, Justine?"

She answers me in a way I never anticipated, but in a manner that may very well kill me if I don't tread carefully.

She kisses me.

32

JUSTINE

I'm shoved off-balance from the sternness of Nikolai's lips. They fail to part to the lashing of my tongue, and his hands remained clenched at his side. His response isn't one I anticipated, but it makes me want him even more. He's wary our exchange has made me vulnerable, and he doesn't want to take advantage of me.

"I want you," I whisper against Nikolai's mouth, my eyes focused on his. "I've wanted you from the moment I saw you. And now that I'm not your attorney, I can have you."

A deep, simpering moan rolls up my throat when Nikolai parts his lips, allowing me to slip my tongue inside his mouth. He doesn't push or deepen our kiss. He holds back, letting my kiss assure him our exchange has nothing to do with vulnerability.

I weave my fingers through his hair to bring our bodies closer together. The heat of his stiffened cock breaks the connection between us. I leap into the air, my clit oversensitive from days of torturous foreplay.

A hint of the Nikolai I've been wrangling the past three days surfaces when his eyes spark with smugness, revealing he didn't miss my body's response to his touch.

Endeavoring to snuff the cockiness from his eyes, I give my hands free rein on a body I've been dying to touch. I run them over the smooth planes of his pecs before dropping them to the hard bumps in his stomach. I glide them across the rough patch of curly hairs in his midsection, scrubbing ever so lightly on the massive bulge too large for my hand before drawing them around to squeeze an ass that feels as good as it looks.

Nikolai keeps his hands at his sides, though they're more tightly clenched than they were minutes ago. "I want to fucking touch you. I'm dying to fucking touch you," he mutters, his words strained like he is in pain.

"Then touch me," I instruct, my voice husky with arousal.

He doesn't respond... unless you include grunting as a form of communication.

My breasts brace against his chest when I drag my arms behind my back to remove my bra. The fabric falls to the ground with a silent whoosh, heightening the sexual tension brimming in the air. I stand frozen for a moment, giving Nikolai the time needed to see my scars without hindrance. If he wants to stop this, this is his final chance.

"You're fucking perfect. If I stared at you long enough, I'm certain I'd come just from looking at you," Nikolai mutters as his cock thickens more.

His compliment awards me with enough heat to see me through winter. His excitement can't be contained when I fall to my knees in front of him. The veins in his cock thicken as the tip glistens with arousal.

"Fuck, *Ангел*. I was trying to fix the wrongs I made, not have you kneeling before me." The strain in his voice is unmissable, heightening my senses even more. "I should be stopping this, but fucked if I can."

I smile, smitten I'm not the only helpless one in our odd duo.

His cock flexes against my palm when I slide my hand down his shaft. My movements are purposely slow, ensuring he knows nothing I do is done under duress. My mouth dries in an instant when a thick, shiny drop of pre-cum beads on his knob. It's such a mesmerizing sight my IQ declines to a disrespectful level. I'm practically drooling, incapable of a better response.

I lean forward, eager to clear away the decadent drop. I wrap my hand around his velvety shaft before my tongue darts out to lap up the sticky bead of moisture. His groan rolls down his chest before vibrating on my tongue.

His wordless response instigates recklessness within me. I glide my lips down his shaft, taking as much of him in my mouth as I can without gagging. His cock pulses as it thickens even more.

"Fuck," Nikolai moans through a roar, his hands moving to clutch my hair. "This is even better than I imagined."

His grip on my hair is firm, but he remains perfectly still, allowing me to worship his cock without any hindrance. I draw him into my mouth again and suck down hard, loving the sting his hold on my hair is causing to my scalp. Pleasure crackles through me as I take him deeper. I'm determined to have him singing as loudly as I did when he took me to the brink.

I tighten my lips and flatten my tongue. At the same time, his hips begin to naturally rock. He pumps in and out of my mouth as efficiently as lust races through me. I've never been good at giving head, and in all honesty, I've never really enjoyed it, but this is a different experience. I love sucking his cock so much my orgasm builds like a tsunami: fast and without warning.

"That's it. Just like that," Nikolai groans, rocking into me faster.

As waves of excitement roll over my stomach, I hollow my cheeks even more, wanting to ensure I don't come before him. He increases his speed as his breathing intensifies. His heavy pants thrill me, thrusting my desire to climax to the forefront of my mind.

Mindless with need, my hand slithers down to my pussy. Air leaves my lungs in a long, brutal grunt when I feel how damp my panties are. I'm saturated.

"Don't worry. I'll look after you. You'll feel me for days once I'm done with you," he guarantees as he gathers my hair to the side, giving himself an unrestricted view of my fingers toying with my clit.

His pledge makes my excitement reach a point I can't ignore. I groan against his knob before sucking down hard.

Just as he wasn't prepared for my surprise attack, I'm ambushed by his sudden climax. Cum spurts out of his cock, sliding down my throat within seconds.

"Mmm," I moan.

Nikolai's taste is so wickedly delicious that I can barely hold back my own orgasm.

After I finish swallowing every drop of his cum, he scoops down and lifts me from the ground. An audible pop bounces around the room when his still erect cock slips from my mouth. I whine softly, my mouth already missing the weight of him. Lust detonates in his eyes when I run my finger over my lips, ensuring I didn't miss a drop of his cum.

"You got every drop," he mumbles, his voice electrified with unbridled lust. "Every fucking one."

The suede on my couch feels smooth against my skin when he lays me down on it. "Too far," he mumbles against my neck when my eyes stray to my bedroom door. "I can't wait another fucking minute."

His erection rubs against my wet pussy as his lips go crazy. He sucks on my neck, chest, stomach, and thighs while his hand snaps away the minuscule article of clothing I'm wearing. My hands twitch to cover my body when he leans back to take in the entire picture, but the amorous flare in his eyes keeps them planted at my side.

"So fucking stunning. If I weren't dying to sink my cock into you, I'd be staring at you all day."

I blink back tears before pulling open the end table drawer next to the couch. Nikolai raises a brow when he sees the twelve pack of condoms resting in the middle of the empty drawer.

"You can never be too prepared," I mumble as embarrassment rolls through me. I purchased those condoms during my trip to the grocery store this weekend. I don't know why. I just did it instinctively.

I'm mesmerized moments later by the visual of him rolling a condom down his cock. Although grateful his eagerness saved me from embarrassingly fumbling through the process of securing protection, my hands are jealous they weren't given the chance to touch him again.

"Oh, sweet Jesus," I mumble when he balances the head of his cock against the entrance of my pussy. "Will that fit?"

A surge of electricity sparks my womb when Nikolai chuckles at my shameful question.

"Yes, it will fit," he assures me, inching the head in ever so slightly. "Because you're so fucking wet, I'll slide straight in."

He slams home, taking me to the base of his cock with one

ardent thrust. My insides clench, equally excited and pained we've finally reached this stage of our exchange. The feeling is odd, an imbalance of pain and pleasure. It feels good and wickedly bad at the same time.

When the pain starts to subside, I expect him to move. Twitch. Do something. He does nothing. He just stares down at me, his eyes as icy as Antarctic waters.

"You know this changes everything, right?" he asks, his voice minus its earlier anguish. It isn't cocky or arrogant, more pleased than anything.

"Yes," I answer, gingerly nodding.

That one thrust changes everything. But I don't care. I'm too caught up in the moment to let anything dampen it.

"Good."

Nikolai's one short word barely leaves his mouth before he pounds into me. He uses every muscle in his body to thrust into me over and over again, only stopping to reposition me so he can take me even deeper.

"Fucking perfect. I knew from the moment I laid eyes on you that you'd feel this good."

His breathing is as hard as his thrusts into me, a controlled, rhythmic pace that showcases his bedroom skills in the most brilliant light. He is a man familiar with fucking, and he does it well. He has me sitting on the brink within minutes, my mind blank, my body shut down. I am so wet I'm panicked about what the dampness will do to the material of my couch.

My worry doesn't linger for long. Not a thought passes my mind when he glides his hand between our bodies to locate my clit. He pinches it with his fingers, sending jolts of ecstasy darting all over me.

"Oh god. Oh god. *Oh god*," I chant on repeat, my intellect too low to conjure a better set of sentences.

"That's it, *Ангел*. Let me hear your screams," Nikolai murmurs as he continues hammering me into oblivion.

My pleasure builds rapidly, scorching my veins and heating my face.

"I'm going to come," I warn, like it's a bad thing.

Something this good couldn't possibly be bad.

I free fall into ecstasy when his rough groan shreds my

eardrums. "Good. Come on my cock. Show me how much you're enjoying this."

He watches me crumble beneath him, the thrill in his eyes undeterred by my withering frame. His orgasm soon follows mine, but his pursuit doesn't weaken. He rams into me with every magnificent spasm jerking through his body.

When the intensity becomes too much for either of us to bear, Nikolai collapses on me, his breathing heavy on my neck. My orgasm sucks the life right out of me, but it can't stop me from smiling.

That was...

I don't have a word to explain it.

It deprived my lungs of oxygen and coated my skin with sweat.

It also made my heart the fullest it's ever been.

I'm so exhausted the rhythm of my breathing soon lowers to a gentle wheeze.

"Oh no, *Ангел*." Nikolai draws me back from my slumbering state. "You don't have time to sleep. I'm not even halfway through with you yet."

He hoists me off the couch before throwing me over his shoulder. My eyes comically bulge when he smacks my backside while charging for my room. His spank was playful but frisky enough to ward off any eagerness for sleep.

"**E**nough is enough. You've had your fun, but now it's time to get back to business." I don't know what's frustrating Vladimir the most. That he's been left in the dark the past twelve hours, or he's realized he needs me more than he will ever admit. It could be a combination of both. "We had a shipment due yesterday afternoon. It never arrived—"

"Because the distribution company had a nark they needed to take care of. Trey updated you about the delay Wednesday afternoon."

"All delays must be justified."

"They were. The Yurys agreed to pay a penalty for the interruption in our schedule, and the crates have been earmarked for immediate approval at Customs. They'll be on the docks early tomorrow morning."

My snappy attitude takes a step back when Vladimir mutters, "Is Adrian's crew ready for the shipment?"

"No." I scrub at the stubble on my chin, tracing the tremor there. "We had some issues at Knightsbridge. I sent Adrian and Lia there to sort it out. Abram is handling this one."

Vladimir's grunt reveals he already knew my reply, but he was testing my loyalty.

He's always testing my loyalty.

"I can't believe Adrian is still with *that girl*. I thought he would have grown bored of her by now."

My back molars smash together from the way he spits out 'that girl' when referencing Lia, but I keep a cool, collective head for Justine's sake. If Vladimir believed Justine was a threat to his realm, we'd be having this conversation in person, not over the phone. His lack of worry proves my ruse is working, and it also verifies that Roman's hacker ensured Vladimir only saw the footage I wanted him to see from my exchange with Justine before I debugged her apartment.

Furthermore, I'm not surprised Vladimir sees his daughter as the lesser-valued commodity in his working relationship with Adrian's distribution company. Adrian makes him money, so that awards him more respect than his own flesh and blood.

The tightness of my jaw is heard in my words when I ask, "Is that all?"

My question stumps him for all of two seconds. "Do what needs to be done, then get back here. We have *other* matters to take care of."

By other matters, he means personal ones that are usually left off the table when discussing business. His demand for me to return to the Popov compound sooner rather than later convinces me his frustration stems more from needing me than being denied the opportunity to watch the nine-hour-long fuck session Justine and I undertook last night. He hates being in the dark, but that annoyance would never overtake his wish for ultimate supremacy.

When Vladimir ends our call without a farewell, I dump my cell phone onto a set of drawers in Justine's room before moving toward the mattress she's resting on. She murmurs into her pillow when I drag my index finger up the leg peeking out of the bedding, but her eyes remain shut.

I can't blame her for being exhausted. I'm usually awake long before the sun, but even I'm dead on my feet this morning. I knew she'd be explosive in the bedroom, but I had no clue it wouldn't be just her bringing the ammunition to the party.

My head must not have been in the game until Justine's pussy was placed up for offer. Usually sex was about getting my rocks off. Last night was nothing like that. I still came—*multiple times*—but since it was occurring with Justine, it felt different. It mattered. If that makes any fucking sense?

I stop reprimanding myself for being a soft cock when a sing-song voice trickles into my ears. "Hey. Everything okay?" Justine's voice is as groggy as her tired eyes.

My finger continues its trek up her leg, only stopping when it reaches the tastiest cunt I've ever eaten. "Everything is fine... *now* that you're awake." The way her body heats up from my comment could convince a devil into becoming a saint. "Oh, *Ангел*. I fucking love the way you blush."

I push on her hip until she falls onto her back, then I spread her thighs wide. Her clit is already hard and throbbing for me, and her nipples are budded.

After unbuttoning the fly in my jeans to give my inflated cock some much-needed space, I lower my head until the tip of my nose is an inch from Justine's delicious-smelling cunt. I'm set to devour her like a crazed, hungry man, but my hunger isn't the only one being announced. Justine's stomach is grumbling loudly.

A smug grin stretches across my face when I crawl up Justine's body until we meet eye to eye. She's inwardly cursing my unexpected chivalry as much as my cock. "Soon, *Ангел*. Very soon." I bite her drooping lip before releasing it with a pop. "Once you've fed me, I'll feast on your tight little cunt as often as you like."

The sticky sheets cling to my body when I slip off the mattress before jerking up my chin, demanding for her to follow me to the kitchen. When she attempts to curl the paper-thin cotton around her body, a growl rumbles in my chest.

Her eyes snap to mine when I snatch the sheet from her hands, bundle it into a messy ball, then toss it into the middle of the bed. When I drag my finger across her collarbone, her breaths shudder as erratically as her thighs. She's not scared. She is turned on from me saying, "I examined every inch of your body last night. There wasn't a single section I didn't like, so don't ever hide it from me. Your body, when it's gripped by ecstasy, is as telling as your eyes. It shows the confidence you fail to exude."

I slant my head to hide my smile when she briefly nods in agreement before slipping her hand into mine to guide me to the kitchen. I'm not laughing at her. It's from realizing she's as clever as the devil, just ten times prettier.

34

JUSTINE

"That is not how you spell fuck. F. U. C. K. Not F. V. C. K," I argue when Nikolai places down the last of his tiles onto an overloaded Scrabble board.

"That's not a V. It's a U." Nikolai chuckles at my assumption he can't spell a curse word he regularly uses.

Even though his laugh hits every one of my hot buttons, I continue to argue, unwilling to back down since this is our third game, and we are tied one all. "No, it isn't a U. It's a V." I point to the offending tile. "That's why it's worth more points."

"You lost, *Ангел*. It's time to pay your debt. Lose the shirt." His words are barely audible since his sexy voice is hindered by laughter.

"No way. You cheated. Cheaters don't prosper."

I cross my arms over my chest, hating that my undefeated Scrabble streak was stolen by a man I never saw as a challenger. If I knew Nikolai's love of language was as extensive as mine, I would have picked another game to keep us entertained during a power-less night.

I hate losing—hate it!

With today's temperatures as scorching as my day with Nikolai, a massive storm rolled over Las Vegas in the late afternoon, plunging my apartment into darkness.

Nikolai and I have utilized the time well. We've spent hours talking, drinking wine, and testing out the sturdiness of every hard surface in my apartment. It has been a day unlike any I've ever had. It's been truly magical.

Away from his crew, Nikolai is an ideal man. He is kind, well-educated, and dominant. He can bring me to the brink of ecstasy as quickly as he can make my blood boil. It feels like a year has passed since our exchange on my couch yesterday afternoon, not just one measly day.

My eyes move like a missile to Nikolai when he warns, "Lose the shirt. Or I'll remove it myself."

Acting like his threat didn't roll through me like liquid ecstasy, I reply, "I'd like to see you try." My voice is crammed with attitude it doesn't usually project.

When his brow arches, I bolt for my bedroom door, certain my years of track will give me a good lead on his agility. It doesn't. He's on my heels in a matter of seconds.

I squeal like a teenage girl when he curls his arm around my waist and hoists me from the ground. It isn't solely the vibrancy firing in the air that's responsible for my playful response. It's my entire day.

A breathless chuckle escapes my lips when Nikolai and I tumble to the floor with a thud, thankfully giving me an excuse for the sentimental tears looming in my eyes. I roll to my side before crawling onto my knees, striving to stop him from yanking my shirt over my head.

It's a pointless endeavor. Nikolai has his target locked and loaded, and like the entire time I've known him, I'm defenseless to his charm.

The steamy conditions turn even more roasting when he drags my shirt over my head, exposing my erratically panting chest to his more-than-eager gaze.

"Now that wasn't so hard, was it?" He glances down at me, his eyes brimming with the natural arrogance I'm growing to love.

By the back of his head, I pull his lips onto mine. He groans against my mouth before he spears his tongue between my lips. I've lost count of the number of times we've kissed in the past thirty-six hours, but they seem to get better with every one we share. That probably has more to do with my rusty kissing skills than Nikolai's prowess.

A few hours ago, I was a novice.

Now I'm a professional.

After kissing me breathless, he withdraws from our embrace and stares at me in silence, his gaze attentive. "I never understood what Rico meant when he said his wife was his reward for years of misery..." –his eyes bounce between mine as the unidentifiable glint I spotted yesterday grows—"until you walked into my life. You're my little slice of heaven in a hot and temperamental place."

I graze my teeth over my bottom lip as I struggle to find words strong enough to express what his words mean to me. Thankfully, I'm saved from embarrassing myself when Nikolai's focus drops to my breasts. It's only been thirty-six hours, but I can confidently tell you that Nikolai Popov is most certainly a breast man.

He kneads my breasts, squeezing and sucking them until my nipples bud to a nearly painful point. The zinging pain diverts to my pussy when he encloses his mouth over my right areola. His mouth is warm and inviting, his tongue, wet.

I throw my head back and moan, overwhelmed by the sensations heating every inch of my body. I've been put through the wringer the past four years, but that is all set aside when Nikolai's mouth is on mine.

I love the dominance he displays in his kisses. The power of his strokes, the taste of his mouth, and how he kisses me as if he needs my lips on his more than he needs air. But more than anything, I love the way he makes me feel like I'm free. It's as if the past four years never happened.

"That's it, *Ангел*. Let me hear you," he requests when my moans ramp up a gear.

I purr softly, adoring the stubble on his chin grazing my stomach when his focus drops to a region of my body begging for his attention. He nips and bites on the squishy skin, enlarging my heart with every playful graze of his teeth. He worships my body as if it isn't covered with horrible scars, treasuring it as if it's perfect.

The heat of his breath fans my pussy when he growls out in a throaty purr, "*Ангел*, you're saturated."

As his fingers trace the seam of my panties, his eyes lift to me, soundlessly seeking permission. He's done the same thing since our first encounter in the bathroom over thirty-six hours ago.

I nod, incapable of articulating speech.

I can barely breathe, much less talk.

He wastes no time slipping my panties to the side before circling his lips around my clit. My hands dart out to secure a hold on something—anything—when he sucks my clit into his mouth.

They come up empty.

The power of his sucks overwhelms me. They're mind-hazing, leaving my mind vacant of cognitive thoughts. I pant, incredibly aroused by the deep groan he releases when his tongue delves into my soaked pussy.

"So fucking sweet. Tangy. Bitter. The tastiest cunt I've ever eaten."

The crudeness of his comment excites me more. I part my thighs before weaving my fingers through his hair so I can hold his mouth hostage to my slicked pussy. My bottom lip drops into a pout when he seizes my hands and pins them to my side. The sting of his fingers clamped around my wrists would usually cause a negative response from me, but since it's Nikolai, it sends my libido soaring.

"A real man eats without assistance," Nikolai growls, his Russian accent more pronounced.

Staring up at me, he devours my pussy without hindrance. His teeth graze my clit as his lips and tongue worship the rest.

"Ride my mouth like you ride my cock," he requests a short time later, his throaty voice sending a pleasurable zing from my nipples to my clit. "Fast and without restraint."

Since my arms are pinned to my side, I raise my backside off the wooden floor to rock against his mouth as requested. The strokes of his tongue and the weird sensation of my clit grinding against his nose drives me so wild I'm sitting on the brink of ecstasy in a shameful amount of time.

Not wanting to make a fool out of myself, I close my eyes and let my mind drift elsewhere.

My eyes pop back open when he bites my clit. "I'm starving to taste your arousal again, Justine. Don't make me wait any longer than I already have."

Blood floods my heart from him using my real name. More times than not, he refers to me as *Ангел*, which is Russian for angel, though his pronunciation is a little off. His nickname is sweet, but I much prefer it when he uses my name.

Then I know he is with me and only me.

Lust deprives the air of oxygen as I watch Nikolai consume me like a man starved of taste. His tongue glides up my pussy on repeat before he circles it around my clit. He sucks and tugs at my clit until a familiar tingle rolls across my stomach. It gains in intensity with every perfect caress, building to a point I can't hold it back.

I arch my back, my race to climax building so rapidly that I feel like I'm spiraling out of control. I'm hot all over and screaming without reservation. My cries of ecstasy spur on his pursuit. He licks, sucks, and worships my pussy like a man out of control—like a man who is insane.

I don't know who moans louder when my orgasm reaches fruition.

"That's it. Come for me, *Ангел*. Give me every scream. Let the world hear what I do to you," Nikolai groans, his voice as rough as my throat.

My head flops back as stars detonate in my eyes. I tremble in ecstasy while panting his name on repeat. The pace of his strokes grows more urgent with every shuddered syllable escaping my lips. I barely register him releasing my wrists from his dominant hold until he grips the curve of my ass and thrusts my hips forward.

"I don't want to miss a drop."

He mushes his mouth against my pussy, stretching my orgasm from one to two. My cries grow louder when he keeps his word. He slurps up every morsel of my arousal, only stopping once every excited tremble coursing through my body has been exhausted beyond reprieve.

When he lifts his head, the grin on his face—my god.

That grin will be the death of me.

"Just like everything you do, you come with perfection."

After one last peck to my pulsating clit, he crawls up my body, his movements effortless and agile. I taste myself on his lips when he seals them over my quaking mouth.

He has only just slipped his tongue between my lips when the buzz of a cell phone shrills through our ears. Nikolai groans. He knows who is calling without needing to look at the screen. It's Roman, making this his fifteenth call of the day.

Roman is more of a father to Nikolai than any man in his life, but I wish he'd quit calling. Every time Nikolai's cell phone flashes, his birthright is thrust back into the forefront of my mind.

Both Nikolai and I know our time is borrowed.

That's why we aren't wasting a single moment.

The past seventy-plus hours exceeded anything I could have imagined when I unknowingly invited a mafia prince to reside with me, but I know it's only a matter of time before the bubble we've been hiding in bursts.

If I could shelter Nikolai from his lifestyle forever, I would, but I can't. Eventually, his past will catch up with him. And with how frequently Roman has called the past three hours, I'd say it will be much sooner than anticipated.

When Nikolai's cell buzzes, announcing he has a new voice-mail message, he stands and heads to his phone resting on my coffee table. Even sexually satiated from two mind-hazing orgasms, I can't help but drink in his delicious frame. His walk is as arrogant as ever, a cocky swagger that leaves no suspicion of his self-assuredness.

I could learn a thing or two from his confidence. His body is as marked as mine, but his confidence exceeds mine tenfold. Although from how many compliments he has given me the past two days, I doubt low self-esteem will be a problem of mine much longer.

After listening to Roman's voicemail, Nikolai heads back to where I'm sprawled on the floor.

"Everything okay?" I ask when I spot the deep groove in the middle of his pulse-quaking eyes.

"Yep. Just laying down some foundations." His tone is as cryptic as his reply.

My body flops hard against his torso when he bobs down and gathers me in his arms. I nuzzle into his chest, loving how easily he carries me as he makes a beeline for my bedroom. My brows furl when his trek deviates from the path I'm anticipating. Instead of dumping me on the bed like he has numerous times so far today, he hooks the bed sheet around his forearm before taking a sharp left.

Balancing me with one hand, he slides open my balcony door. A dash of panic surfaces, but it's hardly noticeable since Nikolai drapes the bed sheet in front of my body before stepping outside.

I purr like a kitten when he sits in the rickety old sun lounger shoved in the back corner of the tiny space. I'm not purring because I'm cold. It's from feeling his monstrous cock brush against my ass when he pulls me to sit on his lap.

After ensuring the bed sheet is covering the intimate parts of my body, he draws me into his chest. "You said you've never seen the lights of Vegas. I can't take you to the strip, but I can show you the best show Vegas has to offer."

He nudges his head to the skyline peeking above the rooftops. With the hours burning away more quickly than I'd like, the black sky is transforming into a mottled gray color as the sun prepares to rise.

I sigh, loving Nikolai's thoughtfulness but hating the reality behind it. Once that sun rises, everything will change. By 9 a.m., I'm once again Justine, a first-year intern at Schluter & Fletcher, and Nikolai will be the man he has always been: a Russian mafia prince.

"Do you know every sunrise is unique? It isn't defined by the night before's sunset. It's free to do whatever it wants." He runs his hand down my arm, drawing me into him even more deeply. "That's what we'll do, *Ангел*. We're going to live every day as if it's a new one."

I smile against his chest, adoring his silent pledge that our bizarre kinship isn't ending just yet. "You know we're going to have an uphill battle. We've got the world against us," I murmur, expressing the concerns lingering in my mind since our run-in with Vladimir yesterday afternoon.

Nikolai said it himself. Anything he wants, his father takes.

Does that include me?

He shakes his head, the determination radiating from him in invisible waves. "I've got it all worked out. You just wait and see."

I peel off his chest to peer into his eyes. "You've got everything worked out?" My voice is jeering even though I see the honesty in his wide gaze. "Am I going to get a say in any of this?"

The murky cloud in his eyes clears away as his cock stiffens beneath me. He'd never admit it, but I'm confident he likes the idea of having a person standing beside him instead of three paces back. That's why he's been striving to rebuild my confidence.

A king needs a queen, not a servant.

Acting like I can't feel an odd sensation sweeping over me, I ask, "What's this brilliant plan you're hiding up your sleeve?"

He adjusts me until I'm snuggled back into his torso, facing the sky that is getting lighter by the second, before saying, "First, my attorney needs to get this fucking thing off me. It's annoying as fuck."

He taps his ankle monitor against my leg, ensuring I know who he wants counseling his case.

When I nod, acknowledging I understand his request, he continues. "Second, we'll get things straight with your brother. If it weren't for him, your fine ass wouldn't be heating my cock right now."

The playfulness of his tone does nothing to dampen the emotional punch his promise inflicts on me. Tears pool in my eyes as my heart triples in size. Maddox needs as many people on his side as possible, but having a man as powerful as Nikolai take up his cause is more than I could have ever hoped for.

"And the third?" My words are brittle, cracked by the sob in the back of my throat dying to break free. Although I'm on the verge of crying, for the first time in years, my tears are not ones of sorrow. They're happy tears. "Everyone knows good things come in threes, Nikolai. So, what's the last item on your wish list?"

His chest rises and falls at a slow, rhythmic pace four times before he mutters, "I'm going to kill my father."

35

NIKOLAI

Have you ever wanted something so bad you're willing to kill for it? That's what I felt the instant my eyes locked on Justine. I could practically taste her innocence on my tongue when she stood across from me, riling me up like the life in her eyes hadn't been snuffed years ago. The thrill of the chase ran through my blood so fast that, for the first time in years, I felt like I had a heart sitting in my chest. Its beat was weak and cold, but it was thumping nonetheless.

It had only been hours since I had a woman's warmth wrapped around my cock, but my hunger for Justine was uninhibited. Her scent was so intoxicating that my arrogance fed off it. I craved it like a drug, willing to give up everything to have it embedded in my skin —even my freedom.

A quick slip of hands was all it took, and my application for house arrest was switched with Justine's. With dollar signs flashing in his eyes, protecting Justine's privacy wasn't on the mind of the corrupt officer when he accepted the terms of our agreement. His buy-off was the cheapest I've negotiated, but it will cost him more than he ever perceived. He is a loose end. One I don't need as I endeavor to fix all the mistakes I've made.

I thought one taste of Justine would be enough.

I had no fucking clue.

She is the worst drug on the market, more potent than the most addictive substances I've sold. Every taste I have of her has me craving another. At a time when I should be most vigilant, I can't think, sleep, or eat, as I'm too busy plotting a way to get another sample of her. I don't wine or dine—fuck, I don't even date—but I'll button up a suit and break out a razor if it guarantees Justine's lips on mine. I'll do anything to get another taste of her.

I'll even slit the throat of the man who raised me.

They say revenge is a dish best served cold, but Vladimir won't be that lucky. I was maimed, beaten, and tortured as he groomed me to be a natural-born killer, and he is going to discover the hard way how precise his tactics were.

Disrespecting my family is as punishable as disrespecting me. Justine is now my family, and I'll spill the blood of a thousand men before I let anyone take her away from me.

This devil needs his rest, and Justine is the angel who can give it to me.

The end... *or is it?*

Nikolai's next story is already available. You can find it here:

Love what you've read? Join my Facebook page to keep updated.
www.facebook.com/authorshandi

Hunter, Hugo, Hawke, Ryan, Cormack, Rico & Brax stories have already been released, as has Brandon, Regan. All the other great characters of Ravenshoe will be getting their own stories sometime during 2024

Nikolai
RESURRECTING
THE BRATVA

USA TODAY BESTSELLING AUTHOR
SHANDI BOYES

COPYRIGHT

© Shandi Boyes 2018

Edited by: Mountains Wanted Publishing

Second Edit: Courtney Umphress

Proofing: Lindsi La Bar

Cover: SSB Designs - edits made to stock photo

Photographer: Ren Saliba

15/02/24

1

NIKOLAI

"Nikolai..." Justine's throat works hard to swallow before she forces out the rest of her sentence past the thump. "You can't kill your father. Y-y-you can't."

My knuckles popping when I clench my fists is the only audible noise over the manic beat of her heart. The lust in her eyes has faded, but that's not what has rendered me mute. I'm silent because of the terror in her eyes. Over the past thirty-six hours, I've worked hard to renew the life our exchange with Vladimir stole from her eyes, and now that prick is once again dousing it.

Vladimir may be the man who raised me, but he is *not* my father. All Vladimir's children have eyes darkened by the ashes they were born in, so my icy-blue eyes had me combatting suspicions most of my childhood. Believing they were spoken by vindictive men wishing they were me, I brushed them off as envy.

Little did I know every sneered taunt was true.

I am the byproduct of a woman pushed to the brink by a man she loved. Desperate and delusional, my mother pledged to birth Vladimir a son at any cost—even her life.

I am the result of that guarantee.

I was raised as a prince in one world, where, in reality, I am king of another.

"It's either me or him, *Ангел*. Who would you prefer?" The tic in my jaw grows. I didn't mean for my tone to come out the way it did, sharp and direct, one I generally reserve for my crew.

Justine isn't a member of my crew. She's unlike any woman I've met. She is smart, has a face that could bring men to ecstasy just looking at it, and has a body more sinful than Satan, but that's not why I'm attracted to her.

It is the woman I see behind the shield. The one who didn't cower when going head-to-head with a mafia prince. The one who battled the most vicious man in my crew and survived without a scratch on her. That's the woman I crave like a drug, not the one staring at me with a pained expression.

Although worry continues clouding Justine's eyes, its rate slows when I run my index finger down her cheek before it drifts along her collarbone. She breathes noisily when my trek moves to the small bite marks gracing the top of her shoulder.

She hates her scars, but I think they're beautiful. They reveal that even angels can be sent to hell and come out stronger than they went in.

If someone so innocent can survive Satan's wrath, who's to say I can't do the same?

"I can't keep my promise if he remains breathing, *Ангел*."

Justine's breathing switches from pants to gasps when my hand drops to her breasts. I glide my finger over her budded nipple. When it hardens more from my meekest touch, the heaviness on my chest is pushed aside for smugness. I love how she responds to my touch, her desires more potent than her worry.

"He'll take this away from me." I lift and lock my eyes with hers. "He'll take you away from me. I'd rather slit his throat than let him come between us again."

Tears glisten in her aquamarine eyes as her teeth graze her bottom lip. She doesn't need to speak for me to hear her internal battle. I can see it in her eyes, smell it on her skin. She isn't worried about Vladimir. She's concerned about what this will do to me.

She doesn't need to fret. Being raised in the shadows of a monster means I learned his greatest tricks. I know how Vladimir thinks. I know what makes him tick. So no man in the world is more suitable for this task than me.

"There must be another way, Nikolai. Murder can't be your only option..."

Justine's words trail off when I shake my head. "There's no other way. What I said was true. Anything I want, Vladimir takes. But I'll be fucked if I let him take you away from me. I will not give you up, Justine. Not in a million years."

An offer sneered in Russian nearly lost me the chance of making Justine mine. I will not fuck it up a second time.

Roman is like a father to me. He's been my "uncle" since the day I was born, but I wanted to slice the tendons in his thighs and watch him fall to his knees when he suggested I use Justine's scars to diminish Vladimir's interest in her.

I should have cut out his tongue for even suggesting Justine was anything but perfect, but instead, I took the coward's way out, deciding Justine's safety was more vital than maintaining her dignity.

I was wrong.

The look on Justine's face when she discovered what I had done cut me raw. I've fought in the most brutal battles—my body wears the medals of my triumphs—but not one scar I've endured my past twenty-eight years maimed me as much as when it dawned on Justine what I had done. The pain in her eyes scorched my soul, issuing me with a wound I'll carry for eternity.

That wound didn't just confirm I have a heart beating in my chest. It struck me down from a god to a mere man. I was raised believing I was a prince and those beneath me were my servants.

Now I realize that isn't true.

There's only one king in this story. I am not him. I'm the pawn he mind-fucked to seek revenge.

I am not his son.

I am not even his sergeant.

I am the man who will teach him his greatest lesson.

An eye for an eye.

A life for a life.

A crown for a crown.

Vladimir fucked with what is mine, and now he'll pay the ultimate price. It's time for the king to be removed from his throne, and who better to do that than the man who will take his place?

2

JUSTINE

Too shocked to express words, I stare at Nikolai. From the information I unearthed about Vladimir over the past four days, I know every word Nikolai speaks is valid, but it doesn't make them any easier to hear.

Vladimir is a reincarnation of the devil. He's a man who'd rather slay the weak than offer them a hand off the ground, but murder can't be the only solution to defeat him.

I know from personal experience how deadly revenge is to an ethical mind. It wreaks havoc with the most honorable men. But more times than not, when the person seeking vengeance doesn't achieve the outcome they set out for, their thoughts turn even more sinister.

I wanted to look Col Petretti in the eyes as he took his last breath. When that opportunity was taken away from me, I felt hollow and bleak. The man who haunted my dreams was dead, but instead of being grateful, I was angry. I wanted to be the one who made him pay his penance. I wanted to show him what he did to me didn't affect me. But more than anything, I wanted to see the look on his face when my brother walked out of prison a free man, because the best revenge you can achieve is showing those who hurt you how great your life is after you've been scorned.

When I say that to Nikolai, the tenseness in his eyes grows

tenfold. Heat crackles in the air as the tic in his jaw turns manic. Although his eyes show he doesn't appreciate my continued arguing, my campaign doesn't falter. I said minutes ago that he needs someone strong enough to stand next to him, not three paces back, so that is precisely what I will do.

"I understand you want revenge, Nikolai—"

"It's not revenge," he interrupts, his voice gravelly and thick. "It's taking back what's mine and proving I'm more of a man than Vladimir raised me to be. You said it yourself, *Ангел*. I may have been born into this lifestyle, but it only became my life when I let it. It's time to take back what's rightfully mine. Killing my father is the only way I can do that."

I freeze, paralyzed by my own words. I didn't realize when they stumbled out in anger that they would significantly impact him. I intended to show him a world outside his family. I didn't expect them to encourage murder.

My lips twitch, preparing to continue my plea, but Nikolai squashes his finger against my mouth. "No more," he commands, his tone gruffer than usual. "We have hours, *Ангел*. I don't want to waste another second debating a matter not up for discussion. I've made my decision. Nothing you could say will change it."

I stare at him as my brain compiles the facts. From the way he pursued me, I can confidently declare he's a determined man who goes after what he wants with a ruthless edge you can't help but admire, so the chance of me altering his mindset is practically impossible, but what sort of woman would I be if I sat back and watched the man I'm growing to admire dwindle into half the man he is?

"You said I'd be worth three days in lockup. You never said I'd be worth a lifetime in hell."

I head for the open balcony door before Nikolai can comprehend what's happening. The sun is barely peeking over the skyline, but the fireworks raging in my gut overtake my desire to witness the ultimate Vegas light show.

After throwing a dress over my shuddering frame, I pack my belongings. I don't know why I'm the one leaving when this is my apartment, but my emotions are in such turmoil my flight mode mechanism has kicked into overdrive.

"What are you doing?" Nikolai asks from his station at the

balcony door. His tone would make grown men wet their pants, but my stupid body reacts on the opposite end of the spectrum.

I'm turned on by his deep timbre, not scared.

Sickened by the lust-craved idiot I've become the past thirty-six hours, I head to my closet to pull down my suitcase stored on top.

I've barely yanked down the heavy object when Nikolai snatches it from my grasp and propels it across the room. It smashes into the far wall with a thud, proving its guarantee to withstand any pressure was fraudulent.

"You are not leaving, Justine," he warns, his words so volatile they are spat off his tongue in rapidly fired hits.

I snap my eyes to him, the anger in them doubling from his assumption I can't leave of my own free will.

There was only one time I was told I couldn't leave—it ended with me being mauled by a dog.

"Don't tell me what to do, Nikolai. You don't own me. Nobody does." My voice cracks with emotions at the end. I know he would never hurt me, but haunted memories are holding my vocal cords hostage.

When Nikolai's face lines with anger, I rush to the door, the value of my belongings not high enough to worry about leaving them behind.

Possessions can be replaced.

Values can't.

A squeal bellows from my parched mouth when Nikolai beats me to the door, snapping it shut with so much violence the wood trim around the doorjamb loosens.

My lungs hunt for air when he curls around my back. His body temperature is as hot and brooding as my mood, a dangerous combination of anger and need.

"I don't take anything not willingly given, but help me god, I will fuck you where you stand if that's the only way you'll learn who you belong to. I may not yet own your mind, *Ангел*, but I own every inch of your body," he hisses into my ear.

I arch my back, despising how my body heightened with anticipation from the fury in his clipped tone. "A weekend fuckfest doesn't imply ownership."

He slants toward me, turning what should be an honest declaration into a lie. "The moment I slipped my cock into you, I asked if you understood what that meant. You said you did. Are you saying you lied?"

"No," I reply with a shake of my head. "I knew what you meant."

In that instant, I became his. My body knows it. Nikolai knows it. It's just my brain failing to get the memo.

"But that doesn't mean I'll sit by and watch you make a mistake you can't take back. I'd rather run through the gauntlet again than have you kill a man for me."

"When the choice is to kill or be killed, I'd rather kill," Nikolai snarls, his words not as volatile as earlier.

"That can't be the only option. That can't be your only choice," I mumble, my voice breaking into a sob.

I'm not tearing up at the prospect of him becoming a killer—his laid-back attitude toward the potential loss of life the past four days leaves no doubt Vladimir won't be his first hit. It is the thought of him being killed flooding my eyes with moisture.

"If there were another option that would guarantee you the same level of safety, I would take it. But there are no other options. You are my weak spot, and the instant Vladimir discovers that, he'll use it to his advantage."

I love how protective he is, and that in such a short period of time, I've crawled so profoundly under his skin that he's willing to do anything to protect me. But do I love those traits enough that I'm willing to let it supplant my morals?

I'd like to say no, but since I value integrity highly, I keep my mouth shut.

Sensing that my fighting stance is weakening, Nikolai continues chipping at my hostility. "I gave you my word that I'd never let anything happen to you." He gathers my hair to the side, exposing my neck to his torturous lips. "I'm going to keep my word," he murmurs into my ear before placing a peppering of kisses down my neckline.

"Are you sure there isn't any other option?" I mumble through a moan.

My contradictory responses can't be helped. Nikolai's lips are as dangerous to my ethics as his handsome face. One touch and my reservations combust as readily as my senses.

"There's only been one time I've been more certain." His

wintry-blue eyes spear me in place with their intensity. "It was knowing I had to make you mine."

I moan again—louder this time.

While lavishing my neck so effectively the turmoil in my stomach drops several inches lower, his fingers skim the side boob my free-flowing dress can't conceal. He's barely touching me, but my skin sets on fire with every movement he makes. I'm practically panting, my eagerness at the swift change in our exchange leaving me breathless.

"I'll protect you and keep you safe." The misting of sweat on my neck amplifies when he slips his hand beneath the loose material of my dress to cup my breast. "I'll stop at nothing to ensure the world knows if they mess with you, they're messing with me." Every word spoken coincides with a tweak of my nipple.

I lean into him more deeply, encouraging his pursuit no matter what objections my brain fires.

I want him—anywhere and anyhow—and no matter the cost.

"But first, before any of that, I'm going to remind you who you belong to." His possessive growl turns me on more than I could ever articulate.

I should be ashamed I'm allowing my desires for this man to overrule my astuteness, but I'm not. Just his lips on my neck make my inhibitions falter, so what chance do I stand after hearing his pledge of protection?

None.

I am defenseless to him.

"Tell me you want this," Nikolai pleads as his hand slithers across my stomach to draw me in even closer. I purr when he grinds his erection against the globes of my ass, ensuring I know what his question refers to.

"I want this," I say in a hushed whisper, my voice full of need. "I want you."

You'd think continued sexual contact over a prolonged period would weaken the hold he has over me.

It hasn't.

Not in the slightest.

His influence over my body is more powerful now than ever. How he switched my devastation to excitement within seconds reveals how significant it is.

"Turn around and face me. I want your eyes on me," Nikolai demands, his voice husky with arousal.

When I do as requested without qualm, his lips curve upward. He isn't shocked by my obedient response. He's pleased.

I learned quickly that passiveness is well-rewarded by Nikolai. The more submissive I am, the more mind-hazing our interactions are.

My heart kicks into a mad beat when he crouches down in front of me. "Put your leg over my shoulder," he requests before fisting the hem of my dress.

Not the least bit concerned two bite marks will be thrust into his view, I curl my right leg over his shoulder, devoid of a negative thought.

His ardent stare ensures not a snick of hesitation thickens my blood. He idolizes me as much as I crave him, so I refuse to let two measly marks hamper our exchange.

"Now watch me eat the tastiest cunt I've ever eaten," he growls out before his tongue spears between the folds of my pussy.

I cry out, my desire heightened beyond belief when he loses control on my pussy. He sucks, licks, and nibbles on my aching clit, causing waves to crest in my stomach before they crash into my womb.

With my clit still sensitive from earlier stimulation, the pressure in my pussy is too great to overlook. "I don't think I can hold back for long," I warn, my voice as colorful as my cheeks.

Nikolai smiles against my soaked sex before his effort to have me spiraling into climax doubles. He sucks down hard on my clit as his fingers join the Derail Justine Train.

He pumps two fingers into me before quickly switching to three. Even stretched to a point where it hurts, I moan on repeat, a more intelligent response beyond me.

The sensation is overwhelming, charging my desire to climax to within an inch of the finish line.

"Oh god, Nikolai. I can't. I don't think I can come. I'm too sensitive," I mumble a short time later.

My words are whimpered with devastation.

I'm so worked up that I feel over-coiled.

Can an orgasm build at a rate so fast it will never break? If so, that's what is happening to me now.

"Ohhh," I moan in a throaty growl when Nikolai's teeth graze my clit before he tugs on it—hard.

The weight of my leg on his shoulder doubles when the sudden arrival of an orgasm blindsides me. My mouth dries as perspiration beads on my skin. I convulse without reservation, my climax too powerful for a restrained reply.

"That's it, *Ангел*. Give it to me," Nikolai murmurs against my drenched pussy. "Give me every fucking drop of your goodness."

I moan on repeat, adoring that he brought my climax to fruition with the same aggressiveness our exchange began with.

Before Nikolai, any type of hostility was a turn-off. Now I can't get enough. I relish every graze of his teeth, mark of his hand, and pounding of his cock.

His touch is like a drug.

The more I have it, the more I want it.

I shudder uncontrollably when Nikolai scoops me into his arms and moves us across the room. With my lungs void of oxygen, all the weight in my body relocates to my eyelids.

I'm exhausted—both mentally and physically.

Not letting my tiredness impede him, he places me on the mattress on my hands and knees. My face smushes into my pillow when he raises my ass high into the air, erotically staging me for his visual pleasure.

Even being the most exhausted I've ever been doesn't stop me from cranking my neck to peer at him as I hear him unzip his pants.

"Oh, sweet Jesus," I whisper when his thick, rigid cock springs free from his jeans.

Every vein in his body is working hard to feed his cock, making it so mouthwateringly delicious that I'm tempted to fall to my knees and devour him with the same wickedness he conveyed consuming me. The only thing stopping me is the image of him tearing open a condom with his teeth.

I stare, mesmerized and shameless when he rolls the condom down his thick shaft. I never knew a mundane task could be so riveting. That thin sheet of latex should offer protection from STIs and pregnancy, but it is much more symbolic than that.

It is the only thing stopping me from being wholly consumed by Nikolai. Without a condom, there would be nothing between us. That is how close we've become this weekend.

I raise my eyes to Nikolai's face when I feel the heat of his gaze on me. He's staring at me, hot and devoted. "I'd give up everything I have before I'd give this up," he grinds out as the head of his cock dips between the folds of my pussy. He coats himself in my arousal, his actions as enticing as his sweet-talking gaze. "A thousand men couldn't keep me from you, Justine." He swipes the crown of his cock over my clit, sending a jolt across every inch of me. "So what chance does one man have?"

He thrusts into me so hard my hands clutch the bedding in a white-knuckle hold as a mangled groan rolls up my chest.

He stills for a moment, giving me a chance to acclimate to his sheer girth—a painstaking few seconds filled with nervous excitement.

Lust has thickened my blood, but I didn't miss the hidden innuendo in Nikolai's statement. Even guiding me through a star-detonating climax hasn't diminished his determination one bit.

He's out for revenge, and his target is his father.

As he has for every second of every minute of every hour since I've known him, Nikolai puts my mind and body on opposing teams. He works my body with the knowledge a man who has only known me for days shouldn't have, immediately blurring the line between right and wrong.

He drives me to the brink, proving lust is more poisonous to an ethical mind than revenge.

He fucks me until I'm as convinced as he is.

There's no other option. His father must die, because falling in love is beautiful, but it is keeping the connection alive that can make things ugly.

3

NIKOLAI

Justine runs her hand down the gold drop earring she threaded into her ear as her eyes lift to the vanity mirror she's been in front of for the past thirty minutes.

She sighs, disappointed by the woman glancing back at her.

With her shorts and casual tee replaced with a knee-length skirt and a shimmery blouse, she's once again Justine, a first-year defense attorney, not a woman who spent the past four days living in a world she knew existed but one she had no idea she craved.

The way Justine talks about her job leaves no doubt she loves it, but her eyes don't hold half the light they do when I'm balls deep inside her. That is when the real Justine comes out to play—when I take her to the brink of insanity.

She says she can't think when I'm inside her. I don't believe a fucking word. I've watched her so intensely the past few days I know what she's thinking at the precise time she is thinking it.

Justine believes she craves normalcy.

She doesn't.

She's desperate to break out of the dull existence she's been living for the past four years. She wants to be free of the burden her brother's incarceration has put on her life.

She wants to live.

And I'll make sure she does precisely that.

Pushing off my feet, I head into the bathroom. Call me cocky, but I know my touch is the only thing needed to weather Justine through her latest battle.

I have the respect of hundreds and am feared by thousands, but I've never felt more powerful than I do when my hands are on Justine.

Her response to my touch is explosive, unlike anything I've ever experienced.

Torture can bend the will of any man, but only my touch can bow the resolve of the most influential woman I've ever met.

That power is addictive.

One I'm growing to crave even more than respect.

Justine's gaze meets mine in the mirror. Her breaths quicken as the natural pink hue of her cheeks descends to her collarbone. "Nikolai..." she breathes out in warning, reading the determination in my eyes. "We don't have time. I have to be at work in under an hour."

Ignoring the silent plea in her slanted gaze, I continue my mission.

I don't need an hour to switch the worry in her eyes to lust.

I don't even need a minute.

The scent of her floral perfume smacks into me when I curl my arm around her waist and draw her to my body. Her soft plea for clemency switches to a moan when she feels the effect only she has on me.

She isn't the only one defenseless in our bizarre union. One sideways glance, one tug of her lips, or one breathless pant, and I'm fucking done.

I want her more desperately than my lungs desire their next breath.

I'm so hard it's the fight of my life not to bend her over the bathtub and replace her scent with my own. But since an hour isn't long enough to get my fill, and the fact our condom supply has been depleted to zilch the past two days, I harness my desire.

Barely.

Instead of devouring her sweet cunt like a man starved of taste, I run my thumb over her plump lips before dipping it into her mouth.

Like the good, obedient woman she is, Justine wraps her lips around my thumb before sucking down hard.

I groan as my cock hardens more. She smiles, loving my unrestrained response. She loves forcing me out of my comfort zone—pushing me into a world I'd prefer to fuck over than live in.

When she worships my thumb with the same attentiveness she usually reserves for my cock, I lose all control. I arch her over the bathtub before running my hand down the bumps of her spine, counting every little groove on my torturously slow trek.

Justine is a fighter, but even she knows every dip, curve, and crevice on her body belongs to me—and only me.

"Ah, *Ангел*. I've barely touched you, and you're already dripping for me," I hiss through clenched teeth when my hand cups her glistening pussy barely concealed by the meager pair of panties she's wearing.

I've already threatened to cut off Carmichael's cock if he gets within an inch of Justine, but her panties have me wanting to issue a whole new threat.

This one is more sinister than any I've given.

Her knees curve inward when I snap her lace thong off her body, my desire to have her shouting my name too urgent to slide it down her thighs.

I tuck her shredded panties into my pocket before yanking at my fly. "Hold on to the bathtub, *Ангел*. This will be hard and fast," I warn her while releasing my cock from the tight constraints strangling it. "I'd like to take my time with you, but that must wait until tonight."

Her molten-red hair falls from her shoulders when she hesitantly nods. My chest puffs high, smug as fuck by her obliging gesture. She's not only a beautiful woman. She is also smart. Her agreement will award her a mind-hazing orgasm and will see her claimed in a way she's never been claimed before.

She'll have all of me—wholly and without restraint.

I'm going to make her mine for life.

Justine's cries of ecstasy bounce around the bathroom when I slam into her in one eager thrust. Her pussy is tight, not the slightest bit damaged from the poundings I've been giving it the past two days. It hugs my cock, clenching around me so firmly I could blow my load right now.

I draw my cock out to the tip before ramming it back in more furiously than my first thrust, agitated at how quickly she makes me lose my mind. I've fucked more women than I can count, but not one has caused me to lose control like Justine does. Like my touch sparks her eyes with life, her touch bombards me with reckless thoughts that could get me killed—thoughts that could get *her* killed.

I thrust into her harder, punishing her with my cock for how weak she makes me. If I want to protect her as promised, I need to be strong. I need to be the killer I was born to be, not a soft cock crippled by a woman.

That is what got my brother killed.

I will not be as stupid as Rico.

I have no intentions of giving Justine up, but I need to play this game with the ruthlessness its brutality deserves. If I don't do that, neither Justine nor I will walk out of this alive.

If it were solely my life hanging in the balance, I'd feed off the torment, but my decisions don't solely affect me anymore.

I promised Justine I'd keep her safe.

I'm going to keep my promise, no matter what the cost.

Skin slapping skin booms around the bathroom as I fuck Justine like a madman—like I am possessed. She takes it all in stride, moaning my name on repeat and begging for me to slam into her even harder. She knows I'm taking my anger out on her, but determined to stand by my side, she's put her body on the line to prove it. She'd let me do anything to her. I can see it in her eyes, smell it on her skin.

She is as far gone as me.

I roll my hips with every pump, raising her throaty moans to ball-clenching screams. "That's it, *Ангел,* scream for me. Let me hear how much you're enjoying this."

My voice is rough with endorphins but doesn't hold its usual arrogance. I'm getting lost in the moment, allowing the thrill of the hunt to overtake my worry.

After tightening my grip on Justine's hip, my other hand moves to her clit. I roll the firm bud, still sensitive from our exchange earlier this morning, in the same rhythm I'm pumping into her.

She moans even louder, washing away some of the chaos tormenting my mind. I love the way my mind is blank of thoughts when I'm fucking her. I've barely had a moment of quiet my entire life, but that is all null and void the instant she caresses my cock.

It doesn't matter if it's her hand, her mouth, or her tight little cunt, nothing but driving her to the brink filters through my mind when she's near me.

"Oh god, please. Oh god," Justine sings as her clutch on the bathtub firms. "I'm going to come, Nikolai. I'm going to..." Her words trail off as her head flops forward.

"Fuck!" I groan when her pussy clamps around my cock, milking it with the same ferocity I'm fucking her with.

I hold on to her tightly, squeezing her clit and pumping into her in the rhythm her body is shaking.

Moaning my name on repeat, she rides the waves of ecstasy. The sight of her in climax is a spectacular visual. She uses every inch of her body when she comes, leaving nothing behind until she is a whimpering, quivering mess.

Feeling like a god, I thrust into her another three times before the tingling sensation in my balls grows too intense to overlook.

My fingers flex against her hip as cum rockets out of my cock in savage, raring spurts. Justine's thighs shake when the heat of my seed coats the walls of her pussy.

She knows what this means without me needing to speak.

She is mine—wholly and without reservation.

She belongs to me.

And I'll slit the throat of any man who dares to say any different.

4

NIKOLAI

I've barely finished cleaning the mess I made in Justine's snug cunt when a doorbell ringing shrills into the bathroom.

Justine stiffens as her eyes rocket to the door. Her uneased response puts me so on edge I reach for my knife instead of my clothes.

Most men think guns are the best defense in any war.

They aren't.

You can't prepare for an attack you don't see coming. More times than not, my knife is pressed against my target's jugular before he even knows I'm in the room.

That's why I'm called The Snake.

You'll never hear me coming, and my strike is deadlier than a cobra's.

Justine sucks in a sharp breath when I snap open the blade of my trusty knife. I've had this knife for years. It's seen me through many battles.

"What are you doing, Nikolai? It's probably just Ms. Aaronson startled by my screams," she theorizes as her wide eyes bounce between me and the open bathroom door.

I nearly laugh at her innocence, but not wanting to scare her before I've fully acclimated her to my lifestyle, I store away my laughter along with my knife before shadowing her into her living room.

My lips arch high from her wobbly steps. If I had it my way, she wouldn't be walking upright for a week, but with Vladimir's suspicions at a pinnacle, I don't have a week to spare.

I need to act quickly, but I also need to be smart. Vladimir doesn't trust his own sons, so I'll have the fight of my life to catch him unaware.

With Justine's apartment being the smallest I've resided in, we reach the foyer in no time. Her guest hasn't even knocked for a second time.

She waits for me to pull my jeans up my thighs before she curls her hand around the door handle.

"Ms. Aaronson, sorry about the noise," she says with a grimace, slowly prying open her door. "I promise to keep it on the down-low from now on."

"No fucking chance," I growl out without remorse.

I wasn't lying when I said she's more potent than any drug I've sold. Her screams give me more of a high than any substance I've taken. I don't care if she wakes up the entire continent. I'd rather be buried in a shallow ditch than have her hold back the power I have over her body.

After issuing me a sneaky stink eye, revealing she heard my mumbled comment, Justine finishes opening her door.

The itch to kill smacks into me when the blemish on the back of her knees spreads to her cheeks. She fumbles out an awkward "good morning" before gesturing for her unexpected guest to enter her apartment.

My fingers skim my knife when the cuff of a black business suit announces who Justine's visitor is before he enters the foyer.

Carmichael I'm-Going-to-Gut-Him-Alive Fletcher.

"Mr. Fletcher. Hi," Justine greets him, tugging on the hem of her skirt, suddenly mindful she's missing her panties.

My jaw tics when Carmichael runs his eyes down Justine's body. His eyes possess the same arrogant assuredness they held when he nibbled at the bait I dangled in front of him four days ago.

He still thinks he's in with a chance of dipping his fingers into Justine's pie. I can't fucking wait to gloat to him that I stole the pie out of the oven before it had even finished baking.

Justine appears nervous in Carmichael's presence, but her stammering composure has nothing to do with excitement.

She's wary of my reaction to his unannounced arrival.

She doesn't need to fret.

As much as I'd love to show Carmichael exactly how under my spell she is, and for him to feel the wrath of my blade, for now, I can't act on either of my desires.

I don't give a fuck about Justine's position being compromised by our relationship—there's nothing illegal about an attorney and a client having a sexual connection. I can't run the risk of my family finding out about how deeply she's crawled under my skin.

Until all my cards have been dealt, and all the chips are on my side of the table, as far as anyone is concerned, Justine is part of my defense team—nothing more.

Carmichael's long strides into the living room falter when he spots me standing at the side, glaring at him. I can smell the fear leaking from his pores, but he greets me with a chin dip like he's not on the verge of pissing his pants before he drinks in the drooping candles Justine lit last night when her apartment plunged into blackness.

When his narrowed gaze stops on a puddle of wax in the middle of the living room floor, my smug grin grows.

Justine and I made good use of that hot wax last night.

I'm hard now just thinking about how delectable she looked with wax dripping over her skin.

Justine is a beautiful woman, but she's an absolute knockout when she lets go of her inhibitions.

The more Carmichael's eyes absorb the erotic-smelling space, the more his eyes slit. He knows I achieved in days what he couldn't do in months. I stole the girl he wants from right under his nose, and there isn't a single fucking thing he can do about it.

Not if he wants to live.

When Carmichael returns his eyes to Justine, she mumbles, "We had a power outage last night." Her usually smooth voice is throaty, exposing I'm not the only one recalling fun memories.

Carmichael's lips crimp as he nods. He isn't buying Justine's excuse for the heady aroma hanging thickly in the air, but my warning glare stuffed his true response down his throat before he could issue it.

His mute response isn't shocking. He knows from experience that one wrong word will render him void of a tongue.

He was lucky he left our last tussle breathing.

He won't be as fortunate a second time around.

"What do you want, Carmichael?" I ask, moving our conversation forward. The sooner he reveals why he's arrived at Justine's apartment unannounced, the faster he can leave and never return.

While folding his coat over his forearm like the pompous snob he is, he says, "It took a bit of wrangling, but I secured you an in-chambers hearing with Judge Marco at 8 a.m."

"Bennett Marco?" I ask, wanting to make sure we're on the same page.

I don't trust Carmichael as far as I can throw him, so I'll always add an extra buffer of arrogance to our exchanges.

If he hadn't arrived with Justine in tow on Friday, his firm wouldn't be associated with my name in any form. Guaranteed.

Hate is a strong word, but I can use it without hesitation when describing Carmichael.

When Carmichael nods, confirming my suspicion, a glint of recognition sparks in Justine's eyes, revealing she knows of Judge Marco's infamous reputation.

Bennett Marco is an extremely wealthy man. None of his capital was amassed legally. He's been an acquaintance of my father's for longer than I've been alive. Their friendship has generated more business opportunities in the past thirty-three years than the entire alumnus of Dartmouth College's renowned school of business.

"Who organizes an in-chambers hearing outside of official court hours?" Justine questions, moving to stand between Carmichael and me, her tone rife with suspicion.

Carmichael doesn't need to answer Justine's question. His deep exhalation tells her everything she needs to know.

This deal is as shady as a used car salesman seeking a Christmas bonus big enough for both his family and the hooker he wants to fuck in the ass.

I wouldn't expect anything less since the meeting was organized by Vladimir at my request.

Justine's wide eyes dart to mine when I ask, "What terms is he requesting?" I asked for Vladimir's help, but that doesn't mean I'll walk into this blind. Especially since I promised to protect Justine with everything I have *after* requesting his assistance.

Dollar signs flash in Carmichael's eyes as he replies, "That we arrive in his chambers no later than 8 a.m." His tone is way too showy for my liking. He thinks he's running the show. I have news for him. The wheels were already in motion. He's just the lackey chauffeuring the big hitters to the game. "He's announcing his retirement before preliminary hearings this morning. He wants all his *loose ends* tied up before then."

Justine sighs, confirming she heard Carmichael as intended. Judge Marco's retirement is being funded by me. "You don't have to go, Nikolai." She slings her eyes to me before stepping closer, wordlessly announcing whose side she's on. "You are within your rights to follow the schedule appointed during your arraignment. You simply need to advise your attorney of your wishes." When Carmichael attempts to interrupt her, she slices her hand through the air, stopping him mid-sentence. "Our client has rights. I'm merely ensuring he is aware of what they are."

My chest puffs high. I'm proud as fuck about her take-no-prisoners tone.

I thought Carmichael's arrival would have snuffed the fire glowing in her eyes over the past thirty-six hours.

It hasn't—not in the slightest.

She's more determined than she's ever been.

Spurred on by her grit, I ask, "What happens if I don't accept Bennett's terms? Worst-case scenario."

Carmichael throws his head back and laughs as if it is ludicrous I'd consider facing my charges in a non-corrupt way.

Usually, my response would mimic his, but not today.

I'm too shocked to do something as pitiful as laughing.

I've never considered manning up to my responsibilities before, but one glance into Justine's eyes has me throwing caution to the wind.

I'm not pussy-whipped. I'm just... ah...

Fuck! I'm totally pussy-whipped.

Carmichael's chuckles simmer when he's subjected to my vicious snarl. I'm pissed from the discovery that I'm being led by my dick, but that isn't the only reason he faces the brunt of my wrath alone.

He's been on my hit list for years, and it's taking everything I have not to drop his smile two inches lower.

Carmichael's Adam's apple bobs up and down before he says, "Worst-case scenario, you'll serve fifteen years in a high-security prison."

"Fuck!" I drawl out in a long, violent roar.

His reply isn't what I anticipated, and it proves I'll be indebted to Vladimir more than I already am. The minimum he demands for any favor invoked is double, so I could be at his mercy for another thirty years.

Fuck that.

A king can't rule when he's under a mountain of dirt, but I'll have no chance to put him there if I'm serving the equivalent of a life sentence to any man in my industry.

Stepping closer, Carmichael adds, "Your best-case scenario isn't much better than that, Nikolai. If you don't accept Judge Marco's terms, you'll serve at least seven years."

"That's not true. Not all the evidence has been processed. We still have witness accounts and surveillance tapes to go through. Circumstances could change," Justine interrupts, her voice lowering with each syllable she speaks.

Carmichael shakes his head. "You've seen the evidence first-hand, Justine. You know as well as I do that Nikolai won't walk away from this charge without handcuffs shackled around his wrists."

Justine's mouth twitches, preparing to cut down his confidence as I wish I could with my knife, but not a word spills from her lips.

I am guilty of assaulting my accuser. I know it. Carmichael knows it, and so does Justine. She's just not ready to follow me fully into the dark just yet. She needs a little more convincing—*and perhaps the removal of a king from his throne.*

Confident the latter is closer to the cause of her uncertainty, I say, "I'll take the deal." When Justine's eyes snap to mine, the moisture in them triples, but it doesn't change my mind. It is made up. "I'm not doing seven years. I can't."

I stare at her, allowing my eyes to express what my mouth can't articulate in front of a two-faced *ублюдок* like Carmichael.

My battle will be the most furious the underworld has ever seen, so I don't need more obstacles placed in my way.

I also can't defend her in a four-by-four concrete cell.

Or touch her.

Fuck that. I don't care how good the deal. I'd never agree to it if it means I'd have to keep my hands off Justine. I only had her beneath me minutes ago, and I'm already craving another hit. I won't survive seven years without touching her—no chance in hell.

"I'll get you off your charges, Nikolai," Justine promises, peering at me with begging eyes. "I just need time to work through the evidence."

"We don't have time. The deal ends at 8 a.m." Carmichael's eyes stray to the clock on the wall, displaying it is 7:30 a.m. "When that clock strikes eight, the deal is gone. You'll be processed like every other prisoner."

Scrubbing my hand over the stubble on my chin, I weigh up my options. I hate the thought of disappointing Justine, but I can't risk a seven-year jail term on the hope it'll continue fooling her into believing I'm half the man she thinks I am.

My life has been a long-ass death sentence, and at the exact moment I decide to take back what's mine, I could lose the opportunity.

I can't let that happen. I didn't send Lia away from no reason. This is my chance to fight back, to bring Vladimir to heel for the cruelness he's instilled on my family. On Justine. *On me.*

This is the opportunity I've been seeking since I was sixteen. I refuse for anything to take this away from me.

Furthermore, corruption is a part of my life.

The sooner Justine learns that the better we'll be.

"How long does it take to get to the courthouse from here?" I ask Carmichael, my voice one I haven't used the past few days. It leaves no doubt who Justine and Carmichael are dealing with.

I am once again Nikolai, Russian Mafia Prince.

"Twenty, maybe thirty minutes, depending on traffic," Justine answers on Carmichael's behalf.

She folds her arms over her chest and returns my turbulent stare. She knows I've made my decision. She's not happy about it, but she recognizes no amount of arguing will change my mind.

I'm a stubborn fucker when I want something.

My rueful chase over the past three days ensures she knows that better than anyone.

Pretending I can't feel my heart beating at an abnormal rhythm, I say, "I don't care what you need to do. Get me to that meeting on time."

Within five minutes, I'm dressed in clothes suitable to face attempted murder charges, shackled, and bundled into the back of a blacked-out SUV. With two armed guards flanking me, and Justine's mentor sitting next to her, the possibility of updating Justine of my plans during our commute is impossible.

That doesn't mean I can't watch her, though.

Like our first ride in a sheriff's vehicle, the air is thick with lust but it isn't as prominent. Don't get me wrong, attraction is still in abundance, but the despair clouding Justine's eyes diminishes their vibrancy, and don't get me started on her boss monitoring her every move with an eagle eye.

I drop my eyes to the floor, doing everything I can to douse the anger surging through me. My fury doesn't rise from the circumstances of my arrest. It's knowing Carmichael is as determined as me when he wants something. He just hides his ruthlessness with a tailored suit and a hundred-dollar haircut.

He shouldn't bother dressing up. Justine is as smart as she is beautiful. She saw straight through his façade as quickly as she did mine.

That's why months of prep work never saw him stepping up to the plate to wield the bat. Justine saw the man behind the shield—the one whose soul is as black as mine.

My focus diverts from haunted memories when I hear my name being called. Carmichael is balancing on the edge of his seat, holding out a piece of paper and a pen for me. Justine is next to him, her face wearing the same mask it had during our first meeting.

I wait for her to acknowledge my heated gaze with a smile before accepting the items from Carmichael. I'm not shocked to discover the document is a long list of monetary transactions scheduled to be transferred within five minutes of me entering Judge Marco's chambers.

Like every exchange my family has negotiated with Bennett, he's coming out of our arrangement with many more digits in his bank account than he woke up with this morning.

"How much are you getting out of this deal?" I ask Carmichael while scribbling my signature on the bottom of the form.

Justine stares at Carmichael, her interest as intense as mine.

Carmichael slips the paper worth nearly a million dollars into the breast pocket of his suit jacket before lifting his eyes to mine. "Nothing," he answers, his tone as shocked as his facial expression. "I... umm..." He rubs his hands together as he contemplates how to say his next statement in a way that won't piss me off. His deliberation is pointless when he says, "I made a mistake, Niki. I'm hoping this will repair the error I made. Clean slate, so to say."

The tic in my jaw turns dangerous. There are only two men in my life who call me Niki. If I have it my way, neither of them will be breathing by the end of the year.

In a traditional family, nicknames are seen as terms of endearment.

In my family, they're insults.

Niki was the name I was called when I was informed of my brother's untimely death. It was the name Vladimir shouted when he demanded I leave my mother's lifeless body on the dirty, blood-spilled floor where she'd taken her life.

It was also the name used when they told me my brother had killed my biological father.

I'm only called Niki by men determined to break me.

The weasel who left me defenseless at sixteen doesn't have the right to call me Niki.

A singsong voice stops me from showing Carmichael my displeasure at his shortening of my name.

I shift my eyes to Justine and arch my brow, pretending I didn't hear her whispered request.

"The pen," she murmurs again, her eyes dropping to the silver-tipped writing instrument I'm clutching so firmly my knuckles are white. "I need to finalize some forms before we arrive in the chambers, and I forgot my pen."

She shakes her head when Carmichael attempts to hand her a

pen from his briefcase, her eyes never leaving mine. "I want *that* pen." She glares at me, letting her eyes speak the words she can't articulate.

Fuck—now I know why I lost my mind to this woman in less than a second. She knows what I'm thinking before my brain has formulated the plot. I told you she sees straight through me. No one has ever seen me as she does. Not even my mother.

"Give me the pen, Nikolai," Justine requests, her voice not wrathful or worried. "We've got this last hurdle to jump, and you'll be scot-free." Her eyes express way more than her mouth ever could. She didn't say I have one last hurdle to jump. She said *we*.

We're doing this together.

With my smirk revealing her body will pay restitution for my obedience, I hand Justine my pen. It's the cruelest battle I've ever endured not to pull her into my lap and ravish her lips when she nods at the silent demand in my eyes. The only reason I don't is because I can't afford to be weak. Not now. Not with the eyes of the devil watching my every move.

I was so entranced by the lust detonating in Justine's eyes that I failed to notice we'd arrived at the courthouse. My father is standing mere feet from my idling transport van, wrangling his way through the media.

Even with the court not officially opening for another hour, the media contingent is out in full force. They'd rather walk the planet like zombies than miss out on seeing a king rule his kingdom.

Although Vladimir's presence is unwanted, it is expected. The family always shows a united front in public. The stronger we appear, the less likely we'll endure an attack.

Although it's been a few years since Rico's death, Vladimir won't take any chances. Our competitors are weak, villainous men who've been in our industry long enough to garner our respect.

Does that mean I wouldn't slit their throats at the first opportunity presented? No, it doesn't. But just like my plans for Vladimir, my tactics for handling them must be methodically planned before they're executed.

Every man knows that preparing for battle is half the fight.

"Niki," Vladimir greets me when I'm ushered out of the transport van by the two armed guards. He kisses each of my cheeks. The clicking of reporters' cameras capturing his charade nearly drowns out his next murmured comment. "She looks how I imagined she would after being thoroughly fucked."

He shifts his eyes to Justine, his stare desolate enough for my back molars to grind together. Anger seeps from my pores as my body shudders with rage.

I don't know what angers me more: my father's comment on Justine's appearance or Carmichael guiding her away from me with his hand on her back.

Considering my molars are gnawed to tiny buds during my last confession, I'd say it is the latter.

"Move aside," my father demands when the paparazzi hover in close, eager to snap a rarely seen sight: a king and a prince in the same realm.

His command is so authoritative even the armed guards move out of his way. We walk the stairs of the courthouse in silence. This isn't unusual. Vladimir isn't a talkative man. He prefers actions over words. Even when a simple sentence could erase a lifetime of torment, he swallows his words and uses his fists.

"Are you done with her?" he asks when we join Carmichael and Justine in the foyer of the courthouse. "Did you fuck her out of your system? Put your needs to rest?"

He speaks as though forgetting a woman like Justine is as easy as failing to recall what you ate for dinner the night before.

I know every word he utters is untrue.

He is a heartless man, but he wasn't always that way.

He gave his heart to a woman years ago—his one true love.

My father killed her.

That's why Vladimir raised me the way he did. I was the ultimate representation of his revenge. I was to confess my real identity to my father in the minutes before I killed him.

I was so fucked in the head I planned to execute his plot to the most stringent detail. I was born a killer, and I was going to honor the title before my brother beat me to the task.

The life expectancy in this industry is already well below national average, but mine is even shorter than that. I've been living on borrowed time for the past four years, my days only increased by shadowing Vladimir's reign.

That's why I've lived my life so carelessly, without constraint or worry. I've been cramming eighty years into thirty, knowing my life could be instantly snuffed out.

I always assumed Vladimir would switch off my lights.

I had no clue a woman would do it.

The instant Justine walked into my life, my view of the world changed. It wasn't solely the thrill of the hunt renewing my heart with blood. It was her eyes.

Although Justine was issued her death sentence years after mine, the burden on her shoulders was just as substantial. But instead of letting her potential demise rule her decisions, her willpower has fed off it.

She believes her attack rendered her half a woman.

She is wrong.

Can you imagine the immense strength it takes to sit across from the men who caused your family's demise and not flinch?

That is what Justine did. She sat beside her attackers every day of her brother's trial with her head held high.

If that wasn't courageous enough, when her brother was sentenced to life without parole, she looked her attackers straight in the eyes and told them she had no intention of backing down and that she would continue fighting no matter the cost.

Half a woman would never have the courage to do that, but Justine did. She's stronger than she realizes, and with me by her side, she'll learn nothing is out of her reach.

I'll give back what my father stole.

I'll give her back her life.

"Niki." Vladimir's deep Russian rumble drags my focus back to the present. "Are you done? Have you finished with her?" he repeats, his voice more demanding than earlier.

"Yeah, I got what I needed," I reply, nodding. "I made the most out of a bad situation. Can't blame a man for that."

I struggle to keep anger out of my voice. Usually I'm the calm, controlled one who can kill a man without flinching, but talking about Justine as if she's nothing more than a whore bombards me with emotions I've never handled before.

She's making me weak, but in a way I can't help but encourage.

Vladimir takes a moment to gauge any dishonesty in my eyes before muttering, "Good." He leans into my side, the twinkle in his eyes one I've rarely seen. "Malvina flew in late last night. She's very much looking forward to seeing you, Son. She's warming your bed as we speak." His volume rises during his last sentence, ensuring I'm not the only one to hear his confession.

Pretending I can't feel Justine's confused gaze boring a hole in the side of my head, I shadow my father into Bennett Marco's chambers, preferring to end one battle before commencing another.

5

———

JUSTINE

"**H**ey," I greet Mr. Fletcher when his frame fills the doorway of my office.

Snubbing the nerves bubbling in my stomach, I set aside the depositions I've been working on the past three hours before gesturing for him to enter.

The natural attraction bristling between us the past three months is still present in abundance, but it isn't as fervent as before. He's angry about the scene he walked in on in my apartment this morning.

Schluter & Fletcher have clear guidelines employees are to follow when it comes to clients. Having your mentor walk in on you in a compromising position with a client isn't on the list.

Nikolai's hearing was finalized four hours ago, and I've been running our conversations this morning through my mind on repeat ever since, meaning I'm not just physically drained—I am emotionally exhausted as well.

Being subjected to Vladimir's evil glare for the twenty minutes he sat across from me during Nikolai's hearing made me see Nikolai's plight to escape his father's clutches in a new light.

Vladimir has orchestrated Nikolai's entire life. From the position he holds, to the charges he faces, he puppeteers every move Nikolai makes.

That's why he arrived at court this morning. He was testing the control he has over Nikolai. If Nikolai didn't respond in a way he deemed acceptable, today's hearing would have ended differently.

Vladimir is one of the most powerful men in his industry, but the one thing he wants more than anything will never be his.

The respect of his son.

That's why Nikolai reacted so brutally during our argument three days ago. He knew my defense of respect was true. He just couldn't admit it.

You can scare a boy into obeying you, but you can't scare a man into respecting you. Nikolai is a man—one of the strongest and most determined I've seen. He will look past any ruse his father dangles in front of him and come out the other end with not only the respect of his crew, but mine as well.

I stop fiddling with the hem of my skirt when Mr. Fletcher places a sheet of paper in front of me. First, I'm worried it is due to breaking Schluter & Fletcher's no fraternization policy.

Only on closer inspection do I realize my assumptions are wrong. This is the form I completed in haste to have Nikolai bailed under house arrest, the document that forced me down a path I never considered walking.

The only thing is, this isn't the paperwork I filled in. The handwriting is all wrong. I write in a cursive font with my E's and L's looped extravagantly. The handwriting on this document is neat, but its E's resemble a backward 3, leaving no doubt it isn't the paperwork I filled in Friday afternoon.

Spotting the confusion crossing my face, Mr. Fletcher hands me another sheet of paper. This one I recognize immediately. It is the one Nikolai completed after he was acquitted of all charges. It has his full name printed at the bottom: Nikolai Elian Popov.

"The E's match," I murmur more to myself than Mr. Fletcher.

Assuming my statement is a question, Mr. Fletcher nods. "I told you once he had his sights set on you, he'd stop at nothing to have you." He nudges his head to the document shaking like a leaf in my hand. "He had you eating out of his palm before he even left the interrogation room."

I drop the sheet of paper onto my desk, not liking his tone. This document makes it look like Nikolai has been playing me from the get-go, but I don't believe that.

Mr. Fletcher is basing his opinion on the evidence presented in front of him. I know the real Nikolai, the man behind the paperwork.

"Things aren't as you're perceiving them, Mr. Fletcher."

He groans, unappreciative of his formal title. "They're not?" he asks, sinking into the vacant chair across from me.

The unease radiating out of him in invisible waves makes me hesitate, but I shake my head, determined to keep my resolve strong. "No, they're not."

His lips tuck in the corner of his mouth, his expression unamused. Prior to this weekend, his arrogance wouldn't have appealed to me. It's piqued my interest, but not in the way one might think. His confidence doesn't turn me on. I'm interested to know why it's grown so rampant since this morning.

He barely uttered a word during Nikolai's hearing. I thought his startled composure stemmed from having a man as infamous as Vladimir watching over the proceedings. But his quiet front continued even after Vladimir guided Nikolai out of the courthouse.

With his silence directed more toward me than his three junior associates, it didn't take long to realize he was giving me the silent treatment.

Although annoyed at his childish behavior, I responded to his silence with the same level of maturity. I'm not a fan of tit for tat. I was just happy to use the quiet to my advantage.

My mind has been so chaotic the past twelve hours that I'm having a hard time remembering which way is up. Having one less issue to tackle has been a godsend.

A short time later, Mr. Fletcher's heavy sigh captures my attention. He's not a sighing type of guy. Other than when he sighed before releasing me from Nikolai's case, I can't recall ever hearing him sigh in the four months I've known him.

While working his jaw side to side, he takes in the depositions stacked on my glass and chrome desk. It was only last week I thought all my Christmases had come at once when he selected me to comb through the evidence of a high-profile murder case.

He has the best paralegal team in the state at his disposal, yet he selected me to work alongside him on this case. And how did I thank him for the privilege? I broke the one rule I swore I'd never break. I mixed business with pleasure.

Swallowing down the anxiety creeping up my throat, I mumble, "Is there something you need? I've begun weeding through the DA's numerous witness accounts, narrowing them by demographics as you requested—"

I stop speaking when Mr. Fletcher slices his hand in the air, ending not just my words but my heart as well. "Trent is here to gather the Hester files. He and Michelle will work toward the preliminary hearing over the next six weeks."

My gaped mouth doubles when he gestures for Trent to enter my office. With my brain on the fritz, I didn't notice him standing outside my door.

"Thank you," Trent mutters when I place my handwritten notes on the Hester file on top of the depositions.

"I don't know if they'll be useful, but..." My words trail into silence when my voice trembles like I'm moments away from crying.

I wait for Trent to leave my office before rolling my shoulders and lifting my chin high. If my four days with Nikolai has taught me anything, it is that I am stronger than I realize.

"Are you firing me?" Even though I'm asking a question, I continue talking as if I didn't. "Because if you are, I am well within my rights to have a union representative present during my unfair dismissal. I haven't done anything wrong. I may have stepped outside the guidelines you deem acceptable for your employees, but nothing I did this weekend went beyond tactics I've witnessed in this firm time and time again over the past three months. You requested I use any means necessary to secure Nikolai as a client. I did as you requested."

Now there's no doubt I am on the verge of crying. While striving to defend myself, I threw my relationship with Nikolai under the bus, acting as if our connection was a ruse to lure him as a client.

I'm a horrible person.

Nikolai is willing to kill a man to keep me safe, but at the first sign of trouble, I throw him to the wolves.

If I didn't have my brother's case occupying my thoughts, I

would hand Mr. Fletcher my resignation instead of waiting to be fired.

My eyes missile to Mr. Fletcher when he says, "You're not being fired, Justine." His tone doesn't match his guarantee, which is gruff and uneasy.

"Then why was I removed from the Hester case?"

The knot in my stomach intensifies when he sighs for the second time in under five minutes. Like when he informed me I had been removed from Nikolai's case, this sigh tells me I won't like what he's about to say.

After licking his dry lips, he announces, "Mr. Schluter requested Trent and Michelle take over the preliminaries on the Hester case, as he requires your assistance with another high-profile client."

A scratch impinges my throat. "Mr. Schluter wants me to work with him?"

My brows stitch when Mr. Fletcher nods.

"Why?" I blubber out, astonished.

I've been with Schluter & Fletcher for the past three months, but I've only communicated with Mr. Schluter once that entire time—when he interviewed me for my position.

I wouldn't necessarily say Mr. Schluter is an old bigot who demoralizes the women in his firm as if we are still in the 1700s ...

Actually, scrap that.

That is precisely how I'd describe Mr. Schluter.

He believes women either belong in the kitchen or his bed—not working alongside him.

Lines crease my forehead. His Stone Age mentality is oddly similar to things I overheard earlier this week.

After breathing out my nerves, I align my eyes with Mr. Fletcher. "What *exactly* is Mr. Schluter requiring my help with?"

"I don't know." His eyes show the honesty in his reply. He is as stumped by Mr. Schluter's request as I am. "But I have a feeling neither of us will like the outcome of his demand."

My eyes follow him when he stands. He tucks his chair in tightly under my desk before returning his eyes to mine. "Grab your coat. Mr. Schluter is waiting for you in the foyer."

Pretending I can't feel my stomach tightening, I secure my

high-waisted jacket from the coat rack before shadowing Mr. Fletcher into the foyer.

The wealth of Schluter & Fletcher is well-displayed by their headquarters. High vaulted ceilings, veined marble floors, and dramatic lighting stun prospective clients so well that they don't even notice the exorbitant hourly rate they're charged.

Although the employees at Schluter & Fletcher are the cream of the crop, it wasn't always this way. Only thirteen short years ago, this place was a dump. Representation rarely extended past misdemeanors or domestic situations and was appointed by the courts for clients who couldn't afford their own defense.

The caliber of clientele didn't change until Mr. Fletcher jumped ship from the DA's office to the defense. I don't know what caused his sudden decision to join the dark side, but it was brilliant. Mr. Schluter and Mr. Fletcher are rolling in dough, and their client list is the best in the country.

My brisk pace down the glistening corridor ends when Mr. Fletcher suddenly stops. He spins around to face me, his expression as unpredictable as my heart rate.

"Remember what I've taught you, Justine. Ethics are the difference between knowing what you must do and what the right thing to do is." He adjusts the collar of my blouse so it sits outside my coat before saying, "Sometimes the lines blur. Whether it is a good or bad blur, you won't discover for many years to come."

I don't know why, but I feel his saying is more for him than me.

Unsure of an appropriate reply, I nod. It is lucky my retort is short, as our private pep talk is interrupted not even two seconds later.

"Yes, well, now his request makes sense." Mr. Schluter shuffles out of his office, instantly changing the bustling space into a graveyard. "That will be all, Mr. Fletcher." He dismisses Mr. Fletcher with a nudge of his hairy chin.

Mr. Schluter has the creepy-old-man vibe down pat. His chin is covered with a ghastly salt-and-pepper goatee, and his expensive tailor-made suit barely covers his expanded midsection.

Although he has a sneer that would have grown men quivering in their boots, he stands at approximately the same height as me without my heels—five feet, eight inches.

His age has never been revealed, but from the information I

unearthed when researching for my interview, he'd have to be at least mid-sixties, if not early seventies. He is a gifted attorney if you can look past his Stone Age beliefs and chauvinistic edge.

"Let's go," Mr. Schluter mutters, snatching his coat from his frazzled receptionist, Sierra.

Not waiting for me to acknowledge his request, he hightails it to a chauffeur-driven Bentley idling at the curb.

After giving Mr. Fletcher one last sideways glance, soundlessly requesting he pray for my safe return, I hotfoot it outside.

The blazing Las Vegas summer temps are even more horrid when I slip into the back of the Bentley. Mr. Schluter's blood must be icy cold, as he has the heat up high.

I tug off my jacket while Mr. Schluter finalizes a call on his cell. With the temperature settings sweltering enough to accommodate Satan, I'm sweating profusely—and it has nothing to do with the compromising situation I've found myself in.

Most of our drive passing beautiful Las Vegas landmarks is spent with me gawking out the window, acting as if I can't understand a word Mr. Schluter is uttering in Spanish into his cell.

I might have been more interested in his discussion if his conversation went beyond reprimanding his housekeeper for purchasing sheets with a thread count of less than a thousand.

"Hmm. Sorry?" I mutter a short time later. I was so caught up absorbing the extravagant houses lining the street that I didn't hear a word grumbled from Mr. Schluter's mouth.

His caterpillar brow bows, unappreciative of my blasé response. "Nationality law, how familiar are you with it?"

"It was covered in my studies, but I've never practiced it. Why?"

Mr. Schluter hands me some documents. "We've been requested to aid a client in their petition to have their spouse nationalized. I'm not up on the current law. I haven't filed a claim since the eighties."

"Schluter & Fletcher is a defensive firm. We don't handle citizenship applications." Confusion echoes in my tone.

His hourly rate is more than I clear in a week, so having him work on a citizenship application would be like asking the president to bag my groceries.

I swallow harshly when his narrowed gaze spears me in place.

His expression shows he doesn't welcome my comment on his firm's legal capabilities. "I suggest you take a moment to remember your place, Justine. When we have a client as influential as the one we are visiting, *my* firm is anything they want it to be," he mutters, overenunciating the word "my."

When his snarl fades, my eyes drop to the document in my hand. I'm interested to discover who is so influential they have him shoving aside high-profile murder cases to aid in their quest to become a US citizen.

"Malvina Smirnov," I murmur to myself.

As our Bentley glides down a street dotted with mansions you'd expect to see in Beverly Hills, I scan Malvina's application for citizenship. She has all her i's dotted and t's crossed, so I'm left baffled as to why she requires our assistance with her application. She's been engaged to her US-born fiancé for four years, she has plenty of capital to live in the US without government assistance, and influential parties have endorsed her application. If I were processing her claim, I'd approve it without a second thought.

I stop assessing Malvina's application when we arrive at a sizable reinforced gate operated by four armed men. After the guards scan the credentials of the driver and both Mr. Schluter and me, the black wrought iron gate slowly chugs open.

The sweat misting my skin from the stifling temperature in the car doubles as the Bentley slowly glides down an asphalt driveway. Hedged greenery edges a manicured lawn that rivals the gardens at Buckingham Palace, and a mansion stands tall and proud at the back of the long, winding road. The number of windows glistening in the bright afternoon sun leads me to believe this property has as many rooms as a hotel. It is massive and utterly jaw-dropping.

"Thank you," I murmur to a man in a black suit when he opens the back passenger door for me.

I smooth the wrinkles from my skirt while shadowing Mr. Schluter up the stairs leading to a pristine double glass door entranceway. Although my outfit is designer, it looks dowdy compared to the glamorous dress the dark-haired beauty waiting for us in the foyer is wearing. From the lack of wrinkles on her face and the aura of wealth surrounding her, I highly suspect this is Malvina.

"Hello, welcome, please come in," she greets us before waving her hand into the foyer. "Maya will take your coats."

A petite brunette wearing a plain white blouse and black skirt appears out of nowhere to take our jackets as requested. I eye her curiously, sure I've seen her before. Although she's malnourished, her eyes, hair coloring, and facial features are familiar. I've never been good at remembering faces, but I'm sure hers is one I've seen before. Perhaps she lives in my building?

Shrugging off my confusion as an effect of minimal sleep, I follow Mr. Schluter and our client into a large library/sitting room at the side of the foyer. The expansive collection of first-edition books and antique furniture leaves no doubts as to the affluence of this family. It is so pungent I can feel it seeping into my skin. This family has wealth most people can only dream about. I doubt anyone in this residence has seen a penny, much less counted them to pay an overdue bill.

"Malvina, this is Justine, the junior associate we were discussing this morning," Mr. Schluter introduces while sitting in a floral-printed chair across from Malvina.

I don't cite an objection to his incorrect use of my title. I'm too stunned by his disclosure they were talking about me this morning to correct him on a formality only he can alter.

Mr. Fletcher is my mentor, but Mr. Schluter solely handles staff hiring. If you don't pass his once-over, you won't be an employee of Schluter & Fletcher.

"It is a pleasure to meet you, Justine," Malvina praises, offering me her hand to shake. Although her greeting is pleasant, her tone is anything but.

The massive diamond rock on her ring finger digs into my palm when I accept her handshake. I don't know if she is left-handed or just wants an excuse to flash her mammoth engagement ring.

Considering that the conceit in her eyes doubles during our awkward interaction, I'd say it is the latter.

Malvina is beautiful—rich chocolate hair falls to her shoulders in effortless waves, perfect, unblemished skin, and fiery blue eyes—but her aura is nowhere near as glamorous.

I don't know her well enough to call her a snob, but her demeanor most certainly implies snootiness.

After ensuring my hair is covering the bite marks the low collar of my shirt fails to conceal, I take the empty seat next to Mr. Schluter.

I've barely begun reprimanding myself for my low self-esteem, when I endure another unexpected blow. The man who called out my marks for their horrid unsightliness enters the library from an opening on my right.

Vladimir's walk is as haunting as ever. He stalks into the room, his steps as menacing as his evil scowl. When he spots me frozen on the couch, the corners of his thin lips tug high.

Like our first meeting, he feeds off my fear, loving every forced swallow I endure.

"Ernest," Vladimir greets, his Russian accent the most pronounced I've heard. He kisses Mr. Schluter's cheek before his eyes turn to me. "*Ангел*, what a pleasure to see you again."

Fear glides down my spine when he squashes his lips to my cheek. The instant his puckered mouth graces my skin, I desperately need a shower, even more so when I see the way Malvina's eyes flare from my wide-eyed expression.

"Everything settled?" Vladimir queries as he moves to join Malvina on a loveseat opposite us.

I become worried for Malvina's sanity when she leans in to accept Vladimir's greeting with overzealous eagerness.

Who cherishes the kiss of death?

"I don't know. They've just arrived," Malvina replies after returning Vladimir's welcoming with one of her own.

She doesn't save her lips for his cheek, though. She kisses him right on the mouth.

I wipe the ghastly expression from my face when Malvina shifts her focus to me. "I'm hoping you've got good news. This wedding is long overdue."

"Wedding?" I query, my tone high.

"Yes," Malvina replies, her eyes sparkling with unbridled excitement. "It is many years later than we would have liked, but you can't force a bull into a china shop."

She slaps Vladimir's chest when he throws his head back and laughs. I'd like to say it is the pleasant chuckle of a man excited at the prospect of being wed, but it sounds nothing like that. It is as evil and vindictive as Vladimir's dark eyes searing my soul from the inside out.

Malvina waits for Vladimir's laughter to settle before asking, "So, what are the chances of a wedding happening this weekend?"

"This weekend?" I choke out.

I don't know what is more shocking: the fact she wants to marry Vladimir, or that she's hoping it can be done as soon as possible.

"You want to wed this weekend?" My eyes bounce between Vladimir and Malvina, utterly shocked and, in all honesty, sickened.

Vladimir is a horrible, vile man. How does his fiancée not know this?

Noticing the direction of my gaze, Malvina giggles. "I'm not marrying Vladimir. I'm marrying his son, silly." She abruptly stands, startling me. "Speak of the devil and he shall appear. Darling, in here." She waves her hand at someone behind my shoulder.

I freeze, suddenly distressed. I don't know why I'm being bombarded with disturbing thoughts—*reckless, distressing thoughts* —but my stomach is somersaulting so fiercely I feel like I'm moments away from barfing on the expensive Persian rug under my feet, and my skin is slicked with sweat.

The reason behind my body's horrid reaction comes to light when, out of the corner of my eye, I catch the quickest glimpse of a profile I'll never forget. Nikolai is entering the library, his swagger as pompous as ever. He's wearing the same clothes he wore this morning, although his shirt sleeves have been rolled up to his elbows, and his hairline is dotted with sweat, as if he's recently performed exhausting activities.

He pretends he hasn't noticed my gawking stare as he crosses the room to join Malvina and Vladimir on the other side.

He's a good actor, but not good enough to hide the tic his jaw gained from my paralyzed state.

The churning of my stomach ramps up a gear when he kisses Malvina's cheek. Malvina swivels her head, unwilling to let her fiancé slip by without a more intimate embrace, forcing Nikolai's lips to land on hers.

She kisses him for mere seconds, but I swear it feels like the sun circles the earth a hundred times.

When Malvina pulls away from Nikolai, her eyes carry the same spark I saw in mine numerous times the past weekend. She's caught in the trap of a mafia prince, too defenseless to fight his charm and too enamored to care.

"Oh, goodness, I got lipstick on your lips. Here." Malvina fusses over Nikolai until every smidge of her vibrant red lipstick has been removed from his mouth.

I try to force my eyes to the floor, but like staring at a car wreck, I can't tear my gaze away from them standing side by side. It is like seeing royalty in the flesh—a prince with a princess worthy of the glamorous title.

The only reason my eyes drift away from the heart-crushing sight is when I feel the heat of a desolate gaze boring into my temples. Vladimir is watching my every move, categorizing me as much as he did when he considered Nikolai's offer of making me his whore.

I force a fake smile onto my face, acting unaffected by the sappy visual shredding my heart into pieces.

It is all a ploy. I'm utterly destroyed.

If Nikolai is the fiancé Malvina listed in her application for US citizenship, she has been his fiancée for four years.

FOUR years!

"Sorry?" I mumble when Mr. Schluter nudges me with his knee, drawing me away from negative thoughts.

He glares at me, demanding I get with the program. "Malvina asked if there was any possibility she and Nikolai could wed this weekend. They have been waiting for this day for years and hope her citizenship application won't stall their plans."

"Oh... umm..." Words fail me when my eyes collide with Nikolai's. He's glowering at me, his anger so potent anyone would swear he just discovered I was the one hiding a secret engagement.

Usually I'd cower from his wrath, but I'm too angry to leash my spiteful tongue. "A citizenship application does not affect their ability to get married. If anything, it may aid in Malvina's application." I shift my eyes to Malvina, the determination in them as vibrant as ever. "You're in Vegas. You can do whatever you want in Vegas."

Malvina squeals as she claps her hands together. "See, I told you no formalities were stopping us from tying the knot." She squeezes Nikolai's hand, firming his fists and making his knuckles white. "I better get planning. Gosh, I only have days." She presses her red-painted lips onto the edge of Nikolai's mouth before her eyes stray to mine. "Thank you. You just made my year."

I bow my head. It's the least I can do after spending the weekend shacked up with her fiancé. "If you have any more questions, please contact the firm via telephone. You don't need to bring us out here for a simple question."

Malvina is discreet, but I don't miss the quickest roll of her eyes. Her reaction isn't shocking. She looks like a woman who is used to having people serve her. I wouldn't be surprised to discover her servants scoop her cereal directly into her mouth.

I inwardly grumble. *They probably chew it for her as well.*

"I'll show you out," Nikolai says, focusing on Mr. Schluter.

When Mr. Schluter stands, I follow suit, happy to vacate a room where the oxygen supply is thinning with every second ticking.

It's the fight of my life, but I muster a forced grin to bid farewell to Vladimir and Malvina. The only reason I do is because Malvina doesn't deserve my anger. She may be unpleasant, but who am I to judge her? She isn't the homewrecker in this situation.

That title solely belongs to me.

"Don't be long, Son," Vladimir demands, his voice gravelly and thick. "We've got lifelong seeds to plant. Ones that should have been sowed years ago." His eyes collide with mine during his last sentence.

Nikolai nods, not the least bit distressed by Vladimir's demanding tone. After returning his eyes to Mr. Schluter and me standing frozen in the library, he gestures to the door. "This way." His timbre is so low it feels like it was delivered straight from hell.

Mr. Schluter and I follow him through his expansive family compound, shadowing him in silence like sheep going to the slaughter.

Nikolai doesn't speak a word. He doesn't need to. I can feel his anger radiating out of him in hot, invisible waves. It is as volatile and temperamental as mine.

Not even thirty minutes ago, I was defending him.

Now, I realize what Mr. Fletcher said is true.

I've been stupidly eating out of Nikolai's palm the entire time I've known him.

Our brisk trek across the glistening tiled floor halts when a non-accented voice at our side asks, "Ernest, can I have a minute?"

My heart pounds against my ribcage when my eyes swing in

the direction of the voice. Roman is standing at the entrance of a long, dark corridor, the dingy design of which starkly contradicts the opulence of the rest of the residence.

"Certainly."

When Mr. Schluter pushes off his feet to head to Roman, I follow him.

"Just Ernest," Roman demands, stopping my steps mid-stride.

I glare at Roman, soundlessly begging him not to do this.

He returns my stare, telling me what I already know.

He doesn't need to speak to Mr. Schluter.

He's setting me up to be left unoccupied with Nikolai.

"I'll be back in a minute, Justine," Mr. Schluter says, peering at me in shock, confused as to why I'm acting so jittery.

Having no idea of the dangerous situation he's leaving me in, he shadows Roman into the dimly lit corridor.

He's barely disappeared from my vision when my elbow is clutched, and I'm dragged into a dining room on my left. The table is so large it could seat hundreds.

"Out," Nikolai demands, his angry snarl directed at a group of women cleaning silverware at the end of the vast space.

They clamber out of the room without uttering a word, their exit soundless and swift.

When a door slamming shut announces their departure, I attempt to yank myself out of Nikolai's hold.

He remains holding on tightly, refusing to relinquish me from his grasp.

"What the fuck are you doing here, *Ангел*?" he sneers, his words hot enough to melt ice.

Although he is brimming with anger, he keeps his volume low.

I don't know if he's quiet because he doesn't want anyone overhearing our conversation or because he is worried his fiancée will discover how he occupies his time when she isn't around.

"I'm striving to keep you off Vladimir's radar, and you walk straight into his fucking trap."

"Don't act angry because you're sheltering me from Vladimir. You're not angry because of that. You're mad because your secret has been exposed." My voice is as hushed as his, but it leaves no doubt of the fury heating me.

Nikolai's grip on my arm firms, but it doesn't compare to the agony strangling my heart. "My anger has nothing to do with my arrangement with Malvina—"

"Arrangement? You're engaged, Nikolai!" My voice breaks at the end.

Just admitting he is engaged cuts me deep, way deeper than I could ever explain.

"So? She means nothing to me. Not a single fucking thing." His whispered roar is so explosive only his Russian accent breaks through.

His reply doesn't fill me with gratitude. It has the opposite effect because he doesn't deny he is engaged. He replied as if he is a coward using any excuse he can to defend his cheating ways.

It's the fight of my life not to retaliate with violence to the pain tearing me apart.

As much as my hands are twitching to slap the arrogance right off his face, I won't strike him a second time. His police record shows he endured enough abuse during his childhood to last him a lifetime, so I will not add more.

Instead, I ask, "The entire time we were together, you were engaged?"

I don't know why, but I wait for Nikolai to nod, to acknowledge what I already know is a true declaration.

When he does, tears burn my eyes.

"But that shouldn't matter because she means nothing to you?" I quote, my words more resilient than I anticipate. With my tight throat, I expected my voice to be hoarse and unclear.

When he nods for the second time, my fight to keep my hands balled at my side ramps up a gear.

"You're a pig," I snarl, my devastation too deep to harness my retaliation. Verbal abuse is as damaging as physical, but I'm so angry I'm speaking before thinking.

"I risked everything for you. My job, my freedom." A tear slides down my cheek as I whisper, "My brother's freedom. And what do I get...? *Nothing.*"

"You didn't get nothing. You got me," Nikolai replies, his voice quickening as his tone deepens. "And I will give you everything. You won't want a thing when you are with me."

"Is that before or after you've married Malvina?" I sneer, sickened at how my pulse began racing at his false declaration.

I don't want to be kept. And even if I did, it wouldn't be by a man who's already taken.

"She is my fiancée, *Ангел*, but she will never be my wife. I live in Vegas, for fuck's sake. If I wanted to marry her, I could have done it years ago."

His words don't stop me from wanting to get away from him. If anything, they make me more determined. His sneered statement confirms what I expected: He has been engaged for years.

"Let me go, Nikolai," I plead, my words as raw as my throat feels from holding back my devastated sobs. "I swear to god, if you don't let me go, I'll scream at the top of my lungs." My voice grows louder with every syllable I speak. I'm two seconds from blowing my top. I've never been so angry. I feel like I'm spiraling out of control.

Nikolai relinquishes me from his hold. It isn't my shouted pledge that has him dropping me like a hot potato. It is the creak of a door sounding into the room.

"Is everything okay?" Malvina asks, gliding into the room with her suspicious eyes darting between Nikolai and me. "I thought I heard shouting."

The influence she holds over Nikolai smacks into me when he replies, "Yes, everything is fine. I was just asking Justine's advice on merging our assets."

My eyes rocket to his, stunned and sickened by his reply.

When his eyes lock with mine, I shake my head, ashamed of the man glancing back at me.

The coward standing next to me isn't the man I spent my weekend with. That Nikolai wouldn't stand down when confronted by a hundred men, much less a woman who has "no right to fracture the rightful order."

"Darling, I told you this morning I'm not interested in a prenup." Malvina glides around Nikolai, her steps so lithe she practically floats. "But you know me, Niki, I'll do anything to make you happy. Anything at all." She purrs her last sentence into his ear as her eyes glower into mine. Her responses couldn't be any more opposite. She adores Nikolai while hating me.

I can't say I blame her.

Nikolai cringes when she grazes her teeth over his earlobe before sucking it into her mouth.

He isn't the only one grimacing.

I'm forced to close my eyes and count to ten to ensure I don't drag Malvina off him by the hair on her pretty little head. And don't even get me started on the slosh racing to the base of my throat.

I feel ill—horribly ill.

Only this morning, Nikolai claimed me in a way no man ever has, and now I'm watching him being doted on by his fiancée.

My grandmother would be disgraced if she could see me now.

Needing to leave before the contents of my stomach see daylight, I connect my eyes with Nikolai and mumble, "It appears you no longer need my services, so I best leave you to it." I clear the nerves from my voice with a quick swallow before my brimming-with-moisture gaze drifts to Malvina. "I wish you the best of luck." *You're going to need it.*

Stealing her chance to reply, I race to the door Nikolai dragged me through mere minutes ago.

"Justine."

Nikolai only says my name, but the demand in his voice speaks volumes. He is as ropeable as I am.

He has no right to be angry. The only thing I've done wrong is to believe he isn't the man his police file portrays.

I've been proven a liar more than once, so I shouldn't be surprised I've been caught a second time. I just never saw this one coming.

I thought Nikolai was different from Dimitri.

Obviously, I was wrong.

"Nikolai... Get back here right now!"

I don't need to spin around to know Nikolai is chasing after me. Malvina's stumbled demand indicates he is on my heels, let alone the prickling of the hairs on my nape.

Trying to forget the horrid similarities between my past and my present, I continue for the door, reaching it in two heart-thrashing seconds. I exhale a harsh breath when my charge through the tight confines has me colliding into a wall of hardness.

My hands shoot up to cover my nose as I stumble backward. As he did the evening he entered my apartment, Nikolai steadies my swaying movements with his torso.

I nearly thank him until the eyes of a devil steal my words.

"I thought you were leaving?" Vladimir asks, his voice brimming with condescending amusement. Not the least bit fazed he nearly sent me tumbling to the floor.

Reaching my quota on arrogant, insolent men, I snarl, "That is precisely what I'm trying to do."

I sidestep Vladimir, ignoring the evil glare Mr. Schluter is projecting at me. I just snarled at a mafia king. I've got far more pressing issues to handle than the wrathful scowl of my employer.

Pretending I can't feel the heat of Nikolai's gaze trekking over me, I snatch my coat out of Maya's hands and gallop down the stairs, my eagerness to leave overruling my manners.

With my mind hazy, neither my career title nor niceties are in the forefront of my mind. I only care about my sanity and getting as far away from this place as possible.

6

NIKOLAI

"Is she like that in the bedroom?" Vladimir asks, his eyes fixated on Justine as she charges down the front stairs of the Popov compound like she's outrunning a bullet. "All hot and temperamental?"

He asks his questions without concern about the pair of ears listening in. His disrespect of women is so great he treats every one of them as if they're whores, even ones he knows are more powerful than him.

When he shifts his eyes to me, waiting for my reply, I answer, "Would I have slept with her if she wasn't?"

Ignoring Malvina's sigh, I pivot and head down the corridor on my left. Although her tactics to make me her husband are as ruthless as a missile locked on its target, she won't dare follow me down here—not if she knows what's good for her.

Malvina is my fiancée, but that doesn't mean I have to like her. She is the beloved daughter of Andros Smirnov, the wealthiest and most influential man in Russia.

In Vegas, Vladimir is a king, but even he knows he is a jester when it comes to a man like Andros.

If I marry Malvina, the Popov entity will become one of the most prominent corporations in the world.

Vladimir has more wealth and power than most men will ever achieve, but it isn't enough for him.

He wants more.

Malvina can give him more.

She's Vladimir's guarantee of ultimate power, the final chunk of concrete he needs to fortify his empire so thoroughly that it will never be demolished. And the fact Malvina is obsessed with me gives him even more incentive to take Andros's place.

They caught me in a moment of weakness. Even the worst ideas sound brilliant when you're as high as a kite and drunk as a sailor.

Malvina was the most convincing of them all. She assured me marrying her would place me higher in the rankings than Vladimir, and I'd finally have an opportunity to rule over him as he has done to me my entire life.

The quest for revenge was blinding. So much so that I agreed to become Malvina's husband.

We sealed our agreement like any soon-to-be-wed couple would—between the sheets.

One night, that was all it took to know I'd never marry her, no matter how grand the prize would be.

Fucking Malvina was like bedding a dead mule. She didn't move or speak. She didn't do a fucking thing. I blame her for my promiscuity over the past four years. If I was going to spend the rest of my life bedding a corpse, I was going to sow my oats—and I sowed them well.

Before Justine's arrival, I thought no woman would quench my hunger. I was wrong. She appeased my thirst and ignited a flame in me I hadn't felt in years.

Although marrying Malvina would be a quick solution to displace Vladimir from his throne, the victory wouldn't be as sweet as what I'm planning.

Hate is a strong word. It thickens your blood and makes the bravest men weak, but it is what has kept me driven for the past thirteen years.

I want Vladimir to feel what I felt when he fed me lie after lie during my childhood. I want him to experience what I went through when my mother killed herself because she couldn't please him.

I want to see his heart break when he realizes he will never be good enough for me, as mine did years ago when I realized nothing I did would ever get his approval.

I maimed for him.

I killed for him.

I forgot who I was for him, yet nothing I did was good enough for him.

Not anymore. I am done. There's only one person I'm going to lose myself to.

Vladimir is not that person.

The look on Justine's face when she discovered I was engaged stripped my lungs of oxygen, but I couldn't do anything to ease her pain. Until I have all my plans in motion, as far as the world is concerned, I am Malvina's fiancé. Her father is a very powerful man, and I plan on using my connection to him to strengthen my numbers as I move forward in my quest to dethrone Vladimir.

Anyone in this industry knows numbers are the most imperative factor. One man can't take down an army, but three thousand men can.

I move through a darkened room, only stopping when I reach a mildew-covered window. With the Popov's housemaids frightened to enter this domain, the numerous rooms breaking off the corridor are dark and sooty. Their lifeless appearance represents precisely what happens down here.

They aren't called torture chambers for no reason.

The muscle in my chest I was certain died years ago kicks into a crazy beat when I peer out a thick pair of pleated curtains. Justine is standing at the base of the Popov compound entranceway stairs, waiting for the dark-colored Bentley gliding down the driveway. Her face is ashen, and her eyes glisten with tears. I don't know what the old geezer standing next to her is saying, but whatever it is, he is adding to the heat flaming her kneecaps.

If I were certain my actions weren't being monitored, I wouldn't stand by and watch her be reprimanded without cause, but since I know her arrival this afternoon was a tactic by Vladimir to test my loyalty, my feet must remain planted.

My disobedience this weekend is why Malvina's visit from Russia occurred two months earlier than usual. Usually she shows up twice a year to strengthen the ties between our families. She's only here, demanding we marry immediately, at Vladimir's request.

If I had turned down her suggestion as I really wanted to, Vladimir would have seen it as a direct insult to him, leaving him free to discipline those involved in the treachery without fear of repercussion.

As much as I can withstand the wrath of Vladimir's fury, Justine isn't prepared for the sting of his madness. She's barely coping after her first tussle with a mafia kingpin. She may not survive a second dose.

Just before Justine enters the idling Bentley, her head cranks back in my direction. Even though she can't see me through the tinted windows, I know she has spotted me spying on her. She can feel it in her bones, sense it with every breath she takes. She knows I'm with her even when I'm not. She knows me better than anyone does.

"Soon, *Ангел*. Very soon," I pledge when she slips into the back seat of the Bentley. "We are not done, because we're not even close to beginning."

What I said to her earlier is true. She will want for nothing when she is with me. When I am king, she will be treated like a queen. The world will be her oyster.

I wait for the Bentley to disappear through the gates of the Popov compound before pivoting on my heels. The scent of fear lingers in my nose when the man lying in bed registers my approach.

I could sneak up on him unaware, but where is the fun in that?

The smell of desecration is nearly as intoxicating to me as Justine's skin. I feed off it. It was the only thing keeping me alive for the past thirteen years—until Justine arrived. Although her attention has shifted my hunger, my determination to protect her is more pressing than anything.

"Sergei," I growl out as I slip my trusty knife from the back pocket of my jeans. "Where were we before we were interrupted?"

Although I'd hoped my intuition was wrong, it was proven deadly accurate when my wander through the Popov compound had me stumbling upon Justine.

I thought my quest to fix the wrongs I committed made me

imagine her presence, but it wasn't my imagination. Just as my body advised, she was close enough for my cock to notice.

The spell that woman has on me—*fuck*.

She has me thinking recklessly. I've never been as unhinged as I am now. Merciless, yes, but never unhinged.

Sergei holds out his shackled wrists in a plea, fighting to express words through the gag stuffed in his mouth.

"Shhh," I say, squashing my finger to his bloodstained lips. "You had one order, Sergei. One. You failed. There's only one penance for failing to adhere to a direct order from your superior. You know that as well as I do."

His pupils dilate as he sucks in a garbled breath, my movements so quick he doesn't have a chance to blink.

"Do you remember this room? How you told me you would beat me until I peed my pants, and when I failed to bow to your fucked mind, you broke my arm instead?"

I slant into him deeper, digging the blade of my knife further into his chest. "Do you remember the smell of my brother's skin burning when you threw acid on his back in this very room?"

Blood gurgles up Sergei's throat as he struggles to breathe through the pain ripping through his body.

For the first time, he's experiencing what many men under him have endured.

He is getting a taste of his own medicine.

"None of that would have mattered. I would have let it slide. It is the way things are in this business. It's who we were born to be. But you couldn't let it go. You had to drag an angel into a fight she didn't belong in. You touched what is *mine*. And that alone will cost you your life."

I stare into his almost lifeless black eyes, watching them darken with every second that ticks by.

"Save a spot for Vladimir in hell. He'll be joining you soon enough," I whisper into his ear as his breathing withers to lifeless gasps.

I wait for his jerking to ease before removing my knife from his perfectly still chest. I stare down at the blood smeared on the blade, shocked to see it is red.

Sergei had a heart as black as Vladimir's, so I was certain it wasn't pumping blood.

I remain standing next to his lifeless body for several minutes, quiet and confounded. I've killed many men, more than I'll ever admit, but this death is different, and it has nothing to do with Sergei having the blood of a Popov. This is the first time I've claimed a life of my own free will.

I killed Sergei for me, not because I was forced to.

I should feel remorse.

I should feel guilty.

But all I am feeling is one step closer to freedom.

After clearing the blood from my blade with the rag stuffed in Sergei's mouth, I exit the room. Roman is waiting for me in the corridor. Although he expressed concern at my decision, he knew nothing would stop my crusade. Sergei was a stupid man, so heedless he assumed he could run his mouth about Justine without it reaching my ears.

His misassumption cost him his life.

His death will serve as a warning to those he encouraged to seek revenge for our exchange on Justine. One wrong glance in her direction will be fatal, so no man in Sergei's crew will be inclined to take it any further than that.

"Get rid of him discreetly enough Vladimir won't find out, but his death will be common knowledge amongst the men. I want this to be a warning, Roman. No one is to touch Justine."

Roman dips his chin, acknowledging my request with a maturity that matches his years. "I understand. The wheels are already in motion."

He sidesteps me to stride down the corridor. He freezes halfway through the door when I call his name. "The jet, is it ready as requested?"

"Yes," he replies, his short reply unable to hide his worry. "It is fueled and waiting for you on the tarmac as requested." His throat works hard to swallow before he adds, "Are you sure you don't want me to come with you?"

I don't like him implying I can't take care of myself, but I appreciate that he cares enough about me to be worried.

"Some things are better handled alone." My eyes drift to the room Roman is entering. "The fewer witnesses, the better."

"Very well," he breathes out heavily, his sigh more forthcoming than his reply. "I shall see you on your return."

I nod before pivoting on my heel. "Watch her for me, Roman."

I don't need to look at him to know he will comply with my request. He's the most loyal man I have—almost to a fault—but his loyalty will be repaid tenfold when I take back what is mine.

Unlike Sergei, his allegiance will give him back his life instead of claiming it.

7

NIKOLAI

Hot, humid air smacks into me when I step out of the twelve-seater jet that landed at a private airstrip in Hopeton, Florida. I gallop down the stairs, the two hours of sleep I managed during the flight lightening my steps.

"Nikolai, welcome to Florida," croons a heavy-breasted female standing next to a shiny black sports car. "We hope you're pleased with our selection." The seductive purr of her voice reveals what she is referring to.

It isn't the sports car.

Before Justine, this blonde would have been sucking my cock during the commute to relieve boredom.

Now my cock isn't even twitching at the idea of having her lips wrapped around it.

I'm a breast man—the rounder the better. Although this blonde's tits are barely contained in her tight cropped spaghetti-strap shirt, they look like clumps of silicone wrapped in over-stretched skin.

If I hadn't spent my weekend smothered by the best tits I've ever seen, her plump lips could have had me looking past her less desirable assets.

Unfortunately for her, I've suddenly developed standards.

The blonde's penciled brows stitch when I slide into the car's driver's seat and crank the ignition. She rattles on the door handle, soundlessly requesting that I unlock the passenger door.

She'll need another visit to the plastic surgeon to smooth the heavy groove in her forehead when I plant my foot on the gas pedal, leaving her in a cloud of smoke in the middle of the tarmac.

I push the rental car to its limit, loving the purr of its high-horsepower engine as I weave through a seaside community.

My resolve is the most determined it's ever been. I've negoti-ated deals worth millions of dollars. Money laundering, drug ship-ments, and weapon exchanges have netted the Popov entity a very impressive capital of possessions and cash. Still, not one deal I've negotiated will trump the one I'll seal today.

If everything goes as planned, I'll fly out of Hopeton richer than I've ever been.

As I glide the murky black car to a stop outside a manned gate, an armed guard emerges from his station. His pupils dilate to the size of saucers when I roll down the driver's side window enough he can see my icy-blue gaze.

I'm not a celebrity by any means, but in my field, I'm notorious.

After parking my car in the spot requested by the guard, I peel out of the driver's seat. I smile, amused when six men brandishing MP5s surround me.

Most people would see their excessive tactics as wasteful—I'm one man, and I'm not even carrying a pistol, for fuck's sake—but I see it as smart.

When you're approached by a man who's never felt fear, you're best to act cautiously.

"Brother," I drawl out in a long, mocking roar when my guided tour of the Petretti compound has me walking past the man I stabbed in the neck last week.

When his eyes drop to his feet faster than the blood drains from his face, I mutter, "What? Aren't we friends anymore? I thought we were family?"

With rumors of my birthright circulating faster than I would have liked, I've had men like that weasel confront me more than a dozen times in the past three years.

Usually I'd handle the situation with more constraint, but his constant referring to me as his brother irritated me.

I don't have a drop of Popov blood running through my veins, but I'm sure as fuck not a Petretti. The Petrettis are my rivals, and I'd rather die than take on their name.

When the man I'm mocking cowardly shuffles into a room on my right, my conceited laughter bellows through the dead-quiet residence.

Although I'm chuckling at his fear, it also hides my shock at the size of the Petretti compound.

When Col died, most of his monetary assets dwindled alongside him, but this residence leaves no suspicion about the empire Dimitri is building.

I'm surprised. Dimitri clearly has an eye for detail, as Justine caught his eye, but he isn't that smart. One glance into Justine's eyes made the adrenaline in my blood surge so powerfully I felt invincible.

How could she not have had the same effect on Dimitri?

My tour of the Petretti compound is quick but long enough to gauge what their business is. There's a small shipment of powder in one room on my right, but it is only enough for domestic use by their crew.

If they plan to distribute coke, they'll need more than a few bricks. The range of accents projecting from the padlocked rooms that leaves no doubt to my assumption. They're pedaling the sex trafficking ring even more than Col did during his final years.

When we enter an office at the back of the compound, testosterone thickens my blood. Dimitri sits behind a large wooden desk, his tapered gaze as smug as his fancy office. He has a lot of similarities to his father. Same dark, trimmed hair, elongated face, and icy-blue eyes. He just lacks the aura of arrogance.

I was the only one gifted with that trait from Col.

"Nikolai, to what do I owe the pleasure?"

He stands before gesturing for the men surrounding me to stand down. They don't go far—only to the corner of the room. Although I can respect his determination to show he isn't scared, I'll never respect him.

He lost any chance of gaining my respect when I discovered he stood by and watched an animal maul Justine and did nothing to help her.

I thought I was a sick man. I've got nothing on Dimitri.

I sit in the chair Dimitri directs me to before shaking my head, denying his offer of a drink.

I'm not here for pleasantries.

I'm here on business.

After filling his crystal glass with three fingers of bourbon, Dimitri joins me on one of the four single chairs assembled around a wooden table. "If this is regarding your exchange with Matthews Friday afternoon, it is being handled in-house..."

His words trail off when I shake my head. "This has nothing to do with Matthews. I handled the situation. I'll handle it more thoroughly if he steps out of line again." My tone ensures he can't misconstrue my admission.

Matthews was lucky he was still breathing Friday night.

"Then what is this about?" Dimitri asks, sinking into his chair. "You made it clear the last time we met that our exchanges from thereon would only pertain to business."

"And that they will," I reply, gliding my hand into the back pocket of my jeans.

My lips curl when his men approach me, mindful of my meekest movement.

They should be on alert. If I weren't spurred on by the desire to give Justine her life back, my meeting with Dimitri might have looked like the one I had with Sergei yesterday afternoon.

Dimitri tries to act unaffected when I slide a picture of Justine across the table, but I see the quickest flare of his nostrils.

He is reacting the exact way I did when I first laid eyes on her. The thrill of the hunt is warming his veins and thickening his cock.

Even through a photo, Justine's attractiveness is undeniable. Although she's sleeping, there's no doubt of her beauty. Her hair has fallen away from her shoulders, exposing every flawless feature of her face, and the drape of her clothes can't hide her alluring curves.

I took this photo the first night I stayed in her apartment, knowing it would be one of many.

"Her debt," I say, tapping my index finger on Justine's photo. "I want it transferred to me."

Dimitri shakes his head, adding to the manic tic in my jaw. "What debt? I don't even know who she is, let alone why she's indebted to us."

I work my jaw side to side, struggling to contain my anger. I want to slit his throat for his stupidity in believing he can lie to me. I want to squeeze his neck until the blood drains from his face. But knowing the rules of our industry, I can't.

If I kill him, I'd be dead before I leave the compound.

Usually that wouldn't bother me, but now I have something I'm willing to live for.

I've got my woman waiting for me at home.

My eyes drift away from Dimitri when a deep voice at my side asks, "How can you not remember her, boss?" A man in his mid-thirties licks his lips as his eyes drop to Justine's photo, utterly oblivious to the murderous glare Dimitri is issuing him. "She's a little older than I remember, and her tits are a little rounder, but man, her screams... I'll never forget them. They would have only been hotter if they were done beneath the sheets. If that dog hadn't fucked her over, I sure would have."

I glare at him, my blood so hot I can feel it reddening my face.

I try to hold in my anger.

I try to remember I am not here for revenge.

I'm here to have Justine's debt transferred to me, but when the unnamed man secures Justine's photo in his filthy motherfucking hands, I lose all sense of control.

A feral grunt rips through my lips as I yank my knife from my back pocket and pierce it through the skin of the man whose taunt maimed me more than any scar I've been given.

The man's eyes widen as his bloodcurdling scream alerts his crew to his distress. I ram my knife down harder, stabbing his hand even further into the wooden table it is pinned to.

I don't even begin to let up when I feel the pinch of a rifle on my temple. I curl my hand around the man's neck before drawing him to within an inch of my face.

"What did she sound like? A wounded animal? Because that is *exactly* what you'll sound like when I pull your stomach out of your throat." My hot breath scorches his face, my Russian accent so pronounced my words are barely comprehensible.

"I didn't mean anything by it. I was playing, man. Calm down," he pleads, his words forced and laced with fear.

I tighten my grip, loving his pulse weakening under my hand. "You're a pathetic piece of shit. The closest you would *ever* get to bedding a woman like that would be in your dreams. Now you've lost any chance you had." I nudge my head to Justine's photo resting next to his bloody hand. "Disrespecting her is as punishable as disrespecting me. Do you know what the penalty of disrespecting me entails?" When the man briefly shakes his head, I snarl, "Death."

His bones creak when I firm my grip even more. I'm moments from snapping his neck. The only reason I don't is Dimitri's warning. "If you kill him, any chance of having Justine's debt transferred to you will be null and void."

My eyes stray to his, wishing it was his pulse fading from my touch. "I thought you didn't know who she was?" I growl, my words as lethal as the Grim Reaper. "Yet you called her by her name."

His Adam's apple bobs up and down but he doesn't stand down. "Her brother repaid her debt years ago. We have no business with her anymore, so I had no reason to disclose old matters," he replies, his tone more composed than the flare in his eyes.

"She's still paying her debt. Every fucking day she lives with the guilt of what your father put her through!"

"Our father, Nikolai. *Our*," Dimitri corrects.

The man I'm strangling falls to his knees when I abruptly stand, thrusting him out of my way in the process. My nostrils flare as my fists firm so tightly that my clipped nails pierce my palms. "I may have Col's blood running through my veins, but he is *not* my father. Just like you're not a man."

Red dots line my chest when I take a step closer to Dimitri. I'm not in fear of my life. There are rules in our industry, ones not even someone as highly ranked as Dimitri can ignore.

"How could you not protect her from him?" I ask, expressing the one question that hasn't left my mind since Justine disclosed the reason for her scars.

I've done some bad shit in my time—stuff that will haunt my dreams for years to come—but you've got to be completely fucked up to watch a woman you care about be mauled by a dog and do nothing.

Dimitri's lips twitch, but not a word spills from his lips.

I spit at his feet, my anger the strongest I've ever dealt with. "You're a fucking coward," I taunt without remorse.

A spark detonates in a set of eyes identical to mine in every way when the reason for my unexpected arrival dawns on him. "You don't want Justine's debt. You want her."

"No," I deny, shaking my head. "I don't *want* her. I already *have* her. She is *mine*. And unlike you, no one will take her away from me. Family or not."

His brows stitch as his face washes with confusion. He stares at me, his composure unreadable.

After relieving his throat with a quick swallow, he gestures with his index finger for his men to leave the room. The armed guards stare at him in shock, certain they misread his gesture.

Strengthening his silent request with a throaty growl, he screams, "Out! Now!" His eyes drop to the man writhing on the ground with my knife still stabbed in his hand. "You too."

He sends a whiskey tumbler flying across the room when his crew still fails to move. Shards of glass and whiskey raining down on his team convince his men to jump into action.

Four men leave without uttering a word while a brute with a face full of tats removes the barrel of his gun from my temple to aid his colleague from the ground.

The man whimpers like a child when his assistant yanks my knife from his hand with as much brutality as I used putting it in there.

The endorphins surging through me triple when his eyes bounce between Dimitri and me before he dumps my knife on the table wedged between us.

Dimitri waits for his crew to leave before he nudges his head to my knife, advising me to take it. It's a foolish move on his behalf but smart at the same time. He knows I feed off fear, so he's doing everything he can to act fearless.

His skills are impressive, but I don't need to see him shaking to know he's scared. I can feel it in my bones, smell it leaching from his pores, taste it on my tongue. There's only been one time he's been more scared—when he thought I'd come to collect my crown.

He had no cause for worry. I had no intention of claiming my birthright when we met for the first time three years ago. I was merely here to conduct business. There has only ever been one throne I want to possess. It isn't Dimitri's.

After throwing down his whiskey as if it is water, Dimitri asks, "How far are you willing to go to secure Justine's debt?"

"That is the equivalent of asking how fond you are of breathing," I reply, my tone laced with arrogance.

It has been mere hours since I've killed, but the desire to watch the life snuffed from someone's eyes still runs rampant. He is the only man who can lessen the guilt Justine has been carrying for the past four years, but that doesn't diminish my wish to kill him.

If it weren't for him, Justine's family wouldn't be in the predicament they are in now. She wouldn't hate her body as if it were anything but perfect, and the spark I see hiding deep in her eyes could finally be set free.

"You started all of this, Dimitri, and you will end it... whether you want to or not."

8

JUSTINE

"So everything's okay? Are they looking after you?"

My brother Maddox's hearty chuckle sounds down the line. "Everything's fine, J. Compared to Wallens Ridge, this place is a country club."

His tone is honest, but it doesn't ease the worry twisting my hair. Maddox has always been the quiet, reserved unit of our family. He could be eating a three-day-old reheated cheeseburger, and he'd still tell you it was the best meal he had ever been served.

"I'm going to bring you home, Maddox." When he tries to interrupt me, I talk faster, wanting to ensure I express myself before I lose the chance. His calls are timed, and our ten minutes are nearly up. "It isn't a possibility. I *will* bring you home. I'll never stop fighting until I've fixed all the mistakes I've made..."

My words taper at the end when my throat clenches tightly. Most of my statement refers to my brother's incarceration, but the small confession at the end was solely for Nikolai.

"J... you better not be crying. My time's nearly up. I've already got the guard glaring at me. Fuck. I can't hang up if you're crying." I hear him cup the phone before he adds, "Can you give me another minute? It's my baby sister. She sounds like she's crying."

The guard mumbles something back, but I can't hear what he says because Maddox has the speaker muffled.

"I'll clean it with my toothbrush if you'll give me another minute. *Please.*" The guard must agree with Maddox's request, as not even two seconds later, he adds, "You've got a minute. Spill. Who made you cry? And don't say you're getting teary over my predicament. You shed enough tears during the first month of my trial. You can't have any left."

More moisture burns my eyes from the protectiveness in his voice. My brothers hate when I cry, even when they are the cause of my tears.

"I'm not crying," I lie, my cracking voice betraying my fib.

"J..."

"I'm just emotional, that's all. I'm a girl. We get emotional."

"Twice in a week?" he questions, his tone relaying he doesn't believe my excuse. "Mom told me you were upset earlier this week. You're supposed to be happy, J. You did all of this." I can't see him, but I imagine him waving his hand around his space. "I've got a color television and phone privileges, and Mom has been to visit twice this week already."

I giggle at the grimace in his tone.

The tension in his voice eases when he hears my laughter. "The guards love her, but if she keeps bringing them baked goods, my reputation is gonna go to shit."

The last part of his confession spikes my interest. "Your reputation? What reputation?"

He breathes noisily down the line, unappreciative of the tsk in my tone. "Things are different in here. You either man up or leave in a casket. I'm not leaving this place in a casket, J."

I don't have a chance of holding in my tears, so I let them free. "You won't leave in a casket if you just speak up. I know you're keeping things from us, Maddox, vital information that could set you free."

"Justine..." he growls in warning, gaining my attention with my full name. He only ever calls me Justine when I'm in trouble. "We're not discussing this again. What's done is done. We can't change it."

"No, Maddox," I reply, refusing to bow to the command in his tone. "Your silence is the only reason you're stuck in that hellhole."

"My silence is the only reason you're *not* stuck in hell," he interrupts, his words quickening. "I did this for you, J. To keep you safe. To keep you away from that monster."

"Col is dead. He can't come back from that, so you have no reason to continue your silence."

My shrieked comments are met with silence—long, uncomfortable silence.

"Talk to me, Maddox. Let me help," I mumble through hiccups a short time later.

"It isn't that simple. I wish it was, but it isn't." He mumbles something to someone in the distance before saying, "I've gotta go. My time is up." A chair scraping across a tiled surface sounds down the line, closely followed by, "You've already done me proud. Your trek across the country brought me closer to home than I've ever been, so don't feel bad. Your boss achieved something no man could do in years, but he wouldn't have done it without you. It's enough, J. It might not be what you want, but it's enough for me."

While wiping away my tears, I nod. I want to tell Maddox that Mr. Fletcher isn't responsible for his transfer, but with our time dwindling to seconds, I settle on, "I love you, Maddox."

"I've never doubted it. Now go and live your life. I didn't plead guilty for both of us to serve life behind bars."

Not giving me a chance to reply, he disconnects our call.

I sit silently for several minutes, recalling our brief conversation. It's the first we've had since I moved to Vegas. I want to tell Maddox who is responsible for his transfer, but I am also apprehensive about what his reaction will be to me seeking aid from a man so similar to the one responsible for his incarceration.

That's why I haven't told my parents Nikolai deserves the praise they've been raining on Mr. Fletcher every time we've spoken since Maddox's transfer.

I don't want my mom to hear my tears for the second time in a week. I pretended my sobbing was due to my happiness about Maddox's transfer, but my mom didn't buy my act. She knows there is more to my fluctuating moods than I let on. And so do I.

I haven't heard from Nikolai for the past three days. Not a peep. I should be happy with his standoffish approach, but I'm not. I'm miserable. Alone. Petrified. I'm not scared about the repercussions my fight with Nikolai may cause to my family. I'm panicked at how insecure I've become.

I only knew Nikolai for four days, for crying out loud—*four measly, pitiful days*—but my heart feels like it lost its lifetime companion.

Nikolai betrayed me. He pursued and bedded me while he was engaged to another woman, but no matter how much my brain rationalizes with my heart, my devastation hasn't diminished. I feel lost—even more than when I left my family and moved across the country.

I gained so much confidence in the four days I knew Nikolai, but that all vanished when his lips collided with Malvina's. My attack years ago made me half a woman, but Nikolai's deceit was even more damaging than that.

The blow was so brutal because of the beautiful thing he did for my family only days before he shattered my heart.

It truly is a double-edged sword. If Nikolai weren't in my life, Maddox's transfer to a safer facility would have never occurred, but his presence stirred up a set of emotions I didn't plan for when I moved to Vegas. I'm supposed to be here for my family, but I want to act selfishly for the first time in a long time.

Is that bad of me to admit? Should I feel guilty I want to put myself first? I would have said a resounding yes if you had asked me before my conversation with Maddox. Now I'm not so sure.

Maddox is the key to unlocking his conviction, but I'm at a crossroads with him refusing to help. I'll never stop fighting to have his conviction overturned, but I can't keep rotting away and not living my life anymore, either.

I've barely lived the past four years, and I focus more on those around me than myself, so can't I put myself first for a little while?

My hands swipe across my face when the awareness of being watched washes over me.

"Margarita Thursday. You coming?"

After ensuring my cheeks are tear-free, I swivel my chair to face the voice. An unexpected giggle spills from my lips for the second time in under ten minutes. Trent is standing in my office door, wearing the most hideous floral shirt I've ever seen. He has a pair of maracas in his hand and a ridiculous straw hat on his head.

"Come on, Justine, five-dollar margaritas. No one can turn down five-dollar margaritas." He shimmies into my office, his dance moves as horrendous as his outfit. "I'm not taking no for an answer this time. You've been at Schluter & Fletcher for over three months but have never come out with the gang for drinks. It's time to put some hair on your chest with the sweet burn of alcohol."

"I can't," I murmur, waving my hand over the paperwork sprawled across my desk. "I have..." My words fade into silence when I fail to conjure a plausible excuse.

After my performance at the Popov compound three days ago, I've been relegated to intern hell. Years of studying criminal masterminds mean nothing when you snarl at a client in front of your employer.

Mr. Schluter's scolding was brief but potent, although he shredded my confidence into pieces, after the shenanigans I pulled, I'm grateful to still be employed—even if I've been demoted to a glorified file clerk.

"Come on, Justine," Trent grumbles, promptly reminding me to save my wallowing until I'm in privacy. "You've always been a stiff, but you've been acting like a corpse this week."

My mouth falls open. I'm battered by his snide remark on my personality. I had no clue that my determination to achieve the goals I made four years ago made me appear like a wet blanket. I know how to have a good time.

Well, I did four years ago.

When Trent peers at me with giant puppy-dog eyes, I mumble, "Fine. Lead the way."

I push back from my desk, nearly running over his toes since he is wearing flip-flops. If I don't put my wheels in motion while my determination is high, I won't leave my office before 11 p.m., just like the past four nights.

"Seriously, you're coming?" Trent asks, his pitch high with shock. He is so startled by my agreement he sounds a decade younger. When I nod, he bolts into the corridor. "Michelle, get those extra clothes from your car. Justine's coming."

Before I can announce I'm perfectly fine wearing the clothes I have on, Mr. Fletcher's impressive frame fills the doorway of my office.

"You're coming out for drinks?" he asks, his voice rife with suspicion.

I nod, adoring his quirked expression.

Although I got hammered by Mr. Schluter Tuesday afternoon, Mr. Fletcher kept his reprimand to a private, mature discussion on how I can better handle the situation next time a problematic client blindsides me. He never directly mentioned Nikolai's name—or the compromising position he discovered me in the morning he arrived at my apartment unannounced—but his pep talk felt more personal than businesslike, leading me to believe he understood why my composure slipped.

"Are you in the mood for margaritas?" I ask, hesitantly pacing toward him, praying my extension of the olive branch won't be rejected without consideration.

Before spending my weekend with a mafia prince, we were close. Now it feels like I'm on the outs, not just with him but everyone on our team.

A smile etches onto my lips when Mr. Fletcher pinches the crease of his trousers and raises the hem. He is also wearing flip-flops. Actually, come to think of it, they are identical to the ones Trent is wearing.

"Even when I'm not in the mood for drinking, I can't pass up five-dollar margaritas."

When Trent appears at his side, lugging an armful of Hawaiian-print clothes, I ask, "What's with the clothing?"

Mr. Fletcher secures a straw hat from the top of Trent's stack, places it on my head, and then says, "Club rules. If you don't wear the outfit, you pay full price."

I grimace. Cocktails in general are outrageous, but they price gouge even more because of our hotspot destination.

As we walk down the hallway, Mr. Fletcher's suit jacket and long-sleeved business shirt are traded for a Hawaiian shirt and a grass skirt. With all the excitement in the air, it isn't hard to tell Mr. Schluter's half of the office is vacant. The pizza and beer Mr. Fletcher rewards us with when we have an all-night cram session never arrives until Mr. Schluter has left for the evening, so I doubt he'd be a fan of the current ruckus. He is as anti-social as I've been for the past four years.

"I don't have any more shirts, but if you whip off your blouse, your cami will go perfectly with this," Michelle says, handing me a plastic grass skirt.

"Oh, it's fine. My blouse will work," I reply, slipping the skimpy accessory up my thighs and over my skirt.

When Michelle's brows become lost in her hairline, I undo the bottom three buttons of my blouse and tie the ends into a knot in the middle of my stomach. With the floral lei Trent handed me, I have the Hawaiian surfer chick vibe down pat.

"Ah, that totally works. Sexy and sophisticated."

I smile, grateful for Michelle's compliment and pleased with my quick thinking. I'm not ashamed of the circumstances that resulted in my scars—having the courage to tell a man no is nothing to be ashamed of—but I am embarrassed about my scars.

Although I doubt any of my colleagues would look at me differently if they knew I was marked, my ego is too fragile to take another hit this week. I'm barely staying afloat as it is. I'm not strong enough to endure another blow.

"Was that Maddox you were talking to earlier?" Mr. Fletcher asks when we merge onto the sidewalk at the back entrance of Schluter & Fletcher.

Smiling, I nod. "Yeah. With Mom visiting him every other day, he used one of her calls on me."

The twinkle in his eyes tells me he didn't miss the sentiment in my tone. "Is he settling in okay? Finding his way around?"

Again, I nod. "As well as he can for the situation."

Placing his hand on the curve of my back, he guides us a few paces in front of the rest of our group. He reveals the reason for his sudden need for privacy when he faintly questions, "Did you ever discover who organized his transfer?"

I keep my eyes facing the front, taking some time to deliberate a response. Mr. Fletcher is a smart man, so I have no doubt he is aware my relationship with Nikolai went further than a standard attorney-client acquaintance, but with my emotions badly faltering, now isn't the right time to admit to breaking company policy. I plan on telling him, but I want to do it in a professional manner—not when I'm a crying, blubbering imbecile.

I don't trust my voice not to squeak, so I shake my head.

Mr. Fletcher's lips crimp before he mutters, "Might have been an old application finally placed in the right hands?" he says, his tone one he generally reserves for clients.

"Maybe," I reply softly, hating how many lies I've told. Not just today but my entire week.

With his hand remaining on my back, he directs me toward a rowdy club far from the strip. The turmoil plaguing me all week lifts instantly when we walk into the vibrant, colorful space. I felt foolish walking down a bustling street in a grass skirt and a lei, but my outfit is tame compared to the many other patrons downing margaritas like their throats are on fire.

One man has the Hawaiian look down to a T. His long brown wig sits on his shoulders, and the black markers used to trace islander tattoos on his biceps could only look more authentic if they weren't intermingled with the sweat dripping from his pecs. He kind of looks like Dwayne Johnson... with hair.

"Margarita?" Kirk asks, glancing in my direction.

I smile before nodding. That is the first word Kirk has spoken to me since I stole his chance to first-chair with Mr. Fletcher last weekend. I had hoped his silence was because he was too busy to chat, but our staff meeting yesterday made me suspicious. He never looked my way when updating our department on incoming cases.

When my hand delves into my purse to secure some cash to pay for my drink, Mr. Fletcher curls his hand over mine. "All drinks are on me," he advises, his tone friendly.

"Oh, no, I can't have you buying my drinks."

I don't know why, but I've always seen the purchase of drinks as something more meaningful than just friends hanging out. It is like when a man pays for a woman's meal—is he just being nice, or is he hoping his gallantry will be awarded in a more intimate way?

Mr. Fletcher leans into my side, ensuring I can hear him over the music thumping around the club. "I'm not just buying your drinks, Justine. I buy everyone's." His tone reveals he didn't miss the hesitation crossing my face.

"Why do you think we do Margarita Thursdays instead of Tequila Saturdays?" Trent shouts, obviously standing close enough to hear Mr. Fletcher's guarantee.

"Because Carmichael is too cheap to pay full price," Michelle, Trent, and Kirk shout in sync, their voices crackling with laughter.

When Mr. Fletcher shrugs, neither denying nor confirming their assertion, I giggle for a third time today. At this rate, I'll make up for my lack of social life in one evening.

"Are you sure?" I double-check. I've caused a lot of trouble for Mr. Fletcher the past week, so I'm not eager to add more drama to his life.

"I'm sure, Justine. It is just a drink. What's the worst that could happen?"

9

JUSTINE

"Oh my god, I never knew Kirk could sing like that. Why is he a lawyer? He could be making a killing on Broadway."

Mr. Fletcher throws his head back and laughs. "I know, right? I guess some of us are just gluttons for punishment." He sidesteps a restaurant owner putting out his trash for the night. "I always thought money was the most important thing in life. Only now am I realizing it doesn't make a difference. Quality of life has nothing to do with assets and everything to do with who you spend your time with."

"That's easy for someone with money to say." I waggle my brows, ensuring he knows my statement wasn't in malice. I'm being as playful as my tipsy state allows.

He laughs again. "True." His eyes lift to my apartment building peeking over the horizon before he returns them to me. "I'm glad you came out with us tonight, Justine. Nights like tonight make our team stronger."

I smile, humbled by him saying "our team." After my foolishness the past week, it's nice to know he still considers me a team member.

"I'm glad I came too. It was a lot of fun."

When my hand reaches out to open the door of my apartment building, he beats me to it. "Allow me. What kind of man would I be if I offered to walk you home but didn't ensure you arrived at your apartment safely?"

Not waiting for me to answer, he heads to the elevator bank and pushes the call button. I breathe out my unease before following him. Although he's been in my apartment before, my stomach has an odd set of nerves. I wouldn't necessarily say it is worry, but my intuition warns me to be cautious.

Mr. Fletcher's flirty tendencies tonight were as vigorous as they've always been but weren't as appealing as usual. I don't know if my lack of interest is because we're not in a work environment or because of Nikolai.

Considering the churning of my stomach ramped up during my last confession, I'd say it is the latter.

Suddenly, my heart launches into a crazy beat, startled by Mr. Fletcher's hand unexpectedly diving into my hair.

"Sorry," he murmurs, clearly stunned by my skittish response. "You have a piece of straw stuck in your hair."

He removes the offending article from my unruly curls, which are extra buoyant from the scattering of rain we dodged on our walk home.

Although his gesture is innocent, I can't lower my heart rate.

He's a mere inch from discovering a gritty scar nestled behind my right ear.

"See? Just a piece of straw."

He waits for me to acknowledge the tiny blade of grass before he releases it from his grasp. It floats to the floor, its whoosh nearly audible in the edgy silence bouncing between us.

"You've got another piece right here."

Air rushes out of my mouth in a hurry when his fingers glide past my left temple before drifting down my inflamed cheek.

To an outsider, it could appear as if he's ridding my hair and face of evidence of our fun night, but I know it is more than that. I can see it in his eyes. He exudes confidence by the bucketloads, but that's not what's lighting his inky-black eyes.

It is the spark of desire.

With his eyes bouncing between mine, he takes a step closer to me, testing if I too can feel the energy bristling between us.

When I fail to protest his intrusion on my personal space, the hankering in his eyes triples.

As much as I know I should be shutting this down, I can't. Has your ego ever been so low you're willing to do anything to regain the smallest slice of confidence? That's what I'm dealing with right now. I know I should stop this. I know I'll regret my lack of worth in the morning, but with my dizzy head and low self-esteem playing havoc with my mind, bad intentions suddenly seem honorable.

My heart smashes against my ribcage when Mr. Fletcher's hand glides over my inflamed cheek before dropping to float past my lips. His touch is gentle and reserved, adding to the giddiness in my head.

My lips tremble when he cups my jaw, but instead of pulling away from his embrace, shockingly, I lean into it.

He stares into my eyes, ensuring the alcohol lacing my veins hasn't caused me to mistake his intentions.

Grazing my teeth over my bottom lip, I faintly nod, acknowledging I understand his objective.

The tightness in his shoulders loosens as relief floods his eyes. When he tilts even closer, bringing his lips to within an inch of mine, the smell of salt lingers in my nostrils. His scent is a unique tangy aroma, amplified by the orange liqueur and lime juice in the margaritas we shared this evening.

It is an intoxicating smell but nowhere near as appealing as Nikolai's masculine scent.

I freeze, suddenly disturbed.

I'm moments away from being kissed by one man, yet my mind strays to another.

God, who am I?

I came to Vegas to coerce the best defense lawyer in the country to work on my brother's conviction, but all I've done the past week is watch four years of hard work circle the drain.

With only a second to spare, I slant my head to the side, forcing Mr. Fletcher's lips to land on my cheek instead of my mouth.

Even with our exchange being as innocent as a schoolyard peck, guilt smashes into me hard and fast. It may be uncalled for and utterly ridiculous, but there is no doubt it is guilt clutching my throat.

When a faint ding sounds in my ears, I mumble, "Thank you for a wonderful evening."

I dash into the waiting elevator car, the timing of which couldn't be more perfect. The elevator attendant, Simon, smiles a greeting before pressing the button for the fifteenth floor.

"It's fine. Simon can take it from here," I advise Mr. Fletcher when he attempts to enter the elevator. "Can't you, Simon?"

Simon's eyes bounce between Mr. Fletcher and me for several uncomfortable seconds before curtly nodding. Although horrified I'm using one man to deflect the attention of another, I don't alter my approach.

When you are backed into a corner, nothing is off-limits, not even your pride.

Mr. Fletcher's brows furrow, his confusion at an all-time high. He knows Simon isn't a threat—his retirement-colored hair and coke bottle glasses ensure he is no competition for a man as handsome as Mr. Fletcher—but he still seems stumped.

"You don't want me to walk you to your door?" The throatiness of his reply wipes the innocence from his question.

The only door he wants to walk me to is my bedroom door.

The lust raging in his heavy-lidded gaze clouds with uncertainty when I shake my head. He eyes me peculiarly, wordlessly requesting clarification on the conflicting messages I've sent all night.

"I can't. I just... *can't.*"

If I could offer him a better reason for my stupidity, I would, but I'm lost for an explanation. I'm the most discombobulated I've ever been. I know it is guilt bombarding me, but it's not the same guilt I've dealt with over the past four years.

Just like your love for your family is different from your love for a spouse, this guilt is different because it isn't associated with my family. It is about Nikolai. He deceived me, but until I understand why he did that, two wrongs don't make a right.

Thankfully, I'm saved from further interrogation when the elevator doors snap shut. Breathing deeply, I balance against the glass wall of the car. I need a moment to ease the pain sitting on my chest before it cripples me.

I know why I led Mr. Fletcher on. I wanted him to ease the pain of Nikolai's deceit. I just wish I was strong enough I didn't need a man's touch to make me feel worthy. I've gone four years without requiring validation from the opposite sex, so why am I suddenly craving it like it's more valuable than life itself?

When the elevator dings, announcing its arrival at my floor, I bid Simon farewell with a chin dip before exiting. My steps down the hallway are heavy, weighed down by the conflict sitting on my shoulders.

I should hate Nikolai for how he betrayed me, but dislike is the last thought to enter my mind when he sneaks into my memories without warning.

We only had four days together, but the shortness of our time can't weaken the impact he made on my life. What he did for Maddox was beautiful, but how he looked at me... *God*... I felt like the most valued treasure on the planet.

After throwing open my apartment door, I toe off my heels and kick them under my entryway table. I smell like cheap liqueur and cigarettes, but I stumble toward my bedroom instead of the bathroom.

With my sleep severely lacking the last three nights, I am exhausted—both physically and mentally.

My sluggish steps stop halfway across my living room when a deep Russian voice asks, "Where have you been, *Ангел*? I've been waiting for you for hours."

The alcohol hindering my smarts burns off in an instant when a dark shadow stands from a chair at the side of my living room. Although the room is pitch black, I know it is Nikolai. I can sense him with every nerve in my body.

He turns on the lamp next to my couch before heading my way. My first thought is to demand an explanation for him being in my apartment unannounced, but I swallow my words, paralyzed by the murderous rage beaming out of him in invisible waves.

His natural arrogance is at an all-time high, leaving no misconception of who is standing before me. He is the man behind his title. He is Nikolai, a Russian mafia prince.

"You have to the count of five to answer my question, *Ангел*. After that, I'll reach my own conclusion," Nikolai warns, his voice as hot-tempered as his face. "I can guarantee my findings won't be as pleasant as yours. Five... Four... Three..."

"I went out for drinks with friends." My voice trembles when I articulate the word "friends."

It isn't the slight deceit in my reply that made me stammer. It is Nikolai stopping to stand in front of me. The darkness of the room can't hide his soul-stealing blue eyes and traffic-stopping face I've missed ogling the past three days. He appears as he does in my dreams every night: perfectly haunting.

I'm freed from being trapped by his entrancing eyes when he grumbles, "Friends?"

His tone is rough, as if his throat was scorched with the same deceit mine was scolded with earlier this week.

I shouldn't get pleasure from his jealousy, but I do.

I want him to be angry, because if he is, I wasn't just a side dish he used to keep himself occupied while his fiancée was away. He was with me because he wanted me as badly as I craved him.

"Answer me, *Ангел*," Nikolai demands.

"Yes," I stammer out, feebly nodding. "I was with friends." Since my statement isn't a lie, it sounds as it should—honest.

Angling his head to the side, Nikolai circles me like a shark, his pace purposely slow. He reeks of pigheaded cockiness, but there is something deeper, more tangible in his narrowed gaze.

In a matter of seconds, the heat in the room turns excruciating, suffocated by both arousal and unbridled fury. I don't know how two such contradicting responses can occur at the same time. I'm just calling it how I see it.

My heart rate spikes when his hand dives into my hair. Unlike my frightened response to Mr. Fletcher's touch, my body reacts positively this time.

Disturbed by my needy response to his touch, I blubber, "What are you doing, Nikolai? You can't just arrive at my apartment unannounced."

Acting like he didn't hear a word I spoke, he leans in and takes a deep and undignified whiff of my hair. Goosebumps prick my skin, my body excited by the throaty growl he releases not even two seconds later.

"What did I tell you, *Ангел?*" Although he's asking a question, he continues speaking, hindering my ability to reply. "I told you I'd know if *he* touched you." Fear and excitement roll down my spine when his gaze narrows. "I can smell *him* on you."

I shake my head, futilely trying to deny his claim. It's a woeful waste of time. Nikolai's eyes reveal his opinion, which is far more sinister than reality. His body is gripped with tension, his eyes as bleak as my heart felt when I realized he is a taken man.

I look away, fighting the bile surging up my throat. I thought it would feel good to see him as pained as I was when I discovered he was engaged.

I was wrong—*very, very wrong.*

This doesn't feel good at all.

"I wanted you to experience what I went through, and I wanted him to take away my pain..."

My words stop when the sound of feet stomping booms into my ears. Nikolai is retreating from me faster than my foggy brain can comprehend.

"I'm going to fucking kill him," he murmurs under his breath, throwing open my front door with so much force the door handle smacks into the drywall, leaving a significant dent.

With four margaritas flowing through me, it takes me a few moments to register who his threat pertains to. When the light bulb finally clicks on, my stomach violently gurgles.

"Nikolai, wait," I say, chasing after him. "You didn't let me finish."

I freeze halfway out my door when Nikolai's furious gaze spears me in place. His nostrils flare as his fists clench into firm balls. "You don't need to finish your story. You confirmed what I already know. *He* touched you. *Carmichael* touched you." His face screws up when he snarls Mr. Fletcher's name.

"Not in the way you're thinking."

"I don't fucking care!" he yells. "I warned him what I'd do if he got within an inch of you. I fucking told him to stay away from you." His face reddens with every syllable he speaks. "Now I will show him I'm a man of my word."

When he stalks down the hallway, I match his steps stride for stride.

"Don't follow me, *Ангел,*" he warns, hearing my soundless steps. "Not unless you want to witness him taking his last breath."

His threat freezes my steps and my heart. I heard the promise in his words—the determination. His warning wasn't idle.

He fully intends to follow through.

Nikolai issues me one last dangerous stare when the elevator arrives at my floor. "Go inside, *Ангел*. I'll deal with you when I get back."

Not waiting for me to reply, he enters the elevator.

10

JUSTINE

I'm grateful for my outdated apartment when I slip into the elevator moments before its doors slam shut. Although panicked about what Nikolai's reaction will be to me ignoring his request, my hesitation doesn't linger for long. Mr. Fletcher may have shrugged off Nikolai's threat from last week, but a kiss on the cheek doesn't equate to a death sentence.

After taking a moment to breathe out my nerves, I scan the elevator car. Nikolai has taken control of the elevator panel. His head is hanging low, his hands fisted at his sides.

With Nikolai bubbling over with anger, Simon has understandably moved to the far left-hand side of the car, the fear of losing his job forcing him to surrender control to a mafia prince.

Jerking his chin, Simon gestures for me to join him cowering in the corner. I shake my head, denying his request. I'm rattled, but I'm not scared of Nikolai.

He can shred my heart to pieces, but he will never hurt me.

My eyes stray away from Simon when Nikolai's anger gets the better of him. He throws his fist into the elevator panel three times, the roar leaving his throat sounding like a wounded animal.

Although panicked he has injured himself, some good comes from his fury. The elevator doors open on the next floor, giving Simon a safe exit.

"No," Simon mumbles under his breath, denying my suggestion he leave. He pushes his thick-rimmed glasses up his nose as his massively dilated gaze drifts to Nikolai.

"I'll be fine," I assure him, my voice hushed. "He won't hurt me." Fortunately, my tone is confident enough to ease the turmoil in Simon's green eyes. When the elevator doors slowly chug closed, I quickly warn, "I can't make the same guarantee for you, Simon. If you don't leave now, I won't be held accountable for what happens next."

I've got enough guilt on my shoulders. I refuse to add any more.

Simon's panicked eyes bounce between Nikolai and me for what feels like hours but is mere seconds before he hurries out the elevator door with only a second to spare.

Nikolai is so engulfed by anger he doesn't register Simon's exit.

His focus is on one thing and one thing only—hunting down Mr. Fletcher.

After breathing out my nerves, I jab the emergency stop button on the cracked elevator panel. "We need to talk."

Nikolai's head rockets to the side. He glares at me, his back molars grinding as erratically as my heart is smashing into my ribs. "There is only one conversation I plan to have... one with my fists."

Snarling at me like I'm gum under his shoe, he pushes the emergency stop button, sending the elevator back into motion.

Matching his immaturity, I once again hit the emergency button.

"Try again," I stammer out, my demand stronger than my words.

Nikolai growls before jabbing the emergency stop button so hard the outer plastic panel crumbles under his touch. Even with the air deprived of oxygen, my insides clench from his seductive purr.

Although ashamed of my body's response, I'm not surprised. Even filing Nikolai and Malvina's application to wed this afternoon didn't loosen Nikolai's hold over me. My heart doesn't want to see sense, even when the evidence is the most damning it's ever seen.

"You're being ridiculous. A man kisses me on the cheek, and you act like the earth is crumbling beneath your feet, but it's perfectly acceptable for me to find out you're engaged from your gushing fiancée, who is so eager to marry you, she can't wait a few measly weeks for citizenship!"

I stare at him, waiting for him to react to my outburst.

He does nothing.

He remains perfectly still.

His silence hurts more than his words ever could.

Fuming with heartbreaking anger, I stab the emergency stop button again.

Putting his open palm on my chest, Nikolai shoves me away from him. "Enough!" he shouts, his loud voice booming around the small space.

His shove barely jolts me halfway across the car, but it is forceful enough for my mood to snap. I've been pushed around way too much over the past four years. I am done being treated like I'm worthless.

I charge for Nikolai, my steps so fast tears trickle down my cheeks. My fists pounding on his back match my heart thrashing against my ribs.

Pain shoots up my arms, but I don't hold back. I express every pain tearing me apart by pummeling his back over and over again.

Maybe if he feels even ten percent of the agony his deceit put me through, he'll have more understanding of why I acted the way I did tonight.

"I risked everything for you, and how do you repay me? By having your *fiancée* flash her ginormous rock in my fucking face!"

Nikolai moves so stealthily that I'm squished between him and the elevator panel before I can comprehend what is happening.

He pins my arms to my sides, tethering my body to him as well as his deceit strangled my heart. "I'm risking everything for you, and how do you repay me?" he quotes, his words as pained as his eyes look. "By letting that *Идиот* touch what is *mine*." He snarls his last word in a possessive, narcissistic way.

"That's not even close to the same thing," I choke out through a sob, my voice surprisingly loud for how hard I'm crying. "A peck on a cheek is nothing compared to how you deceived me. You are *engaged*, Nikolai. You're getting *married*." Anger overtakes my devastation when he shakes his head, denying my claims. "I saw the paperwork. Malvina filed for a marriage license Wednesday afternoon. You're getting married on Saturday." Heartbreak is clutching my throat so fiercely I struggle to force out my last sentence.

"I'm not marrying Malvina," he shouts, making my heart shudder. "How many times do I have to spell it out for you? If I wanted her, I'd already fucking have her. I. Don't. Want. Her." He leans into me deeper, snatching the air from my lungs. "I want you. I've never lied about that." His tone dulls from an angry growl to a slight sneer. "But having you comes at a cost. One Carmichael is going to discover the hard way."

"It was a peck, Nikolai—"

"On a face that belongs to me. On skin that is mine. You're not his to kiss," he interrupts, his words growing as heated as his face. "You are *mine*, Justine." He releases my right wrist to bang his fist on his chest as he growls, "M*ine*."

The rawness in his eyes causes more havoc to my mind than the world's most potent drug, stripping my insecurities as quickly as my anger.

All I see in his beautiful blue irises is a little boy who had his every wish denied—over and over again.

That is why he is so possessive.

In his heart, he believes it will only be a matter of time before I am taken from him as well.

God—why didn't I see this earlier? It could have saved us both days of heartache.

Nikolai's eyes drop to my chest when my hands dart to the buttons on my blouse. His hot breath hits my cheek when I yank open the delicate fabric with so much force buttons shoot in all directions. I slide the shimmery material off my shoulders before tugging my skirt down my thighs. I'm not worried I'm revealing bite marks on my shoulders and legs. Nikolai is the rawest he's ever been, and now I am as well.

"Take it away. Wash it away. Do whatever you need to do to remove his scent from my skin," I say, talking through the lump in my throat.

I stand across from him in nothing but a pair of panties and a skintight cami with my chest rising and falling in the same frantic rhythm as his.

I've made myself as vulnerable to him as I can.

I can't do any more than I have. Now it is up to him. He can continue his quest for revenge or take back what he thinks was stolen from him.

"He needs to be punished. I warned him," Nikolai groans, his words so rough they sound like they were dragged through gravel before he spat them out.

"What about me? How will you punish me?" His eyes snap to mine, their volatility making what I'm about to say ten times harder. "I disrespected you more than Carmichael did, so shouldn't I be the one suffering the consequences of our stupidity?"

"He kissed you—"

"Because I led him on," I interrupt, my voice shaky with tears. "I wanted you to feel what I felt when you kissed Malvina. I wanted you to hurt as much as I was... as I still am! God, Nikolai, how can you not understand how much seeing you with her killed me? You spent the weekend building me up, only to stand back and watch me fall. Why would you do that? Why set out to intentionally destroy me?"

His eyes flare as the tic in his jaw firms. "I'm not destroying you—"

"Yes, you are," I mumble through a sheet of tears gliding down my cheeks. "Look at me. Look at what you've done to me. You've made me so weak I don't even know who I am anymore."

Nikolai balks as if my words physically stunned him. "You are not weak, Ангел. You are the strongest you've ever been." He pinches my chin when I shake my head, forcing my eyes to align with his. "Look at how you came at me, fighting and without fear. Days ago, you wouldn't have done that. You would have bowed your head like you did the day we met. You would have given up before you ever made it this far." His eyes lock with mine, ensuring I can see the truth in them as he adds, "I'm not destroying you, Justine. We're destroying each other... for the better."

I freeze as I'm bombarded with emotions. As much as our argument sliced open my chest for the world to see, what he is saying is true. Before him, I would have never had the courage to battle a man as powerful as him. I would have bowed down and accepted my fate as I did four years ago.

I didn't even fight Col's decision. I completely froze, too scared to even speak.

My silence would have killed me that night if it hadn't been for Maddox.

The veins in my neck twang when Nikolai's thumb drags over the exact spot on my face Mr. Fletcher's lips touched. His accuracy is so precise you'd swear he can smell Mr. Fletcher's scent on my skin. "That's why he wants you, Justine. He sees in you what I do."

"He'll never have me. I am not his to have," I reply, glancing into his bleak, pained eyes. "I'm yours. I will always be yours—"

I stop talking when the most delicious pair of lips press against mine. My eyes snap shut, sending fresh tears rolling down my cheeks.

These are tears of relief, not sadness.

At the request of Nikolai's lashing tongue, I part my lips. The turmoil making my skin a sticky mess fades when my taste buds detect the flavor of his mouth. I thought heartache was playing tricks on my mind. It wasn't. He tastes even better than I remembered. So sweet and oh-so-manly.

Weaving my fingers through his hair, which is damp at the ends from the oppressive heat in the elevator car, I slide my tongue along the roof of his mouth.

Nikolai groans, his excitement as palpable as mine. I curl my legs around his waist before deepening our kiss. I'm so desperate for his lips on mine that I crave them even more than my next breath.

As our tongues duel in a fire-sparking showdown, he fiddles with the fly on his jeans. When the distinct noise of a zipper rolling down sounds through my ears, I drag my mouth away from his.

Air traps in my throat when his glorious cock springs free from its tight constraint. It is thick and jutted, with a bead of moisture pooling at the tip.

I tear my eyes away from the glorious visual when the heat of Nikolai's gaze captures my attention. He's staring at me, his gaze hot and attentive. He doesn't speak. He doesn't need to. His eyes relay his every intention. I am his, and he is taking back what is his.

My head falls back when he slips my panties to the side and impales me in one fervent thrust. The pain of taking a man his size without preparation is pushed aside for sheer pleasure at being the fullest I've ever been. It is a hard sensation to explain, painful and bittersweet at the same time.

Nikolai's throaty growl on my neck reveals I'm not the only one overcome by the utter brilliance of our exchange. He is as taken aback as I am.

"You feel that... how well we fit? That's because you were made for me. This greedy cunt sucking at my cock, begging to be consumed—it's *mine*. You're mine, Justine. *Mine*."

He waits for me to acknowledge his assertive comment with a nod before he draws his cock out to the tip. A pleasurable tingle shoots through my womb when he rocks back into me, his second thrust as perfectly precise as his first.

He pumps into me over and over again, his grinding as uncontrolled as the husky moans rolling up my throat. He works my body with perfection, not only showcasing his impressive bedroom skills but how in tune he is with my body as well. The sensation is amazing, better than any sex we've had.

Every precise thrust of his cock drives me to the brink in a shameful amount of time. He screws my body as well as he fucks with my mind, a mind-hazing exchange that makes my heart swell as much as shatter. Even with my morals blinded by lust, I know I'm still the other woman.

I may be Nikolai's, but I'm not the only woman he has a claim to.

Seeming to sense my resolve weakening, Nikolai grips my nape and soundlessly commands my eyes to his. The churning of my stomach switches to waves of ecstasy when my eyes lock with his. They are laced with natural arrogance and brimming with unbridled possessiveness. He knows only he can drive me so wild I forget the world is striving to keep us apart. He knows I am defenseless to him.

He knows I am his.

"Say it," Nikolai requests, his voice thick and husky.

When I stare at him, confused by his request, he adds a roll to his hips, confident he can destroy my hesitation with nothing but a thrust of his crotch.

He is right. One touch and I'm under his spell. I'm burning up everywhere, my desire for him more potent than my morals.

I moan through the sensation zinging from my clit to my aching breasts, before whimpering, "I'm yours."

"Again," he growls while pulling me away from the wall my sweat-drenched back is braced against.

Considering his jeans are wrapped around his knees, his strides are remarkably stable. I'm not the least bit worried he is going to drop me. He's not solely showcasing the power he has over my body. He is demonstrating his overall strength. And with every perfect thrust of his hips reflected in the mirrored walls of the elevator, it is a brilliant, pussy-clenching sight.

The way he guides me up and down his cock by clutching only my neck drives me wild. He fucks me without reserve, using every muscle in his body to wholly possess mine. The sexy V muscle I'll never tire of seeing grinds into my clit while his densely veined cock dominates every inch of my quivering pussy.

"Again!" Nikolai demands, displeased by my delay.

His loud voice startles me so much my climax is thrust to within an inch of the finish line. I'm panting without constraint, and my body is heightened beyond belief.

"I'm yours," I shout as violent waves sweep across my core, growing in intensity with every magnificent drive of his hips.

Sweat dots my forehead as the coil in my womb tightens to the point of snapping. The sensation is so frantic it is almost dangerous. I've never been woven so tightly before. I'm spiraling out of control.

"Oh god. Please. I need more. Please," I beg, my voice practically a scream.

"Do you feel that, Ангел?" Nikolai asks, throwing his hips forward, ramming his cock even further inside me. "Me inside you. Fucking you. Claiming you. That is all me—not God. It. Is. All. Me." He grinds out his last four words with the unconcealed arrogance I've fallen in love with. It is gruff and dominant, and it has me free-falling into orgasmic bliss.

I shout his name into the air as tingles race the length of my spine. I'm shuddering without hesitation, loving the sensation launching me into a quivering, blubbering mess.

"That's it, Ангел, give it to me. Scream my name for the world to hear."

I am lost, swept away by a phenomenon the world's most lethal substance could never replicate. The highs I experience with Nikolai are like no other: long, sweet, and utterly devastating.

Nikolai's orgasm soon follows mine. He pumps into me another two times before the hotness of his cum lines the walls of my pussy.

I moan, adoring the heat of his sperm filling every inch of me. Before our exchange in the bathroom Tuesday morning, I'd never had sex without protection, but just like Tuesday morning, today's encounter is more significant than just an accidental slip in protection. It is tethering us closer together, making us unbreakable.

It makes him mine as much as I am his.

Nikolai never hid the fact he's never had unprotected sex. He knows a man of his stature and wealth is a prime target for any woman hoping to catch a ride to easy street.

He even bragged about double-bagging his cock. His smile was wiped right off his face when I informed him that double-bagging increases the chances of condom breakages.

That's another reason his deceit hurt so much. We discussed so many things over the thirty-six hours we had together, but he did not mention he was engaged. He told me stories about his eldest brother, Rico, and his death three years ago. He even disclosed the circumstances of his mother's suicide, but Malvina's name never entered the conversation.

Was she not there for him when he needed her? Or does Nikolai not care about her like he says? And if that is the case, why is he still engaged to her?

I grow concerned that I expressed myself out loud when Nikolai says, "Everyone makes mistakes. It is only once we learn from them that we can move on."

When he places me on my feet, I balance on the glass wall of the elevator car. The coolness of the smooth material is wondrous on my overheated skin, and the sturdy surface ensures my wobbly legs keep me upright.

After tucking his half-masted cock into his jeans, Nikolai gathers my clothing from the floor. I watch in silence as he dresses me, confused and suddenly bombarded by panic. Our exchange wiped the turmoil from my eyes, which seems to have increased it for him. I wouldn't necessarily say his anger is as intense as it was when we entered the elevator, but there is a cloud over his alluring gaze. He looks worried, and if I am not entirely mistaken, spooked.

"Nikolai—"

"Don't," he interrupts, pressing his finger to my lips. "Not yet.

I've got some stuff I need to sort out first. Then we'll move on to... *this.*" He waves his hand between us, making me feel like the size of an ant.

"This?" I mimic, my voice surprisingly strong for how hard my heart is hammering.

My boiling anger dulls to a simmer when the corners of his mouth tug into a smirk. I glare at him, equally happy and mortified by his smile. I'm happy, as his smile is genuine and shows what I've always known. He wants a woman strong enough to stand beside him, not three paces back. But I'm mortified he referred to our relationship as "this." If that doesn't make me feel like the other woman, I'm not Catholic.

"Justine," Nikolai grumbles, drawing my focus back to him. "I swear to god, if you don't get that look out of your eyes, we'll never leave this elevator. You are so fucking sexy when you're jealous."

I try to reply that there is nothing sexy about getting jealous over another man's fiancée, but nothing but air bubbles leave my mouth. I'm so stunned at how quickly his composure can switch that I'm left without a retort.

Thirty minutes ago, he was close to detonating. Now he's looking at me like he didn't just drive me to the brink mere minutes ago.

After restarting the elevator, Nikolai shifts his eyes to me. "Come here," he demands, a jerk of his chin amplifying his request.

My body jumps to his command before my brain can cite a single objection. Even though I'm acting like a submissive imbecile, if I could go back in time, I wouldn't change my decision. Nikolai's grin at my obliging gesture—my god. I nearly combust a second time.

He runs the back of his fingers down my flaming cheek before dropping them to my heavy-with-need breasts. Some of the unease in his eyes clears for smugness when my nipples bud under his touch.

"Did I hurt you?" he asks, his voice as low hanging as his head.

"No," I reply without hesitation.

I'm tempted to add "not physically," but I leash my scornful tongue. One glance into his eyes, and the cause of his teetering mood smacks into me. He's not harboring anger at my exchange with Mr. Fletcher. He's petrified he hurt me.

Before I can voice that nothing he could ever do would cause me harm, the elevator dings, announcing its arrival at the lobby. My heart rate I've only just settled kicks into a mariachi beat when my quick scan of the foyer has me stumbling upon an ashen-faced Simon, a tired super, and two snarling security guards.

Crap!

Snubbing the security guards' overzealous holds of their batons, Nikolai kisses the side of my mouth. His manly scent lingers in my nose, his unique smell even more prominent since his body is misted with sweat.

"Go upstairs. I'll be back in a few hours."

My eyes rocket to his. "Hours?" My voice is so loud I'm certain people three blocks over heard my shrieked word.

Pretending he hasn't spotted the mountain load of questions pumping out of me, Nikolai steps out of the elevator. With a jerk of his chin, he demands Simon reconvene his position as elevator attendant. Unlike our earlier scuffle, Simon does as suggested. He dives into the steamy, sex-scented space faster than the Flash, lurching the elevator into gear before a syllable can be fired from my mouth.

"I'll be back," Nikolai assures me moments before the elevator doors slide closed.

I quietly ride the fifteen floors, scrambling to clear the muddled mess in my head. Did my exchange with Nikolai erase his quest for revenge on Mr. Fletcher, or did it simply dull it? Should I warn Mr. Fletcher of the impending tornado set to wreak havoc in his life, or act innocent to save my tail? Does our encounter mean my affair with Nikolai is back on? And if it is, is this something I want? No one craves being the other woman, but am I so hungry for love I'm willing to set aside my strict dating rules?

I would have said no if you had asked me these questions before I met Nikolai. Now I don't know what to think. God, I truly am a different woman around him. One glance into his eyes and I am defenseless.

He owns me.

My heart, my mind, and my body.

11

JUSTINE

By the time two hours tick by, I've worn a hole in the rug of my living room. The confusion I tried to unscramble during my elevator trip with Simon remains unanswered.

I've also dialed Mr. Fletcher's number over a dozen times but failed to hit the call button every single time. Although part of my hesitation stems from ensuring I remain employed—if I'm unemployed, I'll have no chance of getting my brother's charges revoked—but for the most part, I'm hoping my touch is as effective for Nikolai as his is for me.

I also want to trust Nikolai. He said he'd never hurt me. Shouldn't that include hurting people I care about?

Deciding to wash away my confusion with scorching-hot water, I head for the bathroom. I shred my clothes off my body, leaving them where they fall.

I am so exhausted I'm shocked my legs are even moving. This week has been one of the most challenging I've had. I always knew my relationship with Nikolai would be an uphill battle. I just had no clue most of the fight would come from him.

He is engaged—no amount of unscrambling can change that.

I ensure the water is nice and hot before stepping into the shower. Flashbacks of Nikolai doing the same thing when demolishing the surveillance cameras bombard me. The protectiveness he displayed last week reveals that I am important to him, but am I significant enough to tilt the axis of his universe like he has mine? I want to say yes, but I'm so discombobulated I'm wary of trusting my morals. There is no greater poison to an ethical mind than lust.

Groaning, I step deeper into the spray. The more I analyze my relationship with Nikolai, the more confused I become. It would be nice to pretend our time together has been two people working through pent-up sexual frustration, but it feels like more than that.

Nikolai is willing to kill a man to keep me safe, and I'm risking not just my life but my family's well-being for him. That has to be more momentous than two sexually compatible people finding solace between the sheets, doesn't it?

While lathering my body, the hairs on my nape prickle, and an awareness of being watched washes over me. Cranking my neck to the side, I spot the cause of my body's response. Nikolai's shoulder is propped against the doorjamb of my bathroom. He looks tired and frustrated, which worries me more than his anger would have. He isn't the type of man who carries worry on his shoulders, so to see him so quiet is a little off-putting.

"Hey," I greet him as my eyes scan his body, wondering where he's been the past two hours.

He appears as he did when he left. His knuckles aren't showing signs of a fight, and his plain white shirt is clean and without wrinkles. His only change is the stormy cloud in his alluring gaze. It is a replica of the look I've been wearing for the past three days.

Knowing a million obstacles could never keep me away from this man, I pull open the shower curtain, soundlessly offering for him to join me. When his eyes rake the length of my body, the water pumping from the showerhead turns cold. Nikolai's gaze is so heated I feel like I'm standing on the sun. I love how he stares at me as if I am perfect, like my skin is unmarked.

While pushing off his feet, he drags his shirt over his head. The unease swishing in my stomach somersaults when the body I've missed ogling the past week breaks through the steam.

Nikolai's body is pure perfection, with muscles in all the right places, but not those horrid, overdone ones that take hours at the gym to maintain. He is firm under my hand but smooth to the touch. He truly is a triple threat with looks, intelligence, and stamina.

"Hey," I greet him for the second time when he removes his jeans and steps into the shower.

Not speaking, he curls his arm around my waist and pulls me to his thick, tense body. The stubble on his chin scratches my neckline while the heat of his rod scorches my ass. He steps forward until the suds coating my body circle the drainpipe. Although his closeness is heating every inch of me, his reserved response dampens its effect.

"Is everything okay?" I ask, worried by his silence.

He nods before switching places with me so he is under the spray. When he runs his fingers through his hair, it spikes under his touch, making him look like he did the day I first laid eyes on him.

Unable to keep my hands off him, I squeeze body wash into my palm before running my hands over the hard ridges of his chest and stomach.

Groaning, Nikolai opens his eyes and drops them to mine. He doesn't say anything. He watches me nurture him as if it is the first time it's ever happened.

Tears prick my eyes. *It probably is.*

From the reports I read on his childhood, he didn't have his mother's love and protection. Her sole devotion belonged to Vladimir. Although angered she failed to protect her own flesh and blood from a monster, I see some sense in her madness. She was under Vladimir's spell as intensely as Nikolai bewitches me.

It doesn't excuse her behavior, but who am I to judge her actions? I couldn't even muster the courage to inform my mentor and friend of impending danger, and I've only known Nikolai for a matter of days. Oksana was infatuated with Vladimir for well over a decade before Nikolai arrived. She was too far down the rabbit hole to see logic.

After ensuring every inch of Nikolai's body has been cleaned, my focus diverts to his hair. My chest expands with a deep breath when his eyes flutter shut at the soothing massage of my fingertips to his scalp. I take my time pampering him, loving how handsome he is when his face is void of his mafia sneer. He is such a sexually appealing man.

Mannish, yet beautiful.

Stern, yet playful.

Mine, yet not entirely.

Swallowing down my unease, I guide Nikolai's head under the spray. We're standing so close to each other his cock warms my pussy as well as his breath heats my lips. Although I'd love nothing more than to be reacquainted with parts of his body I'll never tire of devouring, now is the time to listen to my brain. Nikolai needs this type of intimacy as much as I do. He deserves to be shown tenderness.

He deserves to be shown he is loved.

As my hands glide down the wispy strands of hair curling around his ears, I notice angry red marks on his neck. They look like scratch marks, like someone got their claws into him and didn't want to let go.

"Malvina wasn't too happy at my request for her to leave. She kicked and screamed all the way to the gate."

My eyes shoot to Nikolai.

He didn't just say what I think he did, did he?

"You asked Malvina to leave." I'm not asking a question. I'm stating a fact. I read the truth in Nikolai's eyes. He asked her to leave.

After closing my gaping mouth, he mutters, "I understood seeing me with her hurt you. I just had no clue how bad the burn was until tonight." His body stiffens as his jaw pulls taut. "Just the thought of you with Carmichael. His lips on you. His hands on you... *Fuck*. I want to kill him, *Ангел*. I want to gut him the way I was gutted smelling him on you."

Although his temper is rising, I get some comfort in his words. He spoke them as if he hasn't harmed Mr. Fletcher yet—like it is a possibility, not a statistic. I just wish he hadn't spoken the last sentence. I hate that I contributed to him feeling "gutted."

Having no words to ease the turmoil in his eyes, I return to pampering him. I condition his hair, being extra cautious not to touch the wounds of a desperate woman. I can't say I blame Malvina. If I had no other option but to claw myself to Nikolai and never let go, that is precisely what I'd do.

When the bubbles from Nikolai's body and head are gone, I switch off the faucet and leave the shower.

"Let me," I plead when Nikolai grabs a towel.

After wrapping a towel around my drenched head and another around my body, I use a third towel to soak up the water droplets

I'm suddenly envious of. I don't think those beads of moisture have any idea how lucky they are. They're running over smooth pecs, gliding down rippling abs, and seeping into an area that is growing larger with every gentle pat.

Seriously, Nikolai's cock is so entrancing, if my heart and head weren't finally speaking the same language, I'd be falling to my knees and devouring him for dinner. But since I'm trying to give my mind the same understanding it is giving my body, I hang Nikolai's wet towel on the drying rack before turning around to face him.

Let me tell you, it is the fight of my life to keep my eyes on his face, even more so since the glorious vision of his naked package is two seconds away from being concealed by his jeans.

That's another thing I love. Since the first night he slept in my bed, Nikolai has forgone briefs, choosing instead to go commando. I don't have proof, but I'm reasonably sure the change has more to do with having one less article of clothing between us than changing preferences.

When the womb-detonating visual is hidden from my perverted gaze, I lift my eyes to Nikolai and ask, "Are you hungry?"

He stops buttoning his jeans and locks his eyes with mine. The hunger in his heavy-hooded gaze intensifies the mugginess in the room. It makes me so hot and oh-so-needy.

"Are you going to feed me, *Ангел*?" he asks, the low roughness of his tone forcing my knees together.

"Yes," I reply, my voice throaty and full of need.

The pulse in my pussy amplifies when a ghost of a smile graces his full lips. His gaze slides over my face when I return his smile. His stare is so wicked it revs up my needs. I fight with all my might not to writhe on the spot, but it is a pointless endeavor. It wouldn't matter if we were in a room surrounded by thousands. My body will always respond to his attention.

His smile turns genuine when he hooks his thumb into the knot of my towel, sending it tumbling to the floor. I ball my hands into fists at my side when his eyes rake my body. Old habits nearly have me hiding myself, but new habits stop me from doing it. This may sound conceited, but I feel beautiful when Nikolai's eyes are on me.

He lowers his eyes down my body in a slow, dedicated sweep, taking in every inch of me as if it's the first time he is seeing me. I remain perfectly still, so ensnared by him nothing could break the hold he has over me. Nikolai loves this.

The power.

The control.

Knowing I am defenseless to him.

Warm breath hisses from my parted lips when he curls his hand around my jaw. His fingers are so long they creep past my ear before weaving through my hair. Although he is touching an area plagued with scars, I don't so much as flinch. The feeling of being desired overpowers any shame.

"When you were a kid, did you ever want dessert before dinner?" Nikolai asks, his voice laced with desire.

Unable to speak through the lust clutching my throat, I merely nod. Our time in the shower was intimate and teeming with mutual respect, but just as quickly as my feelings have developed for Nikolai, a shift in the air has occurred. I want him more than my next breath, not just his body, but him in his entirety. Sex is incredible, but sex with Nikolai is out of this world. It makes me feel whole.

It makes me me.

"Was your request ever approved, Justine?" Nikolai asks, his lowered tone revealing I'm not the only one stuck in a crazy lust vortex. He is as deep as me.

Even though I'm seconds away from lying, I shake my head. "No."

My parents weren't pushovers by any means, but like all responsible guardians, they knew every child needs flexibility. Whether it is taking a gap year to travel Europe before college or skipping school to go to Disney World, a change in routine can be beneficial for a child—particularly one who grew up in a household like Nikolai's.

"Do you want dessert before dinner?" I ask Nikolai, my husky tone leaving no doubt what I'm offering as sweets.

A heated flare scorches my cheeks when he replies, "I guess that depends on what's on the menu."

When he takes a step forward, I take one back. It isn't because I'm scared of the spark brightening his eyes. It is from the seduction revitalizing them. He is a man on the hunt, and I'm his prime target. I can't make things too easy for him. The chase is half the fun.

"Don't run, *Ангел,* not unless you want to be caught, cause I'll never stop chasing you, no matter how fast you run," he warns hoarsely.

I'm grateful for the bathroom sink digging into my back when his threat causes my knees to buckle. It wasn't what he said that has my legs giving way. It was the way he said it. It wasn't a ploy or a line to get into my panties. It was a message directly from his heart.

"Do you want me to chase you, *Ангел?*" he asks as his gorgeous eyes bounce between mine.

I nod without hesitation. "Yes."

His eyes spark, his happiness at my swift response unmissable on his handsome face. "Do you want me to catch you, *Ангел?*" he asks, taking another step closer to me, sweet-talking me with his intoxicating scent.

"Yes," I repeat, my voice more throaty than usual from his big body swamping mine.

Lust zings from my nipples to my pussy when he squashes his lips to the shell of my ear before whispering, "Do you want me to keep you *forever?*"

"Yes," I breathe out heavily, ignoring the tears pooling in my eyes from the emotional punch his question inflicted on my stomach.

His heavenly gruff groan rolls through my ears before he returns his eyes to mine. He rests his forehead against my sweat-slicked one as he drinks in my flushed, emotion-filled face.

Every breath we take is shared, unifying us more than any sexual exchange ever could. We need this, time away from a world determined to tear us apart.

"I don't need dessert before dinner," Nikolai murmurs a short time later, his hot breath hitting my lips. "I already have it. The ultimate treat is already mine." He brushes away a rogue tear rolling down my cheek before saying, "You are my slice of heaven in a hot and temperamental place. My *Ангел,* the sweetest dessert a man can have."

Several hours later, I am woken by Nikolai slipping out of my bed. I didn't think my heart could get any bigger after what Nikolai said to me in the bathroom, but it grew exponentially in the hours that followed.

Nikolai and I did what every standard couple does on a Thursday night. We ate dinner together and watched television snuggled on the couch until the heaviness of my eyelids became too great to ignore. I don't remember coming to bed, but for the sheer bliss heating my skin, I know I spent the last several hours cocooned by Nikolai.

"Are you leaving?" I whisper, my cheek already missing the heat of his torso.

He snags his jeans off the floor before tugging them up his legs. "I've got some business to take care of."

"At 4 a.m.?" My question is muffled by Nikolai's lips pressing against mine.

He runs his finger across my forehead, removing a strand of hair falling in front of my eye, before murmuring, "The devil can't tell time if he's never seen the sunrise."

I sigh, disturbed by his saying but also accepting of it. What I said last week was true. Nikolai is so immersed in his lifestyle he doesn't realize a world exists outside of it. Expecting him to change would be the equivalent of gifting a cat to a dog lover. Furthermore, he is who he is, and I accept that.

"When will I see you again?" I hate how needy my voice sounds, but I can't help it. Just like Nikolai doesn't know life outside of his family, I don't truly live when I'm not with him.

"I'll be back tonight," he replies, his lips quirking, appreciative of my neediness.

He kisses me again, his lips lingering longer than a standard peck. Although we didn't have sex again last night, the teasing touches and kisses we exchanged throughout the night kept the fire in my womb well-stoked. Every new relationship has an exceptional sex life, but my needs are more extensive. I love spending time with Nikolai in and out of the bedroom.

"Be good," he whispers against my mouth before hesitantly pulling back.

"Don't be too bad," I reply through a yawn, the exhausting week taking a toll on my vocal cords.

Nikolai's husky morning voice hits every one of my hot buttons when he replies, "Where is the fun in that? The good girls always want to tame the bad boys, Justine. Except you. You like me just the way I am."

Having no plausible defense to his honest statement, I burrow my head into my pillow, hoping it will conceal my bright grin. I'd give anything to go back and save him from all the heartache he has endured in his short twenty-eight years, but he wouldn't be the man he is today without all the challenges he has faced. And I *really* like the man he is.

"Silenced by the truth, hey?" he mutters, his deep tone brightened by laughter.

My skin bristles with goosebumps when he trails his index finger up my bare thigh, only stopping when he reaches the curve of my right butt cheek. I moan softly, my coil tightening with every subtle touch.

"Oh, *Ангел,* you could tempt a devil into becoming a saint," he murmurs under his breath, loving my body's reaction to his touch. "If you didn't look so peaceful resting in my arms, I would have taken you in your sleep."

My breathing shortens when he cups my pussy from behind, his fingers so long they brace against my thudding clit. Although there is a pair of panties between his hand and my heated pussy, my body responds as if there isn't. My clit is thrumming without constraint, my hunger evident.

"Have this bare and waiting for me tonight, *Ангел.* I want my dessert before my supper," Nikolai requests through a growl, heightening my senses even more. "As much as I'd love to bury my head between your legs and eat your greedy cunt for breakfast, if I want to catch Vladimir unaware, time is of the essence. I can't waste a second."

I crank my neck back to peer at him before faintly nodding. My eagerness at his promise is unmissable, but my worry for him weakens its impact. I want to argue that acts of revenge never end well, but I know this is more than just vengeance for him.

He doesn't want his father to pay penance for years of suffering. He wants to protect me, and in all honesty, deep down inside, I love how protective he is. I don't want him to kill a man for me, but I do love that he will stop at nothing to make sure I am safe.

Nothing in life is free. Even love comes at a cost. We just don't know how sacrificial the amount will be until push comes to shove. My brother gave up his life for me, and now Nikolai is risking the same thing. I just pray the outcome will be different this time around.

12

JUSTINE

"**I** was beginning to think you were avoiding me."

My eyes dart up from the mountain load of paperwork I've been filing the past three hours to the person accosting me. Although I'm glad for a distraction from the most mundane task I've ever completed, my heart slithers into my gut when I see who is approaching me.

Mr. Fletcher's impressive frame fills the doorway, blanketing the room with even more darkness than its dingy, cramped environment already offers. He's wearing the same suit and tie he had on this morning when I snuck into his office to make sure Nikolai's threat of harm went without execution.

Thankfully, he was both unharmed and uninjured. From the half-empty bottle of whiskey on his desk and the paper crinkles on his cheek, it appears as if he headed straight to the office after our near-kiss and never left.

Although a little voice in the back of my head tells me I should have never doubted Nikolai, I can't contain my glee that my intuition was right. Nikolai may be a mafia prince, but leaving Mr. Fletcher uninjured means he knows right from wrong.

When Mr. Fletcher coughs, wordlessly requesting my focus back to him, I stammer, "Umm... not at all. I've just been busy."

I pray for the poor lighting in the room to hide my flaming

cheeks. I've never been good at lying. That is more to do with my face turning the color of beetroot than my poor choice of excuses.

"Did you need me for something?" I ask, my tone hopeful, wishing he would save me from an intern's hell.

He loosens the collar of his shirt as he enters the room. "I think we should discuss what happened last night."

I exhale sharply, unnerved by his tone. This is why I've been hiding in the records room for the past four hours. I wanted to avoid the awkward conversation many colleagues have after work functions that include alcohol.

Mercifully, our exchange was more innocent than the ones I witnessed when working in New York, but it is just as uncomfortable.

"Do we need to say anything? Can't we just let the alcohol speak on our behalf?" I inwardly sigh, grateful my voice came out with the witty edge I was aiming for.

Mr. Fletcher's shoulder lifts into a shrug. "I was planning on taking my rejection like a man, with half a bottle of whiskey, but after discovering this on Mr. Schluter's desk this morning, I decided a more drastic step was required." He hands me a folded-up piece of paper before continuing. "If you're worried I will harbor anger over our exchange, I can assure you I will not. I am a man, Justine, who has no fear of rejection."

Confused by his statement, my face screws up. Nudging his head to the document in my hand, Mr. Fletcher suggests that I open it.

My confusion intensifies when my eyes absorb the exponential amount of a check I'm clutching for dear life. Whoever wrote this check must live on Easy Street, as there is no hesitation in the elaborate flair of the seven-digit number scrawled across the crisp, fresh document.

"When I agreed to counsel your brother's case, it wasn't for a one-way ticket to retirement. I did it for you." Mr. Fletcher places his hand under my dropped chin and raises my head. "Because you're my friend, and I admire and respect you."

Moisture glistens in my eyes, humbled by the honesty in his eyes. "The feeling is mutual, Mr. Fletcher." Pretending I didn't hear him groan at the formal use of his name, I continue. "But I don't understand what this has to do with me or my brother's case."

He recoils as if shocked by my reply. "You wrote the check, Justine. You left it on Mr. Schluter's desk this morning."

I shake my head, my brain scrambling even more hopelessly. "I snuck into your office this morning to ensure you were okay. I didn't go anywhere near Mr. Schluter's office." I snap my lips shut, suddenly mindful I'm spilling secrets I never meant to share.

Thankfully, Mr. Fletcher is too focused on my last statement to absorb my first confession. "Your name is on the check, Justine. It drew from the same account your monthly wages are deposited into. This check is from you."

I stop shaking my head when he points to my name printed in thick black ink at the payer section of the check. A scratch impinges my throat when his finger treks across a sequence of numbers at the bottom of the check—it matches my bank details.

"I hate to tell you this, but there is no way this won't bounce. I don't have that type of funds in my account." My tone is as colorful as my cheeks.

I don't know why I'm embarrassed. He's well aware of my financial situation, but that doesn't mean I want the rest of our team to hear about my dire state.

My eyes snap to Mr. Fletcher when he grumbles, "That is precisely what I said in the minutes leading up to Mr. Schluter's receptionist cashing it. It didn't bounce. The entire amount was deposited in Schluter & Fletcher's account at ten this morning."

I take a moment to absorb all the facts. It is a woeful waste of time. No matter how hard I strive to decode my confusion, I'm left stumped. I'm an online banking type of girl. I haven't had my hands on a check since my grandma updated to internet banking. Now she transfers my birthday money into my account instead of sending me a tea-stained check.

"Did the check come with anything? An envelope? A note? Something?" My voice is so loud it bounces off the walls and shrills into my ears, meaning I hear every ear-piercing syllable twice.

My response can't be helped. My family's home and vacation condo in Miami were sold to fund Maddox's legal fight, so I know this exorbitant check didn't come from any members of my family. Who else would be willing to spend such an extravagant amount on a man they don't know?

When clarity forms, Mr. Fletcher murmurs, "You want dessert, but I own the restaurant. Better luck next time."

"Jesus Christ," I mumble under my breath.

So Nikolai was in the building. He just used words instead of his fists.

Although I'd like to act shocked by Nikolai's generosity, I'm not. The amount he supplied is excessive, but it is nowhere outside of his means. He is a very wealthy man who would have no qualms paying over seven million dollars to fund the legal battle of a stranger.

But in saying that, it doesn't mean I will accept his generosity. Even if I make a name for myself in this business and become as wealthy as Mr. Fletcher, it will take years to repay this debt. Relationships are generally hard, but when money is involved, they're much more difficult.

After exhaling my nerves, I say, "I need you to reserve the funds. As much as I'd love to pay you your weight in gold to work on Maddox's case, I can't afford seven million dollars."

"But you *paid* that amount," Mr. Fletcher replies, his words laced with angered confusion. His anger doesn't stem from me requesting a refund for services rendered. It is because he knows I am keeping something from him. He isn't solely a cut-throat attorney. He is a shrewd businessman and friend.

I lick my dry lips, praying the moisture will help force out my next confession. "I didn't write the check. But I know who did." My heart smashes against my ribs, knowing I'm moments away from risking everything I've been striving to achieve for the past four years. "It was Nikolai."

My last sentence was so faint, if Mr. Fletcher hadn't nodded his head, I would have assumed he didn't hear me.

"So, what I walked in on Tuesday morning was the start of..." He leaves his question open, leaving me to answer it how I see fit.

"It was the start of something... *complicated?*"

I want to say more, but the disappointment flaring through his eyes steals my words.

"Nothing happened until after I was removed from Nikolai's case," I mumble a short time later, incapable of withstanding Mr. Fletcher's demanding gaze. "I was *strictly* professional."

I groan. Even I heard the deceit in my voice. I may not have slept with Nikolai until the board unjustly removed me from his case, but there has always been more than an attorney-client relationship between us.

"It's... just... ah..."

His disapproving glance rams any excuse I'm planning to give into the back of my throat.

"You don't see him like I do," I settle on, giving the most honest answer possible. "You see the man he presents on paper. I see the real Nikolai."

Mr. Fletcher's eyes roll skyward as he briefly shakes his head. "What I see on paper is *immensely* disturbing, Justine." I nod, agreeing with his assessment, but before I can give my side of the story, he keeps talking, nipping my reply in the bud. "But I learned quickly in this business to never believe what is presented in front of me." He nudges his head to the bank check shaking in my hand. "That's *huge*. That's *mammoth*. But it is *not* something an average man would do."

"Nikolai isn't an average man."

"No, he isn't," he agrees. "But there is more to this story than you know, Justine. One I doubt he will *ever* tell you."

The tartness in his tone hackles my spine. "Don't judge someone you don't know. That would be like me telling you if you stopped sleeping in your office every night, you'd have more than a cat to go home to. But I wouldn't say that, as I have no right to judge you any more than you're judging Nikolai."

"A judgment is never given until the defense wades through all the shit. You're not even halfway through the shitstorm he is going to rain down on you, yet you're already defending every move he makes."

"Because he deserves to have someone on his side," I shout, my croaky voice displaying I'm on the verge of tears. "He deserves to know he isn't fighting alone. He did it his entire childhood. He doesn't need to now."

"That's not having your back like you have his. It is a payout, Justine. A bribe. He's buying you," Mr. Fletcher continues to argue, jerking his head to the check in my hands.

"You can't buy something that is given willingly," I reply, defending the first half of his ill-informed bias before tackling the second half. "I asked you to reverse the funds because I have no intention of accepting his money. You and Mr. Schluter may see me as a naïve bimbo with big tits and half a brain, but I'm an expert on dealing with assholes whose assumptions are as ill-advised as their manners." My last statement is for him, not Nikolai.

Loathing the tears pooling in my eyes, I gather the files I've been organizing in my arms before returning my eyes to Mr. Fletcher. He stares at me, stunned by my outburst. He isn't the only one shocked.

I knew my feelings for Nikolai were developing rapidly, but I had no idea they extended this far. By defending him, I'm risking my livelihood and my brother's freedom. But what I said to Mr. Fletcher is true. Nikolai deserves someone on his side. He has battled alone for years; it's time for that treachery to stop.

"I'll make an appointment with human resources when I return to my office," I advise, not needing him to spell out the consequences of our argument. Hopefully he will let me finish the remainder of the month, but I'll understand if that isn't possible.

Before I exit the room, Mr. Fletcher seizes my elbow in a firm grasp, foiling my endeavor to leave before my tears fall. "You are *my* intern, Justine. I handle *my* matters in-house. There is no need to get human resources involved."

His words fill me with both gratitude and panic. The way he growled "my" was way too possessive for my liking, but I'm grateful his first thought isn't to remove me from his firm.

"But..." He waits, building the suspense. "This isn't acceptable. The consequences that follow a matter like this can be substantial. When you make a deal with the devil, no amount of atonement can alter the result. When you sell your soul to the devil, you can't get it back."

"Nikolai isn't the devil—"

"I didn't say he was, but Nikolai's choices aren't his own. The sooner you realize that, the sooner you will understand my concern," Mr. Fletcher interjects.

I peer into his forthright eyes, hoping they will decode his cryptic message. They give me nothing but more questions. His eyes look as haunted as I feel, but they also plead for me to consider his comment carefully.

"Stop payment on the check. I'll handle the rest." When he

attempts to interrupt, I quickly say, "If I get stuck on anything, you'll be the first man I call."

Although my tone is confident, he still hesitates before curtly nodding. I smile, issuing him my thanks without words before entering the corridor.

I've barely trekked halfway down the hall when Mr. Schluter barrels out of his office, his face as red as my fitted skirt. If I hadn't seen his receptionist slipping crushed blood pressure tablets into his coffee this morning, I'd be worried he is about to burst a blood vessel—that is how red he is.

"I've been looking for you everywhere. Where the hell have you been?" he grumbles, his words rushed.

Not giving me the chance to reply, he demands, "Let's move. We're already five minutes late." He continues down the hall, not waiting for me to acknowledge his request.

After dumping my files into Mr. Fletcher's offering hands, I chase after Mr. Schluter.

"Thank you," I whisper to Sierra when she hands me Mr. Schluter's briefcase and a travel mug of coffee before I exit the rotating glass doors. I can only pray she slipped some happy pills into his beloved brew, or my dodge from prosecution a second time may end worse than my first taste.

"Where are we going?" I question, slipping into the backseat of Mr. Schluter's Bentley.

Although I have an inkling about the circumstances of our hasty meeting, I'd rather him spell it out for me. I've barely had a moment of clarity all week. I don't need more confusion.

"Vladimir called an emergency meeting," Mr. Schluter answers, his voice as gruff as his mood. "Did you file Malvina's citizenship documentation as requested?"

I wait for him to take his belongings from my grasp before nodding. "Last I heard, her citizenship application was approved Wednesday afternoon. The formal documentation should arrive within a few weeks."

"And the marriage license, was it also approved?"

I swallow the brick in my throat. "Yes. It's good to go as well. But as I explained earlier, her citizenship application was irrelevant to her quest to wed. Whether she marries or not, by the end of the month, she will be a citizen of the United States."

I breathe out heavily, grateful my voice was professional, even though I'm feeling anything but. Mr. Schluter's questions were brief but revealing enough to divulge he isn't aware Nikolai put Malvina on a redeye to Russia last night. If he isn't aware of that substantial fact, what is the likelihood Vladimir is also unaware?

"Did Vladimir mention what our meeting pertains to?" I keep my voice neutral, hoping my question won't raise suspicion.

He grunts. "Does he ever give a reason for his madness?"

When his focus shifts to his state-of-the-art cell phone, my opportunity to grill him further fades into the distance. With the number of butterflies in my stomach, I'd also like to occupy my time, but with my belongings sitting in the bottom of my desk drawer, I'm left twiddling my thumbs, pretending I can't feel the contents of my stomach winding to the base of my throat.

I'm not worried about meeting Vladimir again. I trust that Nikolai will keep me safe. I'm more concerned about Nikolai's reaction to me arriving unannounced again. I could have warned him of my imminent arrival if I had my cell. I just have to pray he is one step ahead of his evil father.

Every inch we travel down the long Popov compound drive-way, the tighter my stomach knots. My world was upended the last time I stepped foot on this property. I hope today doesn't have the same outcome. I've been in so many battles lately that I should enter every room with my fists swinging.

Hot, bland air greets us when we exit the Bentley to climb the mammoth stairs at the entrance of the Popov mansion. Unlike our first meeting, we are not welcomed at the door. After being shown into the foyer by a man in his late twenties, we are guided into the massive library by the same petite brunette with rich chocolate eyes who took our coats last week.

Since Malvina's beauty is not blinding me, I can observe Maya's features more diligently. She is attractive but successfully conceals her stellar attributes with dowdy clothes and a lowered chin. With her hair pinned back and clothing more suitable for someone her size, I could easily mistake her for one of the beauties parading around my living room last week. She is gorgeous but so shy and reserved she floats around the room like a ghost.

After gesturing for us to sit on the same loveseat we sat on last week, Maya commences serving tea.

"Thank you," I whisper graciously when she hands me a floral-painted china cup and saucer.

"Sugar?" she questions, her accent a unique mix of French and Russian.

"*S'il vous plaît*," I reply, hoping she understands French.

Maya peers up from the tray of tea, her smile as captivating as Nikolai's. She is truly beautiful when she isn't cowering.

"*Lait?*" she asks shyly.

When I nod, she adds a dash of milk to my tea, her smile growing.

As quickly as her smile arrived, it vanishes. I can understand her swift change in composure. I don't even need to look in the direction of her gaze to know why her face is whitening. I can feel the vivacity in the air draining with every creeping step he takes.

Hell has been left unattended today, as the devil is walking amongst the living.

"Ernest," Vladimir greets Mr. Schluter, his voice prominent and booming. After welcoming Mr. Schluter with kisses on his cheeks, Vladimir's attention turns to me. "The Huntress herself," he murmurs under his breath as he presses his lips to my cheek. "As cunning as Satan but twice as pretty. You could only look better blushing beneath me."

Repulsed by his offensive words, I pull back with only a microsecond to spare, forcing his kiss to land midair.

"Ah, such spark," he whispers. "But don't underestimate me, *Ангел*. I do not handle disrespect well. By the time I finish punishing you, your marks will look like child's play. My bite is much harder than a mangy mutt's."

Before I can fully absorb his threat, I'm startled by a much more dangerous, intangible risk. "Father, what is this? You said you'd call them to update them on the situation. Not summon them here."

Nikolai enters the room with his eyes rapt on his father, but his devotion focused on me. How do I know his attention is dedicated to me if I can't see his eyes? I can feel it in my bones.

I didn't need to call him to announce my arrival. He knew I was coming before I even entered the foyer. He can sense my presence as well as I sense his.

"I thought I'd kill two birds with one stone," Vladimir answers, his voice as flagrant as his facial expression. "Advise them of Malvina's departure to Russia last night while also reporting Sergei's disappearance."

Vladimir's blasé response to Malvina's return to Russia fills me with hope that he accepts Nikolai's decision not to wed, but his second admission sucker punches me.

It isn't solely Vladimir's confession that creates fresh wounds. It is Nikolai's reaction. He portrays the role of mafia prince well, but even he balked during his father's confession.

"They're attorneys, not detectives," Nikolai replies, ignoring my questioning glare. "If you want to report Sergei's disappearance, shouldn't you contact the authorities?" His tone dips when he articulates the word "disappearance."

Vladimir throws his head back and laughs. It isn't a genuine laugh packed with sunshine and happiness. It is vindictive and cold —just like its owner. "I'm not reporting Sergei as missing. I am merely initiating a claim on his life insurance policy. Sergei was an asset that grew in value with his death. Whoever got rid of him did me a favor—more than they will ever realize."

"Sergei's dead?" I blurt out before I can stop myself, the hammering of my heart resonating in my tone.

"No," Nikolai answers while Vladimir says, "Yes."

I lock eyes with Nikolai, knowing I can trust him more than any words.

Unfortunately, his eyes are the most guarded they've ever been. He isn't the Nikolai who kissed me goodbye at four o'clock this morning. He is once again Nikolai, Russian Mafia Prince.

I'm not stunned by his swift change in demeanor. The protectiveness radiating out of him is as stealthy as when he sheltered me from Sergei last week. He knows who the real monster in the room is. It isn't him. It's the man glaring at him, goading him into making a mistake, hoping he will expose his hand before all his cards have been dealt.

Vladimir is playing the same tricks on Nikolai he's always played. He is striving to wedge a gap between Nikolai and anyone who dares stand by his side. He knows Nikolai is his greatest contender, so he is doing anything to weaken his resolve.

If Vladimir thinks he can play me against Nikolai, he is sadly mistaken, because:

In every angel, a demon hides.
And in every demon, an angel strides.
—Author Unknown

Nothing is left off the table when you're forced to protect the ones you love. I've only known Nikolai for weeks, but that doesn't make him any less worthy of defense. I will protect him as vigorously as he defends me. I will have his back no matter what because I know if he did kill Sergei, he wouldn't have done it without good reason.

Values are not taught. We're born with them. Nikolai's morals may be misguided at times, but his heart is in the right place for the most part.

After a quick swallow to clear the nerves from my voice, I explain, "Typically, life insurance policies are paid within thirty days of the beneficiary supplying the insurance company with a death certificate. Do you have a death certificate for Sergei?"

"It is a little hard to supply a death certificate when we don't have a body," Vladimir replies, his words taunting and not the least bit upset that a member of his family has passed.

"Without a body, the coroner will not issue a death certificate," Mr. Schluter interjects, finally joining the party, albeit way too late.

Vladimir sits on the chair across from me, his movements as haughty as his arrogant face. "That isn't necessarily true. I know of many cases where a murderer has been convicted without a body being found." He stares into my eyes, ensuring I don't miss the hidden innuendo in his statement.

My brother was sentenced to life behind bars—even with his "victim's" body never being found. He is a prime example of how the justice system rewards some and punishes others.

Although my stomach squirms from Vladimir's malicious comment, it doesn't stop me from saying, "In most jurisdictions, you need to obtain a court order directing the registrar to issue a death certificate in the absence of a physician's certification. However, I don't see any jurisdiction issuing such a request without circumstantial evidence that Sergei has passed. There has to be evidence of foul play. Blood. Body tissue. A crime scene. Do you have any of those things?"

Even though I'm asking a question, I continue speaking,

ensuring Vladimir can't issue the pompous reply his eyes are relaying. "And if you do have any of those things, they will need to be
thoroughly processed by members of law enforcement before a
death certificate can be issued."

"Then perhaps we should call them in," Vladimir suggests, his
tone reeking with condescending amusement. "Get the ball rolling
while the evidence is still fresh." He turns his slanted gaze to
Nikolai during his last sentence.

"You want to bring law enforcement officers here?" I question
as my eyes drift between Nikolai and Vladimir, stunned he'd want
to do something so ludicrous, much less lawful.

Although Nikolai's presence is very much felt, he's too busy
categorizing Vladimir's every move to answer the silent questions
I'm directing at him.

Now his nickname makes sense.

He is as still as a snake, ready to strike at any moment.

When I realize I'm not going to gain anything useful from
Nikolai's stone-hard demeanor, I swing my eyes back to Vladimir.
My heart stops for a second, startled to discover he is watching me.

His skin-crawling scar proves what I suspected—he's testing
both mine and Nikolai's loyalty. I am familiar with how things work
in his industry. One wrong move and he will be free to issue us any
punishment he sees fit.

Usually I'd cower from the prospect of going toe-to-toe with a
mafia king, but with Nikolai standing at my side, primed and ready,
I'm feeling invincible.

"If you want to call in the authorities, go ahead, but considering
the four men you have operating the gates, and the additional six
camouflaged throughout the grounds are carrying firearms illegal in
the state of Nevada, as a member of your defensive team, I strongly
suggest you have them removed from the property beforehand."

His brow quirks, matching his cunning smirk. "You're advising
me against seeking restitution for wrongdoing to a member of my
family?"

"Not at all. I'm merely recommending you consider all your
options." I clear the nerves from my voice before continuing.
"Sergei's disappearance should be investigated, but I am sure you
are more than capable of conducting that investigation without the

authorities being called in. You've managed for decades without their help, so why change something that isn't broken?"

Like all conceited men, Vladimir acts as if my backhanded compliment stroked his ego. He sits up in his chair, his peacock feathers fanning behind his back. "Smart and beautiful. Perhaps I should reconsider Niki's offer of making you my whore."

Although his comment makes my stomach lurch into my throat, I keep my composure neutral, ensuring my fear doesn't encourage his arrogance. His condescending mood is already being fed by Nikolai's unusual silence. It doesn't need any more nourishment.

"I'm not saying anything any other defense attorney wouldn't recommend. I am not here to prosecute you. I'm here to defend you."

Although my eyes are facing Vladimir, my words are for Nikolai. He appears moments away from blowing his top. His fists are clenched at his sides, and his glare at his father is murderous. If I don't say something to diminish his fury, the Popov crew will lose two key members in less than a week.

When the volatility in Nikolai's eyes fades, I know he took my saying as I had hoped. He has my support, no matter how murky the waters get.

"Ernest?" Vladimir asks, seeking his opinion on my suggestion.

Mr. Schluter scoots to the end of his chair, his mood unreadable. "I hired Justine solely on her looks. What can I say? My clients like eye candy..."

I want to act surprised by his revelation, but I'm not. Mr. Schluter is a chauvinistic pig stuck in the Stone Age. That is why I arrived for my interview in a micro miniskirt and a blouse with only two buttons done up. I love my brother so much that I played Mr. Schluter better than he believes he played me.

"But if she interviewed with as much guts as she's showing now, I would have hired her sight unseen. You know the statistics when the authorities are brought in, Vlad. Do you really want to lose that type of capital again for Sergei? He's been a liability since the day he was born. You should be glad to be rid of him, not mourning his loss."

I stare at Mr. Schluter with my mouth hanging open. His reply was way too personal. He spoke as if he is a member of Vladimir's crew—not his defense attorney. Yes, you can have lifetime clients, but not to this extent.

When your personal relationship clouds your ethics, you may as well walk headfirst into a tornado, as there's no coming back from that.

I'm pulled from my thoughts when Vladimir snarls, "Very well. Do what needs to be done, but keep them away from here." How he sneered "them" leaves no doubt to who he is referring.

Mr. Schluter nods, understanding Vladimir's demand to repress law enforcement from his home base.

"And the wedding?" Mr. Schluter asks, unable to harness his curiosity for a moment longer.

Vladimir's eyes lock with Nikolai before drifting to me. I act as curious as Mr. Schluter, pretending I am unaware of the reason behind Malvina's sudden decision to leave.

My acting must be A grade, as Vladimir explains, "Malvina had to return to Russia on family business. The wedding has been postponed—"

"The wedding has been canceled," Nikolai interrupts, his tone shaking my knees. "Malvina had a change of heart. It's best for all involved."

He's lying, not about the wedding being canceled, but about it being Malvina's choice. Her interest in Nikolai was abundant only days ago, so there's no way she canceled their wedding. This was solely Nikolai's doing—and the fact he's so vehemently denying any connection to her proves where his loyalties lie.

A member of his crew is missing, possibly dead, yet no worry crossed his face, but at the first mention of his name associated with someone who could cause me harm, his daggers are out.

Nikolai is on my side as surely as I am on his.

Confused by the silence between Nikolai, Vladimir, and me, Mr. Schluter says, "Either way, your wedding license won't expire for twelve months, so if she has another change of heart, you're good to go." He waggles his bushy brows, compatibility meaningless to a man whose value of women doesn't extend past their chest size.

"I'll keep that in mind," Nikolai replies, acting unaffected by Mr. Schluter's bigoted ways. He waves his hand to the entranceway of the library. "I'll show you out."

When Mr. Schluter stands from his chair to gather his business jacket, I follow suit, faking ignorance to Vladimir's suspicious stare. I've never been more grateful for a knee-length skirt than I am right now. The shaking hampering my body is so convincing that my knees are clanging together.

After dipping my chin in farewell to Vladimir, I shadow Mr. Schluter out of the library. I secure my first breath in what feels like minutes when Vladimir doesn't object to our quick retreat. From the look crossing his face, he appears to want to say something, but thankfully, the length of our strides steals his chance.

My heart rate I've only just settled kicks into overdrive when the warmth of a hand heats my back. Unlike the first time Nikolai guided us out of his residence, he doesn't take charge. He lets Mr. Schluter take the lead, giving his hand unlimited access to my skin.

Although worried our every move is being watched, I can't shut down my body's awareness of his closeness. My desire for this man outweighs any risks associated with being his. Furthermore, I have no reason to fret. Nikolai has angled his body so his touch is hidden from Vladimir's view, and I am also.

"Ah, fuck, woman, I didn't think you could get any sexier," he murmurs under his breath as he shadows me down the stairs to the waiting Bentley. "But watching you put Vladimir in his place. *Fuck*... I've never been so hard."

"I had a good incentive," I murmur, my eyes facing the front. When Nikolai's hand stiffens on my back, revealing his confusion of my reply, I say, "Trouble shared is a trouble halved. You're not fighting this battle alone, Nikolai. I am standing right next to you."

I can't see him, but I know he's smiling. I can sense it with every fiber of my being.

"But in saying that, you should have told me about Sergei. I can't help you if I'm left in the dark. Vladimir was playing us in there. This is all just a game to him."

"My entire life has been a game to him, Justine. One fucked-up day after another," Nikolai replies, announcing I'm not the only one aware of Vladimir's power trips. "But I'm one step ahead of him. I know all his moves. It will only be a matter of time before the slate is wiped clean."

"Until then, we need to even the playing field," I murmur, my voice laced with unusual cattiness. Since I've reached my quota of arrogant men today, my mood is fraying.

Nikolai closes the gap between us, bringing his lips to within touching distance of my ear. "Spoken like a queen ready to rule her empire." He groans his words in a long, wicked purr, hitting every one of my hot buttons. "I knew there were devilish thoughts in your mind, *Ангел*. You just needed the right man to bring them to fruition."

My mouth twitches, preparing to recant his statement, but I'm left void of a retort. Vladimir is a vile, heinous man who is well overdue for a taste of his own medicine. Does that mean I'm on board with Nikolai's decision? No, not entirely. But I understand why he has chosen to walk down the path he has. He has no other option.

After accepting Mr. Schluter's handshake, Nikolai opens my side of the back passenger door of the Bentley for me. "Don't make any plans this weekend, *Ангел*," he says in Russian, his words throaty and full of need. "Your calendar just got blacked out by the man determined to read your wicked thoughts."

I nod eagerly. Even if the twinkle in his eyes didn't dampen his threat, my response wouldn't have changed. I'm under the spell of a mafia prince, trapped without a chance of escaping. And I wouldn't have it any other way.

13

JUSTINE

"Richer than God, but with a heart as black as Satan," Mr. Schluter grumbles, his eyes rapt on Vladimir, who's standing at the stoop of his stairs and eyeballing our car gliding down the driveway. "My mother always said, 'Avoiding temptation is easier than risking it.' I should have listened to her. With an average man, karma will eventually show its hand, but when you deal with a devil, your misgivings follow you to your grave."

"You've represented Vladimir before?" I keep my tone neutral, hoping my impassiveness will be rewarded in the most significant way.

A brick lodges in my throat when Mr. Schluter swings his eyes to me. He doesn't need to answer my question. I can see the honesty in his slit-eyed gaze.

Today's visit was one of many.

"When did representation start?" I ask, stunned by my audacity.

His snarled top lip relays without doubt that he doesn't appreciate being interrogated. His grumpy mood grows more volatile with every second spent in the Popov compound.

Not anticipating a response to my question, I drift my eyes back to the scenery rolling past my window. Mr. Schluter startles me for a second time today when he answers, "A little over thirteen years ago. The firm needed capital. We were one payment from going under. An opportunity presented at the exact moment we needed it. Was it the best decision for the firm? Probably not, but we didn't have any other options at the time."

Returning my eyes to his, I nod, understanding how desperation can force even the saintliest person in a direction they never saw coming. I've come close to walking down paths I'd never expected during my endeavor to have my brother's conviction overturned, so I can't judge his decision.

Horrid unease scorches my throat when Mr. Schluter locks his eyes with Nikolai's file sitting between us. He stares at his record for seconds, but it feels like the moon circles the Earth three times.

"He only had two years until he became an adult. After everything he had been through, what was another two years?" His weak words are more for his ears than mine.

"Nikolai?" I swallow harshly, soothing my burning throat before continuing. "You represented Nikolai?"

He glares at me as if I am an imbecile. "Nikolai wasn't our client. He was the DA's. We represented Vladimir against charges brought forward by Nikolai."

"Nikolai pressed charges against Vladimir? When?" I blurt out before I can stop my words.

I stare at Mr. Schluter, hoping he will answer the questions pumping out of me.

He does no such thing.

He reverts his focus to the scenery outside, acting like he didn't hear a word I spoke. I try to fire off a demand for him to answer me. My mouth opens and closes, but not a syllable escapes. Sick unease clutches my throat so badly I can't force a single word out of my mouth.

With my mouth refusing to cooperate, I sit in silence for the remainder of our trip, repeating the facts in my head.

No matter how many ways I compile the evidence, a clear verdict never presents. I've come up with several hunches—*none of them pretty*. They're as ghastly as the bitter taste in my mouth.

Mr. Schluter said Nikolai was only two years from adulthood when he brought charges against Vladimir, which means he was just shy of his sixteenth birthday. After spending most of my weekend deep in Nikolai's file, I know Nikolai spent his sixteenth birthday in the hospital with a broken arm, three cracked ribs, and numerous other bruises and cuts from a supposed tumble down the stairs.

If that evidence isn't damning enough, thirteen years ago was when Mr. Fletcher jumped ship, leaving the DA's office to become a part of Mr. Schluter's team. He was offered a partnership at the suddenly viable firm only a few months later. It could be a whole heap of coincidences, but my intuition warns me not to be so gullible.

When the Bentley pulls to the front of Schluter & Fletcher, I throw open the back passenger door before it completely stops. After clambering onto the sidewalk, I barge through the rotating glass door, strengthened by determination.

When I first walked into this building, I was in awe of its beauty. In minutes, I was convinced anything was possible with hard work. Its architectural wonder filled me with hope I could get Maddox off his charges within weeks because nothing was unachievable with the right amount of grit.

Only now am I beginning to wonder if all that is a crock of shit. Was anything in this building achieved the hard way? Or was it all funded with money as vile as Vladimir?

Ignoring Michelle's curious glance, I charge into the record office and move to an extensive collection of files in the bottom back corner.

It takes me nearly two hours of combing through encyclopedia-sized archives before I find the evidence I am looking for, but when I do, anger steamrolls into me, making it hard for me to breathe.

I knew Mr. Fletcher and Nikolai had met previously, and now I have proof.

I make a beeline for Mr. Fletcher's office, my steps remarkably stable for how hard my legs are shaking.

"No wonder Nikolai hates you! You sold him out! You had a

chance to help him, but greed trumped your morals," I shout, slinging open his door.

I throw Nikolai's file onto his desk, sending the horrifying images of the numerous injuries Nikolai sustained throughout his childhood sliding across his pristine desk.

Mr. Fletcher's eyes shoot from the ghastly pictures to the usually bustling corridor. When he stands from his chair to close his office door, Michelle, Trent, and Kirk pretend to act busy, loathing that they were caught eavesdropping.

"How much was your soul worth to the devil, Carmichael?" I ask, purposely using his first name. My respect for him has been lost, so there's no reason for me to address him formally anymore.

He shuts his door before turning around to face me. "I didn't sell Nikolai out. I acted in the best interest of my client."

"You acted in the best interest of your client?" I quote, my voice full of disbelief. "Children were being abused! What about their best interest?"

"No evidence of abuse was documented during the preliminary hearing."

The outraged expression on my face reveals how disgusted I am with him as I dig my hand into Nikolai's file. Tears flow down my cheeks, but I don't clear them away. My heart is in shreds for Nikolai, so why shouldn't my outward appearance match my insides?

While slamming down a timeline of photos that represents the unimaginable abuse Nikolai endured the first eighteen years of his life, I say, "Nikolai was maimed, beaten, and tortured his entire childhood, but instead of bringing his abuser to justice, you took the evidence he handed you, twisted it, then used it against him on the witness stand. Do you know how much courage it took for him to talk to you, all to have you use him for your own gain?"

"I represented my client, Justine—"

"You let a child abuser go free. You defended a monster, all to line your pockets with filthy money," I interrupt, angered by his pathetic denial.

I continue slamming down pictures, not stopping until all fourteen of Vladimir's sons are sprawled across Mr. Fletcher's desk. "A broken arm. Thirteen stitches. A grade three concussion. Burns to his back from an *accidental* acid spill." I point to each photo corresponding to the injuries I'm mentioning. "Nikolai proved to you time and time again that Vladimir was a monster, but instead of defending him, you defended the man responsible for his injuries."

"I did my job!" he shouts, his voice as hot-tempered as my face. "I tried to defend him, but the jury would have never sided with the DA. The instant Nikolai attempted to kill his father, he lost any chance of having him prosecuted for abuse."

His voice is as loud as mine, his determination just as strong, but it does nothing to lessen my campaign. I chose to intern at Schluter & Fletcher solely because Mr. Fletcher pledged to protect the innocent. He has often claimed he isn't a defense attorney to get murderers off scot-free. He does it to protect the people wrongly convicted of crimes—men and women like my brother.

I adored that about him. His integrity was his most attractive attribute, but all I see now is a pitiful man who steals from the poor and kicks the weak when they're down.

Grabbing the photo of the teenage boy with half the skin on his back eaten away from acid, I move to stand in front of him. "Nikolai held a knife to Vladimir's throat on June fourteenth—the same night this happened," I say, thrusting the horrifying image to within an inch of Mr. Fletcher's face. "Nikolai attacked his father because he was protecting his brother like you should have protected him!"

His throat works hard to swallow before he turns his eyes away from the image, the sight too gruesome even for someone as heartless as him to look at. "I tried, Justine. I did the best I could."

"You didn't try. You took the money and turned a blind eye." After running my hand across my cheeks to remove my tears, I continue. "Do you know what happened to Nikolai when Vladimir's charges were thrown out of court? Do you know what they did to him? What he went through because of you?"

I point to the photos sprawled across his desk. "That was nothing. Years of abuse were nothing compared to what he endured when he was forced back into the hell he tried to escape. He had to become a replica of the man he hates just to stay alive. All because you wanted a fancy office and a swanky new car!"

"I made a mistake!" Mr. Fletcher shouts, his voice cracking as much as my heart is. "One I've been trying to fix since I made it. I was young and naïve, Justine. I didn't know the consequences of my stupidity until it was too late." The severity of his tone lowers during his last sentence. "I was backed into a wall. I didn't have a choice. I had to either defend Vladimir, or lose my partnership."

"So you're admitting it? You chose money over morals?"

He scrubs his hands over his watering eyes before confessing, "Yes, but if I knew back then what I know now, I would have never gone so hard. I wouldn't have—"

"Made it look like Nikolai was the abuser?" I fill in, anger deepening my tone. "Or that he was a 'psychotic adolescent who manifested lies for beneficial gain?' You portrayed him as if he was more of a monster than Vladimir, and he caused all his siblings' injuries."

I wait a beat, expecting Mr. Fletcher to deny my claims.

He doesn't.

He remains as quiet as he did thirteen years ago when he went from defending Nikolai to prosecuting him.

"You didn't just sell your soul thirteen years ago, Carmichael. You dragged Nikolai to the depths of hell right alongside you. He tried to do the right thing, and what did he get for his effort? More lies. More pain. More heartache. You threw him under the bus for this." I wave my hand around his office, which could house dozens.

After thrusting the piece of paper I'm clutching for dear life into his chest, I say, "Enjoy your pristine office and ninety-six percent win rate. Because I'd rather have morals than wealth gained at the expense of innocent children, I quit."

"Quitting won't help anyone, Justine. It won't help Nikolai, and it most certainly won't help your brother," Mr. Fletcher replies, stopping my angry steps out of his office mid-stride. "Stay and help me fix the wrongs I've done."

"You can't fix this. It's too late for Nikolai. The damage has already been done," I say with a shake of my head. "You threw him to the wolves, leaving him no choice but to be hunted or become the hunter. He became the hunter. And in all honesty, you deserve to be hunted by him because you destroyed any chance he had of a normal life as badly as his father did. He was a boy trying to be a man, but your lies turned him into the monster he didn't want to become."

His eyes bounce between mine, but his mouth remains

tightlipped. He knows every word I spoke is true, so why deny them?

"I will get Maddox off his charges because the truth always comes out. Whether it is three years or thirteen, no one knows, but today proves your past always catches up with you no matter how fast you run."

I exit his office as quickly as I entered it.

14

NIKOLAI

"I f you wish to continue trading with the Popov entity, I recommend you stop considering this as a suggestion. You either move forward with me, or I'll take my business elsewhere."

Asher swallows before saying, "We've been trading with your family for years, Nikolai. We have no intention of changing that."

"Then do as I suggested. Have my father's agreement with the Yurys transferred to me. I'll continue with the original shipment schedule as discussed last month, but I'll throw in an additional five percent in good faith."

"Five percent?" Asher double-checks, his tone high.

I could offer a more substantial incentive, but five percent is the equivalent of over fifteen million dollars annually. Asher would be a fool not to seriously consider my negotiation.

He is a shrewd businessman, so he knows that the initial risk during the transition will be awarded tenfold soon.

"Shipments will remain on schedule?" he asks, his tone conveying his opinion is swaying in my favor.

"Yes. If not, an additional two or three thrown in for good measure."

Asher inhales sharply, dollar signs flashing in his eyes. My capital will take a hit adding more shipments to our already crammed agenda, but if it's the only way I can convince Asher's father to retain me as a client, I'll absorb the loss.

If Vladimir loses access to the weapons, drugs, and money laundering services Yury's crew has supplied to the Popov entity for the past thirty years, he will be financially crippled.

Without adequate incentives, he will soon have nothing to negotiate the loyalty he's purchased over the past seventy-two years. Everyone knows loyalty isn't earned in this industry—it is bought.

"What if I send over payment for the first shipment with Dominique? I heard she has a sweet spot for balding men with limp cocks."

Asher laughs. "Fucking bastard," he replies in Russian, his taunt more in fun than scorn, hoping to conceal his eagerness at my suggestion.

You'd have to be a blind man not to notice his fascination with one of Vladimir's favorite whores. He practically drools over Dominique whenever he visits the Popov compound on assignment from Russia.

He's never acted on his desires for fear of retribution, but with me announcing Vladimir's "retirement," I'm sure his interests are piqued. The Yurys are as powerful as the Popovs, but their strong point is distribution. They don't have the muscle required to turn their entity into an impenetrable force like my crew has become.

I hear Asher scrape his hand along the stubble on his jaw before he mutters, "Father will take a bit of convincing, but I think you are right. It's time for a change in rankings. Send me the documents. I'll handle the rest."

His reply makes me suspicious I'm not the only one in the process of dethroning a king, but I set aside my interrogation for a more appropriate time.

"I'll have the information forwarded by 9 a.m. Monday."

I'm pulling my phone away from my ear when Asher calls my name.

"Yeah," I reply, pressing my cell back to my ear.

"Send Dominique. If World War III is starting, I don't want her getting caught in the crossfire. I can keep her safe here."

My chest puffs, swelling with smugness. "She's already on her way. Her flight will land at Koltsovo Airport within the next hour or two. She's traveling with Malvina."

I can't see him, but I know he is smiling. "So the rumors are true? You sent Malvina packing?"

"It's best for all involved," I reply, giving the same excuse I've given numerous times today.

Asher inhales a sharp breath. "And what's Vladimir's opinion on the subject?"

"Does it matter? He wasn't the one marrying her."

When he swallows, mindful of my short temper, I run my hand over my scalp, aware I'm taking my frustration out on the wrong person.

The trades I've negotiated most of my day have all followed a similar path—they're worried my decision not to marry Malvina will impact our business.

They don't need to worry. The Popov entity was thriving decades before Malvina was in the picture and will continue to thrive for decades after.

"Vladimir isn't happy, but that shouldn't surprise anyone. He's never happy," I mutter a short time later, issuing Asher the first honest answer I've given all day.

He is a business associate, but I also consider him a friend.

"True," Asher agrees. "That's why I want Dominique off his radar. I've seen some fucked-up shit the past twenty-seven years, but your father's antics are by far the worst." He tries to hide the heavy disdain in his tone. He fails.

"Look after Dominique, Asher. She's a gem. She just got snagged by the wrong man." *Much like Justine did years ago.*

He grunts but doesn't reply to my unaccustomed compliment. Happy to let him construe my statement in any way he sees fit, I disconnect our call and return my cell to the pocket of my jeans.

Before Justine, my praise never veered far from throwing hundred-dollar bills onto the bed my female companions were lying on after we'd finished fucking. They weren't hookers, but considering I used their bodies as if they were, I paid them like prostitutes. Now I'm beginning to wonder if my cock has been replaced with a vagina.

Justine is making me weak, but in a way I can't help but encourage. I'm fucking lost to that woman. My desire to have her screaming my name is more persuasive than my need to slit Vladimir's throat.

I never thought I'd be crippled by a pussy, but in all fairness, I never thought I'd meet a woman like Justine. She's smart, beautiful, and strong enough to stand by my side while I take back what's rightfully mine.

Justine thinks she wants an innocent, unadventurous life, but I see the fire in her eyes begging to be released. She was born to lead. She just needs to recoup the confidence stolen from her. Then she will be unstoppable, a queen worthy of the most powerful throne.

"Pull over here," I direct one of the new recruits I've been amassing in droves in the past year.

Although Justine's arrival in my life thrust my quest for vengeance into the forefront of my mind, I've been planning this for years. Her presence means it will happen earlier than initially planned.

I throw a bundle of rolled-up bills over the tinted partition of my car. "There's a parking garage three blocks over. Stay there until I call you."

Not waiting for him to reply, I clamber onto the sidewalk two blocks down from Justine's apartment, knowing he will follow my instruction to the T or lose his life.

The bone-dry heat is disgusting, but my desire to keep Justine's location unknown means I'll share the sidewalk with another three dozen idiots stupid enough to walk in 110-degree heat.

With traffic heavier than usual, traveling from my compound to Justine's apartment building took longer. I was hoping to arrive before her as I had last night, but with Roman advising she left work an hour earlier than planned, I'll most likely arrive after her.

"Where is she?" I ask into my cell, not bothering to issue Roman a greeting.

"She just entered the elevator of her building."

I nod, even though he can't see me. "Was she followed?"

"No, but you should speak with her about increasing her awareness. I walked behind her the entire way, and she never noticed me." I'm not surprised by the worry in Roman's voice. The paternal instincts he usually bestows on me switched to Justine when I placed her on his watch.

"I'll talk to her. Are you heading out?"

"Yeah, I'll be back tomorrow morning. 3 a.m.? Or will you drop the ball again like you did this morning?"

I smile smugly. "Would you leave if you had a woman like Justine lying in your arms?" My cock hardens at the thought of her lying in my arms.

"Fuck no."

My smile turns genuine from Roman's unusual use of an expletive. "I'll be ready for you to take over at three. I've got more foundations to lay."

"The Yurys agreed?" he asks, hearing the underlying message in my reply. "I didn't think they'd ever part ways with Vladimir."

"They didn't have a choice. Asher took the decision out of their hands."

I push through the revolving glass door of Justine's apartment building before heading for the elevator bank. Knowing the car is on level ten, I open the emergency fire stairs and enter the dimly lit space.

"The trade didn't come cheap. An extra five percent and an additional two shipments."

I swear I can hear Roman's brain ticking over as he calculates the loss in production. "With you securing Yadkor yesterday, you'll cover the loss within a month."

"I know. Now I just need to convince Alexei. If he is on board, I'll have over sixty percent of Vladimir's assets."

My words come out hoarse, stifled by my fast gallop up the stairwell and the adrenaline raging through me. My plan to take down Vladimir is coming together better than I'd hoped. What I thought would take months has occurred in days. I want to say the swiftness of proceedings is due to shrewd business dealings, but that isn't the case. It is my determination to keep Justine off Vladimir's radar—my desire to keep her safe.

"You need to tread carefully with Alexei, Nikolai. He's been your father's minion for longer than you've been alive," Roman warns, his tone low.

"Then he knows better than anyone not to underestimate me. He will do well not to cross me." The tic of my jaw matches the beat of my heart, both as dangerous as the other. "Alexei either agrees with my terms or follows Vladimir to hell. The loss in production won't affect us. The Yurys deal will pick up the slack."

Roman sighs heavily, but not a word seeps from his lips. He has warned me numerous times in the past year, but I have never listened. It isn't because I'm stubborn. It is because I am a Popov through and through.

"Let's reconvene tomorrow... after you've been wiped of excessive energy," he suggests, his tone spirited during the last half of his sentence.

I roll my eyes, feeling younger than my nearly twenty-nine years. "I'm not being led by my cock, Roman."

"I never said you were," he intervenes. "But your motives are fueled by the one muscle in your body that pumps just as much blood as your cock."

He laughs at my furious growl. The fucking gall of him. If the thrill of the hunt wasn't coursing through my veins, I'd teach him a lesson on disrespect.

Lucky for him, I have Justine on my radar, pushing aside any negative thoughts. She is moseying down the hallway, the natural swing of her hips seducing me with every step she takes.

Fuck, she is beautiful, an intoxicating mix of innocence and sexiness.

Justine has no idea of her appeal, often missing the numerous glances she gets when she enters a room. I heard for months about the tempting redhead every criminal in the county wanted to work on their case before testing her as thoroughly between the sheets.

I thought her allure was purely due to her being fresh meat. I had no clue every murmured comment was factual. Justine is a knockout—a ten out of fucking ten. The prettiest woman I've ever seen. And if that doesn't already have blood pumping to my cock, there's also the fact she's mine.

"Roman," I murmur into my cell, my eyes not leaving Justine.

"Yes," he replies, his voice still brittle with laughter.

Wanting to wipe the smile off his face, I say, "Tell Lorde I found the package she left in my glove compartment. Although tempting, pink lace panties aren't really my thing."

Air whizzes out of his nostrils. "I swear to god, Nikolai. If I find out you touched my daughter, I'll—"

Happy he is ensnared by the trap I laid for him, I disconnect our call. Roman's twenty-two-year-old daughter is gorgeous, but I see Roman as a father, so I've never taken advantage of the numerous offers Lorde has made me over the past two years.

Roman is a good man who has miraculously kept his family out of our lifestyle, but that doesn't mean I won't use his daughter's interest in me to get a rise out of him. Serves him right for pissing me off.

The closer I get to Justine, the lighter my shoulders become. I've been tackling one shitstorm after another today, but none of that matters when Justine is on my radar. She is my drug, the sole nutrient feeding my ego. If she weren't in my thoughts all day, I would have thrown in the towel hours ago and lost my motivation with a handful of Popov whores, as I've done numerous times in the past twelve months. But the desire to have her beneath me, riling me up like no woman before her, has kept me driven.

I want to dethrone Vladimir, but not nearly as much as I crave Justine. That desire is irrepressible. Whether it is ten days or ten years, I'll never get my fill.

I sneak up on Justine unawares, my steps inaudible. A good hunter doesn't need to chase his prey. He takes what he wants, using his target's weakness against them.

Justine isn't my prey, but she is the greatest game I've ever played. My *Ангел*—the ultimate prize.

15

JUSTINE

While I balance a half-empty box of knickknacks on my hip, my hand delves into my purse for my house keys. Although my employment at Schluter & Fletcher was short, I amassed enough ornaments on my desk to fill half a box.

My items have no monetary value, but their sentimental worth was significant enough to squash the desire for a dramatic exit. It was for the best, as I managed to give Michelle, Trent, and Kirk sneaky farewell cuddles before I left Schluter & Fletcher for the last time.

I'm startled to within an inch of my life when a smooth, cultured voice asks, "Can I help with that?" Nikolai curls his body around mine, his movements so agile I once again failed to register his approach.

After tugging my earlobe with his teeth, he kisses my temple before scooping the box off my hip as if it is weightless. "You're home earlier than anticipated. No trips to Margaritaville today?" Although he keeps his tone playful, there's a snip of jealousy in it.

"Who needs Margaritaville when you can buy tequila by the gallon?" I reply, snagging the bottle of tequila I picked up at the store on my way home and wiggling it in the air.

Mercifully, my voice sounds as playful as Nikolai's, concealing my dire need for a stiff drink.

My steps into my foyer freeze halfway when a disturbing notion smacks into me. "I don't have any shot glasses."

An unexpected giggle rolls up my chest. After everything I've been through today, a lack of kitchen accessories is a disturbing notion.

What the hell is wrong with me?

Nikolai dumps my box of goodies on my entryway table before curling his arm around my waist and drawing me to his torso. "We don't need glasses. I have all the accessories I need right here." His finger glides across the dip in my collarbone before dropping to my inner belly button. "Now I can get high and drunk off your body."

When the stubble on his chin grazes my neck, an excited shiver surges through me, clearing away some of the murkiness lingering from my argument with Mr. Fletcher.

Only Nikolai can make me forget the world is against us.

Only he can make me smile when all I want to do is cry.

If the smile creeping onto my face didn't already justify every decision I've made thus far today, the swelling of my heart is a sure-fire indication I made the right choice resigning from my position.

Being led by my heart and body, I spin around to face Nikolai. The fiery amber darkening his icy-blue eyes simpers when our gazes collide for the quickest second. His jaw muscle spasms as the width of his pupils doubles. My heart rate quickens to a gallop, spurred on by the hasty shift in his demeanor. He went from play-ful, flirty Nikolai to a man prepared to go on a murderous rampage in under two point five seconds.

My confusion intensifies when he asks, "Did someone hurt you?" His voice is as dangerous as quicksand.

"No," I answer with a shake of my head, the shortness of my reply incapable of hiding my bewilderment.

"I swear to god, *Ангел*, after the day I've had, now is not the time to lie to me. Did someone hurt you?" he asks again as his eyes dart between mine.

Even with tension compressing the air from my lungs, the brutishness beaming out of him hits every one of my hot buttons. His eyes are blazing with the same intensity mine had when battling Mr. Fletcher, his protectiveness at an all-time high.

We may have the world against us, but nothing will defeat us when we stand side by side as we are now. That is how determined we are to protect one another, an unstoppable, equally inspiring, and frightening force.

When Nikolai glares, I mumble, "No one hurt me. I just missed you, that's all." Because only half of my statement is a lie, it sounds truthful. He hasn't left my thoughts all day, much less in the four hours since I saw him last.

When he curls his hand around my jaw, I lean into his embrace, needing friction against my skin. His touch can erase all the negativity burdening me, so I need it like my heart requires its next beat.

"Soon, *Ангел,* very soon," he promises, reading the plea in my eyes.

Remaining quiet, he dabs his thumbs into the corners of my eyes, ensuring not a drop of moisture is present.

Thankfully, my tears dried over thirty minutes ago.

Happy my eyes are moisture-free, he turns his attention to the heavy groove between my scrunched brows. He rubs at the spot, soothing it with nothing but careful strokes.

I stare at him in wonder, shocked a man who has endured so much pain knows how to be gentle. Seeing the vulnerability in his eyes as he caresses me soothes me more than I can explain. He will never let anyone hurt me—not even himself.

Satisfied his touch has relieved my tension, Nikolai drops his hands. They soon ball into fists as if he's struggling not to touch me.

Even though he stands across from me fully clothed, heady lust bristles between us, growing every second we spend in silence. I want him so badly I'm feeling greedy.

"Nikolai—"

"No, *Ангел.* Not yet." My clit thuds in response to the rough command of his voice. "I know you're lying to me, so I need a moment to work out whether to fuck the truth out of you or beat it out of Carmichael."

New tears glisten in my eyes. How does he already know me so well he can intuit the person responsible for my bad mood?

Because he knows me better than anyone.

My lips quiver when I begin to speak. "I know why you hate Carmichael. I read the court transcripts today. I know what he did to you."

When a tear spills from my welling eye, Nikolai brushes it

away before it gets halfway down my cheek. My heart doubles when he draws me into his chest, weaving his fingers through my hair.

Inhaling deeply, he drinks in my scent like it is addictive before muttering, "I don't hate Carmichael for what happened thirteen years ago."

When I stiffen, he quickly corrects, "I don't *just* hate him for what happened thirteen years ago. I also hate how he looks at you and wants you to be his. But more than anything, I fucking hate that I wanted to slit his throat last night, but for some reason, I couldn't."

I firm my grip on his waist as my chest tightens. The feelings I've developed for this man in such a short time span are so overwhelming I struggle to breathe through the concept.

"You're making me weak, *Ангел*," he murmurs into my hair, proving I'm not the only one besieged by these feelings. He is as bewildered as me. "At a time when my strength needs to be vital, you're making me weak. He was there, right in front of me, but I walked away."

"That doesn't make you weak. That makes you a man. You knew when to walk away. That's more courageous than fighting a battle unworthy of your time. Carmichael isn't worthy of your time. He wasn't thirteen years ago, and he isn't now."

Drawing back, Nikolai eyes me with amusement. I don't know what he thinks is funny. I can feel the fire in my stomach growing, my annoyance at the injustice he faced stacking my anger with more wood. This is not a laughing situation.

"What are you laughing at? This isn't funny, Nikolai. What he did to you isn't funny."

"I'm not laughing, *Ангел*. I am smiling. Not even twenty-four hours ago, you said I was destroying you. Now you're ready to jump in and defend my honor no matter the cost," he murmurs, his full Russian accent on display.

"I protect what's mine," I reply without hesitation, my voice as possessive as his is when he refers to me.

His grin enlarges. "I'm yours?"

"Yes," I squeak like a mouse, suddenly worried he won't appreciate my clinginess.

I've only known him for a week. Is that too soon to declare him as my own?

"If you want to be..."

My words trail off when Nikolai pushes his finger to my lips. "No, *Ангел*. If you go all in, you go all in, no half-baked shit." His voice is fierce, his earlier amusement null and void. "Am I yours?"

When he stares at me with the same openness his eyes held last night, I realize I misread the innuendo in his voice. He isn't angry. He's worried.

I don't know what he has to be concerned about. He couldn't be more embedded in my skin if he tried. A million years couldn't erase him from my mind, much less a few measly days.

Suddenly, the truth smacks into me.

Has anyone ever claimed Nikolai as their own? Malvina's interests were abundant, but were her feelings directly from her heart? Or was she inspired by the prospect of money?

I already know Nikolai's well-being was ignored by his mother, so who's to say Malvina wasn't dipping her toes into the same murky water?

Determined to show Nikolai I'm not like every other money-hungry woman, I connect my eyes with his before murmuring, "Yes, Nikolai. You are mine, and only mine. I protect what is mine, no matter the cost."

His smile does stupid things to my insides before he seals his mouth over mine.

A groan rolls up my chest when his tongue spears between my lips, his taste too scrumptious for my body to ignore. His kiss is skilled and assertive and proves without a doubt he isn't concerned about my declaration of ownership.

Balancing on my tippy toes, I deepen our kiss. I slide my tongue along the roof of his mouth before dueling with his.

Nikolai draws me in closer before dropping his attention to my neck. He sucks on the delicate skin on my earlobe before possessively growling, "Mine," into my ear.

His voice carries through me like molten lava, stimulating every nerve. I curl my arms around his shoulders when his chin grazes the side of my neck. I'm hot and heavy, my needs more urgent than my next breath.

When he cups my breast in his big, manly hand, I arch my back, coercing him to lose control on my body like he always does.

We move through my apartment like drunken teens, haphazardly shredding each other's clothes like hungry wild animals.

Air hisses between Nikolai's teeth when my skirt slips off my thighs, exposing my lack of undergarments. He stares at my pussy unashamed, the ardor in his eyes as stimulating as the bulge in his jeans.

"You told me to be ready," I murmur against his neck, nibbling at his skin. "You never said when you were arriving, so I pre-prepared." When he stiffens, as if angered by my reply, I announce, "I slipped them off in the restroom of my building. I didn't travel across Vegas without my panties."

He growls at my admission. It is a pleasing growl—*thank god!*

After removing my bra with a flick of his wrist, he traps my erect nipple in his warm and inviting mouth. Sweet tension builds in rhythmic waves in my womb, heightening both my body and my mind with every powerful suck. I love how he consumes my body without reserve, sending me toward a mind-hazing orgasm.

A giggle topples from my lips when I fall onto my mattress, my tumble softened by Nikolai catching our combined weight with his outstretched hand.

"Please, Nikolai... oh god, please," I murmur when I'm trapped under the bliss of his divine body. I love the weight of him against me as he pins me to the mattress in a domineering, controlling way.

When he rocks against me, stroking his cock along my bare pussy, I claw at his back, needing more.

No, wanting more.

He gives it to me. With one hand clutching my hair and the other on my hip, he plunges inside me. Our kiss made me so wet he slides in without hindrance, but it isn't lacking the burn of taking a man his size without preparation.

With my focus on nothing but the insane urge to fuck, I dig my feet into his ass before raising my backside off the mattress. I grind against him in a frenetic rhythm, encouraging him to take me hard and fast.

Nikolai answers my every want with perfection. He pumps into me on repeat, swiveling his hips with every thrust.

"Fuck... you feel so good," he grunts in a low, primitive growl.

He drives into me harder, nailing me to the bed as effectively as he's ensnared my heart. My orgasm builds like a storm, growing more rampant with every thrust of his densely veined cock.

Gripping my thighs, he spreads me wider for him, taking me even deeper. "Your cunt is so tight and greedy. Can you feel the way it milks me, begging for my cum?"

I answer his question by tightening the walls of my vagina, massaging his cock more firmly. His breathing quickens along with his pumps. He grips my ass and thrusts my hips higher, drawing me closer to him.

I moan on repeat when the crown of his cock rubs the aching spot inside of me, my orgasm charging to within an inch of the finish line.

Mindless with pleasure, I meet his thrusts grind for grind. The headboard of my bed smacks into the wall, our pace so out of control. I have no doubt Ms. Aaronson can hear my screams, but I can't hold back. I no longer have command of my body. It has been relinquished to the man fucking me to oblivion.

"That's it, Justine. Nice and loud. Scream my name."

The husky, intoxicating way he purrs my name sets me off. I climax in a hoarse cry, my clutch on his back so firm I'm confident I'll leave scratch marks.

"Ah, fuck, *Ангел*," Nikolai grunts heavily, his hips thrusting violently.

The sensation gripping every inch of me intensifies when his groans vibrate on my neck, spurring my climax to roll on and on. My body tingles as my lungs are relieved of air. I shudder uncontrollably, every muscle in my body exhausted from the brilliance of my orgasm.

"Oh god, Nikolai. Oh god..." I moan when my climax refuses to end, the perfect strokes of his big cock too wondrous to stop the sensations. My orgasm is like a freight train, long, powerful, and capable of destroying me.

I've barely come down from the clouds of orgasmic bliss when Nikolai's dark hair dusts my stomach. My body convulses when his tongue unexpectedly runs along the cleft of my pussy, lapping up the arousal shimmering between my legs.

As I growl his name, my hands shoot down to his head, striving to pull him away from the oversensitive bud he's stimulating so expertly it almost hurts.

He pins my wrists to the bed before ramping up his efforts. He slides his tongue between the folds of my pussy before swirling it around my clit. He devours my pussy like a man starved of taste, like a man who's never eaten.

"Give it to me, *Ангел*. I've been dying to taste your arousal for hours. Don't make me wait any longer than I already have." The heat of his breath adds to the mess between my legs.

My thighs shudder as I fight against the sensation overwhelming every inch of me. "I can't. Oh god, I can't. I'm too sensitive. I'm too..."

My words trail off when an unexpected climax blindsides me. Pleasure racks my body, rendering me a blubbering, incoherent mess.

I was so unprepared for another orgasm to come so quickly that all I can do is surrender to the insanity. I shout Nikolai's name into the night air, loving the buzz lighting up every inch of me. I never knew sex could be like this: mind-blowing and heart-tethering at the same time.

After bringing me down from climax with a gentler approach than he brought it on, Nikolai crawls up my body, swiping my arousal from his mouth on the way.

I taste myself on his tongue when he slips it between my parted lips, which are sucking in air like I'm seconds from fainting.

My lungs' effort to collect air grows when he guides his cock back to the entrance of my throbbing slit. He slides in without hindrance, my two orgasms ensuring not an ounce of friction is felt.

"That's better," he murmurs against my mouth before thrusting into me harder, taking me to the root of his cock. "Now I can fuck you for hours without hurting your tight little cunt."

I nearly laugh at his statement until his heavy-lidded gaze collides with mine. He isn't being deceitful or stroking his ego. He's being as honest as his tone implies.

We may have only entered this room half an hour ago, but we aren't leaving any time soon.

I'd be lying if I said I wasn't tickled pink at the idea.

16

NIKOLAI

"I t's beautiful," Justine murmurs under her breath as she drinks in the sunrise peeking over the buildings neighboring her apartment. "Florida is gorgeous, but I've never seen a sunrise like this."

"It's the wildfires in California giving it a smoky look," I reply, pulling her back to rest against my chest.

I took her to the brink more times than I can count last night, but my need to have her skin touching mine hasn't weakened. I crave her like a drug, one hit only making me crave another.

As I tried to do earlier this week, I'm showing Justine the ultimate light show in Vegas.

I've never been a man who appreciates the beauty surrounding him, but the thirty minutes before sunrise has always held a special place in my heart.

It is the only time I've had a moment of quiet my entire life.

What I said to Justine yesterday morning is true. The devil has never seen a sunrise, so it's the only time I'm guaranteed not to have Vladimir interfering in my life.

"I wish we could stay here forever, cocooned in our own little bubble," Justine murmurs into my chest, her breath fanning my sweat-slicked torso.

My cock stiffens, relishing the neediness in her voice. I'd love nothing more than to lay her out and devour her sweet cunt for the rest of the day, but I'm already hours behind the tight schedule I have planned for today.

I had every intention of meeting Roman at 3 a.m. like arranged yesterday, but my plans altered when I was balls deep inside Justine in the wee hours of this morning.

As she quivered through her third orgasm of the night, a snippet of my conversation with Asher played through my mind.

Asher and Dominique are practically strangers, but he was concerned enough about her being caught in the crossfires of my takeover. He put his business at risk to ensure her safety.

It was in that instant I realized I should be doing the same for Justine.

I crave her like a drug, but shouldn't my desire to keep her safe place my carnal needs on the back burner? I'm not talking weeks, months, or years like Lia's prolonged trip to the UK—just long enough to get Vladimir off her scent.

Then, once everything settles and the throne is mine, she can return to Vegas. She can come back to me without compromising her safety.

I want to pound my chest and act macho, declaring no one will get close enough to Justine to harm a hair on her head, but I know how the men in my industry work. I've lived amongst them my entire life.

When Vladimir discovers how effectively I've shut down his crew in a matter of days, he will be gunning for blood.

With Lia seen as worthless to Vladimir, Justine is my only weakness, one I'm not willing to put at risk for anything or anyone.

I pause for a moment, my mind spiraling. If only things were different. If I could dethrone Vladimir without fear of the repercussions many men suffered during his reign, then I wouldn't need to give Justine up, not even for a second. But nothing is fair in my lifestyle, so I have no choice.

I must let her go.

When I look down at Justine, she glances up at me, her eyes bright and shimmering with lust. My anger frays to the point of snapping, hating that anyone has the power to rule my life.

It's my life, for fuck's sake—*mine*.

And so is Justine.

I stand from the chair we're sitting on, taking Justine with me. She moans, loving my half-masted cock grinding her ass as I move us inside.

The Las Vegas heat becomes a distant memory as I stride through her living room, my focus on her outdated bathroom across from her bedroom. I don't know why I chose the bathroom when her bed was right beside us, but it feels like the right place to do this.

Things changed for us in that bathroom in a way I never saw coming.

Placing Justine on the vanity sink, I peel away the sheet concealing her body from my view. Since this will be the last time I will sample it for days, if not weeks, I don't want a single inch hidden from my eager eyes.

Justine's breathing quickens, her eyes flaring with excitement at my aggressiveness. I'm tugging at the sheet so hostilely that cotton ripping drowns out the mad beat of her heart.

Once she's uncovered, I lift and lock my eyes with hers. "Stand for me, *Ангел*. Show me your beauty," I demand, my voice so husky that my Russian heritage can't be missed.

She hesitates for the quickest second before she slips off the vanity to stand in front of me. Her tiny hands ball into fists at her side as the width of her pupils grows.

I know she finds this hard—being exposed and vulnerable—but we need this more than she realizes. I need her to see what she does to me, to quiver under my hand, but more than anything, she needs to know I'm not sending her away because she isn't perfect.

I'm doing it to keep her safe and to save us.

"Kneel, *Ангел*," I command, noticing the direction of her gaze hasn't veered far from my cock in the last twenty seconds.

Cockiness pumps through me hard and fast when her knelt position brings her mouth to within an inch of my cock. She licks her dry lips before raising her chin.

The pulse in her throat increases when I gather her hair with my fist to pull it away from her face, exposing the bite marks she hides with her long, wavy locks.

My cock thickens more, smug as fuck at the beautiful image of my woman kneeling before me with her eyes sparked with hunger.

"See what you do to me, *Ангел*? What your body does to me? You're not even touching me, and I'm struggling not to come."

Justine groans as she licks her lips again, her desire to taste me evident on her face.

I grip her hair tighter, fighting to express myself before my morals are led astray by my desires. "You want this, *Ангел*." I'm not asking a question. I'm stating a fact.

I swipe the crown of my cock across her plump lips, eliciting a husky moan from her throat. "You want to suck my cock as desperately as I want to keep you safe." The lust in her eyes is exchanged for worry when I mutter, "But we can't have both. It isn't possible."

My balls clench when my swollen crown dips between her parted lips. I know I shouldn't use her attraction to me against her, but when I'm running on empty, I use what I can.

Eager to please, Justine opens her mouth for me but keeps her hands resting at her side.

I told you she was smart.

She knows this is more than me wanting my dick sucked.

"I can't keep you safe if you remain here. I can't keep my promise if you stay in Vegas." Her eyes well with moisture, partly from my cock ramming into the back of her throat but most of it from unshed tears. "I want to keep you safe. I *need* to keep you safe."

She attempts to talk, but I rock my hips forward, stuffing her words back into her mouth with my cock.

Her husky moan vibrates against my knob as her tears moisten my shaft.

Thrusting more shallowly, I coerce the pain in her eyes to switch to lust.

Call me conceited, but I can bend Justine's seemingly impenetrable wall with nothing but my body. She is as defenseless to my touch as I am to hers.

Although the pain in her eyes remains, she works her lips up and down my shaft, sucking my cock like a woman born to bring me to heel. She swirls her tongue around my knob before trailing it down the vein feeding my cock.

My head falls back, and my eyes close when she increases the power of her sucks. I try to remember she's not kneeling in this erotic-scented space to get my rocks off.

I'm supposed to be using my body to lower her defenses before I inform her of my plans to ship her back to Florida today.

I also hope she will remember the energy bouncing between us when she discovers the secret I've been keeping from her.

The heat of her mouth and the firm grip of her hand has my climax building shockingly fast. I roll my hips faster, the need to come so overwhelming I make Justine gag.

I shouldn't love the sound of her choking on my cock, but I do.

With tears rolling down her cheeks, she takes me to the base of her throat. The rush of heat over my knob is too intense to ignore. I grip her hair with fury as cum rockets out of my cock, coating her mouth and throat.

She moans unintelligibly before her throat works hard to swallow my cum. She doesn't miss a single drop with her greedy sucks.

I nearly come for the second time when her tongue licks the underside of my knob, but I hold back the desire, suddenly recalling my objective.

A popping noise sounds from Justine's mouth when my cock breaks free from her suctioning lips.

She groans in disappointment, the glistening between her legs revealing how close to the brink she is.

Unable to deny the silent plea in her eyes, I lift her to the vanity, then burrow my head between her legs. She calls out hoarsely, whispering my name between each pleasurable cry.

I spear my tongue inside her insatiable cunt, not the least bit deterred by the fact my cum was inside her mere hours ago. I eat her like I'm starving, knowing this could be my last taste for weeks.

"Nikolai... oh... god," Justine pants between moans, her thighs tightening around my ears as her screams grow louder.

I slide two fingers inside her before quickly switching it to three. Her screams turn ear-piercing, thickening my cock to a point it is painful.

While thrusting in and out of her, my tongue flicks at her sensitive clit, arousing it more with every stroke I inflict.

Within minutes, she's quivering through an orgasm, her grip on the vanity so tight her knuckles go white.

I wait for every shudder to be exhausted before I line up my cock up with the entrance of her slicked pussy.

We groan in sync when I take her to the hilt, ramming every inch inside her.

I still for a moment, drinking in how good she feels.

There isn't a drug in the world that could replicate the high I get when I'm balls deep inside her. She is the sweetest substance I've ever sampled.

When Justine clenches around my cock, begging to be consumed, I draw all the way out to the tip before ramming it back in. My thrusts are so furious her head smacks into the mirror that I forced her to stand in front of last week.

I can't believe that was only a week ago.

It feels like a lifetime.

The urge to drive Justine to the brink engulfs me when I catch the quickest glimpse of my reflection in the mirror cupping her skull to protect her head.

My eyes are wide and full of life. My lips are swollen and wet with her arousal, and my skin is flushed.

If I hadn't already swept Justine's apartment three times tonight, I would have believed an intruder had snuck into her bathroom. That is how different I look.

I don't recognize the man staring back at me. He is a stranger I never thought I'd see again—one I haven't seen in over thirteen years.

Skin slapping skin booms around the room as I fuck Justine without restraint. I drive her to the brink of ecstasy, unraveling her as forcefully as she does me.

Just like every time I'm inside her, my mind is blank, clear of any negativity.

"Nikolai... oh. I'm going to come... *again*."

I smile smugly at the shock of her last word. If you had told Justine last week that she was only days away from a record-breaking number of orgasms, I doubt she would have believed you.

I knew from the instant I laid eyes on her that something intense was about to happen, but even I had no fucking clue how phenomenal it was going to be.

The chances of holding back my release are lost when Justine's pussy clamps around my cock. She sucks me into her deeper, begging for the heat of my cum to add to the sensation rolling through her.

I pump into her another three times before the temptation becomes too great.

"Fuck..." I growl, filling her to the brim. "Do you feel that, Ангел? My cum inside you? Filling you. Marking you. Claiming you."

"Yes," she answers, her one word quivering. "I feel you. In me. On me. Everywhere." The moisture in her eyes doubles. "I feel you everywhere, even when you're not with me." A tear glides down her flushed cheek as she stammers out, "But that doesn't mean you can send me away. I'm not going anywhere. I'm staying here with you. Fighting at your side."

I brush the tear off her cheek, hating that I'm causing her pain.

I've made grown men cry like babies without feeling any remorse, but one tear out of Justine's eyes feels like a knife stabbed into my chest.

I continue fucking her, knowing she won't give my suggestion an ounce of consideration unless I'm balls deep inside her. "You don't have a choice, Ангел. My decision is not negotiable. You're flying to Florida this afternoon. Roman has made all the arrangements."

Her anger rises from her gut to her face, replacing the lusty heat on her cheeks with fury.

Flattening her palms on my chest, she pushes me away from her. She tries to shut it down, but I see the quickest flare of disappointment dart through her eyes when my cock slips out of her snug cunt.

"Justine..." I growl in caution, warning her I'm not up for negotiating. My decision is final. Nothing she can say will change it. "It's time for you to go home. With you quitting your job, you've got no reason to stay here anymore."

On a shaky pair of knees, she covers herself with the sheet, hiding her body from my view. "Don't tell me what to do, Nikolai," she sneers, her voice cracking with emotion. "I'm not a child, so stop treating me like one."

"I spent all night proving you're not a child, Ангел. That fact has already been established."

She snarls, baring teeth, unappreciative of how my eyes slowly rake her body. "This isn't the time for stupidity. You're in for the fight of your life and acting like it's a game."

"You don't think I know what I'm up against? Why the fuck do you think I'm sending you away?"

"Because you're scared! Because you're worried I'm getting too close," she shouts, her voice shrilling around her bathroom.

"Nothing scares me, Ангел... except losing you," I admit, hating the weakness of my words.

The anger on her face fades as more tears fill her eyes. "Then don't send me away," she begs, her plea low and tainted with sorrow.

I step closer, praying she won't pull away from me.

Although she watches me cautiously, her feet remain planted on the ground. "I'm not sending you away because I'm afraid of what you're doing to me. I'm sending you away because it is the *only* way I can keep you safe. You've got me so unhinged, Ангел, I don't recognize the man I've become. That's dangerous. It could get me killed. It could get *you* killed."

She startles from my confession, but her determination remains strong. "A fight shared is a fight halved."

"It's. Not. Your. Fight," I grind out, pausing dramatically between each word, the tiresome week causing my fuse to grow ever shorter. "It is my fight. One I intend to win without a woman standing at my side."

Justine shakes her head as her face lines with disgust. "So that's what this is all about? I'm just a *woman*." She spits out her last word like it scorched her tongue. "A poor, defenseless *woman* who needs a man to rush in and save her?"

Not thinking, I nod, my protectiveness of her too strong to hear the underlying message in her question.

My back molars slam together when Justine's open palm connects with my left cheek. Her slap is so weak I barely register receiving it, but it's strong enough for me to react.

I clamp my hands around her wrists, my anger reaching its boiling point. "Don't fucking hit me. I told you not to hit me."

I had unimaginable things done to me my entire childhood, but none stung as severely as my mother slapping me when she recalled my true birthright. She hated me because I wasn't Vladimir's son, yet she was the one who lay with his enemy and birthed him a child.

I didn't choose to be born.

I didn't choose this fucking life.

Just like I wouldn't choose to have Justine away from me unless it was completely necessary.

I grew up despising my mother nearly as much as I hate my father. That's why I walked out of the restaurant the night she killed herself. I knew what she'd do, but I didn't stop her. If that makes me a monster, so be it. She deserved to die. Justine doesn't.

New tears spring down Justine's cheeks as she mumbles a string of unintelligible words. Although I can't understand what she's saying, I know she is apologizing. Her eyes are sorrowful.

I want to draw her into my chest and promise everything will be okay. I want to wipe away the tears streaming down her face, but more than anything, I want to keep her safe. So instead of crossing off the first two items on my wish list, I say, "Pack your bags. Roman will be here in an hour."

She won't look at me. She hasn't made eye contact with me in over two hours.

I fucking hate it.

I feed off the sneaky glances she gives me. They stroke my ego and boost my attitude, but she won't look at me, not even for a second.

"Don't block me out, *Ангел*. I'm trying to keep you safe," I say in Russian, knowing Roman doesn't know Russian like Justine and me. "You can be angry at my decision but also accept it."

Her thigh quivers, revealing she heard my mumbled comment, but her eyes remain on the scenery flying past her window.

"Justine," I try again, knowing she always reacts to me calling her by her real name. "Look at me."

She doesn't. She ignores me with the stubborn determination I've been fighting to unleash in her since we met.

This is the grit she should have shown Col when he sentenced her to death.

This is the woman I saw behind the shield.

I crave the persistent, beautiful woman who could bring any

man to heel with nothing but a sideways glance, but right now, I need her to be a woman with understanding.

I'm not doing this to hurt her.

I'm doing this to save her.

Pretending I can't feel Roman's watchful eye glancing at me over the newspaper he's reading, I unlatch Justine's seatbelt and pull her into my lap.

She kicks and thrashes against me, but I remain holding her tightly, my determination spurred on by the driver taking the exit for McCarran Airport.

"Fight me, *Ангел*," I growl into her ear, hating that her last thought of me will be me yelling at her. "Scratch me, hit me, slap me, but know when clarity forms, you'll regret this exchange as much as I will. I am not the enemy, Justine. I'm the man keeping you away from him."

"By sending me back to the place that stole my freedom to begin with," she retaliates, her voice as hot-tempered as her face. "How chivalrous of you."

Her reply shocks me, maiming me more than her silence the past two hours. "Your family lives in Hopeton—"

"But my heart doesn't," she interrupts, her reply loud enough to gain Roman's and the driver's attention. The moisture in her eyes kills me. "God, Nikolai. Can't you feel it? Don't you see it? I can't be the only one feeling the crazy connection we have."

She stares into my eyes, begging for me to concur with her admission, to acknowledge how fucking crazy she makes me, but I can't because if I give in to one plea in her eyes, I won't stop.

I'll keep granting wish after wish until every foundation I laid the past six hours is undone.

Furthermore, I promised to keep her safe.

For the first time in my life, I will keep my promise.

"Your flight leaves from gate fourteen. Roman will ensure you return home safely."

Justine stills as her eyes lock with mine. She doesn't breathe, move, or speak. She stares at me like she can't believe the words that left my mouth.

"When things settle down, then you can come back."

"Come back?" she struggles, her two words expressing way more than any sentence ever could. "Why would I come back,

Nikolai? You said it yourself. I have nothing keeping me here, so why would I return?"

With the mask she was wearing the day we met firmly slipped into place, concealing her beauty from a man she no longer deems worthy of seeing it, she shimmies off my lap.

When she throws open the door with force, it's the fight of my life to keep my ass in my seat. The only reason I do is because I know this industry better than anyone.

My chances of dethroning Vladimir are already slim to none, but if he discovers I have a weakness, they will be non-existent, not only putting my life at risk but also Justine's.

That is not something I will settle for.

I'll kill any man who stands in my way of protecting her—even myself.

When Roman clambers onto the sidewalk on Justine's heels, I hear her mumble, "I thought Dimitri was a coward, but Nikolai just stole his title."

Glancing down at my feet, I fight to keep my anger at bay, my fists clenching the only indication I heard her grumbled comment.

Acting ignorant is pointless. I slide across the seat in under a second, my focus on one thing and one thing only—proving to Justine I am more of a man than Dimitri will ever be.

"No," Roman commands, pointing his index finger at me while blocking my exit with his body. "Finish one battle before you start another."

"I won't have anything to fight for if I lose her," I reply, shoving him out of my way.

He fists my shirt, stepping over a line I deem acceptable.

If he were any other man, my knife would already be pressed against his jugular, but since he is like a father to me, I keep my knife in my back pocket.

"She's not going anywhere, Nikolai. She's angry, so she's lashing out. Give her some time, and she'll realize you made the best decision you could for the shitty situation you're in." Noticing my anger is simmering, he lets go of my shirt. "We discussed every possibility this morning. This is your only option. She'll understand."

"She said she has no reason to come back." I grit my teeth, hating the panic in my voice.

Roman's brow quirks. "She wouldn't have fought you like she did if you aren't who she wants. She'll come back. I'm so confident I'll put money on it."

I take a moment to consider what he's saying. He's been married for thirty years, so he should know how this works, but it doesn't make his knowledge any easier to absorb.

Scrubbing my hand across my unshaven jaw, I slump into my chair. "Look after her, Roman. Treat her like your own daughter."

My eyes lift from my knuckles when the scent of heated skin streams through my nose. "If I did that, I'd have to kill you. No one touches my girls. Not even you," he mutters, glaring at me.

My lips tug at his reply. I should be annoyed, but all I'm feeling is gratitude. If Roman protects Justine as if she's family, nothing will happen to her. He isn't as highly ranked as I am in our industry, but his kill count is just as high.

"Give her this once you're thirty thousand feet in the air," I request, handing him an envelope from my back pocket.

Nodding, Roman places the envelope in the breast pocket of his jacket before shutting the door. I wait for him to guide Justine into the terminal before rapping my knuckles on the privacy partition separating the main cabin of my car from the driver, requesting for him to go.

As my SUV chugs into action, I scan the heavy foot traffic, hoping to distract my thoughts long enough that I don't demand the driver to stop.

It kills me to admit that Justine will be safer in Hopeton. By shipping her home, Vladimir will think I've grown bored of her like I did Malvina.

The soothing effect I was hoping to achieve from people watching is undone when my eyes lock in on a dark-haired man exiting the arrival terminal.

My temples pound against my skull when I shake my head to clear my vision, sure I'm not seeing who I think I'm seeing.

It can't be him.

He's dead.

My brother Rico is dead.

17

NIKOLAI

"**S**top here."

I keep my eyes arrested on the cab we've been following for the past twenty minutes while yanking a bundle of cash out of my pocket.

I only saw the quickest glimpse of the man's profile before he entered the idling taxi at McCarran Airport, but I'm confident he is Rico.

I'd never forget his face, not in a million years.

I track the dark-haired man when he curls out of the taxi and darts across the sidewalk. When he presses a buzzer on a private entrance, I throw a wad of cash at my driver.

"Go," I instruct before sliding out the back passenger door.

The driver peers at me over his shoulder, his expression unamused. "Where?"

"I don't fucking care where you go, just go!" I roar, my loud voice startling a group of people mingling on the sidewalk.

Fortunately, Rico is too busy scanning a list of names at the entrance of an apartment building half a block up to hear me.

My eyes stray to the driver. "I won't need your services for the remainder of the night." I keep my tone neutral, though I'm feeling anything but.

The driver smiles a slick grin, assuming Justine's departure has me returning to old habits.

It doesn't.

I don't care if she is gone for weeks, months, or even years. My cock isn't interested in filling any crevice that isn't hers.

"Enjoy your night," the driver croons, his voice the type that makes me want to slit his throat so that I don't have to hear it again.

After slamming the SUV's door shut, I wait for it to disappear into the sea of traffic before I head in Rico's direction. I keep my interest on the down-low, pretending I'm too busy eyeballing the scantily clad women watching me with zeal to pay him any attention.

It's all a ruse. My interests are so piqued I'm tempted to walk straight up to him and call him out as a fraud.

Things were bad between Rico and me when he died. It probably didn't help that I ordered a member of our crew to rape and murder his wife. I didn't have a choice. I was acting on behalf of Vladimir. But Rico has never heard sense when it comes to Blaire—his little kitten.

Now, I better understand his desire to protect her. I've only known Justine for days, but the short time hasn't weakened my resolve to keep her safe.

I'll take a bullet for that woman.

I'll even slit the throat of the man who raised me.

After scanning my location to ensure I'm not being followed, I shadow Rico down an alley. The adrenaline surging through me is as intense as when Justine quivers beneath me.

It's only been days since I've killed a man, but the urge to inflict pain never tapers... *except when she's with me.*

My hunger for Justine is stronger than any craving I've had.

Nothing can overwhelm it.

Not. One. Single. Fucking. Thing.

With my thoughts locked on Justine, I'm left defenseless when I'm suddenly clutched by the throat. I gasp for breaths through restricted airways when I'm slammed against a stack of bricks robbing my lungs of any oxygen they had left.

I take a second to gather my wits before retaliating. While slamming a hand down on the arm squeezing my neck, I throw an elbow into his midsection.

When he folds in pain, I inflict a left and right combination on his ribs before gripping his head between my hands. I practically climb the wall, giving myself enough leverage to snap his neck.

Expertly slithering out of my hold, he completes back-to-back left jabs to my ribs before ducking low to sweep my feet out from underneath me, sending me free-falling to the ground.

Blood surges to my face when I hit the concrete with a thud, the impact winding me more than his jabs to my ribs.

Gasping for air, I swing my leg out, bringing my accoster down to my level with a grunt. Before he can return to his feet, I crawl over his body and straddle his hips. With his hands protecting his face, I direct my focus to his stomach, spleen, and ribs.

He grunts, accepting each jab as if he is a born fighter.

My intuition is proven dead on point when the man taunts, "Is that all you got, Eli? You still hit like a girl."

If I didn't know I was fighting Rico, I have no doubts now. No one calls me Eli—except Rico. He knows how much I despised my name when I was a child—*who wants to be named after the devil?*—so years before I became the shadow of our father, Rico shortened my middle name.

It was something he only called me in private when we were safe from prying ears, but the name stuck.

Clearly, he hopes exposing himself will stop my onslaught on his body.

He's dead wrong.

I said Rico and I *were* close.

We aren't anymore.

I continue punishing Rico's body with my fists, replicating the fights we'd had many times in our teens. Although brutal, those matches were nowhere near as violent as our bout today.

Rico retaliates to my anger with the same level of viciousness, battering my already aching ribs with forceful hits.

When his hands drop to inflict back-to-back jabs on my spleen, I take advantage of his exposed face. My fist connects with his left jaw with so much force his head slings sideways.

Growling, he throws me off his body as if I'm weightless. I spring to my feet, my determination as strong as it was the night he confronted me with his torture instruments of choice.

I understood why he was angry, but he never gave me a chance to explain why I ordered the hit on Blaire. He came at me guns blazing.

Rico and I stand toe-to-toe with heaving chests and raised hands. We are prepared to fight, but neither is advancing on the other.

Our mutual disdain for one another is unmissable in our sky-blue versus midnight-black stare down. He hates me for what I did to his wife, and I hate him for the years of misery he put me through believing he was dead.

Before his back was burned with acid, I considered him my brother, even without sharing the same blood, but the day he met Blaire changed everything. He protected her—a stranger—from members of our crew, which lost the Popov entity a valuable asset and disrespected our father in front of key members of a rival association.

When you disrespect Vladimir, you must be punished, and Vladimir used Rico's punishment to make an example out of him. His penalty was a clear warning that no member of our entity was to put a woman's needs above their commitment to our crew.

Rico was put through the absolute wringer. I'm still shocked to this day he survived.

Rico thinks his punishment was the end of it.

It wasn't.

I couldn't let it go. If Vladimir could do something so heinous to his own flesh and blood, what chance did I stand of making it past my teens?

I went to Vladimir that night both wanting my freedom and justice for Rico. I was right there, with my knife pressed against his jugular, but no matter how many times I tried to drag it across his throat, I couldn't do it.

Vladimir had fucked with my head so badly, with only a few words, he convinced me Rico was in the wrong and deserved to be punished.

I paid for my wrongdoing as severely as Rico did.

You know your childhood was shit when a two-week-long stint in the hospital was two of the best weeks of your life. Roman never left my side, and I even had the occasional visit from my mother. Having the nursing staff fuss over me like I was a god made me feel invincible. So much so that I believed every dribbled promise spilled from Carmichael's mouth.

"If you just speak up, I guarantee you'll never step foot in his house again."

That was the false promise that sealed the deal for me. That was all I wanted—to escape Vladimir's clutches, so I stupidly believed Carmichael.

I was a fucking idiot.

Even more than I am now.

Rico's dark brow slants when I drop my fists to my sides. I keep them balled, but my stance is nowhere near as irate as it was moments ago.

Running my tongue along my lips, I clear away a smear of blood dripping over them before saying, "You know I didn't have a choice, Rico. Blaire was a liability."

His fists clench more firmly as he glares at me with murderous black eyes. "You had a choice. You could have come to me."

"And say what?" I reply, half laughing. "I've been ordered to kill your wife or be killed? That would have landed us in that dungeon even faster than when you discovered I'd set her up."

He drags his hand under his nose, wiping away the bloody contents before gluing his fists to his sides, loosening his defensive stance. "You could have warned me—"

"I did," I interrupt, glaring at him. "How the fuck do you think you escaped RaRa's clutches so fast that night? I intervened, saving your hide from her infamous thirty-minute ramblings."

Rico stills as his eyes dart between mine. I can tell the moment clarity forms in his mind as his pupils expand and his lips part for air.

"I ordered the hit on Blaire, but I made sure the timeframe matched your return to her room," I admit. "But I didn't factor RaRa into the equation. When your sights were set on Blaire, usually nothing could deter you. I just forgot how fucking stubborn RaRa can be." I stop for a moment, my heart rate lowering. "Could be."

"RaRa's gone?" Rico asks, his low tone indicating I'm not the only one who craved RaRa's attention.

I nod. "A little over three months ago. She went peacefully."

I don't know what compelled me to say my last sentence. Probably something to do with RaRa being Vladimir's first whore. Most of his whores don't make it to the age of thirty. RaRa turned seventy-three the week before her death. In mafia time, that's the equivalent of three lifetimes.

When a tension-filled silence passes between Rico and me, I ask, "What are you doing here, Rico? Why come back now? If Vladimir finds out you're alive, he'll have a bounty on your head by the end of the day."

I step back, stunned by his reply when he answers, "I came to help you. You're ruffling so many feathers you are gonna get yourself killed." He shrugs as if unsure how to say his next sentence. "I don't want that to happen, so I'm here to ensure it doesn't."

I laugh a little, finding the situation amusing. I have blood streaming down my cheek from a large gash on my right brow, and possibly three broken ribs, compliments of his return to Vegas, but I'm supposed to believe he is here because he's worried about me.

For the first time, I lack a retort when he asks, "Is it true? Did you try to kill Vladimir after what he did to me?"

The veins in my neck twang. "How do you know about that?"

"That doesn't matter. Is it true?" His tone is half wrathful, half uneasy.

"Yeah, it's true." The shortness of my reply doesn't lessen its impact.

Air whizzes out of Rico's mouth as if my reply winded him more than my fists. "Jesus Christ, why didn't you tell me, Nikolai?"

I shrug, acting like it's no big deal. "You would have done the same for me."

He nods, not attempting to hide the honesty in his eyes. While scrubbing his hand along his bloodstained jaw, he strays his shocked gaze to me. "Who are you protecting from him now?"

My lips twitch, but before a lie can spill from my mouth, he warns, "If you lie to me, I'll be on the first plane home, leaving you to clean up the bloodbath on your own."

Blood floods my chest, puffing it high. I'm not the same Nikolai Rico left behind three years ago. I can take care of myself.

"I don't need your help, so you're more than welcome to march your ass back to the airport and catch the first flight home."

His brow arches high into his clipped hair. "You don't need my help?"

I shake my head, my arrogance at an all-time high. "Nope. Survived many years without you. Will survive many more just as well."

Rico grins as his coal-colored eyes glare into mine. "You've always been a stubborn fuck. That will be your downfall, Nikolai. You aren't living. This isn't living." He waves his knuckle-busted hand around the alleyway we are standing in. "Whoever has you so twisted up you're making stupid mistakes... that's living. Raising my son far away from this life... that's living. Playing into Vladimir's hand with the same fucked-up games he played on us our entire life... that isn't living. That's surviving... one fucking miserable day at a time."

"You have a son?" I mutter, starting at the only shocking thing in his long-winded statement.

Everything else he said was true, so it doesn't need rehashing.

"Yeah," he replies, his eyes twinkling with a gleam I've never seen in them before. "We named him Eli."

Shock slams into me, blindsiding me. "Why the fuck would you name him after me? That's the equivalent of my mom giving me Vladimir's middle name. You're setting your son up to fail."

Rico shakes his head, dismissing my assumption. "You may have gone way off the tracks years ago, but you were a good kid before Vladimir ruined you." His eyes bounce between mine before he mutters softly, "If only you had gotten out all those years ago."

I stare at him, striving to work out how he knows I tried to leave when I was sixteen. I didn't tell a soul of my desire to leave—*well, except one man.*

Like a freight train crashing into me, the truth dawns on me. "You've been in contact with Erik." I'm not asking a question. I'm stating a fact. "You know he's a snitch, right? He's working with the FBI."

He stares at me, his eyes revealing more than his mouth ever could.

"You fucking traitor!" I shout, my body heating up. "You better get back on your plane before I slit your snitching throat. A tattler can't talk when he doesn't have a tongue."

When I step toward him, he doesn't flinch. He stands his ground, his confidence way too pigheaded for my liking. "If I wanted to take you down, I could have done it years ago. I'm not here on behalf of the FBI."

"Then why the fuck are you here?" I sneer, my words hissing from my mouth like venom. "If you're hoping I'll follow you back to the 'burbs and live in a house with a white picket fence and two point five kids, you're barking up the wrong fucking tree."

"I know. I don't like it, but I understand. This is your life. You don't know any different. But this isn't about you, Nikolai. I'm here to ensure my son doesn't live the life we did," Rico answers, his voice growing alongside his anger. "I'm sick to death of looking over my shoulder every two seconds. I'm tired of hiding in the shadows, waiting for the day Vladimir arrives at my door to claim my son as his own. So, I'm here to do what the FBI won't. I'm here to take Vladimir down. I'm taking back my life."

He runs a hand over his clipped hair. "When I heard you were negotiating trades without Vladimir's knowledge, I knew you were up to something. A man like Vladimir doesn't retire. He'll die protecting his throne before he'll ever hand it over."

"And your point is?" I ask, my tone cocky.

He doesn't flinch at my roundabout way of saying I'm going to kill Vladimir. He takes it in stride, as if he too has dreamed of the day revenge will finally be served.

"Who is she?"

I glare at him, acting confused by his question.

It's all a ploy.

I'm not confused. I know exactly who he's talking about.

Rico never hid the fact his wife was his gift for years of misery, but he also knows if they had never met, he would have followed Vladimir to hell.

Just like me, he was born a mafia prince.

Unlike me, he won't die a king.

Rico's wife doesn't have one-tenth of the intensity Justine has. She would have never survived in our world, so Rico did everything he could to keep her out of it instead of forcing her into it.

"That good?" Rico surmises, noticing the smirk I cannot hide when my thoughts stray to Justine.

"You got the kitten. I got the tiger," I reply, my tone as smug as my grin.

A split in his top lip becomes apparent when he smirks, his

fondness for his wife as strong as ever. "There's nothing more provocative than the woman you love purring beneath you."

I nod, not bothering to correct him on his insinuation that I'm in love with Justine.

To be honest, I don't know what any of the weirdness I feel when I'm with Justine means, but I'm certain it isn't love.

Well, I don't think it is?

Rico laughs, seemingly amused.

"What the fuck are you laughing at?" I snarl, my voice so stern my accent is the thickest it's been.

"Nothing. Come on." Still laughing, he nudges his head to a door a few spaces from where we are standing. "Eli turned three last month. I haven't slept a full night in over three years."

"I don't need sleep, Rico," I inform him, following him to the concealed entrance.

"Who said anything about sleeping?" he questions, heading to a set of stairs on our left. "We need to sit down and devise a plan, or neither of us will get out of this alive. I don't know about your missus, but if I don't keep my word on returning to Kitten in one piece by the end of next week, mafia crossovers will seem like child's play."

"Blaire knows you're here?" I ask, shadowing him up the first flight of stairs.

When he nods, I balk. Blaire has the purity of an angel. She'd blubber nonstop just at the thought of Rico breaking a nail, so I'm somewhat shocked she's okay with his plan.

I've never seen a woman cry as much as Blaire did in the weeks following Rico's supposed death. She's either a good actor or had no clue about Rico's intentions.

"Blaire's a mother now, Nikolai. Nothing stands between a kitten and her cub," Rico explains when he sees the confusion crossing my face. He stops climbing the stairs and spins around to face me. "She was also unaware of my plan. I knew you were watching her, so I had to make sure her grief looked real."

"Once again, it wasn't my choice."

"I know," he agrees, twisting his lips. "Doesn't make me want to smash your teeth any less."

"I'd like to see you try."

He doesn't reply to my statement. He heard the playfulness in my tone. We still have a long way to go, but this is the most we've communicated in over ten years. Although I don't like reaching out for help, I could benefit from his unexpected arrival. Only one other man knows Vladimir as well as I do—he is standing in front of me.

"Is there any reason we can't use the elevator?" I ask when we reach the thirteenth floor.

With my muscles still feeling the effects of the strenuous activities Justine and I undertook last night, I'm dreading every fucking step.

"We could, but considering Vladimir has access to every elevator camera in Vegas, I prefer taking the stairs."

Rico's confession stops me midstride. "Vladimir has access to every elevator camera? Since when?" I try to keep the worry out of my voice. My attempts are borderline.

He stalks down a long, dingy hallway while answering, "Since cameras were invented. Why do you think I always climb the stairs?"

"Sucker for punishment? Fucked if I know. I thought it was part of your fitness routine," I answer, yanking my cell phone out of my pocket.

Laughing, he stabs a freshly cut key into a door and twists the lock. I finish compiling a message to the guy who handles my digital security, requesting he wipe any surveillance footage from Justine's apartment the past week, before shadowing Rico inside the state-of-the-art apartment.

Damn.

From its outside appearance, you'd be none the wiser to the extravagance hiding behind the thick reinforced steel door. This property is pristine, putting the world's most glamorous presidential suites to shame.

"Whose place is this?" I ask Rico, galloping down three stairs leading to a massive sunken living room.

I answer my own question when my eyes lock in on a set of shelves straddling a top-range open fireplace.

Anger overwhelms me, slicking my skin with sweat. "I am *not* a snitch. I'd rather die than work with the FBI." I turn my eyes to Rico, their narrowed width leaving no doubt as to the fury raging through my veins. "Why the fuck did you bring me here?" My voice shakes with the anger I'm struggling to contain.

At first, I assumed this property was one of many Rico amassed in his early twenties, but when the photos of Erik and Rico began intermingling with law textbooks and service medals, the truth smacked into me.

This isn't Rico's property.

It is Erik's crash pad.

"I don't know how far you've gone down the rabbit hole, Rico. I'm hoping you used the FBI to escape Vladimir's clutches, but if that isn't the case, you know as well as I do that there is only one cure for rats. Extermination."

He stands to his full height, bringing him an inch or two taller than me. Although he is larger than me, I don't stand down. I can take him. I've got rage on my side. I've got grit. And I've also got my woman relying on me to bring her home sooner rather than later.

"How many times did Vladimir guarantee you that his last punishment would be the final punishment?" Rico asks, his tone flat and lifeless. "Or that just another year of service would be your final year? How often did he promise you freedom if you did one last task for him?"

I don't need to answer his questions. He knows as well as I do how many broken promises Vladimir issued me during my childhood, as he was served just as many.

"The FBI is no different from the man they're hunting. One more week... a month... a year. It never fucking ended." I clench my fists when he admits, "I gave them enough intel on Vladimir he'd never breathe outside of prison walls again, yet it still wasn't enough. They wanted more." I keep my eyes focused on his inky-black gaze when he moves to stand in front of me. "I'm not here on behalf of the FBI. I'm here to do what I should have done years ago. I'm here to take Vladimir down."

"Then why come here? Why bring me into the home of a man determined to take *me* down?"

Smirking, he showcases a side of him I haven't seen in years. He points a small black remote over his left shoulder and hits a button.

Curious, I spin on my heels in the direction he is looking.

It feels like all my Christmases have come at once when my eyes drink in a wall of weapons. Tommy guns, Smith and Wesson,

Colts, and brand-spanking-new Winchesters—you name it, the secret room Rico just unlocked has it.

Relishing my slack-jawed expression, Rico enters the space that smells like death and money all at the same time. He places a loaded Colt M1911 into the waistband of his trousers before loading the chamber of a dated Smith and Wesson.

"Do you even know how to fire one of those anymore?" I ask Rico, my tone brittle with laughter.

Blaire is a kindergarten teacher, so the closest weapon Rico has most likely touched in the past three years is an electric pencil sharpener. Although a correctly sharpened pencil can kill a man, Rico has always preferred clean kills over gory ones.

Smiling, he screws a silencer on the SIG Mosquito. I smirk when he aims the barrel at the crinkle between my brows. "Do you want an apple on my head? Or are you going in blind?"

Without hesitation, he pulls back on the trigger, sending a bullet whizzing toward my head. With only half an inch to spare, it hisses past the strands of hair curling around my ear before shattering a vase behind my shoulder.

"Does that answer your question?" he asks, his tone smug as fuck.

"Depends. Were you aiming for me or the vase?"

Laughing, he blows on the end of the barrel like the corny mafia movies we watched when we were kids. I have no doubt he loves his wife enough he'd never return to our lifestyle, but a twinkle in his eyes tells me he misses the adventure that came with his previous job description.

You can take a man out of the mafia, but you can't take the mafia out of the man.

Nudging his head to a set of chairs on his left, Rico says, "We've got the weaponry. Now we just need a plan."

"We?" I ask through arched brows.

He glances at me. His earlier amusement has vanished. "You know the way things work in this industry, Nikolai. No matter how badly you want to kill Vladimir, you can't." He sits in one of the chairs before adding, "That's where I come in. You can't accuse a ghost of murder."

Veins pop in my neck as a wounded roar sounds from my mouth. "No, Rico. You're not taking this from me," I reply, shaking my head. "I've been waiting for this day my entire life. I'm not giving it up."

"Alright," he replies, shocking me with his blasé response.

Suburbia has made him soft. The Rico I used to know would never back down so easily.

The reasoning behind his nonchalant reply is exposed when he says, "You can kill Vladimir... but you're gonna need to give up your girl first because you can't have both items on your wish list."

I clench my hands at my sides, fighting to keep from answering his words with my fists.

A deep crease furrows in Rico's brow when he says, "If you break the rules of our industry, you not only put your head on the chopping block, you put anyone associated with you there as well. Once they get you, she'll be kill number two. You know this, Nikolai. You're just assuming the rules don't apply to you. I hate to tell you, but the rules were created for guys like us. Otherwise, Vladimir would have been dethroned years ago."

Blood pumps through me, kicking my heart into a frantic beat. Even knowing what he says is true doesn't make it easier to hear. I promised to slit the throat of any man who dares look at Justine sideways, but that will be hard to maintain if I'm six feet under.

"Fuck!" I growl, angered about the next set of words prepared to leave my lips. Justine makes me unhinged, but I never thought she'd have me saying this...

My cell phone vibrates in my pocket before a syllable can leave my mouth. Hoping it is Justine, I dig it out. Disappointment surges through me when I peer down at the screen to see who is calling me. It is Asher.

"Asher, if this concerns the transfer of Vladimir's account to me, it needs to wait. I'm snowed under," I say in Russian.

Rico tries to show disinterest in my conversation. He's a terrible actor. His lips quirked when I uttered Asher's name, and his watchful gaze alerts me that he's still fluent in Russian.

"This isn't a business call," Asher replies, his tone low for a man who usually exudes confidence by the bucketload.

I remain quiet, waiting for him to elaborate.

I consider Asher a friend, but our alliance does not entail calls out of the blue for no reason.

"It's about Malvina," Asher continues a short time later, leaving me long enough to stew on the reason for his call but not long enough to voice anger over his delay. "She didn't fly back to Russia with Dominique. She said she had business to take care of before returning home."

"What the fuck? Why are you only telling me this now?" I ask, glancing down at my watch to calculate how long Malvina has been left unattended in Vegas.

It's been well over thirty-six hours.

"Dominique doesn't understand Russian, and her English is poor. By the time I remembered Maya spoke French, an entire day had passed," Asher explains, his tone remorseful.

I scrub the back of my hand over my eyes, unhappy but also understanding. Just like Maya, Dominique is of French heritage. She can barely understand a word of English, much less speak it.

A knot twists in my stomach when Asher adds, "That isn't the worst of it. Malvina didn't leave unattended. She was collected by—"

"Vladimir," we say at the same time.

I cuss under my breath as a barrage of disturbing thoughts bombard me. Malvina was spoiled by her father, making her a cold-hearted and vindictive bitch. She's so used to getting what she wants that she threw everything she had at me when I walked her to the private jet myself just to make sure she got on the plane. Money, private dealings with her father—she even tried the dreaded "I'm pregnant" stint I've handled numerous times over the past ten years.

Nothing she could have said would have changed my mind, but her last ploy was the final nail in her coffin. I haven't touched a hair on her head since we sealed our arrangement four years ago, so I knew every word spilling from her mouth was a lie.

Things turned physical when I called her out for the liar she is. She clawed at my neck while calling me every Russian cuss word under the sun.

When anger didn't work, she resorted to tears.

Realizing my heart is as hard as hers, she finally took her seat while threatening retribution for the disrespect my rejection will cause to her family.

Although Andros was displeased when I contacted him upon leaving a private airstrip on the outskirts of Vegas, the cancellation of our engagement allowed him to secure a more beneficial arrangement with a Russian businessman he was knee-deep in negotiations with.

With Andros's approval to end our engagement, I never put much thought into Malvina's pledge for revenge.

Now I'm beginning to wonder if I've underestimated her.

Malvina reminds me a lot of my mother. She'd crawl over a bed of glass on her hands and knees if it guaranteed her more power and money than she already has.

She is the female equivalent of Vladimir.

"Thanks for the heads-up," I say to Asher before disconnecting our call.

It's the fight of my life not to slam my cell against the floor, but I hold the urge back—*barely!* This cell is the only communication I have with Justine and Roman, so as much as I'd like to take my anger out on it, I can't.

"What's going on?" Rico asks, reading the fury radiating out of me.

"Malvina..."

He grimaces, his memories of Malvina as sour as mine.

"I sent her back to Russia last night. Well, I thought I did. She slipped the net before the plane took off."

Rico takes a moment to deliberate before asking, "And your girl, where is she?"

A bit of gratitude eases my anger. "On a plane to Hopeton." *Thank fuck.*

"Have they met?"

My eyes stray to Rico. "Who? Malvina and Justine?" When he answers my question with a bow of his brow, I say, "Yeah. It didn't go well."

He smirks, reading the underlying message in my short reply. "And Vladimir and Justine? Have they met?"

I hold my hands out in front of my body, feigning innocence. "What's with the twenty questions, Officer? Yes, they've met. A few more times than I'd fucking like."

Rico takes my snooty attitude in stride, unaffected by my rapidly building anger. "Were you there when they met?" he continues to interrogate.

"Yes, but why does that matter?" You can't miss the annoyed confusion in my tone.

He scrubs the back of his hand over his mouth, striving to hide his hard-set jaw.

It is a pointless effort. His eyes tell you he's angry even when you can't see his mouth.

"You're a fucking idiot," he growls under his breath, forcing my anger to an all-time high. "You wear pussy-whipped as well as every other male in the population. If Vladimir saw you with her, he knows why you sent Malvina packing. That won't sit well with him. No woman can fracture the rightful order." His words quiver at the end, the tic of his jaw too furious to contain.

I shake my head, denying his accusation. "I led Vladimir away from Justine's scent. He has no clue what she means to me. I don't have a clue what she means to me, so how the fuck would he know?" My last sentence is more of a personal reflection than an actual question.

Rico's brow arches high, calling bullshit.

I return his glare, my desire to kill the greatest I've ever battled. Unlike Justine, being around Rico magnifies my drive to kill. It doesn't suffocate it.

"You need to look at the entire picture, Eli," he says, using my nickname on purpose, hoping it'll lessen my anger. "Vladimir knows about Justine because he knows everything." He waits for me to absorb the honesty in his eyes before asking, "Are you sure your girl is on a plane to Hopeton?"

An uneasy feeling spreads through my gut as I consider his question. I did everything but fly the plane to Russia, and Malvina still evaded me, so who's to say Justine hasn't done the same thing?

Ignoring how my hands have begun to shake, I dial Roman's number. It rings on repeat, making my stomach queasy. I try to convince myself it doesn't mean anything. Roman could have switched off his cell in preparation for takeoff, but the longer my calls go unanswered, the darker the cloud engulfing me becomes.

Pretending I can't feel the fury burning me alive, I say, "It's time."

He nods, understanding my request without another word needing to spill from my lips.

It is time for Vladimir to pay his penance. It is time for justice to be served. It is time for this prince to take his crown.

An eye for an eye.

A life for a life.

A crown for a crown.

It's finally time to take back what's mine.

18

JUSTINE

After accepting my boarding pass from a smiling flight attendant, I make my way down the gangway. I don't bother waiting for Roman, my desire to cry in private misplacing my manners.

I have no clue what the hell is happening. The greatest week of my life was destroyed in thirty seconds. I lost my job, my relationship, and my residential status in the blink of an eye.

Last night was... *god*.

Finding a word adequate to describe it is impossible.

Nikolai was wonderful. He took me to the brink of ecstasy so many times I lost count, but it wasn't done in a crazy-lust-filled romp type of way. It had meaning, like we were *finally* unifying as one. Then, a sunrise unraveled everything.

A new day.

A new beginning.

An ending I never saw coming.

After handing my ticket to a pretty blonde flight attendant standing near a bar at the front of the plane, I scuttle to my seat a few places down.

I want to say I was surprised when Roman handed me a business-class ticket, but that would be a lie. Nikolai is anything but stingy.

Dumping my handbag onto my seat, I move to the closest restroom. I hope cold water will hide the angry red streaks lining my cheeks. I've been eyeballed enough the past hour while waiting to board. I don't desire more curious gawking on my five-hour flight home.

Latching the bathroom door closed, I spin around to peer into the mirror. The heavy crevice between my eyes deepens. I look as terrible as I feel.

I'm not solely upset because I've been forced home against my wishes. I'm devastated for striking Nikolai for the second time in under a week.

I didn't mean to slap him. With my emotions still high from my argument with Mr. Fletcher, and my brain on the fritz from a night of strenuous activities, my hand swung out before I could stop it.

My slap was nothing more than a fairy tap, but the pain it caused to Nikolai's eyes will forever maim my heart.

I'm beginning to wonder if it was why he didn't respond to my taunt about him being as cowardly as Dimitri.

My grumbled comment was another stupid thing I said before stopping to consider the consequences of my actions. My intention wasn't to hurt Nikolai. I was just desperate to force the world-dominating Nikolai from the shadow swallowing him whole.

I came close. He tussled with Roman, but at the end of the day, I still failed. My devastation wasn't incentive enough to bring him out of the blackness. He was too far gone to see sense.

After splashing cold water on my face and using the facilities, I exit the washroom. My steps are sluggish but not as heavy as when I entered the plane nearly fifteen minutes ago.

If I stop thinking with my heart for a second and listen to my brain, I can see the logic in Nikolai's decision to send me home. He promised to keep me safe, and he's doing everything he can to do that. I can't judge him for that, can I?

I want to stand by his side, but if I am as distracting to him as he is to me, perhaps me being in Vegas is more of a hindrance than a help.

I'm not sure what good my presence would be anyway. I don't know how to fire a gun—I haven't even held one—and in all honesty, I don't want to.

I've grown to love being a defense attorney so much because it is one fight that doesn't require a weapon. The grit Mr. Fletcher puts into every case he counsels is mind-blowing. His battles are worthy of the record books. That's why I was so stunned he left Nikolai defenseless like he did.

Greed is a horrible thing, but I had no clue it made courageous men cowards. If I hadn't seen the evidence firsthand, I would have never believed Mr. Fletcher was capable of such a heinous act. And the fact Nikolai was a minor when it occurred makes the matter ten times worse.

With my heart in tatters, I increase the length of my strides down the surprisingly empty aisle. Only minutes remain before the plane is scheduled for takeoff, but I have plenty of time to apologize to Nikolai for the terrible things I said.

I'm angry he took away my right to make my own choices, but I'm not angry enough to let him think I hate him for a second more than he already has.

He isn't a coward. He is the bravest man I've ever met.

"Roman, can I please borrow your phone?" I ask, stopping to stand beside Roman's cubicle, which is positioned across from mine.

With my cell phone battery depleted updating my parents on my unexpected return home, I don't have any other means of contacting Nikolai.

"Roman?" I ask again when he fails to acknowledge my presence, much less my request.

When he neglects to respond for a second time, my stomach gurgles, warning of impending danger. My brief encounters with Roman this week have revealed he isn't overly talkative, but his silence fuels my panic.

"Roman." I shake his shoulder, praying he's just dozing. "Are you okay?"

Snubbing the sick unease spreading through me like wildfire, I crouch down in front of him and lift his dangling head.

Air vacates my lungs in a brutal grunt when a pool of blood slides down his left temple before slithering around my hand. I can't see what has caused his injury, but the blood is coming from the top of his skull.

I stumble back, startled. I can't stand the sight of blood as it is, let alone when it is coming from someone I know.

Fighting through the bile racing up my throat, I press my fingers against Roman's neck to check for a pulse. A dash of relief overrides some of my panic when I feel the faintest flutter beneath my fingertips.

"Excuse me, ma'am," I stammer out, my eyes drifting to the flight attendant who guided me to my seat earlier. "My friend is injured. He's... ah... hurt."

My words are choppy from the worry clutching my throat. If Roman were just unresponsive, I wouldn't be as spooked, but the fact he's been assaulted has my fright escalating to a point I can't contain.

The sheer terror depriving my lungs of oxygen grows when the flight attendant raises her chin high enough that I can see her face. She isn't the same woman who greeted me earlier. She is Malvina, Nikolai's ex-fiancée.

"What are you doing here?" I ask, standing from my crouched position, my body quivering.

When she advances toward me, I shoot my eyes in all directions, praying my full gaze and whitening face will alert other passengers to my distress.

My prayers fall on deaf ears when my quick scan of the cabin fails to locate another presence. The entire business class section of the plane is empty.

My attention reverts to Malvina when she hisses, "Nikolai isn't the only one taking back what's rightfully his." The hatred in her eyes triples as she fans open her lightweight coat, revealing a small pistol strapped around her thigh. "So am I."

I peer at her, oblivious as to what her statement refers to. As far as she and anyone in her entity know, I am part of Nikolai's defensive team, nothing more.

Malvina doesn't buy my act. The snarl on her top lip grows as her eyes narrow into tiny slits. "Don't treat me like an idiot. I saw the way Nikolai looked at you. He has never looked at me like that, not even when I had his dick between my lips."

My stomach lurches into my throat, sickened by the scorn in her voice.

"You were supposed to get him off his charges, not get him off." Her face grows redder with every syllable fired off her tongue.

"I did. I got him off his charges. That's *all* I did," I reply, hopeful she doesn't know me well enough to hear the deceit in my voice.

Snarling so profoundly her top lip is riddled with wrinkles, she snags an outdated recording device from the pocket of her jacket and throws it in my direction.

I barely grab it before it falls to the floor, my shuddering hands impeding my catching skills.

"Press play," Malvina demands, her low tone making my exposed toes shudder.

I lick my parched lips before doing as instructed. My pupils widen to the size of saucers when a recording of my ecstasy-riddled voice breaks through the silence teeming between us.

My fingers fumble wildly over the device, seeking the stop button when Nikolai's throaty groan for me to repeat my pledge of being his rolls out of the speakers.

"That isn't you?" Malvina asks, her tone revealing she already knows the answer to her question. "I'm yours, Nikolai. Yours. Yours. *Yours.*" The fury on her face doubles as she mocks me. She steps closer, her anger so white-hot that sweat beads at my temples. "Four years I invested in him, all to have some little tramp steal him away before I reap the benefits of my effort."

She rakes her eyes down my body, lowering my confidence with every grimaced expression she makes, but I don't back down. I roll my shoulders and stand tall, spurred on by the desire to protect what is mine.

Malvina spoke of Nikolai as a possession, not a person, proving what I suspected. She doesn't love him. She was using him like so many others in his life already have.

"If you had treated Nikolai like the man he is, he wouldn't have looked elsewhere." I don't usually condone cheating, but this is an entirely different kettle of fish. "Your loss is my gain."

Her anger twists from her gut to her face. "Our wedding is merely delayed, not canceled."

"That's not true," I reply with a shake of my head, my tone firm for how intense my heart is hammering. "I'm sorry if our actions hurt you, but you need to accept Nikolai's decision with the grace of a lady. He doesn't want you. You're not who he wants."

"And you are?" Malvina huffs, faking amusement. "I would handle the *postponement* of our wedding with dignity if he had chosen a better whore." Her mocking tone dents my ego, but my dedication to protecting Nikolai remains firm. "But to have something I've been working on for years snatched out from underneath me by a marked-up mangy mutt..." She stops talking, allowing her growl to finalize her sentence. "I won't stand for this!" Her nostrils flare as her eyes widen in a terrifying way. "My father won't stand for this! You disgraced me, and now you will pay the penance for your stupidity." She hisses her words with so much violence that steam billows from her ears.

"You disgraced yourself. Don't put that on me," I mutter before I can leash my vicious tongue.

She lunges for me, squealing like a wounded animal. I stumble backward, tripping over a sizable black instrument I didn't notice on the floor.

Since she thinks she has me at her mercy, a vindictive smirk etches onto Malvina's mouth. "The Huntress being hunted, how fitting."

Excitement blazes in her eyes, and she relishes my forced swallow. My frightened response can't be helped. Only one man has referred to me as the Huntress.

The devil himself—Vladimir.

Although I'm scared, Malvina shouldn't be so cocky. Only last week, I took down a man double her size. She may have a gun, but there's no greater weapon than determination.

Remaining on the ground, I wait for her to be within reaching distance before kicking out my leg with violence.

Malvina sucks in a mangled breath when my stiletto smashes into her knee before crashing into her crotch. The absolute agony hardening her features reveals it isn't just men who are unappreciative of a hit to that region.

After sweeping her feet out from underneath her, I leap from the ground and charge down the narrow aisle.

"Help!" I scream at the top of my lungs, praying Malvina's tumble will keep her down long enough I can exit the plane without a bullet wound.

I'm halfway down the aisle when I suddenly freeze, startled by a gun being fired in warning. My stomach violently rolls, warning me of Malvina's imminent arrival, but I'm void of a defense.

No amount of grit can outrun a bullet.

My hands shoot up to save my hair from being wrenched from my scalp when Malvina fists it in a deathly clutch. She viciously yanks me back, sending horrid pain rocketing through my skull.

"You're lucky he wants you alive, or I'd kill you now," she snarls, her words breathless like she is in pain. "Although, for what he has planned for you, you'll soon be wishing you were dead."

Encouraged by the malice of her words and unwilling to go down without a fight, I drop one of my hands from my head to ram my elbow into her chest.

Upon hearing her winded grunt, I throw my head back with force, crashing my skull into her unprotected nose.

Hair rips from my scalp when I restart my sprint. For how harshly my body is shaking, my strides are powerful. I reach the space separating economy and business class in under two seconds.

Spotting the open plane door, I'm filled with gratitude.

My appreciation doesn't last long.

I've barely crossed the threshold between the plane and the gangway when my brisk pace ends with a collision into a wall of hardness.

Instinctively, my hands shoot up to cradle my nose as I struggle to breathe through the pain radiating across my face.

"Help. You need to help me," I plead to my savior before peering over my shoulder to see if Malvina is approaching me. "There is a woman with a gun... She's trying to kill me. She's already hurt my friend. He's injured. I don't know what's wrong with him, but he won't wake up," I babble between breaths, my panic making me a blubbering, incoherent mess.

The efforts of my heaving lungs double when a broad Russian accent says, "Don't worry, Ангел. I'll keep you safe." His thick, condescending tone doesn't match his assurance.

Scarcely breathing, I raise my wide gaze to the man gripping my arms.

The eyes of the devil stare back at me—as lifeless and hollow as ever.

"Vladimir..." I breathe out heavily before a strike to the back of my head forces me to succumb to blackness.

Thirteen Years Earlier

...

"You better pray he kills me. If not, I'm gonna hunt you down and gut you like a dog. Do you hear me?" I yell while fighting the six-foot-three guard dragging me out of the courtroom. "The lies you told the jury last month will be *nothing* compared to the shitstorm I'm gonna rain on you."

When my father's defense attorney maintains his quiet front, I spit at his worthless feet, wishing we could be left alone for just a minute.

I don't need a week, a day, or even an hour. Just one measly motherfucking minute to show him I'm the monster he portrayed me to be.

I sat by and watched him spill lie after lie to the jury because, at the end of the day, whether I was the psychotic adolescent he was portraying me to be or a boy who had endured an incalculable amount of abuse his entire life, I was destined for freedom. It was so close I could taste it on the tip of my tongue and smell it in the air. I didn't think anything could wipe the victory from my eyes.

I was wrong. *So very fucking wrong.*

The jury believe every twisted lie spilled from my father's defensive team's lips, and stupidly believed he was an honorable man. The man who had abused me for years was seen as a saint when he took the witness stand to beg for the judge to be lenient on me.

"Niki is sick. He needs help. I will get him the help he needs," he said earlier today, urging a deep sigh from numerous female jurors batting their lashes at him. "This doesn't need to go any further than it already has. Nikolai is my son. I don't want to see him hurting any more than he already is. Please, Judge, I implore you to return my son. Let me take him home where he belongs."

The judge soaked up every word he spoke as if it were gospel, not hearing the sneer in his undertone that warned me I'd be punished for disobedience the instant I returned home.

I heard his underlying message, and the three men flanking him perceived the hidden innuendo in his confession, but those most important didn't hear a thing.

All they saw was a father panicked his second eldest son was set to face prosecution for attempted murder. They saw the shiny façade Vladimir wears in front of others—the one that hides his satanic face—instead of the man he is behind the shield.

The monster.

The taunter.

The person I despise so much, if given a second chance, I wouldn't hesitate to slit his throat.

Unaware he was sentencing me to a fate much worse than death, the judge accepted my father's plea for leniency. He spoke as if he were doing me a favor by ordering me back to the hell that had been my life for the past sixteen years, completely oblivious that I'd have chosen a life sentence in maximum security prison over returning to my family compound any day.

And that is how we reached the point of me being dragged from one court to another—the one in which I'm about to face the deadliest trial any man could undergo.

My father is waiting in the car for me, his patience stretched thin at the court's request to secure a tracking monitor to my ankle before returning me home.

He isn't the only one impatient because of the delay. The sooner my probation begins, the faster my quest for revenge will start.

"And it's gonna start with you," I murmur as my icy-blue eyes lock on to Carmichael Fletcher, the recently knighted partner at Schluter & Fletcher defensive law.

Under different circumstances, I'd be impressed that a first-year law student was offered a partnership at any firm, even one on the verge of collapse. But since I know Carmichael's promotion wasn't rewarded for years of gallant service, I keep my accolades to myself.

I wonder how much my soul was worth to the devil? Did my father negotiate a lower rate to have me returned to him by using the statistics of any man in our industry living past their twenties to his advantage? Or was he as blindsided by Carmichael as well as I was?

I should have smelled Carmichael coming from a mile away. Usually I can sniff out a ratty, underhanded man for more than a mile, but Carmichael's scent was suffocated by honest eyes and gifted words. He was a good actor, nearly as skilled as the sheriff strapping on my ankle monitor.

He tries to act ignorant, but I saw the quickest flare of emotion blaze past his eyes when he spotted the numerous cigarette burns and scars running down my left leg.

If he's green at the gills because of the faint marks on my skin, he needs to harden the fuck up. They aren't one-tenth as bad as the ones I keep hidden with clothes.

After giving me a rundown on how the ankle monitor works, the sheriff ushers me toward the back entrance of the courthouse, thankfully saving me from walking through the sea of media waiting out front.

The media contingency is always strong when a high-profile member of my family is in public, but their attention grew tenfold when they caught wind that closed court sessions being held every day the past three weeks were in direct association with members of the Popov entity.

My family aren't celebrities by any means, but the media treats us as if we are. I only turned sixteen three months ago, but that hasn't stopped me from attending nightclub opening after nightclub opening the past two years. I've snorted coke with celebrities and fucked a handful of foreign princesses in the last six months alone, but I doubt one of them remembers my name.

When you have money, people don't care how it is achieved.

They treat you like a god whether you slave over a computer for eighteen hours a day or financially cripple a rival gang.

Money is money—filthy or not.

When we reach a sizable vault-like door, the guard jerks his chin up, requesting me to spin around. Although adrenaline is still coursing through my veins, I'm hyped up for an entirely different reason than earlier. My father's SUV is idling at the curb, waiting for me.

Now the real fight begins.

"Good luck," mumbles the sheriff as he opens the door, freeing me from incarceration but sentencing me to death.

Incapable of a suitable reply, my lips etch into an uneasy smirk. A lack of confidence has never been a weak spot for me, but for the first time in my life, hesitation thickens my blood when I gallop down a set of stairs to the waiting SUV.

How fucked up is the world we live in when it's acceptable to order a sixteen-year-old boy to return to the man who has abused him for years?

I gave the DA enough evidence to convict Vladimir of over thirty charges of abuse, torture, and deprivation of liberty, but instead of the DA prosecuting him, I was the one facing conviction.

I did try to kill my father—I've never lied about that—but it wasn't because I am a beneficiary to his estate like the jury was told. I wanted to kill him for what he did to my brother. The punishments I have suffered under Vladimir's watch were nothing compared to what Rico went through three months ago.

The smell of his skin burning when Vladimir ordered for acid to be thrown over him... *Fuck.* My stomach rolls at the thought. It was terrible, one of the most disgusting scents I've ever had the displeasure of smelling.

I recorded my first kill when I was eight. I've traded in weaponry, drugs, and women since I was eleven, but not one thing I've witnessed the past sixteen years scarred me like watching the skin on Rico's back melt like butter on toast.

He didn't scream or even fight. He just accepted his fate like a man much older than the teenage boy he was. The courage he showed that day was so remarkable that he'll be my model when I face my darkest day.

After dipping my chin in greeting to Roman, who's holding open the back passenger door of my father's SUV, I slide inside. Roman looks tired and withdrawn, his glistening eyes clouded with worry. He would have stopped me if he had known what I had been planning to do.

That's why I kept him in the dark. Even though he is like a father to me, in our industry, that means nothing. It doesn't matter if you have forty years of experience like Roman or sixteen years like me, we were born to serve one man, and we will continue serving him until we are laid to rest.

Favoritism, friendship, or even something as weak as love should never enter the equation.

We are not men. We're soldiers.

"Niki," my father greets me, the word trickling out of his mouth alongside a thick stream of smoke.

He takes a second substantial draw on his cigar while tossing a pack of cigarettes into my chest. He waits for me to gather the packet before signaling for the driver to go.

His gesture could be seen as friendly to an outsider, but to anyone in our industry, being offered anything without a stipulation attached is a death sentence.

Vladimir is not a generous man. If you accept anything from him, even something as cheap as a pack of cigarettes, you better be willing to accept the terms associated with it.

Vladimir watches me intently, his arrogance craving a frightened swallow or a silent plea for forgiveness. I give him neither, refusing to bow at his feet for a second longer than I have my entire life.

My stubbornness nearly kills me.

"No!" I shout, the combination of my angry roar and warning glare stopping Roman's steps mid-stride. "Don't interfere. It's *not* your place to interfere. This is *family* business. It has nothing to do with you."

He stares at me with pleading eyes, the moisture in them

doubling when my back is whipped for the umpteenth time in a row.

I arch my body, resisting the urge to succumb to the pain shredding me to pieces.

Although my battered and bruised body displays signs of distress, not a sigh spills from my lips when I'm whipped again and again and again.

I refuse to add more glory to my father's retribution.

He's watched the entire proceeding with an eagle eye, the glimmer in his sable gaze brightening with every whip, punch, or cut inflicted on my exhausted body.

I don't know how long I've been hanging in this sooty, blood-stained room. The sky has shifted from a murky blue to the color of Vladimir's lifeless eyes, so at least four to five hours have passed since we arrived at this warehouse on the outskirts of Vegas.

I've been beaten to the point of blacking out before being awoken by the slice of my knife. The blood coating the chains wrapped around my wrists has dried, but the pools under my feet are sticky to the touch.

I've nearly broken twice, but with my desire to die greater than my wish to live, I've yet to surrender to the pleas of my body.

Besides, only a coward breaks under pressure. I am not a coward. I'm just a boy who dreamed of freedom.

Gritting my teeth, I struggle to fill my lungs with air when men triple my size and double my age come at me from all directions. I stop scanning their faces for future recognition when the blood streaming from my skull adds to the weight of my eyelids. I am on the brink of death, both exhausted and relieved.

I silently beg for the blackness to take over, to be freed from the hell I've been living for the past sixteen years.

My soundless pleas are answered with more fists, cuts, and taunts.

I don't want them to break my spirit.

I want them to break my soul.

I can't hold up my head by the time my punishment is over. I slump to the ground with a thud. The chains holding me hostage for the last seven hours crank through the hoist mechanism mounted to the ceiling before raining down on me, coating my already purple skin with fresh welts.

A short time later, through the pulse raging in my ears, I hear the scuffling of feet. At first, I pray they're returning to put me out of my misery.

Unfortunately, I've never been lucky.

"You should have let me stop them," Roman chastises, his voice croaky with emotion.

"Then we'd both be dead," I manage to force out, my words barely audible.

Air whizzes between my teeth when Roman curls his arms around my torso to lift me from the ground. "Jesus Christ, Nikolai. How are you still breathing?"

"Maybe I am lucky?" I reply with a blood-streaked grin, my stomach heaving when I attempt to laugh at the madness consuming me.

He mumbles something under his breath, but I can't hear a word he's speaking. My ears are still ringing from the back-to-back hits that battered my brain against my skull.

While I gasp through a collapsed lung, Roman moves me toward a dirty old mattress stashed in the corner of the room. My right ankle is so contorted it drags along the ground, staining the already filthy floor with more of my blood.

After carefully aiding me onto the mattress, he flutters around me, gathering supplies and hot water to dress my wounds. I lie as still as a corpse with my eyes facing the ceiling and my mind shut down. I didn't cry, whimper, or sob during my punishment. I acted like a man, although I am only a boy, but I'm still full of shame.

I did the one thing I swore I'd never do.

The one thing that will haunt me until the day I die.

I broke.

Mentally, not physically.

When your brain is beaten to the point of swelling, you can be excused for a moment of madness, but I know that isn't the case with me. I'm not plotting revenge or configuring a way out of my predicament. I'm strategizing ways to guarantee something like this never happens to me again by ensuring I'm the one dishing out the punishments instead of receiving them.

It is a sick and twisted twenty minutes, even more stomach-churning than the past seven hours.

You'd think I'd welcome a change in perspective. I don't. Because...

There is only one difference between
a madman and me.
The madman thinks he is sane.
I know I am mad.
—Salvador Dali

Present
Day

...

20

NIKOLAI

"**N**ikolai..."

"What?" I reply, my mind drifting from the past to the present.

With my birthday rapidly approaching, my thoughts often stray to memories I'd prefer to forget. Although that day nearly thirteen years ago changed me in a way I'll never forget, I'm not ashamed of the man I have become. I did what I needed to survive. If I hadn't teetered on the brink of insanity, I would have been buried beneath a pile of dirt years ago.

Usually, the prospect of death wouldn't bother me, but I've got someone I want to live for now. Justine's been through enough. She doesn't need more pain added to the weight she's carrying on her shoulders. Furthermore, there's nothing spineless about living. It is the men who give up without trying who are cowards.

Rico waits for me to scrub my hand over my tired eyes before repeating, "Still nothing?"

My chest expands when I suck in a large gulp of air before shaking my head. I've called Roman's cell phone nonstop for the past twenty minutes.

He has yet to answer.

I want to pretend his lack of reply is virtuous, but a weird feeling twisting in my stomach stops me from believing that. I left

Justine and Roman at the airport a little over an hour ago, but their flight wasn't scheduled to depart until ten minutes ago.

Although Roman is cautious of personal security, that doesn't extend to airport protocol. Usually, the flight attendants have to pry his cell out of his hands before takeoff on any flights we've shared, so for him to turn it off before boarding is out of the ordinary.

"Take West Tropicana," I advise my driver when I spot the exit coming up. "It's faster than I15. When tourists invade the Vegas sign, traffic can be held up for miles."

The driver's dark eyes stray to mine in the rearview mirror. "I checked the reports. Traffic is clear."

"I don't give a fuck. Take West Tropicana," I snarl through gritted teeth.

The driver swallows harshly before doing as requested. Frustrated by his delay in following my direct order, I rub my hands together, fighting to keep them away from my knife. The driver may be new, but that doesn't mean his insolence can be forgiven. If panic wasn't clutching my throat, my blade would be pressed against his jugular.

As my SUV glides down West Tropicana, I continue rubbing my hands together, shocked by how frozen they feel. Anyone would swear I am in the middle of the Antarctic, not a desert. It isn't cold today.

Vegas has been hitting record temperatures all week. Even the world's most advanced HVAC systems have had a hard time keeping the conditions below sweltering. The unease suffocating the air of oxygen is responsible for my icy cold response.

The air has the same rigidity it held the night I organized Blaire's attack. It is so dense it feels like it is asphyxiating me one lung-clogging breath at a time.

After loosening the collar of my shirt with a quick tug, I ask, "Did you know?"

When he peers at me unaware, as if confused by my question, I clarify, "Did you know Blaire was going to be attacked before it happened? Did you have a weird sensation in your gut you couldn't shake?"

I'm not a feelings type of guy, much less talkative, so Rico isn't the only one shocked by my question. I am as confused as him.

Rico tries to shut it down, but I spot the quickest flare of emotion pass through his eyes before he answers, "Yeah." He licks his dry lips before adding on, "I don't know what led me to the servants' quarters that night. Maybe it was intuition, or I just sensed Kitten's closeness. Whatever it was, if I hadn't had that sick, churning feeling in my stomach, she would have been dead by the time I found her." He scrubs his hand over his jaw, hiding the manic tic making the taut muscle spasm before explaining, "Matvei barricaded the door with a mattress. I didn't hear Blaire's screams until after I kicked it down." The honesty in his eyes hits me square in the gut. "I wouldn't have broken the door if I hadn't had a feeling something was amiss, so if your gut is telling you something is wrong, Eli, you need to listen to it."

My jaw clenches as I nod. I don't know what my stomach is trying to tell me, but I've got a horrible feeling I won't like its warning once it's been unearthed. If I could just get ahold of Roman, the twisted knot in my stomach would calm down.

The unease I'm experiencing is more about Justine than my quest to dethrone Vladimir. I don't know if it is based on our argument in the minutes leading to her departure, or something more sinister.

From the way bile scorched my throat during my last suggestion, I'd say it is the latter.

I return my eyes to Rico. "Do you still have contact with that hacker you worked with during Callie's sale?"

The tightness in his jaw firms, memories of the day his sister was sold sullying his thoughts. Callie's mother double-crossed Vladimir, but instead of seeking retribution for her treachery directly on her, Vladimir sold their daughter on the black market before ultimately killing Anya.

Although Vladimir didn't pull the trigger on the gun that killed Anya, just like my mother, he is responsible for her death. He taunted her for weeks, revealing in sickening detail what happens to children sold on the black market.

Incapable of seeing past the smoke and mirrors Vladimir placed in front of her, Anya believed every word he spoke, unaware that Rico had arranged for Callie to be bought by his sister's fiancé. I was aware, but since it was a family matter, I didn't intervene. Was that the right decision for me to make? No, probably not. But at the time, it felt right.

For years, I only looked out for myself. It is amazing how much has changed in a week. I will maim for Justine. I will kill for her. I will even slit the throat of the man who raised me to ensure she is safe. Nothing is above me when it comes to protecting her. Not a single fucking thing.

"Yes. Why?" Rico eventually answers, his snappish tone matching the anger burning in his eyes.

"Justine and Roman's flight was scheduled to depart ten minutes ago. Can he check if they are actually on the flight?" I try to keep the hope out of my voice. I miserably fail.

Although we are already en route to the airport, I'll do anything to ease the commotion in my stomach. I've never felt this way before. I am fearless, but what I told Justine this morning is true. Nothing scares me... except the thought of losing her.

That fucking petrifies me.

Nodding, Rico yanks a sleek black cell phone out of his pocket. "Give me their flight details."

After jotting down their names and flight number onto a scrap of paper, Rico raises his cell to his ear. "It's Enrique," he says not even two rings later. "I need you to check the in-flight manifest of a departure that left McCarran Airport approximately ten minutes ago." He recites the information I gave him to the man on the other end.

After what feels like a lifetime, he lifts his eyes to me. The blackness filling them thickens the lump in my throat.

"All right. No, that's all... You don't need to tell him... Because this isn't about Izzy, so it's no concern of his," Rico snaps, his voice stern enough to startle the driver. "All right, bye."

He slides his phone into the breast pocket of his business jacket before connecting his eyes with mine. "They boarded their flight."

I sigh heavily, relieved as fuck. Although I hate that Justine has to be away from me for even a second, she will be safer in Hopeton. Vladimir won't go down without a fight. He'll defend his throne with the same iron fist he has ruled his empire with for the past fifty-plus years, so the more distance I have between them, the better.

My relief doesn't last long when Rico says, "But... their flight never left the tarmac. Authorities were called in thirty minutes ago for a disturbance onboard. Roman is en route to the hospital with life-threatening injuries—"

"And Justine?" I interrupt, hurrying him along.

Don't get me wrong, I'm concerned for Roman, but Justine will always be my priority. Roman is well aware of the hazards of his job. Justine is innocent, so her safety must come first.

Rico's throat works hard to swallow before he discloses, "She hasn't been seen since her boarding pass was scanned forty minutes ago."

Fuck!

Roaring like an animal, I throw fists into the chair in front of me, adding to the bruises scattered across my knuckles. The headrest video monitor is no match for my force. It crumbles more with every hit I inflict, shattering into millions of tiny pieces.

Why did I wait so long to question the knot in my stomach? Forty minutes may not seem long in a traditional industry, but in my field, forty minutes is a torturously long time. The things you can do to a person in forty minutes...

Fuck, fuck, fuck!

I swing my fists harder, battering them as severely as my heart is smashing into my ribs. I should have waited for her plane to taxi to the runway before I left the airport. I should have taken her to Hopeton myself, but more than anything, I should have kept my promise. I promised to keep Justine safe. I didn't keep my fucking promise.

Rico waits for me to finish my outburst before scooting to the edge of his chair, narrowing the small bridge between us. He doesn't say anything. He doesn't need to. His forthright eyes relay the entire picture. His thoughts are as desolate as mine.

"He's got her, doesn't he?"

I already know the answer to my question. I just want Rico to spell it out for me. The pit in my chest grows when Rico nods, not attempting to hide the worry clouding his wild eyes.

"What do I do now? This changes everything. I can't risk her, Rico. I won't risk her."

I hate relying on anyone, but with my mind spiraling, I'm moments away from going on a murderous rampage. That won't help anyone—especially not Justine. If I want to get her out of this situation alive, I don't just need to act quickly. I also need to act smart.

I glare at him, my stare so volatile it could melt ice when he answers, "We wait."

My jaw muscle quivers. "Wait? We can't fucking wait! She'll be dead if we wait!"

He connects his eyes with mine, ensuring I can see the truth in them, before saying, "We don't know where he has her or what he is planning to do with her, so we've got no other choice but to wait. He needs to make the first move." He grips my tense shoulder and squeezes it. "The instant he shows his hand, we'll have him because we've got him at an advantage. There are no two better men for this job, Nikolai, even more so since he's only prepared for one of us."

It kills me to admit it, but every word he speaks is gospel. This is a game to Vladimir—nothing more. If we don't strategize our next move, Justine will be dead before I get within sniffing distance of her.

I won't let that happen, not on my watch, so as much as I want to storm in and rain my wrath down on Vladimir, I can't. Not yet. Not until Justine is safe.

Noticing my brooding temperature is being set aside for scheming, Rico slumps into his chair before asking, "What now?" Although his tone is as commanding as always, it acknowledges who leads our fight.

Justine is my woman, so she is my responsibility.

Pretending I can't feel my knee bobbing up and down, I reply, "First, we need to get to Roman. He could have seen something that will be invaluable. Vladimir may only have his men working with him, but my gut warns me that isn't the case. I will treat everyone as rivals until I rule out all my enemies."

Rico nods, agreeing with my suggestion.

"I'll call in some of my men to run decoy—"

"Do you trust them?" he interrupts, his tone wary.

I take a moment to consider his question before nodding. I can only hope Justine's assurance that respect earned the old-fashioned way exceeds respect acquired by fear. If that is true, I trust my men because they were amassed the traditional way—with dedication and hard work.

Although the Popov entity has been running since the 1700s,

its rules were long overdue for an overhaul. The value and principles of its founder, Altony Popov, are invaluable but clearly show he started as a cloak-and-dagger business. I had to move the Popov entity into the twenty-first century to keep it ahead of our competitors. It was an uphill battle, but that is precisely what I've done for the past three years.

Ever since Rico's "death," my crew's perspective altered. With sex trafficking, prostitution, and lower-range drug trades decreasing in value over the past five years, I directed my focus to weapon distribution and foreign trade.

Although it doesn't have the same cloak-and-dagger feel, the Popov entity has been fueled by the past three hundred years. The capital amassed over the past two years far exceeds the combined total of the previous ten.

Sex trafficking, prostitution, and drugs will always have a place in my industry, but until my latest money pit dries up, my focus will remain on distribution and foreign trade. I'll stay one step ahead of the game by staying where the money is. *I hope.*

"All right, then let's do this," Rico suggests, returning my attention to the present. He snags a duffle bag filled with weapons from the floor before his eyes drift to me. "What do you need?" he asks, gesturing his head to the pile of weapons that would give most men a heart attack from the mass surge of adrenaline pumping through their veins.

Unfortunately for all involved, I'm not an ordinary man.

"I've got everything I need right here," I reply, tapping my hand on the back pocket of my jeans. "Vladimir was spared by my knife thirteen years ago. He won't be so lucky this time around."

21

NIKOLAI

"Where is he?"

Trey extends his finger to a door at the end of a long, dark corridor. "Dok's with him. Not sure what happened yet. We ran logistics as you requested."

His eyes drift to Rico as though unsure he should be speaking in his presence.

With a jerk of my chin, I gesture for Rico to continue without me.

Rico is discreet, but I don't miss his jaw working side to side before he continues down the hall without uttering a syllable.

He's not accustomed to taking orders, much less demands from his younger brother.

When blackness engulfs Rico, my eyes stray back to Trey. "What is it?" I ask, reading the unease in his narrowed gaze.

He's only been a member of my crew for the past three years, but I know him well enough to intuit a reason for the extra crease between his blond brows.

Trey runs a shaky hand over his scalp while saying, "Alexei's men had the hospital barricaded. I had no choice. I couldn't get to Roman without first taking down two of his men."

Air whizzes from my nose. I'd like to pretend I'm shocked Alexei is involved in a war he doesn't belong in, but I'm not. It would have been foolish for him to pass up an opportunity to weaken my crew. If I were allowed to take down one of the top dogs in our industry without fear of repercussion, I'd be there with bells on and guns loaded. Although I'll never have proof, I'm confident Alexei's involvement stems from Vladimir offering him the chance to kill me without consequence.

It's a pity they underestimated the skill of my men. They may not have decades of experience like their crews, but they have one thing their men will never have. They have me as their leader. My men were not born killers, but they are trained killers, and they are undoubtedly the best marksmen in our field.

"Loss of life is a casualty of war, Trey. Alexei knows that better than anyone," I reply, shocked by the dread clouding his eyes.

Trey's kill count over the past three years is as high as mine, so I'm stunned he is concerned about the death of two men. Two lives in a sea of hundreds shouldn't cause the slightest ripple to his seemingly impenetrable ego, let alone instigate something as weak as panic.

"Yeah, I get that," he agrees with a bob of his head. "But I don't see Alexei willing to accept that excuse when he discovers I murdered his son."

My heart beats in an unnatural rhythm as worry thickens my blood. Unlike Vladimir, Alexei treasures his sons. So much so their lives are more valuable to him than his own.

"Which son?" I grit my teeth, loathing that the unease in his voice has crossed to mine.

"Tristan," Trey forces out.

I exhale a relieved breath. Although Alexei will still mourn Tristan's loss with the rampage of a man scorned, I'm glad his loss was a son he birthed with one of his whores instead of his beloved wife.

"Is Alexei aware of the incident?" I inquire, praying he didn't throw years of training down the drain during a moment of panic.

Trey shakes his head. "No, we cleaned the scene as thoroughly, if not better, than you would have. Their bodies are still in my trunk."

"Good," I reply, relief echoing in my tone. "Keep them in there until I say so."

I lift my brow and glare at him when he attempts to refute my direct order. He may be my most loyal man, but that doesn't mean he should test my tolerance when it comes to disrespect.

There are rules in this industry, ones even someone as high as me can't ignore, but if Alexei discovers his son was a casualty of a war he had no right to be in, my effort to find Justine alive will become non-existent.

Considering Justine's well-being is my absolute priority, delaying a father's chance for a proper goodbye by a few days isn't my concern.

"Once Justine is home, I'll deal with Alexei. Until then, his son's body will remain in my possession." I lock my eyes with Trey, ensuring he can see their honesty when I say, "Negotiating Tristan's return is the only bartering chip I'll have for you to see out the week with your pulse not flatlining."

Usually mafia kings retaliate to the death of their children by draining the blood of the men they believe responsible. I won't let that happen to Trey. He was following my direct order, so if anyone is going to suffer the consequences of Tristan's death, it will be me.

After forcefully swallowing, Trey mutters, "All right, I'll gather the men and head to Jim's. Hopefully some ice will keep away the vultures." He murmurs his last comment so quietly I'm confident he didn't want me to hear it.

"Once you've got them on ice, gather the rest of the men from Clarks, and then come back here. Until we know Vladimir's plans for Justine, none of us are getting any sleep." My jaw spasms during my last sentence.

With every hour that ticks by, my chances of finding Justine unharmed dwindle more and more.

I swear to god, if Vladimir has hurt her, he'll wish he had killed me thirteen years ago, as his demise will be the slowest and most torturous death I've ever issued.

After nodding, agreeing with my demand, Trey strays his eyes to Rico standing at the end of the hall. "Is that who I think it is?" he asks, confusion unmissable in his deep timbre.

"Have you ever seen a ghost, Trey?" I ask, my tone as haunting as I feel.

When he shakes his head, I reply, "You have now."

Ignoring his shocked gasp, I push off my feet and head for Rico.

"You're lucky Trey isn't an original member of my crew, or I would have had to shoot you on sight to save the extermination bill. You let one rat in, you risk an infestation of rodents," I mutter, stopping to stand beside him.

Rico brushes off my snide remark with a shrug, intuiting my threat is more based on our situation than actual malice.

Although I hate relying on anyone, it's nice to have someone on my side, supporting me. For now, it's Rico. By tonight, it will once again be Justine. My *Ангел*—the strongest and most determined woman I've ever met.

When I am king, she will want for nothing. She will be my queen.

After glancing over his shoulder, Rico nudges his head to the door we're standing next to, motioning for me to enter before him.

He wasn't joking about scanning every shadow he passes. I don't know if he realizes how often he does it, but constantly checking his surroundings has occurred often enough for me to notice it—*and hate it.*

I get he wanted out of this lifestyle, but is the benefit of living outside this realm worth looking like a coward for the rest of your life?

I freeze for a beat, and my mind scrambles. Rico's quest to escape our father's clutches wasn't any more cowardly than mine. It simply happened years later, so why am I judging him as if he is a deserter?

I shouldn't be, should I?

Setting aside my turmoil for a more appropriate time, I clutch a grime-covered doorknob and swing open the door.

"As stubborn as ever," I murmur when I spot Roman clutching Dok by the throat, his anger so strong every vein in his body bulges. "Sit the fuck down, Roman, and let Dok do what he needs to do," I say, entering the room. "You're not going to be good to anyone if you pass out again."

Forever testing my patience, Roman takes a minute to consider my suggestion before doing as requested. Grumbling a string of curse words under his breath, he drags his bloodstained shirt over his head before lying face-first on a makeshift hospital bed on his left.

Air hisses between my teeth when I spot the dark bruise circling a bullet wound on the lower left quadrant of his back. From the way the skin around the hole is singed and sucking inward, I can quickly ascertain that he was shot from behind.

I'm even more suspicious that Vladimir is the orchestrator behind Justine's disappearance. He's the only person I know spineless enough to shoot a man in the back.

"Just dig it out," Roman pleads to Dok when he sees him loading a syringe with anesthetics.

Dok's eyes dart to me, the anxiety in them indubitable. I nod at his silent question, approving him to remove the bullet from Roman's back minus any numbing agent.

Roman is as stubborn as me. He won't take anything that will impair his mind until Justine is found. This is one of the ways he is loyal to a fault. Even a bullet can't slow him down.

I wait for Dok to dig a set of tweezers into Roman's wound before asking, "Who was it?"

Although I already know the answer to my question, I want Roman to spell it out as well as he did when he warned me that fooling around with Justine would end badly.

I should have listened to him, but with all the blood in my body surging to my cock, I made a costly mistake. Roman knew one taste of Justine would never be enough. He was right.

When Roman shifts his eyes to me, bile surges up my throat. The bitter taste in my mouth has nothing to do with the agony crossing his face from Dok hunting for the bullet. It is the cloud swamping his usually bright eyes. He doesn't need to speak to answer my question. His eyes tell the entire story.

"I wasn't standing down this time," he murmurs through clenched teeth, his volume increasing at the exact moment Dok drags a 185-grain bullet from his back.

Roman bites his palm to muffle his screams when Dok pours alcohol-based disinfectant over the gaping hole. His wounded cries mimic the ones I made when he cleaned and stitched my injuries in a similar room nearly thirteen years ago, and his eyes are firing with as much vengeance.

In hours, my quest for revenge has been sliced into three neat pieces, equally shared between Rico, Roman, and me.

Vladimir has no idea of the wrath about to descend on him. He has not only awakened the devil he resurrected years ago. He has awoken a man hungry for revenge. A man ready to take back what is rightfully his. A man who will make him wish he had never been born.

My desire to kill has always been rampant, but now it is unquenchable. Just as Vladimir beat me into submission thirteen years ago, I will make him pay for his error in judgment. I just need to find him first.

I lock my eyes with Roman's tormented gaze. "Do you know where he took her?"

My back molars grind together when my voice comes out laced with arrogance. Now is not the time for defiance to get the better of me.

If I want to bring Justine home in one piece, I must keep a calm, collected head. This isn't a standard game of cat and mouse. This is my life being played out for the world to see. If I fuck this up, there is no going home a second time.

I will be done.

Hanged by my own noose.

If you go against your creator, you can't lose. There is no option B or second chance, so you either give it your all or walk away before the game even starts.

Considering I'd rather suffer a dozen deaths than be seen as a coward, I'll face Vladimir head-on. I'll play his game with the underhanded tactics he used on me my entire life, and I'll win. That is not a probability. It is a confirmation. This isn't just about me anymore. This is about Justine—the woman I'd slay a thousand men for.

"They popped one into my back before clocking me over the head, so I've got nothing useful," Roman answers, drawing my focus back to him.

"Haven't got anything useful, or don't want to share?"

I'm shocked by the sneer in Rico's voice. He isn't usually so hostile. He could kill a man without flinching before he met his wife, but he never slayed without cause, so the icy brutality of his words is shocking.

Roman shoves Dok away from him before rising to a sitting position. The handful of stitches Dok sutured in his wound only closes half the hole in his back, but it looks better than it did minutes ago.

"If you've got something to say, *boy*, I suggest you say it."

My lips tug at the fury in Roman's tone. He hasn't even glanced in Rico's direction yet but still knew he was in our presence. That is just like Roman, always one step ahead of the game.

Rico crosses his arms in front of his chest, not fazed by Roman's anger. "Vladimir shoots to kill. If he wanted you dead, he would have shot you in the head. He hates wasting a bullet, so why did he keep you alive?"

Roman laughs, seemingly amused by Rico's assumption he is a snitch. "You've got some hide coming in here and accusing me of tattling. How many years were you working against us? Four? Five? Six?" He hits the nail on the head when Rico's jaw clenches on six.

Fuck—I had no clue he was in so deep.

Although I am pissed he betrayed men who are like family to him, my anger is only a simmer, not a full boil. The fact the Popov entity has continued trading without incident since his death three years ago proves what he said earlier is true. He never intended to take us down. His sights were set on one man, and one man only—our father.

Suddenly, the knowledge of Roman's comment smacks into me, slackening my jaw and halting my breathing. "You knew Rico was working with the FBI, but didn't tell me?"

I try to keep my anger at a simmer. I miserably fail. I tell Roman *everything*, so the fact he kept this from me not only pisses me off, it places doubt on every conversation we've had.

Even though he is nearly double my age, he is my number one man. If I can't trust him, I can't trust anyone.

"I had my suspicions," Roman replies, gingerly standing. "But without concrete evidence, there wasn't much I could do about it. You idolized your brother, so the chances of you believing me were slim, to say the least."

My lips twitch. I want to refute his insinuation, but I'm left void of a retort when I see the honesty in his eyes. I did idolize Rico. I still do. He is my brother, even if we don't share the same blood.

Satisfied he's calmed the storm looming on the horizon, Roman's eyes stray to Rico. The pain in his glistening irises deepens when their gazes collide for the quickest second. "You should have told him your plans. That boy went to hell for you, and what did he get in return—"

"A set of fucking ears. I'm standing here, so stop talking about me as if I ain't."

I appreciate that Roman is looking out for me as he has done my entire life, but now is not the time to hash out old shit. Justine has been taken. We have our suspicions about whom, but nothing is set in stone. For what reason, we don't know. But there's one thing I do know—until she is returned to me safe and in one piece, nothing else matters.

Not revenge.

Not condemnation.

Nothing.

Stepping into the path of Roman's slit-eyed gaze, I silently demand the devotion of his eyes. When I get it, I ask, "Tell me what you do know. Even the shit you don't think is important."

Sick unease flows through me when the moisture in his eyes triples. Only one time I've seen so much wetness in his eyes. It was when he coerced my dislodged fingers back into place following my punishment thirteen years ago.

"Tell me," I demand, speaking through the lump in my throat.

He breathes heavily before muttering, "When I was drifting in and out of consciousness, there was a mix of murmured voices. Most were male, but one distinct voice broke through the darkness more consistently than the rest." His Adam's apple bobs up and down violently before he adds, "Justine was a fighter, Nikolai. She fought to the very end."

I balk, physically shunted by the remorse in his voice. "End?" I ask, my eyes bouncing between his. "What do you mean 'the end'?" When he remains quiet, the veins in my neck twang and my fists clench tightly. "You have five seconds to answer me before I finish what Vladimir started," I warn through gritted teeth, my anger growing like an out-of-control wildfire.

Roman would have given it his all to protect Justine, but it doesn't lessen my fury. I can see in his eyes he is keeping something from me, and considering it is about Justine, my anger is hitting a record-breaking high.

"What the fuck do you mean 'she fought to the very end'?" I ask again, the hostility of my words leaving no mistake that this will be the last time I'll ask my question without violence.

Roman waits for me to read the warning in his eyes before

disclosing, "When I started coming to, there was a commotion, like someone was in a fight. Not long later, I heard a gunshot, closely followed by a wounded cry. Everything went silent after that."

"No," I deny, shaking my head at the silent admission in his glistening eyes. "I'd know if she were dead. I would fucking know it. She's not dead!" I scream my last sentence, despising the sorrow in Roman's eyes.

I'd know if Justine were dead. That weak, pitiful beat my heart has been thumping since she walked into my life is still cranking its own unique tune. That wouldn't be happening if she were dead. It would have died right along with her.

Furthermore, Vladimir wouldn't kill her without making a mockery of her death. He's a bully, a man who feeds off fear. A clean death without a parade is worthless to him.

I know Vladimir. I know he doesn't do a single thing without fanfare. He needs the attention. He *craves* the attention. Killing Justine in a non-dramatic way makes no sense. He wouldn't get any benefit out of it, so he wouldn't do it.

I look at Rico, praying he will back up my admission. He does no such thing. His focus is fixated on a sleek black cell phone in his hand, his eyes as wide as the bullet wound in Roman's back, and his face as white as a ghost.

"We found Justine," he murmurs, his low tone revealing I won't like what he's about to say next.

Deciding actions speak louder than words, he swivels his cell to face me. Blood roars heat to my cheeks when an image I'll never forget burns into my retinas.

My *Ангел* has walked through the gates of hell, and I'm the devil responsible for her incarceration.

22

JUSTINE

When the creak of a door sounds through my ears, I stop scrubbing my wrists along a switched-off wall heater.

Scarcely breathing, I roll onto my back, praying the person approaching me won't discover the rips my hour of hard work has caused to the duct tape circling my wrists.

I don't know how long I've been held hostage in a space that smells like the locker rooms at my high school. It's long enough that my stomach grumble has switched from a faint purr to a growl, but not long enough for the ghastly Vegas daytime temps to become comfortable nighttime lows.

If I had to guess, I'd say I've been held against my will for three, possibly four hours.

I don't recall the trip from the airport to my current location. Whoever struck me hit me so hard I've spent the last several hours catching flies.

Although I'm panicked at the length of time I was unconscious, my dozing lessened the severity of the knock to my skull, mercifully leaving me relatively uninjured.

Well, as uninjured as I can be while bound and gagged to a bed.

After leveling my breathing, I prick my ears to count the steps of the person approaching me. With my vision blurry from a silk material draped over my eyes, my unimpeded senses must pick up the slack for their weakened counterparts.

One, two, three, four, five.

With my guest's strides long enough to reach me with only five steps, I'm guessing he's male. Although my vision remains hazy, enough light is shining through the thin material to indicate the size of my room. It's larger than a master suite but not quite the size of a loft apartment.

"Up. Now," grunts a heavily accented male voice.

Not waiting for me to respond, he hooks my ankle and drags me across the stinky mattress. Because his pull is so rough, the scarf covering my eyes falls from my face, exposing the only boarded-up window in the room.

With the sky a murky blue, my initial assumption about the length of my captivity appears to be corroborated. Roman and I boarded the plane at 10 a.m., but there's no doubt the sky is currently ruled by a late afternoon sun.

When my bare feet land on the ground with a bang, I sway like a leaf on a hot summer's day. My weak state can be traced to the combination of a hard knock to the head and excessive hunger. I went straight from my argument with Mr. Fletcher to a night of lovemaking with Nikolai, so I haven't eaten since yesterday morning. I am beyond starving.

Not speaking, a man with dark hair and a full beard directs me across the room. His swagger is as jagged as the vicious snarl on his face, and his strides are so long that I have to jog to keep up with him.

Thankfully, my feet are bare, so the sky-high stilettos I smashed into Malvina's groin aren't hindering my effort to stay glued to his side.

"All this effort for a whore," the stranger mutters under his breath, annoyance echoing in his tone.

I don't bother informing him I'm not a whore. It would be a waste of air. As far as any member of the Popov crew is concerned, women are either whores or housemaids, and no amount of arguing will alter a lifetime of misconceptions.

Even with the man's voice too low for me to pick up his accent, I know he's one of Vladimir's goons. I only glanced into my attacker's eyes for a second before I was struck from behind, but it was long enough to see his blackened soul.

I have no doubt I'm being held hostage by Vladimir. I can feel it in my bones and sense it with every fiber of my being. My skin has also never crawled so much in my life.

After tugging the gag out of my mouth, the stranger throws open the warped door we're standing next to. "Get in there and clean up. He's asking top dollar for you, so his buyers will want their money's worth."

I stare at him, my scrambled brain struggling to absorb his confession. "Buyers?"

He smirks, amused by my lack of knowledge, but not a word spills from his hard-lined mouth.

"Move it. We haven't got all day," he demands a short time later, peeved by my delay.

With a grunt, he shoves me in the direction he nudged. I stumble haphazardly into the damp-smelling space, stomping on his boot-covered foot.

After I regain my balance, I stray my wide gaze around the scarcely lit room. A cracked toilet, a soot-covered vanity, and a shredded shower curtain add to the horrifying image of numerous blood splatters coating mildew-covered walls. This bathroom looks like a set in the world's most horrific horror flick. It is stomach-churning and nightmare-inducing at the same time.

"You're not expecting me to get clean in here, are you?" I ask, the clanking of my knees heard in my tone.

I'd have more chance of getting clean in a bucket of dirty dish-water than in this dingy, bloodstained room.

My eyes rocket to the unnamed brute when he snarls, "You either clean up in there, or I give you a sponge bath. The choice is yours." There isn't an ounce of humor in his voice... *or yearning*. He speaks as if seeing me naked is as ordinary as cheese on a pizza.

Swallowing down the bile creeping up my esophagus, I whimper, "Can you at least untie my hands?"

He takes a moment to contemplate my suggestion before jerking his chin up, wordlessly requesting me to spin around.

In different circumstances, my chest would puff high at his pause for deliberation, but since I'm being held against my will, I'll save my cockiness for a more appropriate time.

My heart freezes when the coolness of a switchblade slides between my wrists. With a grunt, he drags the knife along the seam of the tape, proving I was hours away from freeing myself.

"Thank you," I murmur when my hands fall to my sides.

While rotating my wrists to encourage blood flow back to my hands, I merge deeper into the gore-scented space.

The fear clutching my throat increases with every hesitant step I take. I don't know if a murder occurred in this room or if it is merely the clean-up location for vile, heinous men, but the scent of death is undeniable. No amount of bleach can rid the smell of desecration. The only cure for the stench lingering in my nostrils is a flamethrower and half a gallon of gasoline.

When I spot the cracked toilet, my bladder niggles, silently pleading to be relieved of the liquid it's been holding for hours. After knocking down the lid with my elbow, I drop my hands to the waistband of my skirt. I stop lowering its concealed zipper when awareness of being watched overwhelms me.

Lifting my gaze to the door, I spot the stranger watching me. Amusement sparks his eyes, and his lips are tugged high in the corners.

"Do you mind?" I nudge my head to the door hanging by a thread, requesting him to close it.

Angling his head to the side, he arches his brow in a condescending, jeering way. I spread my hands across my waist and cock my hip, determined to maintain my dignity. The room is windowless, and his massive frame blocks my only viable exit. How far does he think I can get?

Seemingly relishing my fighting stance, a blistering smile stretches across his face. "You don't have a fucking clue about the shitstorm set to rain on you, do you?"

Unsure if he's asking a question or stating a fact, I hesitantly shake my head.

The stranger's smile grows while he runs his hand over his clipped hair. "You don't need to be worried about me watching you use the washroom, because you're minutes away from being broadcast to the world as naked as the day you were born."

"What?" I stammer out through sawing lungs.

My hands shoot up to cover the scars on my shoulders with my hair as my brain struggles to compile the facts.

Surely I heard him wrong.

He couldn't have said what I thought he said.

I must be mistaken.

Not trusting the dangerous spark detonating in the stranger's murky eyes, I fist my shirt close to my body when he heads my way. He walks slowly on purpose, stalking me like a tiger on the hunt.

"I don't usually pay for whores. Why pay for something I can get for free? But your feistiness is inspiring me to branch out. The fighters are always more fun to play with." He growls his last sentence with a throaty groan.

My worry triples when he weaves his fingers in my hair and yanks my head back. Although part of my response is due to discovering a blinking red light in the corner of the room, most of it is from the heat of his body curled over mine.

Even being in a room that represents death to a T, his cock is primed and bracing against the zipper of his pants, and his breath is heavy on my ear.

"If he didn't threaten to slit my throat if I sampled the merchandise before paying for the privilege, I'd give you a play-by-play rundown on what your *adventurous* night will entail," he hisses into my ear, his voice as dangerous as my heart rate. "But since I value my life more than any whore, I'll let you get washed up." He fists my hair more firmly, forcing tears to prick my eyes. "But don't test my patience, Justine. I'm not a patient man. Do you understand?"

I nod the best I can from his hold on my hair.

"Good. Now let's get this shit wrapped up. The quicker we get this over with, the faster the party will start." A shiver rolls down my spine when he presses his lips to the shell of my ear. "I just hope whoever buys you likes to share. It's been a while since I've had a redhead screaming my name."

Satisfied I've absorbed his threat with the malice he intended, he shoves me away from him. His jolt is so forceful I crash into the vanity with a thud, sending pain rocketing through my hip.

The sparkle in the stranger's eyes brightens when pain touches my face. "I don't know what the men will pay for more... your feistiness or your screams. I might make you perform both."

Clutching the frail vanity in a white-knuckled hold, I keep my chin close to my chest. Although my fighting instincts have kicked into overdrive, with my body weak from malnutrition and my heart on the verge of coronary failure, I shut down the desire to respond to his taunt. I don't know why, but my intuition is warning me Mr. Dark and Dangerous isn't my biggest battle tonight.

Once the tattooed man returns to his post at the bathroom door, I lift my eyes to the grime-covered mirror. With my pupils filling my corneas, my eyes are barely recognizable. They are as dark and lifeless as Vladimir's were when I crashed into him earlier today.

A smear of dirt is covering my right cheek, and blood streaks smeared through my hair have added more vibrancy to its bright-red coloring. Considering I'm being held captive in an unknown location by numerous gun-wielding men and the deranged ex-fiancée of the man I'm falling in love with, I look remarkably put together. Sane, even.

After splashing my face with water, I use a stack of napkins resting on the vanity to clear away the mascara smeared under my eyes. The material's roughness boosts the natural rosy hue on my cheeks, giving me a sexed-up look typically produced by hours of strenuous activities.

Hating that my outside appearance doesn't reflect how I feel on the inside, I switch off the water faucet and spin around to face the unnamed man.

"Bathroom?" he asks, nudging his head to the toilet I attempted to use earlier.

I shake my head, my determination to preserve my dignity strong enough to ignore the niggle in my bladder.

The man's brow is lost in his hairline. "Are you sure? If I'm made to return to this room for the second time, our next exchange won't be as pleasant as our first."

I glare at him in shock. If he thinks our exchange was full of niceties, I feel sorry for any woman he has ever dated. Dragging a woman around by her elbow before tearing her hair from her scalp is not my idea of a fun time.

"I'm sure," I reply, my throat as dry as his apparent humor.

"All right, then, let's go." He jerks up his chin, suggesting I exit before him. "Ladies before gentlemen."

I save my eye roll until I'm out of his line of sight. Either the water I splashed on my face was from the fountain of youth, or the person I heard screeching in his ear via a radio transmitter changed his mindset quickly. If I had to pick, I'd rather have the arrogant, pigheaded man he was earlier.

You can't prepare for an attacker you don't see coming.

"This way," the unnamed man demands when I head for the bed I've been bound to for several hours. "The beds are reserved for one thing and one thing only..."

He aligns his eyes with mine as his lips tug into a smirk, the remainder of his sentence revealed without words. Under different circumstances, I'd not hesitate to say he is a handsome man, but as he stands before me now, smirking with so much arrogance my teeth ache, he is as ugly as the back end of a dog.

Keeping my prying eyes on the down-low with a narrowed chin, I count the number of rooms we pass as we trek down a long, dark hallway. At least half a dozen rooms filter off the corridor we are walking down, and another two dozen break off the main one.

Considering every door we pass is sealed with large, industrial padlocks, it isn't hard to determine the extreme security measure isn't to keep people out of the rooms. They are to keep the women I hear whimpering locked in.

"Who are these women?" I murmur to myself, my voice breaking into a sob.

I loved being multilingual until now. Every heartbreaking plea for help, whether mumbled in Russian, French, or Czech, breaks my heart more and more.

"*To je v pořádku. Přichází pomoc,*" I promise to the bright-blue eye peering at me through the keyhole of a door we have stopped across from.

Although she has no reason to believe my guarantee that help is coming, the woman responds, "Thank you," in Czech.

"Get back in bed," the unnamed man demands, banging his fist against the lock. "You've got another three visits before your night is over."

His fists hit the door so forcefully that she scampers away in fright, but it doesn't stop her from warning, "*Ďábel. Pozor na ďábla.*"

My heart smashes against my ribs as her words repeat in my ears.

Devil. Beware of the devil.

If her warning doesn't foreshadow who's waiting for me behind the engraved door I'm standing in front of, the creeping of my skin is a surefire indication.

I'm about to meet the spawn of all evil for the second time in my life.

My lungs saw in and out when the door slowly glides open, revealing a room fit for a king. As I'm guided into the spice-scented space, my eyes go wild, absorbing all the unique features of the extravagant room.

A four-poster bed covered with satin sheets and leather shackles sits in the middle of the vast area. Wooden trunks line the walls with recently replaced wallpaper, and a crystal chandelier hangs awkwardly out of place in the far right-hand corner.

If it weren't for the scent of cigars lingering in the air, the opulence of the room would be overwhelming. Its wealth is in such abundance it is gag-worthy.

My neck cranks to the side when a deep Russian voice greets me. "The Huntress herself. Welcome to my abode."

Vladimir emerges from the shadows, his creeping steps as slick as his gelled-back hair. He rakes his eyes down my body, his stare as desolate as the one he gave me when he considered Nikolai's offer of making me his whore.

"I get it. I do." Although his eyes haven't left mine, his words aren't for me. They're for the man standing behind me. "It's not solely her face that hardens men's cocks. It is the fire in her eyes."

When Vladimir heads in my direction, I step back, the danger in his eyes destroying my confidence in less than a nanosecond.

Smirking, he inhales deeply, as if he's drinking in my fear. When a flare fires through his eyes, I realize that is precisely what he's doing.

He wants me scared and at his complete mercy.

He wants to break me.

It is a pity he failed to realize I broke years ago, so there is nothing left of me to break.

Standing tall, I roll my shoulders and lock my eyes with Vladimir's lifeless black gaze. His arrogance doesn't yield in the slightest. If anything, it grows, feeding off my determination.

"That's it, *Ангел*. Just like that," he commends me, his voice the kind I never want to hear from a man his age. It is throaty and full of need, the type that should only be used behind closed doors.

"Stay back," I warn, my voice surprisingly strong for how hard my heart is hammering.

Clenching my fists, I brace them in front of my body, silently warning him I'm not going down without a fight this time around. I may only get in one hit before I'm taken out, but I'll make sure it's a good one.

The crazy thud of my heart is deafening but not loud enough to miss a male voice on my right shout, "Ten thousand dollars!"

My head slings to the voice so fast that my neck squeals in protest. The air is sucked from my lungs when I discover the sound didn't come from a man. It came from a bank of computer monitors filled with the faces of men of all ages and ethnicities.

With their gazes locked on Vladimir and me, it doesn't take a genius to realize they are watching our charade with eagle eyes.

My stomach gurgles when a second heavily accented voice roars, "Seventeen thousand dollars." His accent is so unique I'm confident it is either Scandinavian or Norwegian.

Not to be outdone, a distinctively Asian voice counterbids, "Thirty thousand."

Vladimir smirks, seemingly pleased. "They haven't even seen you naked, yet they've come out of the gate firing." He keeps his voice low, ensuring the men gawking at me through video surveillance can't hear him. "Let's see if we can entice them some more."

Before I can comprehend what is happening, he grips my blouse and thrusts it open. Tiny pearl buttons fly in all directions as my hands dart up to cover my erratically panting chest.

Reading the turmoil of my expression, Vladimir mocks, "Don't worry, Ангел, not every man bidding on you will be turned off by your scars. Some may add to them." I gasp in a mangled breath when the blade of a knife digs into my back. "Now be a good girl and smile at the camera before I'm forced to increase their bids with your blood instead of your smile," he commands in my ear, his hot breath adding to the sweat beading on my nape.

Ignoring the pain of the knife piercing my skin, I muster a fake smile. The sudden incline of my cheeks squeezes the first tears from my overfilled eyes.

My pained response incites the men more.

Their bids turn frantic, coming in by the droves.

"Thirty-five thousand," shouts a man from a computer speaker on my right at the same time another man bids, "Forty thousand," from a screen on my left.

And so the bids continue until I'm sold to the highest one.

23

NIKOLAI

With my fists clenched and my back molars gnawing together, I stare at the live video of Justine playing on the screen of Rico's phone. She appears relatively unharmed, but the clothes she wore this morning when I dropped her off at the airport have been cut open, exposing her pale-blue undergarments and wobbling knees to the world. Her face is ashen, enhancing the angry red streaks streaming from her eyes, and her gaze is wide and terrified.

Although the man standing behind her has his face hidden by shadow, I can testify it is Vladimir. The quickening of my pulse and the red-hot fury bubbling in my veins leaves no doubt about his identity.

The weak beat of my heart strengthens when a shouted, "Sixty thousand," shrills through the speaker of Rico's phone.

Like a freight train crashing into me, reality dawns.

He's selling her.

Because Vladimir thinks Justine's scars make her imperfect, he doesn't want her for himself. He just doesn't want me to have her.

He has been this way my entire life.

Anything I want, he takes.

If not for him, then for someone else.

"Counterbid," I order when the amount rises by another ten thousand dollars.

Rico shakes his head. "I can't."

I storm toward him, preparing to knock two of his teeth into the back of his throat before using his phone to submit my own bid.

"We can't bid because we haven't been invited to the party. Justine's sale is by invitation only. We can only see proceedings because we're tailgating off an FBI feed," Rico rushes out, stopping my steps mid-stride.

"Jesus fucking Christ," Roman sneers under his breath, drawing my focus to him from his rare use of an expletive. Recognizing he has the devotion of both Rico and me, he mutters, "Listen," while nudging his head to Rico's phone.

The room falls into resolute silence. I don't even breathe for fear that my expanding lungs will drown out the bidding war over Justine.

With bids increasing by ten-thousand-dollar increments, her sale soon reaches the high six figures, but that isn't what has us shocked into silence. It is the range of accents blaring through the speakers.

"There are no Russians," I mutter more to myself than Rico and Roman.

Roman nods, agreeing with my assessment. "That's why he made her sale invitation only, so neither you nor anyone associated with you could bid on her."

Shifting my eyes to my floor, I struggle to subdue the anger tearing me in two.

I want to kill.

I want to maim.

I want to unleash the pain shredding me to pieces onto some poor, unsuspecting bastard, but if I do any of those things, I'll never get Justine back. So instead, I graze my teeth over my bottom lip before asking, "Can Hunter get me a list of the men bidding on her? Their IP addresses? Names? Something?"

I'd prefer to gain access to Vladimir's location, but knowing how tight his online security is, I'll start with a less challenging task.

Rico's brows stitch for the briefest second before he nods. "You know his skills as well as I do, so I'd say so, but why?"

I smirk to hide the callousness stewing in my stomach. It is a pointless endeavor when I reply, "Because I'm going to hunt down the man who wins her and slit his throat before he has the chance to touch her. Then I'll do the same to Vladimir. There are rules in this industry, but the instant Vladimir dragged Justine into our fight, they became null and void."

Rico must be on board with my plans as he slides a second, more outdated phone out of his pocket without any hesitation crossing his face.

What I am saying is true. The Popov founder was a bigamist but loved his wife without question. So much so, his protectiveness of her is undeniable in the rules the Popov empire has abided by over the past three hundred years.

A king is untouchable until he messes with another man's queen.

By taking Justine, Vladimir made a fatal error, because not only can I now kill him, but I can do it without fear of repercussion.

My eyes drift to Rico when he says, "Hunter can't access the server Justine's auction is being held on. The security is so encrypted it will take days to bypass. We're only in now because he is piggybacking off an FBI surveillance device tracking one of the bidders."

Hearing a "but" hanging in the air, I verbalize it.

"But..."—Rico waits, building the suspense—"he can supply us with a list of bidders from a sale held last weekend."

He stares at me as if I should know what he is referring to.

I don't have the faintest fucking clue.

"It was the sale of a Czech woman," he advises, his tone as high as his arched brow. When I remain quiet, still stumped, he growls, "The Czech woman you bid on and won last weekend. Hunter has access to *that* list."

"One, I don't pay for whores," I grind out, annoyed at his accusation. "Two, I most certainly don't take anything not willingly given, and you know better than anyone that the instant Vladimir's whores submit, he gets rid of them. His clientele doesn't appreciate passive women. And three, why would I pay for half a meal when I own the restaurant? Justine isn't half a woman, Rico. She is all woman, and she is all *mine*. I can barely keep up with her insatiable needs as it is. I don't need any more than she's giving me."

Rico keeps his narrowed gaze locked on me, either reading the truth from my eyes or silenced by my rare pledge of monogamy.

His slacked-jaw response isn't shocking. Before Justine, exclusivity wasn't my strong point. But with my desire for Justine more powerful than the world's most potent drug, I'd never risk losing her for a measly few hours between the sheets with a woman who wouldn't shine half a light on her.

"When all of this is over, you need to apologize to my wife," Rico demands, his tone stern. "She went through hell because no one in our family understood her importance to me. I have a feeling things have now changed." He waits for me to nod, before squashing his outdated phone to his ear. "Send the list," he requests, accepting my silent pledge with a confidence I don't deserve.

I was acting on behalf of Vladimir when I arranged for Blaire to be raped and murdered, but I'm man enough to admit I did treat her wrong. I could justify my malice because I was raised believing women are worthless, but that would be a pitiful excuse. The way Rico looked at Blaire left no doubt she was important to him. I just chose to ignore the obvious.

"Hunter is emailing us a list of names now," Rico informs us, then returns his second cell to his pocket.

Not even thirty seconds later, we're pursuing the possible names of the men bartering to make Justine their newest whore. Just as Roman had suspected, every nationality is represented in skin-crawling detail, except Russian. Vladimir did this on purpose. He must be aware of the connections I've made in the industry the past year, much less the past week, so he's publicly announcing his defiance to the change in guard.

He is a foolish man.

Denying a Russian man the chance to bid on a woman with qualities as fine as Justine's is as disrespectful as calling his бабушка a whore. Russian men are very protective of their grandmothers, their possessiveness nearly as strong as their love of a good woman.

Vladimir will pay for his insolence, but his punishment will be nowhere near as brutal as the wrath I will bring down on him.

The pit in my chest I've been struggling to ignore the past five hours grows when the reason for Justine's low reserve suddenly smacks into me. Although the bids for Justine are still coming in hard and fast, Vladimir generally starts bidding in the high six figures. A woman of Justine's caliber would quickly sell for over a million dollars, so there is only one reason Vladimir would start bidding at such a low amount.

"He's doing a totem auction," I murmur, my tone laced with fury. When Rico peers at me unaware, I explain, "Vladimir isn't selling Justine. He's loaning her out. Every man who bids on her will have an hour with her. The highest bidder goes first. Then, they continue down the list until every offer is exhausted." My words are brimming with so much anger they sound like they were delivered straight from hell. "If Justine recovers from her first auction, he will commence proceedings again. He's been operating totem auctions for the past six months. It's netted him massive capital and a heap of criticism."

"What the fuck, Nikolai?" Rico mutters, clearly shocked at the direction our entity took after his death. "There is wrong, and then there is *wrong*. This is way past fucking *wrong*."

"This wasn't me. This was all Vladimir's undertaking. He saw an opportunity to make money and ran with it."

Rico glares at me, not accepting my piss-poor excuse.

I deserve his wrath. I knew what Vladimir was doing, but I never voiced concern about his proposal because his distraction opened up business possibilities I never had the opportunity to pursue previously.

When the heat of Rico's gaze becomes too great to ignore, I shift my eyes to Roman.

His stare matches Rico's. He glares at me, allowing his eyes to convey words he'll never be game to say out loud.

I told you so.

Roman expressed concern over Vladimir's dealings for months, but with Vladimir's new venture keeping him well-occupied, I took advantage of his absence. That's how I amassed so many of his associates in such a short period. I've been strategizing my takeover since the day I turned sixteen, but the wheels were never set in motion until Vladimir's interest moved from the weaponry trade to prostitution.

While he coerced our associates into purchasing women they

could have for free, I convinced them they needed a stockpile of weapons to keep their newly acquired possessions safe.

With one exchange came another, closely followed by another and then another.

Within six months, my capital was doubled.

Although no amount of money will ever make Vladimir happy, it does make the world go round.

Ignoring the manic tic of my jaw, I drop my eyes to the sheet of paper. With the bids in Justine's auction still coming in hard and fast, I scan the list of names three times before clarity finally breaks through the anger engulfing me.

How did I not think of this sooner?

It is the perfect solution to my predicament. I just need to tread carefully so Vladimir won't hear my steps.

"I know a way to get us in." I turn my eyes to Roman, the hope in them unmissable. "I need to borrow your phone."

24

JUSTINE

When Vladimir removes his knife from my left rib, I clutch my shredded clothes close to my body. Tears roll down my cheeks unchecked, but I don't brush them away. My desire to cover the scars Vladimir has been eyeing with disgust is more urgent than my need to clear the devastation from my face.

I've never been more humiliated in my life. I thought the laughter I endured when mauled by a dog would be the worst thing I'd hear in my lifetime.

It wasn't—not even close.

The taunting I encounter between bids has made the slosh in my stomach race up my windpipe more times than I can count.

If the fact I was being sold wasn't already outrageous enough, hearing detailed descriptions of what the men plan to do to me when they win is horrendous.

They speak about me as if I'm a piece of meat—a mere pawn to play with before being tossed aside like trash—making me scared. Angry. Lost.

My conflicting emotions peak when Vladimir rolls his index finger across my cheek, gathering a hot, salty tear. "You'd do best to save these for your new owners. They love collecting tears from pretty little dolls." His words are laced with warning, but the covetousness in his tone doesn't relay the firmness of his threat.

Watching me through heavy-hooded eyes, he pops his wet finger into his mouth. He licks away my tears with a slither of his tongue, making my stomach roll. When he releases a throaty groan, bile scorches my throat. The thought of any part of my body, even something as simple as my tears, giving him pleasure makes me violently ill.

"It is such a pity you have these," he murmurs, trailing his finger over a scar my ruined clothing fails to conceal. "If you were unmarked, nothing would have stopped me from having you beneath me."

"Thank god for mangy mutts," I mumble under my breath before I can stop my words.

His dark eyes flare, apparently more welcoming of my spiteful tongue than his lifelong rival Col Petretti.

It was my inability to stop my reaction to a snippy remark Col made that led to my being mauled by a dog four years ago. Since I grew up sheltered by my four older brothers, I thought I was invincible.

The fall from grace was very hard and extremely painful.

Col and Vladimir have a lot of similarities. Both are mafia king-pins. Both value the lives of their sons over their daughters, and both make my skin crawl with an equal amount of disgust and repulsion.

There is only one difference between them.

I am not here because I rejected Vladimir's son.

I'm here because I accepted him.

"He's going to kill you," I mutter, my fear of retribution not enough to prevent my warning.

I don't need to use Nikolai's name for Vladimir to know to whom my threat pertains. The darkening of his eyes and the pulse in his nape tell me he is aware.

His frightened response spurs my determination, fueling me to warn, "When he discovers you've taken me, he won't stop hunting until he finds me. And when he finds me, which we both know he *will*, I suggest you fall to your knees and beg for mercy. Because this time, when he holds his knife to your throat, nothing will stop him from removing your crown. Not me. Not you. Not anyone."

My head slings to the side when Vladimir backhands me with force. His hit doesn't weaken the vindictive grin spreading across my face in the slightest. If anything, my smile grows.

He lashed out because he knew every word I spoke was gospel.

Circumstances beyond Nikolai's control made him a hunter years ago, but this hunt is different. This hunt is personal. Just like there is no greater power than a lioness protecting her cub, nothing will stop Nikolai's pledge of protection. He promised to keep me safe. He will keep his promise.

Vladimir's slit-eyed gaze drops to the rippled skin on my ribcage. Its ghastly appearance is compliments of cartilage being torn from my bone during my mauling four years ago. "Get her out of here before I damage the merchandise more than it already is."

The brute who lugged me into the room clutches the top of my arm and roughly drags me to the door. I don't know if he's being extra aggressive to put on a show in front of the numerous men watching the spectacle unfold from the corner of the room, or because his patience is as thinly stretched as mine. But whatever it is, his manhandling stacks the fire in my stomach with more wood, growing it to a point I can't ignore.

"*Если вы не хотите умирать, я предлагаю вам уйти сейчас,*" I warn, my enunciation leaving no doubt to the honesty in my threat.

If they want to survive, they better leave before Nikolai arrives. Nikolai has never hidden his protectiveness of me. He has openly said on numerous occasions he will kill a thousand men before he'd let anyone between us, and that is what he will do if they don't heed my warning.

"Nikolai is coming. He will kill you all if you stand in his way," I warn in Russian, my arrogance feeding off the panic flaring in the eyes of the men tracking me.

"Get her out of here! Now!" Vladimir shouts, his voice so loud the women trapped behind the padlocked doors scream in panic.

Although his frightened response is unexpected, it mimics those of half the men surrounding him. Most are staring at me with wide, panicked eyes, but a small handful are glancing at Vladimir, stunned by his outburst. They can smell his fear as effectively as I can.

He should be scared. He raised Nikolai to be a killer, and he is mere hours from discovering how precise his tactics were.

Fighting with the strength Nikolai has always seen in me, I continue issuing threat after threat until my throat is as raw as my heart feels. I know Nikolai is coming. I can feel it in my bones and smell it on my skin. And now that I've warned them of his arrival, my conscience is free of guilt. They either leave or suffer Nikolai's wrath.

If they're smart men, they will leave.

"You either stupidly believe you have a golden pussy, or a lack of nutrients has made you crazy," grunts the blond man clutching my arm when we're halfway down the hall. "Nikolai would never challenge his father's title over a whore."

"When did I say this fight was solely about me?" My words come out garbled, forced through overworked windpipes struggling to keep up with his fast pace down the hall. "Revenge has always been a dish best served cold. Thirteen years couldn't make it any colder."

The man stops walking, his hand moving for my throat so fast that I fail to secure a breath before my ability to breathe is lost.

"How do you know what happened thirteen years ago?" he hisses, his voice as hot-tempered as his face. "Nobody knows what happened thirteen years ago. Not even the men in the room know what happened thirteen years ago."

The fury of his tone can't hide the panic dangling on his vocal cords. He is more frightened than I was when my skirt was shredded from my body by Vladimir's knife.

"Answer me!" he roars, his empty hand crashing through the drywall at the side of my head, showering my shoulders with fragments of dust and gypsum.

My fingernails dig into his leathery skin when he firms his grip on my neck, which lowers my wheezy breaths to barely a trickle.

Realizing I'm no contest for a man his size, I drag out, "Niko... lai." My confession snatches the last of the air in my lungs.

The stranger glares into my eyes, gauging the truth from them. He must see something in them, as he loosens his grip on my neck, freeing me from asphyxiation with only a second to spare.

"You're Nikolai's girl."

Even though his tone relays he isn't asking a question, my head bobs up and down.

"Jesus Christ," he murmurs as his eyes sling sideways. "We're all fucking dead."

"You don't have to be," I propose, my bloodshot eyes bouncing between his. "If you let me go, I'll tell Nikolai you saved me, that you were the one who set me free."

His brows stitch together as unease clouds his eyes. "You think that will stop him? He won't stop hunting until every man who saw you like..."—he stops talking to rake his eyes down my scarcely covered body— "*that* is dead. We were ordered not to share the same air as you, much less look at you when you entered a room. That's why he killed Sergei, because the dumb fuck wouldn't give up his quest for revenge no matter how stern the warning."

His admission shocks me, but not in the way I anticipated. I should be mortified that Nikolai killed Sergei to protect me, but all I am feeling is gratitude. If Sergei had heeded Nikolai's warning, his life would have been spared, just like every man in this warehouse.

"Sergei only died because Nikolai was protecting me. That won't happen to you if you let me go."

When the man contemplates my reply, I know I'm getting through to him.

"Nikolai promised to keep me safe. Help him keep his word, and I will do everything possible to get you out of this situation alive..."

My words trail off to silence when a snarled, "How precious," thunders through my ears. "A pledge of protection. It must be true love."

My eyes slit as they rocket to the voice. Malvina is sauntering down the hall, the jaunty sparkle in her eyes not matching her battered face. I should feel guilty that a thick coat of makeup has failed to conceal the bruise extending from her nose to her left ear, but I don't. She attacked me. I merely defended myself. No guilt is to be felt.

After stopping in front of me, Malvina spreads her hand across the unnamed man's chest to push him away from me. He steps far enough away I can gauge her importance in this industry but not far enough for me to miss the smell of worry seeping from his skin.

With the glare of a shark, she rakes her beady eyes down my half-naked frame. Her desolate gaze adds to the heat Vladimir's slap caused to my cheek, but I don't back down. I roll my shoulders and stand tall, my stance warning her the loss of our first tussle hasn't dampened my campaign.

I will protect Nikolai as fiercely as he protects me.

I will defend him until my heart thumps its very last beat.

"Oh, you poor child. You have no clue about this lifestyle, do you?" Malvina sighs, feigning sorrow. She will never be an A-grade actress. Her performance is the worst I've seen.

"You realize Nikolai's interests only last as long as his latest high? The instant he comes down from whatever substance he's been tripping on the past two weeks, he'll drop you faster than a hot potato before moving on to the next flavor of the month." She laughs as if humored by her reply. "When I heard you were a lawyer, I thought I'd have to up my game." She rolls her eyes, bringing her IQ closer to her age. "I shouldn't have bothered. You're as dimwitted as every other whore Nikolai has bedded the past four years." Her lips curl into a sly smirk when the color drains from my face.

"Oh goodness, you thought you were the only one he fooled with during our engagement? I hate to tell you this, but you are no more important to Nikolai than the many other whores he keeps locked in this very compound for personal use."

After Malvina revels my wide eyes and shallow breaths, her eyes stray down the long line of doors. "I heard he took quite a liking to Kristina last weekend. Perhaps you could share notes on his likes and dislikes. She doesn't speak English, but that shouldn't bother you since you understand Czech."

Her eyes remain focused on one door, ensuring I know exactly who has her utmost devotion. It is the blue-eyed female who earlier warned me of my meeting with the devil. The woman who accepted my promise of help at face value.

After returning her eyes to mine, Malvina discloses, "Kristina wasn't warning you about Vladimir. She's only had the pleasure of meeting one Popov member. Vladimir isn't him. That obsessive showering routine you witnessed from Nikolai last weekend... Kristina is to blame for that."

"Like I'd believe a single word fired from your mouth," I snarl.

I'm smarter than she thinks I am.

The cockiness in her eyes brightens, illuminating her icy-blue gaze. The reason for her boastful swagger comes to light when she pulls a delivery confirmation form from her pants pocket and hands it to me.

Although the document is printed in Russian, my love of language also extends to written text, so I have no problem deciphering it.

Auction Date: July 2nd
Slave Sold: Kristina Svoboda
Winning Bidder: Nikolai Popov
Amount: $1.3 Million
Funds Transfer: Approved
Slave Collected By: Nikolai Elian Popov

A dash of hesitation weakens my resolve when my eyes scan the signature scribbled on the bottom of the form. The flare of the elegant E matches Nikolai's signature on his court documentation earlier this week, but something is off with this document. It looks authentic, but my intuition warns me not to be so gullible.

My narrowed gaze darts to Malvina when she sneers, "Still want to protect him?"

I nod. "This doesn't change anything," I reply, my tone neutral and without jealousy.

Her eyes lift from the document I'm holding out for her, returning to mine.

She tries to act unaffected by my nonchalant response.

She miserably fails.

"How doesn't it change anything?" Her pitch is so high the man standing at our side gawking at our exchange cringes.

"It proves what I've always known." I wait for her interest to switch from eager to annoyed, before saying, "If you weren't so pathetic, Nikolai wouldn't need to stray."

The blond man coughs to hide his chuckle while Malvina slaps me. Since I am prepared for her outburst, the sting of her hit is nowhere near as bad as Vladimir's.

Although shocked by the vindictiveness of my words, I'm glad I couldn't leash my tongue. Malvina wants to pretend this fight is personal, but I don't believe that. Her quest for revenge is more profound than a woman scorned by deceit. She doesn't just hate me. She hates society in general. Outside of this realm, I may have believed her jealous lover act, but the money-hungry, power-Nazi vibe pulsating out of her is too intense to discount.

She doesn't want Nikolai.

She wants his birthright.

Pinching my chin between her index finger and thumb, Malvina returns my eyes to hers. "Why would I fake interest in a prince when I can have the king?"

Goosebumps creep across my skin as I'm bombarded with disturbing thoughts.

Who in their right mind would pick a man like Vladimir over Nikolai?

A sick and highly disturbed individual, that's who.

Mercifully, I'm saved from issuing a response to Malvina's question when a thick Russian accent bellows down the corridor. "Take her to Nikolai's room. Her buyers are on their way."

Unease surfaces when the unnamed brute resumes dragging me down the hall, sidestepping a grinning Malvina on the way.

"Word to the wise, don't fight. It only turns them on more," she snickers evilly.

I wait until we're out of earshot before continuing my ploy to change the stranger's mindset. "You don't have to do this," I whisper when we take the corner of a dark and dingy hallway. "Let me go, and I'll pretend I never saw you."

The man smirks. It isn't a rainbow-on-a-crystal-clear-blue-sky type of grin. It's cold and reserved, adding to the clamminess of my skin. "When you create a storm, you can't cry when it rains. You just whip out an umbrella and pray it passes quickly."

My chance to reply is lost when he unlocks a room on our right and shoves me into a pitch-black space. I scamper backward when the darkness swamping me forces a collision with a recurring nightmare.

Although frightened beyond belief, I charge for the door, praying I will reach the opening before I'm left trapped and help-less. The last time I was thrown into a pitch-black room ended with me being mauled by a dog. The darkness left me defenseless to stop the dog's onslaught, as I had no clue where he was coming from. The louder I screamed, the harder he came at me.

My heart falls from my ribcage when I fail to reach the door before it slams shut, and blankets the room with dancing shadows and painful memories.

"Please," I beg, pounding my fists on the thick reinforced door. "Please don't leave me in here. I'll do anything you want. Anything at all!"

I claw at the door, the pain of my nails tearing from my skin not incentive enough to stop my wish to escape. While issuing plea after plea, I pound on the door repeatedly, not giving in until exhaustion inevitably kicks in.

Hours pass before the pleas for help projecting from the rooms surrounding mine stop. I think. It could have been minutes, hours, or days. I honestly don't know. I've been immersed so profoundly into this insanity that the ability to keep time is beyond me. I'm scared and hungry and would give anything to return to my family.

Col's revenge was horrendous, but at least it was quick. He didn't hold me hostage for hours with nothing but bitter memories to keep me occupied. His punishment was issued within minutes of his verdict being served. If I could choose between a long, torturous death or a swift one, I'd always pick the latter.

Pain isn't torture. Silence is.

When the jingling of keys rings through my ears, I firm my hold on my legs. I'm in the corner of the room with my back braced against the wall. My body is rolled into a ball, replicating the position I took to protect my face from being torn to shreds four years ago.

Thankfully, my visit to the brink of madness is minus a vicious animal this time.

I blink several times to clear my vision when a fluttering of light scampers into my room. Although grateful my visitor could locate the light switch I frantically searched for hours ago, I'm not as welcoming to the brightness as I should be.

I wasn't a fan of blood before I was mauled, but my dislike grew rampant after my assault. And considering there's a massive amount of old, dried blood pooled at the bottom of a pulley-like contraption, no amount of denial can push my disdain aside.

Because I am incapable of removing my eyes from the horrid image, the man entering the room sneaks up on me unnoticed. He hoists me from the ground as if I'm weightless before spinning me around.

With one hand pinning my head to the wall, he demands I place my hands behind my back. Too exhausted to fight, I do as requested without protest. I can barely stand, much less fight a man double my weight.

"*Come sottomesso come sempre,*" he murmurs, amused by my lack of fight.

I roll my eyes, not bothered by his snooty comment. He hasn't been locked in a dungeon-like chamber for several hours, so his opinion on my submissiveness is the least of my worries.

Suddenly, I freeze, disturbed.

He didn't grumble his remark in Russian like the many other accents I've heard today. He spoke in Italian, his pronunciation so precise I wouldn't be shocked to discover he was born in Italy.

"*Per chi lavori?*" I ask, demanding to know who he works for.

When he spins me around to face him, the grin cracking onto his face answers my question without a word spilling from his lips.

He is a Petretti crew member.

"No," I mumble, my one word barely audible, torn from my throat with a sob.

This can't be happening again.

I won't let this happen again.

With my mind hazy between the past and the present, my survival mode kicks into overdrive.

If Dimitri expects me to submit in silence as I did years ago with his father, he has another thing coming. I'd rather be killed than go down without a fight for the second time.

Stomping on the brute's foot, I bite at the bandaged hand closing in on my face. The man squeals like a girl when my teeth gnaw through his skin so forcefully blood tingles my taste buds. My stomach rolls with queasiness, but I keep my determination strong. I'm not the same woman I was when I last wrestled with the Petretti crew. I am stronger and more determined.

After ramming the man with all my might, I charge for the door he left hanging open. My steps are remarkably strong for how hard my legs shake, and I reach the opening in two heart-thrashing seconds.

I nearly lose my footing on the polished wooden floors in the corridor when I take the corner at the speed of a rocket.

Thankfully, I keep upright and moving with my fighting spirit surging past my panic.

Ignoring the pleas for help shouted from each room as I race by, I sprint down the hallway lined with dozens of doors.

"I'll come back. I promise I'll be back," I pledge to the numerous pairs of eyes watching my escape through the keyholes of their room, their pupils as wide as mine.

When I reach the end of the corridor, my frantic pace comes to a dead stop. Two armed men are guarding the stairwell, blocking my only viable exit.

Crap!

Incapable of giving up, I return to the direction I just came from. The squeak of my sweaty feet twisting on the shiny floors alerts the guards to my presence.

They fire a warning shot, forcing the hallway into pin-drop silence.

I freeze halfway down the dimly lit corridor. I'm not freezing in fear of being shot. It's from unveiling a sight more frightening than my most horrendous nightmares.

The Devil and Satan are standing side by side, their amused expressions as dangerous as my heart rate.

"Is she as you remember?" Vladimir asks Dimitri, his tone reeking of condescending arrogance.

After angling his head to the side, Dimitri's eyes scan my body in a long, dedicated sweep. He assesses my half-naked figure as if I am dripping in precious gems, not shredded clothes and soot-covered skin.

"Yes," he eventually answers. His reply is for Vladimir, but his eyes are for me. "You can stave off your hunger for years, but it doesn't make your desire to eat any less rampant."

Vladimir grunts, his expression a cross between agreement and disgust. "Even knowing she is marked?" He sounds repulsed, like he had to force his question past a clump of vomit in his throat.

His disgust doesn't faze me. I'd rather him find me repulsive than enticing.

Dimitri considers Vladimir's question for a second before nodding. "Scars don't bother me. The marks you can't see are the hardest to heal," he murmurs under his breath as he stalks my way.

I inch back, not trusting the gleam in his eyes.

Something has changed in him since I last saw him. He isn't the same man he once was. He's different. I just can't figure out how.

Vladimir grunts again, assuming Dimitri's quote was for him.

It wasn't.

He was staring directly at me when he said it.

"To each his own. Just don't mark her any more than you already have. A long list of men are waiting their turn."

Vladimir's sneered comment makes bile race up my throat, but it doesn't stop me from saying, "He will kill you if you touch me."

It's only fair I issue Dimitri the same caution I gave Vladimir hours ago, because this will be his only chance to leave this warehouse unscathed.

"When Nikolai discovers what you have done, he will kill you both."

While filling the last bit of air between us with his large build, Dimitri mutters, "We can only hope."

The snarl of his words doesn't match the twinkle in his eyes. His heavy-lidded gaze is brimming with excitement, a stark contradiction to the emotions he should be feeling.

He should be scared, not eager.

My head snaps to the side when a roared, "He's here! Nikolai is here!" bellows up the stairwell.

Gunfire breaks through the silence encompassing us, closely followed by a wounded cry. More bullets soon follow, growing louder with each one dislodged.

The noise is more bone-rattling than any high-definition action flick I've watched. From the number of shots and the volume of accented voices, I'd guess at least three to four dozen men are storming the lower level of the warehouse where I'm being held captive.

I swing my eyes to Vladimir, who's standing as frozen as a statue, when the unmissable sound of machine guns booms into my ears.

Even afraid, I can't help but smile at the panic masking his disgusting face. He looks more frightened than I did when Col threw me into a room with a vicious animal trained to kill.

He should be panicked.

Retribution is about to be served, albeit years too late.

"I told you he'd come," I sneer, my voice as high as my confidence surges. "It's time to pay your penance, Vladimir. The prince has arrived to collect his throne."

My head brutally slings to the side when he backhands me, slapping me so hard my brain rattles in my skull.

"The sale has been canceled. I'll refund your money by the end of the week," Vladimir snarls to Dimitri, his words spitting out of his mouth like venom.

The heavy thud of footsteps racing toward the commotion drowns out my screams when he fists my hair in a firm hold. Tears spring to my eyes when my hair rips from my scalp, but with my arms tied behind my back, I'm defenseless to ease the pain.

When Dimitri steps toward us, Vladimir yanks an ancient-looking revolver out of the waistband of his pants and directs it at his chest. "I said the sale is canceled," he snarls, his voice leaving no misgivings about his annoyance.

If Dimitri fails to meet his demand a second time, he won't leave this hallway breathing.

Holding his hands out in front of his chest, Dimitri cowardly bows out.

Vladimir smirks arrogantly.

Victory is all over his face.

My bare feet scuttle across the floor, and I struggle to keep upright when Vladimir drags me down the hallway by my hair. For a man of his age and size, his strength is remarkable.

"Go! Now!" he screams in Russian to a group of men huddled in a room similar to the one I was in earlier. When I spot the pool of dried blood circling the floor, I realize it is the same room.

Vladimir grips the collar of my shredded blouse in a white-knuckled hold while his other hand strikes me across the face. His hit is so brutal I'm overcome with nauseating dizziness.

Using my lightheadedness to his advantage, he paces to the other side of the room to gather a rickety old chair.

White spots are still floating in my eyes when he places the chair over the puddle of old blood. With a yank of my arm, he forcefully shoves me into the chair.

"I should have killed that bastard years ago," he hisses through clenched teeth while gathering something from the floor.

Fear engulfs me when he circles a noose around my neck. "No, please," I beg, my words as stuttered as my heart rate.

Remaining quiet, he tightens the rope around my neck, allowing his actions to answer my plea on his behalf. He has no intention of letting me go.

Not alive, anyway.

Not willing to give up without a fight, I push onto my feet and rocket out of the chair.

I don't even make it two steps before Vladimir yanks on the rope, jerking me backward. I land on my backside with a thud, but I barely register the pain. I'm too engulfed by panic to respond to something as weak as pain.

The terror ripping through me grows when he feeds the rope into a metal pulley contraption bolted to the ceiling.

Happy everything is in place, he yanks down on the rope. For every inch I'm hoisted into the air, the wooziness in my head grows, as does the sting of the rope burning my neck.

My only saving grace is the brittle wooden chair under my feet. Although I'm precariously balancing on my tippy toes, if I didn't have that small piece of wood keeping me upright, I would have been strangled by now.

Hearing my ragged gasps as I fight through the fear eating me whole, Vladimir raises his eyes to mine. The grin on his face triples as he watches me struggle to fill my lungs with air.

"Don't pass out yet, *Ангел*," he mocks with an arrogant wink. "You don't want to miss the miracle of the devil being reincarnated into hell for the second time in his life."

26

NIKOLAI

W ood splinters fly in all directions when two of my men ram open a reinforced door on one of the many compounds Vladimir has amassed separately from the ones owned by the Popov entity.

I prick my ears, praying our quest to gain access goes unnoticed. Failing to hear any noise creep through the quiet space, I lift my gun high and enter the concealed back entrance.

At my request, Rico shadows closely behind me. With this compound being my home base during the ten weeks of my recovery thirteen years ago, I know the floor plan better than anyone.

I should have realized Vladimir would bring Justine here. He always loves adding a mind-fuck element to every punishment he serves. He knows I haven't stepped foot in this warehouse since I left it with more than just physical scars. But not even incapacitating flashbacks will stop me from entering this property tonight.

Nothing will prevent me from protecting Justine—not even the risk of being tortured as I was here thirteen years ago.

After Rico and I sweep the first floor, I glance back at my crew, anticipating their panic over who we're about to storm in on. But they aren't panicked. They are ready to fight with their guns braced and their eyes blazing with grit. The support I've been shown today is shocking. My men think I'm either delusional or intelligent. Either way, their respect will be rewarded tenfold once Justine is returned to me.

Spurred on by a mass surge of adrenaline racing through me, I gesture for my men to enter the compound. They quietly move into the property, their steps soundless on the cracked concrete floor.

Hours of painstaking deliberation gave us plenty of time to devise a plan of attack, and for the first time, my crew's vote was unanimous.

We agreed on a stealthy approach because the closer I am to Justine before Vladimir is aware of my arrival, the better chance I'll have of saving her.

Vladimir is a coldhearted man who has no trouble putting a bullet through the heart of an innocent, but this isn't the standard game of cat and mouse we've been playing my entire life.

It's personal.

Vladimir wants revenge.

He wants to maim me like I've crippled his empire the past week, so he won't go for a standard bullet-through-the-heart kill.

He wants a messy, gruesome death that will warn others of the consequences of double-crossing him.

He wants to make an example out of me as he did to Rico all those years ago.

There's just one difference.

Instead of taking his anger out on me, he unleashes it on a woman undeserving of his wrath. It is a foolish move on his behalf. My heart has never thumped in the rhythm it's been pounding for the past seven hours. I've also never experienced the massive surge of testosterone racing through my veins like I have today.

I feel like King-fucking-Kong.

I want to bang my chest and shout my invincibility to the world. I want to burn off my excess energy between the sheets with the woman who proved I have a heart in my chest. It may have been a weak and pathetic organ mere days ago, yet it is still a heart, nonetheless. But more than anything, I want to show Vladimir there are some things he can't take from me.

He can steal my power, my wealth, and even my sanity, but he cannot take Justine from me.

She is mine, and I will stop at nothing to bring her home.

My focus returns to the task at hand when a murmured voice breaks through the padded-cell silence surrounding me. I raise my hand in the air, requesting my men be quiet.

The faint hum of energy dulls to complete silence, revealing what I thought I heard the first time was correct. Justine's singsong voice is echoing in the silence.

Locking my eyes with Rico's, I nudge my head to a set of stairs on our left. Justine's voice is faint, but I'm confident it comes from above us.

Rico nods, reading the command in my eyes before signaling for half my crew to follow us to the stairwell. The remaining twelve will keep watch with Trey on the first floor, ensuring our approach isn't interrupted by one of our own.

With the wood on the stairwell in desperate need of repair, we take the stairs one at a time, not trusting it to hold the combined weight of me and over a dozen of my men.

The cockiness heating my blood spikes when I hear Justine growl, "When Nikolai discovers what you have done, he will kill you both."

Blood rushes to the lower extremities of my body from the confidence in her tone. She's been missing for over twelve hours, but her spirit remains intact, proving what I've always known.

She was born to lead.

My *Ангел* is a queen, and she's mere minutes from receiving her crown.

My cock's primed stance doesn't last long, only long enough for me to recall what Justine said.

When Nikolai discovers what you have done, he will kill you both.

Vladimir better not have touched her. If he has, his death will be the most painful thing he's ever experienced. His wish for a bloody, torturous death will be granted, as it will be his own.

Our chance to confront Vladimir unannounced is thrown out the window when one of his long-serving goons gallops down the stairs. He's almost halfway down the rickety stairwell before he spots Rico and me crouching in the shadows. He is close enough I can smell the fear leaching from his pores, but not close enough for me to silence him with my knife.

"He's here!" he screams in Russian, his voice bellowing up the stairwell. "Nikolai is here—"

Bang, bang. The remainder of his sentence is silenced by a bullet between his eyes and one through his heart.

His death is as hushed as the life in his soulless eyes, but it comes too late. His cowardly cry already alerted Vladimir's crew to our presence, much less the heavy thump of his body crashing into the rotted wood.

"Move, move, move," I command when Vladimir's men swarm the stairwell from all directions. They swell in size with every bullet dislodged, outnumbering my men three to one.

Guns fire around me as I continue scaling the stairs, taking down four of Vladimir's men in the process. The smell of lead burning through skin is intoxicating, stimulating my veins with massive amounts of endorphins.

This is the one thing I would have struggled to give up if I had been freed from this lifestyle thirteen years ago. The rush that comes with a raid like this is addictive. It turns boys into men and men back into boys.

It's like competing in one of those video games teenage boys love, but in graphic detail no amount of high definition could produce. It is gory and thrilling at the same time.

This is me.

I am in my element.

Even though our crews aren't evenly matched, with my men being younger and fitter, we soon have the advantage over Vladimir's more mature crew. I'd like to say my team's tactical response has eased the panic raining down on me, but that would be a lie. Until I take down Vladimir, Justine's life is still at risk.

"Go. I'll handle things down here," Rico assures me when I peer back at him, knowing I've only got seconds to get to Justine before Vladimir kills her.

He directs his Smith and Wesson over my left shoulder and guns down an old crew member with precise accuracy before returning his eyes to me. "The longer she's alone with him, the less chance of survival. She's counting on you, Eli. Don't let her down."

That's all it takes for my protectiveness to reach fever pitch. I climb the stairs two at a time, dropping men like flies every four to five steps.

By the time I get to the top landing, I'm covered with sweat, and my heart is pounding against my ribs, but my grit hasn't lessened.

Real men thrive on danger.

Only cowards weaken.

With my gun braced in front of my chest, I scan the long corridor of doors, praying one will give me an indication of which room Justine is in. There are over a dozen of them, all closed and all reinforced with industrial-sized padlocks.

Realizing nothing but determination will alter my predicament, I move toward the first door. My boot makes quick work of its locked status. I check each corner of the room. They are all empty.

Suddenly, I jerk to my right, startled by a shadow lurking in a doorway halfway down. I don't need to see the face of the man sheltering himself in the darkness to know who he is. His icy-blue eyes tell me everything I need to know.

"Where is she?" I ask, knowing we've only reached this stage because Dimitri texted me Justine's location a little under an hour ago.

Although protecting Justine was never part of the agreement we negotiated earlier this week, I'm glad my threat to skin him alive if anything happened to her was enough incentive to secure his loyalty today.

With the Petrettis' focus centering around sex trafficking, requesting Dimitri's assistance was the smart thing to do. It killed me asking for his help, but when I'm backed into a corner, I use anything I can to get out. I was backed so far into a corner I didn't think I'd ever get out. I used what I could. I sided with an enemy.

Dimitri could have exploited my desperation to advance his crew to a level his father never achieved, but my agreement last week to grant his crew unlimited prostitution operations on the West Coast for the next three years without paying distribution rights to the Popov entity helped his focus remain firm.

He will still garner the same level of power and respect. He will merely achieve it by his actions instead of having it handed to him. In different times, his valor would have gained my respect. But since I can't get over him not protecting Justine, he remains on my shit list. I will continue negotiating trades with him, but I will never respect him.

When Dimitri nudges his head to a door three spots up from him, I ask, "Do you have a gun?"

I cuss when he shakes his head. The manic tic in my jaw grows when he murmurs, "Vladimir's men disarmed me half a mile out. Besides, this isn't my fight. I got you this far. Now I'm walking away."

My teeth grit as anger lines my face. This is the exact reason I will never respect him. He is a coward.

"Bet that isn't the first time you've said that line, is it? Is that what you told Justine before your dog mauled her? 'I got you this far, now I'm walking away'?" I mock his Italian accent, the scorn in my tone my only readable defense. Since Justine must remain my priority, I will deal with him and his bad choices later.

Not waiting for Dimitri to respond to my taunt, I head for the door he nudged his head at. My steps are soundless, the thumping of my heart the only noise I hear.

Bracing my gun in one hand, I check if the door is locked with my other.

It is.

Pop. Pop. Pop. I destroy the deadlock with bullets before kicking open the door with force.

The room is shrouded in blackness, adding to the scent of death lingering in the air. I run my hand down the wall, seeking the light switch.

When I find it, fire rages through me, and my anger surges to a record-breaking high. Justine is dangling in the middle of the space, suspended from the ceiling by a noose wrapped around her neck.

Her face is red and stained with angry, salty tears, and her body is stretched to its limit. She's only breathing from the faintest touch of her tippy toes gliding above a frail wooden chair.

"Do you remember the fun we had in this room, Niki?"

My eyes shift sideways when a monster emerges from the shadows shrouding Justine.

"How many times did you pass out in this room? Four? Or was it five times?" Vladimir ridicules me.

I aim the barrel of my gun at the crinkle between his lifeless eyes, my anger so violent I feel my hands shaking all the way up my arms. I'd take him out right now if I hadn't seen his gun jabbed into Justine's ribs.

If I was assured my bullet would be dislodged and wedged between his eyes before he shot her, I'd be issuing him his last rites. But the way he has his gun angled at Justine's heart, she'd bleed out in under thirty seconds. Since we're miles from the nearest medic, I can't risk her being shot.

I won't risk it.

"Watch out," Justine gasps through the pain clutching her throat.

I don't need to turn around to know who's approaching me. The sheer panic in her eyes reveals who it is. She looks more fearful now than she was when Sergei attacked her last week.

"Look at me, *Ангел*," I instruct, my tone comforting even though my mood is volatile.

In any other situation, I'd crave a bloodbath, but this is Justine —my *Ангел*. My desire to protect her is stronger than any craving, and I'll stop at nothing to keep her safe.

"It's okay. Dimitri won't hurt you," I assure her when the fear in her eyes grows.

Justine shakes her head as violent shuddering hampers her tiny frame. Panic shreds through me when her sudden movements nearly make her lose her weak grip on the chair. New tears spring down her face as she struggles to regain her balance.

"Look at me!"

The fury in my roar demands her utmost devotion. Although I hate adding pain to her terror, her frozen stature stops her fidgety movements, which in turn decreases the chance of her being asphyxiated.

"He won't hurt you. I promise you, Dimitri will *not* hurt you."

Justine's eyes remain wide with panic, but she faintly nods, accepting my guarantee with the strength of a tigress, demonstrating what I saw in her the first day we met.

She is a fighter through and through.

"Oh, isn't this sweet? Two brothers fighting side by side," Vladimir sneers.

I keep my eyes on him, but my devotion is on Justine. With her concentration focused on keeping her grip on the wooden chair, she seems to have missed Vladimir's admission that I am a Petretti.

Although I'm planning to tell her my DNA matches the man she hates, I'd rather do it when her life isn't hanging by a thread.

Justine's eyes snap to mine when Vladimir digs the barrel of his gun further into her ribs, stopping my slow advance mid-stride.

"No woman has the right to fracture the rightful order," he growls, his fury uncontained.

"That's not true. Otherwise, I wouldn't be here. You raised me to kill my father, all to seek revenge on an injustice he committed against a woman who has 'no right to fracture the rightful order,'" I interrupt, my words so sneered, my Russian accent is thick. "You're a hypocrite who changes the rules to suit yourself."

"And you are a disgrace to *my* name! After everything I have done for you, you disrespect me on *my* turf, using *my* weapons and standing next to *my* enemy!" Vladimir shouts, the anger in his eyes tripling. "I should have drowned you the instant you left that whore's womb."

I want to smash his face in. I want to ram his callous words down his throat with my fists, but since Justine's safety means more to me than any amount of revenge, I keep my feet planted on the ground and my gun pointed between his brows.

"This is between me and you, Vladimir. It always has been. It always will be. Let Justine and Dimitri leave. Then we'll fight this battle like the men we are."

He has the respect of thousands and the fear of millions, but he loses the ability to lead our crew when he shakes his head at my request.

Turning down a direct challenge equates to instant dismissal. You can't be entrusted with the lives of thousands of men if you fear one. That is the number one rule Anatoly Popov laid down when the Popov entity was founded in the 1700s.

"If a direct descendant of your throne challenges you, and you deny it, you must stand down," I quote, reciting the rules Vladimir has quoted to me time and time again over my past twenty-eight years. "I am challenging you, Vladimir. Man versus man. Popov versus Popov. Father versus son."

Vladimir's thin lips crimp in the corner as he spits in disgust, "You are *not* my son." He shrugs, his nonchalant response not matching the tension bristling in the air. "Besides, I much prefer this predicament."

"Don't," I beg when he leans on the chair Justine is balancing on, leaving only the slightest sliver of wood under her big toes.

Vladimir laughs, finding my plea amusing. "Don't what?" he taunts, slanting into the chair even more.

The rise and fall of Justine's chest barely registers as she struggles to maintain her balance on the portion of wood just out of her reach.

"You're going to be okay," I promise her when our fearful gazes collide for the briefest second. "I'll get you out of here. You just need to trust me, okay?"

Although she can't answer me for fear of being strangled, I don't need her to nod her head to know she trusts me. I can see it in her eyes, smell it on her skin. She knows I'll never stop fighting to keep her safe. I will protect her until the day I take my last breath.

After issuing Justine a final guarantee solely using my eyes, I swing my wide gaze to Dimitri. His stance mimics mine to a T. His gun is facing Vladimir, but his eyes are on Justine. From the width of his pupils and the low hang of his jaw, you'd swear this is the first time he's seen her in distress.

Suddenly, the truth smacks into me. He didn't stay to witness Justine's punishment. Whether that was by choice or not, I don't know, and right now, I don't fucking care. I just need him to give me the same amount of faith Justine has. To trust me with his life.

"We need to lower our weapons."

Dimitri glares at me like I am insane, his trust not as easy to secure as Justine's. "He will kill her the instant we surrender," he whispers, expressing my exact concern. "This isn't about us. He can't touch us, but the rules he lives by don't apply to Justine. He will kill her, Nikolai." His last sentence is delivered without hesitation because every word he speaks is true.

"I know," I reply, the shaking of my heart echoing in my tone. "That's the idea."

Dimitri's dark brows cinch together when I empty the chamber of my gun and place it on the bloodstained ground. "Fuck," he murmurs under his breath before he follows my lead.

Victory gleams in Vladimir's eyes when we kick our guns out of our reach. "Why am I not surprised?" His tongue clicks against his teeth when he mocks us with laughter. "When you're born a coward, you die a coward."

His eyes drift between Dimitri and me as he devises his next move. I can only pray I am one step ahead of him. I know how he thinks. I know what makes him tick. I just hope he reacts as I am predicting. Otherwise, I risked Justine's life for nothing.

As suspected, Vladimir plays right into my hand. A condescending grin etches onto his face as he kicks the chair out from under Justine's feet.

My worst nightmare comes true when Justine's body stills for two terrifying seconds before it convulses through the pain shredding her lungs of oxygen.

Although the image of her shuddering will horrify me for years to come, I'd rather her shake than be completely still.

Disappointed Justine's initial plunge didn't snap her neck, Vladimir releases a deep sigh before pivoting on his heels, planning to leave.

Just as Dimitri had predicted, he has no intention of killing us. He knows Justine's death will be punishment enough for us both.

The scene plays out like a perfectly rehearsed skit in terrifyingly haunting detail. Justine's fight to live diminishes at the exact moment Vladimir's quick exit falters. The only difference is that Vladimir's eyes bulge when they lock on to a shadow blocking the doorway, whereas Justine's slowly taper closed.

Like the Grim Reaper exiting hell, Rico steps out of the darkness, revealing a set of eyes even someone as corrupt as Vladimir couldn't deny.

Rico's eyes are identical to his father's in every way—scorched from the ashes of the hell they were born in.

"Hello, Father," Rico greets him, his voice a vicious snarl when he reaches Vladimir's title.

Vladimir only balks for the quickest second, but it is long enough to set my wheels in motion. I push off my feet with a roar, my strides so long I'm halfway to Justine before my knife is yanked from my back pocket and snapped open.

Before I launch into the air, I fling my knife in Vladimir's direction, taking advantage of his frozen state gawking at his resurrected son.

As gunfire rings around me, I leap into the air, praying the old rusty mechanism on the hoist pulley has frayed the rope enough that my sudden collision with her body won't impact Justine's neck. Although I don't want to cause her any more harm, I have seconds to get to her before she is asphyxiated.

Any air left in Justine's lungs vacates in a fierce grunt when I crash into her midair. Our brutal impact tethers the brittle rope more, snapping it in half. As we hurtle toward the floor, I roll with only a second to spare, ensuring my body subdues the impact of our fall onto the floor.

Pain rockets up my spine when we hit the ground so hard I'm confident we've added more cracks to the already fractured floor, but I ignore it, my desire to save Justine too extreme to let something as weak as pain slow me down.

Although I can see the faintest flutter of Justine's pulse thrumming in her neck, my panic hasn't weakened in the slightest.

The beautiful skin on her nape is contorted by the rope strangling her, and her left cheek is covered with a nasty bruise the poor lighting concealed from a distance. Her eyes also remain closed, adding to the manic feeling tearing me in half.

If my knife hasn't already ended Vladimir's life, I'm seconds away from shredding him to pieces with my bare hands. I should have run faster. I should have protected her neck better during our collision. I should have never coerced her into this lifestyle to begin with.

"Here," Rico mutters, sliding a switchblade across the floor to me.

He's standing next to Vladimir's lifeless body with his gun hanging at his side. His eyes are teeming with a unique mix of relief and alarm, and his jaw is twitching.

I don't know if it was my knife or Rico's gun that ended Vladimir's reign, but right now, I don't fucking care. As long as he is dead, and Justine isn't, that's all I care about.

After flicking open the knife, I dig two fingers under the rope still strangling Justine to protect her skin before dragging the blade upward. The knife's edge is blunt, but the rope gives way without too much effort.

"You're okay. You're okay," I assure Justine on repeat when she suddenly arches her back.

She gulps in air at a rate faster than her heaving lungs can handle as her pupils expand even wider.

"Slow, deep breaths, *Ангел*. One breath at a time."

Utter relief echoes in my tone, killing my itch to go on a murderous rampage. Just hearing Justine's wheezy breaths weakens my urge to kill, let alone witnessing her beautiful eyes slowly fluttering open.

When her gaze meets mine, the panic on her face immediately washes away. "I knew you'd come," she murmurs, her voice husky from her near-death experience. "I warned them you wouldn't stop hunting until you found me." .

I run my thumbs across her cheeks to remove her tears while saying, "No one could keep me away from you, Ангел. Not a hundred men or even a thousand. No matter how far you go, I will always find you."

It is the fight of my life not to seal my lips over hers when the most stunning smile stretches across her face.

Fuck—no wonder I'm so lost to this woman.

She's been put through the absolute wringer the past twelve hours, yet she can still smile like she has the world at her feet.

"You are so strong, Ангел. So fucking strong," I say before tackling her tethered hands.

The shaking wreaking havoc on my body impedes my ability to untie the rope encircling Justine's hands. Rope has been one of my torture instruments of choice for many years, so something as simple as an anchor knot shouldn't faze me in the slightest.

It is not the knot daunting you, Nikolai. It is how close you came to losing her.

Seeing my struggle, Dimitri drops to his knees to untie the knot. Although Justine acts unresponsive to his closeness, I hear her take in a sharp breath when his fingers briefly touch the indented skin on her wrists. It isn't the same needy, husky response her body produces when I touch her. It is more like wariness.

"You're okay, Ангел. No one will ever hurt you."

Once Dimitri has her hands free, I scan every inch of her body to ensure she doesn't have any life-threatening injuries.

Confident most of the marks on her skin are from the dirty conditions, I drag my shirt over my head and drape it over her shuddering frame.

My blood chills from how much she's shaking. I don't know if she is bombarded with adrenaline or shock.

I just hope it isn't fear.

"He is dead, Ангел. He will never hurt you again."

The urge to protect Justine as if she is my own has been with me from the first moment I saw her. I'll never let anyone hurt her—not even me.

"I know," she replies, accepting my admission without any remorse crossing her face.

Although we're in the middle of a war zone, I hold her close to my body for several long minutes. My mind is in overdrive, calculating how to exact revenge on the men who bid on her. But since her well-being is my utmost priority, I remain seated on the floor, snatching a rare moment of peace.

The immediate danger is over, so I can take a moment to gather my thoughts. To breathe without fear. To hold my woman in my arms.

Like it does every second I spend with Justine, the negativity engulfing me soon disappears. The hold this woman has over me is miraculous. Not revenge, not power, not a single fucking thing matters when she is in my arms. Living a peaceful life isn't a prospect for a man like me, but when I am with Justine, I am as close to peace as I will ever be.

"It's true, isn't it?" Justine asks a short time later, her voice still raw.

When I glance down at her, her eyes lift to mine. She's still shaking uncontrollably, but the fear in her eyes has diminished.

Slanting my head to the side, I arch a brow, wordlessly requesting further information about her question.

After her eyes bounce between mine for two heart-clutching seconds, she swings them to the side of the room.

Following her gaze, I spot Dimitri standing on my left, speaking into his cell phone.

"He's your brother, isn't he?" she questions, her tone low.

My eyes fall back to hers, panicked and on edge. I can see in her eyes that she knows my secret. She knows whose blood is running through my veins. But instead of issuing me a look I've seen many times over the past twenty-eight years, she looks at me the same way she did only minutes ago. She peers at me without an ounce of hate or disdain crossing her face.

"Yes, he is my brother." Shock echoes in my tone. I'm stunned at how calm she is.

I was anticipating a more agitated response to her discovering my true identity. That is why I cowardly issued the task to Roman when I dropped them off at the airport this morning. The envelope I handed him told Justine everything she needed to know. It revealed my true identity in sickening detail, leaving nothing off the table.

Although it was a spineless way of exposing myself, I didn't want to witness her response after discovering firsthand I have the blood of the man responsible for ruining her family running through my veins. I crave the sneaky glances Justine gives me. My ego feeds off them, so I did everything possible to ensure nothing tainted them.

I had nothing to fear. The look of adoration in her eyes hasn't faded in the slightest. If anything, it's grown more rampant.

"You have the heart of a warrior, *Ангел*," I whisper in Russian. My words are only for me, but they trickle from my mouth before I can stop them.

I'm glad I couldn't hold them back when Justine replies, "Only when I'm with you. You give me strength I didn't even know I had."

While running her thumb over the crinkle in my brow, a commotion in the corridor gains our attention.

"We need to go," Trey advises, his words breathless, as if he has been sprinting. "Spotters have detected movement at the station. We've got approximately ten, maybe fifteen minutes before this place is swarming with police."

Nodding, I stand, taking Justine with me. I head for the door on the heels of Dimitri and Rico, leaving Vladimir to rot in the hell where he belongs. I don't even look in his direction as I stride past his still body. He doesn't deserve an ounce of sorrow, much less one final glance.

My heart's weak, pitiful beat strengthens when Justine nuzzles her nose into the groove of my chest and inhales deeply. The metallic scent of blood in the corridor is as pungent as the room we're exiting, but that isn't why she is smelling me. She's as addicted to me as I am to her. Not even something as vulnerable as fear can harness her desires.

"Soon, *Ангел*. Very soon," I promise, the change in the air so swift it is almost palpable. It has gone from being shrouded with devastation to sparked with yearning in under two point five seconds.

Justine locks her eyes with mine, the promise in them thickening my cock. She stares at me as if I am her savior, when in reality she is the one who saved me.

My body wears the medals of my triumphs, but the thump of my heart is proof of my biggest victory: my *Ангел*—my slice of heaven in a hot and temperamental place.

My strides halt halfway down the corridor when Justine unexpectedly shouts, "Wait!"

She glances over my shoulder before wriggling in my arms, requesting to be placed down. Although confused by the sudden change in her demeanor, I do as asked. I will never shelter her strength. I will only ever encourage it to be released.

Her steps into the room that held her captive are frail but remarkably determined for what she has endured. At first, I assume she's heading for a stack of towels in the bottom left-hand corner of the room so she can maintain her modesty. I realize what she is doing when she stops halfway across the bloodstained floor.

She's protecting me as fiercely as I defended her.

She is saving my life for the second time.

27

JUSTINE

Bile surges up my throat, adding to the burn in my esophagus when I lean over Vladimir's corpse to grasp Nikolai's knife in my hand.

After scouring Nikolai's police records in great depth last weekend, I know firsthand his knife has been logged into evidence numerous times in the past five years, so it won't take the authorities long to match him to the weapon used to kill Vladimir.

I'm not going to let that happen.

Just as Nikolai risked his life to save mine, I will risk mine to save his.

Even discovering Nikolai was sired by a man I hate hasn't weakened my feelings for him. He just killed a man for me. How much more does he have to sacrifice to prove his devotion?

Nothing.

Not a single thing.

I am his for eternity, and he is mine.

I protect what is mine.

The chance of holding back the contents of my stomach is nearly lost when the last bit of air in Vladimir's lungs releases as I pry Nikolai's knife from his chest. The amount of blood seeping into his shirt makes determining his cause of death difficult, but with most of the blood pooling around the area Nikolai's knife pierced, I would say a fatal knife wound to the heart will be cited on the coroner's report.

Pretending the blood dripping from the blade of Nikolai's knife is jam, I head back to him and his crew frozen in the hallway.

Nikolai gawks at me, the sparkle of awe in his eyes amplifying with every step I take.

"You can't leave any evidence you were here," I say, thrusting his knife toward him. Although my words are strong, my shuddering heart is evident in my tone.

The corners of Nikolai's lips tug high as he accepts his knife from my grasp. He wipes the blade with his shirt, not the least bit worried he's smearing the blood of the man who raised him onto his clothing.

After storing his knife in his back pocket, he cups my jaw, being extra careful not to graze the bruise throbbing on my left cheek. I realize I'm not the only one overwhelmed with emotions when I feel how shaky his hands are. He is as shattered as me.

He stares at me like he doesn't have a dozen of his men waiting for him, ensuring I can't miss the gratitude in his heavy-hooded gaze. Even with tension suppressing the air of oxygen, his stare makes me needy and hot.

"Come, Ангел. It's time to take you home," Nikolai murmurs, his deep timbre intensifying the heat on the back of my knees.

I nod, striving to ignore the feelings I shouldn't be experiencing in a hallway that reeks of death. Smirking at my agreeing gesture, he curls his hand around mine, and we begin exiting.

My stomach rolls on multiple occasions when we dodge bullet casings strewn between numerous bloodied bodies. I don't know how many men were killed tonight, but I do know one thing. This bloodbath was inevitable—whether I was in the picture or not.

Well, that's what I plan to tell myself when guilt eventually steamrolls into me.

My mind strays from dangerous thoughts when the faintest hum trickles into my ears. I abruptly stop at the crest of an old stairwell and prick my ears.

"We need to go, Ангел," Nikolai advises when my brisk halt jerks my hand out of his.

Ignoring both his plea and the insanity of his men pouring

gallons of gasoline over the wooden floors we've just walked, I listen for the noise again.

My suspicion is set aside for shock when I hear the faint cry of a woman over the sloshing of liquid. The swirling of my stomach escalates when a second plea joins the first, closely followed by another and another and another.

Shockwaves jolt through me.

The women! Oh my god, I forgot about the women.

The width of my pupils doubles when I swing my eyes back to Nikolai. "There are women trapped in rooms. We need to free them," I say, pointing in the direction the murmured voices are coming from. I spin on my heels, my objective spurred on by massive amounts of adrenaline thickening my veins.

Nikolai grips my wrist, foiling my endeavor to return to the hallway we just left. "We don't have time, *Ангел*. We have to go."

"No," I reply with a shake of my head. "I promised I'd help them. We can't leave them here."

"We don't have time," Nikolai replies, more firmly this time, his dangerous tone kick-starting both my heart and my libido.

"Then make time," I reply, the plea in my voice unmissable. "I promised I'd help them. Please don't make me break my promise."

Tears glisten in my eyes, but I don't do anything to discourage them. My heart is breaking for those women, so why shouldn't my outside appearance match my insides?

Nikolai tries to shut it down, but I see the quickest flare of emotion blaze through his eyes when he spots the sorrow creeping across my face. I don't want him to feel guilty. I simply want him to understand if he hadn't saved me like I'm striving to save those women, I would have become one of them.

"Please, Nikolai," I beg, incapable of ignoring the glint in his eyes that reveals he isn't the man his police record portrays. A monster raised him, but he is not a monster. He knows right from wrong.

"*Ангел...*"

His tone indicates he doesn't appreciate my continued arguing, but I don't back down. The women trapped don't deserve to be imprisoned by Vladimir any more than he did his entire childhood.

He is now free from the torment, so can't they be as well?

I glance up at him with the same promise in my eyes I had

when he carried me out of the room where he claimed a life just to keep me safe. I issue him silent pledge after silent pledge that his gallantry will be rewarded tenfold if he does this one last thing for me. He already owns my body, mind, and spirit, but if he does this, he will also own my heart.

"Please." I give it one last shot.

Relief floods me when he nods for the briefest second. After muttering a Russian cuss word under his breath, he diverts his focus to a group of men surrounding him as they wait for further instructions.

Faster than I can blink, three members of his crew start clearing the first two corridors on our right, and Nikolai and I head for a third bank of rooms on our left.

"We have five minutes, Justine. Any longer than that, they'll have to defend themselves." His tone is a cross between the man who makes me swoon beneath the sheets and the one who makes my knees clang together when he is engulfed by darkness. One is as appealing as the other.

Nodding, I direct him toward the doors I know have women trapped behind them because they're the ones I issued promises to during my daring escape.

The gasoline smell in the confined space is nauseating, but I press on. When we release them, the sheer relief on the ladies' faces makes more adrenaline surge through my body than it can handle. I'm physically shaking, but the tremors racking my body have nothing to do with fear. I am excited and, in all honesty, turned on.

There must be something wrong with me. Hours of solitude in the dark, damp-smelling room must have wreaked havoc in my head. Otherwise, what plausible reason could I have for my disturbing response?

I should be scared—or at the very least mortified—but no matter how hard I try to ignore the sensation thrumming in my veins, there is no denying it. I am far from scared.

I'm excited.

Shutting down my inner monologue for a more appropriate time, I follow Nikolai to a door that hasn't left my mind all night. The same frightened blue eye peers out of the keyhole, but she remains as silent as a mouse, fear rendering her speechless.

"Move away from the door," I instruct her in Czech when Nikolai points his gun at the large padlock holding her hostage.

Nikolai waits for the keyhole to darken before he pops a bullet into the lock. He then kicks open the door, leaving it hanging by its hinges. Seeing his strength in the flesh adds to the frantic quiver of my pulse.

"Stay behind me, Justine," he instructs before he enters the sooty-smelling space. My safety is always his utmost priority.

When I enter the room on his heel, I spot a very skinny and grubby young girl, who couldn't be any older than nineteen, sitting in the corner of the room. Her arms are curled around her shuddering legs, and her face is buried between her knees.

"It's okay. We won't hurt you," I assure her in Czech, cautiously approaching her.

"Not too close, *Ангел*," Nikolai warns, cautious about what her response may be.

Nodding so he's aware I heard him, I slowly close the gap between the blonde and me. Although she remains huddled on the ground, the absolute terror blanketing her eyes dulls every second we share the same air. She knows we're not here to hurt her. She's just lost the ability to trust anyone.

"The devil is dead. He can't hurt you anymore." I glance into her eyes, issuing my promise with the same guarantee Nikolai gave me.

Her hollow eyes bounce between mine for what feels like hours, but it is mere seconds before she accepts the hand I'm offering.

Tears prick my eyes when I feel how brittle her skin is. I don't know how long she's been trapped here, but if her sunken eyes and translucent skin are anything to go by, she's been trapped in this room for weeks, if not months.

"*Děkuji*," she praises on repeat, her thanks completely unnecessary but beautiful to hear.

She glances into Nikolai's eyes without any hesitation crossing her face, proving today is the first time they've met. "*Děkuji. Děkuji mnohokrát*," she thanks him, her eyes brimming with tears.

The pure joy on her face when she gingerly walks into the corridor forces moisture to my eyes. Her steps down the rickety stairs are frail... until she spots an equally battered and wide-eyed female standing at the warehouse's entrance.

Gasping loudly, she gallops down the last three steps before throwing her arms around the shoulders of a woman with undeniably similar features.

Curling his hand around mine, Nikolai directs me toward Trey near a bank of blacked-out SUVs at the front of the property. Although I want to learn the identity of every man who saved me, I can't take my eyes off the women we rescued. Even with the threat of danger still prominent, they are all smiling, their happiness too immense to contain.

They're not the only ones looking like lunatics.

I can't stop grinning either—or shaking.

"Is this everyone?" Nikolai asks Trey, who I'd guess to be in his mid-twenties.

Trey ushers two frazzled women into the back of the SUV he is standing next to before nodding. "Yes. But we need to move quickly." The ringing of sirens in the distance underscores his request. "Where do you want them taken?"

"Take them to Clarks, but no one is to move until I say so," Nikolai instructs before he scans the dozen or so men surrounding us. "Where's Rico?"

My eyes rocket to Nikolai. Shock is all over my face. He didn't say Rico, did he? That's the name of his brother—his deceased brother. Rico is a common name, but Nikolai's tone dipped when he articulated it, indicating that Rico is more important to him than a standard member of his crew.

Smiling at my slack-jawed expression, Trey replies, "He's getting our guest ready for transport." His smile increases as he nudges his head to his right.

My heart kicks into a mad beat when I follow the direction of his gaze. Malvina is guided down the stairs by a handsome man with inky-black hair and defined facial features. Her hands are bound behind her back, and her mouth is covered with the same industrial-strength tape used to tether my hands together earlier today.

Even with Nikolai's impressive body sheltering half her face, I can't miss her eyes widening with every step she takes. She is panicked, and rightfully so. She should be.

The furious growl Nikolai releases while guiding me into the lead SUV reveals he's aware Malvina's role in my kidnapping was as big as his father's. It also adds to the excitement caking my skin with sweat.

Just like with the women smiling in the middle of a war zone, the responses he elicits from my body could never be harnessed no matter how dire the conditions. Nothing could scare me away from Nikolai—not even witnessing him killing the man who raised him. He killed Vladimir to save me. I can't judge him for that.

It's the fight of my life to keep my backside glued to my seat when Malvina is shoved into the space across from me. The only reason I do is because the shriek of sirens grows louder with every second ticking by. We have mere minutes before this compound is inundated with police.

Once the dark-haired man with piercing brown eyes slides into the vacant seat next to Malvina, Nikolai signals for the driver to go. The tires of the SUV spin on the mud-slicked surface for several seconds before we rocket into the pitch-black night.

For every quarter of a mile we travel, the fainter the sound of police sirens becomes. I writhe uncontrollably in my seat, powerless to ignore the excitement lacing my veins, much less the heady smell of testosterone lingering in my nostrils. I thought I understood Nikolai's world, but the thrill of it is beyond anything I've ever experienced.

It's like watching a horror movie right at the gory part. You know something terrible is about to happen, but no matter how often you beg your eyes to look away, they remain glued to the screen, fearful of missing a moment.

The events leading to us fleeing the scene of a crime were immoral and unjust, but I can't act innocent. I knew what I was signing up for the instant I laid eyes on Nikolai. I was just unaware I'd be open to the violence I knew he was a part of.

28

NIKOLAI

Resolute silence falls over the Popov compound when I walk into the foyer hand in hand with Justine.

Seeing Justine alive and in one piece tells my crew everything they need to know.

A new king has been crowned, and he has his queen at his side.

Any chance of misconceiving the new reign flies out the window when Rico enters the foyer, lugging a red-faced Malvina.

Shock hangs heavily in the air as the silence shifts to murmured hums, my crew equally stunned and frightened by Rico's return.

"Go." Rico nudges his head to the stairwell that leads to the sleeping quarters on the second floor. "Take care of Justine. Trey and I will get everything under control down here."

Trey's lips quirk as he nods his agreement with Rico's plan. "We know where to find you if we need you."

I nod at their suggestion, not the least bit concerned by the demand in Rico's tone. He must be on his toes, or my men will eat him alive. It's lucky he's more than capable of taking care of himself. Justine, on the other hand, hasn't stopped shaking since we entered the SUV nearly thirty minutes ago.

I don't know if she's in shock or having a hard time working through the adrenaline pumping into her tiny frame.

Whatever it is, I won't leave her side until the woman I see behind her shield reemerges, hopefully more potent than ever.

"Take care of everything but her," I demand, my eyes straying from Trey to Malvina. "We've got a few matters to discuss before she returns to Russia. *If* she returns to Russia."

Malvina swallows harshly, her pupils expanding.

I wait for Rico and Trey to acknowledge my command before I lead Justine toward the stairwell.

Although Justine weakens me, I keep my head high as we move by the thirty or so suspicious pairs of eyes gawking at us. Now is not the time to show vulnerability. Vladimir is dead, but the fight is only just beginning. My family has lived by the same rules for the past three hundred years, but all good leaders know rules are meant to be broken.

As news of Vladimir's death circulates, my list of challengers will grow. This is not an assumption. It is a given. My opponents are smart men, but they will do their best not to underestimate me. I am well aware they only encouraged me to oust Vladimir with the hope it would open opportunities for them in our industry.

It won't.

I didn't solely dethrone Vladimir as a means of keeping Justine safe. I intend to take his place, meaning the Popov entity will continue to rule the West Coast and thrive under my command.

If my competitors believe removing Vladimir from his throne has compromised my crew, they will be taught a harsh lesson. My men are the strongest they've ever been, an unstoppable force that will have no qualms reminding those who double-cross me of the consequences of their disrespect.

Whether I'm seen as a mafia prince or a king, disrespecting me carries the punishment of death. Vladimir's dethroning hasn't altered that fact.

"Bring us food and water," I instruct a group of housemaids watching my trek across the expansive foyer with ashen faces and moisture-filled eyes.

Don't underestimate their dour response. They aren't shedding tears of sadness—they're relieved. Vladimir was a cruel man who had many enemies. Most were direct descendants. He governed our family with an iron fist, meaning not even those closest to him will mourn his loss. He raised me, yet I feel nothing.

Not remorse.

Not guilt.

Nothing.

I don't know what I expected to feel upon confirmation of his death, but I anticipated it to be something greater than nothing.

Upon entering my bedroom, Justine gasps. That's the first noise she's made in the past forty minutes.

The reason for her sigh is exposed when I spot some of her belongings scattered sparingly around my space.

"Roman," I explain to her shocked gaze.

The instant I denied Roman's repeated request to join our raid tonight, his focus would have shifted in another direction. He knew I would stop at nothing to bring Justine home, so he made sure everything was ready for her return.

"My parents," Justine garbles when her eyes zoom in on her family portrait sitting on my bedside table. She swallows several times to relieve her parched throat before asking, "Do they know I'm still in Vegas? My dad was going to pick me up at the airport. Oh god, I need to call them. They'll be panicked out of their minds."

She stops scanning my room for a phone when I dig my cell out of my pocket. Although I had Roman update her parents on the delay in her return home, I'm sure they'd rather hear it directly from Justine.

"Thank you," she faintly whispers, accepting my phone.

While dialing a number she knows by heart, she paces to my bed and then sits down. I watch her in silence, both proud and in shock. I'm proud of how controlled and serene she is, but shocked at how naturally she fits into my private space.

It's so natural seeing her here. It is like she has always belonged here—a queen in her palace.

Over the next twenty minutes, I try to keep my interest away from Justine's conversation. I fail. Discretion has never been a strong point for me—most notably when it comes to Justine. She tells her parents on repeat that she is safe and blames her lack of contact on a dead cell battery.

Every white lie spilled from her lips adds to the red hue on her nape. I don't blame her for lying, though. With one child already incarcerated, the last thing her parents need to hear is that she was just freed from her own prison.

After promising to call them at a more appropriate time tomorrow, Justine disconnects her call. Hating the tears glistening in her eyes, I stab out my half-smoked cigarette into an ashtray before pulling her into my chest. She is shaking even more now.

"They were so worried," she murmurs, her warm breath tickling my neck.

"They weren't the only ones." I keep my tone low, ensuring she won't hear me. She doesn't need more weight added to the guilt on her shoulders.

We stay huddled together for the next ten minutes. I've barely had a moment of quiet my entire life, so this should feel out of the ordinary. It doesn't. It's nice. Actually, it's more than fucking nice. It's great. I've got my woman in my arms, my crown on my head, and my life back.

It can't get better than this.

At one point today I was worried I'd never hold her in my arms again, so even with lust building between us like an out-of-control wildfire, I keep my arms glued to her waist and my lips pressed against her sweat-slicked temple.

It's a fucking challenging feat.

I crave this woman like a drug, and every hit adds to my addiction.

"I can't stop shaking," Justine murmurs a short time later, her jitters resonating in her tone.

"It's the adrenaline. I didn't sleep for three days after my first raid because I was so hyped up."

She peels her head off my chest. "So this is normal?" she asks, her eyes bouncing between mine. "I'm not... *weird?*"

The unease in her voice makes me smile. "No, *Ангел*, you are not weird." I stroke her cheek with my finger, easing the worry in her eyes. My chest puffs high when my meager touch heats her face enough that the faint bruise on her left cheek fades. "Why would you think you are weird?"

The deepness of my tone can't hide the desire in my voice. My response can't be helped. I'm barely touching her, but her body is responding as if I'm balls deep inside her. Her eyes are wide and brimming with lust, and the intoxicating scent of her cunt is lingering in the air. If her mental well-being wasn't my primary focus, the only shaking she'd be doing would be the result of ecstasy.

"I'm just... Ah..." Justine grazes her teeth over her bottom lip, causing my cock to twitch. "I'm kind of horny," she murmurs in quick succession, her words coming out in a flurry.

A growl rolls up my chest as my cock flexes against my zipper.

That wasn't a response I was anticipating.

Upon hearing my growl, Justine stills, her seductive scent amplifying. She fists my shirt, the yearning in her eyes indisputable.

"No, *Ангел*. Not yet." My words are rough, strangled by the lust clutching my throat.

Denying her is more complex than any challenge I've faced, but her needs must be placed before my own. She walked through the gates of hell today, so until I'm confident the endorphins roaring through her body are solely due to lust, I can't answer the silent plea in her eyes.

I know from experience that one wrong move tonight could set her recovery back by months, so I'm not willing to risk her sanity just to have her screaming my name.

"Nikolai—"

"No, *Ангел*," I interrupt, my tone leaving nothing off the table. My reply wasn't a suggestion. It was a command. "I will feed you, shower you, then put you to bed, but I will not fuck you. Not tonight."

Justine groans, making my cock thicken more. It wasn't a groan of disappointment. It was a groan of a woman on a mission. She knows what she wants and is as determined as ever to get it.

I love that about her. Her spirit. Her fight. Her insatiably greedy cunt that gets needier with every pounding I give it.

Mercifully, I'm saved from breaking my pledge when a knock at the door breaks through the heady silence teeming between us. Justine groans for the second time in under a minute. This one is a groan of disappointment.

Smirking at her needy response, I move to the door. "By the bed," I instruct the two Popov housemaids on the other side.

Justine's eyes bulge when they wheel a large selection of food and beverages across the wooden floorboards of my room. The wheels on the trolley have barely stopped spinning when she plucks a bread roll out of a basket and tears it apart.

"Mmm..." she moans as her eyes lift to the women serving her. "This is so good. Thank you so much."

The two stout ladies balk for the quickest second before dipping their chins in thanks for Justine's praise.

Compliments are a rarity in the Popov compound.

Once they remove the protective film from the mountain load of food they've supplied, they exit the room without so much of a glance in my direction.

Eye contact has never been highly favored, either.

"Not too much sugar." I command, pacing over to stand next to her. "Sugar and adrenaline are a lethal combination."

Justine rolls her eyes before popping a *картофель пирожное* into her mouth. The moan she releases when the fatty carbs melts on her tongue has my cock thickening all over again.

"Oh my god, what is that?"

She doesn't wait for me to answer her question before she devours another *ккартофель пирожное*, closely followed by another, then another.

"You better hurry, Nikolai, or you'll miss out," she garbles through a mouthful of food, her husky tone revealing food isn't the only item she is offering for me to devour.

Pretending I can't feel my cock knocking against the zipper of my jeans, I sit on the edge of my bed, happy to watch her eat. With my stomach still dealing with that weird, twisty feeling I've had most of the day, I'm not hungry.

Furthermore, I need a moment to determine why my hands are still shaking. Justine is alive and well, standing right in front of me, but the shudder in my hands is undeniable. It is as strong now as when I first saw her with a noose around her neck.

Maybe that's why my adrenaline is the strongest it's ever been. From seeing Justine taunted to the brink of insanity in the same room that drove me insane.

"A new dawn, a new day," Justine murmurs.

With her eyes glued to the sun rising on the horizon, she nuzzles into my chest. Since I don't have any patio furniture, we're sitting on the concrete floor of my balcony, taking in the sunrise as I have nearly every day for the past thirteen years.

It is barely 5 a.m., and the heat is disgusting, but nothing will stop me from watching the sunrise this morning. The only time I missed seeing the birth of a new day were the days I spent with Justine last week. I didn't need to appreciate another day amongst the living when the very definition of life was directly in front of me.

Curling her arm around my waist, Justine draws herself closer to me. She burrows her head into the groove in the middle of my chest, the hunger for friction on her skin unmissable in her fire-sparked eyes. I run the back of my fingers down her arm, relishing the goosebumps that follow in my wake.

I kept my word of feeding her, showering her, and putting her to bed without fucking her. Let me tell you, it was a fucking hard feat. Justine is my drug of choice. The more I denied myself, the greater my cravings became. But I did it. I kept my word—*barely!*

Although we didn't sleep, the past five hours were as beneficial to Justine as rest. The shakes hampering her tiny frame have eased dramatically, and the adrenaline in her blood began tapering off nearly an hour ago. We haven't directly discussed the outcome of tonight's event, but we worked through Justine's concerns in a remarkably mature way.

I'm not a fan of Q&A. I generally avoid interrogations like they're the plague, but my stomach became less knotted for every question I answered. The shake in my hands remains, but that could be due to keeping them away from Justine. I crave her more than my lungs wish to breathe. One taste will never suffice.

"Nikolai?" Justine croons, her voice as sweet as the treats she devoured earlier tonight.

I hated my name growing up, but I love how it rolls off Justine's tongue. Her voice is sweet and sexy, and it sends a pleasing zap straight to my balls.

"Yes, *Ангел*," I answer, my restraint pulsating in my tone.

She peers into my eyes, the lusty gleam in them as pleading as ever. There's a slight variation to the look they've held all night. They don't solely have the glimmer of a lady being led by her desires. They're pleading on behalf of her heart as well.

Fuck—she is beautiful.

Innocent, yet tempting.

Dangerous, yet safe.

Mine, and only mine.

When she feels the effect she has on my body digging into her curvy ass, her cheeks inflame with heat. She runs her teeth over her bottom lip, acting innocent.

She can't act coy. She knows the power she has over me, as she has relished every shameful squirm I've done while fighting the urge to touch her.

That's why she doesn't need to utter a syllable for me to hear her thoughts. I can see them in her eyes and smell them on her skin. She craves me as addictively as I need her.

"I always knew there were devilish thoughts in your mind, *Ангел*," I mutter, my tone half wrathful, half playful.

I'm not angry at her. I'm just annoyed by how weak she makes me.

For the first time in my life, I'm trying to treat her with the respect I've never shown women, but instead of encouraging my honorable intentions, she is rebelling against them.

I understand her motives. I know better than anyone the struggle of denying yourself your greatest wish—I did it numerous times the first night I stayed at Justine's apartment—but I also know if I make one wrong move, I could fuck everything up. I don't want to do that, so I will keep my word no matter how often she begs.

"Please, Nikolai. I need you," Justine murmurs, issuing the same heart-stabbing plea she's given many times tonight.

"No, Ангел. Not yet," I grind out, my short reply incapable of hiding the volatility in my voice. "I will take you when I am good and ready, not when I'm forced to."

My back molars smash together. I didn't mean for my words to come out as they did. They were rough and full of command, not a tone I should be using on a woman I'm trying to keep away from the edge of insanity.

"Justine," I mutter when she pulls away, the look on her face anything but pleasant. "I'm tired and lashing out."

"Tired?" Justine replies, the anger in her voice shocking me. "Or are you just not liking what you see anymore?"

When I remain quiet, unsure of what she means, she unknots the satin belt cinched around her waist. Her kimono slips off her body with a soundless whoosh, amplifying the pin-drop silence surrounding us.

I fist my hands at my side, my fight not to touch her ramping up to a level I've never experienced. Her lush tits fall heavily to her chest, and her wet slit is displayed in ball-clenching detail directly in front of me.

I want to eat her until she is screaming my name. I want to fuck her until her nails make my back bleed, but I also want to protect her from the torment I experienced thirteen years ago.

So instead of crossing the first two items off my wish list, I stand from the ground and then say, "No, Ангел."

Grief crosses her features as her lips quiver. "I knew it. You're embarrassed that everyone knows you sacrificed everything for me, a marked-up half a woman."

"What the fuck?" I reply, my voice so loud I'm confident the entire compound heard it. "Nothing about you embarrasses me."

"Then why won't you touch me?" she sobs, her voice as loud as mine.

"Because I am doing everything in my power to keep you sane! That's why I won't touch you! It has nothing to do with the way you look and everything to do with keeping you out of the hell I've been living the past thirteen years!"

A tear rolls down her cheek when she shakes her head, denying my defense with stubborn determination. "If you don't like what you see, Nikolai, we may as well end things now..."

Her words trail off when I yank at the waistband of my boxer shorts, dropping them to my knees. When my cock springs free, it slaps my stomach, its firmness so uncontained that the veins feeding it are as furious as my heart rate.

"Does this look like the reaction of a man who doesn't like what he sees?" I ask, my words as hot-tempered as my face. "I'm not torturing myself because I don't want you. It is because your well-being is the *only* thing stopping me from hunting down the men who bid on you and slitting their fucking throats."

Justine doesn't balk at my confession. She doesn't even glower at me. She keeps her eyes locked on me, the lust in them deepening with every syllable I speak.

"And believe me, I won't kill them because I'm embarrassed they saw your scars, you are way beyond fucking perfect. I'm going to slit their throats because they saw in you what I see. They saw what is only *mine* to see. They saw you—my *Ангел*!" I bang my chest with my fist, its hollowness unknown from the rapid beat of my heart. "Mine."

She stills as the tension in the air turns roasting. I don't need to say any more than I have. She knows I'm telling the truth. That's why my hands won't stop shaking. My desire to kill is at its greatest. I'm not embarrassed my competitors have seen her scars. I'm mad as hell she was in that predicament to begin with.

But since my desire to protect her is more intense than my wish to kill, I can't react to their insolence.

Not yet.

Not until I'm assured she is safe.

Then they will regret the day they ever placed a bid on her.

I will hunt down every one of them, and I will kill them. It isn't a probability. It's a fact. Protecting Justine doesn't just extend to those who physically harm her. It is also for the men and women responsible for keeping her guarded. I want her free, and no amount of bloodshed will stop me from achieving that.

"The men who bid on you will pay for their error, but not until I am assured you are okay first. You are my number one priority. Nothing will *ever* change that. Not revenge. Not power. *Nothing.*"

Justine connects her eyes with mine, the adoration in them thickening my cock to the point it is painful. "Just like nothing can lessen my desire for you, Nikolai. Not insanity. Not a man with the heart of Satan. *Nothing.* I am not me unless I am with you, so not touching me in the hope of keeping me sane is pointless because not having your hands on me is enough to drive me mental."

As quickly as our disagreement began, it ends. Our bodies collide with brutality, our hunger for one another no longer capable of being restrained.

I growl into Justine's mouth, equally annoyed and relieved she broke my restraint. I'm dying to touch her, but I must tread carefully. At the first sign of distress, I'm out. I can't hurt her any more than I already have.

When we fall to the floor, I stretch out my arm, catching our bodies as we tumble. Justine's giggles tickle my mouth before her tongue adds to the tingling sensation dancing across my face. She darts her tongue between my lips before dragging it along the roof of my mouth, tasting the cinnamon roll we shared while watching the sunrise.

After I finish yanking my boxers down my legs, I assault her mouth with the same eagerness she is bestowing on me. Our kiss is as frantic as my need to drive her to the brink of ecstasy. One hit is never enough.

My toes flex on the polished wooden floor as I jerk my hips forward, ramming my cock inside her. Her breaths fan heavily on my neck when she moans through the sensation stealing the air from her lungs. Even with my desire to have her screaming my name at fever pitch, I watch her intently, evaluating every look crossing her face.

Assured I see nothing but pleasure beaming from her gorgeous features, I draw my cock back out of her tight pussy. Her insatiable cunt sucks at me, begging me to stay immersed in the warmth more capable of crippling me than my greatest enemy.

After adjusting the tilt of her hips, giving me unrestricted access to her lavish slit, I ram back inside her. Her nails claw at my back when I take her to the root of my cock. I slam into her harder, wanting her to mark my skin as deeply as she has scoured my heart.

To replace his scars with ones less painful.

"Your body was built for me. To be fucked by me. That's why we fit together so well. Your cunt was crafted by God for me, Justine."

The urge to drive her to climax triples when she huskily moans at the mention of her name. She loves it when I use her real name, but I prefer calling her *Ангел*, as she truly is my gift from heaven.

My *Ангел*—the only person capable of keeping me sane.

Cupping Justine's ass, I lift it off the ground, the inane need to fuck spurring me to take her harder and faster. I grind into her on repeat, loving the throaty moans rolling up her chest. The more I urge her to climax, the less knotted my stomach becomes. Only Justine can make me forget. Only she can strip revenge from my mind as quickly as she clears me of thoughts. When I am inside her, nothing but having her scream my name is on my mind.

Not. A. Single. Fucking. Thing.

"That's it. Nice and loud."

As Justine's clutch tightens on my back, her screams grow louder. I plunge into her faster, ensuring I roll my hips at the exact spot that drives her wild.

"Oh god, Nikolai. Oh..."

Her moans are muffled by my neck when she burrows her head under my chin to gnaw on my shoulder blade. I love fucking her so wildly she becomes senseless with lust, but I need to see her eyes to ensure I'm not hurting her. One wrong glimmer and our exchange will be over, no matter how much my cock objects.

Careful not to irritate the nasty bump on the back of her head I assessed in the shower earlier, I coerce Justine's eyes back to mine. She complies with my request without too much protest.

Cupping my sweaty jaw, she draws my head down to rest on hers, giving me unlimited access to her beautiful eyes. The love projecting from them doesn't match our exchange.

The speed of my pumps and the sting of her nails in my back

leave no doubt I am fucking her, but she is staring at me like I'm making love to her—like every pound of my cock is freeing her from insanity.

Perhaps what she said is true? Maybe my touch is the only thing needed to ensure she doesn't break as I did thirteen years ago.

Ignoring the urge to bang my chest like a caveman, I grip her slender thighs in my hands and guide them around my sweat-slicked waist.

The change in position allows me to drive into her deeper, ensuring every inch of my cock is caressed by her greedy cunt. Although we are fucking on the floor like wild animals, there's no hesitation in Justine's eyes. They are too filled with lust to let something as weak as worry enter the equation.

When her cunt ripples around me, squeezing the last of my constraint, I demand, "Give it to me. Come for me. I need to feel you quivering beneath me while screaming my name. I want your cunt milking my cock for its release as I pound into you."

Justine arches her back with a moan, her heels digging into my ass as she matches my thrusts grind for grind. A rough groan leaves my mouth when she cries my name on repeat, her wish to come resonating in her breathless moans.

"Nikolai..."

Pinning the top half of her body to the ground by her shoulder, I drive into her harder. I fuck her with violence, my hips like a piston, lethal and without constraint.

She grows slicker, hotter. As her cunt tightens around me, the lust in her heavy-lidded gaze grows and grows and grows until it reaches the point of detonation.

She orgasms with a hoarse moan, growling my name in a way that feels like hot lava is rolling through me. As an orgasm steam-rolls her into a hot, sticky mess, the heaviness of her eyelids becomes undeniable, but she keeps them open, electrifying the air with palpable energy.

"Fuck," I groan, fighting against her cunt tightening around me and wordlessly begging for my cum.

Incapable of denying her every wish, I grind into her another four times before the tingles gripping my sack eject into her in raring spurts.

"Nikolai..." Justine whispers in a soft cry as my climax stretches hers from one to two.

She stares up at me as her body works through the shudders enveloping every inch of her, the utter bliss on her face unmissable.

Fuck—why didn't I see this sooner?

Vladimir didn't make Justine crazy. I did.

30

NIKOLAI

My head lifts from glaring at a pack of cigarettes on my desk when awareness of being watched washes over me. Rico has his shoulder propped on the doorframe of my office. His eyes are drifting around the vast space, categorizing the changes I made to his domain after his "death" three years ago.

"Didn't like the glass furniture?" he mutters, stepping into the room.

I wait for him to slump into the chair across from me, before shrugging. "It was all right. It just didn't look too good after I took a bat to it," I reply, stabbing my half-smoked cigarette into an ashtray. When his dark brow slants, showcasing his confusion about my reply, I add, "Everyone handles grief differently."

My tone is low, hating the soft cock I've become the past week. I thought Justine was the only one who could alter my mindset. I realize now that isn't the case.

Rico has nearly as much influence over me as Justine does. He just does it in the same mind-fucking way our father always does.

Did, I mentally correct.

Rico's brows stitch as guilt crosses his face. "If I had known my decision would haunt you, Eli, I would have gotten word to you... *somehow*. I just didn't realize what was happening behind the scenes. I only saw what Vladimir wanted me to see."

"I know," I reply, my lips twisting as I struggle to hold in the rest of my retort. It's a pointless endeavor when I say, "But right now, none of that matters." I scrub my hand over my tired eyes before they drift to the wall separating my office from the room Justine is sleeping in. "She needs to remain my number one priority."

Even though I'm not looking at Rico, I know he is smiling. I can feel it in my bones.

"Never thought I'd see the day."

When my eyes swing back to Rico, he says, "You finally got your gift from heaven."

His shit-eating grin turns blinding when I nod. "Stick a fork in me. I am fucking done."

When he throws his head back and laughs, it feels like we've stepped back in time. I haven't heard him laugh like this since we were teens. Even then, it was infrequent.

Our childhood wasn't filled with trips to the playgrounds or fond memories. We were groomed to be killers with rules designed to break us more than teach us.

"Do you feel different?" I ask Rico when his laughter settles down, wondering if I'm the only one not registering Vladimir's death.

Don't get me wrong, the air of the Popov compound is the most vibrant it's ever been, but that hollow nothingness I've felt since we left the warehouse last night is still present.

Rico begins answering my question with a shrug. "I'll still check Eli's closet every night for the next few months. It all seems a little surreal at the moment."

I nod, agreeing with his assessment. I coasted past Vladimir's room twice this morning to ensure it was vacant, and I even made Maya sit in with Justine while she was sleeps to ensure her safety.

"Talking about surreal," Rico mutters, drawing my attention to him.

He balances on the end of his chair, his large frame looking oddly out of place on the rickety dining chair where Roman usually sits.

Roman wasn't happy when I ordered him home to rest this morning. He wanted to stay. He soon discovered that my change in title hasn't weakened my resolve in the slightest. He left with his front teeth—*barely!*

After digging out a piece of paper from his pants pocket, Rico slides it across the thin wooden desk between us. "Trey found this yesterday. Thought it might be of interest to you."

I take a moment to read his forthright eyes before glancing down at the sheet of paper. Although I never ventured into Vladimir's latest money scheme, I know what this document is. It is the contract Vladimir exchanges when buyers purchase his whores.

"What the fuck?" I growl when my eyes scan my name at the top of the contract.

Although my first question should be how over a million dollars got transferred from my account without my knowledge, it isn't. I'm just praying Justine never sees this document.

Justine was remarkably open about my business during the many discussions we had last night, but I could see in her eyes there was a fine line she will never cross when it comes to certain aspects of my lifestyle—most notably the whores we freed last night.

She asked at least five times what I planned to do with the women amassed by Vladimir's takeover. I answered her as honestly as I could. For now, they will sit at Clarks until the heat from Vladimir's dethroning dies down.

Although she wasn't happy about my plans of keeping the women detained, my promise that they will not be touched while under my watch eased her worry.

"This isn't me. I don't pay for whores," I defend, throwing the slip of paper onto my desk.

"I know. I've seen the way you look at Justine. You're as pussy-whipped as the rest of us." The seriousness of our conversation doesn't match Rico's snickering tone.

His grin grows larger when I immaturely roll my eyes. My eye roll stops halfway when he adds, "If you had heeded my warning four years ago, none of this would have happened. I always told you she was a money-grabbing whore."

I snap my eyes to his, wanting to ensure I'm not mishearing the accusation in his tone. "This was Malvina?" I ask, distrusting the story his eyes are relaying.

Rico's eyes drop to the document sitting between us before nodding. "Yep." His tone is as cocky as his facial expression.

Blood roars to my ears as I clench my fists. At Justine's request, Malvina's punishment wasn't going to be as severe as Vladimir's. Now, she may not be so lucky.

My mind strays from dangerous thoughts when Rico says, "You're not the only schmuck Malvina was pedaling money from for the sex trafficking trade. She's got a few men under her belt."

"Who?" I ask, incapable of harnessing my curiosity.

I barely know the man in front of me, but before our relationship went sideways, I knew Rico well enough to detect when he was hiding something from me.

Our relationship has a long, winding track to drive before it can be restored, but I'm confident he is keeping something from me.

He scrubs his hand over the stubble on his chin, its unkept appearance compliments of two days of no sleep. He's like me, incapable of sleeping until all our ghosts have been laid to rest. It's been a long-ass twenty-eight years.

"Andros," Rico eventually answers.

"Her father? Malvina has been swindling money from her father?" My tone is high with shock. Double-crossing Vladimir carries a sentence of death, but double-crossing Andros... There isn't a punishment worthy enough for that.

When Rico nods, I mumble, "She's dead. Andros loves his children... until they steal from him. Did she not learn from Marko's demise?"

"That's what Andros said when I updated him this morning," he informs me, his tone wary of how I will react at discovering he's been communicating with an associate behind my back.

I'd be worried if I hadn't seen the flare that brightened his eyes when he spoke of his son earlier. Furthermore, his wife would never survive in our industry, and he loves her enough he'd never force her into our life.

Rico was born a mafia prince.

Unlike me, he won't die a king.

"What terms did Andros state?"

I try to keep annoyance out of my tone. My attempts are below average. I'm not worried Rico wants his rightful title. I'm frustrated Malvina's punishment is being snatched from my grasp. Andros is a powerful man, one I want on my side as I transition from a prince to a king, so I have no choice but to accept any conditions he invokes.

"He wants you to send Malvina home." When I attempt to interrupt, he waves his hand through the air, cutting me off. "He said he understands your objective, but guarantees returning Malvina to Russia will be the best outcome for all involved. If you truly want to succeed Vladimir's reign, Eli, you must think smart. I know you want revenge for what your girl went through, but you've already got the sweetest reward." His eyes stray to the wall I was staring at earlier. "You've got your *Ангел*. What more do you need than that?" His accent is so thick his Russian heritage echoes in his tone.

I slump in my chair while considering his request. I want Malvina to feel the pain I went through watching Justine lie lifeless on the bloodstained floor that nearly claimed my life thirteen years ago, but I also promised Justine that she would want for nothing when she is mine. I can't keep my promise if I go against a man as powerful as Andros. Besides, the less cleanup I'm required to do from Vladimir's dethroning, the better.

"Very well. Send her home."

My eyes snap to Rico when he says, "Already done." My narrowed squint widens when he cheekily adds, "I may have taped her to the chair to ensure she didn't go anywhere this time." A pompous wink increases the gleam twinkling in his eyes.

I laugh. "What's your kitten going to think when she discovers you've been tying women up... *again?*" The jeering of my tone leaves no doubt of my playfulness. He may now be a family man, but he wasn't only a few short years ago.

His growl rumbles through my chest. "Blaire knows there's only one kitty I want purring beneath me. I don't care if it is three years or three hundred, I'll never get enough of her sexy purr."

His eyes are as dark and haunted as Vladimir's were, but when he talks about his family, a flare breaks through the darkness encompassing him.

He truly looks free.

"Then don't let me stop you," I say, standing from my seat. "Go get your kitten."

He hesitates for the quickest second when I offer my hand. It is unusual for me to show any signs of affection, much less release a man from this madhouse without chastisement, but the more Justine's attention pumps blood to my heart, the further I tiptoe away from insanity.

Accepting my gesture, Rico pulls my body into his chest. Although a desk is between us, the sentiment of his gesture can't be missed.

We're two brothers hugging out our indifferences.

"I can stay if you need me. Wait for the dust to finish settling," Rico murmurs into my ear, his tone conflicted. He hates being away from his wife and son as much as I hate being away from Justine for even a second.

"I'll be fine," I assure him. Thankfully, my tone is confident.

I've got a shit ton of rebuilding to do and a few matters I'd rather ignore for the next century, but nothing I'm set to face the next week will be more challenging than what we tackled head-on yesterday. With Rico's help, I got Justine back. He doesn't need to help me any more than he has already.

"If you change your mind, I gave Roman all my details."

I nod before slapping his back three times, requesting to be released from his firm grip. He holds on a little longer, either hoping I'll react to his jeering or not as eager to step away from our lifestyle the second time around as he was the first time.

After holding on to me long enough it starts getting awkward, he finally pulls away. "I'll give you a week," he advises, his tone a complete contradiction to the man who was practically humping my leg thirty seconds ago.

"For what?" I ask, unable to read the demand in his eyes.

He gathers a bag I didn't notice sitting at the entranceway of my office before returning his eyes to me. "To apologize to my wife. If you haven't called within a week, I'll be back, and this time, I won't go easy on you."

I huff as my ego awakens. He might be a few inches taller than me and a few pounds heavier, but I can take him. I've got grit on my side. I've got determination. I've also got my queen to protect. No one will take Justine away from me—not even myself.

A little over an hour has passed since I walked Rico to his car. His departure caused as many hushed whispers as his arrival did, but this time, they were void of malicious taunts.

He isn't a part of our business anymore, but he is my family, and disrespecting anyone in my family is as punishable as disrespecting me.

My men can be annoyed at Rico's deal with another devil as evil as Vladimir, but at the end of the day, his negotiation was no more disrespectful than the ones many of them have made over the years.

He wanted out of this lifestyle. He found a way out. That's courageous, not fearful. So, if anyone has a problem with me issuing him a full pardon from our family, they can bring it up with me. I'll be more than happy to show them what I think of insolence.

A tap at my door draws me out of my thoughts. I'm hoping it is Maya advising me Justine is awake, but I'm left disappointed when my eyes lock on Trey.

"We've got a problem at Clarks."

"Handle it," I demand, unwilling to leave Justine's side for even a minute.

Clarks is an off-site compound approximately two miles from the main house. With my crew amassing new members faster than the principal residence could handle, a set of bunker-type dorms were built on land fringing the property's borders.

Although the facilities at Clarks aren't as lavish as their original living conditions, my men prefer it over the massive mansion Vladimir commissioned in the early nineties. They have unlimited booze, drugs, and women. What more could they need?

"Can't," Trey replies, drawing my attention back to him.

Dropping my pen on the paperwork in front of me, I slouch back in my chair. This is the one thing I've always hated about my... *job*. It doesn't matter how my fortune is amassed. It is never done without a paper trail.

Even the shadiest men won't consider a deal unless they see a contract. It may be written in the blood of their loved ones, but they don't care. They still want everything in writing.

Although I'd like to forget this side of my industry for a week or two, my wealth is already taking a hit with the deal I made to secure the Yurys earlier this week. And considering my conversation with Alexei about his son being caught in the crossfire of a war he didn't belong in didn't go as well as I was hoping, I need to keep my associates happy.

Furthermore, Justine needs her sleep, so anything I can do to stop me from taking her while she is resting, I will do it. Even something as mundane as paperwork.

"Why can't you handle it?" I ask Trey, my tone jeering.

I've been grooming Trey as my second-in-command since the day he joined my crew. If he is incapable of handling a dozen or two whores, we're going to have an issue.

Trey swallows harshly, his Adam's apple bobbing up and down. "Because we need you... and your girl."

31

JUSTINE

"*Ангел...*"

I snuggle deeper into my pillow, praying the trickle of light filtering through my eyelids won't wake me from the deliriously intoxicating dream I'm having.

My fantasy is so believable I can smell Nikolai's virile scent lingering in my nostrils. It kicks my heart into a crazy beat and reawakens my libido.

Last night was tense, but it was also magical.

I was devastated when I thought Nikolai wasn't attracted to me anymore. I understood having his competitors see me in such an unflattering light would have been hard for him. I just hated that it drew a line between us.

Nikolai is often misunderstood, and that's what happened last night. I misread him completely, believing his desire not to touch me was more sinister than it was.

What he said last night, and the protectiveness radiating from his eyes... *Jesus*.

Discovering he was holding back his quest for revenge for me was mesmerizing. I've never felt more cherished than I did in that instant.

He wanted to hunt, but instead of tracking down the men who

caused me pain, he stayed with me. That proves what I've always known. He isn't just a man. He is an honorable one as well.

"Ангел..."

A trail of goosebumps rolls across my shoulders when a fingertip glides over my bare skin. Usually being snuck up on would cause me panic, but not an ounce of worry bombards me. I have no doubt who is touching me, as my body only responds like this to one man.

After taking one last long breath to relish Nikolai's unique scent, my eyes flutter open. The heat lighting up every inch of my body surges when my full gaze collides with his icy-blue eyes.

"Hey," I greet him, my voice groggy from just waking up. "How long have I been sleeping?"

I stop scanning the room for a clock when he replies, "A while. I didn't want to wake you, but I need your help."

I rise to a half-seated position. Nikolai isn't the type to need help, so the fact he needs mine immediately piques my interest.

He brushes a wayward curl from my face before saying, "The woman we released last night, the young blonde girl..." He waits for me to nod, acknowledging I'm aware of whom he's referring to before adding, "Could you understand what she was saying?"

Worry glistens in his eyes when I hesitantly nod. "She speaks in the Czech language."

When his brows tighten, I explain, "I can understand her. I'm just not as fluent in Czech as I am in Russian."

The crinkle between his brows smooths as a smile etches on his mouth. "Thanks for the reminder to be cautious about what I say in front of you," he mutters with an impish wink.

He rises to his feet and heads into his walk-in closet. The mattress creaking at the loss of his weight drowns out my disappointed moan.

There must be something wrong with me. The knock to my head yesterday must have screwed with my senses.

Yesterday was... *God.*

How do you put something so mammoth into a short sentence? It was frightening, electrifying, pulse-quickening, terrifying, inspiring, wrong, good, evil, bad. That's just a small handful of words I could use to describe the range of emotions I went through yesterday.

The first half of my experience was horrible, but deep down inside, I always knew Nikolai would save me, so it hasn't affected me in the same manner my first tussle with a mafia kingpin did. I feel invigorated, like nothing can tear me down.

Sliding across the mattress, I join Nikolai in his expansive walk-in closet. He rummages through a set of drawers at the end of the ample space but stops when he detects my presence.

Air hisses between his teeth when his eyes rake over my naked form. His reaction shocks me. He put me to bed naked, so he is more than aware I'm without clothes.

His gasping response makes sense when his eyes stop on my hands resting at my sides. For the first time since I was mauled by a dog four years ago, my hands aren't balled into fists. I'm standing before him as naked as the day I was born, but I don't feel an ounce of shame.

Wow.

"Look at you. Graced with the confidence of a queen." Nikolai's voice is so rough nothing but his Russian heritage rings true in his tone.

My heart smashes against my ribs when he heads my way. His steps are slow and tempting, and they set my pulse skyrocketing. He walks with arrogance, but in a way I can't help but swoon over. He is the true representation of good and evil wrapped up in one sinfully delicious package.

"Come to me, *Ангел*. Meet me halfway," he croons, his tone half demanding, half pleading.

My feet jump to the command in his voice before my brain can cite an objection—not that it was going to. My heart and head are still speaking the same language. They both want the same thing. They want Nikolai.

When I stop to stand in front of him, he curls his hand around my jaw before sealing his lips over mine. Unlike last night, we don't attack each other like wild animals. Our kiss is controlled and precise, tethering my heart to him even more.

It also proves I'm mentally unstable.

I've only known this man for weeks, but I am already falling for him so unequivocally I'm willing to do anything to have him in my life.

You'd think I'd be nervous about my silent pledge. I'm not.

Nikolai has proven time and time again he will stop at nothing to protect me, so I'll replicate his dedication. I protect what is mine, and Nikolai is mine.

After kissing me senseless, Nikolai aids me in getting dressed. I've lost count of the times I've smiled at his struggle to do the simplest tasks. It isn't that he finds zippers and buttons difficult. It is putting my clothing on me instead of ripping it off that he finds challenging.

"Soon, Nikolai. Very soon," I mock, mimicking his accent.

He rolls his eyes, acting unimpressed by my goading. It's all a fib. I saw the faintest tug of his lips, revealing he wasn't annoyed by my comment. He took it as a guarantee.

Curling his hand around mine, he guides me through his vast residence. There's a vivacity in the air that was missing last night. It reminds me of the first day of spring. Warm, yet not overbearing. It's quite peaceful, which is odd considering the events of last night.

As we exit a large flight of stairs, I smile a greeting to the two ladies who served me supper last night. I don't know what those little chunks of sugar and butter I consumed were, but they were delicious.

When the housemaids' eyes lock on mine and Nikolai's conjoined hands, they giggle like schoolgirls. Their laughter is infectious, spreading through the small group of women gawking at us like wildfire.

"If you're void of a task, I'm sure Igor can find you one," Nikolai grumbles in Russian, his tone a stark contradiction to the man kissing me speechless mere minutes ago. It is rough and full of command, leaving no question of his anger.

The foyer falls into silence as the women dart in all directions. I don't know who Igor is, but his reputation is fierce enough to scare the women.

"Don't defend them, *Ангел*," Nikolai warns when he spots the contempt brewing in my eyes. "If you lose the respect of one, you risk the respect of thousands. They're not employed to be your friends. They are here to serve you."

I'm not going to defend them. I just want to... ah... Okay, I was going to defend them. But not because I feel sorry for them. I merely wish to remind Nikolai not all women belong to one of two categories.

The more I drum that into his head, the better chance the women we rescued last night will be set free. Nikolai promised they would be unharmed and untouched under his watch, but the twisting in my stomach won't be relinquished until they are released from captivity.

I know deep down in my heart that Nikolai's reasoning for keeping the women isn't as sinister as some may believe. He isn't interested in using them for financial gain—the fortune he's amassed over the past ten years is mind-boggling. It is the repercussions he could face if he is seen as weak by his enemies.

So, although I'd like him to release the women without delay, I also understand his objective. I always knew our relationship would be an uphill battle, so I won't throw more obstacles in our way. Not yet.

My curiosity increases when our trek down the stairs of the Popov compound veers to the left. Usually we continue straight ahead. The smell of gasoline filters into my nose when we enter an industrial-sized shed hidden behind hedged greenery. The cause of the strange smell becomes clear when Nikolai directs me to a set of ATVs in the back right-hand corner.

After I close my gaping jaw, he says, "It is quicker to go over than around."

If he's anticipating his reply will ease my confusion, he needs to devise another tactic. I'm more confused now than ever.

Remaining quiet, Nikolai gathers a helmet from a stack on our left and then places it over my head. My heart gains an extra beat when he's extra attentive not to touch the bump Malvina's knock to the back of my head caused.

"What happened to Malvina?" I ask, incapable of harnessing my curiosity for a second longer.

Nikolai finishes securing the helmet to my head before answering, "I sent her back to Russia."

"You did?" I ask, astonishment echoing in my tone.

The retribution he issued his father was quick and precise, so I'm stunned he didn't handle Malvina in the same manner. Don't get me wrong, I don't believe he would have harmed Malvina. I just didn't think she would get off scot-free either.

Nikolai throws his leg over one of the ATVs before assisting me onto the seat behind him. Once I have my arms wrapped around his waist, he says, "The punishment her father will serve her will far outweigh any penalty I could have invoked."

His tone dips during his confession, indicating part of his statement was a lie, but since I can't see his eyes, I cannot determine which part.

"If I feel her punishment isn't severe enough, I will intervene, but until then, we must wait." He squeezes my thigh with his big, manly hand, shifting my focus to more pressing matters than his ex-fiancée and her poor judgment. "If you wish to speak with Malvina, I can arrange it."

Even though he can't see me, I shake my head. "I said everything to her I needed to say. Some of our conversation didn't need words, though."

The veins in my neck thrum. I am shocked by the cattiness in my voice. I'm glad yesterday's circumstances didn't result in a lapse of the confidence I've been accruing by the bucketloads the past week, but I'm still stunned by my self-righteousness.

My worry is pushed aside for need when he laughs. My god his laugh is sexy. It is deep and manly, and it encourages recklessness in me that I've never experienced.

"So you're the one responsible for the bruise on Malvina's face?"

Nikolai's tone indicates he's well aware of my answer, but feeling coy, I reply, "She attacked me. I retaliated."

I shrug like it's no big deal. At the time, being shot at and having my hair wrenched from my head wasn't my idea of fun. But right now, yesterday is far from my thoughts.

Nothing worries me when I'm with Nikolai. I know he'll always protect me. That and his soul-stealing eyes are two of his most beautiful assets. For a man raised without morals or integrity, he has them in abundance. He just doesn't realize it.

"Oh, *Ангел*," Nikolai growls, causing my pussy to quake. "You're even naughtier than I first perceived."

Gripping my thigh, he drags me forward, pinning my body to his. My erect nipples graze his back when I inhale deeply, sucking in his seductive scent.

Drunk on his intoxicating smell, I press my lips to his ear and whisper, "The good girls always want to tame the bad boys, but what happens when the good girl isn't quite as saintly as the bad boy believes?"

The throb in my pussy reaches fever pitch when Nikolai growls for the second time. I feel the rumble from my nipples to my aching pussy, making me needy and hot.

I writhe in my seat, my excitement uncontained, when he replies, "Then that makes the bad boy the luckiest motherfucker around."

32

NIKOLAI

Justine remains quiet most of our trip. Although the landscape surrounding Clarks isn't as lush as the rolling turf and edged greenery of the Popov compound, it has its own unique qualities that make it just as appealing.

The rough Las Vegas conditions and I have a lot in common. We are both harsh and rugged on the outside, but we could be something great with a little bit of TLC.

Hearing my ATV rolling over the dirt hill that shrouds Clarks from prying eyes, Trey and an additional dozen or so members of my crew emerge from the main living quarters.

Although I haven't officially taken stock of the number of men I lost last night, I'm glad to see the morale of my crew is as strong as ever. They're smoking cigars and drinking whiskey, a regular Sunday afternoon occurrence in this neck of the desert.

After pulling my ATV to the side of the compound, I assist Justine in removing her helmet. Her pupils are massive, nearly filling her entire cornea, and her mouth hangs ajar.

Her response is understandable. Clarks looks like a government agency set up shop in the desert. If she is worried she's about to have a run-in with the law, she doesn't need to be concerned. Nothing lawful is done here.

Not a single fucking thing.

I place Justine's helmet on the seat of the ATV before gathering her hand in mine. My men act as shocked as the Popov housemaids when they saw me walking through the Popov mansion with Justine. Just like the whores who transitioned into housemaids, my crew has never seen me with a woman before—well, not holding her hand, anyway.

Their shock isn't only from my unusual display of affection, though. It's from bringing someone I've only known for a little over a week into an area reserved solely for people I trust.

Usually no one gets within sniffing distance of this compound without my thorough once-over. And even then, the chances of them gaining access are still low. But Justine has my trust. I don't know when she gained it or how long she has had it, but I trust her.

Justine's eyes go wild as we shadow Trey to the back of the compound. My interests are as piqued as hers. I'm not just scanning our surroundings, though. I'm watching Justine, gauging her reaction to a side of my life she has yet to experience. She's about to see me at my worst: warts and all.

Just like the first time I laid eyes on her, Justine continues to surprise me. She doesn't bat an eyelid at the obvious drug shipment in the first lot of shipping containers we stroll by.

Her nose screws up at the scantily clad whores entertaining a group of men in a resort-sized hot tub, and her grip on my hand tightens when we proceed through the weaponries room, but not once does a look of disgust cross her face.

I told Rico I got the tiger. Justine just sealed my pledge.

When we enter a bunker in the bottom left-hand corner of the compound, I yank Justine behind me, blocking her view of the blonde Czech woman we rescued last night holding a shard of glass to her neck. She has stabbed the jagged edge into her throat so profoundly that a large puddle of blood is circling the collar of her shirt.

"What the fuck, Trey?" I growl, furious he'd put Justine in this situation.

I'm not worried about Justine's safety. My men stationed in the corner of the room will take out the blonde in an instant if she moves for Justine, but after everything Justine went through yesterday and last weekend, I don't want more gore added to her memory bank.

"She doesn't speak English, and your girl speaks multiple languages, so I figured it wouldn't hurt to know what her demands are," Trey answers, his rattling tone advising he is aware we'll have a word after this. Like Justine's conversation with Malvina, not all our talk will involve words.

"We don't negotiate with whores." I lower the severity of my tone when Justine's nails dig into my palm, her annoyance at my response issued without a syllable slipping from her lips. "We tell them what to do, and they either listen or die."

My growled reply is slightly exaggerated, but I give it my all since I'm testing Justine's reaction to my lifestyle. I haven't dealt with the sex trafficking trade in years. It's not that profitable, and in all honesty, it's never interested me.

I don't understand why men pay for women when there are plenty willing to submit of their own free will. Some even enjoy being smacked around, so they can't use that as an excuse for opening their wallets.

I stop glaring at Trey when Justine's singsong voice trickles into my ears.

"What?" I ask, the blood roaring through my veins affecting my hearing.

She licks her dry lips before repeating, "She wants her sister. She keeps saying *sestra*. That means sister."

Justine's brows inch together as she pricks her ears. Although my body is sheltering her from the visual of the blonde attempting to take her life, her repeatedly shouted pledge can't be ignored.

"Her sister was here last night but vanished this morning. She wants to know where she went," Justine mumbles a short time later.

"Her sister was here last night?" I double-check, wanting to ensure she's confident in her interpretation. The blonde is speaking so fast I'm shocked Justine can understand her words.

Justine takes a moment to listen to the woman's pleas for the second time before nodding, the confidence in her eyes undeniable.

"She's adamant her sister was sleeping next to her last night, but when she woke this morning, she was gone."

I wait for Justine to see the gratitude in my eyes before they drift to Trey. Her eyes reveal she's uncomfortable but has set aside her fear of blood to help both me and the blonde.

"Where is her sister?" I ask Trey.

While rubbing a kink in his neck, Trey shrugs. "I don't know. Nearly every nationality is covered in this room, but none of the girls speak English."

"How many women did you bring here last night?" I continue to interrogate, my voice speeding up with annoyance.

I'm not pissed at Trey. I'm annoyed I've been left to clean up Vladimir's mess. This is one of many I'll face in the next six months. I had no idea how much of a shamble our operation was in until I started looking at the paperwork this morning. It will take me months, if not years, to get things back on track.

"Seventeen," Trey answers after a quick mental calculation. "Six each in the first two SUVs and four in the last."

"That's sixteen." I glare at Trey, allowing my eyes to issue my scorn. *Fucking moron.*

Trey's throat works hard to swallow before he mumbles, "One rode with me."

I arch my brow, shocked by his admission. Trey would never disobey my direct order, so I know he didn't keep one of the whores for himself, but the fact he's segregating one woman from the group is unusual for him.

"She reminded me of India," he admits softly, his words only for my ears.

The weak, pitiful beat of my heart grows an extra thump from his admission. India is the one girl Trey wanted but could never have. He nearly died trying to make her his. I benefited from India's family's stupidity. After nursing Trey back to health, he rewarded my dedication with his full loyalty.

After dipping my chin in understanding, I run my eyes over the room, counting only sixteen women in a space that could house thirty.

I can tell the exact moment Trey reaches the same number as me. His pupils widen as his throat works hard to swallow.

"I told you not to move until I said so."

My furious growl startles the fifteen women huddled in the corner of the room. The only person who doesn't balk is Justine. Her pulse raging through our conjoined hands quickens as her warm breath hits my neck.

If I didn't know any better, I'd swear my anger turns her on. It's a pity I know better. I promised her the women we saved last night would remain untouched under my command, and Justine is aware I am a man of my word.

"I didn't," Trey replies, the truth in his eyes strengthening his admission. "I told Rory to sit on them until you gave us word on what you wanted done with them."

I scan the room, seeking Rory amongst my men. He's nowhere to be found. The tic in my jaw turns manic as anger reddens my face. If Rory has denied my direct order, I'll fucking kill him, because he isn't just stopping me from keeping my promise to Justine. He's making a mockery of me in front of my men. That isn't something I will stand for. Not in a million years.

"Watch Justine," I command Trey before pivoting on my heels.

Justine tugs on my arm, but I shrug out of her hold. I'm not angry at her. I'm fighting to keep my crown. In this industry, you're nothing without respect. If I let one man get away with disobedience, I'll be dethroned by the end of the week.

Rory's punishment will warn my crew. They will be punished if they fail to adhere to my direct order. I don't care if they're ranked number two or two hundred. If I give them an order, they better follow it or lose their life.

I search nearly every room in the compound before I find Rory. As suspected, he's holed up in bed with a petite blonde who looks similar to the one holding a shard of glass to her neck.

The anger blindsiding me doubles when my eyes zoom in on a singed spoon and used needle on a bedroom dresser.

"So you didn't just ignore *my* directive. You spaced her out on *my* drugs as well?"

Rory jackknifes to a half-seated position, batting the barely coherent blonde away from his hardened crotch in the process. "Ah... Nikolai. This isn't what it looks like," he stammers out, his words laced with fear.

I slant my head to the side and arch my brow. "It isn't?"

He shakes his head, the terror on his face unmissable. He should be scared, because no matter how many times I tell my brain the woman lying half-lifeless on the bed isn't Justine, it doesn't listen.

If the FBI hadn't been surveilling one of my competitors, Hunter might have never discovered Justine's auction. Then, if I hadn't gotten to her in time, she could have been that blonde or one of the other sixteen women sitting scared in the bunker.

Just the thought of her being drugged and treated like a whore has my anger reaching a record-breaking high.

"You not only disrespected me, you disrespected my *Ангел*. Disrespecting her warrants the punishment of death." My words are so volatile I don't even recognize my own voice.

I charge for Rory before he has a chance to blink. He barely puts up a protest when I drag him out of his bed by clutching his throat. Pinning him to the wall with one hand, my other throws back-to-back jabs into his unprotected face.

The brutal connection of my fist to his cheek makes blood gush from his nose and mouth, but I don't back down. He isn't merely being disciplined for denying my order. He's being served the punishment I was unable to give Vladimir.

Vladimir is dead, but his sentence wasn't severe enough. I wanted him to feel the pain I went through when he ordered my torture all those years ago. I wanted him to experience the agony that shredded my heart into pieces when I saw Justine with a noose around her neck. But more than anything, I wanted to look him in his eyes when he took his last breath so he could see the relief in mine.

I'll never regret putting Justine's safety above my need for revenge, but I'll always regret that Vladimir's death was painless. He deserved to be tortured. He deserved an inhumane death. He didn't deserve to go as easily as he did.

I continue pummeling Rory with my fists, my strength growing with every hit I submit. From the way he's choking on the blood flooding his lungs, I know I'm moments away from killing him, but I don't stop. I can't stop. The devil within me has been unleashed, and nothing can stop it.

Nothing but her.

"Enough, Nikolai," commands a voice at my side.

The shakiness of Justine's words is incapable of hiding her strength. She is so strong that even seeing me at my worst can't weaken her resolve.

"You taught him a lesson. He won't defy you again."

My next two hits aren't as robust as my prior two. I'm not tired of the fight—a natural-born killer never grows weary of the hunt.

I'm exhausted from the mental strain. Staying one step ahead of the game is fucking exhausting, and I've been striving to stay ahead for over thirteen years. I'm tired.

"Nikolai..." The plea in Justine's voice stops my fists midair. "I need you."

Rory slumps to the floor with a thud when I release him from my grasp to turn toward Justine. The spark her eyes held last night remains resilient as she silently coerces me to her will.

Only she can break through the evil encompassing me.

Only she can make me see sense through the madness.

Justine walks into the room that smells like death and desecration, her eyes never leaving mine. Her face pales with every step, but the fire within her roars. The woman I see behind her shield is thriving, dying to break free.

"Come to me, Nikolai. Meet me halfway," she pleads, her voice as heavenly as ice-cold lemonade on a scorching-hot day.

I head for her before I even register my legs are moving, my desire to grant her every wish greater than my quest for revenge. Rory's blood smears on her cheek when I cup her jaw in my quivering hands. I stare into her eyes, reminding myself over and over again that she isn't the woman lying drugged on the bed. She is here, and she is safe. I saved her from him. *Me.* I saved her. And I'll never let anyone hurt her.

"She's not me," Justine murmurs, her breath tickling my lips. The dark cloud engulfing me thins when she presses her lips against mine. "They're not me. I'm here and I am safe," she assures me, her voice nurturing and without hesitation.

Fuck—no matter what shield I wear, she sees straight through me.

She doesn't see the mafia prince, the madman, or the boy who wished for freedom.

She sees me.

33

JUSTINE

As Nikolai moves us through the secret compound nestled at the back of the Popov property, from the corner of my eye, I spot Trey assisting the man he attacked off the floor. Although his face is bloody and bruised, the fact he's still breathing is good enough for me.

Initially, I assumed Nikolai was punishing him because he failed to comply with Nikolai's directive. It was only when my name tore from his throat in a mangled groan did I realize what was happening.

I wasn't the only one who walked through the gates of hell twenty-four hours ago—so did Nikolai.

I called him a coward. He discovered his deceased brother was alive and well. His ex-fiancée and his father kidnapped me before selling me to his rivals. Then, he ultimately killed his father to save me.

He had endured enough pain in his childhood to last him a lifetime, so I'm certain yesterday's adventures would have topped the cake.

How many more coals can he be dragged over before he inevitably snaps?

When we reach a room far from the others, I fist the hem of my shirt and drag it over my head. Since my legs are curled around Nikolai's waist, my jeans must remain in place.

Peering into Nikolai's violent eyes, I thrust out my chest in offering. I'm giving myself to him, allowing him to use my body to work through the anguish tormenting him as I did with his body this morning. I didn't just want him to make me feel whole. I wanted him to wash away the torment crippling me.

His touch did that. It freed me from suffering and cleared the negativity from my mind.

I can only hope my body is as wondrous to him as his is to me.

With a flick of his wrist, my bra falls to the floor with a whoosh. Goosebumps rise to the surface of my skin when Nikolai burrows his head between the valley of my breasts and inhales deeply, drinking in my scent.

After dragging his cheek over the swell of my bosom, he sniffs me again, more deeply this time.

I know what he's doing. He is intermingling our scents, making us smell like one.

Once he is happy he has achieved what he set out to do, his attention diverts to my puckered nipple. He sucks the hardened bud into his mouth as he continues pacing through the room, only stopping when we reach an extravagant bathroom in the far right-hand corner.

He swirls his tongue around the stiff peak before grazing his teeth over the little grooves straining for more attention. I softly sigh when my nipple falls from his mouth as he sets me on the vanity. He blows on the budded nub, stimulating it with his warm breath before his devotion switches to my other breast.

He devours my left nipple with as much attention as he gave the right. The visual of his bloodstained hand cupping my milky white breast is oddly erotic. It's a strange sensation that adds to the waves cresting in my stomach.

I'm not usually a fan of blood, but like every moment I am with Nikolai, I'm unearthing facts about me I never knew.

"Keep your eyes on me," Nikolai demands when the power of his sucks overwhelms me so greatly my eyelids flutter shut. "If your eyes aren't on me, I'll stop."

Panicked that he will end our exchange when it's only beginning, my eyes rocket open. Nikolai smirks against my breast, relishing my eagerness to please. I'm not stupid. The more submissive I am, the more mind-blowing our exchanges are. Furthermore, I'm supposed to be aiding him through his latest crisis, not chasing my next orgasm.

A brilliant idea formulates in my head, but Nikolai's hair dusts my ribcage before I can set my plan in motion. He places a trail of kisses down the skin of my stomach, not the least bit daunted by the horrid scars mottled throughout.

Any worries about the ugliness of my body fly out the window when he reaches the button on my jeans. He pops it open before lowering the zipper, his eyes never leaving mine. The anguish in his beautiful arctic gaze is gone, leaving nothing but a man spurred on by desire. His eyes relay his every intention, making me wiggle embarrassingly in my seat.

"Soon, *Ангел*. Very soon. We need to shower first," Nikolai informs me as he peels my jeans and panties down my quaking thighs. "Then I'm going to lose myself in you. There isn't a drug in the world that can replicate the high your body gives me."

Grazing my teeth over my bottom lip, I nod, a better response beyond me.

My eyes bulge almost comically when he drags his blood-splattered shirt over his head before removing his jeans. Once again, he's commando, and his body makes my eyes go wild and my mouth dry.

My god, he's a beautiful man. Not even the mafia sneer our exchange has yet to erase can dampen his appeal. His muscles are extra tight from their exertion from punishing Rory, and a mist of sweat enhances the impressive grooves carved in his formidable torso and stomach. It's a glorious visual that could only look better if his hands weren't bloodied and battered.

Like he can hear my inner monologue, Nikolai moves to the large walk-in shower on his right. He switches on the water full blast before shoving his hands under the penetrating spray. The faint pink water rolling off his bruised knuckles circles the drain for seconds before clearing away.

Once all the blood from his hands has been removed, he cups the water before splashing it over his face. He runs his fingers through his hair, giving it the same sexy, messed-up look it had the day we met.

Confident all signs of a fight have been removed from his body, he spins around to face me. The blaring Las Vegas desert temps have nothing on the heated look he is giving me. His stare is enough to make me combust into ecstasy without any additional stimulation.

With every step he takes toward me, his facial features soften. He's once again on the hunt, but this time, his target is an entirely different kettle of fish. He wants to be freed from the torment, and he's going to use my body to achieve that.

I'd be lying if I said I wasn't tickled pink by the idea.

Banding his arm around my waist, Nikolai lifts me from the vanity. Steam billows around us as he walks us into the shower stall. The muggy conditions amplify the red-hot energy bouncing between us.

I can feel him heavy and thick against my stomach, but that isn't the sole cause for the lust bristling between us. It's the look in his eyes. I calmed the storm bubbling in his veins with nothing but a brush of my lips and the scent of my skin.

That makes me feel invincible.

Knowing I can lasso a rope around his waist and tether him down when he's floating away makes it feel as if I have the world at my feet, as if I'm unstoppable.

Spurred on by a mass surge of confidence, I squeeze a blob of shower gel into my palm before working on cleaning Nikolai's body as thoroughly as he cleaned mine last night. I glide my hands across the smooth planes of his pecs before dropping them to the six clumps of muscle in his midsection. My hands trail over the fine hairs on his lower stomach before scrubbing over the bulge growing in size with every second we stand across from each other.

"Ангел," Nikolai grinds out in warning when my attention fails to deviate from his crotch.

The huskiness of his voice inspires me more. I lock my eyes with him, and then my hand glides down his thick cock. The bubbles coating his skin make his shaft smooth, easing my quest to unravel him. I slide my hand to the base of his cock before dragging it back up.

When my thumb flicks over his knob, it becomes evident that not all the wetness coating the crest of his cock is water. A sticky drop of pre-cum is beading on the tip, begging to be consumed.

Dying to taste him, I lower to my knees.

Nikolai bats the showerhead to the side, stopping the torrent of water gliding down my cheeks. "Keep your eyes on me," he demands, eagerness in his voice.

Nodding, I drag my tongue over his knob, lapping up the delicious goodness pooling there. His groan rolls through his body until it vibrates on my tongue, activating every one of my hot buttons.

The combination of his lust-sparked stare and his deliciously virile smell forces my thighs to squeeze together. He tastes manly, sweet, and oh-so-dangerous.

While Nikolai gathers my hair into his fist, I work his thick cock into my mouth. I draw him to the back of my throat, taking him as far as I can without gagging.

Although his hips naturally rock in a rhythm matching my pumps, he leaves the pace of our exchange up to me, trusting me enough to know I can please him without hurting myself.

"Ah, fuck, *Ангел*," he growls through a moan when I suck harder, wordlessly praying for more of his delicious cum.

My cheeks hollow as I take him even deeper, wanting to unravel him as effectively as he unravels me. Keeping my eyes locked on his is challenging, but it intensifies our undeniable connection.

This man's hold on me is already wondrous, but it grows tenfold with every moment we share. He went to the depths of hell for me, and now I'm using my body to bring him back.

My nipples tighten when Nikolai inhales a deep breath, sucking in the scent of my arousal lingering in the air. Bringing him to the brink of climax has my orgasm loitering, and I'm praying for the chance to be unleashed.

Fisting his cock, I work the parts of his shaft missing out on the warmth of my mouth. My speed is as uncontrolled as my heart rate, a manic pace that makes my and Nikolai's conjoined moans bounce around the steamy space.

It's quite frightening how unhinged he makes me. My desire to taste him is more rampant than my urge to breathe.

"Eyes, *Ангел*," Nikolai demands when my eyes drop for the quickest second to take in the spectacular visual of his cock pumping in and out of my mouth.

My response can't be helped. The vision is awe-inspiring and sexy enough to bring my climax to within an inch of the finish line.

Raising my eyes to his, I roll my tongue over the thick vein feeding his magnificent cock before sucking down hard on his knob. The combination of my greedy suck and my squeeze of his sack sets him off.

Cum rockets out of his cock in uncontrolled spurts, coating my tongue and the back of my throat. I struggle to keep up with the thick stream, but I give it my best shot. I swallow on repeat, moaning through the sensation igniting every nerve ending in my body.

Nikolai's cock has barely finished pulsing when I'm hoisted off the ground and pinned to the spotlessly white tiles. "My turn," he growls before burrowing his head between my legs.

I call out, the sensation of his tongue flicking my clit over-whelming. He sucks the pulsating nub into his mouth as two of his fingers slide inside me.

"So fucking wet," he murmurs against my pussy, heightening my senses more. "And so fucking tasty."

My breasts jiggle up and down when he pumps in and out of me, his pace as uncontrolled as mine was earlier. He works my body with a knowledge only he has, bringing my climax to fruition so fast it utterly devastates me.

Clamping my eyes shut, I shudder through the wonderment bombarding me. I repeatedly shout Nikolai's name, ensuring he knows who I'm thanking for the revitalization zapping through me.

Nikolai wasn't lying when he said there's no better high than this. I'm overwhelmed by the emotions that swamp me when he brings me to climax. I feel wicked and naughty but sexy and cher-ished at the same time.

I genuinely feel like a queen when I'm quivering beneath him.

After a final lash of his tongue on my clit, Nikolai rises from his crouched position. I taste myself on his mouth when he spears his tongue between my lips. He kisses me until the blurriness in my head is the least of my problems. My knees are wobbling so severely they are moments away from collapsing.

Like he can sense my worry, he tightens his grip around my waist before guiding my legs around his sweat-slicked hips. Air is sucked from my lungs when his cock sits heavy between us. He's as hard as he was before I took him to the brink of ecstasy.

"Are you ready?" he asks, his voice full of warning.

"Yes." The throatiness of my reply leaves no doubt to my mental state. I am lost. I've completely fallen down the rabbit hole.

In the past two weeks, I've witnessed him do unlawful act after unlawful act, yet my feelings for him continue to grow. I don't think there's anything he can do that will stop me from falling in love with him.

I want to protect him from the world. I want to save him from the men determined to tear him down. But more than anything, I want to love him like he's never been loved.

When Nikolai locks his eyes with mine and I see the utter adoration beaming from them, it dawns on me that my earlier assumption was wrong.

I'm not falling in love with him.

I love him.

34

JUSTINE

As my eyes continue to explore the opulent space surrounding us, I snuggle into Nikolai's chest. Since my focus was so fixated on Nikolai's well-being when we first entered this domain hours ago, I never took in its extravagance.

This room is nearly a replica of Nikolai's room in the Popov mansion. It just has a cozier vibe. The photos of family members scattered between numerous knickknacks stop it from feeling like a hotel room, and the way Nikolai's shoulders have loosened reveals he's comfortable here.

"Is this your place?" I ask Nikolai, balancing on my elbow to peer at his spent face.

Sexually satiated is a good look for him.

I hope he likes it, as I plan to make him wear it for many years to come.

He takes a moment to consider my question before answering, "More like a safety net. Vladimir was unaware of this property's existence. I paid for it with my own money and had the deed filed under an alias he was unaware of."

My heart rate kicks into overdrive. "So Clark isn't an actual person?"

He smiles before shaking his head. "No. It was the last name of the person lodging my development application."

His smile makes me giddy, but not in the way you're thinking. His earlier anguish has been forgotten, torn from his mind as effectively as his name was shredded from my throat multiple times in the past three hours.

I'm glad my wish to give him a moment of peace was successful. I don't doubt quiet is a rare commodity for him.

"Can I ask you something?"

I drag my fingertips over his dragon tattoo, hoping my touch will ease the severity of my nosiness. Nikolai doesn't like being interrogated, but one question hasn't left my mind for the past two days. After everything we've been through, its persistence should mean something, shouldn't it?

Nikolai locks his eyes with mine to gauge the seriousness of my question. He must see something in them, as he nods not even two seconds later, albeit hesitantly.

"Why didn't your threat of retribution ever surface for Mr. Fletcher? I read the transcripts from your trial. You were pretty convinced he wouldn't walk amongst the living for much longer."

Don't misinterpret me. I'm glad Nikolai's quest for revenge never surfaced. If it had, I would have never come to Vegas, which means I would have never met Nikolai. I'm just stunned that years of being raised by the devil didn't snap his levelheadedness. He was only a boy during his trial, but his actions were those of a man—a mighty and determined man.

I return my cheek to his sweat-slicked chest to ensure he knows *exactly* whose side I am on. I'm not judging his actions. I simply want to know every aspect of his life: the good and the bad.

While running his hand down my arm, causing the fine hairs to prickle, Nikolai mutters, "Last week wasn't the first time Carmichael was spared my wrath. I came close a little over ten years ago."

Since his reply seems unfinished, I lift my head off his chest and sheepishly peer into his eyes. The pulse in my neck twangs when I spot a gleam in his eyes I've never seen before. It is the gleam of sorrow.

"What happened?" I ask, incapable of holding back my curiosity for a second longer.

He arches his brow, silently announcing his annoyance at my eagerness. I'm not impatient to discover why Mr. Fletcher evaded

Nikolai's wrath twice. I'm eager to find out what has caused the glint in his eyes. He isn't overly emotional, so when I get the faintest glimmer outside his usual realm, I must run with it.

"If the last twenty-four hours hasn't proven to you where my devotion lies, Nikolai, I don't know what will. If you don't feel comfortable telling me what happened, don't. It's no skin off my back." I keep my tone low, portraying disinterest. My acting skills are pathetic.

A stretch of silence passes between us. I wouldn't necessarily say it is uncomfortable, but a peculiar feeling looms in the air. I'm sure Nikolai finds trust hard, but I had hoped our interactions the past few days would have awarded me his faith. I would never do anything to hurt him, much less break his trust.

After a deep sigh that raises his chest high, he asks, "Have you ever met Carmichael's family?"

Keeping my head glued to his chest so he won't see my smile, I shake my head. I'm not smiling at his mention of Mr. Fletcher's family. I'm grinning with glee that I can alter the mindset of a mafia prince—*or should I now say king since Vladimir is dead?*

Shaking off my confusion, I utter, "Mr. Fletcher and I were more work acquaintances than anything."

"Not by Carmichael's choice," Nikolai grumbles under his breath, revealing the cause of his delay.

He's worried his confession will swing my opinion of Mr. Fletcher back into a favorable light. He doesn't need to worry. Unless he's going to tell me he orchestrated for Mr. Fletcher to jump ship from the DA to the defense, nothing he could say will change my opinion on the matter. What Mr. Fletcher did to Nikolai was wrong—no debate required.

"I know he has four older brothers like me," I reveal, pushing Nikolai to continue our conversation minus any unnecessary jealousy.

He has no reason to be jealous.

No man could ever steal my attention from him.

Ever.

My persuasive efforts are better than my acting skills, prompting Nikolai to say, "Then you know how far people will go to protect their brothers. Nothing is above a man's desire to protect the ones he loves."

The pain in his voice shreds my heart to pieces. Our conversation, however, centers around Mr. Fletcher and how Nikolai's childhood factors into his story. He didn't want to become a monster all those years ago. He just didn't have a choice. He had to hunt or be hunted. He chose to hunt.

Unable to speak, fearing he will hear my voice crack, I nod.

After a deep sigh, Nikolai discloses, "Carmichael used me to protect his brother."

I wait, praying he will fill in the gaping holes in his story. Thankfully, he doesn't leave me hanging for long.

"Carmichael's brother was a gambler, a bad gambler. He was in the hole for millions. When he failed to pay his debt, Vladimir's men paid him a visit." He locks his eyes with mine so I can see their honesty before revealing, "They sent Carmichael his finger."

"Jesus Christ," I murmur under my breath, unable to stop my words. I like to think I'm well-educated on all parts of Nikolai's life, but there are some things you can't study for.

"I didn't know about Carmichael's dealings with Vladimir until the day I went to seek retribution for the lies he told." He smirks, his smile not matching the heavy sentiment in the air. "I didn't believe him, but for some reason, I left him breathing." He drops his eyes to mine, the worship in them unmissable. "Now I know why. If I had killed him, I would have never met you. You're my gift for my atonement."

I don't have a chance of concealing my smile, so I set it free. His reply mimics thoughts I was having mere minutes ago. It also proves we are on the same page. We will both stop at nothing to ensure the other is safe and protected.

Leaning over, I press my lips to Nikolai's. The growl that rolls up his chest stimulates every nerve ending in my body.

"Ah, fuck, woman, your smile is already deadly to my sanity, and then you go and kiss me. You're supposed to be bringing me back from insanity, not pushing me toward it," Nikolai utters in Russian, heightening my excitement even more.

"Don't you know insanity is the definition of fun? People are most creative when they're insane," I reply in his native tongue, reminding him of my fluency in Russian.

The smirk tugging his full lips and the thickening of his cock reveal his delight at my reply. They also display I responded as he had hoped. I feel sorry for what Mr. Fletcher and his brother went through, but Nikolai is still the innocent in their exchange.

He was a child who should have been defended, not thrust into a fight he didn't belong in.

"*Ангел...*" Nikolai moans in a throaty groan when my lips drop from his mouth to his chest.

Locking my eyes with his, I continue my trek to the ultimate prize, encouraged by the lust detonating in his eyes. I never knew I craved power, but the more control he awards me, the more I want.

It is dangerously addictive.

I don't want the power needed to lead a country. I just want enough to influence the man I'm in love with to see sense through the madness surrounding him.

With the gleam in Nikolai's eyes brightening with every kiss I press to his skin, I can confidently declare I have that and so much more.

My advancement toward his jutted cock is interrupted when a knock sounds at the door. After grumbling a Russian cuss word under his breath, Nikolai requests for his guest to leave in a manner that leaves no uncertainty of his displeasure. It's as stern as his mouthwatering cock sitting a mere inch from my mouth.

"Can't," says a voice through the door, a distinctively male voice that sounds much like Trey.

I only interacted with Trey for the twenty minutes he watched over me while Nikolai searched the compound for Rory, but his accent is distinctively unique. Unlike his many counterparts, his heritage isn't Russian. He is British.

"Birds have word of a takeover bid."

I don't understand a syllable of Trey's cryptic message, but Nikolai does. He dives out of bed like he is on a mission while grumbling another Russian cuss word under his breath.

Thrusting his feet into the opening of his jeans, he yanks them up his legs with violence. After ensuring a bed sheet covers every inch of my naked form, he swings open the door. As I had anticipated, Trey is standing on the other side.

Ensuring he doesn't stoke Nikolai's anger with more wood, he keeps his eyes glued to his feet. It isn't because he is scared of Nikolai—although I'm sure a small dash of fear is surging through his veins—it is because the noises coming out of this room the past three hours leave no doubt about how Nikolai and I have occupied our time.

I should be disturbed his men have heard my cries of ecstasy, but for some reason unbeknownst to me, I'm not. I genuinely forget who I am when I'm with Nikolai. Embarrassment, shame, or any other weak confidence slayer are kept at bay when I'm trapped in a Nikolai trance. My self-esteem surges when I am entranced by a mafia prince. It doesn't diminish.

Pretending I can't feel greedy heat creeping across the back of my knees, I return my focus to Nikolai and Trey. Worry brews in my gut when I see the concern masking Nikolai's features. I can't hear a word they're speaking, but all the anguish I stripped from Nikolai's features hardens with every second he interacts with Trey.

"Is everything okay?" I ask Nikolai when he closes the door and heads back in my direction.

"I need you to get dressed," he responds, not looking at me.

My stomach gurgles violently as I slip off the bed to gather my clothes from the floor.

Nikolai's movements mimic mine, although his are more constrained. I'm jittering so much I can barely fasten the button on my jeans.

Seeing my struggle, Nikolai gathers my shoes from the floor before aiding me with my clothes. He drags my shirt over my head before pulling my hair from the collar. For the quickest second, flashbacks of the Nikolai I've been besieged with the past three hours break through the turmoil engulfing him. He runs the back of his fingers down my inflamed cheek before they drift over my lips.

"No one will take you away from me," he whispers ever so quietly. "Not even me."

Denying my chance to reply, he curls his hand around mine and heads for the door. His strides are so long that I must jog to keep up with him.

"I need you to stay here with Trey, and no matter what you hear, you are *not* to leave this compound," Nikolai demands, assuring I understand it is an order, not a suggestion.

Tightness spreads across my chest when a member of his crew hands him a weapon similar to the one he was holding when he entered the room I was held hostage in last night.

After checking the chamber to ensure it is loaded, Nikolai slides it into the back waistband of his jeans.

"What's going on?" I ask anyone listening.

Over three dozen men swarm around us like bees circling a honeypot. All hold weapons, and their faces are as hard-lined as Nikolai's.

The carefree sentiment lingering in the air when I arrived at this compound nearly four hours ago, has been snuffed, replaced with the horrid scent of battle. Not a drop of blood can be seen, but I'm confident it is the scent of death I am smelling.

"Nikolai, please tell me what's going on," I demand, my voice shaking as I follow him into a room full of weapons. When Nikolai continues barking orders at his crew, ignoring me, I shout, "I can't help you if I'm left in the dark! Tell me what is happening!"

The room falls into silence as shock descends over Nikolai's men. They aren't the only ones glowering at me in disbelief. The half-dressed women I spotted floundering around the hot tub earlier are gawking at me with their mouths hanging open and their eyes bugged.

Clearly no one in this room has ever been brave enough to go against Nikolai.

Usually I'd cower from a fight as well, but my interactions with Nikolai the past week have boosted my confidence to an uncontainable level, leaving me free to say, "Please, Nikolai. I want to help."

His attention shifts to me after telling his men to prepare to leave. The anger in his eyes fades when he spots the sheen glistening in mine. "*Ангел*—"

"What's going on?" I interrupt. An explanation for my tears can wait until four dozen gun-wielding men don't surround us.

Nikolai's chest rises and falls two times before he utters, "The Popov compound is moments from being stormed." His tone is as rough as the expression on his face.

"By whom? If it's the authorities, I can help. They need a warrant, and don't even get me started on the number of books I'll throw at them if they don't have one."

Nikolai smiles, pleased by my offer of representation. It isn't his genuine smile, but with how thick the tension is hanging in the air, I accept it as if it is.

"We aren't being raided by the police. It's a rival, unhappy with the consequences of joining a war he didn't belong in." His words come out hurried as he races to the entrance where his men are gathered.

I quickly follow him. "What do you mean? What war?"

He signals to a group of men straddling ATVs to move before swinging his eyes back to me. "Vladimir sought help with your kidnapping. My men couldn't get to Roman without taking down members of their crew. A man lost his son. Now he's coming to get answers."

I try to reply to his statement. I try to express that no amount of fighting will give him the answers he wants, but no matter how often I open and close my mouth, nothing but air bubbles come out.

I'm swimming way out of my depth. Mafia takeovers and war games were not covered during my studies, and my brief interaction with Dimitri circled around his family, not rivals set for revenge.

My head snaps to the side when Trey says, "Let me come, Nikolai. Let me speak to Alexei. He just wants to bury his son."

"No." The shortness of Nikolai's reply doesn't weaken its impact. It was direct and to the point, kickstarting my heart and libido. He straddles the ATV we rode to Clarks earlier, before locking his focus on Trey. "He will kill you, and then he will bury his son. You were acting on my orders, Trey, so the blame for Tristan's death is on my shoulders, not yours."

Bile burns my esophagus. If the man storming the Popov compound wants to avenge his son's death by claiming the life of the man he holds accountable, that means he wants to kill... I can't say it. I won't say it.

"Please don't go," I beg, my fearful eyes bouncing between Nikolai's. "*Please.*"

I'm on the verge of falling to my knees when he replies, "I have to. These are *my* men. That makes them *my* responsibility."

The honesty in his eyes strengthens the truth in his statement, but it doesn't stop me from saying, "What about me? I'm your responsibility too. You promised to keep me safe. You can't do that if you are dead." A sob muffles my last word.

Acting like he didn't hear a word I spoke, Nikolai kicks over his ATV before saying, "Keep her safe, Trey. That is your *only* job. Keep my *Ангел* safe."

"Nikolai, please!" I scream when he pulls back on the throttle at the exact moment Trey's arm wraps around my waist. "Don't leave me! I love you!"

I fight with all my might to escape Trey when Nikolai's ATV roars through the pitch-black night. His speed is so out of control that he's nothing but a speck on the horizon within seconds.

"Let me go!"

I stab my nails into Trey's arm and throw my legs into his shins, but no matter how much I fight, he holds on tightly, not the least bit deterred by my vicious wailing.

"Nikolai!" I scream at the top of my lungs, my throat raw from the sobs tearing from it.

My panicked cries echo through the dead-quiet space, alerting the women trapped in the far back corner of the compound to my distress. They call out in a similar fashion as they did last night, their screams complemented by their fists banging on the walls of the dorm they're housed in. They are endeavoring to protect me as fiercely as I protected them last night.

Trey remains holding on tightly, taking my battering with a silence that switches my devastation to anger. I grunt, kick, and wail until my body is covered with a dense layer of sweat and my lungs are relinquished of air.

My efforts are pointless. Trey is too large for me to contend with.

He releases me from his grasp only once the taillights glowing in the distance fade to nothing. I pivot on my heels, my fist slinging out before I've stopped to consider the consequences of my actions.

The half-naked women watching our charade with eagle eyes gasp in sync when Trey's head rockets to the side. The viciousness of my hit even shocks me. Mere minutes ago, I strived to argue that violence solves nothing, but at the first opportunity I have to back that up with action, I lash out with my fists instead of words.

While returning his head to its original position, Trey runs his thumb over the trickle of blood oozing from his left nostril. I blink several times in a row, preparing for him to react to my viciousness with equal aggression.

He does no such thing.

He just peers into my eyes before muttering, "I deserve that... and so much more."

35

NIKOLAI

The body count of our battle is high. Thankfully, Alexei's men bore most of the brunt of our exchange.

It didn't have to come to this.

I reached out to him this morning regarding Tristan's death. I respectfully offered my condolences and expressed remorse for his loss.

I had hoped we could work through our differences like men, but Alexei has never been merciful. He sent his men here to exact revenge.

They left with a legacy.

"Get word to Dimitri. With Alexei's attempt at dethroning me unsuccessful, he may seek another outlet for his anger."

Although the Popovs will never work side by side with the Petrettis, Alexei's crew's knowledge of yesterday's events was too informed to ignore. They weren't aware of solely Vladimir's death. They knew the people involved in his downfall.

"And Rico?" my third-in-charge, Mikhail, questions.

I freeze for the quickest second, still not accustomed to Rico's name being freely used by my men. Within weeks of his death, Vladimir ordered for Rico's name to be struck from any conversations held. He never spoke of his son or the circumstances that resulted in his death. He acted as if Rico had never existed.

I guess that's why my men haven't mentioned Vladimir's name today. He set the benchmark on how we mourn vital members of our family, and my crew is following it to a T.

"Leave Rico out of this. Alexei isn't aware of his involvement, and I want it to stay that way."

If Rico catches wind of my altercation with Alexei's crew today, he will return to Vegas.

I don't want that.

If I want to succeed Vladimir's reign, I must do it on my own accord.

Besides, our fearless battle with Alexei's men proves how strong my sanction is, so I don't see us being re-challenged anytime soon.

When Mikhail nods, advising he heard my reply, I throw my leg over my ATV and shoot out of the Popov compound.

My hands shake as I merge from one battle to another just as fierce.

The look on Justine's face when I left her at Clarks hours ago will forever haunt me. Although I hated leaving her, I had no choice. I promised to protect her, and that's what I did tonight.

I not only protected her from a man who bid on her, but I also sheltered her from a man threatening to take her honor away.

Alexei didn't send his men here solely for Trey's blood. They came for Justine. Alexei paid his dues to Vladimir, so he wanted his men to collect his prize.

His crew learned the hard way that Justine was never up for negotiation.

When the brightness of the Clarks compound breaks over the horizon, I switch off the headlights of my ATV and lower my revs. If I know Justine like I think I know her, she will come out either fists swinging or shedding tears.

I really fucking hope she comes out guns blazing.

I'd rather her slap me again than see tears in her eyes. I hate seeing her cry, especially if I'm the reason for her tears.

In all honesty, not all my panic is from wondering what Justine's reaction will be upon my return. It is from trying to decipher if the three little words I heard whispered through the warm night air when I left was just my mind playing tricks on me or if Justine said what I thought she did.

Does she love me?

Surely I'm mistaken. Nobody loves me. I'm the byproduct of a woman pushed to the brink by the man she worshipped. I wasn't born to be loved. I was born to be feared. Not even the woman who gave birth to me loved me, so why would someone as beautiful and perfect as Justine want to?

At the edge of the compound, I shut down my ATV and then dismount. My steps into the serenely quiet space are heavy, weighed down by the confusion muddling my brain.

Mafia takeovers, bloodbaths, and slaying men like they're flies is nothing out of the ordinary, but dealing with emotions I never knew I wanted but suddenly crave is way out of left field. I'm out of my fucking depth, even more so since I'd give anything to hear Justine tell me she loves me again.

Fuck, I hope it wasn't my mind playing tricks on me.

My long strides into the central area of the Popov compound halt when I spot a pool of red on the deck surrounding the hot tub. Following the sticky red drops oozing down the wooden shell of the hot tub, my eyes lock on the haunted and bleak eyes of one of my crew's whores. Her slumped form can't hide the bullet wound between her eyes.

Fuck! Fuck! Fuck!

As my hand slips into the back of my jeans to remove my gun, my eyes assess the scene. Numerous wet footprints are racing from the hot tub's edge to the compound's side entrance.

Considering the puddles of water are void of any red coloring, it appears as if one woman was sacrificed to scare away the rest.

Although grateful I'm not arriving at a scene that mimics the one I just left, anger thickens my blood.

Where is Justine?

I want to believe she escaped with the other dozen or so women who call Clarks their home, but the weird, twisting knot in my stomach isn't letting me believe that, much less the fact I can sense her presence. I know she's here, waiting for me. I just need to find her.

Hoping my body's awareness of Justine's closeness doesn't lead me astray, I move through the compound, my steps as quiet as the Grim Reaper. I hold my gun up high as I make my way through the corridor the sleeping quarters break off from. My heart is smashing into my ribs, but my resolve remains strong.

My *Ангел* is counting on me.

I will not let her down.

As I creep past the dorms housing the women we saved from Vladimir's wrath, a bright-blue eye gains my attention. It is peering out of the keyhole of a locked door, staring straight at me.

"Where is she? I ask, unsure of the hushed words she is whispering to me.

I don't understand Czech, but even if I did, I still wouldn't be able to understand her. She's crying too hard to articulate clear speech.

Dragging my hand along the doorframe, I pray Trey's knack for leaving keys in plain sight remains true. Thankfully, it is.

Upon spotting the key, the blue eye disappears from the lock. My hands noticeably shake when I stab the freshly cut key into the lock and twist.

When I swing open the door, I'm not surprised to discover the remaining sixteen women housed in this room are huddled in the corner of the vast space. Their arms are wrapped around their legs, and their heads are burrowed between their knees.

The only one brave enough to face me head-on is a petite blonde with bright-blue eyes—the same blonde who held a shard of glass to her neck earlier today.

Although her eyes are wide with panic, they also reveal she knows I'm not going to hurt her. She saw me defend her sister. That issued me her trust.

Do you know where Justine is? I silently mouth, bringing my hand to my chest. *My Ангел. Do you know where they took her?*

The blonde nods eagerly.

Can you show me?

When she nods again, I press my finger to my lips, demanding her to remain quiet. Catching my enemies unaware is my only chance to get Justine out of here alive.

Although I'm sure there are watchers on the main roads surrounding this compound, I'm confident they are unaware of my arrival through the desert-like conditions separating the Popov property from Clarks. That's why I purchased this property—for its multiple access points.

After gesturing to the women at the side of the room to remain quiet, the Czech woman returns her attention to me. She waves her hand in front of her badly malnourished body, signaling for me to follow her. Her steps down the dark corridor are as weightless as mine—her buoyancy compliments of her famished frame.

A few paces down from her dorm, she stops. Peering into my eyes to express their urgency, she points to a door three feet down.

"Justine is in there?" I question, my words not even a whisper.

Her throat works hard to swallow before she nods.

The fighting glint in her eyes brightens when I mouth. *Thank you.*

I gesture to the room we just left before pointing it to the back entrance of the compound. Her head slings in the direction I'm pointing before she nods again, understanding my request to relocate the women in her dorm into the darkness of the night.

They will be safer there.

Before she can reply, a roared, "What do you mean? You were told to keep him there until I gave word I had finished here," bellows up the hall, startling both the blonde and the women trapped three doors down.

The sound of flesh connecting with flesh booms into my ears, closely followed by a gargled groan.

"Go," I instruct the blonde before heading to the door she gestured to.

"This is why I don't send you to do anything... If I want something done right, I have to do it my fucking self... I don't want to hear your excuses, Clancy," the male voice shouts.

If I didn't already have my suspicions about who entered my property without an invitation, mentioning his number-two sergeant tells me everything I need to know.

Alexei is not only a stupid man.

He's a dead one as well.

Tilting my head to the side, I glance inside the room Alexei's voice is booming from. Trey is sitting bound and gagged in a chair left of Alexei, who is talking on his cell. Every inch of Trey's body is covered with cuts, welts, and bruises. His head is hanging low, showcasing the numerous cracks in his skull. If I couldn't see the faint flutter of his breath fanning the blood dripping from his mouth, I would assume he was dead.

"How long do I have before he arrives...? Don't give me an assumption. Give me facts..."

While Alexei waits for his number two to update him on my expected arrival time, I continue scanning the room, seeking Justine.

"Fuck!" Alexei swings his eyes to Trey's half-dead form. He's so motionless that I'm not sure if he's still breathing. "I'll head out now... No, I don't need a bullet. He'll bleed out long before Nikolai arrives." The conceit on Alexei's face triples when he shifts his focus to the side of the room. "But I'm going to take my time with her. She's too feisty to fuck over in an hour. I'll need at least a week or two to work her over as good as I did his second-in-charge. I'll enjoy this even more than I did gutting his dog."

When Alexei moves to his right to gather a pair of tin snips from a silver gurney, I spot the cause of his excitement. Justine is lying hogtied on the floor, her body as still as Trey's.

Anger clogs my heart. If he has killed her, the punishment he's in the process of issuing Trey will look like child's play.

I realize Justine is alive and well when Alexei diverts his focus back to the cell phone squashed against his ear.

Confident Alexei isn't paying her any attention, she slips a tiny shard of glass between her fingers before setting to work on cutting the tape circling her wrists and ankles. She's been working on her escape for some time, as she's already nearly three-quarters through the three-inch-wide tape.

Although her eyes are wide and brimming with terror, the determination on her unmarked face is as robust as ever.

That was Alexei's first mistake. He underestimated Justine's strength.

His second: he forgot why my crew calls me The Snake.

He has no idea of the wrath I'm about to rain down on him.

After slipping my gun into the waistband of my jeans, I remove my trusty knife from my back pocket. A mass surge of testosterone pumps through my veins when I flick open the switchblade as Justine's eyes collide with mine across the room. Her nostrils flare when she inhales a sharp breath. She knows she is seconds away from witnessing me kill again.

I don't want her to see me do this. I crave every sneaky glance she gives me, so I'll do anything I can to not taint that, but she knows I don't have a choice. Alexei came to my home turf to kill my man and take my woman. His punishment can't be any less severe than death.

He should be grateful for how fast I will take him down.

If Justine's wellbeing wasn't my utmost priority, we'd spend the next several hours becoming well-acquainted.

With my desire for Justine greater than my urge to maim, I silently mouth, *Close your eyes.*

When Justine does as requested without hesitation, my killer instincts kick into overdrive. The air in Alexei's lungs vacates in a rush when I yank his head back by his hair and then familiarize his jugular with my knife. I've snuck up on him so stealthily the tangy scent of urine loiters into my nostrils when he pisses his pants at my abrupt arrival.

"Nikolai, please—"

"Say hello to Vladimir for me," I interrupt before dragging my knife sideways.

One Year Later

...

36

NIKOLAI

"Objection, Your Honor. The ADA is badgering the witness." I slip into a pew at the back of the chambers as Justine stands from her seat. "The defense already disclosed the accused's extensive criminal history. Does the jury need to hear it all over again?"

She waves her hand at the dozen men and women filling the jury box. The strain on their faces shows they fully agree with her objection.

"Objection sustained. Move on to your next question, Mr. Gregor."

When the ADA attempts a snide remark at Judge Morrison's ruling, the judge glares at him, stuffing his reply into the back of his throat.

I've not yet had the pleasure of being seated in front of Judge Morrison, but I've heard numerous reports from Justine and affiliates of my industry that his rulings are stern but fair.

Unlike the judge he replaced, he's not susceptible to bribes. I'm sure it will only be a matter of months until he eventually succumbs to greed. Until then, I will continue my negotiations without burden.

I've always been a stubborn bastard.

Over the next hour, I continue watching Justine in her element.

Just like my strengths are best used in the underworld, Justine's are revealed in glorious detail in the courtroom. She's a tigress inside these walls, protecting her clients as if they're her cubs.

After taking a few weeks of leave to work through circumstances beyond her control, Justine jumped back onto the bandwagon. Her decision to stand behind a prosecutor's desk was her own choice, but unfortunately, that wasn't the case.

When a shipment of drugs went wayward, two of my men needed representation. Justine was my first choice. It was a brilliant move on my behalf. Not only did I get to work side by side with her for weeks on end, but she agreed I could pay her clients' fees in a non-monetary way.

It was a fucking awesome three months.

I didn't think my infatuation with Justine could grow any more rampant than it did during our first two weeks together.

I was wrong—*so very fucking wrong.*

Justine is the worst drug on the market, more addictive than any substance I've sampled. Her strength continues to amaze me every day, which in turn feeds my infatuation. Whether she was quivering beneath me thirty minutes ago or three days ago doesn't matter. I can't get enough. Every hit makes me crave another.

"Hey there, sorry things ran a little longer than anticipated."

I lift my eyes, taking in the super-tight knee-length skirt and shimmery satin blouse Justine is wearing. When my gaze lingers on her perfect tits longer than socially acceptable, heat flashes across her neck.

"Oh, *Ангел*," I croon, my deep tone leaving no doubt as to my aroused state. "You can't blush in the very room I've fucked you in... *twice*."

Her teeth graze her bottom lip. "Who said I was blushing with embarrassment? I could simply be recalling fond memories."

Her thighs press together when I growl, her body incapable of ignoring the excitement blazing through her veins. "There was nothing *simple* about what we did in this room."

I slide out of the pew she stands next to. Her eyes blaze with unbridled anticipation when they drink in the black trousers, button-up long-sleeve shirt, and vest I am wearing.

"Nikolai, you look—"

"Out of place? Like a fucking imbecile?" I interrupt with a grumble while yanking on the collar of my shirt.

Usually I wouldn't be caught dead in this outfit, but I did as requested when Justine asked me to dress nicely this morning. I wasn't lying a year ago when I said I'd button up in a suit for this woman. Anything she wants, she will have—even me in a monkey suit.

"Fucking hot," Justine fills in, shocking me with her language.

My cock hardens to the point it's painful. It's so rare to hear a cuss word leave her pouty lips. I relish every one I get.

"But if you don't feel comfortable, Nikolai, you don't have to wear it. I love you, not the clothes you wear."

My cock thickens even more. What I thought I heard Justine say all those months ago was true. She did tell me she loves me. Although I'm sure she only blurted it out in a moment of panic, the hundreds of times she has said it since can't be misconstrued.

For some inane, stupidly crazy reason, she loves me. And I love her too.

"You asked me to dress nicely. Usually I don't follow commands... unless they're given by you. I'll do anything for you." I kiss the shell of her ear. "I'll even slit the throats of a thousand men to keep you safe."

A chill runs down her spine, causing her tiny frame to shudder. If I didn't know her as well as I do, I'd be worried she is scared.

Pity for Justine, I know her better than anyone.

She's not scared, frightened, or remorseful.

She's turned on.

"Soon, *Ангел*. Very soon," I promise, curling my hand over hers.

Her disappointed groan is nearly drowned out by her client calling her name. From the information Justine gave me this morning over brunch, Frederick McClare is a nineteen-year-old West Coast native who has lived in Vegas for six years. Although he moved here with his parents, he's been raising his four-year-old sister alone for the past two years.

In desperate need of supplies, he robbed a liquor store at gunpoint three months ago. Stupidly, he got caught with not just the money he stole but with his balaclava and gun in his possession as well.

"Hey, I'm glad I caught you before you left," Frederick greets, his eyes locked on Justine.

Although his heavy-hooded gaze mimics many I've seen eyeing Justine the past year, his stare doesn't bother me enough to spark a reaction out of me—*not yet!*

"I just heard from Mercer. They're going to let me see Talia this weekend. It's a supervised visit, but I'll take anything I can get."

Justine's smile quickly reminds me of the organ beating in my chest. "That's wonderful, Frederick. I'm so glad. Talia must be missing you a great deal."

When she runs her hand down Frederick's arm, wordlessly relaying her excitement, I tighten my grip on her hand. Frederick is barely a man, but nothing can harness my jealousy regarding this woman. She's mine and only mine, and I don't give a fuck how old you are—if you don't learn that fast, I'll beat it into you.

Frederick is smarter than I first perceived. His eyes stray to me as he says, "Oh, hey, man. You must be Nikolai. I've heard a lot about you. Justine talks about you all the time."

I jerk up my chin before accepting his offer of a handshake. I squeeze his hand, strengthening the warning my eyes relay with a bit of muscle.

He doesn't glower at me or even give an indication to Justine about the pain jolting up his arm. He accepts his punishment like a man much older than his years.

It is inspiring, and it has me thinking reckless thoughts.

"Don't even think about it," Justine grumbles when Frederick saunters away. Frederick impresses me further by waiting to check his hand for broken bones until after he's walked through the swinging doors of the chambers. "He only robbed that store because he didn't have a choice. He isn't a criminal."

Placing my hand on the curve of Justine's back, I guide her into the courthouse foyer. "He didn't rob that store because he had no choice. He did it for his sister."

When she nods, agreeing with my assessment, I say, "If he worked for me, he wouldn't need to be a petty criminal to ensure her needs are taken care of... I'll make him a master crafter."

Her elbow pops into my ribs. "It's not funny, Nikolai. If you keep *mentoring* my clients, I'll run out of clients to represent..."

Justine's words trail off as her brows stitch. She knows as well as I do how false her statement is. When she's with me, not only will her every wish be granted, but she will also never be exhausted of clientele.

Lia has kept her on her toes the past nine months, let alone my extensive list of men.

"Give me a minute to freshen up," Justine requests, her eyes straying to the ladies' room.

Nodding, I wave my hand to Roman, who is sitting at a bank of chairs on our right. "I've got a few calls to make before we head off, so I'll wait for you outside. Make sure you stay with Roman."

Although my vicious yet triumphant battle with Alexei and his crew ensured my sanction hasn't been targeted in the past twelve months, there's no such thing as too much caution when it comes to protecting Justine.

Anywhere Justine goes, Roman follows, even five-second restroom visits.

Knowing no amount of arguing will change my mindset, Justine presses her lips to my mouth before signaling for Roman to hurry.

I wait for them to enter the ladies' room, before slipping my cell phone out of my pocket and exiting the courthouse.

"Did he talk?" I ask, not bothering to issue a greeting.

"He sang like a fucking canary," Trey answers, the lisp he picked up after his assault barely audible. "I've got an address for a vacation home on the Puerto Rican coast. Do you want me to handle it, or...?"

He waits for further instructions, identifying this isn't a standard run-of-the-mill business negotiation. This is as personal as it gets.

"Send me the info. I'll handle it in the same manner I handled the rest."

Trey chuckles before making a throat-cutting noise. Although I can't see him, I imagine him dragging his thumb across his jugular.

After promising to send me the info, he disconnects our call. As my hand slips into my pants pocket to house my cell phone, my fingertips drift over a ratted piece of paper stuffed in the corner. There isn't anything overly significant printed on the thin document. It is just a list of names, but its importance to me is undeniable.

It contains the names of the men who bid on Justine last year— my list of targets.

As the months have moved on from Justine's sale, the number of names on my list has shrunk. Thirteen men have dwindled to two. One belongs to the owner of the safe house in Puerto Rico Trey just uncovered, and the other belongs to the only man who won't be scratched off my list with my knife.

It belongs to Dimitri—my brother.

Without his help, Justine's location would have never been unearthed, so he will be spared my blade for that alone.

I told Justine the men who bid on her would pay for their insolence.

I've kept my promise.

I arch a brow in suspicion when the group of men standing next to me stop gibbering legal bullshit mid-conversation. Peering over my shoulder, I spot the reason for their gaping jaws and bugging eyes.

Justine is sauntering down the stairs of the courthouse, the natural swing of her hips entrancing every man within a five-mile radius. Unlike the shimmery blouse she wore five minutes ago, the red spaghetti-strap bustier shirt she's wearing showcases every inch of her beautiful frame. Her lush tits bounce with every step she takes, and the slight roll of her hips hints at the seductiveness she exerts under the sheets.

She is a knockout.

A ten out of fucking ten.

"Ангел..." I don't say any more. I don't need to. Justine knows the effect she has on me. She can feel it in the air, smell it on my skin. I am fucking gone. Done and dusted for this woman.

Her long, wavy locks are pinned back in a messy bun, and her delicate neck and shoulders are on display for the world to see. I run my index finger over one of the scars on her right shoulder, smug as fuck at how confident she has become over the past twelve months. My Ангел is a goddess, and she is finally learning that.

"You look fucking ravishing," I mutter to Justine, incapable of holding back my praise.

When she smiles at my compliment, I want to smash the teeth

in of every man gawking at her with drool pooling in their mouths, but I won't. Her confidence is the highest it's ever been, but she still has a little ways to go before the woman I see behind the shield fully emerges. She's damn close, just not quite there—yet.

After hooking my arm around her petite waist, I guide Justine down the stairs of the courthouse on the heels of Roman. Just as they do every time they are in my presence, the paparazzi go crazy. They repeatedly call out my and Justine's names, praying they will get a money shot.

When I arrived at court months ago, they assumed I was here via a legal ramification. They had no clue I was merely picking up my woman after a hard day at the office.

As the months rolled on, Justine's importance in my life was broadcast on every news channel on the entire West Coast. It doesn't bother me that her face is associated with mine in every printed article in the past nine months.

Her gorgeous face is well-recognized. To the media, she's the woman who tamed the notorious murderer, thief, and cheat. To the men in my industry, she's known as the untouchable—one wrong glance, comment, or insinuation means lights out.

To me, she is my *Ангел*—the sweetest dessert any man can have.

My cock braces against the zipper of my pants when Justine slips into the SUV in front of me. When I notice her skirt is minus a panty line, memories of our conversation during brunch today filter through my mind.

I want your cunt bare and ready for me, Justine. If we're going to spend the day apart, I don't want anything in my way.

Spreading my hand across Roman's chest, I stop him from following Justine's lead into the SUV.

"I'll meet you at the restaurant," he grumbles.

His tone amuses me. From the day I told him to protect Justine as if she's his daughter, he has. Which means I've been on the receiving end of many stern looks and lectures over the past twelve months.

Roman will never admit it, but his grumpy attitude is a ploy. He loves riling me up as much as I love stirring him.

As sworn, I attempted to release Roman from obligations with my family the week following his shooting. He wouldn't hear of it.

He was adamant he was born for our lifestyle, and no amount of arguing would change his mindset.

Although it was drummed into me my entire life that favoritism, friendship, or even something as weak as love should never enter the equation, Justine has taught me that isn't necessarily true. Roman may be a member of my crew, but he is also my family.

After slipping into the back seat of my tinted-out SUV, I signal for the driver to go. The pulse thrumming in Justine's neck increases when I slide up the privacy partition between the driver and us. The generous swell of her chest rises and falls as every inch of the thick-paneled glass lifts into place.

It's barely locked into position when Justine slips onto my lap. Her knees straddle my hips as her mouth seals over mine. The heat of her bare pussy scorching my cock increases its thickness.

I love how insatiable she is around me. Her desire for me is strong enough to misplace her morals. Streams of cars are on each side of us, but Justine's hunger is too intense to let something as weak as shame harness her desires.

"Hold on to the handle. This is going to be hard and fast."

I'd like to take my time with her, but we only have fifteen minutes before we arrive at the restaurant she made reservations at earlier this week.

Although we usually eat privately, Justine wished us to dine out tonight. Considering it is the Fourth of July weekend, who was I to deny her request? It is our anniversary, after all.

While Justine loops her hand through the leather brace hanging above the back passenger door, I free my cock from its tight constraints. The veins feeding my cock pulsate when Justine releases a throaty moan. Her eyes are locked on my cock, the hunger in her heavy-hooded gaze unmissable.

"Did you take your little white pill this morning?" I ask her as I drag my cock along her wet cunt, coating my knob with evidence of her excitement.

Justine purrs softly before connecting her eyes with mine. "No."

My cock pulses. "Is that by choice? Or because you want to please me?" I ask, guiding the crest of my cock into the entrance of her greedy cunt.

She swivels her hips, opening herself for me before answering, "Both."

The shortness of her response can't lessen its impact. A little over a month ago, I expressed a desire to have an heir. I want someone with my blood running through their veins to inherit my legacy when I can no longer rule.

Unlike Vladimir, I won't decide my heir by gender. If we have a girl, she will rule my empire with strength garnered from her mother. If we have a boy, he will be shown that rules and discipline aren't the only factors required to make him a man.

Honor, trust, and integrity play a part as well.

When I take Justine to the root of my cock, I wait a beat, giving her time to acclimate to the pain stretching her wide. Although I crave this woman more than my lungs require air, I'll never hurt her —not in a million years.

Too impatient to wait a second longer, Justine clenches the walls of her pussy, wordlessly requesting me to move.

Gripping one hand on her waist and another around her neck, I do as asked. With my eyes locked on the enticing visual of her pretty pink cunt full to the brim with my cock, I glide her up my shaft before ramming her back down.

"Again," Justine demands before rising to her knees to give herself the leverage needed to draw my cock out to the tip.

A tingle races through my balls when she slams back down, her thrust more violent than my first.

Our pace is frantic in no time, adding to the lust teeming in Justine's eyes. Skin slapping skin booms around the cabin of my SUV as I fuck her without hesitation—like I am a man possessed. I drive into her even harder when my thoughts drift to her lips wrapping around my cock this morning.

She swallowed my cum with more eagerness than she polished off her plate of breakfast treats.

I've taught her well over the past twelve months. She knows she doesn't need to ask permission to slip under the breakfast nook and eat me for breakfast.

I'm hers whenever she needs me—in public or not.

"Oh god, Nikolai. Oh god..." Justine moans in a long, throaty groan. "I'm going to come."

I grip her neck more firmly as I lift my ass off the seat. I'm fucking her so furiously her glorious tits are mere moments from breaking out of the confines of her top. They inspire me to unravel her even more. I love her tits—nearly as much as I love her insatiable cunt.

"Give it to me, *Ангел*," I command, my tone rough. "Give me every fucking drop."

She grows hotter, wetter. I grind into her another four times before the most seductive fucking purr I've ever heard rips from her throat.

Rico was right. It doesn't matter how many times I drive her to climax, hearing my name purr from her throat will never grow old.

The sight of her beautiful face etched with ecstasy is enough to set me off. I slam her down to the base of my cock before letting the sensation gripping my sack eject.

My cum surges into Justine's pussy in raring spurts, intensifying the vicious shuddering wreaking havoc on her tiny frame.

Wondering if this could be the moment that ties her to me for eternity prolongs my orgasm.

By the time my cock stops jerking, Justine is slumped on my sweat-slicked torso. Our desire to fuck was so unquenchable we are both still clothed from the waist up.

"You all right?" I ask, hoping my need to drive her to the brink hasn't hurt her.

She doesn't answer unless you include a throaty moan as a response.

If she didn't feel our SUV come to a stop at the front of the restaurant we're eating at, I don't think she'd move at all.

"We're here already," she mumbles under her breath, her eyes widening.

I groan when she slips off my lap, pulling my half-masted cock from her snug cunt in the process.

When evidence of my cum slips onto her thigh, I snag a handful of tissues from a box at my side and place them between her legs. My cock twitches when she's incapable of holding back her moan from my meekest contact.

"Soon, *Ангел*. Very soon," I promise. "That was just the beginning of our night."

After cleaning up Justine the best I can with limited supplies, we exit the SUV.

If Justine's ruffled hair and flaming cheeks weren't enough of an indication to Roman of how we occupied our drive, the intoxicating scent of lust is a surefire indication.

"She's not your daughter, Roman," I remind him when he glares at me.

His chance to reply is lost when we enter the restaurant, and a large group of people screams a massive, "Surprise!"

My fingertips stop seeking my knife when my eyes scan the people approaching me from all directions. They are my crew, my men, my family.

What the fuck?

Justine curls her arms around my neck before pressing her lips to my ear. "Happy birthday, Nikolai," she whispers breathlessly. "I know it isn't your birthday for another two weeks, but after learning the hard way last year you aren't a fan of birthdays, I brought your celebration forward a few weeks." Feeling my pulse surging through our hands, she glances back into my eyes. "Don't be mad. Everyone here loves you, and they want to celebrate with you."

Stealing my chance to reply that she's the only one stupid enough to love me, Justine nudges her head to the right. I'm shocked for the second time in under a minute when I spot Rico, Blaire, and their four-year-old son, Eli, standing at the side of the restaurant with Lia and Adrian.

Although this isn't the first time I've interacted with my brother since he left Vegas a year ago, it's our first meeting on my home turf.

Usually I travel to him.

Our first meeting was when Justine and I arrived on his doorstep so I could apologize to his wife in person. Blaire was apprehensive but accepted my apology with a small snip of the feistiness I'd always seen hidden within her.

Things are still rocky, but my relationship with Rico is solid.

His kitten will come around—eventually.

"Hey, sorry I'm late. I was a little tied up."

Trey enters the restaurant with the same dramatic edge he always has. The limp he gained as a consequence of Alexei's retribution adds to his natural swagger, and the scruffy beard he grew while recovering has the whores at Clarks in a tizzy.

Unfortunately for the numerous women eyeballing our

greeting with batting eyelashes and tempting grins, he is as taken as me.

"Kristina, hi," Justine greets eagerly, leaning in to kiss the petite blonde with bright-blue eyes cradled under Trey's arm—the same blonde who aided me in saving Justine nearly a year ago. "How are things? I hope Trey is treating you well?" I don't know what Kristina replies to Justine in Czech, but Justine approves, as her smile lights up the room. "Good. I told you he was a keeper."

After greeting Trey with a kiss on his cheek, Justine scrubs her thumb over the area her lips touched, believing the bright-red spot on his face is a lipstick smear.

It isn't.

He has matching splotches dotting the collar of his shirt and the cuffs of his sleeves.

"What? I didn't have time to shower," Trey mutters under his breath when he catches my glare. Justine is well aware of our industry, but that doesn't mean she wants it thrust in her face multiple times a week.

Rolling my eyes at his pathetic excuse, I curl my arm around Justine's waist and guide her toward Rico and Lia.

Our long strides stop halfway across the crowded space when Justine's cell phone vibrates in her purse.

My interest piques when a cute little groove crinkles between her brows, which deepens when her eyes lower to the screen of her phone. My blood thickens when I learn the cause of her dour response.

Carmichael I'm-Going-To-Gut-Him-Alive Fletcher.

Although Justine has been working independently for the past nine months, she has maintained an amicable working relationship with Carmichael.

This kills me to admit, but I understand why she didn't cut him off cold turkey. Carmichael is a sleazy, underhanded, lying motherfucker, but he is also a brilliant defense attorney.

Besides Justine, he is the only lawyer on this side of the country capable of getting Maddox off his charges.

Since having her brother released from incarceration is Justine's greatest wish, I set aside my dislike of Carmichael for her benefit.

It is a fucking hard feat.

"Take it," I suggest to Justine when she hesitates in answering his call.

She shakes her head. "No. It's your birthday. He can wait." She waves her hand through the air like she's shooing away a fly.

"It's not my birthday for another two weeks," I reply, tugging her close to my side. "Take your call. I'll wait for you over there." My eyes drift to Eli, who has his little arms curled around his father's thigh.

He looks scared, and rightfully so. Half the men in this room plotted his demise before they knew he existed. Lucky for him, he is sheltered under the pardon I gave his father.

No one will ever hurt him—not if they want to live.

When Justine nods, I press my lips to her temple. My chest swells with smugness when I feel how damp the roots of her hair are. We only had fifteen minutes, but we rocked every minute we had.

Roman shadows Justine when she slips into the restaurant's foyer, seeking quiet for her call.

Happy Roman is forever on guard when it comes to Justine, I make my way to Rico, Lia, and their families.

It takes me nearly ten minutes since I'm stopped by numerous partygoers wishing to bestow their birthday greetings upon me.

If I wasn't so lost in Justine, I'd be pissed she organized this party.

I was born in hell—that shouldn't be celebrated.

Rico greets me like he did when he left a year ago, by using my handshake offer to draw me to his chest.

"Happy birthday, Eli."

I smirk, amused by his tone.

He hates birthdays as much as I do.

After pulling back, he drifts his eyes past my shoulder. "Is everything all right with your girl? She's looking a little white."

Following the direction of his gaze, I spot Justine heading in our direction. Her steps are slow and wobbly, and her face is marked with big, salty tears. I race for her, my legs thumping the floorboards faster than my heart is smashing against my ribs.

If someone has hurt her, I'm going to fucking kill them.

"What's wrong? Did someone hurt you? Are you hurt?" I question, pulling her into my arms.

Her skin is clammy and cold, and the red hue of her cheeks gained during transport is no longer visible.

When her mouth opens and closes but not a syllable slips through her lips, I lift my eyes to Roman, anticipating his white dress shirt to be absorbing blood.

Like me, he won't go down without a fight. He will protect Justine until his very last breath.

Roman isn't injured.

He's perfectly fine, unharmed, and as confused as me.

Ignoring the itch to slit the throat of every man in this room until they snitch on who harmed my *Ангел*, I lower my eyes to Justine.

She glances up at me, the lively sparkle in her eyes a stark contradiction to the expression on her face. "My brother," she croaks through tears, her words brittle. "He's coming home."

Goosebumps race to the surface of my skin as I struggle to understand what she's saying.

"Maddox?" I ask, still confused.

Justine nods, sending fresh tears rolling down her cheeks.

"The woman he was convicted of murdering isn't dead. She was arrested in my hometown for attempted murder. She's alive, Nikolai. Maddox's victim is alive. He's coming home. Carmichael has filed the paperwork. He's being released this week."

Jesus fucking Christ.

My *Ангел's* greatest wish was just granted, but I wasn't the man who granted it.

Now I have even more reason to slit Carmichael's throat.

Are you desperate for more? Readers begged, and I listened. A third and final instalment of Nikolai and Justine's story is available now.

Find it here: Nikolai: Ruling the Bratva

. . .

Facebook: facebook.com/authorshandi

Instagram: instagram.com/authorshandi

Email: authorshandi@gmail.com

Reader's Group: bit.ly/ShandiBookBabes

Website: authorshandi.com

Newsletter: https://www.subscribepage.com/AuthorShandi

Nikolai
RULING THE
BRATVA
USA TODAY BESTSELLING AUTHOR
SHANDI BOYES

COPYRIGHT

Editing: Mountains Wanted Editing

Editing: Courtney Umphress

Cover: SSB Covers & Design

Photographer: Ren Saliba

Proof read by: Lindsi La Bar

1

NIKOLAI

A battle is coming.

I can sense it in the air, feel it quivering over my skin as my blood furiously pumps to cool my unnatural body temperature. I want to pretend my unease arises solely from Justine's brother's impending release, but my gut warns me to remain cautious. This feels bigger than that, as if I'm about to face my deadliest battle to date.

This frustrates me more than it excites me.

Only a year ago, I would have craved a bloodbath. I had nothing to lose and no fear of dying. Now I have more than my reputation at stake. I have my *Ангел* to protect, my gift for years of suffering.

Fools may say the odds are stacked against me, but I wouldn't cut off my nose to spite my face. Justine may be my only weakness, but the lengths I'll go to protect her are well-known by my enemies.

I killed the man who raised me to keep her safe, and I'll do the same to any *идиот* stupid enough to take up the challenge Vladimir's death instigated.

If Alexei's death isn't proof of this, I'm sure I can find more convincing factors.

Alexei arrived on my home turf to kill my man and take my woman.

He left with not even a legacy. His family moved on from his death as quickly as the Popov entity recovered from Vladimir's dethroning.

Both losses were scarcely registered.

Their deaths are proof that what Rico said earlier tonight is true. "Good leaders don't tell you what to do. They show you how it's done."

If I hadn't seen the glint his eyes got every time he caught his kitten's eye, I would have mistaken his comment as him forging a way back into an organization that's profited more the past year than it did the prior ten, but that wasn't what he was doing.

He was commending me.

I've learned many things in the past year, but accepting praise isn't one of them. More times than not during my childhood, commendations arrived with painful citations. The more ruthless you are in this industry, the greater your reputation becomes.

Because Vladimir never wanted to be seen as weak by his enemies, he wasn't just the patriarch of our family. He was the governor who ruled it with an iron fist.

Although I have no intentions of following in Vladimir's footsteps, a weak leader will be quickly weeded out, meaning I must not only remain on my toes when it comes to Justine, but I have to continually peer over my shoulder, keeping watch for the next challenger to bid for my throne.

My crew is the strongest it's ever been, but that doesn't mean I shouldn't remain on alert. Vladimir was pushed from his perch because he became reckless. He thought the reputation Rico and I had developed was enough to stop his reign from being challenged.

He was an idiot.

If anything, it should have made him warier.

He abused Rico and me for years, believing fear would stop us from demanding our share of the glory.

That was his first downfall.

I was plotting his demise years before Justine entered the picture. My desire to protect her merely sped up the process. If I'd had the means after my sixteenth birthday, I would have initiated my takeover bid earlier, but with patience came a greater reward.

By waiting, I not only dethroned Vladimir, I took his place.

I now sit on his throne with my queen by my side.

For how long, I don't know.

Justine only moved to Vegas for one reason. Although I have no doubt of my importance in her life, I'm also confident about the bond she has with her family.

She wants to go home.

The pleading looks she's given me the last three hours assure I can't be mistaken.

Unfortunately for her, a trip to Hopeton is not on our agenda in the foreseeable future. There have been no bids on my empire since my knife claimed Alexei's life, but fools aren't known for their smarts.

Furthermore, I can protect Justine here.

I can't issue the same guarantee in Florida.

Vladimir's death barely created a ripple in Vegas, but the flow-on effect could still inflict a bitter taste in the back of my throat. I challenged the rules and won, which has only encouraged men in my previous predicament to do the same.

For that reason alone, I won't approve the numerous silent requests Justine has been issuing me every hour on the hour since she discovered her brother is being released from incarceration later this week.

My enemies know she's my only weakness, but they're also mindful of how far I'll go to protect her. Nothing is above me when it comes to protecting her.

My urge to kill grows when the natural swing of Justine's hips seduces the men surrounding us so well that they fail to notice the sheen on her cheeks that hasn't dried in over three hours. I know the tears are there because I counted every one she shed.

They were produced in happiness, but there'll be hell to pay for every one fallen. My *Ангел*'s greatest wish was granted, but I wasn't the man who awarded it.

That alone guarantees vengeance.

I didn't ruthlessly pursue Justine because my cock was cold and she had the means to keep it warm.

I hunted her—that is what men like me do.

We pursue.

We kill.

Then we devour.

I just had no clue that one taste of Justine would never be enough.

One hit had me craving another.

And another.

And another.

Before I knew it, she was my addiction—my queen.

Many men in my industry were fooled with promises of power and wealth, but Justine didn't need smoke and mirrors to secure my attention. She merely played the role she was destined to fulfill from the moment she entered my realm with a warrior's heart and an angel's face.

Growing accustomed to the envious glances she's forever subjected to, Justine returns the men's admiring stares, but her eyes aren't glazed with the poisonous snake venom mine are laced with. She shows them a side of her I've always seen, that she's a gift from heaven, the reason I wake every day and rest every evening.

She thinned the black veins woven around my heart just enough to keep me from fully succumbing to the darkness that enshrouded my life twelve months ago, but she kept them thick enough that no man will be game to test my devotion to her.

If Justine can't read my every thought, my demand for Roman to travel with us will have her hearing them loud and clear. Her enticing cunt is still bare as per my request this morning when I discovered our day would be spent apart, but the wishes of my cock can't enter the equation.

Justine's safety must remain my utmost priority. She comes before anything—even my cock's insatiable need to be surrounded by her warmth.

Once she spots my wordless request, I expect Justine to come out fighting like she did when I shipped her to Hopeton a year ago, to argue that not even I have the right to tell her what to do, but shockingly, she slides into the back seat of the SUV without uttering a syllable.

The lack of panty line on her skintight skirt has me detesting my somewhat manic protectiveness. My cock was only surrounded by her heat a mere three hours ago, but the marathon of events we take on each day made our hard and quick fuck during our trip seem the equivalent of foreplay.

I'm dying for another hit of my greatest addiction.

A growl rumbles in my chest when I slide into the SUV on Roman's tail. My battle just grew tenfold. The interior of my car smells like Justine's skin intermingled with mine. It's an intoxicating scent that has my cock bracing against the zipper in my pants.

I still can't believe I'm wearing a monkey suit. I said months ago that I'd don a jacket and tie if it guaranteed me a taste of Justine. Our fuck on the way to the restaurant made my effort worthwhile.

I'd test the theory again if Justine weren't so deep in thought. Alas, even with our SUV surrounded by goons paid to protect her, in her head, she's already halfway to Hopeton.

Justine continues her silent stance for our thirty-minute trip to the Popov compound. Her lips don't even twitch when the house-maids fuss over her as they do every time she's in their presence. The only time she's drawn from her thoughts is when they remove her handbag and shoes from her grasp before advising her our room has been set up as specified.

That piques my interest as much as it does Justine's. While her throat works hard to swallow, her wide-with-lust eyes wander to mine. They have the same doe-eyed look they held in the seconds leading to us entering the restaurant with members of my family and crew lying in wait to surprise me.

"How many more surprises are you hiding up your sleeve, *Ангел?*" My tone is huskier than usual, my accent more pronounced from the lust heating my blood.

Justine's eyes flare, thickening my veins even more. She's on the hunt, and she has her sights firmly locked on one man: me.

"More than you'll ever realize," she whispers as her fingers interlock with mine.

Smiling sheepishly, she guides us toward our bedroom. Although her brother's impending release had her forgetting what established tonight's celebration, her focus has returned more vital than ever.

I wouldn't have been bothered if it hadn't. Men in my industry don't celebrate birthdays—not when they represent surviving another year in hell—but things are different now. Each day I have with Justine is a blessing because she doesn't strive to save me from my miserable existence. She merely removes me from it.

That's why I requested that she stop using contraception over a month ago. I want an heir, not solely to take over my reign when I'm no longer capable of leading my crew, but so I can have someone I can love and protect as much as I do Justine.

For my entire childhood, anything I loved, Vladimir took. It didn't matter what it was: a soft toy, a friendly housemaid, or an uncle who wasn't blood related. If I cherished it in any way, he took it from me.

Initially, I thought his disdain resulted from me taking more of my mother's genes than his. As the years passed, so did my stupidity.

Vladimir knew all along that I wasn't his son. He only raised me as if I were because he wanted to brainwash me into killing my real father. Although I don't have a drop of Popov blood in my veins, I did precisely that when Vladimir fell victim to my knife a little over twelve months ago.

Blood doesn't make you family. Respect and honor do. Vladimir garnered the admiration of his followers the wrong way. He forced it with fearful tactics I was too young and foolish to comprehend.

You can guarantee I won't make the same mistake.

I have the respect of thousands and the fear of millions, but none compares to my love and adoration for Justine. She taught me that you can scare a boy into obeying you, but you can't scare a man into respecting you.

I plan to instill those values into our child when he or she is born. I'll show them how to lead without the sadistic, body-maiming tricks Vladimir used on me my entire life. It won't be easy —I'm a natural-born killer—but with Justine guiding me, I have no doubt I'll achieve a once seemingly impossible task: rule with respect and fear.

My eyes lock with Justine's when our trek down the deserted corridor stops at our door. "Oh, Ангел..." I could say more, but I don't need to. If the thickening in my pants doesn't expose what I'm thinking, the lust firing from my eyes is a sure-fire indication.

My childhood bedroom has been gutted. Not a single piece of its original furniture remains in place. Even though the palette is feminine and girly, the pieces Justine has refurnished it with cause a manly scent to seep from my pores.

They're items from her apartment: the sofa I first claimed her on as mine, the rug I tackled her on when she tried to chicken out of our game of strip Scrabble. She even has the funky retro wicker seat we sat in when I divulged to her my plan to kill Vladimir.

We were supposed to watch the sunrise. Instead, I claimed her in a way I never knew I wanted but now crave more than anything. I made her wholly mine. There was nothing between us that morning, just as there will be nothing between us this evening.

Although the desire to hunt pumps through my body hard and fast, I can't act on it. I have to settle a critical matter before I can get lost in the deadliest drug I've ever sampled.

When my hands are on Justine, she strips my insecurities as quickly as she does my anger, but I refuse to let that happen. Not until she knows the rules and how far I'll go to protect her.

"You can't go home. It isn't safe." I keep my tone stern yet understanding.

Justine's unique green-blue eyes snap to mine. Their apprehension weakens my arrogance, but not enough for my campaign to lose its steam.

"Let's not do this now, okay? It's your birthday. Any discussions about my return home can wait a few more hours."

"No, *Ангел.*" I follow her into our giant walk-in closet. "It's not my birthday for another two weeks, but even if it were today, nothing is being saved for tomorrow because there's nothing to discuss. You're not leaving Vegas. No negotiation needed."

She takes on the fighting stance I fell on the knife for long before her beautiful face. I can tell from the apprehension in her eyes that she wants to delay our argument for a few more hours, but the fire in her gut is too intense to ignore.

"You didn't have any issues shipping me back to Hopeton when it suited you—"

"That's right. When it suited me." My voice is nowhere near as calm as hers. It's wilder and more strained. "Now doesn't suit me."

Her teeth grit as she struggles not to throw her hands into the air. "What about the numerous trips you've taken the past year? You've been all over the globe without me."

"Because you were here, with Roman—safe. Those weren't vacations, *Ангел.* I was working."

I'll never see those trips as a chore, though. They were more a requirement than anything, a prerequisite to the pledge I made to Justine twelve months ago.

I told her every man who bid on her would pay for his insolence.

I've kept my word.

Thirteen men have dwindled to two. If news of Maddox's release hadn't altered my plan of attack, the final man would have been dealt with by the end of this week.

Although I vowed to personally deal with every man on the list Rico supplied me last year, one name will forever remain: my brother Dimitri. Without his help, I may have never located where Vladimir had taken Justine. That alone will spare him the wrath of my blade.

I had once hoped when my list was depleted, the tight reins I've had on Justine the past twelve months would slacken. Regrettably, with every curve in this industry comes new challenges.

Before we were interrupted by Rico and Lia checking if Justine was okay, Justine mentioned Maddox was released because the woman he was accused of murdering was arrested.

If that's true, an entirely new set of rules have been brought into play, ones I'd rather die from than abide by.

Col only issued Justine a pardon from her punishment because Maddox pledged to do anything he wished. Col needed a woman to permanently disappear, and he needed it to appear as if a member of the Federal Bureau of Investigation killed her.

Col died years ago, but if Maddox didn't fulfill his pledge, Justine is still in debt to the Petrettis. Even though Petretti blood runs in my veins, I'll never be a Petretti. They're my enemy, meaning not only is my queen on their radar, but they also own her.

The thought has the black veins around my heart re-surging stronger than ever.

"Maddox may be walking out of prison in a few days, but he is far from free. I don't want you anywhere near him until the shit stops hitting the fan from his release."

Justine glares at me, pretending she hates my somewhat manic protectiveness.

It's a woeful waste of time. I know she fuckin' loves it. Her confidence has grown tenfold over the past twelve months, and although some of her new boldness can be attributed to the role she's taken on at the Popov compound, most of it is accredited to me.

Can you imagine the relief from knowing you have a man who is confident and brave enough to protect you? She knows I'd slit the throats of a thousand men before I'd let anyone touch her, so she has nothing to fear.

I'm not so lucky.

Why do you think Roman tracks her every move? I'm not a pedantic asshole who wants to gouge out the eyes of any man who dares look at her with interest. I'm keeping my greatest asset safe. Before Justine entered my life, I had nothing to lose. Now I have everything, and the odds are even more stacked against me.

"When things settle down, you can travel to Hopeton, but until then—"

"He's my brother, Nikolai," Justine murmurs in disbelief as her wild eyes dart between mine.

"And you are my queen!" I hiss back in Russian, my anger reaching a point it hasn't seen in over twelve months, fueled by both panic and fury. "That means I should rank more highly to you than he does."

"Nikolai..." She stops, then breathes deeply, aware her actions are not hers. We're two people fighting to stay together in a world determined to keep us apart.

Although Justine will never say it, I'm confident her family believes she's only in Vegas to have Maddox's conviction quashed. Now that it's been achieved, her father's already numerous requests for her to return home will double. They have no idea about the life she has created here with me. They know of me, but the industry I'm in, what Justine does for my crew, and the target our relationship placed on her back are concealed with fancy titles and legal talk. They're unaware of how far into hell Justine traveled for me, much less how far I'll go to protect her.

Family or not, no one will be spared my blade if they come between us.

I stop clenching and unclenching my fists when Justine murmurs, "This isn't my family versus yours, Nikolai. It's just..."

"What, Ангел? You don't want them to know you sleep in the same bed as a liar, a thief, and a murderer? You're ashamed of the life you've created here, with me?"

Loose strands of red hair fall down her practically bare shoulders when she shakes her head. "That's not it at all. You misinterpreted what I said."

Not thinking, I brush away the curl hiding the bite marks on her shoulder. She flinches, but not in a bad way. She loves that I love her scars, and that makes me want to love and protect her even more fiercely than I already do.

I can still recall the testosterone that pumped through my veins the first time I saw her in a spaghetti-strap top that exposed her scars. Fortunately, my head was in game mode, or nothing would have stopped me from taking her on the hood of my car at the front of the compound.

Her outfit was simple: a pair of white cuffed shorts with a fitted red shirt, but the confidence radiating out of her sent my head into a tailspin. She was fucking ravishing, as beautiful as an *angel—my angel*.

"Don't ever hide from me," I whisper in Russian.

The anger in Justine's eyes transforms into love. "Never, Nikolai. Just like I'd never hide you. I love you. Nothing will *ever* change that." She wraps her arms around my waist before burrowing her head into my chest. "I talk about you all the time. My mom is dying to meet you. I just don't want it to happen here." She waves her arm toward our room. "Even if you're born for this business, it's a lot to take in."

Hearing nothing but honesty in her tone, I try to lighten the mood. "What's wrong with our home?" My question is more facetious than angry. "You seem to have forgotten how many times you've screamed my name in this very room the past twelve months." Her fist lands in my stomach. Because she's only playing, I let it slide. "Do you need a reminder of all the fun we've had here?"

The lust thickening my tone quickly changes our confrontation from volatile to needy. I'm not the only one noticing the change in temperature. She raises her eyes to mine as her teeth rake her bottom lip. Just like her gallop down the courthouse stairs earlier tonight entranced every man within a five-mile radius, I'm under her spell within seconds.

Recognizing she has me trapped, she murmurs, "I don't need a reminder. I just need a little understanding."

"*Ангел...*" I drawl out in warning at her attempt to revisit our conversation.

My blood pumps hard and fast when she steps back to wrangle the hidden zipper in her skirt. Even knowing she's using my attraction to her against me, I watch her with reverence.

With my eagerness to fuck her earlier tonight keeping her clothed, my eyes missed scanning a body too stunning to be deemed anything less than perfect. I'm not willing to set aside my desires for a second longer.

After she slips her skirt off her milky-white thighs, Justine's attention shifts to her red bustier shirt. Since it has a built-in bra, her lush tits fall to her chest within seconds of her unknotting the red material binding it together.

Striving not to interrupt her sexy striptease, I clench my fists at my sides. Thank fucking fuck I'm the only one showing restraint. She is as eager to get this party started as I am.

Faster than I can growl at the wetness between her legs, she dumps her bustier onto her skirt, then raises her eyes to mine. The desire to hunt and conquer smacks into me hard and fast when she stands before me as naked as the day she was born, with her hands as free and relaxed as her eyes.

Not an ounce of coyness has invaded her.

"Look at you, with more confidence than a queen." My voice is rough, as if I've just woken. I've been awake longer than the sun, so it's not the cause of my groggy tone. It is her, my gift from heaven for surviving years of atonement, lowering herself to her knees in front of me.

"Yes, because of you. The way you make me feel, the way you cherish me. I wouldn't be half the woman I am without you." I almost interrupt, but she continues talking, foiling my attempt to tell her she's always been perfect. My attention merely revealed the woman hiding behind her strong, determined eyes. "And tonight, I will worship you just as eagerly."

Her eyes lift to mine as her hands work on my belt. They relay her every thought: her hunger, her wish to make me feel as revered as only she can, but unfortunately they also expose that her earlier pleas haven't been forgotten. They've been merely placed on the back burner while she succumbs to the heady scent of lust brewing between us.

Although I'm seconds from having my cock sucked, our conversation can't wait. "I can't protect you there. I can't keep you safe."

"Yes, you can," Justine replies before lowering my pants' zipper. "Because you're the king, and I am your queen. We kneel for no one but each other."

She frees my cock from my pants, its thick buoyancy complementing the fire in her tone. She spoke like a woman born to lead. She took her place at my side the instant she removed my knife from Vladimir's chest, but tonight is the first time she's sat on her throne.

After taking in a bead of pre-cum cresting at the peak of my cock, Justine's eyes return to mine, wordlessly seeking permission to unleash her innermost desires.

"Take what you need. I'll never keep anything from you." My last three words come out in a groan from her tongue skimming across my knob.

Her velvety tongue flicks the slit in my cock four times before she guides her pillowy lips down my shaft. She takes me into her mouth as far as she can without gagging before drawing me back out.

While her hand works the sections of my cock missing out on her mouth, I gather her wavy locks in my fist, revealing a visual capable of bringing the strongest man to his knees.

My woman is on her knees, sucking my cock so fiercely she's seconds away from extracting the marrow from my bones.

A lesser man may confuse her eagerness to give head as a tactic to force me to submit, but that isn't the sole reason she's devouring me like she can't get enough.

Right now, she's responding more to her body's needs than her heart. Furthermore, she knows she doesn't need to get on her knees to have me grant her every wish. She merely needs to ask.

My lips part for much-needed air as my body stiffens. It isn't the delicious gag tearing from Justine's throat causing my body's response. It's from realizing I'm a hypocrite. I begged for understanding when Justine discovered I was engaged to Malvina, and how do I repay her for weeks of torture and months of understanding? I fail to give her the same level of empathy.

That's fucked. I was raised on broken promises and misguided morals. I won't let the same issues stain my relationship. I've pledged time and time again that Justine will want for nothing since she became my queen. Now I must uphold my vow.

"If I agree to this, there will be no holds barred. We'll take a crew with us. A full team of my best men. You won't be out of my sight for a minute, do you understand?"

When she fails to respond to my question, I tighten my grip on her hair, weakening her greedy pace. Her tongue swirls around my knob as her lusty eyes lift to mine. She's so hungry for my cum she's forgotten why she's on her knees to begin with.

"Soon, Justine. Very soon," I growl in ecstasy, the yearning in her eyes deserving of an unrestrained reply.

A deep groan vibrates my knob. She isn't growling in agreement. She's moaning because I used her real name. She has said many times in the past year that she loves her nickname, but she prefers me to call her Justine when we're behind closed doors.

I had hoped when the number of whores in the Popov compound dwindled from hundreds to a mere dozen, her worry I'd grow bored of her would lessen.

Regrettably, no matter how many times I assure her that her tight cunt is the only one my cock wants to pound, her panic hasn't receded in the slightest.

It's not all bad, though. The harder she fights to keep me on the straight and narrow, the more savage my addiction becomes.

I extract my cock from Justine's mouth with a pop when I take a step back. She groans before raising her eyes to mine. I thicken even more. Her eyes are wide with lust and nearly black from how dilated her pupils are. Little beads of sweat dot her hairline, and the smooth panels of her stomach can't hide the wetness between her legs. My *Ангел* is saturated and ready to be devoured.

I've just got one matter to settle first.

2

JUSTINE

The frantic quiver of my pulse triples when Nikolai steps back far enough to get undressed without bumping me. I was so blinded by lust that the instant his cock was removed from his pants, I had it in my mouth.

I thought I would have him so spellbound by my impressive cock-sucking skills he'd grant my numerous pleas to return home without his usual overprotectiveness, but all I did was prove I'm defenseless when it comes to anything associated with him.

My appetite for him has always been feverish, but it's grown worse in the past month.

I can't get enough of him.

After removing his boots and pants, Nikolai shrugs off his vest before working on his button-up shirt. Even with my mind blitzed from the call I took at the beginning of our celebration, I can't stop drinking him in. He is an extremely handsome man. The sneer of a madman, the body of an Adonis, and the stamina of a Greek god. He truly is every woman's fantasy and the man I'd go to hell for without a second thought.

That's why I can't comprehend his worry about me returning home. I don't want to go back to Hopeton permanently. I just want to witness my brother walk free.

Two weeks after a dog mauled me, he was arrested and charged with murder. He's not been home since. His release has been years in the making, so I refuse to miss it for anything or anyone.

My campaign to make Nikolai see sense through the madness is pushed to the side for the second time in less than thirty minutes when he stops to stand in front of me. From his recently trimmed hair to the widespread stance of his feet, he's exposed and unguarded.

Entranced by the heat bouncing between us, I track my eyes over him, taking in the rigid bumps of his stomach, stacked thighs, slim waist, and banging guns. My inappropriate thoughts about him the first time I saw him are accurate. He is the reason women buy sex toys and fathers buy guns. He is the representation of good and evil in one incredibly alluring package.

Not even the scars mottled throughout his vibrantly colored tattoos can deter his appeal. If anything, they make him more attractive. They show how strong he is—how he walked through the gates of hell and survived.

For each day that passes since Vladimir's death, Nikolai emerges further from the darkness he was born in, although I don't ever see him being fully freed from it. He was born into this industry. He doesn't know life outside of it, and in all honesty, I don't mind.

This industry isn't for the weak, but I've seen it in a different light over the past twelve months. Every person has good and bad points. The same can be said for mafia men.

Nikolai may not have directly organized Maddox's release, but I'm confident he's the only man capable of keeping him safe as he reintegrates into society. He will protect my family as fiercely as he guards me because he knows how much they mean to me.

My swollen chest puffs more when Nikolai demands, "Eyes on me." His voice is hardened with lust, making his Russian heritage more notable.

The vein inflating his cock pulsates when my eyes rocket to his in an instant. Nothing has changed from the weekend we danced our first two-steps-forward, three-steps-back routine. The faster I submit, the brighter the passion in his eyes burns.

Peering down at me with arctic-blue eyes, he completes the short two steps between us. A dash of coyness invades me when his eyes lower to take in my naked frame. It doesn't last long. His cock thickens more with every inch his eyes travel, proving he likes what he sees.

As I see his scars as medals of honor, he sees mine the same way. For some stupid reason, he believes they make me more attractive. Although I doubt that is the case, the glint in his eyes is undeniable.

"I'm going to lose myself in you. There's no drug strong enough to replicate the high I get from your body."

I smile, adoring that even after twelve months, he's yet to grow bored. Roman has often said the Popov housemaids are the pick of the bunch. Unfortunately, so are their whores. Nikolai had their devotion in bucketloads before he was crowned king of their empire. Now their wish to be beneath him has grown rampant. They'll do anything to secure his attention.

Although I trust Nikolai, I didn't just nearly lose my life five years ago. I lost a part of who I was. While Nikolai's devotion has helped me regain the confidence I lost, watching him being propositioned is a knock even the biggest ego would struggle to tolerate.

I understand the whores' plight. Witnessing Nikolai dote on me firsthand reveals he isn't just a powerful man. It shows that his heart is as devastatingly beautiful as his panty-wetting face.

He truly has it all: looks, power, and stamina. I just thank god he wants me at his side, protecting and loving him as ravenously as he does me.

"Then..." Nikolai waits for my eyes to float to his before finalizing his statement. "We'll continue our discussion on the possibility of you seeing Maddox when he returns home."

My brows furrow. "Continue?" I question, utterly lost.

His grin sends my heart racing. When he nods, I stare at him in shock and awe. I've been known to act like a naïve nymphomaniac in his presence, but this is ridiculous. Tonight isn't supposed to be about me, but here I am, spaced out on lust.

I shouldn't be so hard on myself. I've always said I feel like a queen when I'm bombarded by his affections. Whether quivering beneath him or helping a member of his crew with a legal matter, I've felt more at home the past year than I ever have.

This industry isn't for the faint of heart, so I'm quickly learning how strong I truly am. I may be on my knees, but I have the world at my feet.

As if he can read my thoughts, Nikolai cups my chin and raises my head high. "You are my queen, Ангел. With me at your side, you'll never want for anything."

The combination of his words and his virile scent has my thighs squeezing together. A year ago, he promised me the world. He's given me precisely that. He is a dangerous man, but only when you side with the wrong team.

A squeak pops from my lips when Nikolai hoists me from the ground with a jerk on my wrist. Not speaking a word, he moves us into our room at the back of the Popov compound. He doesn't need to talk for me to hear his every thought, though. My king is on the warpath, ready to conquer any man who dares step between us.

Twelve months ago, I would have shivered at the thought.

Now, I'm shuddering in excitement.

After laying me down on the same sofa on which he first claimed me, Nikolai kneels between my splayed thighs. His hot breaths quiver against my drenched pussy as his equally heated gaze slowly rises to mine.

"My men. My crew. No holds barred. I won't give this up for anyone. Not a million bullets or the Almighty himself can take you away from me."

The urge to pull my knees together grows rampant when he runs the back of his hand down my moist slit. He stares at my body in fascination, as if ugly scars don't mar it.

In no time at all, his adoring glance has my thighs sweeping wider, my confidence at a pinnacle it hasn't reached in years. I'd agree to anything at this point, and Nikolai knows it. That's why he flipped the coin.

Our exchange started with a plea for understanding, but it will end in the most brilliant way.

My body clenches in euphoria when he slaps my clit, awakening it with a hunger no one but him can quench. "But before any of that, you're going to watch me eat the tastiest cunt I've ever eaten."

My back arches off the couch when his tongue spears the folds of my pussy. He drags it up my glistening slit in a slow, dedicated lick before circling his lips around my clit. I shout his name into the sticky night air when he sucks my throbbing nub into his mouth.

My senses are heightened beyond belief when he murmurs against my drenched lips, "I can taste myself in you."

His confession doesn't lessen his eagerness to devour me in the slightest. He continues nibbling, sucking, and licking my pussy as if his cum didn't spill in me only three hours ago. I'm not surprised. He has always said nothing will come between us, so I doubt a little bit of cum will stop him.

The naughtiness of our exchange sends my mind into a tailspin. I clamp my eyes shut as a roaring sensation pummels my smarts into mush. Like every moment I am with him, this feels wickedly deviant and shamelessly arousing at the same time.

"Ride my tongue, *Ангел*. Fuck my mouth hard and fast like you do my cock."

He tightens his grip on my hips before raising my ass off the couch so I can rock against him. The feeling is phenomenal, and it quickly has me coming undone.

"That's it. Nice and loud. Let me hear how much you love this."

I moan his name on repeat, not the least bit worried his crew may hear me. Something so brilliant deserves more than a discreet response.

The screams ripping from my throat jump a few decibels when he slides two fingers inside of me. While his tongue hardens my clit to the point it's almost painful, his fingers replicate the movements his cock makes when he fucks me.

His pace is as wild as the fire in his eyes, a dreamy, hot tempo that makes my orgasm crest at a speed I should be ashamed of.

"I can't hold back." My words shudder as much as my thighs.

Nikolai's lips lift against my pussy before his Derail Justine Train kicks into overdrive. His fingers pump in and out of me at a rapid pace as his tongue flicks my clit on repeat. I moan, loving that every second he spends devouring me loosens the knot my stomach has held since I spoke to Carmichael earlier tonight.

Don't get me wrong, I'm over the moon that Maddox is being released—this is something my family has been striving to achieve for half a decade. I'm just panicked about the repercussions it could cause to Nikolai's reign.

He already sided with his enemy once for me. I'd rather deter a second collaboration than encourage one.

"Give it to me, *Ангел*," Nikolai growls over my slicked pussy. His husky groan gives my orgasm the final push it needs to reach fruition. "Give me every drop of your goodness."

I still as a wave of beautiful devastation spikes through my veins. My thighs clamp around his head as a tingling sensation activates every sensory button in my body.

My climax is long and painstakingly perfect. It frees me from the madness in my head by assuring me I have nothing to worry about. As Nikolai has protected me and my family the past twelve months, I have no doubt he'll do the same for the next several years, if not forever.

My legs have barely stopped shaking when Nikolai flips me over. A long, unsteady breath parts my lips when his thumb skims past my climax-slicked ass.

"I want all of you, *Ангел*," he murmurs while placing pressure on my clenched back entrance. "I want to possess and own every inch of you. You were my reward for surviving years in hell. Now I want the ultimate prize. I want you to be mine, fully and unrestrained."

Not giving me a chance to protest—*not that I was going to*—he slides his index finger into my ass. The oily residue of my climax makes it an easy feat. He slips in without any resistance, the sensation it creates unbelievably enjoyable for how wickedly naughty I feel.

"What did I tell you? I told you it would feel so good you'd soon beg for it."

I answer him with a lustful moan, the nerve endings tickling my back hole too pleasing to release my lust's firm clutch on my throat. This isn't the first time we've done anal play, but it is the first time I've been overwhelmed by a rush of excitement. This is way more pleasurable than it is painful.

Caught up in the thrilling sensation, I sway my hips back and forth.

"That's it. Nice and slow. Your ass is as tight as your cunt. It needs to be stretched before it can take my cock."

The temperature in our room turns roasting when he adds a second finger into the mix. The girth of his fingers and the pace of their pumps should bombard me with worry, but all I feel is excitement. Every thrust, every groan, and every wickedly naughty sentence Nikolai produces has the coils in my womb tightening to the point of detonation.

"But don't worry, by the time I've finished prepping you, your ass will be dripping as freely as your greedy cunt. I promise you, it'll feel so good you'll beg for me to take you in the ass as often as your cunt."

My head falls forward as a throaty groan rolls up my chest. His dirty words have my body sinking into euphoria, meaning his fingers can dip inside me even deeper.

He scissors them gently, widening my once-clenched hole before increasing the speed of his pumps to match my rocking hips grind for grind. The sensation is unlike anything I've ever experienced. It is both manic and possessive.

"Oh god," I moan when his other hand skates around my shuddering body to toy with my clit.

The buzz darting through my womb from him finger-fucking my ass while pinching my clit is mind-boggling, equally shocking and mesmerizing. I've never been coiled so tight before. It truly feels like I'm losing my mind. I'm seconds from exploding, my moans as erotic as the grunts Nikolai releases when I surrender to the madness.

"Louder, *Ангел*. Let them hear you," Nikolai demands as my ass milks his fingers as if they are his cock. "Maybe if everyone hears how much you love this, you'll answer your body's pleas faster next time. It wants me any way it can get me. It just needs your mind on board with its plans."

My orgasm lengthens when he slips a finger inside my pussy. The sensation of having both holes penetrated at once is excruciating but in a good, roguishly unexpected way.

Knowing what we are doing is taboo makes it even more arousing. Sometimes it truly feels good being bad. Nikolai's crash into my life proves this without a doubt.

"Please," I mumble a short time later, my morals lost in a lust-filled trance. "I need... I want..."

"What, *Ангел*? Tell me what you need." Nikolai's voice is thick and manly and oh-so-dangerous. "I'll give it to you. I'll give up everything I have before I *ever* disappoint you."

He scissors his fingers faster, matching the frantic rock of my hips as I strive for my ass to feel the same full feeling his cock gives my pussy. "You, Nikolai... Please... I want you."

"Where?" His hand moves to my hip to grip my waist, slowing my frantic pace that has the couch feet jumping across the carpet. "In your mouth? Your wet cunt? Or here...?" He finalizes his question by doing a prolonged swivel of his fingers in my ass.

"There... I want you *there*."

His husky growl rushes my third climax to within an inch of the finish line. "Say it. Tell me what you want. I'll never take anything not willingly given, so you need to give it to me."

"I want you to fuck me in the ass," I answer without delay, my mind too fritzed with yearning to let an ounce of embarrassment fill me. "I want you to own every inch of me, to have me as no other man has. I want you to claim me wholly as yours."

"Oh, *Ангел*..." He could say more, but he doesn't need to. The veins throbbing through his cock as he coats it in my juices reveal everything he wants to say. He's been waiting for this moment for months and is unwilling to delay it for a moment longer.

"Eyes on me," he requests as his throbbing cock moves from my drenched pussy to my equally glistening ass. "Let me see what I've always seen in you. Let me see your eyes while I claim you like no man has."

His cock tenses against my butt cheek. After slowly removing his fingers from my rear entrance, he yanks open the side table next to the couch. His eyes rocket to mine when he spots a tube of lube nestled next to an unopened box of condoms.

"You can never be too prepared," I murmur, quoting what I said to him exactly twelve months ago today.

With a seductive wink, he snags the anal-recommended lube from the drawer, coats his cock in the slippery substance, then braces it against the area pulsating with both eagerness and worry.

I lick my parched lips when he slowly notches in the first inch of his cock. He's covered with both my arousal and a mammoth load of lube, but the contrasting width between his fingers and his penis is undeniable. Our exchange is now bordering closer to pain than pleasure.

After flattening my torso so I lie smooth across the couch, Nikolai returns his eyes to me. "Breathe and relax. I'll never hurt you, so you don't need to worry, but if you don't relax, I'll never get in."

Breathing out slowly, I do as instructed. I want this. Not because I want Nikolai to claim me as no other man has, but because there's more than just pleasure at stake here. I'm giving myself to him wholly and without restraint. I'm becoming his even more than I did a year ago. We are now one.

Butterflies tap dance in my stomach as the dangerous ride I've been on the past twelve months reaches a hairpin curve I never saw coming. Thankfully, no matter how sharp the curve, the thrill at the end of every ride is always present, making it not just worthwhile but joyous.

"That's it. Accept me nice and slow."

The muscles around my ass stop clenching, allowing the first half of Nikolai's cock to enter me without the pain I felt accepting the tip. Since I am lying flat, I can't take all of him as I generally do. I think he positioned me like this so I have time to adjust before being fully hilted.

After giving me time to acclimate to his girth, he withdraws. Mercifully, he takes it slow, ensuring I don't feel any of the ripping sensation I'm secretly panicked about.

It took my pussy time to adjust to the size of him, so I can't expect a hole that's much tighter to adjust without any pain. Although this hurts, it also feels freakishly good.

Hearing the feverish grunts the couch pillow is failing to stifle, Nikolai says, "Talk to me, *Ангел*. Tell me how it feels. If it hurts, I'll stop."

"Don't stop," I beg, shocked I'm more worried he'll stop than I am about the pain I'm feeling. "It feels good. Foreign, but so very good."

My knees wobble when his growl rumbles to the tip of his cock. "I told you it'd feel good. Nothing we could ever do would feel bad. Unless you want it to." I can't see his face, but I can imagine his cheeky grin during the last half of his statement.

The zing of pain I'm experiencing dulls to barely a buzz when his cock dips in and out of me another handful of times. By the time his hand skirts around to stimulate my clit, all pain is forgotten, and my moans become more vocal.

"Yes... Please... Oh god."

When he slips two fingers into my pussy, a scream shreds from my throat. The sensation is nearly overwhelming. The fullness of his cock in my ass while his fingers grind into my pussy is extremely overstimulating, but in a way I can't help but moan, shout, and demand for him to fuck me faster.

"Louder. Let the world hear what I do to you." His voice is rough, hardened with both lust and euphoria.

"Oh god. Oh god," I chant on repeat, my mind spiraling.

"Can you feel what my body does to you, *Ангел?* Your greedy cunt milking my fingers? Your clit buzzing against my thumb? Even your tight little ass is milking my cock, begging for my seed. All I need is your tit in my mouth, and I'd have every inch of you covered."

"Mmm..." A more intellectual response is above me.

This is wickedly wrong but oh-so-right at the same time. I'm sweating profusely, but the hot Las Vegas night is not responsible for the beads of sweat rolling down my nape. It is the man whispering dirty thoughts in my ear as he fucks me to oblivion.

"More. Faster. Please."

Long, prolonged breaths separate my demands. My breathless response is compliments of my frantic rocking. I want him inside me deeper, to claim every inch of me, and the harder I sway, the better my demands are answered.

"I want all of you, Nikolai. Please."

The crack of a container popping open sounds through my ears mere seconds before the coolness of lube drips past my hole, which is burning with excitement. Nikolai adds a healthy dose of slickness between us before gripping my hips to raise them high into the air.

I scream in ecstasy when he plunges back inside me. My change in position allows more of his cock to slip into my ass. He's even deeper now, more deep-seated, almost fully hilted.

"Talk to me, *Ангел.* Tell me what you need, where you need it, and how you fucking need it."

Since I am still incapable of speaking, my moans talk on my behalf. I purr on repeat, ensuring he's aware I'm loving everything he's doing.

Although he can hear my excitement, his pumps remain slow until my shouts reach an ear-piercing level. They quicken with every desperate scream ripped from my throat.

He rolls his hips at a speed slow enough that he'd never hurt me but fast enough that my third quest for orgasm makes itself known within minutes.

"I'm going to come," I warn a short time later, shocked by my climax's quick arrival but not the least bit embarrassed at its eagerness. Multiple orgasms aren't uncommon when I'm with Nikolai. They're more customary than infrequent.

The veins pulsating in Nikolai's cock are reflected in his groan. "Good. Come on my fingers while screaming my name. Squeeze them like your tight little ass is strangling my cock, and then I'll come in your ass, coat your no-longer-virginal hole with my cum."

The dirtiness of his words is extremely erotic, so much so they push me into my third climax of the night. I slam back, fully hilting his cock inside me before allowing the quivers of my pussy to clamp his fingers.

With my body overstimulated, my orgasm is utterly blindsiding. It takes everything from me, equally brutal and wondrous. Its robust and blinding strength is fueled by Nikolai's cum shooting from his cock in raring spurts.

"Ohh..." I growl in a long, purring moan, loving the frantic pulse of the vein feeding his cock as he struggles to maintain control.

He continues pumping in and out of me until every drop of his cum is dispersed, and we collapse into a heap on my old, frayed couch.

"Fuckin' hell, *Ангел*. I think I just died and went to heaven."

I roll over until my chin is balancing on his sweat-slicked thrusting chest. "This isn't heaven, Nikolai." My eyes bounce between his icy-blue gaze. "You're just no longer in the hell you were born in."

3

NIKOLAI

Trey slumps into the chair across from me. His blond brows are furrowed, and the thick beard that's had the whores' heads in a tizzy the past three months can't hide the tick in his jaw. He's unhappy about my request to cross the country, but he knows better than anyone the consequences of second-guessing my decisions.

"I told Justine she'd have the world when she claimed her throne. I am a man who keeps his word."

Trey's lips quirk as he struggles to hold back a grin.

"*Now* I keep my word," I amend. "Things change." I give him a look that reveals I'm on to him. "You know that better than anyone. We don't marry whores, Trey. We fuck them, spill our seed inside them, then go home—*alone*."

"*Fucked* whores," Trey corrects. "We don't fuck them anymore."

I nod in agreement. Why would I settle for half a dish when an entire restaurant at home is waiting to free me of my every craving?

My thoughts stray back to Trey when he continues. "Besides, K wasn't a whore."

I raise my brow but remain quiet. Even though everything he says is true, I can't help but rib him a little. Kristina wasn't a whore because anything she did under Vladimir's watch wasn't done of her own volition.

The whores at Clarks, though... they don't prance around in micro skirts with no panties because they're ordered to be there. They show up every day of their own choice. They hope limber bodies and perky tits will see them become a lady of the house for one of my men. It's unfortunate for them my crew has more of a clue than they give them credit for.

No matter how well she gives head, a whore never becomes a housewife.

Scrubbing the bushy beard on his chin, Trey slumps deeper into his chair. "Don't fucking start, Nikolai. I'm taking enough shit from the guys. I'm not up for more crap."

His grumbled comment wipes the smirk from my face. "What shit?"

My confusion is genuine. I haven't heard any rumblings, and I keep my ear close to the ground with matters like this. It only takes one man to rule an empire. The same can be said for its downfall.

He makes a *pfft* noise with his lips. "Just the same shit we've been hearing the past twelve months. The whores are whispering in the men's ears, worried your relationship with Justine hasn't just seen their nail marks removed from your back."

His response stumps me for all of two seconds. "They're worried they are being replaced?" When he nods, I say, "They're not going anywhere. Whores are a part of our industry. Justine understands this."

My pulse spikes when Trey halfheartedly shrugs. I'm not selling him anything, but he's still not buying my reply.

"What?" My short tone is incapable of hiding my fury.

Although this contradicts everything I just said, Justine is my woman, so if she suddenly developed a problem with the whores my men lose themselves in every night, they'd be gone faster than I can snap my fingers.

Fortunately for all involved, what I said to Trey earlier is true. Justine has no issues with me keeping my men happy. An endless supply of whores keeps them happy.

As long as their needs aren't shoved under Justine's nose like they were the first month she resided here, she has no issues with how my men relieve their tension.

If only the same could be said in reverse.

The Popov housemaids took an instant like to Justine. She filled them with the hope that the Popov entity was moving away from the bigamist rules Vladimir controlled it with. The whores and a handful of my men were not as welcoming of her arrival.

Almost all the whores see her as competition, believing my addiction will be cured as quickly as I lost interest in them. My men see her as a threat to their livelihood.

Both are learning the hard way what I think of their insolence.

"The main compound is off-limits because it is our home. I want Justine to feel comfortable here. But there are no limits at Clarks. If they want to fuck a whore an hour, so be it."

I've recited the same thing to Trey many times in the prior twelve months, and quite frankly, I'm over their concerns. Drugs, guns, money, and women are supplied to my men at my expense, yet they still whine about my request that they keep their drug-fueled gang bangs on the down-low.

"If any of my men have an issue with my rules, they can bring it directly to me. But be warned, they won't be breathing when I'm done with them. Everything they have—*whores included*—is because of me. I also don't take kindly to assumptions that I'm being led by my cock."

Trey smiles a pompous, revealing grin.

He isn't here on behalf of my men.

He's stirring the pot.

His grin drops an inch when I growl, "You won't be smiling when I slit your throat for goading me."

He holds his hands up in defeat. "I wasn't goading, just testing a theory. Your reply pocketed me two freshly printed Benjamin Franklins."

"Testing a theory? Whose theory?" I'm more annoyed than amused. I don't like being placed under the spotlight, especially if the light is coming from men beneath me.

I'm forced to swallow some of my anger when Trey replies, "Rico. He's so convinced you're under the thumb, he bet two hundred dollars that you'd have the whores deported to Russia before sundown." His eyes lift to mine. They're sparkling with concealed amusement. "He seems to have forgotten he's the only one bedding a kitten too timid for our way of life."

If it were any other man comparing Justine to a tiger, he'd be taking his last breath. But since this is Trey, a man I trust more than I detest, I let his comment slide. *Just.*

Besides, I did get the tiger—more than anyone will ever know.

After adjusting my position so Trey won't see my raging boner, I ask, "Speaking of playthings, where's Rico? I thought he and Blaire were traveling back to Ravenshoe this morning."

"They are," Trey agrees with a nod. "He just had some old memories he wanted to recreate before his flight." He gives me a spirited wink, ensuring I can't miss the innuendo in his thick British tone.

Now I'm more amused than annoyed. The night they married, Rico's little kitty convinced him to buy a brand-new bed so they could consummate their marriage on unstained sheets. Forever under the thumb, Rico did exactly that.

The amount he paid to have their mattress delivered before they arrived from The Little White Chapel they wed at was highway robbery. But from the stories I've heard, he got his money's worth and then some.

Although Rico officially "died'" four years ago, his room still sits the same as the day he left to uphold a promise he had made to Blaire months earlier. I knew possessions would never bring him back, but I couldn't forget him as quickly as Vladimir did.

Vladimir didn't even attend Rico's funeral. He was his firstborn son, yet he dishonored his life as if he were nothing more than a gofer.

In a way, it was a godsend. Vladimir's lack of empathy freed me from giving him a proper send-off when he fell victim to my knife. He was cremated in the house he was killed in, forgotten as quickly as he'd disregarded the years of torture Rico and I had suffered under his reign.

Vladimir was born a king, but he died a pauper. His name has not been uttered in my presence since his death. And if I have it my way, it will never be mentioned again. He haunted me relentlessly when he was alive, and I refuse to let him continue the torture after his death.

Annoyed by my thoughts straying, I get back to the task at hand. "Have the men traveling with Justine and me ready to move by this evening. I want to touch down in Hopeton before sunup because every man knows a devil has never seen the sun rise."

Trey nods. "Who do you want at the helm while we're gone? Zyren has shown great improvement since Andros gifted him to us. He still has a long way to go, but it might soften him up."

A dusting of dark hair falls into my eyes when I shake my head. "Zyren is a good kid, but he doesn't have the balls needed for our line of work. I need a man who will kill without thought. One who will never second-guess any decisions I make. I need a man as ruthless and brutal as me while also understanding that my greatest asset has blood running through her veins, not white powder, lead, or liquid gold." He looks stumped on who could fulfill my requirements until I murmur, "I need you to cover me while I'm gone, Trey, to keep our ship on course."

"I can't. That's not allowed." He cocks his head to the side as his brow arches. "I'm British, not Russian."

I laugh as if his thick accent and pasty-white skin weren't already critical factors in his reply. "I'm well aware of your heritage. It's one of the reasons I made you my number two."

He straightens his dark shirt as if he is wearing a suit. "And here I was thinking it was because of my roguishly handsome face."

I lower my chin, barely concealing my smirk. Although now isn't the time to act heedless, I can appreciate his attempt to stifle the tension thickening the air. It's been stale since I forced Adrian to carry Lia onto a private jet, kicking and screaming. She wanted to stay for the fireworks. I convinced her husband otherwise.

He picked right when he secured Lia to her seat with more duct tape than Rico used on Malvina a year ago.

Once the pompous grin on Trey's face fades, I say, "I need someone I can trust. We're still on un-solid ground since Alexei's death. If a second takeover bid blindsides us, I need someone at the helm who'll maintain control. I trust that man is you, Trey."

He remains quiet. He'll never openly admit it, but my rare commendation was as shocking for him to hear as it was for me to deliver it. I respect and trust him—he wouldn't be my number-two guy if I didn't—but the rules he speaks of are well-known in our industry.

The Popov entity has never been left in the hands of a non-

Russian. This is as controversial as Rico and me banding together to kill the patriarch of our sanction. It is unheard of.

I nod when Trey asks, "Are you sure this is what you want?"

I don't appreciate him questioning me, but only a fool would take this position without some hesitation.

"It's only for a few days. I'm certain even an *идиот* like you won't fuck things up that quickly."

"Ah, you make my heart tingle with your sweet words."

I toss the letter opener on my desk in his direction, smirking when it nicks his neck hard enough to cause a trickle of blood. I wasn't even aiming, yet I still hit my mark.

While Trey tends to his wound, I stand to my feet. "Offer Rico to travel with Justine and me, but warn him I'm traveling heavy. His little kitty might faint when she sees how things truly operate in our industry."

Trey gives me a look as if to say, *and Justine won't?*

"My woman was born to lead. She doesn't kneel for anyone." My smirk finalizes the rest of my sentence: *except me.*

Leaving Trey to string together my demands as specified, I make my way to the room I've shared with Justine for the past twelve months. She's bunked with me since the day I saved her from the hell I was tortured in fourteen years ago.

Unlike my wish for her to birth my child, we never discussed sharing residences as we got to know one another. Our relationship has been full steam ahead since we met, so why would a small detail such as an address on a driver's license change that?

Justine became mine the instant I took her on the couch I claimed her ass on last night.

Nothing will *ever* change that.

The scent of the bath oils slicking Justine's skin lingers in my nose when I enter our room. She's sleeping peacefully in the bed I placed her in after I bathed her last night. Although she was a very willing participant in our exchange, her willingness to submit didn't come without pain.

I've been prepping her ass for months, but fingers, anal beads, and butt plugs can't replicate the size of my cock when it's on the hunt. He was even thicker last night, Justine's eagerness to please me adding to his girth.

"*Ангел.*"

I track my hand down Justine's silky red hair before rolling my fingertip over a dog bite on the back of her shoulder. I'm not sure she's aware of this one's existence. It isn't in a place she can see without being a contortionist, and she doesn't readily cover it as she does the others. If she did, I wouldn't have noticed it when I pinned her to the door of her apartment within a minute of the sheriff deputies leaving us alone.

I don't know what it is about Justine's scars, but I can't get enough of them. They show how strong she is, that she can walk through the gates of hell and come out the other end stronger, but I see more than that when I look at them.

They reveal she's a fighter, a woman above the greatest man. But more than anything, they show that perfection comes in all shapes and styles.

For too long, man has believed perfection is only seen.

They're wrong.

It's felt and heard even more than it's witnessed.

Justine is living proof of that.

Don't get me wrong, Justine isn't close to ugly. She hardens the cock of every man when she enters a room, but her insides are even more spectacular than her cock-thickening body and face.

After watching goosebumps rise on Justine's skin from my touch, I say, "It's time to wake up. We've got matters to attend to before our trip."

That arouses her from her slumbering state. She raises her head an inch off her pillow before her eyes slowly flutter open.

"Good... *afternoon?*" she greets me, aware it is past midday but unsure of the exact time. "Everything okay?"

My eyes drop to her chest when she rolls over to inspect the groove between my brows more intently.

"It is now."

Her nipples bud when I brush my hand over them. She's always been responsive to my touch, but I've noticed she's been even more receptive in the past month or two.

"Are you still bare?" My voice is rough, dense with lust.

Too impatient to wait for her to answer me, I tug down the bed sheet covering the lower half of her body.

My cock thickens when her beautiful curves are exposed to my avid eyes. The Popov housemaids' adoration has added an appreciative layer of meat to her scarcely covered bones. Now the smooth swell of her hips matches the generous size of her tits.

"Don't tempt me," I growl when she gives me a heated look, one that begs to be consumed. "You're still recovering from last night. If I trusted myself to go gentle, I'd get lost in you, but an addict can never be accused of being modest when dabbling in their drug of choice. You are my addiction, Justine. One hit never suffices to curb my habit."

I don't often make mistakes, but I did just now.

Justine is no longer looking at me in reverence. She's glancing at me as if I'm her savior, as if I pulled her from the depths of hell instead of the other way around.

The cause of my error?

Calling her Justine instead of *Ангел*.

When her eyes blaze with lust, my infatuation gets the better of me. "Are you sore?"

A growl rumbles through my chest like thunder when she shakes her head. My heart isn't pumping faster because of her quick response. I'm pissed she's lying. She didn't speak, but I don't need to hear her words to know of her deceit. I can see it in her eyes, smell it on her skin. I can even taste it.

Spotting my slit lids, Justine pulls me down until I'm lying next to her. Remaining quiet, she plasters her gloriously naked frame to mine before balancing her chin on my thrusting chest.

The anger burning me alive soothes when her bliss-filled eyes lock with mine. She's sorry for her fib but not apologetic about her insatiable appetite.

With a rake of her teeth over her lower lip, she murmurs, "I'm a little tender, but it's nothing I can't handle." Her words are as confident as the woman I see in her eyes.

Heat creeps across her cheeks when I brush away the curl hiding her eyes from my view. "Because you're so strong, *Ангел*. So fucking strong."

Smiling in a way that stops my heart, she weaves her fingers through my hair that's been recently trimmed. "Because of you. Only you."

Stealing my chance to rebut her inaccurate statement, she seals her mouth over mine.

Our kiss starts tender until she unleashes her naughty side. She nips at my lips, cheeks, nose, and chin before lowering her mouth to mark me with her "taken" stamp.

Whether it's scratches from her nails dragged down my back or a hickey on my neck, I proudly wear her marks.

While she sucks on my skin as eagerly as she does my cock, her hands fiddle with my belt.

Because she is unaccustomed to me wearing a belt, it takes her longer than she'd like to undo the clasp.

Pulling back, she stares at me with wild, lusty eyes. "You may not take anything not willingly given, but I swear to god, if you don't hurry up and give me your cock, I'm going to scream."

Smiling at her eagerness, I murmur, "There are devilish thoughts in the most angelic mind, *Ангел*. Yours are clearly no different."

Teeth, lips, and hands go in all directions as Justine strives to strip me as bare as her kisses make me. My defiance of her every command increases her eagerness. She tugs at my shirt violently, popping several threads of cotton in the process.

"About time," she grumbles when my shirt is the first thing to go.

My cock is aching to be inside her, but I'm enjoying the fruits of my labor too much to free it from its confines. She is ruling her empire, taking charge of her realm.

I'm not going to interrupt this for anything.

While her needy eyes bore into mine, her hands skate across the ridges in my stomach that have grown astronomically from the numerous workouts she instigates daily. We fuck like rabbits yet still crave one another more than anything.

After tracing the head of my dragon tattoo with her fingertip, she refocuses her attention on my belt. Her cock-thickening scent increases with every loop the black leather slides through.

Once the belt is removed, she dumps it on the ground before wrestling with my zipper. My jeans have barely hit my knees when she straddles my hips. She wastes no time gripping my cock to guide it toward her drenched slit.

When her wetness hits my knob, I bite out a string of curse words. "Oh, *Ангел*, you're fucking saturated."

Any reply she's planning to give switches to a moan when I jerk my hips upward. I love that she's taking charge, but I can't help but demand my share. The sting of her nails digging into my pecs is only one-tenth of the heat radiating from her cunt when I take her to the base of my cock.

I loved fucking her ass. It was tight and hot, and just the fact I was claiming a part of her no man ever has made it even more enjoyable, but nothing can compare to the greedy sucks of her cunt while begging for my cum.

I'm under her spell in a minute, the sensation of her riding me from above mimicking the euphoria I felt the first time I claimed her as mine.

Unlike last night, this fuck is hard and violent. Justine slams down on me repeatedly, our bodies moving in sync despite our frantic speed. Our rhythmic movements prove what I've always known. We were designed for one another. Her body was crafted to be devoured by me, and my body was machined to drive her to the brink over and over again.

As sweat dribbles down Justine's cheeks, I raise my ass off the bed. I widen her thighs with my hips, allowing her to take even more of my cock. Satisfied her new position will have her screaming my name in no time, I jackknife my hips on repeat. Her moans ramp up to a level I haven't heard in weeks.

"Ah... Shit... Christ."

Her moans are lyrical gold to my ears. It pushes me harder—recklessly and without constraint. I fuck her greedily, endeavoring to mark her body with my scent before filling her with my cum.

"Come on," I beg a short time later, incapable of holding back for a second longer. Her cunt's frantic quivers have cum sitting at the crest of my cock, begging to be released. "Give me what I want. Scream my name while your cunt milks me of my cum."

With a breathless moan, Justine shatters like glass dropping on a tile floor. My name tears from her lips as her eyes roll into the back of her head. I watch her in awe, the urge to bang my chest the strongest it's ever been. It must wait, though.

She deserves more than a man who fucks her purely for his own pleasure. This isn't about me and my ravenous need to have her constantly screaming my name. It's about giving her what she deserves. Whether fucking her to the point of exhaustion or slitting the throat of any man who dares look at her the wrong way, she comes before anything and anyone—myself included.

4

NIKOLAI

Several hours later, Justine enters my office on the heels of Roman. He's slimmer than he was six months ago, which is how much time he took off to recover from the gunshot wound Vladimir inflicted upon him.

If Roman's warning glance doesn't indicate I'm in trouble, the fury in Justine's eyes is a sure-fire sign. "Ten men, Nikolai! Seriously? If that isn't already absurd, when Landon questioned their unannounced arrival, he had a gun drawn on him."

My eyes shoot to Roman during the last half of Justine's statement.

He shrugs, aware of the heavy tactics of my men when protecting my realm, but not willing to take sides in what he knows will be a mammoth battle.

It's a smart move on his behalf. Only a stupid man would place himself between a battling king and queen.

Rounding my desk, Justine brings herself close enough to me I can smell her skin but not close enough she's within touching distance.

If it didn't frustrate the hell out of me, I would commend her for her bravery.

Locking her eyes with mine, she huffs. "You said we were

taking men with us when we traveled. You never mentioned anything about sending a crew to my home before us."

"They need to sweep the area to ensure it's safe before you arrive. I will not have you enter an arena unprepared."

The protectiveness in my voice halts her campaign for barely a second. "It's not a fight arena, Nikolai. It's my family home. I'll be as safe there as I am here."

When I pardon Roman from our conversation with a flick of my wrist, Justine slices her hand in the air, demanding that he stay with as many words as I used to dismiss him.

She is as clever as she is beautiful.

She knows she doesn't stand a chance against me in general, much less when we are the only two people in the room, but it doesn't lessen my agitation in the slightest.

Roman's eyes bounce between Justine and me as he contemplates whose demand to follow. If it were any other woman but Justine standing across from me, he'd pay for his indecisiveness with his life. Luckily for him, he's aware Justine rules this sanction alongside me, not three paces behind me.

"I said no holds barred, *Ангел*," I mutter in Russian, conscious Roman isn't multilingual like Justine. "I would have *never* agreed if I knew it was under the guise of less security."

Justine splays her hands across her cocked hips. "You didn't agree because I said I'd bow to your every whim. You did it because I suck your cock better than any woman before me."

I take note to look further into Roman's claims of only speaking one language when he chokes on his spit.

Justine didn't say her comment in English.

She replied to me in Russian.

Missing the signs of treachery flashing in Roman's eyes, Justine steps closer to me.

Wrong move—now she's within touching distance.

Before a protest can squeak from her lips, I seize her wrist and pull her into my lap. The slow thrusts of her chest double when I press my lips to the shell of her ear and growl, "I wanted to send thirty men. Roman suggested I knock it down to ten. I don't compromise, but I did for you. Don't make me regret my decision."

This time, when I demand for Roman to leave, Justine lets him go. The needs of her body are overruling both her heart and her head.

The instant Roman closes my office door, Justine's lips twitch. Although confident nothing but lust is on her mind, I press my finger to my mouth just in case. This needs to be said before I too become lost in her body.

"The man who drew a gun on your brother will pay for his stupidity. You name the punishment, and I'll ensure it's handed to him, but I will *not* remove my men from their posts. They are there for a reason. If you want to protect your family as fiercely as I'll forever protect you, this needs to happen. We're stepping out of my territory, *Ангел*, meaning we must remain vigilant."

She breathes out noisily before dipping her chin in defeat. She knows that my pledge of protection doesn't stop at her. It includes anyone vital to her. My oath to guard her is the only reason Carmichael didn't perish by my blade the past year. He's an insolent, foolish man, but Justine also considers him a friend —*regrettably*.

"Now go and pack. We leave in thirty minutes."

My voice is more commanding than the one I generally use on her, but with my worry rising, so is my impatience. I trust my team. They're stronger and more ruthless than ever, but that doesn't mean I can relax.

With a chunk of my crew following our expedition to Hopeton, my empire will be left open for infiltration.

Unfortunately, that isn't my greatest worry.

My reputation is notorious in my industry, but a new fool is born every hour. They'll be quick to jump if they believe they can succeed me, but they'll discover just as quickly what happens when you provoke me.

My skin won't be the only thing I'll shed if they put Justine at risk. Bucketloads of blood will be shed along with it.

My tightened jaw slackens when Justine presses her lips to mine. Her kiss is only a peck, but it wipes the worry from my gut as quickly as it raises my cock. Only she can free me from the turmoil I've lived in since birth. When I am with her, nothing but her matters.

Not a single fucking thing.

Justine pulls back from our embrace by standing to her feet

after sensing my swift change in composure. Ignoring the growl quickening her pulse, she makes a beeline for the door. She's halfway across the room before she abruptly stops, then spins around to face me.

Although she doesn't speak, I can hear the words her mouth is failing to produce. She doesn't want the man responsible for scaring her brother punished, but she's not letting him off scot-free either. She's merely giving him a chance to prove himself, her wish to see the good in everyone awarding him mercy he'd never see from me.

I've executed men for less, but that's not how queens garner respect. Justine will gain his honor, and he'll serve her all the better for it.

"He won't disappoint you again. I'll make sure of it."

My cock hardens to the point it is painful when Justine mutters, "If he does, I'll serve him his punishment directly."

My chest swells with savage pride. There she is. My woman is on her throne, ready to rule our empire alongside me.

God help any man who dares cross her.

5

JUSTINE

Two SUVs lead a fleet of five through the streets of Las Vegas as we make our way to a private airstrip on the outskirts of the city. The number of armed men surrounding us is nothing out of the ordinary—Nikolai is as pedantic about security as he is about fucking me to the brink of insanity—but his silence isn't a regular occurrence.

He hasn't spoken a word in over forty minutes. At first, I thought his silence centered around my anger over one of his goons rough-handling my brother, but as the minutes ticked by, I realized I had it all wrong.

He isn't angry.

He's panicked.

That's as foreign for him as the pleasure I got from anal penetration.

I guess I shouldn't be surprised. I have a heap of unknown hormones running rampant through my veins, so additional nerves are bound to be present.

Realizing now is as good a time as any to share the secret I've been keeping the past twenty-four hours, I hand Nikolai the box I slipped into my purse upon exiting the courthouse late yesterday afternoon.

He stares at it for several moments, unsure of what it is.

"It's your birthday present. I meant to give it to you last night, but with everything going on, a suitable time never presented."

When he gives me a look, attempting to tell me for the tenth time in the past twenty-four hours that his birthday isn't for another two weeks, I cut him off with a glare.

"I can't hold this secret for another two weeks, Nikolai. I'm shocked I've kept quiet this long."

With his curiosity as piqued as his brow, he pulls off the scraggly piece of string curled around the box before prying off the lid. Time stands still when he glances down at the white stick with two blue lines glowing in the middle.

"It's a pregnancy test," I advise him, unsure if he's seen one before.

He probably has, but I prefer keeping my head stuck in the sand when it comes to him and any woman he associated with before me.

I don't handle jealousy well.

The longer Nikolai stares at the pregnancy test, the redder his cheeks glow. They match the color Roman's held when I asked him to purchase me a test while Frederick's trial was in recess.

He wasn't happy with my request, but when I said he could either purchase the test for me, or I would sneak away from his watch to buy one for myself, he chose the option that was less likely to have him slayed by Nikolai.

Away from Nikolai and Roman, I'm inconspicuous to the media, but when I'm in their realm, I am hounded as viciously as the paparazzi forever tailing Nikolai.

In the beginning, it was great for business. Wrongly believing I had Nikolai's conviction quashed, clients came out of the wood-work to secure my representation, hoping I'd achieve the same outcome for them.

It's a pity for all involved they didn't have access to the substantial lump sum payment Nikolai required to walk free from conviction.

Although I could have accepted the numerous offers handed to me, there's only one set of clients I've stepped outside of the Popov entity to help. They're the ones who can't afford the representation they deserve, boys like Frederick whose hearts were in the right place, but they couldn't find a legal way out of their situation.

My work is pro bono, but the satisfaction I get standing at their side, supporting them, far exceeds any monetary value.

Who knows how different Nikolai's life could have been if Carmichael had helped him instead of going against him when he was Frederick's age?

I understand why Carmichael did what he did—I'd go to any length to save my brothers as well. It's just unfortunate Nikolai was caught in the crossfire—*again*.

Nothing will fix the injustices Nikolai suffered during his childhood, but I stand by his side every second of every day, propping him up. The pain in his eyes dampens as the confidence in mine flourishes.

A king needs a queen at his side, someone strong enough to show him there's a light at the end of every tunnel.

I am that woman for Nikolai.

He's often said once I took my throne, I'd want for nothing.

The same can be said for him.

I'll never stop fighting to show him he is worthy of the greatest treasures and the gifted life his heir will live. The Bratva made Nikolai a man, but only I will make him a father.

I lick my dry lips before saying something I never anticipated. "It's a *positive* pregnancy test. *Our* positive pregnancy test. We're having a baby."

Nikolai's wintry-blue eyes lock with mine, but not a word spills from his lips. Worry stirs in my gut that I jumped the gun too early in our relationship. He dropped hints numerous times over the past few months about his wish to have an heir before he straight-up asked me to stop using contraception, so I seized control of our destiny by skipping my pill a good six to eight weeks ago.

Now I'm panicked out of my mind. What if I don't know him as well as I think I do, and his hope to become a father wasn't an immediate wish?

"Nikolai..."

My words fall short when our SUV arrives at the side of a private jet. It is probably for the best, as I'm honestly lost on what to say. I thought he wanted this. If I knew this would be his reaction, I wouldn't have been so gung-ho to fulfill his every desire.

While a group of heavily armed men creates a walkway from our SUV to the lowered stairs of the jet, Nikolai places the lid back on the box and then slides it into the pocket of his jacket. Roman gives us the nod of approval to leave the safety of our car not even two seconds later.

Remaining quiet, Nikolai swings open the back driver's side door, clasps my hand in his, and slips out. I'm not being cunning when I say it would take a missile to get through the guard of honor flanking us.

The men who work alongside Nikolai are the highest ranked in their industry, but their integrity is even more impressive than that. Since they were acquired with honor instead of the fear Vladimir worked with, they'd never let anything happen to Nikolai. They don't just respect him. They care for him as well.

The heavy stomp of a dozen men follows us up the stairs of the jet, but Nikolai doesn't pay them any attention. He even waves off the stewardess clamoring for the chance to answer his every whim. She flutters her eyelids at him excessively as the heat raring through her body overrules the blush on her cheeks.

Usually my hackles would bristle from Nikolai being ogled so intently, but with my mind shut down with worry, I let her pathetic attempts to seduce a taken man roll off my shoulders like water off a duck's back.

Like Nikolai, my focus is on one thing and one thing only: the bedroom at the back of the jet. I do not want to have this conversation in front of his crew. I don't want to have it at all, let alone while surrounded by men who both love and detest me.

Don't misconstrue. For the most part, Nikolai's crew welcomed me with open arms, but Rory's punishment last year displayed a side of Nikolai his men have never seen. Half were confused by his protectiveness of me, unsure what it meant for their positions, whereas the other half saw my inclusion in his life as a positive.

The latter now form Nikolai's innermost circle, their trust rewarded in the greatest way. Once Nikolai revealed his true self to the men who trust him with their lives, his group has grown tenfold over the past twelve months.

It's funny how life can change in an instant. Whether a niggle in the gut warning you to end a date earlier than your acquaintance is hoping, or falling in love with a mafia prince, you'll never fathom the outcome of your decision until it is too late.

Five years ago, a man's decision altered my life in a way I never saw coming. It tore my family apart, and it shredded my heart into a thousand pieces, but it also brought me Nikolai. His life is as dark and corrupt as the man who tried to destroy mine, but by accepting him and loving him as he is, I had the oxygen in my lungs revived and am discovering not all men in his industry are like Col Petretti and Vladimir.

Whether good or bad, everyone has a place.

Mine is beside Nikolai, and I won't give up my spot for anyone.

"I know this is daunting, Nikolai. I nearly puked when I saw the results. Not in a bad way. I just didn't expect it to happen so soon."

I stop blubbering, realizing I'm doing a terrible job explaining myself.

After a big breath, I try again. My second attempt isn't any better than my first. "It's kind of scary realizing how quickly life can change. For years, my focus centered on one thing, and then you came into the picture and flipped everything on its head. Some-days, I don't even know who the hell I am, so it's okay if you're having a hard time registering this. I won't hold it against you. Just don't block me out—please. I'm scared, but I know we'll be okay. We can get through anything if we do it together."

I stop droning on when a lock sliding into place booms into my ears. I was so fixated on lessening the tension between us that I failed to notice we've entered the private sleeping quarters at the back of the jet.

When I attempt to continue my plea for understanding, Nikolai presses his finger to my lips. "Enough talking."

The pulse in my neck twangs when he guides me into the middle of the room. His natural arrogance is at an all-time high, leaving no doubt who stands beside me.

The king is walking the halls, his head not weighed down by the hefty weight his crown carries.

His pigheadedness shouldn't appeal to me. It shouldn't sing a sweet serenade of love and devotion that has my heart taking notice even more than my pussy, but it does.

The fire in Nikolai's eyes, the sneer on his face, and even the slight flex of his fists as his eyes rake my body reveal truths I've heard many times over the past twelve months.

Men want to be him. Women want to bed him, but there is

only one person worthy of the king's time. The woman who spoke to the king inside of him long before he took his reign: his queen.

Goosebumps prickle my skin when Nikolai slides the straps of my free-flowing shirt off my shoulders. The lightweight material rolls down my quivering stomach until it stops at my frilly skirt. With summer in full swing, I chose a light, breezy outfit to easily go from a dry Vegas night to a humid Florida morning.

Air hisses between his teeth when his eyes take in my scarcely covered breasts, but it's barely a blip on the radar compared to the heavy incline of his chest when his eyes lower to my stomach. I'm only a few weeks along, but I have no doubt he has spotted the slight curve in my stomach I noticed while dressing this morning.

I never believed in instant love, but Nikolai and our baby have made a fool out of me twice in under a year.

Wanting Nikolai to see the entire picture, I tug on the waistband in my skirt. I've barely yanked it past my panties when Nikolai's impatience gets the better of him. With barely a grunt, he shreds my clothes off my body, their sturdy material no match for his strength.

Even though I heard a lock click, my eyes rocket to the door to ensure it is closed. My confidence has grown to a point I never thought achievable, but there are a handful of neuroses I'm still working through. My most driven is subjecting Nikolai's crew to the ugliness of my scars. The last thing I want is for them to think Nikolai sacrificed everything for a marked-up mangy mutt.

All the stupid thoughts clouding my mind leave in an instant when Nikolai falls to his knees. He stares at my stomach for several long seconds before lifting his strong, firm hands to cup my barely existent baby bump. "*Привет мой малыш.*" Tears burn my eyes from him greeting our baby as his. "*Твоя мать спасла меня от адских глубин. Теперь ты воскресишь мои вены кислородом.*"

I attempt to correct him, to tell him the oxygen in his veins will be revived long before our little bundle joins our duo, but the quickest flash of his eyes steals my words. He truly thinks I saved him from the hell he was living in and that our baby will be his final reward for the years of turmoil he suffered during his childhood.

His eyes also reveal the reason for his earlier silence. Although his crew has seen a different side of him in the prior twelve months, they've never seen him like this. His heart is open and exposed for the world to see. He's the most vulnerable he's ever been.

"*благодарю вас.*"

I dip my chin, wordlessly advising him his thanks are not required. I'm the one truly blessed here.

Before I can assure Nikolai of that, he cups my cheeks as tenderly as he did my stomach, then seals his lips over mine. I want to say the warm and fuzzy sensation fueling our exchange keeps our kiss at a PG rating, but there isn't a single thing about Nikolai that could be called innocent. His kisses are like a thunderous summer storm—deadly and awe-inspiring. He doesn't kiss gently or tease me to highlight what I'm missing out on. He takes as much as I'm willing to give, then gives back even more.

His kiss steals the air from my lungs as quickly as his attention rebuilds my confidence. By the time he pulls back, I'm utterly breathless, and my panties don't have a chance in hell of hiding how aroused he makes me.

I'd never hide, though.

Not from him.

Not even when I should.

He saw the butterfly too scared to escape the cocoon she sheltered herself in long before anyone else, so shouldn't he reap the benefits of her metamorphosis?

My lips arch high when Nikolai roughly yanks my lower lip with his teeth before growling, "Now I wish I had sent thirty men instead of ten." His warm breaths flutter my kiss-swollen mouth. "Your news also explains your insatiable appetite of late."

He's not referring to food. There's only one thing I've craved the past week. It's the same thing I've desired relentlessly the prior twelve months: him—my prince of darkness.

When I tell him my greedy urges have nothing to do with my pregnancy and everything to do with him, some of the pride in his eyes shifts for lust.

"How far along are you?" he asks while guiding me to the bed squashed against the side wall.

I shouldn't say "squashed," but compared to the monstrous four-poster bed in the middle of our chamber-like bedroom, it's a little underwhelming.

The rest of the features, though... I only have one word: wow.

My jaw falls open as my eyes absorb the luxurious fittings I was too twisted up in knots to appreciate earlier. If money talks, the Popovs won't be silenced for centuries to come. White-and-gold-print bedding contrasts against the dark wood lining the walls. A partially cracked-open door on our right displays a bathroom fitted with the same pricy features, but the stark-white towels are missing the gold emblem the bedding has. Although, I don't see that being an issue. I can forgive plain towels when I have access to a walk-in shower.

The opulence of the jet leaves no doubt of Nikolai's wealth. This ride is truly worthy of a king.

When Nikolai growls my name, reminding me I failed to answer his question, I shrug. "I have no clue. I had an inkling yesterday morning, so I took a test before we left for the restaurant..."

I stop talking when Nikolai's shocked gaze collides with mine. His Adam's apple bobs as he struggles to maintain his composure. I stare at him in silence, utterly lost on what has caused the quick shift in his composure.

Five seconds ago, he appeared to have the world at his feet. Now he has the same expression his face held when he discovered me with a noose wrapped around my neck.

He's genuinely mortified.

He works his jaw side to side before easing out his next words. "You mean you knew when I... when we..."

"Fucked?" I fill in.

I try to hide my smile at his uncomfortable swallow. My efforts are less than stellar. I'm not a Goody Two-Shoes who despises swear words. I just never get a chance to use them. Between Nikolai and his crew, a lifetime of profanities is depleted in a week.

Nikolai tries to act annoyed at my rare use of a cuss word. His acting skills are as poor as mine. He can't help but smirk while warning, "Watch your tongue, *Ангел*. Now that my cock has achieved its goal, I won't hesitate to use it to wash out your filthy mouth."

"Please," I murmur before I can stop myself, more turned on by his threat than concerned about it. "I'll take you any way I can get you."

His groan is the equivalent of foreplay to my body. We've been sexually active four times in under twenty-four hours, but my hunger for him is still rampant. If I wanted to excuse my nympho tendencies, I could blame new hormones for my syrupy veins, but anyone who knows me knows that is a lie. Nothing we've done the past year has been against my will. Not even the wickedly naughty events of last night.

Although painful, last night was beyond enjoyable. I saw a new side of Nikolai and fell in love with him even more deeply than I thought possible. He was tender and loving while rocking my world as he always does.

If last night was a true indication of what anal sex will be like with him, I have no doubt his cocky remark about me begging him to take me that way more regularly will occur. I should have trusted him sooner. Done right, everything with Nikolai is pleasurable.

I'm pulled from my wicked thoughts when an even more desirable view enters my peripheral vision. Nikolai is undressing. His pace is as reckless as it was when he shredded my clothing as if it were tissue paper. He throws his shirt over his head, exposing his rippling abs and tattooed torso to my view. His jeans are next to go, their swift removal unearthing the dragon tattoo that began my downfall a little over a year ago.

I can't believe I stupidly fought my feelings for him. It was a battle I was never going to win, so I don't know why I bothered. Some would say I never truly tried, but they couldn't feel the conflict that stirred every time I thought about him. I was genuinely torn between what I thought I knew and what was right.

Nikolai soon showed me the way.

The speed at which our relationship progressed is unnatural, but it is the most worthwhile thing I've ever done. Without sacrifice, we'll never have anything, and with Nikolai having more than his share of unfairness, it's only fair that he discovers what it feels like to be the center of someone's world. I'll give him that—our baby and I will give him the world.

Within seconds, Nikolai's clothes sit on the floor with mine, as tangled and messy as he forever makes my heart. As his cock reacts to the undeniable heat teeming between us, he removes my bra and panties before guiding me onto the bed.

Panic floods me when he handles me as if I'm a fragile piece of glass that could shatter at any moment. Although my first thought is my scars, not once in the past twelve months has he treated me delicately, so it can't be that.

My spine straightens as reality zaps down it. Only one thing has changed between this morning and now. He discovered we're having a baby.

Before I can assure him nothing we did the past twenty-four hours could have harmed our little cherub, Nikolai places a peppering of kisses down my neck, across my torso, and over my rapidly swelling chest. His pace is slower than we've gone before, but it is out-of-this-world perfect. His nips and licks remain the same. His steady pace awards me more time to appreciate every seamless bite, lick, and suck.

My chest inflates to accommodate my swelling heart when he places a succession of kisses on my non-existent bump. He refers to our baby as "his greatest gift" before his attention drops a few inches lower.

I can barely contain my excitement when his heavy-hooded gaze makes the wetness between my legs sizzle. I am bare and exposed, yet I feel more beautiful than I've ever felt. The pre-cum pooling at the crest of his cock advises he likes what he sees, much less the admiration in his lowered-with-need gaze.

Scissoring my legs together, I ease the tingling sensation stimulating my pussy. My clit is pulsating so fiercely I'm confident it won't take much for me to come.

One touch and I'll be free-falling into pure bliss.

When Nikolai's eyes rise to mine, the beautiful ruckus sitting low in my stomach stirs. His eyes speak words his mouth doesn't need to verbalize for me to hear. *Now watch me eat the tastiest cunt I've ever eaten.*

My back arches off the bed when his tongue spears the folds of my pussy not even two seconds later. He consumes me with the same dedicated sweeps of his tongue, grazes of his teeth, and sweet movements of his lips he used on my chest and stomach, but his pace is slower, less aggressive.

His self-control doesn't dampen my excitement in the slightest. If anything, it makes me more unhinged. I'm quivering in orgasm only minutes later, its strength stealing the last of the air from my lungs.

The weightlessness of our bodies from the jet taking off adds an excited thrill to my climax, extending it from a mind-hazing orgasm to a body-paralyzing one. I still as excitement rips through my body, equally devastating and exhilarating me.

It is too good, almost too perfect.

The thrill of knowing this is the only time Nikolai will ever let me fall is inconceivably liberating. I broke five years ago, but I'm confident the only time I will shatter from here on out will be when I'm trembling beneath my king.

Nikolai maintains his slow, dedicated pace. His lazy licks and gentle sucks bring me back from hysteria with the same controlled tempo he used to instigate it. He eats me as if I'm a meal fit for a king, as if he'll never crave any woman but me. Only once every muscle-exhausting shudder has been extinguished does he rise to his knees.

"Nikolai," I murmur, half breathless, half laughing.

Confirmation of my earlier assumption rings true when he uses his cock as a measuring stick to gauge the distance between my pussy and my belly button. He's panicked out of his mind that sex will harm our baby.

An adorable crinkle pops between his dark brows when his cock extends well past my tiny bump low in my stomach. "Where does the baby sit?" His tone is deadly serious since it's infested with confusion.

I'm as lost as him, but it doesn't stop me from saying, "On the right. Somewhere around here." I point to the very far right of my stomach.

Nikolai's lips curl into a lusty grin. He knows I'm lying, but he's pleased I'll say anything if it guarantees him being inside of me —*again*.

When my lie fails to immediately grant me my wish, I try another tactic. "Nine months." Nikolai's confused eyes drop to mine. "That's how long pregnancies last. Are you willing to wait nine months before coming again?"

He cocks a brow as his grin picks up. "Why can't I come? Your hand, mouth, and tight little ass aren't out of commission until our baby is born. Just your pretty pink cunt."

His filthy words make my clit ache, but I keep my focus on the task at hand. "If I'm being denied my every desire while pregnant, so the hell are you. This is *our* baby, Nikolai, which means we both suffer any consequences associated with him or her."

"Ангел..." His growl is more in warning than lust. "Nothing about our baby will be done in suffering. Just like his mother, he's a gift. He'll never be a burden."

Ignoring his assurance our peanut is a boy, I reply, "A gift that'll make me miserably depressed if I'm denied having you. We've fooled around more the past twelve months than I thought I'd achieve in my lifetime, but I still need more, Nikolai. I need you."

When he remains quiet, I realize I'm getting through to him. He is only ever silent when he's contemplating.

"Please. I assure you it's safe. He's well protected in there." I purposely say "he," hoping his belief our child is a boy will assure him he'll never come to any harm. "He has his daddy's blood, meaning he's already as strong as an ox."

My lower lip drops to a pout when Nikolai scoots off the bed. With his hooded gaze locked on me, he shoves his feet into the opening of his jeans before yanking them up his thighs. Once the zipper is pulled up to cover his cropped pubic hairs, he scans the bedding puddled around my feet.

The low hang of his brows doesn't budge an inch until the dark bed sheet covers my naked frame. Happy all my naughty bits are covered, he throws open the highly varnished door separating the main cabin of the jet and our room. He speaks to his crew in Russian. Although I'm multilingual, I don't hear a word he's saying. Lust rages too hard and fast to hear anything except my pulse shrilling in my ears.

I get the gist of his conversation when Dok enters the room a few seconds later. He startles when he notices me splayed on the bed, my post-orgasmic face incapable of hiding my flaming cheeks.

Dok stops glancing at an imaginary dot on the wall when Nikolai asks for the statistics of babies being injured in the womb from "vigorous physical activities."

Yes, that's precisely how he said it.

"You're pregnant?" Dok's face holds the same shocked surprise Nikolai's held when he peered down at my positive pregnancy test.

Smiling, I nod. I'm still in shock, but for once, it's a positive surprise.

"How far?"

"We don't know," I answer, bringing Nikolai into our conversation.

What I said earlier was true. This is our baby—not mine.

"Is there a way we can find out?"

Dok's brisk nod makes me dizzy. "There are a few ways. Do you know when your last period was?"

I grimace. I stopped paying attention to my cycle months before Nikolai suggested I quit taking birth control pills. My monthly bleed didn't interfere with our relationship. It just meant we had to be more inventive for a few days each month, so it never held much importance.

"Around twelve weeks ago," Nikolai answers on my behalf.

He gifts me a wink, revealing he appreciates my bugged eyes. I don't know why I'm surprised. He knows all aspects of my life, so I shouldn't be stunned he keeps up to date on my period.

Dok pulls a phone out of his pocket. After a few taps on the screen, he lifts his eyes to me. "Okay, that will make you due around the seventeenth of January, but we'll schedule an ultrasound when we return to Vegas. It will give us an exact date to work with." He exchanges his phone for a notepad he stores in the breast pocket of his suit. "You should start prenatal vitamins and iron tablets as soon as possible. We'll do a blood workup when we land to see if there's anything else you're lacking."

My wide eyes bounce between Dok's when he hands me a prescription for the vitamins he recommends. "Okay." I'm equally stunned and surprised. I thought Dok was a nickname Nikolai's crew calls him because he stitches up their wounds. I had no clue he was an actual doctor.

Suddenly worried he's overstepped his mark, Dok returns to his post at the door. "Was there anything else you needed?"

He shouldn't be panicked. Nikolai is as thankful for his diligence as I am. Knowing we're not the only ones on our baby's side is nice.

"Only for you to answer my original question."

The need in Nikolai's reply reddens my cheeks with heat. I'm not embarrassed. I love that his sexual appetite is as intense as mine.

Dok's face turns the color of a beetroot, matching mine to a T. "No harm can be done to a fetus during... *sexual activities*."

My lips tug high from the uncomfortable delivery of his last two words. Dok is a handsome man. Blond surfer boy locks float around his ears. His face is both handsome and well-carved, and his body could rival Nikolai's if I could ever demand my eyes to drink him in. Although he doesn't have a dangerous aura like Nikolai does, he handles himself well around members of the crew who are more built than he is, so to say I'm shocked about his shyness would be an understatement—a major one.

My smile enlarges when Dok's answer coincides with Nikolai shoving him out the door. He slides the lock back into place before spinning around to face me. If the sparkle in his heavy-hooded gaze is anything to go by, he doesn't just trust Dok with his life; he'll place our unborn baby's life in his hands as well.

He slowly bridges the gap between us, his walk as arrogant as ever. It is a cocky swagger that reveals my every desire is about to be answered.

I'd be lying if I said I wasn't tickled pink by the idea.

6

JUSTINE

Nikolai wakes me an hour before we're scheduled to land. The scrumptious feast the stewardesses prepared while I napped is visually appealing, but my stomach isn't interested. Hormones aren't wreaking havoc with my gut. It is the early hour. It's barely 4 a.m.

The reason for the odd hour of our trip comes to light when Nikolai murmurs, "The devil can't tell time if he's never seen the sunrise."

Vladimir has been dead for nearly a year, yet Nikolai still struggles to comprehend it. It is understandable. Vladimir ruled with gritty, devious tactics that burned fear into the hearts of every man beneath him, but he was killed in a humble, barely spoken-of way.

His death has never been discussed out loud, and no funeral was held to honor his life. He was merely forgotten, laid to rest in the very room he sent his son to hell in. If he weren't such a vile, indecent man, I'd feel sorry for him. It's unfortunate for him empathy was the only thing he stole from me a year ago.

I'm drawn from my thoughts when Nikolai says, "Eat, *Ангел*. You need to keep your strength."

His eyes drop to the plates of food spread out in front of us before he nudges his chin to the seat across from him. He waits for me to sit, before slipping into his chair. His shirtless torso and bare feet have my mind straying from the delicious treats in front of me to the one responsible for the true awakening of my hunger.

"*Ангел...*" Nikolai growls in warning while loading my plate with pancakes, bacon, and sausages. "*Ты и твоя жадная пизда будут смертью меня.*"

I give him a frisky wink. "There are worse ways to die."

"There are." His smile competes with mine. "But I'm already facing an uphill battle keeping you alive. I don't need more obstacles."

That takes care of my rampant horniness by securing it in a dark, tormented place. This is the first time he has voiced concern about protecting me.

Usually his confidence reeks of so much attitude I'm certain nothing will stand in his way of keeping me safe, so his reply is as foreign as his denial of my wordless request for him to take me hard and fast on the table we're dining at.

His eyes stalk me when I fill the gap between us. Something in my eyes must give me away as he pushes his chair far enough from the table that I can slip into his lap. My hair is a mess from our tussle between the sheets, and my eyes are puffy from a lack of sleep, but he still scans my face as if I'm the most sought-after trinket on the planet.

"If this is too dangerous, turn the jet around and go home. We'll devise a new tactic in the morning."

A fire burns in Nikolai's eyes. "And be seen as a coward? Never."

"Being smart isn't cowardice." My raging heart is heard in my voice.

He huffs as if he doesn't believe me. "That's not the theory you ran with when you demanded to go home."

My lips twitch, but words fail me. I was so excited about Maddox's release that I didn't stop to assess the consequences of a trip home. All I wanted to do was celebrate his return with my family.

"I was one of the last faces Maddox saw before his incarceration, so I wanted to be one of the first faces he saw upon his release. I was being selfish, and I'm sorry for that."

"*Ангел...*" Nikolai waits, exhales deeply, then continues.

"You're not selfish. You don't understand the meaning of the word. I just need to stay on my toes."

He gives a look, one that reveals what his riddled comment means. He can't keep me safe and answer my every whim at the drop of a hat. One must be sacrificed for the greater good.

If this doesn't prove how self-centered I am, nothing will. The first thought I had when the reason behind his response dawned on me was to demand our jet return to Vegas this very instant. Maddox lost years of his life for me, but I'm struggling to harness my desires for Nikolai for a few days.

I'm a horrible person.

"Don't." Nikolai's tone is full of warning, proving he knows me better than anyone. "The only selfish person in this room is me." When I attempt to interrupt him, he presses his finger to my lips. "If I truly wanted to keep you safe, I shouldn't have sided with the devil like I did twelve months ago."

My brows furrow as confusion makes itself known in my gut.

What deal did he make? The only one I can recall is the pledge he made to kill his father, but that was vowed to me, not the devil.

I still as recognition dawns. He isn't referring to the moments after we succumbed to the inane sexual chemistry firing between us. He's referring to the home arrest documentation he switched so he'd be placed under house arrest at my apartment instead of the Popov compound.

A year ago, I was mortified I had unknowingly invited a mafia prince to spend the long weekend with me. Now I gobble up every second he's willing to give me.

It's amazing how differently you see someone when you truly look at them instead of judging them on who they're believed to be.

"I'll never regret your decision that day, Nikolai. As you always say, every sunrise is unique, meaning every day is a new beginning. You breathed life back into me that weekend. That's something I'll never regret."

I burrow my nose into his neck to breathe in the scent of our skin mingled together. When his head flops to the side to give me unlimited access to a scent I'll never grow tired of smelling, my heart gains an extra flutter.

His hand traces the bumps in my spine as his nose gets lost in waves of unruly red curls. He drinks in my scent as readily as I'm devouring his. We're truly addicted to one another.

This is conceited for me to say, but Nikolai deserves to have someone like me in his life. He lived in hell for years before I dragged him from the trenches. That's why I know beyond a doubt his worry is unnecessary. He'll protect me and our baby as fiercely as I'll protect him. Nothing will stop me from keeping them both safe.

After a few more deep breaths, I say, "If I'm being honest, I don't want my face to be the first Maddox sees upon his release. I have so many questions I need answered. For example, why was he at the Petretti compound the night Col sentenced me to run the gauntlet? How did he know he could claim my punishment as his own? And although I never believed he killed Megan, if he is responsible for her disappearance, where did he hide her all this time?"

Nikolai murmurs, "All questions I want answered as well. Although I doubt mine will be asked as pleasantly as yours."

The mirth in his tone shelves my retaliation. He will never hurt Maddox. He's a member of my family, which means he is sheltered under the same protective umbrella as me. I'm more concerned about Maddox's answers than how he's forced to give them.

I accept who Nikolai is because he was born into this lifestyle. He doesn't know any different. Maddox can't use the same set of excuses. If any theories running through my head are true, he has a lot to answer for.

7

NIKOLAI

Justine and I walk down the stairs of the private jet before the sun has even risen. The fanfare for our arrival starkly contrasts with the lackluster one I had when I visited her hometown twelve months ago. Although the busty female greeter men in my industry love gifting remains, my method of transportation has altered. Now instead of a topless ride that showcases more grunt than security, we have a fleet of SUVs armored to withstand an AK-47.

A leggy blonde in a tight miniskirt and barely there shirt greets me with a grin when I break through the men swarming my every move. She's the same blonde who had hoped to suck my dick during my last visit.

"Welcome back to Florida, Nikolai."

The high-end whore chokes on her words when she spots Justine at my side. I don't know how she missed her. With beauty no women could compete against, Justine stands out in a crowd.

A grin furls my lips when I take in the blonde's shocked expression. A dozen heavily armed men, a fleet of armored vehicles, and the early hour didn't faze her in the slightest, but witnessing me gripping anything but the hair of the woman sucking my cock is shocking for her.

You'd think my last dismissal would have clued her in that I'm now a one-woman man, but if her clenched jaw and narrowed eyes are anything to go by, tempting assets are the only thing she has going for her.

"So the rumors are true? You now travel with your whores instead of fucking them and dumping them as you usually do?" She drags her narrowed eyes to Justine before sneering. "Don't get comfy, sugar. He'll palm you off to his understudies within a week." She drags her eyes down Justine's frozen frame. "If you're lucky."

My hand rises to backhand the sneer from her face, but something stops me. I want to pretend it is because I'm an improved man who no longer sees women in two categories—whores and housemaids—but that isn't the case.

Years of bad guidance can't be undone in twelve months. Justine is responsible for extinguishing my retaliation, not a new moral compass.

"Did you hear what happened to the last woman who disrespected me?" My blood thickens from the sheer confidence in Justine's tone. My queen is ruling her empire, her stance strong and hardened by jealousy.

The blonde shakes her head, the fire in her eyes doused by Justine's fury.

With a smirk, Justine says, "Exactly. No one knows what happened to her. Not even Nikolai." She whispers her last three words, highlighting their threat.

The blonde scoffs, unsure if Justine is being honest, but before she can voice her uncertainly, Justine warns, "Unless you want to take her place in my story, I suggest you climb aboard your broomstick and leave."

Her tone is calm and unwavering. The same can't be said for the blonde's thighs. Her eyes widen as they dance between Justine's to gauge the authenticity of her threat.

She reaches her decision quickly. Her dash through the men hovering close to watch the spectacle unfold causes her to bump shoulders with Justine. This isn't the first time my men have watched women go to war over me, but it is the first time I haven't sat back and enjoyed the show with them.

With Justine's attention rapt on the blonde, she fails to notice the dip of my chin to a crew member. Justine might be willing to let her disrespect slide, but I'm not as inclined to issue her a pardon.

Her punishment will ensure the Popov entity isn't the only associa-tion aware of the repercussions of disrespecting my *Ангел*.

I wait for Justine and Roman to join me in the middle car in a fleet of three before locking my eyes with Justine. My cock braces against the zipper of my jeans, the leadership in her eyes too invigo-rating not to respond to.

"Soon, Nikolai. Very soon," Justine says in Russian, hardening my dick even more.

With a pleased smirk, she shifts her focus to the scenery whizzing by the window. I take in an equally pleasing sight. My eyes don't focus on the hues of orange and yellow dancing across sandy meadows, though. I peruse something much brighter and more dazzling than the sun's slow rise. I have my sights set on the woman gifting me a direct descendant of the empire we're ruling side by side. A son as strong as his father and as smart as his mother. My urge to protect Justine has always been obsessive, but now it will be downright manic.

Our trip from a private airstrip in Hopeton to Justine's parents' house is short. Before Maddox's arrest, the Walshes had a large, sprawling family home in an oceanic town not far from here. But with legal expenses beyond their means and a willingness to give up everything to see one of their own freed, their family home was sold, and they downgraded to a modest four-bedroom property four miles from the airport.

The only benefit of their downsize was an increase in property. My men have used its vast span to create a safe yet amicable barri-cade around their home, hopefully keeping their neighbors and law enforcement officers off our radar.

"Wait for my men, *Ангел*," I demand when Justine's hand curls around the door handle the instant our car stops at the front of a set of dark stairs.

Her nose screws up, but she nods all the same. The dozen armed guards we're traveling with aren't here for me. I can take care of myself. They're here for Justine. Their orders are simple. Use any means necessary to keep her safe.

Shoot to kill, then take names for later retaliation.

Alexei's son Tristan lost his life when he sided with the wrong team during Justine's kidnapping. Any fool stupid enough to go against me again will suffer the same fate.

Once my men have cleared the area, I permit Justine to leave our SUV. Her feet landing on a rickety porch coincides with an entranceway light being switched on. With details of our arrival on the down-low, her family knew of her return today, but they had no clue it would occur before dawn.

"I haven't seen you up this early since you attempted to sneak Brax into your eighteenth birthday party."

My eyes rocket to Justine's as quickly as hers dart to mine. She gives me a *please be patient* look before greeting the man standing behind the cracked-open screen door with a hug. If I hadn't recognized the murky blue eyes glaring at me from beneath lowered lashes, I would have had my knife pressed to his jugular before he got within an inch of Justine. Fortunately for him, he's her older brother, the gatekeeper when it comes to anything involving Justine or her family. He's Landon Walsh: dedicated pilot, all-around sportsman, and fucking thorn in my backside over the past twelve months.

When Justine presses her lips to Landon's ear, the knife in my pocket grows heavy. Brother or not, Justine is mine and only mine. You either learn that fast, or I'll beat it into you.

"Unless you want Brax to lose the ability to breathe, I suggest you remain quiet about him—"

"Or if you don't want to be tortured, speak up. I'm traveling light, meaning I'm without my instruments of choice, but that doesn't mean I can't get inventive," I interrupt, my tone not as playful as intended.

I know Justine has a past. I fuckin' hate it, but I entered our relationship with more than my share of baggage, so I can't expect her to have none. As long as Brax is a thing of the past, I have no issues with him. *Mostly.*

"Nikolai," Roman grumbles only loud enough for me to hear when he spots my second silent demand for the night. "Let it go."

His glare says more than his words ever will. He voiced numerous concerns about my quest to rid the world of the insolent men who bid on Justine, so he won't remain quiet when my focus shifts to a man whose only crime is associating with Justine long before I entered the equation.

When Diak seeks further instructions, I reluctantly shake my head. Brax should consider himself lucky I'm traveling with Roman instead of Trey. Brax would already be chewing on his intestines if Trey were my moral compass this week.

"He's joking." Justine's pleading eyes stray to mine. "Aren't you, Nikolai?"

"Of course." My voice reveals I'm full of shit, but it weakens the deep groove between Justine's brows. "Nikolai. It's a pleasure to meet you."

Yep, that sounded as awkward as you'd expect. I'm not a meet-and-greet-with-a-handshake type of guy. If you don't know who I am, it won't take long to discover I'm not made out of rainbows and sunshine. Landon learned that fact firsthand nearly a year ago.

The sour expression on Landon's face reveals he's still harboring issues about our last tussle over his sister, but he's not eager to bring it up.

I won our battle back then, and he knows I'll win the second, third, or however many fucking times it takes him to get the hint that I'm not going anywhere.

A thousand men couldn't keep me from Justine, so what chance does one man have?

Continuing with our ploy of deception, Landon thrusts his hand toward mine. "Landon." When I accept his gesture, he adds, "I'd say the pleasure is all mine, but we both know that would be a lie."

A smirk tugs at my lips when he squeezes my hand. His firm hold displays what I've always known. He doesn't care who you are or how dangerous you appear, his family comes before anyone.

Good. Justine is carrying my family, and the more people she and our baby have on their side, the better. Landon isn't on my team, but he isn't my enemy either.

"Is everyone here?" Justine steps into the foyer. Although the house she grew up in was sold to fund Maddox's legal expenses, their temporary abode still has a homey feel. The Walsh kids may not have been raised here, but someone's kids were.

"Yeah." Landon opens the door wide enough for me and the six men behind me to enter. "Dad canceled his next three flights. Mom is between jobs, and Sebastian and Caidyn flew in yesterday afternoon. Celebrations ran late. I'm only just falling."

I try to hide my smirk at Landon's grimace, but it curls my lips too quickly for me to shut down. His whitening gills show he is in desperate need of some hair of the dog.

"Mom set up your room for you and..." Landon nudges his head at me instead of saying my name. "Her study has a cot for Roman." Roman smirks like a smug fuck, pleased he was addressed by name. "And the den looks like a bunker for the remainder of your entourage." This comment is more for me than Justine—as is his sneer.

"And the men I sent here this morning, where are they?"

Recalling that Landon isn't a member of my crew—*yet*—I keep my tone friendly. He's adamant no amount of money will ever have him siding with a man like me, but I'm a stubborn fuck who refuses to back down. Everyone has a price. I just haven't worked out what Landon's is yet.

Landon scrubs the stubble on his chin, barely concealing its frantic tick, before jerking his chin to the left. "Half of them are in the den. The other half are on watch outside."

When I shift my eyes to Justine, she hears my words before my mouth delivers them. "My room is upstairs, third on the right. I'll meet you there once you've updated your men."

She kisses me. The sugary syrup her pancakes were slathered in flavors our kiss.

I've barely sampled half her mouth when she withdraws from our embrace. I am not happy I'm being denied a taste I'd kill for, but I let it slide since my crew surrounds us. My men are horny fucks who would feel not an ounce of shame using my exchange with Justine to relieve tension while they're without their whores.

Justine rolls her eyes when I demand Roman to shadow her to her room before calling it a night. She doesn't give me any lip, though. She's aware anywhere she goes Roman goes.

Justine is barely out of earshot when Landon grumbles, "Is this really necessary?"

"Yes," I answer. "If your sister's scars aren't proof enough, the events you witnessed during my last visit should clue you in."

Without men on hand for the negotiation I forged with Dimitri to have Justine's debt forwarded to me and needing to keep my relationship with Justine out of the limelight, I sought help from someone I knew would protect her as honorably as I would.

One of her brothers was an obvious choice.

Sex trafficking isn't for the weak at heart, but Landon took it in stride. He didn't flinch when he saw the amount of money I was leaving on the table from allowing Dimitri to run a West Coast prostitution operation without paying distribution rights to the Popov entity. I'm not talking about a small seven-figure amount. It was well into the high eights.

The only time his gills got a little green was when he saw a name scratched on the bottom of an old transfer form from years earlier. Katie O'Neill. Her name was most likely an alias, but Landon's whitening cheeks and dilated pupils had me taking note of her sale documents for future exploration.

My search didn't produce many results. Most of the documents after Katie's sale were heavily blacked out. She either got snagged by the FBI, or her buyer didn't want anyone tracking her down. With how pedantic men in my industry are at keeping their virginal whores hidden from their wives, I'd say it was the latter.

Not waiting for Landon to show me the way, I head in the direction he nudged earlier. "Is Dimitri aware of my arrival?"

I can't see Landon, but I can picture him shaking his head when a whoosh sounds through my ears. "But I'm certain he's aware of Maddox's impending release. His crew's presence in Hopeton has doubled in the past month."

My teeth grit. I was hoping our agreement last year would have kept Dimitri out of this, but clearly it was just garnish on his overflowing plate. I'm not shocked. Greed is a major part of my industry, but that doesn't mean I'll take Dimitri's disrespect sitting down.

My steps into the den stop when an accented voice mocks, "For a man who flies all over the world, your geographical knowledge is shit."

When a pair of icy-blue eyes stray to mine, my hand slips into the back pocket of my jeans. The blade of my knife is cool compared to the fury raging through my body from spotting Dimitri sitting across from Gavril, my number-four-ranked soldier.

A hopeful smirk lifts my lips when Dimitri's goon sizes me up. It's the same fool who learned the hard way what happens when you disrespect my woman.

I can only hope the large diamond-shaped scar on his hand doesn't have him cowering away. It's been weeks since I've killed, and my urge is at its greatest. One wrong word, one wrong move, or even so much as a wrong swallow will have my knife getting friendly with his neck.

My hope for a bloody evening is dashed when Dimitri demands for him to wait outside. When the tatted-up hothead fails to immediately jump to Dimitri's demand, Gavril helps him see sense. He's tossed to the curb in under ten seconds, his removal coming with the loss of three teeth.

After taking in a bloodstained tooth discarded halfway down the hall, Dimitri returns his eyes to me. "He's lucky I don't pay him for his looks."

"Then what are you paying him for? It can't be his smarts."

Smirking, Dimitri grumbles something about honoring family values while shadowing me into the den. Landon wasn't joking when he said it's been set up like a fortress. It reminds me of the bunkers my crew slept in while waiting for Clarks to be built, just minus the whores my men trade more regularly than drugs.

I take a seat in an empty chair before gesturing for Dimitri to sit in the one opposite me. It's an amicable gesture, but it doesn't simmer my annoyance. Hoping a hit of nicotine will keep my hands away from my knife, I tap a cigarette out of a half-empty packet, place it between my lips, then light it.

Smoke bellows between us when I mutter, "You shouldn't be here without an invitation."

I say my comment only loud enough for Dimitri to hear. If my men discover he's here without the right protocol being followed, he won't leave breathing. And although I'll always class the Petrettis as my enemy, the one sitting across from me deserves a little leeway.

He helped me save Justine. If I could set aside a lifetime of hatred, I'd award him more than a half-assed mercy bid.

Unfortunately, morals were the first thing I discarded when I lost faith in mankind.

That's why you can be assured if Dimitri is here for any other reason than to give Justine a full pardon, he'll discover how the rules of our industry changed the instant Vladimir fell victim to my knife. Nothing is below me when it comes to protecting my queen —not even century-long traditions.

Dimitri adjusts his position so his back faces my men, before replying, "I could say the same for you, Nikolai. You don't belong here any more than I do."

I admire the grit in his voice. He's seated in a room full of men who'd give anything to kill him, yet his confidence hasn't wavered in the slightest. Either he's a stupid man or he believes he has nothing to worry about. Both expose his recklessness. The fact he's here, in the home of the woman carrying my child, means he's on my turf. Being here without an invitation is as disrespectful as me arriving at his compound without notice a year ago.

My disrespect can be easily excused. I'll never be accused of being a rule follower. Dimitri, on the other hand, follows protocol to the wire—even when it could cost him his life.

Dimitri's dark eyes stop focusing on the ember of my half-consumed cigarette when I disclose, "Justine is with child. My child." The pride in my voice can't be missed during my last two words.

I thought I said my statement only loud enough for Dimitri to hear, but Landon's near-choke on his spit proves I didn't. Although Justine requested we keep news of her pregnancy a secret until after Maddox's release, it is too critical to ignore. Whether a wife or a whore, any woman carrying an heir to a legion is given a full pardon.

I know this because it's how my life was spared when Vladimir caught wind of my mother's floundering ways. If I hadn't been conceived by Col's seed, my blood would have been shed on the concrete floors of the Popov compound long before my sixteenth birthday. Vladimir despised me so much I wouldn't have been shocked to discover he requested to carry out my termination himself.

The rules we live by are as misguided as the man who founded them, but this is one I plan to follow to the T. Even though our baby won't protect Justine's heart, he'll keep her physically safe. That in itself is worth a thousand lives.

I watch Landon's brisk exit from the den while stubbing out my cigarette on the sole of my boot.

Once he's out of my view, I ask Dimitri. "Why are you here?"

My question is short and to the point. If Landon is heading where I think he's heading, I have mere minutes before my battle shifts to one even more detrimental than the one I'm striving to avoid.

My brows furrow when he answers, "I'm here to issue a warning."

"A warning for what?" He could be referring to the last time I entered his realm unannounced, but my gut is steering me in another direction.

Dimitri scoots to the edge of his chair, ensuring his words are only for my ears. "The men Landon mentioned in Hopeton are not my crew. They're a sanction hoping to get a foothold in my area without my approval." I'm about to rib him about keeping tighter reins on his entity, but his next words free the wind from my sails. "They're Russian."

"Russian?" My accent is more pronounced from my anger rising. He didn't directly say he suspects I'm encroaching on his turf, but his snarl sure as fuck did. "Why the fuck would I be interested in a two-bit operation with a main focus on sex trafficking?" Although I'm asking a question, I continue speaking, denying him the opportunity to rebut. "Despite what your daddy told you, there's no money in the prostitution conglomerate."

Dimitri's sixty-thousand-dollar watch reveals my comment is off the mark, but my ego won't accept my reply.

His usually docile face lines with wolfish satisfaction as his lips tug upward. "Rumors are that you're getting soft. That your focus has shifted away from the game."

"Soft?" Anger chops up my growl. "The only thing about to get soft is your cock when I cut it off and feed it to you." I nudge my head to his right ankle. "That piece you *think* I'm unaware of wouldn't be there if it weren't for me." I turn to face him head-on, letting my fury be seen on my face. "The guns your crew carries when shipping whores between states are marked with my brand. Even the coke your men sniff off their breasts between shipments was purchased from me."

My stare goes black. I've reached the end of my tether. "Disrespect me one more time with claims I'm not running *my* organization to *your* specifications, and we'll soon discover who's soft." My eyes stray in the direction his goon went. "This is your final chance to leave before you discover how hard it is to wipe your ass with your non-dominant hand."

My knife feels heavy in my pocket. It's begging to be released, to be used as it was intended. My urge to kill is intense, but I've got more urgent matters to deal with than a rival mistaking determination as weakness. Dimitri's rile exposed more than his ability to piss me off. He said the men setting up shop in Hopeton are Russian.

Considering all Bratva crews on this side of Russia are under the umbrella of the Popov entity, Dimitri's assumption they're a part of my operative is true. It's the fact I'm unaware of their bid for Hopeton that's frustrating the hell out of me. I may not rule my entity with Vladimir's iron fist, but I run a tight ship. A slip like this is not acceptable.

Dimitri stands to his feet before fiddling with his jacket. The cufflinks shining on the sleeves of his dress shirt reveal his entity has jumped leaps and bounds from the ruins Col left it in, but his visit also shows he's aware of his place.

Mafia kingpins don't warn rivals to steer clear of their turf. They squash them, then use their punishment as a warning to anyone stupid enough to follow in their footsteps. In this industry, actions will always exceed words.

"I came here as a mark of respect."

His eyes, identical to mine in every way, float to the stairwell Justine climbed only minutes ago. His prolonged stare advises where his admiration stems. He isn't here to make amends with me. He's here to soothe volatile waters with Justine.

His life expectancy just halved.

The chances of reaching middle age in this industry are already slim. Now Dimitri's are even slimmer than that.

His next words reduce my violent temper. "Words that should have been spoken years ago never were, resulting in an outcome that will haunt me the rest of my life." His shoulders stiffen as he looks up at me. "I decided to try a different route today. Don't have me regretting my decision, Nikolai. We may have the same blood pumping through our veins, but we will never be family." His eyes return to the stairwell, albeit a little glassy. "If it weren't for her, I wouldn't have allowed you within an inch of Hopeton."

When my warning snarl fails to gain his attention, I shift my eyes in the direction he's peering. My heart kicks out a new tune when I spot Justine standing at the foot of the stairs. Her eyes are as wide and frightened as they were the last time she stood across from the man responsible for her scars, but thankfully, this time around, her throat is void of the noose that bit her skin.

Although my intuition tells me I have nothing to fear, I creep up on Dimitri in less than a second. My movements are so meek that not even Justine registers my approach. If she so much as blinks in fear, I'll take down Dimitri as unrepentantly as I did Alexei.

A snake never stops shedding its skin, but it is still a snake at the end of the day. Dimitri is two seconds from learning how lethal my bite is.

Justine's eyes lift to mine when Dimitri says, "*Non ha nulla da temere. Forse non hai pagato il debito che voleva Col, ma hai pagato più di quanto volevo che pagassi. Per quanto mi riguarda, non mi devi niente.*"

She stares at me for several long heartbeats, aware I'm seconds from requesting she close her eyes, but unsure if she wants Dimitri to suffer the same fate as Alexei. There are rules I must follow for men in similar positions as mine, but they're null and void the instant Justine's safety is compromised.

Besides, I don't speak a word of Italian, so the skate of my knife across Dimitri's jugular could be easily excused. How am I to know if his words are threatening or not? I have to rely solely on my gut, which I rarely do. The only time I've let my instincts take over was during my quest to bed Justine. Although I came out of that game a winner, my life has never been more complicated.

Before I can work through half the commotion twisting my gut, Justine shakes her head, wordlessly requesting me to stand down. If her eyes weren't locked on mine, I'd assume her demand was for Dimitri. Unfortunately, words aren't needed to see the white flag she's waving my way.

Don't misconstrue the strength of my queen. She's not surrendering. She's forgiving.

What the fuck?

The demand in Justine's eyes switches to a plea when I'm reluctant to house my blade. My desire to kill has always been rampant. It's not something I can switch off in an instant. But I'm open to change for this woman, my slice of heaven in a hot and temperamental place.

A bead of sweat rolls down Dimitri's nape when the *snick* of my blade announces its return to my knife's handle. He shouldn't be so quick to suck in a relieved breath. I recorded my first kill at the age of eight, which means I've learned many ways to take down a man without a weapon. He isn't out of the woods just yet.

After a quick swallow, Dimitri says, "*Digli che non sono il suo nemico.*"

"Tell him yourself." My admiration for Justine grows when she skirts past Dimitri without the slightest wobble in her stride. She's strong and powerful, even more so when she takes her rightful spot at my side. "He's right here, willing to listen. You just need to speak to him in a language he understands."

Dimitri spins around to face us. His focus isn't on me. His attention remains fixated on Justine. It's both a smart and stupid move on his behalf. He knows she's the only one capable of bringing me out of the darkness my life is filled with, but bringing her into a fight she doesn't belong in displeases me greatly.

Neither ploy will gain him my merits.

"*Questo non è il modo in cui le cose funzionano nel nostro settore. L'unica volta che si diventa amici con il nemico è quando si prevede di portarli giù.*" Dimitri's eyes are missing the pompous flare I expected them to have. "*Egli può essere il Spawn del diavolo, ma è anche mio fratello. Non gli auguro nulla di male.*"

With a dip of his chin—more a bid of farewell than bowing out of our fight like a coward—he leaves Justine's family home under the shadowed watch of three of my men.

My first thought is to go after him. Instead, I circle Justine like a shark. The wish to kill is still intense, but something about Justine is off, and I can't help but devote all my attention to her.

She smells different. Whole. As if she's no longer fractured.

"What did he say to you?"

"Who?" Heat springs to the back of Justine's knees. She's not ramping up for a fight. My arrogance turns her on.

The good girls always want to tame the bad boy... except her.

My nostrils flare when I suck in her scent like an addict hitting three lines. "The person responsible for the change in your scent. You smell different."

Her quick exhale fans my cheeks. "I smell different?" Her words quiver as the tension between us turns rampant.

The last time we played this game, she smelled of another man.

This scent isn't that. It's a feminine scent, both arousing and unique.

"Yeah. I can't tell what it's closest to. How you smelled when you stood across from me with the heart of a warrior but no knowledge of its existence, or the scent that leeched from your pores the first time I fucked you without a condom." My long, purposeful strides come to a stop in front of her. "It might be a combination of them both."

Justine's scent is capable of buckling my knees.

Maybe Dimitri was right. Perhaps I have let this woman soften me. I have enough adrenaline coursing through my veins to take down a thousand men, yet there's only one person I plan to conquer tonight.

Her.

8

JUSTINE

Nikolai's arrogance is at an all-time high, but not all of its boost is compliments of the lust raging in his eyes. I only arrived in the den because an odd sensation was twisting my stomach. I tried to push it aside as excited butterflies, but the longer I denied my feelings, the greater they became.

Ignoring my instincts was the catalyst of my family's downfall five years ago, so I have no intention of ignoring them again.

The further I traveled down the spiral staircase, the tighter the knot in my stomach grew. I couldn't see the man Nikolai spoke to in a hushed tone, but something deep inside me knew their conversation wasn't good.

I didn't mean to startle when my eyes locked on Dimitri, but old habits die hard. His family took more from me than you can imagine, and although he helped in my rescue, I doubt that would have been the case if it weren't for Nikolai's request.

The Popovs are a highly ranked entity in their industry, and Nikolai's reputation is unsurpassed. If you can't play with them, you play beside them with the hope you'll be picked for their team during their next selection process.

That's what Dimitri did that night twelve months ago. He chose a path that would put him in Nikolai's good graces. It was a smart move from both a business and personal standpoint.

Well, so it seemed at the time.

Now I'm not so sure.

His expression when he said my punishment was worse than he ever wanted was the same one his face held when Col sentenced me to run the gauntlet. He seemed in pain, as if his heart bore the scars my body embraces. If I didn't know any better, I'd swear his visit today centered more around me than patching the rift between Nikolai and him.

I attempt to confirm my suspicions by asking, "Why was Dimitri here?"

With a grunt, Nikolai begins circling me again. "No, Ангел. That's not the way things work."

A year ago, I would have believed his sneer was in regard to the unjust rules men in his industry expect me to follow, but I've learned a lot in the past twelve months. His attention isn't fixated on the men pretending not to watch our charade through lowered lids. He has a union much more vital in his sights. He's talking about our relationship—*about us.*

"He said I don't owe him anything and that he's not your enemy."

My breaths come out in a quiver when Nikolai's nose dives into my hair to take a long, undignified whiff. "Is that all?"

The shake of my head amplifies the smell he is intoxicated by. "Although he wishes things were different, he said the only time he sides with an enemy is when he's planning to take them down."

My knees meet when Nikolai splays his hand across my jugular so he can pull my head closer to him. Even over the smell of smoke, his scent is hallucinogenic. He didn't shower after our escapades, so he still smells of my arousal and sweat-slicked skin. It's a sweet, tangy scent that pairs well with the cigarette he just finished.

Recognizing that now isn't the time for lust to get the better of me, I straighten my spine before stammering out, "Dimitri doesn't wish you any harm. He said even though the devil raised you, you are still his brother."

Nikolai growls. I'm unsure if my comment is responsible for his wordless reply, or the fact my hair hasn't been washed since our rigorous activities during our flight to Hopeton.

I assume it is the latter when he gathers my wild curls to one side of my neck. Although there's an inch of air between us, I know he is hard. The blood whizzing through his body isn't just warming his breaths. It is thickening his cock as well.

I gasp in a sharp breath when his fingertip traces the bite marks on my shoulder. "Is that why you smell different? Because *he* set you free?"

Loose strands of hair fall to my shoulders when I rigorously shake my head. "If freedom came with a new scent, you would have smelled it months ago."

"Why?" His voice is jagged, as if his throat is being scorned by the same furious bout of lust charring mine.

A second growl ruffles the fine hair on my nape when I answer, "Because you broke through my cocoon with nothing but the tap of your knuckles on a tabletop."

Nikolai's men stand and leave when a whoosh sounds behind me. He doesn't need to voice his demand for them to leave. They're familiar with his silent commands because he issues them a minimum of three times a day.

Once we're alone, Nikolai bands his arm around my stomach to draw me into his body. He is hard as anticipated, the length of his thickened cock extending well past the curve in my lower back.

"Men in my industry are growing restless. They think I'm being led by my dick. What are your thoughts on that?"

His brutish tone shouldn't turn me on, but it does.

"I think they are foolish, impudent men whose stupidity will soon have them bowing at your feet, pleading for their lives."

I'm not being facetious. Only a fool would accuse him of being spineless. If anything, our relationship should make them fear him more. The strong are brave because they were once weak. The fearless are no longer afraid, because they've already been frightened, just like the men who were denied love stop at nothing to keep it once they have it.

"A real man does whatever it takes to protect the ones he loves. That doesn't make him weak. It makes him fearless. Smart. It makes him the man I fell in love with in less than a second. You are the strongest you've ever been, Nikolai, so I don't just find their remarks laughable—I believe they are punishable. They need to learn your crown isn't emblazoned with fancy jewels and rhinestones. It is spiked with grit, discipline, and bravery."

His cock flexes against my ass when he growls, "Spoken like a true queen." The zipper in his jeans must be biting his cock, yet it continues to grow, showing it hasn't even reached half its strength yet. "The only person I'll ever kneel for."

Although it takes one hell of an effort to pull away from his embrace, I do. He wants me to stand at his side, not three paces behind him. I can't do that if I continually follow the pleas of my body instead of my head. His responses tonight show he's struggling, and although he prefers to keep me out of the gritty elements of his "family business," we're a unit, meaning I have to accept both the good and bad parts of his industry.

"Ангел..." Nikolai's disappointment weakens my campaign, but only a little.

I don't want the power to rule a nation. I merely want enough to influence the man I'm in love with to see sense through the madness surrounding him.

I'm confident I have that... I just have no clue how to use it.

"Why was Dimitri here? It must have been important since he didn't wait for the sun to rise."

Bile burns my esophagus when Nikolai answers, "It's no concern of yours." He isn't rude, but he's giving clear signs that Dimitri's visit isn't up for discussion.

It's a pity for him that my urge to protect him has grown as strong as my confidence over the past year. "If it affects you, Nikolai, it affects me. We're a team." My hand drops to my stomach. "All of us."

Nikolai was raised on hate. I will not have our baby reared the same way. There are parts of his industry I never want our baby subjected to, but I also understand that once you're Bratva, you're always Bratva.

Even when you leave, it follows you.

Nikolai's brother is living proof of this. He gave Rico a full pardon, yet he continually peers over his shoulder, waiting for the day he'll be forced to answer for his desertion.

The worry in Nikolai's voice startles me when he discloses, "Dimitri was here to issue a warning. He doesn't appreciate the Russian stamp my entity is forging on his turf."

I balk, my mouth dropping in bewilderment. I'm not solely stunned he yielded to my demand so quickly. I'm shocked by his confession.

"You assured Rico you'd never set up shop in Florida. You may not have promised, but your word alone holds merit."

"I know." Nikolai scrubs the stubble on his chin before taking a seat on one of the cots his men vacated in a hurry. "And I intend to keep my word." He lifts and locks his eyes with mine. "I am many things, *Ангел*, but I'll never be accused of being a cheat."

His reply has a double meaning—both for Rico and me. Although the eagerness of the unnamed blonde earlier tonight caught me at a low point, I trust him with every fiber of my being. He'd never break mine or his brother's trust.

After removing his hand from his chin, I slip into Nikolai's lap. I am defenseless to his charm, but my obsession has as many good points as it does bad. My body pressed against his is enough to bring him back from the brink of insanity, so imagine its strength when he's gifted my eyes at the same time.

"Do you trust Dimitri?"

Nikolai's fingertip counts the bumps in my spine before he shrugs. "He's yet to give me a reason not to. But..."

He leaves his answer open for me to finalize how I see fit. Trust is not an easy thing for him to give. That's why I'll never break it, because I know how difficult it was for him to give it to me so early in our relationship.

"It was a great risk for him to come here."

He jerks his chin up, agreeing with me.

"He wouldn't have done that if he didn't believe what he was saying."

Nikolai's agreeing gestures keep coming, although this one isn't as smooth as his first.

"If it is true, who do you think the Russians are?"

He smirks, amused at my endeavor to talk shop. He generally uses a *charge like a bull in a china shop, ask questions later* tactic. Not once in the past year have I seen him sit down and work through his confusion. Any "talks" he undertakes are usually done with his fists, so I'm certain this is as foreign to him as it is for me.

Hoping he'll see the good that can come from a new approach, I ask, "Have you spoken to Trey? He might have heard some rumblings."

"These aren't my men." His eyes go a little murky with anger.

"I trust them with both my life and yours. They wouldn't be a part of my crew if I didn't." The conviction in his tone can't be missed.

"Then who could it be?"

I'm not being nosy. I genuinely want to help him with this. Besides, isn't this my role? A true queen doesn't sit back and watch the royalties roll in. She brings an equal share to the table.

My breaths shorten when Nikolai mumbles, "Perhaps Asher."

His reply shocks me. Asher is his friend more than an associate, so for Nikolai to suspect him isn't just outrageous—it's utterly blindsiding.

His suspicion makes sense when he says, "Asher has been off the radar since Dominique's death. A grieving man could never be accused of being reasonable."

A moan vibrates my lips. "But shouldn't Dominique's death keep his focus in Russia? He wants revenge, not a life in a foreign city."

Although details are short, I am aware Nikolai used Asher's infatuation with one of Vladimir's whores to establish negotiations with Asher's father last year. Nikolai wanted the Yurys' business trades to be conducted through his entity instead of Vladimir's. Dominique sweetened the deal at the start of their negotiations.

Unfortunately, she was killed in a coup gone wrong a little over six months ago. Asher has been off the grid ever since.

Recalling a conversation between Nikolai and Asher, I say, "You offered Asher an outlet months ago, Nikolai. He doesn't need to go against you to develop ties here."

He remains quiet, but I know in my heart he believes me. Like Dimitri, Asher respects Nikolai too much to disrespect him like this. He may be mourning, but his grudge isn't with Nikolai or his family.

"You should call him."

When he peers at me as if I'm crazy, I give him my *look who's talking* glare.

With a grin and perhaps a touch of reluctance, he pulls his cell phone out of his pocket. Any worries that he's annoyed at my nosy nancying fly out the window when he purposely brushes my needy pussy in the process. He could have secured his phone without his hand diving between my legs, but the day he stops teasing me will be the day he takes his final breath. He lives to rile me up.

Staring at me, he dials a known number. His widening pupils expose how he wants his obedience rewarded. He's going to get lost in my body, get high on it as if I'm the most potent drug on the market. My body will pay the restitution for his wavering on the rules he generally toes like a tightrope.

It takes Asher a few seconds to answer, but when he does, his greeting exposes what I suspected. He isn't Nikolai's enemy. He is his friend.

"Still chasing the sun?"

A grin tugs at Nikolai's lips. "It's better than chasing a receding hairline."

Even if Nikolai's phone wasn't on speaker, I'd still hear Asher's laugh. "Fucking bastard." He curses Nikolai in Russian. "Just like my cock, my hairline is well-stocked."

"The magic of little blue pills." Nikolai scans my face, ensuring I'm aware I am his Viagra of choice. "I've heard they do wonders. I'll be sure to test them out if I ever get as old and limp-dicked as you."

Their conversation would be amusing if it didn't have a snippet of honesty behind it. Both Nikolai's and Asher's lineage reveal the rarity of any member of their family living past the age of forty. Vladimir had such a long campaign because he was at the top of the food chain.

The soldiers underneath him weren't as lucky.

At the ripe age of twenty-eight, Asher is already in his prime. If this doesn't make me immensely grateful for Nikolai's high role in his industry, nothing will.

Their conversation steers in a new direction when Nikolai asks Asher if he has any men in Hopeton. Asher's tone doesn't falter when he denies the accusation in Nikolai's tone. "I'm fighting my own war, so why would I join yours?"

"Dimitri said—"

"There's your first error. Wasn't it you who told me brothers don't carry the same blood in their veins? They stain their hands with it?" Asher's voice isn't laced with the annoyance Nikolai's has. His is more truthful than anything. "Who stood at your side when you claimed Emil's life for bidding on your queen?"

Nikolai quickly switches his cell to the regular setting, but it doesn't stop me from hearing what Asher says next. "And who will stand at my side when the men responsible for Dominique's death pay their penalty?"

"I will always have your back," Nikolai quotes in Russian, his accent deepening as his desire to kill grows.

He feels every inch of Asher's pain because he experienced the same torturous emotions when my body convulsed after Vladimir kicked out the chair saving me from being hanged.

I want to act surprised by the heaviness of their conversation, but I'm not. Nikolai has never hidden who he is from me. His wish to rid the world of the men who bid on me has not been concealed. I just hate having it thrust in my face like this. Keeping my head buried in the sand may make others see me as a coward, but I'd rather be seen as spineless than heartless.

The flaring of Nikolai's nostrils stops when Asher replies, "As I will forever have yours, Nikolai. Change makes people nervous, but order keeps them in line. My men are in the process of learning that. Yours are already aware. They wouldn't disrespect you like this."

9

NIKOLAI

J ustine's hopeful eyes shift to mine when a gate creak sounds through the eerie quietness surrounding us. She's been on edge since our conversation early this morning, but with Maddox's release being years in the making, she's not letting anything dampen her joy.

Harbortown Medium Security Prison has more men on guard outside its walls than inside. My conversation with Asher verified it isn't his crew aiming for a foothold in Hopeton, but that doesn't mean I'll lower my guard.

If it isn't Asher, who is it? There isn't another operative strong enough to bid on my title, much less have the gall to go against me. The Popov entity is the largest and strongest it's ever been. Only a fool with a death wish would dare test its strength.

"*Ангел...*" I growl when the flash of a grin has Justine racing away from me.

When Roman attempts to follow her, I hold him back. Landon is already on her tail, but if he weren't, the three snipers I have hidden in the dense forest surrounding us would take care of any unwanted visitors.

A medium-built man with reddish hair and a sleeve full of tats dumps a duffle bag on the ground a mere second before Justine launches herself into his arms. The grin on Maddox's face when he twirls his baby sister in the air reveals he never thought this day would come, but a wary, unsure smile exposes his cautiousness.

He knows as well as I do that the agreement he made with the Petrettis was voided the instant he stepped foot outside prison walls.

Maddox's grin jumps onto the faces of a handful of my men. They're not smiling at Justine's overly friendly greeting. Witnessing the Walsh clan's teary response is causing their peculiar reaction.

My men have witnessed many things: pleas from teary-eyed fathers begging for the lives of their sons to be spared, wives begging to save their husbands, and even whores offering favors in exchange for their favorite clients' clemency. But this is the first time they've witnessed a joyous reunion. No blood has been shed, no lives claimed, only enough tears to flood a river.

When Justine returns to my side, her cheeks are lined with vibrant red streaks, and her nose is running. "Maddox, this is—"

"Nikolai." I freeze when Maddox throws his arms around my torso to pull me into his chest. I'm five seconds from showing him there is only one Walsh family member I'm willing to accept affection from, but his next words steal mine. "Dimitri sends caution. The flock is about to fly."

His warning thickens my tongue with hate, but before I can act on it, a police siren shrills through my ears. An unmarked cruiser is gliding down the road my heavily armed men line, the frantic swallows of the two male occupants inside viewable from a distance.

"Stand down." Justine's demanding tone is more for me than my crew. "They're practically family."

"Practically family isn't family, *Ангел*." My voice is hostile, my worry fraying my mood. "So, which are they? Friend or foe?"

Justine's eyes stray to mine. The anxiety in them quickly dries her tears. "They're *my* family, Nikolai, which means they are now also *yours*."

She slips her hand into mine, stopping its frantic clench-and-unclench routine. With my hands losing their ability to expel my anger, the focus shifts to my jaw. Its ticks are barely audible over the gravel crunching under my boots as I follow Justine and Maddox to the stalled police cruiser, but I still feel every grind.

With a lopsided grin, Maddox greets the two plain-clothed men with a handshake before moving away from the object of their focus. I want to pretend they're staring my way because my reputation is known across the globe, but unfortunately, that isn't the case. Their eyes aren't locked on me. They are fixated on my queen, her beauty too pronounced to manifest a guarded response.

"Hi, Ryan," Justine greets a brown-haired man.

In an attempt to return her welcome with equal excitement, Ryan's lips arrow toward Justine's cheek.

They land midair when I yank her out of his path with barely a second to spare.

His chance of being killed for his near miss is halved when recognition dawns on why the blond man smirking behind him seems familiar. He's the man from the dossier I had Roman compile first thing this morning. He's Justine's old flame.

Brax unlikely-to-make-it-to-this-afternoon-alive Anderson.

Dust kicks up around my feet when Justine pivots around to face me. Since she washed her hair this morning, it's extra voluminous, meaning I can no longer see Ryan and Brax through her thick, luscious curls. She stares me straight in the eyes, her pulse working extra hard to convince me there is only one man on her radar.

"I love you." She says her bold statement loud enough that anyone within a five-mile radius can hear it, but her next words are solely for me: "I've never spoken those words to another man before. And I never will again unless he is you. Please remember that."

Bestowing upon me an immense amount of trust I don't deserve, she returns her attention to her guests. This time, it's her dragging me across the asphalt. My back molars crunch when she greets Brax with a peck on the cheek before offering an introduction. Ryan's hand will throb for a week from my firm grip.

Brax's... let me just say, I hope his field of expertise doesn't rely on his hands.

"What are you guys doing here? I thought the authorities wanted to keep Maddox's release on the down-low?"

My smirk at the authoritativeness in Landon's tone sags during the last half of his statement. If my desire to kill the two men standing across from me wasn't already rampant, knowing they are a part of law enforcement triples the odds.

"They do. I'm not here officially." Ryan's reply exposes he's the only one wearing an invisible badge. "Although this case was handed to the Feds years ago, I've kept an eye on it. I've been waiting for this day as long as you guys have. Savannah wanted to be here, but Rylee has chickenpox, so she didn't want to risk... you know."

My brow cocks when his eyes sneakily drift to Justine's non-existent baby bump.

How the fuck does he know she's pregnant?

When reality smacks into me for the second time in under a minute, my slit-eyed gaze snaps to Landon. He forcefully swallows, conscious I'm on to him. He didn't go and rat me out to Justine. He went and tattled to a cop.

Something is very wrong with this picture.

Hating the suspicious glance of her parents, Justine endeavors to switch the focus away from her. "Did you guys want to join us? We're having celebratory drinks at my parents' house." She cozies up to Maddox's side so they know who the celebration centers around. "It's a few miles from here, but you're more than welcome—"

My firm squeeze of her hand cuts her off. I'm not telling her I don't appreciate her extending the olive branch—*even though I do.* It's because she's unaware our celebration has been relocated.

Only Roman and I are aware of that fact.

"If you wish to join us, Gavril can travel with you."

A smug grin etches on my face when Ryan's and Brax's cheeks whiten from Gavril stepping forward. He's tall, large, and Russian: the most lethal combination on the market.

Ryan makes a half-assed excuse about spending time with his family before a week of night shifts. Brax's reply sounds similar, but I miss exactly what he says since I'm so fixated on his sneaky steps toward Justine. She breaks out a smile I've only seen a handful of times in the past twelve months when he whispers something in her ear.

When he shifts his attention to me, he doesn't say anything. He doesn't need to. I can see the suspicion in his eyes and smell the protectiveness on his skin. He's sizing me up, making sure I have the goods to deliver the promises I've made Justine.

I don't know what he sees in my eyes, but it extinguishes the worry in his within seconds, and his hand thrusts my way for the second time in under three minutes. I won't lie. It's the fight of my life not to squeeze his hand as firmly as I did earlier, but I manage —*barely!*

"If you ever want to finish that piece, I know a guy who could help you out." Brax drops his eyes to the snakeskin dangling off an unmarked family crest on the lower half of my right arm, unaware the crest is empty for a reason.

I didn't discover my true birthright until I was well into my teens, but even before then, I never felt like a Popov. That's why the family crest in my tattoo is void of an identity. I want it to represent who I am, not the lie I was born into. That emblem will now include Justine and our baby... and perhaps my trusty knife.

"Maybe one day."

Justine's smile makes it seem as if I said more than I did. She knows I'm not a fan of small talk, particularly with a man not related to her by blood, but her smile exposes my efforts will be well rewarded. That alone lightens the weight of my knife in my pocket.

The dust has barely settled from Brax and Ryan's departure when Justine slings her arms around my neck to seal her lips over mine. She kisses me greedily as if she has been deprived of my taste for centuries instead of minutes.

"I knew there was a good man hiding inside of you," she talks over my lips before playfully nipping at their slight curve.

Dropping my hands to her ass, I squeeze her rounded globes softly, almost teasingly. "You won't be saying that when I take you on the hood of my car in front of your parents."

Her mouth gapes. "You wouldn't dare be so crude. My father would have a coronary."

With a wink revealing that she's secretly hoping I'll make good on my threat, she skips toward the SUVs waiting for us. My acceptance of her past makes her even more eager to get the party started. We have matters much more exciting than Maddox's release to celebrate.

Although we had planned not to share news of Justine's pregnancy until after the scan Dok scheduled, Landon isn't known for his secret-keeping. Aware it will only be a matter of time before her family is updated, Justine would rather she tell them instead of Landon, so we've decided to announce our news after dinner.

It's going to be a night of surprises in the Walsh household.

10

NIKOLAI

Not willing to put Justine in the line of fire, I demand she travel with me instead of her family. While Roman updates the drivers on our new location, Justine hugs Maddox goodbye as if she'll lose the opportunity for another five years.

Although Maddox has a lot of questions to answer, his years in hell are over. I've never seen Justine's eyes as intense as they've been this morning, so you can be assured I'll do everything to keep them as lively. The happier my drug is, the stronger my addiction will become.

Justine's excitement thrums out of her in invisible waves the first ten miles of our trip, but her mouth remains tightlipped until our driver misses the exit for Hopeton.

"That was our exit." She nudges her head to the A345 slip road our SUV is whizzing past before focusing her attention on the driver. "Take the next one, then make a U-turn. We can only get to Hopeton one way."

My teeth grit as I'm reminded why my endeavor to keep her safe has been so time-consuming. I don't know what fuckwit thought it was a good idea to have only one entrance and exit point for Hopeton, but it's been a thorn in my ass the past three days.

It's fortunate there are several airstrips located within the town borders, or Justine's wish to go home would have never been granted. If I had no backup plan to evacuate her in case of an emergency, our travel plans would have ceased in an instant.

Justine stops glaring at the ignorant driver when I disclose, "We're not going to Hopeton."

The veins in her neck flutter as her head cranks back to check if her family's SUV is still following us. Upon spotting its close tail, her eyes return to me.

"Then where are we going?"

She answers her own question when our driver pulls down a familiar street. Manicured lawns, glistening lead windows, and pricy rides sitting in long driveways lead the way to a secret I've been holding for the past six weeks.

"Nikolai..." Justine chokes on a sob when her glimmering eyes take in her childhood home sitting tall and proud on its oceanside perch. "You didn't, did you?"

Her low tone confirms that I don't need to answer her, but I still dip my chin. "You've created a life with me, but my home is anywhere you are, have been, or will be. Although you now reside in Vegas, it hasn't always been that way. This was your home, your safe haven. No man should have taken that away from you. Not even me."

Tears glide down her cheeks as she presses her lips to mine, their quiver uncontained. "I love your mind, body, and spirit, but even more than that, I love your heart." I'm about to tell her I don't have a heart, but the lowering of her hand to her stomach stops me. "What Asher said is true. Family isn't blood, Nikolai. It is pride, honor, and mutual respect. Mercifully, our baby will have both your blood and your dignity."

Years of torment, hurt, and pain are erased in an instant.

I am, for once, complete.

When the tap of a tiny hand rattles the window next to my head, Justine jumps out of her skin. The smile she gave Brax earlier can't compete with the one she flashes when she discovers who is interrupting us. Her mom is standing at our door, her eyes as wide and in disbelief as Justine's. The wisps of red curls around her mother's ears don't have a chance in hell of hiding the tears staining her milky-white cheeks, but she doesn't care. She carries her happiness with pride, unashamed to admit she too is overcome with emotion.

"Is it true?" Justine's mother, Karan, jangles a set of keys. "Is this really our house again?" She giggles nervously, as if she's afraid she might wake up.

Although her questions are directed at me, Justine briskly nods. Aware I'm uncomfortable with the heavy PDA common in her family, she's quick to accept her mother's screams of jubilation on my behalf as well. They jump and squeal in the driveway for several long minutes before they're joined by the male members of their family.

While they tour the home they know like the back of their hands, Roman and I shadow them. Our faces reflect the jubilation theirs hold, just in a more reserved, uncomfortable way.

"Any news from Trey?" My tone is mellow considering the topic.

Roman twists his torso to the right to ensure business matters don't steal Justine's devotion from her family. I understand his quest. I love seeing her like this—happy and without worry.

"He's as unsure who the Russians could be as you are. He put out some feelers, but nothing concrete has been unearthed."

I nod, grateful for Trey's diligence but pissed I'm being forced to act on rumors.

"What about Gavril? Did anything come from his outing last night?" My tone dips on the "outing" part of my comment. Gavril doesn't do teacups and cucumber sandwiches. If he is in town, the entire town is aware of it.

Roman's shoulder notches up. "Same. You know how much Russian men love to drink. He went to every bar in Hopeton. Not a single accent was heard."

I'm about to respond with anger, but Justine entering the walk-in pantry on the heel of her mother to check if the height chart scribbled on an internal wall is still there steals my attention as swiftly as it does my anger.

Her childhood growth chart better be there. I paid top dollar to have their home returned to how it was the day it was sold. No detail was to be missed, not even the pink bedspread Justine's bed donned in the family albums I combed through last week to make sure every detail was right.

Smirking at Maddox's eye roll from being asked to stand next to the wall he was last measured on at the age of thirteen, I shift my focus back to Roman. He has a corny smile on his face. I'm about to rib him until I catch my reflection in the mirror we're standing next to.

I'm wearing the same stupid-ass look.

After grumbling about how Dimitri may be right, I get back to the task at hand. "There has to be something we're missing."

Roman murmurs in agreement. He's not a man of many words —unless he's telling me I fucked up—but his moan reveals he is as cautious about Dimitri's warning as I am.

"Maddox's release was too simple. There should have been more to it. Not necessarily from the Petrettis, but from anyone wanting to make an example of what happens when you don't follow the rules."

I'm not craving a bloodbath. I just know silence never ends well. With the exception of Ryan and Brax's unwanted presence, Maddox's release occurred without a single hiccup. If that doesn't have my men on edge, nothing will.

My eyes lock with Roman's murky green eyes when he says, "Perhaps Dimitri lied."

A snarl forms on my top lip. It's not an angry snarl. I'm more unsure than anything. "For what reason? If he'd kept out of it, we would have arrived and left Hopeton without incident. Now—"

"Exactly," Roman interrupts. "Now he has you worried. You've run your crew with honor the past twelve months, Nikolai."

His praise puffs my chest, but I know there's more coming.

"But you've always been a hothead."

There it is.

I growl, warning him to watch his next set of words. He may be like family to me, but that doesn't mean I'll tread lightly if he disrespects me.

"You can't stand, even for a second, the thought of Justine being hurt."

The honesty of his words ignites something inside me I haven't felt in years. The thought of her being hurt in any way kills me. She's crying now, but only happy tears. If they weren't, there'd be hell to pay.

"Think about it. He said you'll never be family mere seconds before he told Justine he wishes you no harm. His emotions are as contradicting as yours the past few months."

I backhand his chest, my caution coming with violence this time around. "You shouldn't be preaching flawlessness, Roman. A snake has never killed a dragon, but that doesn't mean the dragon shouldn't be wary of the snake's bite." Wanting to test a theory, I say my last comment in Russian.

My assumption about him being bilingual is proven accurate when he replies, "*То, что собака старая, не означает, что ее не научат новым трюкам.*" His rickety comment on old dogs being taught new tricks reveals his venture into bilingualism didn't come easy, but he gets an A for effort.

"Why learn Russian now? It never interested you earlier." Deceit rings in my tone, but it's more aloof than I expected.

His lips furl as he jerks his chin to Justine climbing the sprawling stairwell in her family mansion. "She thought it would lessen my 'disadvantage' with the men."

His grimace when snarling "disadvantage" forces a smile to my lips. Roman could never be accused of being modest, so being told he lacks anything would have been a huge knock to his ego.

"Did it work?"

With a huff, he shakes his head. "I just discovered they're a bunch of dirty fucks who spend more time combing porn sites than they do showering." He steps away from me to sweep Justine's bedroom before allowing her to enter. Once it's clear, he returns to my side. "I've also advised Lorde she's no longer allowed to use the hot tub at Clarks."

His grin drops an inch as anger makes itself visible on his face. He's spotted the pompous glint in my eyes that reveals his daughter's multiple visits to Clarks were never for the facilities.

His teeth grind together when he spits out, "I swear to god, if I discover you or any of your men have touched my daughter, I'll skin you all alive."

I hold my hands in the air, acting innocent.

It's not an easy look for me to pull off.

11

JUSTINE

"**I**s everything okay with Roman? He's been a little quiet tonight."

I slip into the vacant seat beside Nikolai, my head resting on his shoulder. I'm exhausted, both physically and emotionally. Today has been a wonderful day. Nikolai found out he's becoming a father early next year, Maddox was released from incarceration, and we celebrated at a property that will forever hold a special place in my heart.

What Nikolai said is true; my home is anywhere he is, but this is where I was raised. I lost my first tooth here, screamed my first words in anger at my brothers on the very porch Nikolai and I are sitting on.

I even lost my virginity here—although I'd rather Nikolai not become aware of that.

Brax barely left with his life intact earlier today. I don't see him escaping conviction if Nikolai discovers how close we truly were.

He has no reason to be jealous, though. Brax is a great guy. He made me smile when I wanted to cry, and treated me like a princess, but there was never anything more than a physical attraction between us. That's why our flame died within weeks of being ignited. We went our separate ways a few weeks after I left for college. Our friendship was more important than constantly searching for a spark.

Like this house, Brax has a special place in my heart, but it will never be close to how much space Nikolai has taken. He didn't just complete me. He makes me a better woman than I was before I was mauled by a dog.

Even Brax couldn't help but comment on my change today. I'm stronger and more determined than ever, and that's all compliments of Nikolai.

My head pops off Nikolai's shoulder when he responds, "He's dealing with some family issues."

I arch a brow. If Nikolai wasn't smirking like a cat eyeing a bowl of milk, I'd push the matter with more urgency, but his reply was more playful than worried.

"Lorde?" I predict while recalling how much Nikolai loves using her to rile up Roman.

Nikolai's smile triples as he nods. "We better not have a daughter, *Ангел*, because if anyone taunts me about her as I do Roman, I'll be up on a murder charge before she turns one."

"Again," I add before I can harness my vicious tongue.

Thankfully, he isn't the least bit worried about my snappy attitude. "You can't accuse a man of murder when there's no body."

I know for a fact his comment is riddled with errors, but it doesn't stop my elbow from getting cozy with his ribs. "You won't need to worry about that if we keep the rules simple. No official dates until she's thirteen. No serious boyfriends until she's sixteen, and she has to keep her wildness on the down-low until she leaves for college."

Nikolai looks seconds away from coronary failure. "So lock her in a tower on her twelfth birthday? Got it." He says his comment in jest, but the fire in his eyes shows he isn't being entirely facetious.

Our alone time is interrupted by Sebastian breaking through the screen door. He's barely sprinted to the manicured grass edging the front porch when he's dragged to the ground by Maddox launching himself onto his back. They throw fists at one another, their hits mimicking the noises Nikolai's men make when they get a little hot under the collar.

"Should I break them apart?" Nikolai sits straighter in his chair when Sebastian and Maddox's grunts ramp up.

"Nah. The harder they fight, the quicker they'll fall."

The need in my voice says more than my words ever could. Today has been an extremely long day, even more so since I've spent every hour glancing at the clock, counting down the minutes left before I can thank Nikolai for his generosity in a way not suitable for spectators.

I'm still in a dream-like state, shocked by his big heart. I've always known he was a generous, kind man, but today's gift blew my mind, and it made me fall in love with him even harder.

When Landon attempts to pull Sebastian and Maddox apart, he ends up in the middle of their brawl. His groan of annoyance when he hits the ground with a thud alerts the remaining Walsh clan to a ritual that used to be performed here at least once a month.

It also gains the devotion of Nikolai's crew. Money is thrown at my feet as they take bets on who will win. With Maddox fresh out of prison, a majority of their wages are placed on him.

I still as a commotion stirs in my gut. I never thought I'd utter the words I just did. Maddox's conviction was overturned, but a pardon can't reverse the years he spent in prison—away from his family.

Although Maddox has been brutally honest about things that occurred while he was locked up, some questions about events before his arrest remain unanswered. The main two: why was he arrested for Megan's murder to begin with? And why was he at the Petretti compound the night I was sentenced to run the gauntlet?

I could ask Nikolai to force the truth from Maddox, but I've yet to succumb to the pressure. It was a close call when I walked in on him and Maddox having a private conversation before we sat for dinner, but Nikolai's silent request for understanding held back my demand.

Furthermore, Maddox has only recently returned home after years of absence. Tonight is not the time to grill him for information. Tomorrow... that's a different kettle of fish.

My focus returns to the present when cheered roars boom through my ears. Being late to the game, Landon has come out of tonight's exchange victorious... although the shiner on his cheek displays it was a close call.

"Some things never change," I say with a smile.

Nikolai grins. "Are you saying I should have Popov housemaids hide the liquor before their visit next month?"

My eyes snap to his. This isn't the first time he's mentioned a Walsh trip to Vegas, but it's the first time he's said it so matter-of-factly.

After tucking a wayward red curl behind my ear, he twists his torso until he's facing me head-on. "We should start plans soon. You're already showing."

Because his eyes drop to my stomach so quickly, he misses mine widening in shock.

What the hell is he talking about?

After a longing glance at my belly, he returns his devotion to my face. The confusion heating my cheeks jumps to his when he spots my stitched brows and quirked lips. He's truly stumped about why I look so dumbfounded.

With a smirk, he informs me, "Our wedding, *Ангел*. If you don't want your stomach seen in your dress, we should plan to wed before the end of summer. I don't mind either way, but I figured the sooner the better."

I choke on my spit. "Our wedding?"

He nods, his smirk picking up from my high tone.

The arrogance on his face subsides when I ask, "What wedding? You have to ask someone to marry you before you can wed them."

My thighs quake when he growls, "No, I don't. You are carrying my child in your womb and my heart in your chest. Your fate has already been decided."

His entitled sneer has my pulse quickening, but it doesn't stop me from saying, "Like hell it has."

My kidnap may have had us jumping the gun with the move-in part of our relationship, but just like our baby, retirement funds, marriage, and additional children will be discussed at great length before any of them occur. I am Nikolai's as much as he is mine, but I'm not being told I'm marrying someone. I want to be asked.

My anger loses some of its steam when Nikolai growls, "I was born a bastard, Justine. I will not have my child born the same way."

"Then you should have thought about that before voicing your wish to have an heir." My voice isn't as volatile as his, but it reveals

I'm not a pushover either. "If you want to marry me, you'll have to ask the old-fashioned way."

When he attempts to interrupt me, I squash my finger to his lips. I bet he wishes I wasn't so strong and independent now. "Bended knee, permission from my father, and doves flying in the sky. Hell, I'll even take a flash mob if that's all you can think up, but I want..." I stop, realizing my error. "I *deserve* more than a demand to become your wife."

My last comment steals Nikolai's words right from his lungs. For the first time, he's speechless. It's probably for the best, because the last thing I want to hear is his thoughts when I grumble, "And even after all that, I may not say yes."

I'm such a liar. If hormones, a lack of sleep, and a shit ton of emotions weren't fueling my responses, I would have suggested we wed the instant we touch down in Vegas at the little white chapel Blaire and Rico were married in four years ago, but if today has taught me anything, it is that we should never take life for granted.

Maddox's freedom was snatched away in an instant. Friends he'd had since childhood forgot about him the moment his police record included the word "murder." His much sought-after scholarship was given to another. Even the girl he thought he loved vanished from the picture.

My family has sacrificed so many moments of happiness in the past five years that I'm not willing to ransom any more. Our child will be a blessing, and so will the marriage of his parents, but not until I am asked the right way.

12

NIKOLAI

I stop watching Justine's brisk exit from the makeshift office I set up in her parents' home when Roman says, "She's right, Nikolai. There hasn't been a single incident in four days. Perhaps Dimitri's intel was off."

Usually I'd agree with him—men in this industry could never be accused of being slow off the mark—but with my gut advising me to remain cautious, I must.

Just because no incidents have been recorded doesn't mean there won't be.

"Dinner with my brother is not imperative enough to put Justine's safety at risk."

"Yes, it is," Roman disagrees. "It will show her she's not a pawn in your game. She's your queen, Nikolai, so start treating her like it."

"She is my queen!" My fist thumps my chest as wildly as my heart whacks my ribcage. "I'd give my life for her, so how can I be accused of treating her as anything less than my other half?"

Although I'm asking a question, I pray for Roman not to answer me. My mood is fragile, so any reply he gives will only make matters worse.

Justine and I have interacted the past four days, but the intensity hasn't been close to the level as when we were in Vegas. She's my drug of choice, so being denied her attention for even a minute is the equivalent of a death sentence to me. I'm struggling, my temper as volatile as the unsolid ground I'm walking on.

Justine is distant because she's hormonal and pissed I refuse to ask another man's permission for her hand in marriage. I am not standing my ground because I'm stubborn. It's because I'd rather die than admit she belongs to anyone but me.

I understand she wants to be asked to become my wife instead of being told, but why can't that occur without begging another man for permission?

I am the king. I answer to no one—*except her.*

My molars grind to stubs when Roman mutters, "You're treating her as if she'll break at any moment."

"And how do you suggest I change that, Roman? Should I sit back and watch her get hurt just so I can say, 'I told you so.'" I stand and head to the door without waiting for him to reply. "How about you do the job I pay you to do instead of counseling my relationship?"

His reply is barely a grumble, but I still hear it. "You won't have a relationship if you don't pull your head out of your ass."

If I were worried about my status in Justine's life, I would retaliate to his sneer with violence. Fortunately for him, I have no doubt about my influence in her life. Justine is carrying my child, and her finger will soon bear my ring. Away from people who don't understand how we operate, our relationship is solid.

Maddox knows the rules. It's why he hasn't snitched a syllable to anyone since his release but me. Landon and Sebastian, though... they're thorns in my ass. Their numerous comments about my job being a choice is frustrating the fuck out of me.

My position can't be filled by any man. I was born for my role and killed to get where I am. I even butchered the man who raised me for it, so to have its importance brushed off as if it's worthless doesn't just annoy me, it pisses me the fuck off.

If they were any other men, their foolhardy remarks would have been snuffed out by the loss of their vicious tongues. Mercifully for them, just like Roman, I consider them family.

Family is not flesh and blood. It's people who honor and respect you.

Justine's family gained my respect for the admiration they have for their sister, but they'll lose it just as quickly if they continue their attempts to drive a wedge between us.

If I had it my way, Justine and I would have returned to Vegas four days ago. Alas, my woman is as stubborn as she is beautiful. She's confident I misunderstood her brothers' sneers, that they respect me and my line of work.

I think she is full of shit.

Her brothers don't want me marrying her any more than they want me fucking her. Why do you think I'm so hesitant to seek her father's permission for us to wed? He'll never give it to me if his thoughts match his sons'. And since he's sheltered under the same umbrella as Justine, he can't be punished for disobeying my direct order.

It's a lose-lose situation.

If I retaliate, I'm asking Justine to give up the people who guarded and loved her before me. If I let their comments slide, I'm seen as weak by my men and others in our industry.

I don't want either of those things to occur, but I'm at a loss on how to stop it.

Cursing the humid afternoon air, I dig my cigarette pack from the pocket of my jeans. The unlit cancer stick sits between my lips until I break through the back door of the patio. I'm dying for a hit of nicotine, but since Justine's mom asked for my men and me to smoke outside, I have to wait. My men rarely follow the rules, but since Karan's request was more a suggestion than a demand, they've happily obliged.

I freeze with a lit match an inch from my cigarette when a heavy set of double standards smack into me. Something as simple as not wanting cigarette smoke absorbed into replaceable fabrics can be upheld without asking, but I expect Justine to become my wife without so much as a discussion.

I'm a fucking asshole.

I told Justine she'd want for nothing when she took her throne, yet I'm holding her greatest wish hostage because I can't wrap my head around the idea of other people having an influence in her life.

I'll never kneel at the feet of my enemy, but I can bow for my queen.

I'm drawn from dangerous thoughts when shouted words

capture my attention. One voice I immediately recognize, although I prefer hearing it rise in ecstasy than in the anger it's holding now. Justine's fury is undeniable in her low tone.

After stubbing out my cigarette with my boot, I round the corner where the voices are coming from. Justine's voice grows with every step I take, which in turn quickens my pace. I'd sprint if I didn't recognize the uneasy tone of the man she is tussling with. It can only be one of three people: Landon, Sebastian, or Maddox.

My questions are answered when Justine sneers, "I swear to god, Sebastian, if you say one more bad word about him, you'll not only have Nikolai purged from your life..."—the way her tone dips during the last half of her comment reveals she's repeating something Sebastian said earlier—"you'll also lose me. Is that what you want, Saint?"

Her use of Sebastian's nickname reveals her anger will be quickly set aside if he gets with the program. It also proves without a doubt that she loves her brothers, but her love for me is even greater than that.

That alone should have me stepping away from their exchange, not toward it, but I never back down when challenged. Justine is more than capable of handling herself when it comes to her brothers, but I'll never be too cautious when it comes to her.

Justine's flaming-with-anger face enters my peripheral vision at the exact moment Sebastian grips her arm. His firm hold sends my anger to a point it hasn't reached since I was sixteen.

"You can't be serious, can you? He's the same as the monsters who did *that* to you."

I picture my knife skating across his jugular when his eyes drop to Justine's scars. He glares at them as if they are imperfections, as if she is maimed with hate instead of the badges of courage I see every time I look at her.

My hand stops seeking my knife when Justine retaliates, "Nikolai is *nothing* like them." As the woman I forever see in her eyes awakens, a rod hardens her back. "And my scars are a part of who I am. I'm sorry if they make you uncomfortable, but I'll *never* be ashamed of them."

Remorse floods Sebastian's eyes so fast that not an ounce of hostility can be seen, but it does nothing to harness Justine's campaign. The fire inside her resurrects my queen from the shallow hole she's been hiding in the past four days.

"Just like I'll never side with a team that doesn't have Nikolai at the helm. I love him, Sebastian. More than you could ever comprehend."

When she chokes on her words, my first thoughts are to go to her. I nearly do, but Sebastian's quick snag-and-yank routine keeps my feet planted on the ground. His whispered apologies save him from being tortured as painfully as Justine's pledge scarred my heart.

I'd never ask her to pick me over her family, but her reply proves I never had any reason to fear her decision. For years, anything I loved Vladimir took, but even he can't take this away from me. Love doesn't die when you do. It's only at risk of being extinguished when the fear of being unloved suffocates it.

I won't let that happen to Justine and me.

Whether innate or taught through years of misguidance, hate weaves through your veins so hard and fast that you barely recognize yourself in a matter of months. Over the past year, Justine has proven love has the same toxic effect.

She has softened me, as Dimitri said, but not in a bad, villainous way. She has me seeing both sides of the coin, the good and the bad. I want to be a better man for her, which in turn will make me a better leader to my crew.

I'll never stop being the man I was born to be. Justine understands it's a part of who I am. She accepts all of me—annoyingly frustrating parts and all—just as I do her.

Certain I'm making the right decision, I return to my station at the end of the porch. I trust that Justine has a firm hold on the ropes. My queen never does anything with half a heart. Even when she is up against a fiercer foe than any man she's ever met, she doesn't back down without a fight.

The way she removed my knife from Vladimir's chest proves this without a doubt.

13

NIKOLAI

I'm barely through my second cigarette when a scent I'll never forget overtakes the smell of burning tobacco. I watch Justine's brisk pace from the corner of my eye. She's spotted my watch through lowered lashes.

Her throat works hard to swallow, fearful I overheard her conversation with her brother but incapable of hiding her excitement at seeing me again. Even annoyed, she can't deny her attraction to me. I am her addiction as much as she is mine.

After dragging her eyes down my body, she purses her lips as she fights desires greater than us both. They want to be kissed—to be bitten. She just can't work out how to fill the gap between us without feeling as if she's giving in. She doesn't want to win, but she doesn't want to lose either.

A tiny vein in her neck flutters when I bridge the gap between us. She seems shocked I'm making the first move, as if I wouldn't shift mountains to reach her.

I hate that.

I promised her the world and intend to keep my promise—*for once.*

"No distance will ever be too great for me to travel to you, *Ангел.* Water divides land, but nothing can separate souls destined to be together."

Justine's eyes grow wide as she sucks in much-needed air for her overworked lungs. She looks seconds from crying, but instead, she pushes off her feet, reaching me in less than three heartbeats.

With the determination of a tigress, she snatches the half-smoked cigarette from my lips. Orange embers float in the humid night air when she flicks it off the porch before attaching her mouth to mine. My lips part when she drags her silky-smooth tongue along the seam of my mouth.

Her eagerness leads to us crashing into the railing my men spend hours guarding like castle walls. She takes all the control, demonstrating that she'd move more than mountains to keep us together.

As her tongue duels with mine, her hand slips under my shirt to trace the fine hairs above the bulge in my jeans. I had wondered if hormones were at play when she demanded we leave the confines of her family home to accept Rico's invitation for dinner. Now I'm wondering if her eagerness was an excuse for some alone time. She's practically stroking me through my jeans, awakening a beast no amount of armor could contain.

If she isn't careful, I'll bend her over the railing and take her in front of my men. A dragon can be calmed with a sword to his chest, but a snake can never be subdued. No matter how long you feed, love, and take care of a snake, you should always anticipate its bite.

The most poisonous people in my life learned that the hard way. They were weeded out by my venom. Only one person has survived the wrath of my bite: my slice of heaven in a hot and temperamental place.

After kissing me until nothing but having her beneath me is on my mind, Justine withdraws from our embrace. Her lips are swollen from our kiss, and the scent of her needy cunt is lingering in the air, but it's the ownership in her eyes I'm paying the most attention to. They're holding the same possessiveness they held when she told her brother she'll never be on any team I'm not the captain of.

They also expose without a doubt that she'll fight for me as fiercely as I will her. That I am hers as much as she is mine. That the only thing between us right now are the values of a misguided man and the damaged boy he left behind to pick up the pieces.

Vladimir may have raised me, but Justine raises me up. Those are two uniquely different things that deserve equally distinct responses.

The free-flowing white dress Justine is wearing swishes around her knees when I grasp her hand in mine before hightailing it inside. She giggles like a schoolgirl when we race through each room on the lower level of her house. We only stop weaving through the numerous highly decorated rooms when we reach the man I'm hunting as aggressively as I did the men who bid on Justine.

I'm not seeking a member of my crew or Roman. I'm after the man who will be incapable of denying me my greatest wish when he sees the devotion in his daughter's eyes. It's her father. The only man I plan to triumph over without my blade.

I lower myself onto my knees in front of Justine's parents before raising my eyes to my ultimate gift. When Justine mumbles something about it only needing to be one knee, my brow arches in silent question.

She slices her hand in the air, her eyes shining with unshed tears. "It's nothing. It is fine. Please continue."

I swish my tongue around my mouth to loosen up my words before saying, "Devils are angels who fell through the cracks, misunderstood rejects who won't find their place until they're guided toward the light by someone much stronger and more powerful than them. You are my light, *Ангел*, my beacon to good. You understand me like no one ever has, as you too are an angel who fell through the cracks."

She nods, wholeheartedly agreeing with me.

"Your wings never broke as mine did, though. They wrapped around you like a cocoon, protecting and sheltering you from those who wished you harm. You never wanted to escape, to trust again, but your wish to stop others from being hurt led to your metamorphosis happening before my very eyes."

Pride swells in my chest when a timeline of our relationship rolls through my head. She was so shy and timid at the start, an angel trapped by the devil determined to devour her, yet she fought the undeniable pull and my unbendable demand. She was determined to show me a life I never knew existed.

She made me whole.

"You emerged from your cocoon to protect a man unworthy of you long before you considered leaving to save yourself. Now he must do the same."

I notice several members of my crew, Roman, and Justine's brothers surrounding us when my eyes drift to her father standing gobsmacked at the entrance of the kitchen. I expect their faces to be riddled with disgust or, at the very least, amusement. That's not what I am seeing. They appear as joyous, shocked, and happy as me.

"Please."

I have a trillion more words in my head, statements on how I'll never let his daughter come to harm and that I'll protect and love her and his grandchild for the rest of my life, but additional pledges are not needed. The quick dip of Nathaniel's chin assures me he heard the words I failed to verbalize.

Seeking a guarantee that I didn't misread his silent approval, I return my eyes to Justine. Her smile at my stunned expression squeezes the first lot of tears from her eyes. I almost stand to wipe them away but am reminded of the reason for my rare public display of affection when Roman removes a black box from his suit jacket to hand it to me.

I've had this ring for weeks. I had planned to ask Justine to marry me during our celebration dinner earlier this week, but I was the one left grappling for a sense of normality when family and friends emerged from the woodwork shouting "happy birthday." Roman has been the guardian of her ring since that day.

"I don't have any doves. It's probably for the best. I don't think your mother would appreciate them crapping on the carpet." Justine's giggle is barely heard over the uproarious laughter bellowing around us. "But I do have a ring and a promise..."—I wave my hand around her family home, which is dramatically different from the one we arrived at four days ago—"to give you everything and anything your heart desires. You just need to say yes, *Ангел*. Say yes, and I'll give you the world. You'll want for nothing when you are my wife." I lower my eyes to her tiny belly. "Neither of you."

Justine's hand envelops mine when I cradle the tiny bump in

her stomach. She doesn't care about the ring or the size of the diamond in the middle of it. All she cares about is me and the promises she knows I'll never break.

And perhaps granting me my greatest wish with the simplest dip of her chin.

14

NIKOLAI

"He asked like that? In front of everyone?"

When Justine nods at Blaire's question, Blaire's shining eyes rocket to Rico. She glares at him with her blonde brow raised, her large smile weakening her angry sneer.

"What?" Rico chokes on his whiskey, as incapable of harnessing his body's response to his wife's smile tonight as he was years ago. "You barely remember the night we got married, Kitten, much less the words we spoke before it happened. For all you know, I could have delivered a speech much more heartfelt than his."

His Russian accent is more pronounced as his urge to hunt grows rampant. Like me, Rico is a natural-born killer. Unlike me, the only person he hunts these days is his wife.

I give Rico a cocky wink when his narrowed eyes swing my way. It rubs salt into wounds I wish he didn't have, but he'll get the fuck over it. I thought I'd see my deathbed before being awarded a noble look from his little kitty, so I will milk it for all it's worth.

Justine's eyes flare when Blaire locks her lips with Rico's. With her body overrun with hormones, she adores the sickening lovey-dovey stint Rico and Blaire have been working the past four hours. I swear she's had love hearts in her eyes half the night.

If I chopped off my cock, I could understand her eagerness.

Her past year has been surrounded by men who treat women how I used to: as disposable whores. Although I'll never be ashamed of my men's barbaric ways—they work hard, so they deserve to unwind any way they see fit—I'm glad Justine is seeing another side of the coin.

She's fought a good battle, but I know she's struggled with jealousy for the past twelve months. It hasn't been all bad, though. I assumed the day I was crippled by a pussy would be the day my reign would topple. I was so far off the mark that I'm beginning to wonder if it was just my heart Justine stole when she waltzed into my life with the core of a fighter hidden by the face of an angel.

She and her insatiably greedy cunt have kept me so entertained, not a feather has ruffled when my men rib me on fucking the same pussy for the remainder of my life.

If given a choice, I'd sign up to be Justine's cunt's slave for eternity.

My nostrils stop flaring from the thrill of the chase when Blaire snickers, "I remember the good points from our wedding night."

Through a shit-eating grin, Rico swallows a mouthful of his drink before placing an empty coffee mug on the table. "Uh-huh. Like your ability to make balloon animals with condoms?"

Blaire's hand slaps her eyes as embarrassment reddens her cheeks. Unfortunately for her, she doesn't need to see our smiles to know of their arrival. She can hear them in the laughter bouncing around the room.

The heat on her face turns blistering when I snicker, "Oh, Kitty, I knew there were devilish thoughts hidden in you somewhere. With a little more practice, maybe you can change those kiddie tricks into more entertaining ones."

A dishcloth smacks me upside the head at the same time Rico whacks my chest. His hit is soft enough to advise that it was a cautionary hit but strong enough to steal some air from my lungs.

"What?" I give him another wink, switching the leftover mirth on his face to full-blown anger. "Better to be the wolf than the sheep who hides from him."

Rico looks seconds from starting what we didn't finish years ago, but his retaliation is halted by Justine propping herself between us. "Tonight was a lot of fun. We should do this more often."

After issuing me a warning glance to behave, she stands to her feet to help Blaire clear away dessert plates smeared with cheese-cake crumbs.

Her suggestion sounds good, but I don't see it as viable. For one, Rico and Blaire live in Ravenshoe—thousands of miles from Vegas. And two, I'm not a dinner party type of guy.

Although I enjoyed myself tonight, I'm only here because Justine's agreement to become my wife put me in a good mood.

That and the fact we fly home tomorrow.

My curve in protocol hasn't come cheaply, though. I have three men in the hall, four monitoring the street, and Roman faking a placement with the security firm that monitors the surveillance devices planted around Rico's apartment building.

Speaking of Roman, I haven't heard from him since he swept Rico's apartment hours ago. Although ordinary men see silence as gold, it's unlike Roman to maintain radio silence. He knows how pedantic I am about Justine's safety, so he keeps me thoroughly updated. He has always run with the same motto. It's better to know than assume, just as it's better to ask than imply.

With that in mind, I dig my phone out of my pocket.

It's barely halfway out when Rico growls, "Thanks for that, Eli. Kitten won't let me live down my half-assed proposal for weeks, if not months."

I try not to smirk at his annoyed tone, but the high curve of my lips reveals a true smile.

"It's about time I did something better than you. I've only been waiting thirty years."

He struggles to accept my praise as much as I strive to disregard it. Compliments are not given in our industry... and neither are dinner parties.

"Do you do this often? Floral teacups and homemade cheesecake?"

The waggle of my brows lessens the sting of my scorn. I never thought I'd be envious of any man living a humble, meek existence. Rico is proving me wrong. I don't want to emulate his life, but I'm glad he's found peace in the tumultuous world we were born into.

My smile stretches from ear to ear when Rico mumbles, "If it makes my kitten purr, sign me up."

He takes a hefty gulp from his recently replenished drink, the tingling of my lips the only indication he swapped the brown liquid in our cups for something more tempting than brewed leaves while Blaire wasn't looking.

When he sets down his once again empty cup, I notice a baby monitor on the side table next to his chair. I nearly rib him about cutting the apron strings—Eli is four, making the need for a baby monitor pointless—but I hold back my jeering.

I know as well as anyone how hard it is for old habits to die. I struggle every day remembering Vladimir is gone, and up until last week, I only had Justine to protect.

Rico has so much more to lose.

Years ago, he made a decision no boy his age should have been forced to make. He paid for his bend of the rules in the cruelest way, so I have no doubt he'll stop at nothing to ensure his son isn't prosecuted under the same laws.

As I will for my child.

I stop peering at the swinging kitchen door, craving a quick glance at Justine to weaken the knot in my gut, when Rico murmurs, "I'm proud of you, Eli. I'd prefer you step away from the industry altogether, but I understand that isn't something you're likely to do."

I halfheartedly shrug. "You got the kitten. I got the tiger."

I'm not looking to start a fight. I'm just reminding Rico why it's easy for me to stay. I have a woman strong enough to stand at my side. If I didn't, who knows where I'd be right now.

"Your girl has been good for you." Rico's comment proves he understood the gist of my remark, but that doesn't mean he'll tread lightly with me. "She must see something in you no one else can."

I laugh, taking his comment as he intended: playfully. "Every good person has a bit of bad in them. I'm just a bad guy who has a little bit of good." My tongue peeks out between my teeth as I struggle to hold in my shit-eating grin. "Thankfully, Justine has the ratios mixed up."

Any reply Rico is planning to give is snuffed by a hushed whisper. The low, thigh-quaking tone isn't responsible for his frozen stance.

It's the words the man is singing in Russian. "Send the angel to the devil's bed, hold her, cherish her, then cut off her head. She danced with Satan and now she is dead, all for lying in the devil's bed."

The dessert we consumed an hour ago rushes to the base of my throat when panic makes itself known. Only one man sang that song to us during our childhood. He was killed by my knife twelve months ago today. It was our father, the man who sent us to hell long before he groomed us to be as evil as him.

With his heart beeping in his neck, Rico charges for the room his son is sleeping in. I bolt toward the kitchen just as fast. The nursery rhyme came over the baby monitor, meaning the threat is in the opposite direction of Justine, but I can't help but move for her first.

Eli is my family, but Justine is my everything.

"Get Eli to safety while I grab the girls."

Rico's nod barely registers before he's lost in the darkness of a long hallway. I was impressed by the size of his home when I first arrived. Now I fucking hate it. I should have never allowed so many steps between Justine and me. My gut has been twisted up in knots all week, and right when I should be more vigilant, I let my guard down.

I am a fucking idiot.

My feet stop stomping the floorboards when Justine exits the kitchen on the heels of Blaire. She stares at me in shock, stunned by the lack of color in my cheeks. "Nikolai—"

A loud ricochet rolls through Rico's apartment, shredding my eardrums of anything but Justine's panicked squeal.

"Get down!" I demand while diving for Justine.

I only just reach her when a big blast lights up the servants' entrance to Rico's kitchen. The explosion of the grenade-like weapon is so intense that it propels Justine forward at a faster rate than I can shut down. She lands in the dining room with a thud, the sound of her torso hitting the tile floor haunting me more than real-life nightmares.

Pop. Pop. Pop.

Gunfire rattles around me as men swarm through the demolished reinforced door. With the accuracy of a madman, I take down a frontrunner with my knife.

As the life in his eyes vacates, I clamber across the floor littered with metal shards to reach Justine, who's lying still and face down.

Like something out of a police rescue show, I drag her behind the dining table before upending it as if it's weightless. The thick wooden material hides her from the men swarming Rico's apartment while also allowing me to assess her for injuries. Her shirt has holes the size of dimes in it from wood and metal shards pelting across the room during the blast, but her wounds appear superficial. *Thank fuck.*

Grabbing her cheeks with my hands, I lower my forehead to rest on hers. The assurance in my eyes that I'll never let anything happen to her helps quell the violent shakes hindering her tiny frame. She presses her trembling lips to mine, acknowledging my oath with as many words as I used to deliver it. Her strength inspires me. It also ensures nothing is below me when protecting her.

After mouthing to Justine to keep her head down, I remove the gun strapped to my ankle. I don't usually carry a weapon, but Dimitri's warning earlier this week convinced me to step outside the box.

Once again, thank fuck.

A monster awakens inside of me when Justine asks, "Where's Blaire?"

Keeping my surveillance on the down-low, I do a quick head-count. At least a dozen men are racing up the servants' stairwell in Rico's kitchen, and another half a dozen are lying in wait in his kitchen.

Three men lie lifeless within touching distance of a motionless Blaire curled in a ball halfway into the living room, proving I'm not the only one packing heat.

Even with a white picket fence and a humble family life, Rico has kept his gun safe well stocked.

When I catch the quickest glimpse of his murderous eyes as he rains gunfire on the men threatening his very existence, I know what I must do. I break into a sprint without a second thought, knowing without a doubt he'll protect my Ангел as fiercely as I'm endeavoring to save his kitten.

While Rico covers me with the heavy discharge of a fully automatic 9mm Glock, I drag Blaire behind the table Justine's back is propped against, praying the heaviness of her body is because she and Rico have been trying for baby number two the past six months, and not the result of a bullet.

When Blaire remains motionless, I slap her cheeks. "Come on, Kitty. It's time to play."

The sting of my palm reddens her lifeless cheeks, but it barely rouses her. Not willing to give up without a fight, I begin CPR. My compressions are hard but necessary. I don't like rough handling my brother's wife, but if it gets her out of here alive, I'll use any tactic necessary.

Within seconds, a gurgling noise sounds from Blaire's throat. Unsure if it's the right response—I've only ever taken lives, not revived them—I balance on the balls of my feet. The gagging sounds continue as the color spreading across Blaire's cheeks reveals her silent fight.

"She's choking."

With a gusto I didn't know she had, Justine tilts Blaire's head back, props open her mouth, then shoves two fingers down her throat. I stare at the chunk of chicken Justine extracts, praying it isn't one of many, when the noise of a woman fighting to stay alive breaks me from my trance.

With the gasp of a woman seconds from asphyxiation, Blaire's back arches off the tiled floor. Her wide-with-panic eyes stare up at me for several long seconds, as if confused as to why my eye coloring doesn't match her husband's.

Although I'd love to relish her shock for a few seconds longer, now is not the time. She may be breathing, but we are far from safe.

"Watch her?"

Justine agrees to my request without worry, strengthening my belief she was born for this role. She's shaking like a leaf, but that could be her body's only defense to cool the fire in her eyes.

My queen is rising from her throne, ready to defend it as readily as she is me.

"Three on your right." I'm yelling, but I doubt Rico can hear me. There's too much gun power being exchanged between us and the balaclava-clad men overwhelming us eight to one.

Bang. Bang.

Two men approaching Rico's right fall victim to my wrath, the gush of blood running over their eyes the only pops of color in their all-black outfits.

I'm about to take down the third when Dimitri enters the living room. His dark hair is slicked with sweat, and he has a gun in his hand. I'm about to fire at him, when he takes down a man sneaking up on Rico unawares.

His aim is so precise his bullet crinkles the man's brows. After watching him fall at Rico's feet, Dimitri swings his wide eyes my way. "They're swarming you from all angles. You need to get into the open before they kill you all."

He spins on his heels, his second life claimed with a murderous grin that shows he's not happy his turf is being overrun by Russians.

He slices the perp's chest so viciously it appears as if he's prepping him for open heart surgery. Like Rico and me, Dimitri was born for his role. He'll also die for it.

After slicing the tendons on the knee of an unnamed assailant, Dimitri devotes his attention back to me. A year ago, his job was to do anything and everything to take me down. Now he only has one task on his mind: getting us both out of here alive.

It doesn't ease the hostile waters between us, but it does award him my trust.

"Take them."

After clearing the living room of the men crossing it, I thrust Justine toward Dimitri. She's so stunned by the turn of events she doesn't realize who has ahold of her until I shout, "Go with Dimitri. He'll keep you safe."

She's frightened, but she still manages to nod.

As I'm about to launch Blaire in their direction, I spot a man charging for Justine. He has a machete in his hand and the face of a murderer.

With a roar, I line up the barrel of my gun over Dimitri's left shoulder, then fire. When the perp's eye meets his brain, the blood splattering from his mouth adds to the vibrancy of Justine's hair.

It also shreds the confidence from her eyes.

Screaming, she crouches down to cover her ears with her hands. She's not bowing in fear. She's striving to avoid the numerous bullets being fired her way.

Her drop saves her from injury. Dimitri isn't as lucky. He spins in a circle, the bullet rocketing through his shoulder responsible for his ballet move. Although he's been bitten by a bullet, he manages to take down an additional three assailants before a second bullet to the stomach silences his fight.

I watch him fall to the ground, cradling his stomach before peering over my shoulder. Bullet casings litter the floor where Rico once stood, but he is nowhere to be seen.

It's now me versus an army.

My life or my *Ангел's.*

When forced to pick one or the other, you can be certain only one decision will ever be reached. I'll kill a thousand men before I'll let anyone hurt Justine. I'll even die if it guarantees her safety.

With my heart hammering my ribs, I sprint in the direction Justine is crouched. Another three men's eyes blacken with death before an empty magazine changes my crusade from a gun battle to an all-out brawl.

The death toll from my hands is as high as my knife and gun combined, meaning another two men lie lifeless on the floor in Rico's kitchen by the time I get within an inch of Justine, but my endeavor comes too late. A man has her by the hair, his hold so tight her tippy toes struggle to scrape the ground.

The knife piercing the tender skin on her neck has me on edge, but the numerous red dots lighting up her shirt are the biggest cause of my panic. The fear in her eyes makes my anger so white hot, even with them locked on me, I still snap the neck of the man kneeling in front of me. I hate her seeing me like this, but I need the men swarming her to be on guard. Because

> ***There is only one difference between
> a madman and me.
> The madman thinks he is sane.
> I know I am mad.***
> **—Salvador Dali**

As I step over the man's lifeless body, the tick in my jaw grows as frantic as the pulse in Justine's neck. "You have to the count of five to let her go, or I'll hunt down every member of your family, gut them like dogs, then hang them throughout your hometown as a warning of what happens when you disrespect me." My voice is one I haven't heard in years. It was last used the day I realized I was only a boy living the life of a man. "Five. Four. Three—"

"You can't threaten a man who is an orphan. You should know that better than anyone, Niki."

The interrupter's mocking scorn didn't come from the man clutching Justine's hair. It came from my left, from the direction Rico was once standing.

After assuring Justine with my eyes that she has nothing to worry about, I swing them in the direction the voice came from. Although the man's face is covered with a thick balaclava, I know who he is. I thought his voice was the voice of reason when I admitted to killing his father, but tonight's exchange isn't just teaching me to always trust my gut. It's reminding me why I should never show mercy.

I spared Maxsim's life when his father orchestrated a takeover bid on my compound, believing he had nothing to do with it. He won't be so lucky this time around.

"My warning is not just for your goon. It's for every man in this room. Don't make the same mistake your father did, Maxsim. Stand down, and then I'll kill only you instead of your mother, your brothers, and your sisters. I may even spare the bitch you call your wife."

Realizing his cover has been blown, Maxsim tugs off his balaclava. He has the same deadly cat eyes his father had and the same abhorrent sneer. He's just twenty years younger and a lot more reckless.

He moves closer to me, his steps much too haughty for a man minutes from death. "Sansi was nurtured to be just like you. Born into a broken, violent marriage, he was raised by a monster to kill on command and show no mercy." He smiles a lopsided grin when his eyes absorb the clutch his beast has on Justine. "A snap of my fingers will have your queen slumped at your feet before you complete an entire blink. You like killing pretty little white women, don't you, Sansi?"

The brute fisting Justine's hair laughs mockingly, unremorsefully. It isn't the snicker of a sane man. It's similar to the sound I made when I was beaten to within an inch of my life. It proves the man standing before me isn't a man. He's merely a shell for the monster hiding inside of him.

"There are rules you cannot cross, centuries of guidelines that protect her from men like you." I suck in a grateful breath when surging fear isn't heard in my voice. I shouldn't be surprised. I don't bow for anyone who isn't my queen.

Maxsim's chest thrusts as recklessly as mine, his sneer just as violent. "Rules you broke when you slit my father's throat."

He doesn't sound heartbroken. Far from it. If anything, he seems pleased my blade ended his father's rule. Still, I shake my head, denying his claims.

"Alexei broke the rules first. He came onto my turf to kill my man and take my woman. I was well within my rights to kill him. He knew the rules. He knew the consequences of playing outside of them, so he knew his penalty would be his life. Just as you do."

Maxsim's seedy grin barely conceals the panic igniting in his eyes. I can smell his fear and taste it on my tongue. He came in heavy because he thought I'd back down without a fight. He vastly underestimated me.

"It wasn't the first mistake my father made—"

"But it can be your last."

My heart drums into my ribcage as I struggle to keep a rational head. I don't negotiate. I conquer. I maim. I kill as I was taught. Talking never entered the equation, but I'm willing to try anything if it stops fear from overtaking Justine's usually impenetrable smell. The scent I was intoxicated by last week is barely recognizable as terror engulfs her.

"Tell your men to leave. I'll let them walk out of here alive. Then we will settle this like men."

Maxsim laughs as if his life isn't hanging on by a thread. "You'll *let* them walk? Newsflash, Nikolai. You're no longer running the show." His wide eyes stray to the hall he's in the process of exiting. "He is."

I expect his goon to bring a bludgeoned Rico onto the playing field, so you can imagine my shock when the eyes match the ones I'm expecting, just several decades younger.

A man as wide as Rico has Eli pinned to his chest. A gun is pinching his temple, and the dark material of his pajamas is incapable of hiding his fear. He shouldn't be ashamed of his response. Alexei pissed his pants when I ended his life, and he was the mafia boss of over a thousand men. But if it makes him feel any better, Maxsim is about to follow his legacy. I'll make him bleed from every orifice, ensuring the viciousness of his death deters men in our industry from a takeover bid for years to come.

His father got off easy.

Maxsim won't be so lucky.

The flare of my nostrils doubles when Maxsim quotes, "In the wake of my death, I, Anatoly Popov, founder of the underworld association known as the Popov entity, request all my residuary estates, including any corpus that may fall after my death, be divided into one part with the sole beneficiary to be a direct descendent of my bloodline."

He folds up a tattered piece of paper before raising his eyes to me. "A *direct* descendent. As in someone with Popov blood." He snatches Eli from his goon's clutch. His brutal rip sends Eli's tiny cries bellowing around the dead-quiet room. "It could have been Rico, but I knew he'd never come willingly. This little guy, on the other hand, is young enough to train and will soon be old enough to kill."

The gleam in his eyes matches the evil glint Vladimir's got when sending soldiers into a rigged battlefield. "You should have seen the way his eyes lit up when I stabbed his father in front of him. If you had a drop of Popov blood in your veins, I would have said he picked up a few traits from his uncle, but we both know that would be a lie, don't we, Niki?"

His question stumps me for all of two seconds. There are only a handful of people who know my true lineage. One of those people's wife is damaging my hearing with her frantic screams as she struggles to free herself from a goon stopping her from reaching her crying son. Another is staring at me without fear, even with her hair being wretched from her scalp, because she knows I'll never let anything happen to her. And the other is most likely bleeding out in the security office I demanded he station himself at.

Besides Rico, Justine, and Roman, only one other man knows my secret: Carmichael I'm-Going-To-Gut-Him-Alive Fletcher.

Needing to end one fight before starting another, I say, "Anatoly's rules were rewritten months ago. They're no longer valid." When confusion washes over Maxsim's face, a mocking grin lights up mine. "Really, Maxsim? Do you know me at all? As my *Ангел* likes to say, 'Modern men need modern rules.'" I take a step closer to him, confident I have him by the throat. "Anatoly may have founded the Popov entity, but *I* rule it. A scrap of paper won't gain you the respect of my men. It won't secure you the ties I founded through years of negotiations, nor will it see you taking my place. All it will award you is a price for your head and centuries of fear for your descendants as they peer over their shoulders, waiting for my inevitable revenge."

Maxsim's face lines with anger as he snarls, "At least I have descendants." He glances over my shoulder before jerking up his chin. "It's more than you'll ever have."

Anger. Fury. Hate so black I can barely see through the cloud bombards me when the goon clutching Justine's hair throws his fist into her stomach. His hit is so fierce Justine skids across the floor like a limbless ragdoll.

"No!"

Roaring like an animal, I charge for the man who's going to die a death more painful than a thousand. I see nothing but red during my sprint, colored with both anger and blood. They can stab me, shoot me, and beat me until I'm hanging as lifeless as I did on a warehouse floor years ago, but they'll never slow me down.

My acrobatic routine matches my leap into the air to free Justine from the noose wrapped around her neck twelve months ago, except this time, I'm not aiming for her. I have my sights on the man responsible for her fetal curl six feet away from me, for the one striving to end my life without siphoning blood from my veins.

My fists land on the laughing hoodlum's jugular, collapsing his windpipe. I stab my foot into the back of his kneecap, forcing him to topple to the ground in a heap. His drop is too simple. I want him to howl in pain, to experience half the hurt shredding me into pieces.

He does no such thing. He squeals like a child learning to ride a bike for the first time before returning himself back onto his feet. Even my unnatural twist of his neck doesn't dampen his smile.

When Sansi swats me off him like I'm a fly, I don't give in. I'm back up in his face in an instant, my fists raining down on him as relentlessly as the bullets flying past my head.

I want him to cry for forgiveness.

To beg for his life before I end it without mercy.

I want him to suffer.

It seems my wish is about to come true when Sansi howls in

pain two seconds later. I want to say my fists have done the job they're trained to do, but that would be a lie. He's not buckling solely because of my wrath. His rib caught a bullet intended for my head.

Taking advantage of the situation, I jab two fingers into his gushing wound. I scissor them, mimicking the movements Justine's legs do any time she catches my heated gaze. His pained wails are the equivalent of angels serenading me, his fall to the ground the icing on the cake.

With Sansi double my size, it will take everything I have to snap his neck, but I give it my all, my anger not even half depleted. As the beast inside me rises from the ashes he was buried in twelve months ago, I feel the cervical vertebrae in Sansi's neck compressing, dangerously close to slicing the spinal cord they're there to protect. He is moments from death, yet my punishment is only beginning.

If he has harmed my baby, his death will be a blessing. Every man in this room will feel my wrath for years to come before my focus switches to their families. I won't hurt them or make them cry. I'll only kill them with the silent pain currently ripping through my heart. Hell hath no fury like a man scorned.

Even in a room full of noise, I hear Sansi's final breath leave his body... but I somehow miss the bullet fired to kill me.

15

JUSTINE

A buzzing sensation drones through my ears, waking me from my restless sleep. It's the hum you get after a rock concert when you've sacrificed your hearing to watch the latest music icon strut their stuff on stage.

The last time my hearing buzzed with this much static was the night Brax invited me to see a revival of a band we loved in our teen days. It was a disappointing show, but some good came from their pathetic attempt at a resurrection. That night was the first time I was seen in public since I was mauled by a dog. It was awkward and highly emotional, but a necessary step in my rehabilitation.

It was also the night I decided to change my major to pre-law. Brax wasn't convinced I was making the right decision, but he respected me enough not to say anything. I transferred to my new, law-focused university the following week, meaning our first "official" date was also our last.

Last week was the first time I've seen Brax in years, but neither of us have any regrets. He's madly, deeply in love with a woman he swears is way out of his league, and I'm head over heels in love with a man who deserves better than me.

I'm not surprised Brax finally found his Achilles' heel. He's a brutish, rough, filthy-mouthed man, but he has a massive heart. The contrast between his outside appearance and his super shiny insides reminds me a lot of Nikolai.

If Nikolai could look beyond our past, I'm confident he and Brax could become friends.

Or hell could freeze over.

I'm drawn from my slumbering state when my breathless chuckle sends pain skating across my stomach. It's a sharp, intense pain that makes me crave a hot water bottle and a long soak in a tub... *and perhaps a trip to the drugstore for womanly supplies.*

Groaning, I roll onto my side. I've barely stuffed a pillow between my aching legs when a distinct voice calls my name. It's not the deep Russian timbre I'm praying for, but Trey's British twang is welcomed after a week of silence.

When I slowly flutter open my eyes, he smiles. "Hey." His greeting rolls off his tongue slowly, as if he is worried it will pierce my ears more painfully than the hammers pounding my head.

The reason behind his panic comes to light when I attempt to rise to a half-seated position. My ears aren't just throbbing. They're bleeding.

"W-w-what happened?" I wiggle my tongue around my bone-dry mouth before articulating my question for the second time, this one missing the immature stutter.

"You don't remember?" This question isn't from Trey. It's from Maddox, whose backside is propped on a couch that looks oddly similar to the one I used to have in my apartment.

What the hell?

I shake my head. Bad move. Bile scorches my throat mere seconds before the dinner Blaire slaved over for hours sees daylight in the most horrific way.

Maddox catches my slop-laced vomit in a bucket leaning at his side before shifting his eyes to Trey. "Where was she found again?"

"By Interstate 95. One of our couriers thought he was seeing things." His words are as violent as my body's heaves.

When the entirety of Trey's statement smacks into me, I hold my hand over my mouth to conceal my ghastly breath. "Hold on. I was found along a highway?"

Trey nods. "You were a few miles from the private airstrip you used last week. We figured that was the location Nikolai told you to use in case of an emergency."

His reply makes sense. Nikolai has a strict protocol I must follow when traveling interstate, but the rest of Trey's statement is confusing.

"Why was I on Interstate 95? Blaire and Rico's apartment is miles from there."

"Blaire and Rico?" Trey sounds as confused as I feel. "What do they have to do with anything?"

My brows stitch. "We had dinner with them last night. You know this because Nikolai called you on our way." My words lose confidence with each one I speak. Both Maddox and Trey appear utterly flabbergasted.

Undeterred by a bucket filled with sickly smelling vomit, Maddox fills the seat next to me before clasping my hands in his. "You had dinner with Rico and Blaire three nights ago. You've been missing ever since."

I want to call him out as a liar, but his honest eyes stop me. He's being one hundred percent serious.

My eyes bug when he adds, "You're also in Vegas. Trey meant Interstate 95 on the California border, not the one in Florida."

"That can't be true," I murmur, stunned. "You don't just lose three days of your life. Where's Nikolai? He'll prove we were with Rico and Blaire last night."

I scan the room, praying Nikolai will miraculously appear. He is nowhere to be found.

"That..."—my watering eyes lower to the vomit bucket—"is the rosemary chicken Blaire prepared for us. She used herbs that would help my queasy stomach."

I suck in an exhausted breath when my hand cups my tiny stomach. I'm barely touching myself, but my stomach feels as if I'm pounding it with my fists as hard as my heart is hammering my ribs.

Sickened with worry, I raise the hem of my shirt. Tears burn my eyes when I spot how battered my stomach is. Dark bruises mottled through my skin appear as if I trekked through a desert in the peak of summer. Come to think of it, the portions of my legs not covered by the ruined hem of my skirt also appear sunburned.

Jumping to my feet, I race into the bathroom. The confusion fogging my mind thickens when I enter the opulent space I've shared with Nikolai for the past year. With my memories still hazy,

I expected the small, cramped bathroom my family of six shared after Maddox's arrest.

It takes me a few seconds to gain the courage needed to peer at my reflection in the mirror. When I do, I balk. My cheeks are as red as my wild, unbrushed hair. My lips are cracked and bleeding, and I have an extensive abrasion under my chin. With my pupils as dilated as a drug addict's, I appear more like a homeless beggar than the ruthless defense attorney I've falsely portrayed the past year and a half.

Stepping back, I lower my eyes. The portions of my body exposed through my ripped shirt and shredded skirt are dirty, bruised, and blistered. I have a large gash down my right thigh littered with wood splinters, and my stomach has a circular bruise beneath the right side of my rib.

The only good aspect of my disheveled appearance is the brightness of my tan distracting from the redness of my scars. They're barely visible beneath layers of dirt and battered skin.

I aggressively yank down my shirt when I sense I'm being watched. Trey is peering at me in the mirror, cautiously watching me. His blond brows are pinched together, and his fists are clenched.

"You truly don't remember, do you?"

I shake my head. "All I remember is having dinner. The rest is blank."

When Maddox joins Trey in the doorway, he gives him a pleading look. He's not impressed when Trey shakes his head, denying his silent demand, but he does a good job hiding his annoyance. He became a master of his emotions when he was arrested for murder at his girlfriend's place of employment.

Acting like Trey isn't in the room, Maddox turns on the shower faucet before spinning to face me. "Why don't you shower while I get you something to eat? Your confusion may lift once you've filled your belly and taken a nap."

I cowardly nod, bowing out of the fight as quickly as I did when I was released from the hospital years ago. There's just one difference this time around: I don't want to bury my head in my mother's chest and hide from the world. I want Nikolai.

I don't understand what's happening. Why isn't Nikolai here?

How did I lose three days of my life in the blink of an eye? And why is Maddox treating me like he did the days before his arrest?

My thoughts return to the present when Maddox soothingly rubs my arm. "We'll be just outside."

He barely makes it halfway out the door before Trey bombards him with questions. I hear my name numerous times through the partially closed door, but I'm too stunned to string his words into sentences. I feel like I'm dreaming, trapped in a nightmare too debilitating to be real.

After fixing the bathroom door latch, I remove my clothes. I feel like I've stepped back five years, back to the time when I hated my body so much I covered every mirror in my house with sheets. Back to the shy, scared girl who woke up screaming in the middle of the night, convinced a dog was chasing her through a pitch-black field.

Back to the woman I was before I met Nikolai.

Breathing out my nerves, I straighten my spine before removing my clothes with more force than is necessary. Even with my clothes covered with sweat and mud, they peel off my body within seconds.

Steam covers every inch of the glass on one wall when I step into the shower. I'm grateful it hides my battered body from my reflection in the large vanity mirror, but it's a painful reminder of the truth I'm hiding from.

There is a heart etched in the right-hand corner of the shower door. Nikolai drew it there after I blew him a kiss from the bath he ran for me the night before we left for Florida. He wouldn't join me because he didn't want "smelly girly shit" coating his skin, so he showered instead.

He voiced a similar complaint when Blaire set a generous serving of "floral-scented chicken" in front of him last night.

I freeze as reality dawns. According to Trey and Maddox, that wasn't last night. It was three nights ago. If that's true, why can't I remember anything? I remember Blaire's scrumptious food and how she glanced at Rico to gauge his response to every mouthful he ate. I even remember that a lack of blood ties won't stop Nikolai and Rico from being brothers.

Nikolai admires Rico so much he didn't hesitate to place his life on the line to drag Blaire out of harm's way when we were attacked.

I stop lathering my skin when a generous pump of my heart

revitalizes my brain with oxygen. With a towel barely covering me, I dash into the main section of the bedroom I share with Nikolai.

"We were attacked, bombarded without warning. Men came from all angles. They were wearing balaclavas and knew things about Nikolai not many know."

"What type of stuff?" Maddox asks at the same time Trey prompts, "Then what?"

Beginning at the more important question, I reply to Trey, "A battle ensued. Nikolai and Rico were outnumbered, but they held their ground until..."

Air hisses between my teeth when my hand shoots up to my hair. The sting of the brute's hold is still burning my scalp. "A man grabbed me. He was so large he didn't need to extend his arm to hoist me from the ground."

"That's good, Justine. Keep going," Trey encourages, stepping closer to me.

My hand falls from my head. "Nikolai threatened him, told him he'd kill his family if he didn't let me go." Trey nods, aware Nikolai would go to the ends of the earth to protect me. "That's when another man entered the equation." I stop as my brain struggles to clear the fog in my mind. "Maxsim. Nikolai called him Maxsim."

"Maxsim?" Trey checks, his tone high. "Are you sure?"

"If he's Alexei's son, then yes, I'm sure." My voice jitters with panic. "They argued about Nikolai killing Alexei and how Maxsim was going to use Eli to take Nikolai's place."

"How did Nikolai respond?"

"Umm." I stop, my memories still hazy. "He said he had changed the rules, that Anatoly's rulings were no longer relevant." Tears prick my eyes when the cause of the large bruise on my stomach dawns on me. "His reply angered Maxsim so much he signaled for his goon to hit me."

Maddox's and Trey's eyes follow my hand when it lowers to shield my stomach. Even with the incident happening three days ago, I can still recall the bile that scorched my throat from his hit. He held nothing back, maiming me as badly as his hit stole the life from Nikolai's eyes.

I sit on the edge of my bed, not trusting my legs to remain upright. It's not the large king-size bed Nikolai and I have shared the prior twelve months. It's the dilapidated mattress my internship salary struggled to cover.

I wanted to gift Nikolai something unique to celebrate our one-year anniversary. That's virtually impossible when you're dating a man who has everything. After a few days of deliberation, I realized there was one thing I could give him that money could never buy. Happy memories.

That's why I had our room transformed into my apartment. Our time there was short, but we amassed a vault-load of memories we added to only a week ago.

"Do you know what happened to the men Nikolai and you traveled with? Roman? Rico?" I stop shaking my head when Maddox adds, "Dimitri?"

My pupils turn massive. "Dimitri was shot."

When Maddox shifts his eyes to Trey, Trey discloses, "Dimitri is under watch at an undisclosed location. He was found by the Feds, surrounded by numerous deceased members of a Russian association. They're seeking the death penalty."

He appears to want to say more, but his lips remain shut.

Mine aren't as willing to ignore the massive elephant in the room. "What aren't you telling me, Trey?"

Most of my interactions with Trey have occurred while Nikolai is in my presence, so I'm often distracted, but I still know him well enough to know when he's skirting important issues.

"Don't lie to me, Trey. You know the consequences if you do."

Who the hell am I? I may be the most scared I've ever been, but I don't threaten people. I guess what Nikolai said is true. When forced to pick between leading or being led, you pick the one you're most likely to survive.

Failing to hear the deceit in my tone, Trey squawks like a canary. "Nikolai's DNA was found at the scene. A pool of his blood was located next to a man only known as a myth: *убийца.*"

"Murderer," I translate.

Sick unease melds through me when Trey nods. "Rumors are his father was a Ukrainian weightlifter, and his mother an operative in the Russian Soviet. With his childhood devoted to beating his mother's lineage into him, his seven-foot-eight height never matched the maturity of his brain. His mental capacity only reached that of a young teen."

"Was he the man who held me hostage?"

Trey nods again. "We believe so."

With both Trey and me stunned into silence, Maddox joins our conversation. "What are you saying? Nikolai killed a man, and in retaliation, he was killed?"

Trey's shrug has him missing my paling cheeks. "We don't know. Dimitri was the only man found alive."

"Because he was too injured to flee?"

My optimism is dashed when Trey shakes his head. "He was left as a warning. If this was a takeover bid, Maxsim needs the word spread that he toppled the king. Dimitri is his equivalent of a town crier."

"But Maxsim didn't topple the king. Nikolai isn't dead."

When Maddox moves for me, I yank away from him. "J—"

"No!" I scream, refusing to acknowledge the remorse in his eyes. "Nikolai isn't dead! I'd know if he were dead. I'd fucking know it."

My unusual use of a curse word doesn't lessen the impact of my statement. It is the most confident one I've issued in the past five years. Nothing can take away from my certainty.

"I somehow got from Florida to Vegas with my life intact. That wouldn't have occurred without Nikolai's help."

Trey steps closer to me, his eyes as repentant as Maddox's. "The Vasilievs used a subsidiary entity to bid on you last year. You're only alive because they see you as an asset."

"What?" I have a million questions streaming through my head, but with words eluding me, I went for the easiest one.

"I'll call a physician to check you over. He's very discreet. I assure you, nothing you tell him will *ever* leave this room."

Trey's words sicken me even more than the thought of my baby being injured from Maxsim's goon, but it does nothing to douse the rage bubbling through me. "I don't need a doctor!"

My brisk leap to my feet nearly slips the towel off my body, but I don't care. Just like I know Nikolai isn't dead, I'm confident the worry in Trey's eyes holds no merit.

"I also wasn't *raped*." My last word is barely a whisper. "Nikolai would *never* let that happen. He'd kill any man stupid enough to get within an inch of me."

My eyes rocket to Maddox when he mutters, "He can't protect you from the grave, J."

"Then I'm lucky he isn't dead, aren't I?" Anger minces up my words, making them more hostile than confirming.

Hating the incredulous look on Maddox's face, I charge to my dresser in the corner of the room. Even with his belief Nikolai can't punish him for seeing me in a vulnerable state, Trey's eyes snap to the ground the instant my towel slips from my body.

Not the slightest bit worried he may see my scars, I yank a pair of sweatpants up my legs. The fleece material lining the pants is a poor choice considering how blistering hot my skin is, but they're the closest article of clothing I have, so they'll have to do.

After throwing one of Nikolai's shirts over my braless torso, I twist to face Trey. "Where are the men?"

When Maddox steps forward to baby me as he did earlier, I yell, "Where are my men?"

"They're in the den."

I'm out the door before half of Trey's reply leaves his mouth. And even faster than that, he's at my side like he usually is at Nikolai's when they're preparing for battle.

"What are you planning?" Trey's words are chopped up by his giant galloping steps as he follows me through the Popov mansion.

I already have a bucketload of determination fueling my steps, but the large diamond on my left hand strengthens my reply.

"I'm going to fulfill the role I was born to live. I'm going to be Nikolai's queen."

16

JUSTINE

M y willpower gets bitch-slapped when I enter the den in the middle of the Popov compound. It's clear the men filling the space are in mourning, but that isn't the cause for my backpedaling. It is the whores easing their heartache. There are as many scantily clad women as there are men and just as many empty bottles of whiskey.

The scandalous scene matches the ones I walked in on many times after Nikolai's blade ended Vladimir's reign. It's just missing the all-in orgies that resulted in their celebrations being banned from the main compound. For the past twelve months, this filth has only occurred at Clarks.

"The man responsible for your unlimited shots of whiskey, endless whores, and *god knows what else* is missing, yet instead of trekking to the end of the earth to find him, you take advantage of his generosity. You should be grateful Nikolai isn't here, because none of you would be spared his wrath."

My voice doesn't quiver in the slightest, not even when a long-term associate of the Popov entity stumbles my way. He's older than most men in the room, hitting close to mid-sixties. I've seen him around a few times, but it is generally when Nikolai is on overnight trips.

Kliment was one of Vladimir's advisors before he was removed from his position for getting friendly with two of Vladimir's favorite whores. Vladimir was a vile, abhorrent man, but he was as possessive of his whores as he was of his wives.

"Perhaps you should join us. It appears as if you're enjoying the view."

Kliment raises his hand to brush it down the bud pressing against my shirt, but before he gets within an inch of my chest, Trey seizes his hand, yanks him forward, then whispers in his ear.

I assume Trey's hushed words are the cause of Kliment's whitening cheeks, but I'm proven wrong when Kliment takes a step back. Even the dark coloring of his shirt can't hide the massive bloodstain seeping into it. He's been stabbed in the chest, his punishment delivered by Trey in the exact manner Nikolai would have requested.

When Kliment falls to the ground, Trey's wide eyes scan the now-silent room. "Does anyone else have anything to say?" He stares at the shocked men with murderous eyes, hoping someone will take up his challenge.

When they fail to fall victim to his trap, he sneers, "Disrespecting Justine is as punishable as disrespecting Nikolai. Both will result in death."

Because I don't want to risk fainting, I keep my eyes locked on the group of men as stunned by the turn of events as I am. Don't get me wrong, I'm grateful for Trey's protection, but I fear how many more lives will be lost between now and when Nikolai regains his throne.

"Now clean up this mess." Trey's glare at the dozen whores frozen mid-hump discloses what mess he's referring to. "Gather the remaining men from Clarks and return here within the hour. You will be considered a deserter if you're not primed and ready to fight."

Not waiting for them to respond to the threat in his tone that reveals what happens to AWOL Popov members, he guides me over a lifeless Kliment before directing me down the hall where Nikolai's home office is.

My skin quivers more with every step we take. Not because I'm frightened but because the blood on Trey's hand is seeping into my shirt. I'm seconds from passing out. I most likely would if soul-hardening adrenaline wasn't surging through my veins. Now is not the time for me to act weak. Once Nikolai is safe, I can panic as much as I want.

After guiding me into the chair behind Nikolai's desk, Trey lifts my eyes to his.

"Don't," I murmur upon spotting the apologies brimming in his. "He broke the rules and was used as an example of what happens when you do that."

He stares at me, equally stunned and amused. "Nikolai always said he got the tiger. I never would have believed it if I hadn't seen it with my own eyes."

I smile, accepting a compliment I never knew I wanted but secretly needed.

"So, what's your plan?"

Now it's my turn to glare at Trey.

What does he mean? I'm not running this show.

"Ah, yeah, you are," Trey responds to the unvoiced words streaming from my eyes. "What you said earlier is true. Nikolai rewrote the rules we live by months ago. In the event of his death..." —I nearly cut him off, insisting that Nikolai isn't dead before his next set of words steal mine—"or if he is incapable of ruling, the guardianship of the Popov entity is to be bestowed upon you."

He flips open an old, leather-stitched journal until it stops three-quarters in. Although my eyes are too blurry with tears to read the ink scribbled across the time-stained paper, I don't need to know what it says to know who wrote it. It was Nikolai. If the E's appearing as backward threes isn't enough indication, an identical signature to the one he used when altering his home arrest documentation is a sure-fire indication.

My eyes lift to Trey when he says, "Even if Nikolai hadn't changed the rules, you're still the best person to run this operation. You know Nikolai. You know how he thinks, how he acts, and what makes him tick." My nod of agreement ceases when he adds, "You're also the only person capable of telling us what happened at Rico's."

"I don't remember everything—"

"But you remember some things. That's better than what we've had the past three days."

A huff parts my lips. It arrives seconds before my halfhearted nod.

After he removes the planner from in front of me, Trey's backside takes its place. "You mentioned that Maxsim knew stuff about Nikolai no one else knew. What type of stuff?"

"Stuff I can't repeat without Nikolai's permission." My tone reveals I'm not trying to be coy. I just refuse to disclose private information about Nikolai without his knowledge. "Let me just say, only a handful of people know the information Maxsim was slinging at Nikolai."

"Okay. Good. Anything else? Even something that seems insignificant."

I shake my head for barely a second before a small memory breaks through the fog in my head. "When Blaire and I were cleaning up, she broke a cup. The rhyme spoken through the baby monitor in the kitchen was odd but not disturbing enough for the response it elicited from her. I thought that was strange."

"A nursery rhyme?"

I shake my head. "It wasn't a nursery rhyme. Only a monster would sing something so villainous to a child—" I still as commotion causes havoc with my stomach. I wouldn't be shocked to discover Vladimir's style of parenting included scary, death-like rhymes.

Goosebumps break across my skin when Trey sings, "Send the angel to the devil's bed, hold her, cherish her—"

"Then cut off her head," I interrupt. "She danced with Satan and now she is dead, all for lying in the devil's bed."

Trey rakes his fingers through the thick beard on his chin. "Fuck!"

"What?" I scoot to the end of my chair, assuring myself that even if his reply is a whisper, I won't miss it.

Although the name he says is who I expect, it's still a bitter pill to swallow. "Vladimir."

"He's dead."

He gives me a look as if to ask, *Are you sure?*

"I pulled Nikolai's knife from his chest myself, Trey. I heard him take his last breath."

He slices his hand through the air, cutting me off. "What? You *heard* Vladimir take his last breath."

When I nod, he forces out in a hurry, "What did it sound like?"

I do a weird shrug. "I don't know. Like someone taking their final breath."

"Was it wheezy? Gargling?" He stands to his feet. "Did it sound anything like the breath Kliment just took?"

I shake my head. "It was more a..." I make a noise similar to the one Vladimir made when I saved Nikolai from prosecution by placing myself in the DA's sight. "But why does it matter? Even if Vladimir survived a knife wound to the heart, nothing would have saved him from the inferno that followed our departure."

Trey's brow bows. "The inferno that occurred twenty minutes after you removed Nikolai's knife."

He's not asking a question. He's stating a fact. Nikolai had every intention of cremating Vladimir in the hell he was tortured in fourteen years earlier, but my wish to help the trapped women meant a change to the game plan. Nikolai delayed Vladimir's undeserving memorial for me.

Shit.

Spotting my downcast lips, Trey murmurs, "Twenty minutes is plenty of time for an injured man to seek cover."

"No." I shake his horrid words from my ears. This is not a notion I'm willing to consider. "Vladimir is dead. Nikolai killed him. End of story."

"You said Maxsim knew stuff about Nikolai only those closest to him know. The rhyme you heard is one Vladimir sang to Nikolai when he was a child. What more proof do you need?"

"A solid one!" I cradle my head in my hands, striving to ignore the clump of vomit in my throat. "Why now, Trey? If this is true, why would Vladimir wait so long to act?"

"That's like asking how long a piece of string is. Nothing Vladimir did made sense. He wasn't known for rationality."

I take a deep breath before forcing out, "Maxsim wanted Eli so he could raise him to take Nikolai's place."

"Or... Maxsim took Eli for Vladimir so Vladimir could return the Popov entity to its true heritage."

My spine snaps straight as my eyes rocket to Trey.

How does he know Nikolai isn't a Popov?

Hardly anyone knows that.

Trey's throat works hard to swallow. "Carmichael."

"What?"

He points to the journal he showed me earlier. "Nikolai needed documents notarized. The beneficiary couldn't notarize them, so he called a man he knew could. Carmichael."

"So he just told you Nikolai's secrets?" I swear I'm as furious now as I was when I discovered how Carmichael double-crossed Nikolai when he was only a boy.

"Not exactly."

My glare ramps up.

"I overheard some things."

"You spied on Nikolai? Are you insane? He's had men killed for less."

I'm not lying. If you deceive Nikolai, expect to pay for your error with your life.

I swallow my anger when Trey whispers, "I needed to protect K." His wide eyes dance between mine when he adds, "I couldn't have her sold again, Justine. I love her."

I release an exasperated breath. I'm annoyed he spied on Nikolai, but I understand why he did it. Nothing is off-limits when it comes to protecting the people you love.

With that in mind, I scoot in close to Nikolai's desk. There are several men who can help me right now. Unfortunately, none of them are men Nikolai would approve of.

17

JUSTINE

"Trey has arranged for a doctor, but you don't need to worry about that right now, Maddox. I need you to focus on the documents Carmichael supplied us. If Nikolai is being held captive, he's at one of those locations. Find which one it is."

Maddox isn't used to taking orders from his baby sister, but the command in my tone can't be denied. We've been working on Nikolai's disappearance for hours, meaning I'm not solely tired. I'm panicked out of my mind. Time is of the essence when it comes to matters like this.

Trey's recollection of events was proven true during my conversation with Ryan. Dimitri and two-dozen deceased Russians were discovered at Rico's apartment. No members of Nikolai's crew were found. The Feds have kept the incident so under wraps it took Ryan over an hour just to find Dimitri's location.

Although unheard of—and highly illegal—members of Nikolai's crew are in the process of extracting Dimitri. Our covert operation will likely cost Nikolai's entity a great sum of money, but Dimitri stepped up to the plate for Nikolai first, so it's only fair we have his back too. Furthermore, I'd pledge allegiance to Satan himself if it guaranteed Nikolai's safe return.

Unfortunately, Ryan's discovery of Dimitri's location came with a bitter blow. His inquiries unearthed the number of men killed while trying to protect Nikolai and me. Most were the standard foot soldiers Bratva clans use for protection, but a handful of names were recognizable. The most obvious: Dok. He died on the operating table. The three bullet wounds in his chest were too extensive for his trauma surgeons to repair.

Although devastated by the high list of casualties, I'm filled with gratitude that neither Nikolai's nor Roman's names were mentioned. I know deep down inside Nikolai is okay.

He has to be.

I crank my head to the side when the clank of a cell phone landing on a table sounds through my ears. "What did she say?"

A sigh parts Trey's lips. "Not much. She hasn't seen Maxsim in over a year. She rambled some shit about his wife leaving him when he impregnated his whore. I tuned out not long after that."

My shoulders slump. Maxsim's extramarital affairs aren't any concern of mine, but if his mother is out of the loop on his whereabouts, how the hell will I ever track him down?

"Get Carmichael back on the phone. If Maxsim isn't operating on behalf of his family, perhaps he is working with someone else."

I refuse to say Vladimir's name, but Trey doesn't need me to verbalize it to hear it.

"Carmichael won't talk to—" I hold my hand out palm side up, cutting off his accurate statement that Carmichael won't converse with anyone but me.

After dumping his pre-dialed phone into my hand, Trey moves to assist Maddox in sorting the massive stockpile of land Alexei acquired before his death. I want to pretend he's keeping himself busy, but in reality, he just keeps his snooping on the down-low. His work on Nikolai's behalf doesn't stop at Nikolai's crew. It extends to any man threatening him or his relationship— Carmichael included.

"Any word?"

The fact Carmichael fails to issue a greeting shows he is as intrigued by Nikolai's disappearance as I am. I'm just hoping his motives are noble.

"No." I only say one word, but how it was delivered says so much more. "Trey talked to Maxsim's mother. He's not working with them."

"I'm not surprised. The Vasilievs have barely operated since Alexei's death."

My back molars are nearly ground into stubs when I grind out, "How are you aware of that? Are you working with them?"

Carmichael huffs, disappointed at my distrust but also anticipating it. "I've never worked *with* them, Justine... but I haven't *represented* them lately, either. You know the amount of legal work entities like theirs require each month. When things go quiet, you know it only means one thing."

"Dissolution," we say at the same time.

An agreeing noise vibrates Carmichael's lips. "The Vasilievs were going under years before Alexei's death. His death just steamrolled the process."

"So you could say members of his entity are desperate?"

When Carmichael makes another agreeing gesture, I add, "Desperate enough to side with Satan?"

"What are you getting at, Justine?"

I should be shocked at his bluntness, but my short stint as his intern familiarized me with his forwardness. If Carmichael wants you to know something, he'll tell you. Just as if he wants to keep it a secret, you'll be left in the dark for eternity.

"*If* Vladimir were alive, do you think Maxsim would be desperate enough to work with him?"

For the first time in history, Carmichael is stumped. "What...? You can't be serious... Please tell me I misheard what you said." Before I can repeat my inane comment, he says, "Things are tight for the Vasilievs, but I don't see them ever being *that* desperate. Partnering with Vladimir would be as odd as the Popovs siding with the Petrettis."

Ignoring the lump in my throat, I ask, "But it's not entirely unthinkable. Right?"

"I guess." The tapping of a keyboard almost drowns out what he says next. "But none of Vladimir's accounts have been accessed in over a year. If he's paying Maxsim, it's not in money..."

His words trail off, replaced by a massive gasp.

"What is it?"

Carmichael sounds distant when he answers, "A parcel of land the Popov entity has held since the seventies is scheduled to be transferred next week."

"To whom?" My voice is as high as my brows.

"Hold on."

Stomping sounds down the line. I'm shocked I can hear it for how hard his lungs work. He sounds as if he is running.

I push Trey's cell close to my ear when he sneers, "You did it again, didn't you?"

A man replies, but I can't hear what he's saying.

"For fuck's sake, Jeremy! Did the loss of your finger not teach you anything? They'll kill you this time when they discover what you've done."

My heart twists from the concern in his tone. He loves his brother, but he's struggling not to strangle him right now.

"Where are they?"

A commotion sounds down the line before heavy breathing follows it.

"You won't need to worry about him once I'm done with you. I nearly lost my license to practice because of you. I'm not risking it twice."

Carmichael's voice softens, as if he's set his phone down.

My assumptions are proved right when a phone being scraped across wood sounds down the line seconds before I hear Carmichael's dejected tone. "Send your crew to Centennial. There's a dirt road hidden by bushes off Kyle Cannon. I don't know if Nikolai is there, but you may find the answers you're seeking."

I don't get a chance to offer my thanks before Carmichael disconnects our call.

"Kyle Cannon." I leap to my feet before charging toward where Trey, Maddox, and a handful of Nikolai's crew sit.

Trey's finger circles the area I'm referencing on an aerial map. "Except for a few housing developments, there's nothing out there."

"Carmichael said there's a dirt road hidden by bushes."

Trey's lips quirk. "I'm not seeing any roads."

I snatch the map to my side of the desk. "Because most men can't locate their nose. Give it to me."

There are several clumps of shrubs on the map, but none show a clear road veering away from them. "What's this?" I point to a shimmer on the map. If the map were old, the glimmer might be thinning paper, but these were recently printed.

"A dome?" Maddox suggests before raising his eyes to Trey. "What material was used to build Clarks?"

"Anything we could get our hands on, but a majority of our supplies came from a decommissioned airstrip on the outskirts of town. Others were shipped in."

"Decommissioned?" Maddox's finger stretches from the area I'm pointing at to a barren strip of land nestled at the back of it. "Or still in operation?"

All eyes in the room snap to me when I say, "Maxsim had to get me to Vegas somehow. What if he didn't use a commercial airstrip?"

They remain quiet, unsure of what to say. What could they say? My theory is plausible. So much so that Trey barks at the men to be ready for combat before he's even halfway out of his chair. His stomps only cease when he spots me on his tail.

"No, Justine. Just because I didn't send you away with K doesn't mean I shouldn't have. You can't come with us. It isn't safe."

Snubbing the fury radiating from my eyes, he rifles through the gun cabinet hidden behind paneled walls in Nikolai's office. He does a good job of acting ignorant, but his next words reveal his worry about the repercussions of disrespecting me. "Talk some sense into her, *please*." His words aren't for me. They're for Maddox.

Maddox takes up Trey's plea in an instant. "J—"

"No."

He exhales deeply before trying again. "Mom has been through enough—"

It is hard for me not to clutch my chest from the devastation in his voice. "I feel for her, truly I do, but her pain isn't even half of what I'm being pelted with right now."

I'm not lying. Hope is the only thing stopping me from folding in two right now.

"If you go, you could get killed." Maddox's lack of debate reveals he understands the level of hurt I'm experiencing. "Do you understand that, J?"

I nod, aware of what I'm up against. "At least I won't die a coward. Col stripped the life from my veins years ago. He made me hate everything I was and everything I had once hoped to be." Tears pool in my eyes as I force out words I never want to express again. "If I lose Nikolai, I will once again lose every part of who I am. I won't survive going through that again, Maddox. I was barely living before Nikolai came into my life, so I refuse to live a life without him in it."

"J..." Maddox stops, screws up his face as he struggles to remain passive like he has the past five years, then starts again. "Dad is going to kill me."

Once again, I nod in agreement. This goes against everything our father instilled in his sons since the day they took their first breaths—but so does my focus. Our parents taught us to chase our dreams no matter the consequences. That's what I'm trying to do.

Shaking his head, either admiring my stubbornness or in disbelief, Maddox returns his eyes to Trey. "I'll keep her out of harm's way."

Trey chuckles. It's not his happy-go-lucky laugh. "Do you truly believe *you* have what it takes to keep her safe? These men are like me. They don't have morals."

Maddox accepts Trey's knock to his chin like a man, but it doesn't sway his resolve. "Do *you* truly believe Justine would still be here if I couldn't protect her from men like you?"

Maddox's saying appears pompous, but it is one hundred percent authentic. He might look like a humble man, but he's been my family's keeper for years longer than that. Nothing can deter him when it comes to protecting the ones he loves. The five years he spent in prison proves this without a doubt.

"I took one night off, and look what happened. Men trained to keep my sister safe didn't, yet you feel you have the right to judge me."

Their pissing contest ends by Trey shoving a loaded gun into Maddox's chest. "I don't have time for this shit. If you want to walk into your death head-on, who am I to stop you?" He drops his eyes to the semi-automatic weapon Maddox is holding at an odd angle. "The safety is on the tang. If you don't know what that is, you shouldn't be carrying a gun."

I inch back when his murderous eyes shift to me. He isn't happy about my decision, but he's aware he either follows my orders or loses his life. He's going with the former. "If you so much as get a scratch on you, you're going to take Maddox's gun, aim it at my head, then fire. Do you understand?"

"Yes," I reply, comprehending his riddle.

By letting me go with him, it isn't just his livelihood on the line. It's also his life.

"But I won't need to borrow Maddox's gun to take you down. I'll use mine."

The low hang of Trey's jaw grows when I swing open the bottom drawer of Nikolai's desk to remove a Sig Sauer P365 Nitron. He stares at me in shock when I load the ten-round magazine with bullets. I don't know why he's stunned. The first thing Nikolai taught me after Alexei raided his compound was how to fire a weapon. We've had weekly target practice ever since.

Maddox thinks he's keeping me far from the action, but I have news for him. A true queen doesn't sit and watch the royalties roll in. She brings home the bacon as well.

18

JUSTINE

Nerves take flight the further our SUVs travel down a dusty, bumpy road. The airstrip Maddox discovered is a few miles from the location Carmichael suggested we search, but deeper intel discovered an off-road track that weaves throughout dense woodlands separating the dome-like building and the airstrip.

I'm not nervous we're heading to battle unprepared. I'm petrified about what we may unearth. Things are still hazy, but the snippets of information I uncovered over the past seven hours haven't filled me with hope. If anything, they've had the opposite effect.

Preliminary findings on the blood pool located near the myth only known as "Murderer" confirm it was Nikolai's blood. It had shards of muscle and bone mixed in, meaning his injury shredded through his muscle and quite possibly nicked his bone.

That can only mean one thing.

He was shot.

With no bullet located with his DNA, either it's still lodged in his body, or Maxsim's crew combed hundreds of bullet casings to locate his.

The latter is highly unlikely.

With how heavily they came in, it would have only been a matter of minutes before stunned bystanders called the authorities.

They would have left in a hurry, having no time to seek one bullet in a sea of many.

Knowing Nikolai is injured has me twisted up in knots, but adding that to recalling Maxsim's claim he killed Rico in front of Eli, and you have the perfect recipe for a swirling stomach.

And don't even get me started on what damage Sansi's hit could have caused our baby. I just wish I could wake up from this nightmare. I'd give anything to discover that the pelmeni we consumed at lunch caused my delusions and this is all just a long, recurring nightmare.

Before my head can burrow into the sand, I shift my eyes to Trey. "If this is Vladimir, what are we walking into?"

With our SUV brimming with the foot guards Trey ordered to track my every move, my question instigates a collective gasp. Nikolai's men never speak Vladimir's name. It is as if he never existed. But my use of his name isn't the only reason they're gasping. It is my assumption that Vladimir is alive.

"The fact Maxsim orchestrated a takeover bid on soil not commanded by the Popov entity shows he's scared."

Maddox adds to Trey's reply. "That's why he came in hard. Even with Nikolai traveling light, he knew the odds were stacked against him."

Trey nods, agreeing with him.

I'm not as eager to side with either of them. "That wasn't what I asked. I want to know the repercussions if Vladimir is alive. What does it mean for Nikolai and the rules he's forced to abide by?" My words choke at the end.

"Forced" is too kind a word to describe how Nikolai was coerced to toe the line.

"Tortured" is more suitable.

Trey's chest rises and falls three times before he shrugs. "I don't know."

It isn't the answer I'm hoping for, but it is better than the theories running through my head. Vladimir believes in the rules Anatoly enforced when founding their dynasty, but only because they were created in favor of the ruler. If that man is no longer him, I have no doubt he'll skirt them just as he has prosecution the past fifty-plus years.

Any chance for more chitchat is lost when our SUV stops

behind a dense layer of trees. Although the airstrip on our right is battered, there are signs it has been recently used, most notably: the twelve-seater front propel aircraft tucked into a hangar concealed with camouflage tarps and tree limbs. The poor condition of the plane proves the Vasilievs have fallen far from the power Alexei once commanded, but it's more than some crews have.

My eyes drift from the plane to Trey when he updates the men. "Infrared sensors indicate a dozen and a half men in a room at the back of the hangar." He points to the far-right corner of the hand-drawn map he's holding. "There are another half-dozen circling the premise. They need to be taken down first—in silence."

Two men strapped with high-caliber weapons and face paint dip their chins before disappearing into the forest flanking our SUVs. For the direction they're heading, I can only assume they're going to take out the men with long-range rifles.

"The dome on the main property appears to be a bunker, but no visible signs of life have been noticed. But just in case, we'll keep three men on the main road and another two on this little side track. We all know how fond Nikolai is of going over a mountain instead of around it, so we need to keep our minds open."

I smile, grateful he said how fond he "is," not "was."

"What is this?" I point to a clump of red in the middle of a green-and-yellow space.

Trey breathes out deeply. "From their lack of movement the past hour, we assume they are hostages."

"They? As in more than one?" Maddox asks, beating me to the punch.

Trey nods, then screws up his face. "That or someone with a large body mass."

"Could it be Nikolai?" The hope in my voice can't be denied.

My eyes burn when Trey replies, "How about we find out?"

I nod so hard tears roll down my cheeks. The tension teeming from the men flanking me will quickly dry them, but I drag my hand down my face just in case they don't. They're already annoyed at Trey's request to babysit me. I don't want to give them more reasons to hate me.

"Not a scratch, Justine," Trey warns for the final time.

He waits for me to nod before signaling for his men to move. As we race across waist-high grass, I brace my gun high as I've been taught. My determination to protect myself is utterly pointless. The number of men surrounding me means the only people at threat are the ones sworn to protect me. Even Maddox can't see past their guard.

It's probably for the best. The noise is nearly deafening when we reach the hangar. Bullets whizz in all directions as the smell of death amplifies.

I want to say my heart is sitting in my throat because I'm mortified by the pained cries shrilling through my ears, but that would be a lie. It's our approach toward the room I pointed out minutes ago—the one Trey believes may have hostages inside.

Please let Nikolai be alive and safe in there.

"Drop!"

A man named Zoran grips my head, pulls me into his chest, then fires a shot over my right shoulder. He then spins me like a ballerina until I land into Maddox's chest, before executing a man charging toward our huddle with a machete in his hand.

Clearly he's insane. Who in their right mind goes against men brandishing guns with a handheld weapon?

Zoran's break from the circle allows me to catch a glimpse of the carnage occurring outside of my safety bubble. Nikolai's men have a clear advantage over the dozen or so men ambushed without warning. Half lay slayed on the ground, whereas the other half are in the process of surrendering—their fight over before it truly began.

"Wait," Maddox warns when I attempt to break free from his hold to move toward the padlocked door on my right. "Let Trey clear the room first."

I glare at him in stunned horror when he gestures silently to Trey. If I didn't know any better, I'd swear he's participated in mob ambushes before.

Although I have a million thoughts streaming through my head, none matter when Trey and three men make their way to the locked room. With all threats neutralized, Maddox and I can trace their footsteps.

The swirls of my stomach ramp up with every inch of ground we cover. I don't pay any attention to the deceased men lying lifeless on the bloodstained concrete or hear a word Trey is saying as he directs his men to swarm the room after a bullet buckles the padlock. The only thing I can hear is my raging heart and the prayer I've said on repeat since I woke up dazed and confused over seven hours ago.

Please let Nikolai be alive.

Some of my prayers are answered when I enter the room on the heels of Maddox, but they aren't my greatest wish. With the eyes of a murderer and a clutch on Trey's throat that reveals he's minutes from killing him, Rico pins Trey to the inner wall of his room. His hold is so firm Trey's feet dangle midair, and the life drains from his eyes in under a second.

"Stop!" I demand, shocked I'm the only one acting on instincts.

Several armed men are in the room, but not one attempts to stop Rico's wrath. I understand their objection. Nikolai gave Rico a full pardon, which means no one can touch him, but that doesn't mean they can sit by and watch Trey be attacked—*does it?*

"He's one of us!" My endeavor to pry Rico's hand from Trey's neck has my nails piercing his skin, but I don't back down.

As blood trickles down Rico's wrist, his almost-black eyes drift to me. I swallow numerous times in a row, shocked by the intensity bursting from his eyes. He appears as though he's been swallowed by a giant black hole.

"It's me, Justine." Big breaths separate my words. I'm genuinely panicked. "We're here to help you. Where are Blaire and Eli?" When Rico blinks at the mention of his wife, I know I am getting through to him. "Where is your kitten, Rico?"

Trey's windpipe squeaks when Rico suddenly releases him from his grip. He falls to the ground in a heap, torn between breathing and ending Rico's ability to breathe. The tension brimming between them is so intense it's even hard for me to breathe.

"It's okay," I assure both men, although I'm truly unsure if it is.

The width of Rico's eyes reveals his actions aren't his own, much less the puncture wounds in his arm. He's injured, drugged, and fighting the urge to go on a rampage. He's the most dangerous he's ever been.

My brows furrow when my scan of his body reveals a snapped chain on his left wrist. The width of the chain should have made it impossible for a human to snap, but I'll never underestimate the determination of a man trying to protect his family. Nikolai could be on his deathbed, and he'd still fight to keep me safe.

When Rico moves to the side of the room, his steps sloth-like and pained, I signal the men surrounding him to stand down. He could have snapped Trey's neck, but he didn't. That proves the man inside him is stronger than his outer shell.

"Jesus Christ," I murmur under my breath when Rico tosses a king-size mattress across the room as if it is a feather.

His strength isn't what has me choking back tears. It's the image of his wife and son huddled together causing my sobbing response. From how the dirt around them is swirling, it is evident that Rico used his body to shelter them.

"Get the SUVs," I demand before racing across the room. Blaire and Eli aren't moving, but they both have a pulse. It's faint but there all the same. "We need to get them medical treatment ASAP."

Recognizing we're here to help them, Rico lifts an unconscious Blaire into his arms. In comparison to his wide, heavily panting chest, she looks like a tiny, fragile doll.

"It's okay," I assure Rico when he also tries to pick up Eli. "We've got him."

I'm sure he can handle both of them, but with his shredded shirt incapable of hiding the large knife wound in his stomach, I'd rather he didn't.

I signal for Maddox to help me with Eli. He's not heavy. My body is just shaking so much that I don't trust myself not to drop him.

As we make our way to the SUVs Trey ordered to the front of the hangar, Rico eyes the man kneeling at the feet of their captors. His glare warns them their surrender will not be the end of their fight. He's out for blood. He's just putting his family first—for now.

I've only just closed the car door with a safe Rico, Blaire, and Eli inside when someone darting past me captures my attention. I should demand Trey to come with me, but with my instincts in overdrive, I take off after the person breaking through thick scrub at the side of the hangar.

"Maya?" My voice is weak, as unsure of my question as my hazy mind's assumption it is her.

Why would Maya be here? It makes no sense at all.

Seconds before a thick tree trunk hides her from my view, Maya cranks her neck back to peer at me. I chase after her, certain no amount of haze would make me mistake her face. I've interacted with her numerous times in the past twelve months and see her more as a friend than a member of Nikolai's staff.

My mad dash through the heavily treed property stops when accented voices capture my attention.

They're not French like Maya.

They're Russian.

"Whoa there, little lady. Slow down."

A man with a half-smoked cigarette hanging from his mouth grips Maya's shoulders, stopping her endeavor to reach a group of all-terrain vehicles in the far back corner. They're grouped behind half a dozen tents.

"Why are you in such a hurry? Anyone would swear you're outrunning a ghost."

When his eyes stray in the direction Maya came from, I step back. A thousand belligerent rants run through my head when a tree limb snaps under my boot.

In a standard setting, the crack of a branch wouldn't be a concern. But here, surrounded by members of the crew we've just taken down, it is the equivalent of a death sentence.

"What was that?" The same man holding Maya hostage wiggles his fingers at two men slouched in lawn chairs who have seen better days.

"It's probably a squirrel," Maya suggests, her tone panicked. "You know how rampant they are around these parts."

Her reply reveals that they've been camped out here for a while. I don't know if that is a good or bad thing.

The man's lips purse. "Probably, but there's no harm in checking. We don't want your toes getting nibbled while you're sleeping." He taps Maya's nose with his index finger. It isn't a flirty gesture, but it isn't how a captor would treat a hostage either.

Panic sets in when he releases Maya from his hold before nudging his head my way. "Sweep the area."

"If we find anything?"

The man asking the question smiles a slick grin when the commander replies, "Kill it, skin it, then bring it back here for me to marvel at."

A dark-haired man cleans a butcher knife on his jeans while muttering, "It'll be my pleasure."

Even with a thick layer of bush between us, Maya's eyes lock with mine. She gives me a warning look that advises me they'll follow through with their threat if they catch me. It has my feet moving faster than my heart, concern about snapping branches the last thing on my mind.

Hearing my brisk departure, more than a dozen men chase me on foot while another three fire up their all-terrain vehicles. The gun I tucked into the back of my pants feels heavy, but I can't summon the courage to pull it out and fire it. I need to keep running, to reach Trey and Nikolai's men before they're ambushed without notice.

"Trey!" I scream at the top of my lungs, his short name coming out as if it is ten times longer. "They're coming!"

My last word is sliced in half when I'm suddenly clutched from the side. I'm thrown against a tree trunk so forcefully any air left in my lungs evacuates in a sharp breath.

Pop. Pop.

The man about to grab me falls to the ground with blood trickling between his eyes.

I'm grabbed, dropped to the ground, and then squished by a firm body before another three bangs set my hearing back a decade.

Bang. Bang. Bang.

My heart rate skyrockets when the man lying on top of me snarls, "*Убейте их всех, но спасите ее.*"

He rolls us three times, our tumble looking like a couple rolling down a meadow field on a cloudless romantic day.

Pop. Pop.

Roll.

Pop. Pop.

And so the pattern continues until the man's raging heart is replaced with the panicked shrill of my brother calling my name.

"I'm over here. I'm okay." Although I'm on the verge of being squashed to death.

As if he heard my private thoughts, the man sheltering me with his body tilts back. My brows furrow when I take in his features. His shaggy dark hair, icy eyes, and chiseled jawline aren't registering as familiar, but I swear I've seen him before.

"Are you okay?"

I grimace, hating that his deep timbre was felt on a region of my body that shouldn't be attached to his.

Worry that we look intimate flies out the window when I shift my head to the side. There is a deceased body directly beside us. How do I know the man is dead if his green eyes are open? The perfect circle singed between his blond brows.

"Not a bad shot for a limp-dicked balding bastard, hey?"

My eyes snap forward as my heart stops beating. "Asher?"

With a cocky wink, the man lying on top of me nods.

"Is Nikolai with you?"

The smug expression on his face fades before he shakes his head. "But we're clearly on the right path."

He rolls off me before standing to his feet. Leaves fall from my back when he hoists me off the ground without seeking permission.

While Trey and Maddox silently reprimand me for leaving their post, Trey requests an update from his crew. My interest piques when he asks, "Any signs of Maxsim?"

A ginger-haired man with pasty-white skin shakes his head. "No, but I bet she knows where he is." He yanks Maya forward, his shove so aggressive she falls to her knees.

"I don't know anything—" Maya's words are cut off by the butt of the ginger's gun skating across her temple.

"Don't!"

The man's furious growl at my demand simpers to a purr when Asher growls at him in Russian that he'll slice his tendons if he so much as looks at me in the wrong manner.

"Nikolai may not be here to punish you, but that does not mean I won't," Asher continues to warn, unaware I am multilingual.

After swallowing harshly, the unnamed man asks, "Nikolai's?"

"Yes," numerous men reply in sync.

When the man steps back in fear, I approach Maya. The blood streaming down the left side of her face makes me squeamish, but I push aside my annoying neurosis. I don't have time for childish responses.

"This wasn't supposed to happen," Maya whispers in French when I raise her head via her chin. "He said he loved me and that he was going to give me what I deserved." She hiccups numerous times in a row. "No one was meant to die. It wasn't meant to be like this."

"Who promised you, Maya? Maxsim?"

Salty water mingles with blood when she nods.

I take in a relieved breath. This explains how Maxsim knew so much about Nikolai's private life. Maya's presence at the Popov compound is so ghost-like that everyone talks freely around her. It isn't that they trust her. They just never saw her as a threat. Enslaved women aren't known for their gusto.

Not wanting our conversation overheard, Maya communicates with me in French. "I tried to help. I-I promise. When I heard what was happening, I tried to stop it." Her stuttering makes it hard to decipher what she's saying, but I get the gist of it.

I squeeze her hand, believing the honesty in her eyes. "This was too big for you, Maya. You should have reached out to Trey or me."

Her lip quivers as she replies, "I was going to, but when you and Nikolai escaped, I thought you'd come back for Rico."

My heart rate jumps. "Nikolai? He was here?" In my excitement, I express my question in English.

When Maya nods, Trey steps forward. "When?"

"*Il y a trois jours.*"

"Three days ago?" I double-check.

Maya nods again.

"Was he okay?" Nothing but hope rings in my tone.

Color drains from her face before she shakes her head. "He wasn't well." Confusion crosses her features before she asks, "How do you not know that? You were with him. You were the last person to see him alive."

The confused suspicion in her voice makes the wooziness clouding my head double. What she is saying can't be true. I'd remember. Nikolai isn't a man you easily forget. She must be mistaken. If Nikolai had been with me three days ago, he would have been found with me. I wouldn't abandon him—especially if he's injured.

Maya isn't the one peering at me in skepticism. Several pairs of eyes are glaring at me, some more angry than wary.

"If I knew where he was, I'd tell you," I half sob, half shout to the men glaring at me through lowered lashes. "I don't know where he is. I don't remember anything!"

Recognizing that I'm struggling to keep it together, Maddox

aids me to my feet before guiding me back to our idling SUVs. I hear a handful of men snicker about this being the first time a queen has beheaded a king, but they're too cowardly to say it loud enough for Trey or Asher to hear.

I'd retaliate, but I'm too tired, hungry, and heartbroken to deal with their stupidity. They'll suffer for their idiocy when I return their king to his throne. Their punishment will be as ugly as the bloodstained soil squishing beneath my feet.

They'll pay for their stupidity with their lives, and I'll be their executioner.

19

JUSTINE

The further our SUV travels down the unbeaten path, the thicker the black veins strangling my heart grow. They're treating me like a fool, like their death will be the first one I've orchestrated.

They shouldn't underestimate me. Nikolai was right. When forced between killing or being killed, you must always choose the former. That's what I did during our escape. I placed us above anyone. I chose to fight instead of cowering like I did five years ago. I killed a man to save the one I love.

Trey's eyes shift to me when I sit straighter in my seat. That's my first memory since I was found, and it opens a floodgate for many more...

"Ангел..." Shuffling rings through my ears seconds before wetness hits my cheeks. "Wake up. You need to be ready to move. This could be our only chance to escape."

Worried by the panic in Nikolai's voice, I flutter open my eyes and rise to a half-seated position. My throat burns like it's on fire, but it has nothing on the pain spasming in my stomach. I feel like I've taken a cannonball to my gut. It is warm to the touch and back-bending painful.

"Are you sore?"

Not waiting for me to respond, Nikolai counts my pulse thrumming in my neck.

"Your cheeks aren't as red as earlier, but I'd say you still have a fever." He snags an untouched bottle of water from his side before rolling it to me. "Drink only a little, okay?"

Nodding, I do as requested. The water is heaven to my parched throat but wreaks havoc on my stomach. It makes my cramps so intense it takes all my effort not to bend in half.

After forcefully swallowing the water with a grimace, I lower the bottle from my lips and return it to Nikolai.

"Better?" he asks.

Although I'm unsure what the hell is going on, I nod. "I think so. What's that smell?"

My eyes snap to him when he says, "Jet fuel."

Spotting nothing but honesty in his eyes, I scan our location. We appear to be in a tin box. Discarded ropes scratch my left thigh, and some blankets that most airlines used in the nineties are spread across the metal floor I'm sitting on.

The knocks keep coming when Nikolai advises, "We're in the stow of a plane. They started their descent approximately ten minutes ago. I've been trying to wake you since."

My stomach launches into my throat when he gathers a shank-like instrument in his hand. The metal has been sharpened so profoundly that I wouldn't be shocked to discover he's been working on it for hours.

"How long have we been in the air?" I choke on the last half of my statement when he spins to face me. He's bleeding—a lot!

"You're hurt!"

Air whizzes between my teeth when the clanging of metal thwarts my attempt to assess his wound. I'm chained to the underbelly of the plane. When my wide eyes return to Nikolai, I notice he too is detained.

"If I weren't afraid of puncturing the shit-box we're in, I would have removed them hours ago. Alas, their lack of funds forced me to be more inventive." His voice is deeper than usual, and his struggle is physically seen on his face. He's with me, but his mind is in a very dark, tormented place.

The thick material circling my wrist digs into my skin when I stretch with all my might to plant my lips on Nikolai's. His deep *exhalation when my mouth lands on his dries the moisture on my cheeks. It also reveals I made the right choice.*

The briefest alignment of our lips brings him back to me. Not wholly, but he's more recognizable than he was mere seconds ago.

After staring into his eyes so he can see the faith I have in him, I ask, "What do you need me to do?"

"Kiss me again," he answers without delay.

With a smile, I do precisely that.

We're detained, but nothing can keep us apart.

You can't break two souls destined for one another.

Our kiss is barely a peck, but the emotions it ignites make it seem so much more.

"Now?" I ask after drawing back for the second time.

Nikolai appears to want to kiss me again, but our bumpy return to solid ground keeps his focus on the task at hand. "When they come to collect us, I need you to distract the guard."

"Okay... Why?"

With the grin of an insane man, Nikolai waves his shiv in the air.

His smile sags when I ask, "You're just going to stun him, right?"

"When forced between being killed or killing, you must always choose the latter, Ангел. These men are going to kill us. Or worse..." The panic in his eyes reveals the words his mouth refuses to express. Death will be the kindest thing they'll do to us tonight.

"Okay. I'll do it."

I've barely talked my heart into my plans when keys jingling sounds through my ears. Someone is unlocking the cargo hold of the plane.

Seconds before the hatch opens, a name is called. "Maxsim!"

The door slams shut, partially blocking out the female confronting him. I can't hear what she says, but I'm reasonably sure her accent is French.

Fighting the cramps shooting across my stomach, I scoot closer to the escape hatch. The chain circling my wrist pinches my skin, but my new position awards me snippets of the couple's conversation.

"What did you do? This wasn't our plan. You said no one would get hurt."

Maxsim mutters something back, but his words are too low for me to hear them. *They appear commanding yet sorrowful. Perhaps even torn.*

"No! This isn't what I wanted. I only ever wanted you, but you've let greed get the best of you by becoming someone you swore you'd never be. You are your father!"

My heart shatters when a slap breaks through the shouting. It is so loud my cheek stings.

Feet shuffling breaks over my raging heart before I hear, "Maya, wait!"

My eyes jackknife back to Nikolai. His ticking jaw and narrowed eyes reveal that Maxsim's scream was loud enough for him to hear. It also reveals the unlikelihood that he'll believe my claim that there are thousands of Mayas in the world and that she may not be Nikolai's half-sister.

That may be true, but one with a French accent in the middle of a mafia war is highly improbable.

Another ten minutes pass before the jingling of keys returns to our ears.

"Convince him to get close enough to us that I can grab him," *Nikolai instructs as he primes himself to appear as if he's unconscious.*

I nod mere seconds before the hatch swings open. The man entering isn't Maxsim, but I recognize him. He's the goon who held a gun to Eli's temple earlier tonight.

"Come on, wake up, pretty boy. It's time to get the party started." *He tosses a can of beer at Nikolai's head, too scared to approach him even with him being shackled and injured.*

"Argh!" *I clutch my stomach, finally acknowledging the pain tearing me in two.*

I wish this was part of my ploy. Unfortunately, that isn't the case. I'm in immense pain and suddenly in grave fear for our baby.

My screamed howls gain me the attention of both Nikolai and the guard. Nikolai eyes me cautiously, unsure if I have exemplary acting skills or if I'm in genuine pain.

The guard is nowhere near as worried. He saunters my way, his steps as arrogant as the expression on his abhorrent face. He's relishing my pain, loving it as much as Nikolai despises it.

"Save your tears, princess. We don't want them all used up

before we've had our fun. Some whores' tears are tastier than their cunts."

When he leans in to gather a blob of moisture sitting high on my cheek, Nikolai makes his move. He rises from the ground as if weightless, his movements so sleek the guard is none the wiser to the fact that he's about to be struck by a cobra.

It only dawns on him he's being stalked when the metal knife Nikolai crafted with his bare hand colors the steel walls surrounding us with his blood. He falls to his knees, his hands shooting up to clutch the vibrant red line stretching from one of his ears to the next.

When he continues dropping, I shuffle back. The blood seeping from his wound warrants a frightened response, much less the gargled screams tearing from his throat. Even seconds from death, he hasn't forgotten his honor. He's calling out for help, alerting his crew of our plans to escape.

Nikolai attempts to silence his warning with his fists, but with his chain only allowing him to reach his legs, the task is left to me. With our baby's safety at the forefront of my mind, I curl my hands over the unnamed man's mouth and nose. He thrashes and kicks against me, but nothing will stop me from silencing him. If I don't seek medical attention within the hour, I doubt our baby will make it through the night.

Tears roll down my face unchecked when the stranger gives up his will to live. His legs are the first thing to still, closely followed by his chest. By the time his hands flop from his neck, I've shed enough tears to fill a river.

I just killed a man.

Me.

Nikolai may have slit his throat, but I placed the final nail in his coffin.

Sickened with remorse, I slump against the wall I'm chained to. I can't breathe through the guilt clutching my throat. I'm seconds from asphyxiation.

"Ангел." Since I'm at the furthest point of my tether, Nikolai can't reach me... but his words can. "You did what needed to be done. There's no shame in that."

My drenched eyes stray to his. "I-I-I killed him."

"No," Nikolai denies, shaking his head. "You saved me. And our baby. You did what needed to be done. You chose right."

If I had the strength, I'd argue with him, but the cramps that rendered me near unconscious minutes ago haven't weakened in the slightest. I'm either miscarrying or bleeding internally. I really hope it is the latter.

"What now?" *I ask, desperate to get out of here.*

He nudges his head to the frozen goon. "Check his pockets. He came in here to collect us so he'd have keys for our locks."

I lick my dry lips before doing as instructed.

Nikolai is right. He has a set of rusted padlock keys in his pocket.

"Toss them to me."

Not even two seconds later, Nikolai frees himself from his constraints before falling to his knees beside me. He removes the chains from my right wrist before pulling me into his chest.

His familiar scent causes a flurry of new tears to sting my eyes. It hurts knowing I ended the life of another, but in all honesty, I'd do it again if it achieved the same outcome.

Nikolai's hot breath fans my temple when he murmurs, "Let's get you out of here."

He waits for me to nod, before gathering my hand in the one not clutching his weapon. He holds it as possessively as he does me. It may only be a shard of metal, but it is the only thing we have standing between us and a dozen men determined to kill us.

While pressing his finger to his lips, he peers out the partially cracked-open door. I hear his teeth grind together when the door gives out a squeak upon opening. It's loud but not loud enough to be heard over the jubilant cheers of drunken men celebrating a victory they have not yet won.

After crawling through the tight opening, Nikolai helps me out. In silence, he surveys the area. Since most of the noise comes from our left, we head to our right.

Blood is pumping through his veins so hard and fast I can feel it through our conjoined hands. He wants to go on a rampage, but since getting me to safety is more critical than his need to kill, he's moving away from the men he wants to maim.

As we weave through the industrial-sized airport hangar, I try to get my footsteps to match Nikolai's noiseless ones. It's virtually impossible. I sound like an elephant trampling through Africa. It isn't because the Popovs' housemaids have added a few pounds to my frame in the past twelve months. It's because every step I take is done in pain.

"Just a little further, Ангел," he assures as his hand clutching his shiv darts up to slow the blood oozing from his wound.

I'd caution him to be careful, but I doubt his knife could inflict any more damage to his shoulder. It's hanging by a thread, the mottling of his skin indicating it's infected.

Our stomps across the sloshy ground quicken when a Russian cuss word shrills through the night. It's closely followed by the news that we've escaped.

We're about to dart through a stack of old airplane parts when a mouse-like voice says, "This way."

Maya is standing in the shadows, gesturing with her hand for us to follow her. Her face is marked with tears, but their angry red streaks can't hide the handprint covering the majority of her left cheek.

With my trust low but my desperation high, I wordlessly suggest Nikolai accept Maya's assistance. We're already in dire straits, so I can't see matters getting any worse.

"Quickly," Maya begs in French while steering us through the dense forest next to the hangar.

I understand her urgency. The further we travel, the louder the barks of angry dogs become.

My worst nightmare is coming true. I'm running in the dark, striving to outrace the beast who's already scarred me.

And that's not the worst of it. Nikolai is losing a lot of blood— more than enough to kill him.

"Here. Go." Maya shoves a set of keys into my hand before nudging her head to an old truck barely visible in the pitch-black sky. "Quickly."

With Nikolai barely coherent, I clutch the keys, hug Maya for some inane reason, and then make my way to the driver's seat. Nikolai attempts a protest, but a bullet whizzing past his head steals his words. He lurches into the passenger seat before demanding that I floor it.

For an old truck, it's quick off the mark. We shoot down a bumpy dirt road within a nanosecond, our tails chased by men on all-terrain vehicles.

"Keep your eyes forward," Nikolai instructs when my constant staring in the rearview mirror nearly makes us crash into a tree.

He yanks on the steering wheel, straightening our tires, before he searches the truck for a weapon. His hunt comes up victorious when he finds a Glock in the glove compartment. From a distance, it would be pointless. But for the vehicle approaching on our left, it will come in handy.

"Lean back."

I sink into my seat a mere second before Nikolai fires the Glock. Even with his pupils filling his corneas, his aim is perfect. The driver's slumped frame sees his four-wheel-drive veering to the left before it bursts into flames upon impact with a large tree trunk.

The scene continues to unfold like an action-packed blockbuster. Nikolai takes down another three men in a similar fashion, his fight only ending when he runs out of bullets.

"What now?"

"Keep driving."

Nikolai dumps the empty Glock on the truck's floor before searching its interior for the second time. I don't know what he is looking for, but I doubt he'll find it here. There is nothing but a torn picnic blanket, a pack of half-smoked cigarettes, and a metal gas can.

"Seriously?" I screech when he gathers the three items I mentioned in his hands. "You're not MacGyver."

He flashes a grin that shows why I fell for him so quickly. He has a devilish and highly appealing body and face, but his insides reveal nothing but a little boy dying to be loved. "Who do you think I learned the statistics of killing a man with a fork from?"

"Ah... your criminally insane father?"

Nikolai's grin doubles. I really wish he'd stop smiling. I'm already lightheaded from eyeing the copious amount of blood seeping into his shirt. I don't need more distractions.

Recalling our dangerous situation, I return my eyes front and center. They've just adjusted to the darkness when a dog darts across the dirt road we're traveling.

I yank my steering wheel to the right with barely a second to spare.

It isn't the best decision I've ever made.

We're heading straight toward the edge of a cliff.

As I slam on the brakes, we're bumped from behind by the SUV *tailing us. Fear surges through me when they plow into us a second time. I maintain pressure on the brakes, but my willpower has nothing on the goons' determination.*

They've spotted an opening to end us without bullets, and they're running for it.

I stop clutching the steering wheel the instant the truck's front tires careen over the gorge. I can't steer us out of this, but I can protect my stomach from additional impact. It won't do our baby any good if I'm dead, but at least the baby will know I did everything in my power to protect him or her.

The world slows as we roll to our imminent deaths. Nikolai's roared shout of my name, his clamber across the cracked vinyl seat separating us, even the weaving of his fingers through my hair occurs in slow motion. His hold is peaceful—almost surreal.

I'm so out of my mind I don't realize what Nikolai is doing until hot Las Vegas air streams through my nostrils from him throwing open the truck's door to propel us out of the wreckage.

We sail through the air like hang gliders, the brutal impact of Nikolai's back with a tree trunk the only thing slowing our descent...

My thoughts return to the present when my temple collides with the window of the SUV.

"Damn dog. Get out of the fucking way." Trey corrects the swerve he took to avoid a white dog sitting in the middle of the road, before lifting his eyes to the rearview mirror to ensure I'm okay.

The bones in my neck squeal when I crank my head back to the dog. He's one of those shepherding breeds, bred to protect herds of sheep. He's big and white and seems oddly familiar.

"Stop!"

My scream scares the living daylights out of Trey. He slams on the brakes so fast the SUV tailing us nearly rearends us.

The dust kicking up from the abrupt stop scratches my eyes when I fling open my door. I dash through the dust cloud to scan the surrounding area.

For the most part, it looks like barren land, but there are telltale signs corroborating my belief that this is the land Nikolai and I raced across during our escape. There are small tire marks similar to the ones of the all-terrain vehicles that chased us down. A tree on the horizon has char marks halfway up its trunk and is missing a chunk of bark right at the spot where a vehicle may have impacted it. And bullet casings are glistening in the low-hanging sun.

"There's a gorge somewhere near here. Nikolai is in that gorge."

Not having the time or the eagerness to answer the numerous silent questions being slung at me, I return to the SUV to gather the maps inside. The useless ones roll off the SUV's hood, but I firmly grip the topographic map. It shows the elevations and falls of the land surrounding us, meaning within seconds, I have a better idea of which direction we should be heading.

"Here. Our truck went over the edge around here." I circle a section of the map with the biggest change in altitude.

When Trey demands the men reenter the SUVs, a handful of voices grumble a protest, but one is too loud to ignore. "Are you all fucking clueless? Can't you see she's taking us on a wild goose chase, hoping we won't realize she's orchestrated all of this?"

"That's enough, Ethan."

I swipe my hand through the air, cutting Trey off. "Let him speak." I step closer to Ethan. The fight I displayed when silencing the guards' screams is all over my face. "Because they may be the last words he ever speaks."

When Ethan attempts to get up in my face, Trey and Maddox step into his path. Asher doesn't budge an inch, but he does unholster his gun. Ethan may be a member of Nikolai's crew, but that won't stop Asher from taking him down if he steps out of place.

"I get it, all right? You want your king back." Tears spring in my eyes when a collective hum sounds through the thirty or so men circling me. "So the fuck do I. That's what I've been trying to do since you found me. I don't want to take Nikolai's place! I want him to come home! If you don't want the same thing, then leave, go, but be assured, if you do leave, you'll *never* be welcomed back."

My eyes drift around the men watching me with interest. "The instant I became Nikolai's, I became a Bratva. That means I'm as much your family as I am Nikolai's. When one of us goes down, we all go down. That's the Bratva way. So you need to make a choice. Either fight alongside me to bring Nikolai home, or walk away like a coward. Those are your *only* options."

I dart into Trey's car, denying anyone the chance to see my tears. I'm not crying because I fear what state I'll find Nikolai in. It is the growl of his men as they prepare for battle.

My speech inspired them as much as Nikolai's honor does. They're going to bring him home no matter the cost—either dead or alive.

The last part of my statement kills me more than the pain stabbing my stomach.

20

JUSTINE

"There!" Maddox points to a divot in the dusty field. It's a similar groove to what tires make when the driver brakes hard.

"Does anything around here seem familiar?"

I leave the vehicle to deliberate on Trey's question more thoroughly.

The landscape is different from what I recalled in my memory, but we did flee in the middle of the night, so the visibility was poor.

"Over here," Zoran shouts from his post on the edge of a deep gorge.

Rock crumbles beneath my feet when I and thirty of Nikolai's men lean over a crumbling rock face to take in a burned-out truck a hundred yards down.

"He's here," I whisper when a sense of home overwhelms me.

"Be careful," Asher demands when I track down a narrow path on the side of the gorge.

"Get rope, water, and a hoist," Trey instructs him before following after me.

Although Asher isn't a fan of being bossed around, he takes Trey's dominance in stride—*barely*.

Since Trey's feet are wider than mine, he has to use the vines and trees growing out of the rock sideways to maintain his footing.

Watching him trudge through the hostile landscape has my second memory of the day smacking into me...

"*Don't move.*" *Painful breaths separate Nikolai's words, but they also can't hide the urgency of his statement.*

My head is thumping so bad you'd swear I've been knocked out for hours, but the Russian accents above my head prove that isn't the case.

The men responsible for forcing our truck over the edge are shining spotlights down on us, wanting to ensure the gorge did what they couldn't. They would have spotted us if it weren't for a group of trees growing through the cracked rocks.

Unhappy with the crumpled remains of the truck, a thick voice says, "Send someone down there to make sure they're dead."

The crunching of rocks underfoot sounds through my ears a few seconds later. A young boy barely of teen years slowly makes his way down a goat track etched in the side of the gorge. He has a rope wrapped around his waist, but that's as far as his safety measures go.

"Shh." Nikolai squashes his finger to my lips.

When I nod, he sneaks closer to the boy minutes from discovering our hidey-hole. I have no clue what his plan is, but I'm reasonably sure it won't end well for the teen.

As Nikolai is about to pounce, a massive explosion lights up the gorge. The blast is so epic the smell of singed hair lingers in my nostrils.

"Woo-hoo!" The teen throws his arms into the air.

He acts like an grade-A asshole, like the loss of our lives is worth celebrating.

He's lucky the explosion coincides with his exit, or it would have been me pouncing on him unaware.

The flames roaring up the gorge dim to barely a campfire brightness before the spotlights shining above our heads fade.

Within seconds, we're left in silence. All I hear is the noise of Nikolai collapsing.

"Nikolai."

I race to him, the uneven ground not enough of a deterrent to stop me from reaching him.

"Oh god." My visual of his thigh bone piercing his jeans is too sickening for a mature response. "Why didn't you say something? You're hurt. You can't walk with a bone sticking out of your leg."

My panicked rant stops when he says, "I had to protect you. Nothing will stop me from keeping you safe."

His sentence ends in a growl from me applying pressure to the top half of his thigh. "You need to suck it up. You're bleeding from too many areas. You'll bleed out if we don't stop it."

I don't know whether to kiss him or punch him when he laughs. "You can't get rid of me that easily. You're stuck with me for eternity, remember?"

God, I hope so.

After bracing his back on the wall, he says, "We need a splint, something to hold the bone straight and stop the bleeding."

I don't want to know why he's so knowledgeable on broken bone management, but unfortunately, I already am. His medical records expose how many horrible injuries he suffered during his childhood.

"Will this work?" I hold up two decently wide sticks lying on the ground next to us.

Nikolai nods. "Now we need something to strap them to my leg."

I scan every inch of the land visible in the moonlight. A handful of vines are lying around, but I don't see them helping. They're too fragile to knot.

"What about my skirt?" I suggest, waving my hand over the material covered with soot and ash.

"No, Ангел. When my men come, I don't want to send them packing so they don't see you like that." His hot breath fans my lips when he growls, "I don't share," in Russian.

"Seriously?" I roll my eyes. "You're being ridiculous. You either rip it, or I'll remove it entirely."

Glaring at him, I shove the hem of my skirt into his hands. I'm cramping and hormonal.

Now is not the time to mess with me.

Realizing I'll never scare a fearless man into obeying me, I try another tactic. "Come on, Nikolai, don't act like you haven't been fantasizing about tearing it off me all night."

Just when I think he'll never agree with my demand, the sound of cotton ripping echoes in the silence of the night. He doesn't shred my skirt off me like he did in the plane earlier this week. He just weakens the hemline enough that a rope-like material hangs halfway down my thighs a few seconds later.

After an additional tug, he hands the shredded material to me. "Now we both win."

I roll my eyes while circling it around his leg.

"Sorry," *I repeatedly apologize when I use it to constrict the blood flow to his thigh.* "Is it too tight?"

Nikolai shakes his head, preferring to lie without words. I don't need to hear his words to know he's in pain, though. I can see it in his eyes. He's hurting badly, both physically and mentally.

I remove a bead of sweat from his brow before asking, "Now what?"

He balances his back against the rock face he had me pinned to minutes ago before drawing me into his chest.

I accept his comfort but do it without placing any of my weight on him. He has a broken leg and a bullet wound in his shoulder. He shouldn't be sitting upright, much less sheltering me.

"Now we rest until our men find us." *His low, shallow breaths as he struggles to remain conscious lull me to sleep within minutes...*

"This way. He's over here."

Trey signals to the men watching our every move from above to make sure we're heading in the right direction before he follows me to the ledge Nikolai and I spent the night huddled on. The only thing is, Nikolai isn't there.

"Are you sure this is the right spot?"

I nod before all of Trey's question leaves his mouth. There's a strand of cotton the same color as my skirt floating between the leaves of the tree we camped under, and the blood Nikolai's shirt failed to absorb gives the earth-toned rock a red tint.

"He was here. This is where we rested last night."

"Three nights ago," Trey prompts, reminding me of the lapse in my timeline.

I nod, truly confused. "Despite our conflicting times, Nikolai should be here. He has a broken leg. He couldn't travel far."

Air leaves my lungs in a hurry when Trey says, "He would for you."

My heart squeezes in my chest. "He would," I agree. "As I would for him."

As the low-hanging sun casts hues of orange around me, I return to my earlier memory. It's just several hours later...

"Nikolai." Not wanting to agitate his wounds, I gently shake his uninjured shoulder. "It's morning. We need to wake up."

Fear rains down on me when he fails to answer. Nikolai has been called many things, but ignorant isn't one of them.

I shake him again, a little harder this time. "Nikolai. Please wake up."

My hand shakes furiously when I raise it to his neck to check for a pulse. He has one, although it is incredibly faint.

"You need to hold on a little longer, okay? Help is on its way." I hope.

Peeling his shirt back from his chest, I check his bullet wound. The blood trickling out of the hole is only lukewarm to the touch. He's going into shock.

Oh god. This isn't good.

With my mind spiraling, I scream, "Help!"

I don't care if my alerted cries make the men trying to kill us return. Any help is better than none.

"We're down here! We're alive! You didn't kill us!"

Nothing but the echoes of my words pierce my ears.

While circling my temples, I pace the minimal ground I have access to while contemplating what to do. Nikolai said we must wait for his men, but what if they don't arrive in time? He needs surgery and, at the very least, a blood transfusion. They're not things that can wait. He needs them now.

Recognizing what I must do, I crouch down in front of Nikolai. "I'm going to get help, okay? I know you said we should wait, but I don't think that's a good idea."

I know I've made the right decision when I press my lips to Nikolai's. His mouth is as cold as ice, and his breathing barely registers on my trembling lips.

"I'll be back soon. I promise," I say over his lips.

After removing my overshirt to prop Nikolai's head against the rock, I map my course. Not eager to head in the direction we fled from last night, I cross the gorge via a small track etched on the lip of blasted rock. The terrain is more hilly on this side, but it keeps Nikolai in my line of sight most of the way.

I only lose him from my view when I start an eighty-foot climb. I was an adventurous teen, so things like rock climbing and hiking *were regular activities for me, but this is the first time I've attempted to scale a cliff edge without safety equipment.*

"I know, baby. Just a few more hours," I promise to the stabbing pain in the lower right quadrant of my stomach. "Once we get Daddy out of here, we'll have every inch of you checked over."

I could blame a lack of sleep for my delusional state, but I'm reasonably sure that isn't the cause of me talking to our baby like he or she can hear me. I'm on the verge of a breakdown, my symptoms oddly familiar to the ones I endured after being mauled by a dog.

If Nikolai doesn't survive this, I won't either—not mentally, anyway.

A grunt rumbles in my chest when I grip the final rock needed to hoist me over the cliff edge. With recent rains loosening the ground, it isn't as firmly embedded as I'd like, but it will have to do.

I sigh in relief when the rock maintains its clutch on the ground. Sweat and dirt grind into my cami when I roll onto my back. I am relieved I've climbed the wall without incident. I take a few minutes to suck in some much-needed breaths before commanding my wobbly legs to commence my mile walk to a line of trees on the horizon.

Pain twinges in my stomach with every stride I take, but I don't slow down. A twinge will be nothing compared to the pain I'll endure if I lose Nikolai.

Halfway across the grassy field, my brisk pace slows. Noisy engines are zooming my way, the rowdy cheers of their riders indicating their heritage.

They're Russian.

I sprint faster, praying I'll reach the safety of the trees before they spot me. My lungs scream for air, and the burn of my muscles is excruciating, but I don't give up.

I'm running so fast that my break through the line of trees nearly costs me my life.

I inch back with barely a second to spare. The double-trailer semi whizzing down the highway misses me by an inch.

But that isn't where my story ends.

My sweat-soaked shoes lose footing on the uncut grass lining the road's edge. Add my slip to the pressure of the truck speeding past, and you've got the equivalent of a flameless blast.

I land in the ditch separating the road from the field with a thud.

Although my body absorbs most of the impact, my head connecting with an exposed rock makes stars dance in front of my eyes and steals my memories...

Air whistles through my circled lips when my hand darts up to cradle the back of my head. I have a bump the size of a baseball covering most of my occipital bone. Its nasty size reveals the reason for my lack of memory of late. I wasn't drugged or being purposely deceitful. I was knocked out.

"When Nikolai wouldn't wake, I went to get help." I point to the exact location where I left him. "I left him right there with my shirt as protection for his head."

"Okay." Trey rubs his hands together, as unsure as I am about where we go from here. "Which way did you travel when you sought help?"

I shift on my feet to face the cliff I scaled.

A whistle rustles Trey's lips. "Could you see Nikolai the entire time?" When I nod, he moves to stand next to me. "If you could see him, that means he would have been able to see you if he woke."

Not waiting for me to reply, Trey pushes off his feet. He scales the rock edge with less care than I used days ago. Seeing a roughish bearded man trek through the wilderness shouldn't be odd, but it is.

"That's my shirt." I nearly lose my footing when I charge for a piece of the blouse I left with Nikolai. It's tied around a bush halfway down the trail. "He's leaving us clues."

I burst into tears. Now is not the time to cry, but if he's marking his movements, he's alive.

When I say that to Trey, he squeezes the living shit out of me. His firm hold adds to the pain rocketing through my stomach, but my excitement is too blistering to let a little pain dampen it.

We find the other half of my shirt under the rock face I climbed without a harness, but Nikolai is nowhere to be found.

When Trey shelters his eyes to peer up, I say, "He couldn't climb that. I barely made it, and I don't have a broken leg."

Trey looks at me like I'm an idiot. "Nothing would stop him from reaching you, Justine. Not a single fucking thing."

When he hands me his shirt and phone, I thrust them back into his chest. "I'm coming with you."

"No, you're not."

I begin my warning with a glare. "I'm not seeking your permission, Trey. I'm telling you this is what I'm doing."

After rubbing my hands together to rid them of sweat, I grip the first rock. While grumbling about opinionated women, Trey stuffs his shirt and cell into the back pocket of his jeans before tracing my steps.

With sheer determination fueling our climb, we reach the summit with minutes shaved off my already impressive time and lungs void of oxygen. I'm not the only one wheezing. Trey holds his ribs while he sucks in much-needed breaths. They're expelled in a flurry when his eyes sling to the side. A black blob is in the far-right corner of the grassy field. Although distance makes the person's features unrecognizable, I know it is Nikolai. I'd sense him anywhere.

"Nikolai!"

I sprint toward him, my legs moving faster than my brain can command. My gallop looks like a newborn foal learning to stand, and my excitement is delivered with a bucket of tears.

I lose the ability to breathe when Nikolai spins around to face me. He stares at me as if I'm a mirage, as if he too is waiting to be awoken from a dream too surreal to be true.

"Ангел?"

Crying, I nod before starting my sprint again. In my elation, his injuries are forgotten. I throw myself into his arms, my heave brutal enough to send us hurtling to the ground.

Nikolai's midair twirl saves my stomach from any unnecessary impact. It does little for his poor lungs, though.

"I'm so sorry. So, so, so very sorry," I apologize between frantic kisses. "I shouldn't have left you. I should have done as you asked."

"Shh. It's okay. You're here now." He scans my face, seeking confirmation of his wary words.

He still thinks he's dreaming.

"I'm here," I assure him before lowering his hand to my stomach. "We're here. We are safe. You saved us."

"No, Ангел," he denies, shaking his head. "You saved me. More than once."

His eyes reveal he means long before this weekend.

I maintain my strength for the twenty minutes it takes for paramedics to arrive on the scene, gurney Nikolai, and ship him to the closest hospital.

I maintain a brave front while doctors update us on the surgery Nikolai will require to extract the bullet from his shoulder and set his broken leg. I even manage to hide my pain while shadowing Nikolai's bed in the operating room prepped especially for him.

It is only once he disappears from my view do the cramps ripping through my stomach nearly have me kissing the hard tile floor outside of the surgery department.

If it weren't for Trey, the bump on my head would be the only bump I'd be cradling for the next nine months.

EPILOGUE
NIKOLAI

Four and a half years later...

Blood gargling in a windpipe is a fascinating noise. It sounds like death but from a person who hasn't yet submitted to the fact they're going to die. It's their last beacon of hope. Their last endeavor to fight.

You shouldn't delay the inevitable, though.

Death will find you no matter how many years pass.

You can't hurt a man's family and not suffer the consequences of your actions. It might take them a year to find you—it might even take four and a half—but no matter how often you glance over your shoulder, no matter how well you cover your steps, death will always be there, waiting.

Revenge isn't something that must be immediately executed, but be warned, the longer revenge festers, the louder the monster inside a once-subdued man will roar.

The man hanging bloody and bruised in the basement of my compound was given plenty of notice. He was stared down and warned that his actions would not be forgotten. But instead of acting like a man, he hid like a coward.

It did him no good.

His day before the judge, jury, and executioner has arrived.

Rico is about to get his revenge.

Rico's eyes hold the same devilish appearance they had when Justine discovered him barricading his family in a dingy room at the back of an old airport hangar. They're just filled with hate now instead of the toxic mix of drugs the Vasiliev crew tried to subdue him with.

The dose they gave him should have been lethal. He had more drugs in his system than I sampled during the entirety of my teen years. He should have been dead, not pinning one of my men to the wall by his throat.

It's a pity Maxsim's men misunderstood the strength of a man in love. Just like my Ангел went to the depths of hell for me, Rico stopped at nothing to keep his family safe. Delusional nightmares, a knife wound to the chest, and half a dozen men couldn't stop him from safeguarding his family.

He did his job.

Other than a slight case of dehydration and malnutrition, Blaire and Eli were given a clean bill of health after their ordeal.

Only Rico was left suffering.

He wanted to hunt and kill. He wanted the men who hurt his family to suffer. Instead, he set aside his feelings for the greater good. He was so determined to stay by his wife's and son's bedsides, he made the doctors stitch his wound in their room.

They thought he was stubborn, that they'd never handle a more irrational man in their lifetime. They had no clue of the meaning of "neurotic" until I entered their realm...

Just as my instincts saw me following Justine's steps, they warned me something wasn't right the instant the anesthesiologist began placing an oxygen mask over my mouth.

I'd had a countless number of operations in my childhood, so panic about going under the knife wasn't the cause of my sweaty palms and erratic heart rate. It was something much greater than fear eating me alive.

My intuition was proven right when Trey burst into my operating room only seconds later. He didn't say anything, but his ashen face spoke volumes. He had an expression on his face that could only mean one thing. My woman needed me.

I'd removed only half the cords dangling out of me when a much more urgent case was rushed into the operating room next to me.

Justine lay lifeless on a stainless-steel table. Her pants were covered with bright-red blood, and her arm was flopped over the side of the gurney.

The pain rocketing through my body relocated to my heart when I raced to her bedside. I was about to demand an update, when a gloved-up and ready-to-operate doctor entered the room. "What are we looking at?"

The man inserting a cannula into an extremely shallow vein in Justine's arm replied, "Internal bleeding from a mass on the lower right side of her abdomen. Believed orthostatic hypotension. Blood pressure is seventy-five over forty-three, and oxygen levels are mid-seventies."

"Any allergies we're aware of? Current medical conditions?"

The second man shook his head, forcing me to interject, "She's pregnant."

Both men's heads jackknifed to me in sync. They were so caught up assessing Justine, they hadn't noticed me in the room.

Their diligence has served them well to date.

The head surgeon wasn't pleased by my appearance, but he used my knowledge to his advantage. "What caused her injuries?"

I rattled off everything that happened the prior four days.

He was shocked. "And this?" He pointed to the rippled skin covering a majority of Justine's right ribcage.

"She was mauled by a dog."

"A dog?" His remorse couldn't be missed.

It had nothing on mine when I replied, "Yes. Five years ago."

Justine made a low, painful groan when the surgeon pushed on her stomach. I hated that she was in pain, but the fact she made a sound was promising.

My eyes danced between the surgeon's when he headed my way. "We need to stop the bleeding. The blood in her abdomen is compromising her organs. If we don't control the flow, she could go into cardiac arrest."

I nodded, understanding him. I underwent a similar operation a few weeks after my sixteenth birthday.

"And the baby?"

The surgeon's face went a little white. "We don't know yet. We'll do everything we can to stop further impact to the fetus, but our efforts will be focused on Justine's well-being."

I felt like I was sucker-punched. His hit was so forceful, before I could comprehend what I was doing, I was standing on the other side of the swinging operating doors...

I lose my train of thought when a grunt sounds through my ears. The noise didn't come from the man shackled to the ceiling as he watches Rico unroll his bag of tricks. It came from behind my shoulder.

"Eww. Why is his head hanging like that?"

I leave my front-row seat to a private execution when a pair of icy-blue eyes swing my way.

"Is he a bad man, Daddy?"

With a growl warning her it's way past her bedtime, I scoop Mila into my arms and briskly exit the room.

We walk the halls commonly referred to as the "dungeon" without a word spoken between us. Mila is just like me—*a rule breaker in every sense of the word*—but she knows some rules can never be broken, such as interrupting me while I'm at "work."

When we step over the threshold no woman in the Popov household is game to cross, a handful of housemaids rush to my side, more than eager to take Mila off my hands.

I shoo them away without words.

Daddy's little girl is in his arms, and I'm not giving her up for anything.

"Where's Mama?" I ask Mila as we climb the large spiral staircase that leads to the main sleeping quarters.

Mila lets out a big yawn. "She's sick again."

"Is that why you came to find me? Cause Mama is sick?" My hammering heart is heard in my low timbre.

Mila's big blue eyes seek mine as she contemplates whether to tell me the truth or not. She doesn't deliberate for long. "No. I wanted to play with Uncle Rico and you."

She's only four, but I know she isn't referring to the Barbie dolls Justine attempts to entice her with every day. Mila is an exact replica of me.

Same eyes.

Same hair color.

Same black-veined heart.

There's just one difference. She walked through the gates of hell while in her mother's womb. I marched through them after I was born.

Mila is the baby Justine fought with all her might to save four and a half years ago. A little dark-haired girl with the smile of Satan but the beauty to lure an angel into believing she's a saint.

She's a female version of me.

Toby, on the other hand, is just like his mother. He's shy and reserved, preferring to watch from afar before putting his precisely thought-out actions into play. His hair is as red as his mother's, and his face just as sweet. He's such a laid-back little guy who has never once voiced annoyance that Mila snagged the title of "heir" by racing into the world seven minutes and thirteen seconds before him.

There's no jealousy amongst them or hatred that the four years they've had on this earth have been shared with one another. They love each other as siblings should, their bond assuring me that they'll have each other's backs as I will always have Rico's and Lia's... and perhaps Maya's.

If Maya hadn't learned from her mistakes, the results may have been vastly different. But Justine was right—discovering the man she was in love with wasn't who she thought was punishment enough.

Maxsim could have saved Maya the heartache. He could have proven without a doubt that she was worthier than any possession he could have wished for, but it was proven without a doubt that greed was his priority.

He wasn't going to give Maya the life Vladimir withheld from her because she was a girl. He wanted to rule a kingdom he had no right to reign. He wanted to step into my shoes.

He lost the chance to discover that the greatest gift you can have doesn't have a monetary value when I demanded he choose between his life or Maya's.

He chose wrong when he picked himself.

Maya hasn't looked me in the eye since she witnessed firsthand what happens when you double-cross me, but that doesn't mean I can't feel the heat of her gaze.

Don't misconstrue. She isn't eyeing me with hate but, rather, remorse. She's aware how different circumstances would have been if Justine and the twins didn't make it out of the fire she sparked.

Maxsim's blood wouldn't have been the only blood shed that night if Justine hadn't exerted the strength I've always seen in her eyes. She fought like a tigress, her fight still inspiring me to this day.

My queen was worthy of her throne the day she was born, but the grit she showed that weekend sealed her fate for eternity.

My chest swells when I enter Mila and Toby's room. Roman is fast asleep on the rocking chair Justine used while nursing. He has a book of nursery rhymes splayed across his chest and a pair of glasses he swears he doesn't need balancing on the tip of his nose.

If I hadn't given him the weekend off, he'd be punished for sleeping on the job, but since he's here more in a grandfather role than as a guardian, I'll let his punishment slide.

Over two weeks had passed before anyone heard from Roman after the incident at Rico's apartment four and a half years ago. Things didn't look good, but my crew was ordered to continue searching until he was found and returned to his family.

We could only hope he wasn't returned in a body bag.

The discovery of his whereabouts was far from the notions running through my head. He wasn't buried in a shallow ditch or under police watch. He was doing the job I pay him to do. He was bringing the men responsible for our near downfall to justice.

I can still recall the sparkle in his eyes when he stood at the entrance of the dungeon upon his return. His boots were as muddy as the sneer on his face, but they had nothing on his eyes. They were worn by Satan himself—deadly and without fear.

His time off the grid served me well. Maxsim's knowledge assured Roman he wasn't the only one working against us.

His theory was correct.

Four snitches, three members considering jumping ship, and one captain were brought to justice in the two weeks Roman went rogue.

All were dead—except the latter.

Roman kept Maxsim alive for me, knowing I have no qualms about getting my hands dirty while seeking retribution for the ones I love.

I was on the verge of snapping as I had all those years ago when I was only a boy. My men were bombarded. My brothers were injured, and my queen was lying in a hospital bed.

It was all forgotten in those hours I spent with Maxsim.

Sergei's death was hidden to protect my *Ангел*.

Maxsim's was paraded for the same reason.

His death gave me back the fear and respect I crave, and then Asher and Trey returned my entity's honor.

It took a few months, but the Popov entity returned to the glory it once held. Both Asher and Trey can be thanked for its resurrection. While I tended to private matters, they held down the fort.

Now not only do the Popovs hold ranks across a majority of America, we've jabbed our foot in the door of a Russian stronghold we never fathomed we'd own. Soon, we will be unstoppable.

Rumors have circulated about upcoming takeover bids, but none have been implemented. Our enemies are wary of the union we've founded with Asher's crew, but even more than that, they're fearful of the powerful couple helming our crusade.

I thought I was invincible before Justine came into my life. I was a fool.

A king can't be a king without his queen at his side.

After tucking an almost-passed-out Mila into her bed, I make my way out of the room she shares with Toby. There are over a dozen spare rooms in the Popov mansion, but Mila and Toby are adamant about sharing the same one. If that doesn't reveal their closeness, nothing will.

Usually the urge to kill would have me returning to the show I was in the process of watching before Mila arrived, but years of observation award me the knowledge that this is a different adrenaline thickening my blood.

I'm not on the hunt for a bloodbath. I'm craving something much more potent than the high you get watching a monster be silenced. I want my drug. My addiction. The woman I crave more than the greatest drug on the market.

Mila's comment about Justine being sick is proven accurate when I enter our bedroom. Justine is rolled on her side with a pillow stuffed between her legs. Her face is paler than usual, and an empty bucket sits inches from her head.

Goosebumps break across her milky-white skin when I creep up behind her. She purrs a soft moan when the bristles on my chin graze the dog bite on her shoulder.

"The baby still upsetting your stomach?"

I cup the tiny curve in her lower stomach when she groans. "He's not a fan of shellfish."

"I don't blame him. It's stinky and gross."

I'm tempted to pinch myself when Justine giggles before rolling over to face me. The visual confronting me is too soul-stealing to be classed as anything less than perfect. Big, unique green-blue eyes on the face of an angel, and a body that only grows more appetizing the rounder her stomach becomes.

She is truly stunning.

Recalling my request for her to be bare and waiting for me, I tug on the satin belt cinching her kimono close to her body. It gives way without too much effort, exposing a body I've killed for and will continue killing for, for years to come.

"How sick are you?" I ask before lowering my mouth to circle my tongue around her budded nipple.

"Not *that* sick." She arches her back, revealing not even the worst case of morning sickness could curb her desires.

"Are you sure? I don't want you throwing up on me."

Laughing, Justine pushes my head toward the scent I'm sucking in like an addict hitting three lines. In all honesty, the smell of her cunt when she's horny is the most delicious thing I've ever smelled.

"Like a little vomit would stop you."

"True," I agree with a chuckle. "Nothing could keep me away from you, *Ангел*. Not a man or a mountain. Not even an atom bomb." I place a kiss on her chest for each word I speak next. "Not. A. Single. Fucking. Thing." Her thighs sweep open when I lower my lips to her midsection and whisper, "*маленький воин папы.*"

She loves the nicknames I give our babies while they grow inside her. This one is Daddy's little warrior. He'll be stronger than both Mila and Toby combined. Not because he hasn't faced the struggles they did in the womb, but because he's both Justine and me conjoined.

Mila and Toby share our blood, but they represent us as individual people. Mila is strong and protective, whereas Toby is an observer with a massive brain—a.k.a me and Justine.

This baby will have equal parts of us both. He'll be both smart and strong like his mother, and a natural-born leader like me.

As my attention to Justine's body drops lower and lower, she stuffs a heap of pillows under her head. She doesn't want her belly hiding a visual she'll never grow tired of watching. She loves watching me devour her so much I don't need to say my next words, but I will, because not only does she love me, she also loves my filthy mouth.

"Now watch me eat the tastiest cunt I've ever tasted."

THE END!

Asher's story is available now:
Asher: My Russian Revenge (Asher & Zariah)

Trey's and Maddox's stories are also done. Join my readers group to stay up-to-date.
bit.ly/ShandiBookBabes

Also, Nikolai's series is a spin off of the *Enigma Series*. His brother, Rico, already has a book. You can find it here: I Married a Mob Boss

If you want to hear updates on the next story in the Russian Mob Chronicles, be sure to like my Facebook author page.
www.facebook.com/authorshandi

Join my READER's group:
https://www.facebook.com/groups/
1740600836169853/

Rico and Nikolai's stories have already been released, but Trey, Maddox, and Asher's stories will arrive at some point during 2019/2020.

Join my newsletter to remain informed:
https://www.subscribepage.com/AuthorShandi

If you enjoyed this book - please leave a review!

ACKNOWLEDGMENTS

There are so many people who deserve to be mentioned when writing a book. The main: my family! This doesn't just mean the adorable man I married twenty years ago or my five kiddies. I mean my readers as well. They've followed me through this journey just as much as my family. They watched me grow and saw me stumble, but they stuck by my side. For that, I will be forever grateful.

Then there are people in my community who have my back no matter what. Bec, Krista, and the hundreds of authors who know firsthand how much effort it takes to produce a story, much less be brave enough to share it. This industry isn't easy, but my love for it continues to grow everyday.

And lastly, Nikolai. It isn't everyday you stumble upon a character like him. I'm just so damn grateful I got to share his story with you.

You beg and pleaded for this final instalment. I hope I did it justice.

Much love,

Shandi xx

ALSO BY SHANDI BOYES

*** Denotes Standalone Books**

Perception Series

Saving Noah *

Fighting Jacob *

Taming Nick *

Redeeming Slater *

Saving Emily

Wrapped Up with Rise Up

Protecting Nicole *

Enigma

Enigma

Unraveling an Enigma

Enigma The Mystery Unmasked

Enigma: The Final Chapter

Beneath The Secrets

Beneath The Sheets

Spy Thy Neighbor *

The Opposite Effect *

I Married a Mob Boss *

Second Shot *

The Way We Are

The Way We Were

Sugar and Spice *

Lady In Waiting

Man in Queue

Couple on Hold

Enigma: The Wedding

Silent Vigilante

Hushed Guardian

Quiet Protector

Enigma: An Isaac Retelling

Enigma Bonus Scenes (Two free chapters)

Twisted Lies *

Bound Series

Chains

Links

Bound

Restrain

The Misfits *

Nanny Dispute *

Russian Mob Chronicles

Nikolai: Representing the Bratva

Nikolai: Resurrecting the Bratva

Nikolai: Ruling the Bratva

Asher: My Russian Revenge *

Trey *

Nikolai: Bonus Scenes (10+ chapters from alternative POVs).

The Italian Cartel

Dimitri

Roxanne

Reign

Mafia Ties (Novella)

Maddox

Demi

Ox

Rocco *

Clover *

Smith *

RomCom Standalones

Just Playin' *

<u>Ain't Happenin'</u> *

The Drop Zone *

Very Unlikely *

False Start *

Short Stories - Newsletter Downloads

Christmas Trio *

Falling For A Stranger *

Enigma Bonus Scenes (Two free chapters)

Nikolai: Bonus Scenes (10+ chapters from alternative POVs).

One Night Only Series

Hotshot Boss *

Hotshot Neighbor *

The Bobrov Bratva Series

Wicked Intentions *

Sinful Intentions *

Devious Intentions *

Deadly Intentions *

Omnibus Books (Collections)

Enigma: The Complete Collection (Isaac & Isabelle)

The Beneath Duet (Hugo & Ava)

The Bad Boy Trilogy (Hunter, Rico, and Brax)

Pinkie Promise (Ryan & Savannah)

The Infinite Time Trilogy (Regan & Alex)

Silent Guardian (Brandon & Melody)

Nikolai: The Complete Collection (Nikolai & Justine)

Mafioso (Dimitri & Roxanne)

Bound: The Complete Collection (Cleo & Marcus)

Printed in Great Britain
by Amazon

47833080R10453